NOT BETWEEN BROTHERS

An American Epic

David Marion Wilkinson

A SIGNET BOOK

For Bonnie

SIGNET
Published by New American Library, a division of Penguin Putnam Inc., 375
Hudson Street, New York, New York 10014, U.S.A.
Penguin Books Ltd, 27 Wrights Lane, London W8 5TZ, England
Penguin Books Australia Ltd, Ringwood, Victoria, Australia
Penguin Books Canada Ltd, 10 Alcorn Avenue, Toronto, Ontario, Canada
M4V 3B2
Penguin Books (N.Z.) Ltd, 182–190 Wairau Road, Auckland 10, New Zealand

Penguin Books Ltd, Registered Offices: Harmondsworth, Middlesex, England

Published by Signet, an imprint of New American Library,
a division of Penguin Putnam Inc.
This is an authorized abridged reprint of a trade paperback edition published
by BOAZ Publishing Company. For information address BOAZ Publishing
Company, P.O. Box 6582, Albany, California 94706

First Signet Printing, June 1999
10 9 8 7 6 5 4 3 2

Copyright © David Marion Wilkinson, 1996

*The author wishes to thank the following for permission to quote brief excerpts
from their work. All quotations appear on page vi.*

T.R. Fehrenbach, from *Lone Star: A History of Texas and the Texans,* reprinted
by permission of the author and the author's representatives, The Scott Mere-
dith Literary Agency, 845 Third Avenue, New York, NY 10022.
B.W. Ife, from *Christopher Columbus: Journal of the First Voyage,* permission
granted by the author and by the publisher, Aris & Phillips, Ltd.
Donald E. Chipman, from *Spanish Texas, 1519–1821,* by Donald E. Chipman,
Copyright © 1992. Courtesy of the author and the University of Texas Press.
Cormac McCarthy, from *The Crossing,* permission granted by International Cre-
ative Management, Inc. Copyright © 1994 by Cormac McCarthy.

CONTENTS

No human beings were native to the New World;
every race of men entered as invaders.
—*T.R. Fehrenbach*

Thursday 11 October 1492
They [the natives] ought to make good slaves . . . and I
believe that they could very easily become Christians,
for it seemed to me they had no religion of their own.

Monday 15 October 1492
I called the island Santa María de la Concepción. . . . I
did not wish to pass by any island without taking
possession of it, although it might be said that once one
had been taken, they all were.

And so I shall take him [the native captive] across to
Fernandina and give him back all his belongings, so
that he will spread good news about us, and when, God
willing, Your Highnesses send others here, those who
come will be received with honor and the Indians
will give us everything there is.
—*Christopher Columbus*

This federal republic [United States] is born a pigmy.
[But] a day will come when it will be a giant, even a
colossus. . . . Liberty of conscience, the facility for establishing a new population on a new land . . . will draw
thither farmers and artisans from all the nations. In a
few years we shall watch with grief the tyrannical
existence of this same colossus.
—*Count of Aranda* (c. 1783)

The past, he said, is always this argument between
counter claimants.
—*Cormac McCarthy*

BOOK ONE

The Hunger

1816

Chapter One

Remy first saw him as the sun set, a dark silhouette emerging from the soft green of new growth. He raced through the pastures, thick with winter stubble and emerging weeds, to the homestead that lay on the hill.

"He's back!" he cried, bursting through the door. His mother sat expressionless in her rocker, which did not rock, her eyes sunken deep in their dark sockets. She was like cold ashes, listless and gaunt. Remy didn't understand it. For the better part of six weeks they'd been waiting for this day. All would be well, he thought, now that it'd come.

Remy stepped closer, cautiously almost, as one would approach a small wild animal come across in the woods. It might lick his hand, or it might bite it. He rested the back of his fingers against her brow, coarse like weathered canvas, to test for fever. Instead it felt almost chilled. "Are you still ailin', Ma?" he asked.

She moved his hand away. "Are you sure it's your father, Remy?" she asked blankly, never once looking at him. Her distant tone both confused and concerned him. He thought his father's arrival, of all things, would make her happy.

"It's him, Mama," he said more clearly now in an attempt to reach her. "I can see his red cap clear as day. He's back. Things'll be better. You wait an' see."

He watched her eyes, cloudy gray, as they shifted back and forth nervously across the cabin, pausing at nothing, until at last the focus returned and their gaze fell solidly on him.

"Now you listen to me, boy," she said. She spoke slowly, methodically, with the dull resonance you hear if you kick a rotten, empty stump. "I want you to go to your Aunt

Helen's place. If'n you don't dawdle, you can be there 'fore
dark. You stay there a couple of days till someone comes
for you. If no one comes, send your Uncle Will." She
paused, deliberating a moment longer, her eyes lost again
to the distance, and then added, "You don't come with
'im."

What was wrong with her, he wondered? It was dangerous for anyone, let alone him, a boy, to go anywhere at
night. Normally she'd never ask such a thing; she'd always
babied him, if anything. "I'm afraid of the woods at night,
Mama," he protested. "Aunt Helen's farm is better'n six
miles away."

"All the more reason to go now while there's still some
light. You know the trail well enough, be it night or day.
On your way, and be quick about it." She sighed deeply,
as if she'd taken her last breath. "I didn't raise no coward, Remy."

Her insistence did not assuage his anxiety and doubt and
his fear of being swallowed by those dark, brooding woods.
"I won't go, Mama," he said with a sniffle. "I wanna see
my pa."

He waited for her response, to acquiesce with a tight-
lipped smile, just like she always did when he asked for
another slice of cake after he'd already eaten two. Instead,
she just slowly shook her head. Something was terribly,
terribly wrong.

"Mama, I . . ." Before he could speak further, she
snatched him by his shirt collar with her left hand and
slapped him sharply twice with her right.

"I said git, boy! Now! Don't you sass me no more, and
don't you look back!"

Remy glared at his mother. His cheek throbbed warm
and numb, his whole body trembled. His mother's crazed
eyes seemed to look right through him. What in God's
name was wrong with her? She'd never struck him in the
face before. And she'd never, ever, said such mean things.
Only yesterday she'd held him to her chest sobbing for
hours as they rocked together. He had been uncomfortable.
He was too old for that, but when he'd attempted to leave,
she'd only gripped him tighter. It went on the better part
of a whole wasted day. And now this! He was sick of her

moodiness and inconsistencies. All winter long there'd been no way to please her. He'd never once awakened to her hymns or heard those woeful highland ballads she hummed as she went about her daily chores. It seemed that his world had fallen silent, like the pause just before first light when even the birds refuse to sing. That letter, addressed in his grandmother's hand, was the beginning of her blackness. But when he'd reached for it to read it for himself, his mother had tossed it in the fire and never spoken of it again. That same night, however, she'd wailed so terribly that he wept too. And now, she'd slapped him with no cause.

He broke free from her grasp, so furious that he could not stem his tears, and ran from her. If that was what the witch wanted, he thought, that was what she'd have. When he reached the timber line, he collapsed into the deep weeds and lay there in shudders. He wept between gasps of breath that vaporized on the chill evening breeze.

From the high ground to the east, he watched his father approach their home. Remy could tell that he was tired by his stooped gait. He'd come far. In the past, his mother would have gone out to meet him in the pastures, Remy at her side, a smile on both of their faces. He would have helped his father proudly with the stock. Then they would all three sit in front of a warm fire while his father pulled out his map and showed them where he'd been, told them of his travels, displayed his furs, demonstrated the odd object he'd traded for. Remy would've watched him meticulously clean his rifle and pistols, his reassuring pipe smoke hanging in the air, fuzzy like a wool blanket. Their house was not complete without the smell of his father in it. There was comfort in his musky odor.

But this time his father, occasionally casting a wondering eye toward the house, worked alone. One by one, he dropped the packs from the mules with a tug at the leather thong that held them, and then hauled the bundles to the porch, letting the animals wander off toward the barn where the last of the brittle winter hay still waited. His father followed them into the weathered structure to hang his tack on familiar pegs.

When darkness fell Remy crept back toward the farmhouse. She had no right to keep him from his father. All winter long he'd waited to see him, and she couldn't keep Remy from him now that he was here. His father would protect him from her until she came to her senses.

Once he reached the house, Remy hung shivering in the shadows where the light from the oil lamps could not find him. He crouched behind the rain barrel when his father emerged from the barn and entered the cabin. The warped, wavy lines of the window pane that had rattled all winter distorted his father's image as he stepped through the threshold and rested his rifle on the deer-hoof rack above the door.

"Ah, Elizabeth," he heard him say. The voices were muffled, but he heard them clearly enough. His father, arms outstretched, grinned warmly. "I've made it back at last. I've missed you." Remy watched as he pulled her to him to kiss her, but she turned her head and then jerked away. His father's grin faded as quickly as it had come.

"Where've you been all this time, Norbert?" she asked. So often in the past, when he was supposed to have been asleep in his loft, Remy'd heard her purr his father's name, "Nor-bear." Her tone was crisper now, cooler even than it had been with him, her expression more aloof. He knew then that she was angry with his father and not him.

"North, to the foothills of the Ozarks," he answered, his jaw set just like he did before he stepped out into a cold, north wind. "Good hunting there," he offered. "The winter was mild this year." He watched her briefly and then shook his head. "Are you unhappy with me again?"

"The fields should've been ready for plantin' by now, Norbert," she told him. "It's too late, I'm afraid, to make a crop. It'd be a waste of our time."

"There're other ways to live than by farmin'."

"Then why'd you let my father buy us a farm?"

"That was his idea," he snapped. "You married a Frenchman. I've always hunted and trapped for my living. I belong in the woods. I don't like being cooped up in one place, strapped to a plow like an ass."

"You told me that's what you wanted to do."

"An' I tried it with everything that I have," he shot back, making a fist as he declared it, his face stiff like a weathered board. Remy's mother never looked. "It wasn't for me, Elizabeth," he said, his tone calmer. "My furs'll provide for this family. You can be certain of that. They're excellent this year."

"A father away for months at a time can't provide for a family," she said coolly. "More than just money's needed around this place. The boy needs a father. Remy doesn't mind me anymore."

"That's your own fault, woman. You spoil him." He looked around. "Where's that boy, anyway?"

"I've sent him off to Will and Helen's place."

"That's too bad," he said. Remy saw that he studied her blankly. "I'm hungry," he finally murmured. "Is there nuthin' for a man to eat in this house?"

"Sit by the fire, Norbert," she said. Her words were more tender now. Remy thought he'd not have to wait outside much longer. He shifted his weight, placing his palms against the rough-hewn window trim and leaned closer, careful not to leave the shadows. "Warm yourself," his mother said. His father moved toward one chair. She reached swiftly, her hand to his shoulder, guiding him to another that faced the stone hearth where the coals still smoldered beneath a layer of warm, white ashes. "Sit here, husband," she said. "It won't take me long to take care of you."

"You were worrying me, Elizabeth," he said. "It shouldn't be like this between us." Remy saw him look carefully at his mother the same way he studied an empty, sprung trap. "Are ya ill, woman?" he asked in such a manner that Remy knew any answer would displease.

"Well enough," she answered. "Just a touch of fever, I think. It'll pass soon enough."

"You should take better care of yourself."

"It doesn't matter what I do," she answered.

His father settled in, resting his elbows, his fingers meshed, on the table. Remy shuddered, wondering how much longer he must wait in the chill. "I know what you want, Elizabeth," his father said. "Next year, I'm willing to give this farming another try." This was a concession, Remy knew. He'd heard his father make many before. Yet it pleased him to hear his father attempt to console her. That,

Remy knew now, was what she wanted. "I can trap and hunt, too. Remy's ten years old now, isn't he?"

"He's just turned nine, Norbert," she replied, her eyes closing.

"Well, all the same, I'll teach him what little I know about it, and then make sure he learns from others. He'll be your farmer."

Remy saw the glint of his own teeth mirrored in the window. To hear his father promise to spend more time with him meant everything. They were apart so much of the year. But he saw right away that it made little difference in his mother's mood. It should've made her happy that he promised change. She should've stepped closer to him in gratitude. Instead, she stepped away. "I don't see how we can hold out another year, Norbert." Her voice was steady now, almost reassuring, strange given the subject at hand. Remy had no idea they were stuck for money.

"Helen Marie's husband had business in New Orleans in November," she said. "I sent him by the bank to get a little cash for us. We needed some things, and I had no idea when you'd return. It seems that you'd been there before him."

His father did not lift his gaze from the rough, grease-stained table. The color left his cheeks. "I meant to explain that to you, Elizabeth," he said quietly, "when the time was right."

"When would that be, Norbert?" she asked grimly. "All of the money's already gone."

His father rolled his eyes. "I needed supplies," he explained, his voice low, "a fine Christian Gump rifle and there's none better, and goods to trade with the savages. Don't worry about the money," he said with a flick of his wrist. "I admit that it was a bit of a gamble; I've had losses in the past. But this year went very well for me. I've several fine furs and a little silver ore. I wish you'd come and looked like you always do. When these things are sold, most of the money'll be returned to our account. All will be well."

"Maybe," she said. "And maybe not."

"I can't abide your naggin', Elizabeth," his father snapped.

"A man need not explain his business activities to his wife. It's none of your affair."

"It was *my* money, Norbert!", she said curtly. Her tone grated on Remy's ears. "My father gave it to me."

"The more you complain, the more justified I feel in takin' it. That money was to be used to care for you. That's exactly what I did with it. Just give me a little time, woman. In a year or two, I'll put back more than I took."

"You never put back more than you take," she said in a low growl.

"Enough of this now," he said, and Remy knew that was the end of the argument. His father would sit and stare at the fire until his mother gave up. Remy'd seen many arguments end that very same way. "Hurry with that food, woman. I'm starving."

She rattled a pot or two against the griddle as if to appease him, sawed through a loaf of stale bread, the whole time staring at the back of his head. "Were you amongst the Chickasaws, Norbert?" his mother asked. He could tell that she already knew the answer.

"Them, and others," he said beneath his dark scowl, the fire's flames glistening in his eyes.

"I ran into the magistrate at the settlement. He told me that he'd seen you with a Chickasaw woman in Little Rock. He saw but you two alone comin' in for supplies."

"What he says is true," he admitted, grinding his palm into the socket of his eye. "She was my guide."

"A *woman* guide, Norbert?"

"Why not?" he asked impatiently. "She knew the country. She cooked, and prepared the hides. Best of all, she didn't complain. Who'd have been better?" He smashed his fist against the solidity of the oak. "Why all these damn questions, Elizabeth? I want my supper. The rest can wait."

"I just wanted to be sure, I guess, 'fore I made my decision."

"Decision? What decision? Do you want to go home to your father again, Elizabeth? Are you that unhappy?" His face was pale and pudgy, like a fat table candle that had been allowed to burn too long, its true shape lost. Remy hoped he would find the patience to go to his mother and comfort her. Had he not said himself that she looked ill?

She needed to be hugged. But he would not even look at her, let alone attempt to soothe her. He just stared into the fire like he always did when his mother was angry, just like she knew he would.

"I am that unhappy," she told him, "and yes, I'd like to return to my father's house."

Remy's heart sank at the thought of separation. More time apart. His father rolled his head back to gawk crudely at the rafters. Then, at last, he turned to her. "*Go* then, damn you!" he said, his raucous voice low and mean. "I don't want you here to pester me! You should know that my Indian guide's also my wife. I traded for her like I traded for you. Like I said, she suits me better. She's not a sickly Scot, like you. You should see yourself, for God's sake! There's not a trace of color in your face. You look like you're dead! There's cows in the pastures more attractive than you. If it weren't for the boy, I'd spend no time here at all."

His father's words should've crushed her like they crushed him. Never had Remy heard him be so cruel. But if she heard them as he did, they did not seem to matter. She waited calmly for him to turn away from her again, his cheeks flushed and teeth gritted, then she reached for the double-barreled shotgun that rested in the crack between her cupboards and the pie safe. Remy knew it was too heavy for her to handle. She was always dangerous with that thing, unable to steady the bore to the point that she could hit anything further than a few feet away. Uncertain, Remy watched as she silently wrestled with the hammers until she cocked one. She checked to see if his father had heard it, which apparently he had not. Then she cradled the gun in her unsteady arms and drifted closer.

"That's just it, Norbert," she said, her voice slow and steady. "I wrote to my father in October. My mother answered for him just last month. She tells me that he doesn't wish me to return. He remains unhappy with this marriage, saying that he's done all for me that he's willing to do. He'll not take Remy either, or even see him. We've got nowhere else to go."

"I'd think about that, then, if I were you."

"I have," she muttered. "May God help me, I have."

She briefly closed her eyes as she seemed to gather herself. His father must've sensed something. Remy thought he saw his head start to turn when she raised the shotgun barrel to the base of his neck, bit her bottom lip, and pulled the front trigger.

Remy saw the hammer fall, the flash of the primer, the flame erupt from the long bore. The clap of thunder rattled the window panes. Remy snapped back from the window in shock. He'd gripped the wood so tightly that splinters tore into his finger tips as he snatched them away. Then he froze at the image clearing before him. Beneath the cloud of white smoke, his father's chest had slammed flat against the table. He did not move. Only his mouth and nose remained intact; the rest of his face was blown away. His blood spilled from the head cavity, dripping on the dirt floor. A thin web of white smoke danced where his brain used to be. There was the slightest tremor in the clawed fingers of his left hand that lay next to an empty plate.

Remy felt his heart pound as he stared in disbelief at his mother. The rest of him was numb. His mother never looked at the man she had murdered. She was frantic now. She dragged a chair next to her husband's lifeless body. Then she ripped the curtains from the windows and the sheets from the beds, tossed them to the floor and doused them with a tin of kerosene. She took the lamp from the table, increased its flame, and lit the sheets before she tossed it into the stack of kindling she had stacked near the wall. Once she seemed satisfied that the fire would catch, she cocked the hammer of the remaining cylinder, rested the butt of the gun on the floor, and stretched her mouth over the barrel.

Shaken by an instinct deeper than shock, Remy reacted. He darted first one way, then another, gasping for breath. He raced around to the front of the house, fumbling with the latchstring with trembling, bleeding fingers, finally crashing through the stubborn door. Before it opened he screamed, "Nnnooo!"

He flinched at the percussion. The blast rocked his mother's body backwards in the chair where it crashed to the floor. Her body twitched as flames spread to the fabric of her sprawled dress. The last thing Remy saw of his mother was her auburn hair, withering around what was left of her skull, her blood boiling on the floor around it. Remy's hands shot up wildly of their own accord, fingers spread and shaking violently, as a cloak of fire and thick, black smoke rose between him and his dead mother. The flames licked his bare arms and he screamed again as pain replaced panic.

He grabbed a stool and positioned it where he could get to his father's rifle. It was the one thing, Norbert had always told him, that no man alone should be without, and the first thing he thought to salvage. The possibles bag and powder horn, their slick, leather straps wrapped around the rifle's stock, came with it. The bag, he knew, contained his father's crumpled map of the western frontier.

Once he held these things, he turned to see what else he could take. His lungs ached from the heat and the thick smoke. He coughed violently, the mucous dripping from the corners of his mouth, his skin blistered and his hair singed, the acrid smell of burning flesh embedded within his drooling nostrils. The flames snarled at him again, and he turned away and dashed out of the crackling house.

He ran toward Helen's farm too scared to stop. The briars clawed his arms and legs until they bled. He felt warm blood on cold skin. He heard branches snap back defiantly in place, sealing the trail behind him. The laden darkness of an overcast, metallic night smothered the domed glow dying in the distance. His scorched lungs ached for breath as he ran on, the sound of his hollow footsteps on soggy ground echoed in his ears.

Somewhere behind him a hoot owl cried murder. The swirling night wind dallied with the chattering leaves of live oaks to confirm the rumor of blood, overtook him in a solid wave, and then swept past to carry the black tidings ahead. Remy felt the chill of its gossip on his sweating neck. He screamed to no one and ran on, hoping the night would absorb him as it had everything else.

Chapter Two

Little Hand led his mare through the encampment to the river bank. Across his saddle lay an antelope doe, fresh blood still dripping from its nose. Little Hand watered his horse, then made his way back through the rows of teepees to find the smoke lodge where he knew the old men gathered in the late afternoon. He circled the structure and worked the smoke flap closed at the top. Then he waited. Momentarily, he heard the occupants begin to cough. Soon they emerged for fresh air. His grandfather was the third man out.

"Ah, here's the problem, my brothers," gasped Cold Knife, wiping the tears from his eyes. "As always, it's my grandson." His grandfather turned to him. "Little Hand, why this?"

"I'm not allowed in, so you had to come out," he said.

"Why not just call out next time rather than embarrass me like this?" he said. "Oh, well. It's easily fixed," and he knocked the flap loose from the vent by means of the long cedar pole and kicked back the door covering. "A moment or two," he explained to the others, "and it'll be all right. I'm sorry. Boys will be boys."

"Old men get no respect among the People any more," one of the elders said. "These boys are awful these days. Last week, someone shit at the door and covered it with dirt, knowing that we go barefoot inside. We all stepped in it. It'd have been better to die young."

"Then you shouldn't have been such a coward," Cold Knife answered. "You'd have gotten your wish. You may get it now if you don't quit complaining." He coughed, waving his hand in front of his face. "The smoke's going. A moment more and you can get back to your story, which was all lies anyway."

"What do you know about greatness?" his friend sneered.

"I know you don't have it, you old fool," Cold Knife said, and then he thumped Little Hand on the back of his head. "Always trouble from you," he told him, and then that stern, stone face eased into a smile. Little Hand pointed to the

13

antelope, and his grandfather stepped over to admire it. "That's a nice fat doe, Little Hand. Where'd you get it?"

"On the plains near the water hole," he answered proudly. "She came in mid-morning, when the heat got up, just as I knew she would. I was waiting to the east, covered in the brush. She did not smell me, although she came very close. The arrow passed cleanly through her lungs." He showed his grandfather the shaft, its turkey-feather fletching matted with dried blood. "She didn't run far."

"That's good. I'm proud of you."

Little Hand turned his attention away from the doe. He had something else on his mind. "Where's my father?" he asked.

"He and your uncle left last night with Half Moon's raiding party. They'll be out several days, I think."

"Red Sky has asked me to go with him on a raid this very evening," he explained casually. "I wanted to ask his permission." A frown came to his grandfather's face.

"Red Sky has no sense," the old man said, "and you, my young friend, have no medicine. You're too young to raid. Keep hunting for your family. Ride with the other boys your own age. You'll be a warrior soon enough, but there's much to learn and it takes time. Be patient, Little Hand. Cold Knife'll teach you what you need to know."

Little Hand felt that he had a number of promising attributes, but patience was not one of them. Many his own age had already left for the raiding trail that led to honor and prestige. They taunted him with their prizes, calling him a mama's boy, which, to some degree, was probably true. He was small for his age. His manly hair and voice had come on late. Not too long ago he'd been ashamed to swim naked with lifelong friends in the river. He'd have been content to hunt and play as his grandfather suggested, but he could no longer abide the insults of his peers, and he said so to Cold Knife. "Boys my age are already on the raiding trail, Grandfather. I have to go with Red Sky. I can't wait any longer. It's a matter of pride."

He sensed Cold Knife's tone stiffen. "What's your spirit, Little Hand?"

He did not answer at first. His grandfather's words stopped him cold. "I have none," he finally admitted.

"Of course not," Cold Knife agreed. "First, you find your

medicine spirit. Then you can ride with Red Sky, or maybe somebody else not quite so stupid." His face turned solemn. "If you insist on this thing, I'll go and see Three Bears. There are a great many fools practicing around this tribe these days, but I've got faith in him. Three Bears knows the old ways. We'll see what he's got to say about your problem and whether or not he thinks you're ready to follow the warrior's trail. If so, he'll tell you how to find your spirit so that your path'll be straight and clean."

Little Hand felt his grandfather's hand on his shoulder. He turned to meet his benevolent gaze. "He's expensive, Little Hand. I want you to think this thing through a little more. I'll handle the payment, of course, but I don't want to meet his price if this is a boy's silly notion."

A smile came to Little Hand's face. He loved his grandfather dearly. He always knew the old man would help him. "I'm ready, Cold Knife, and I'm committed. I feel it in my bones."

"All right, then," his grandfather said. "Go to your father's lodge and make ready. Begin to fast. Stay clear of women. And by all means avoid hotheads like Red Sky. Have your sisters bring hot stones to your lodge so that you'll sweat tonight. At dawn tomorrow, you should bathe in cold water and then come and find me. We'll travel up river to see Three Bears after that." He paused to re-light his pipe. "You'll abide by his determination, yes?"

"Yes."

"All right. Go now."

Little Hand said he understood, and thanked his grandfather dearly for his concern. Then he walked off to do as he was told. When he was certain that his grandfather had had time to re-enter the lodge, he returned and covered the vent a second time. Before he had gone thirty steps he heard the old men coughing.

Little Hand found relief from the afternoon heat in the shade of a large cedar thicket on a rise just east of the

Tsoko-ka'ani-humo River, the one he knew the Spanish called the San Sabá. The elevation provided him full benefit of the thermal breeze as he lay on the soft brown carpet of cedar mulch. In this way he waited, preparing himself for what was to come. His anticipation was great, but diluted to some degree by a creeping sense of doubt. He'd known other boys, older than he, who had failed to find their animal spirits. He'd watched their confidence erode before his eyes as they stumbled along the path to manhood. On the other hand, the young men who were successful had become unbearable, loud and boastful. If he failed initially, they would chide him to no end. Yet it had gone well for his father, who was adopted by the buffalo bull, and his uncle, who was watched over by the resourceful raccoon, and so Little Hand prayed that success was an inherited trait, like the big feet at the base of his skinny frame.

His reverie was disrupted by the crack and pop of brush limbs as someone approached. It was Morning Song, carrying an empty water bag made from the treated stomach of a buffalo.

"Hey, you," she called. "Silly boy. What're you doing up here alone? Playing with yourself again?"

"The river's down there," he said, annoyed at the intrusion at such a private, special time. Morning Song had a talent for it. She walked up to his side.

"I thirst for something else," she answered. She dropped the container and reached for him. Out of duty, Little Hand pulled away.

"Not now, Morning Song. I'm preparing to meet my vision."

Morning Song shimmied enough to allow her buckskin dress to slip from her shoulders past her waist. Her bronze skin was smooth, her breasts rounded and firm. She swung her hair, which was shorter than Little Hand's and partly daubed with plant dyes, over her shoulder. Her raven eyes were accentuated with yellow lines that crossed at the corners. The inside of her ears were painted red and a small red circle adorned both of her cheeks. She stepped out of the dress and stood naked before him. He'd seen nothing in the world more beautiful.

"This is the only vision you need to become a man, you

fool," she said, and then she knelt beside him and kissed him.

"I'll never get anywhere like this," he said. He couldn't help but smile. He'd loved her as long as he could remember. She kissed him again. This time he responded, and she worked his breechcloth down his legs and swung one of her legs across his waist. He reached his hands around her back to stroke her a moment before they each settled around opposite sides of her hips. She pressed him to the ground and slipped him in with a moan. Suddenly, his spirit quest seemed a long way off.

When it was over, they lay side by side, Little Hand stroking her hair.

"I love you, Morning Song," he said.

"Then take me to your lodge as your wife."

"They'll never let us marry."

"Let's elope, then," she suggested, sweeping the hair back from her face. "My aunt married a Quahadi. We can live amongst them for a while. They wouldn't care."

Little Hand knew that this would never do. "It's scandalous," he protested. "Our families would never forgive us. We've just got to wait a little bit. That's all."

"For me there's no waiting. Other Penateka warriors have sent messengers to my father to ask for my hand. He wants me to marry."

This angered him. "Don't even think about it! You need to wait for me."

"It's not my decision alone," she sighed. "My father and brother might kill me if I don't honor their wishes."

"They wish for you to be happy. All you have to do is make it known that you want me."

"My mother knows."

"Good," he said. "Have her whisper your desires in your father's ear. I'll send my grandfather around to make an offer for you as soon as I'm ready. But the quickest I can do it is later in the year. I've got to find my animal spirit, so I can go on the raiding parties. That way I can get horses to trade your father for you. I just need a little time. Be patient. Encourage no other warriors."

"I can't help it if they look at me."

"You can help it by not looking back."

"Maybe. Maybe not." She raised her eyebrows and grinned.

He turned away. "Don't aggravate me, Morning Song. I've got enough things to worry about for now."

"Oh, don't beat your chest so much, boy," she scoffed. "I'll wait. I love you, Little Hand."

"Good. Stop making me so nervous. I want no other woman but you."

"And you'll have me. Just hurry up." She reached for her buckskin dress and draped it over her. "I'd better go," she said, "or else they'll start talking again." She collected the skin, kissed him again, and had started back for the river when she turned back. "Be sure and bathe well, Little Hand. I wouldn't want the animal spirits to know that you've been with a woman."

He nodded and rolled his eyes. "Good luck," she said, and he watched her disappear through the cedars.

Little Hand did his best to think about his purpose, but all he could do was think about Morning Song. He went down to the river and bathed again; then he returned to his spot on the hill. He concentrated as best he could to push out all thoughts of love and focus on becoming a warrior. It was no use. If she were still here, he'd take her off somewhere and spend the day with her. That's what he'd prefer to do. This warrior business could wait.

As the day passed on, he felt distracted and guilty at a time that called for discipline and devotion. He felt he was the child they'd accused him of being, and could not help wondering if he was setting himself up for an abysmal failure. He knew he could not overcome shame easily. Tomorrow he must go with his grandfather and see the shaman Three Bears. That was the only given. The rest was chance.

But he loved that girl and always had. He thought now he should've told her what this was all about. What he was doing, he was doing for her.

Chapter Three

Remy sat in a comfortable spot in a pile of hay, a borrowed book, Mrs. Mary Rowlandson's captivity narrative, open between his legs. Its worn pages, soft like cloth, were illuminated by a shaft of light that pierced the gap between two warped pine boards of the old barn. Mrs. Rowlandson, a New England Puritan and a minister's daughter, had been captured by Metacomet's Wampanoag warriors in what was known as King Phillip's War. It was a story of trials and tribulations of the old frontier, the magnificence and ferocity of savages, the endurance of the human spirit, the retribution of a vengeful God who purified by fire and pain. What a life that woman had lived! Remy could not flip the thick pages fast enough.

The doors burst open, startling him. The book slipped from his hands open onto the hay.

"There you are, you French half-breed bastard!" The words slapped Remy's ear like a callused hand. "I sent you back to shoe the mule and here I find you! We're out in the fields, waitin'!"

"It was late, Uncle," he offered in explanation. He was terrified. Mrs. Rowlandson's problems were nothing compared to what he faced. "The mule'll be rested and shoed for tomorrow's work," he said, a prayer disguised as a promise.

"Don't toy with me, boy!" his uncle snapped. "We work till dark in the plantin' season. That's a lesson you won't soon forget."

His uncle ripped a harness from the barn wall, wrapped the bit around his hand, then swung the loose leather straps in a circular motion above his head. When the orbit was fixed, he brought the straps down hard against Remy's back.

Remy screamed at the instant burning pain and rolled violently to his side to avoid the next blow. The handle of an old pitchfork, propped up against the wall, fell across Remy's chest. He picked it up, hoping he could hold his uncle at bay. When he advanced, Remy lunged. The points of its rusted prongs buried in his uncle's thigh and then it was his turn to scream. His eyes flashed as red as the blood that gushed from the wound.

"I'll beat you within an inch of your life, boy!" Remy's eyes popped opened, his jaw dropped. He hadn't meant to hurt his uncle. He let the pitchfork slip from his sweating hands. He crawled away until his back came against the barn wall, his uncle closing step by step. Remy braced for the worst.

Only his aunt could save him now and Remy prayed she'd come. Certainly she must've heard the screams.

His uncle's arm was raised when beneath his elbow Remy saw a flash of bright cloth, and then the whites of Helen's startled eyes. She ran between Remy and his uncle, her back to him.

"William! No!" she shouted, thrusting one hand against her husband's chest. "For God's sake, let 'im be!"

His eyes never left Remy's. "Step out of my way, Helen! I've had it with this boy." He pointed to his wound. "Look here what he's done to me! It'll be septic by mornin'. You wait and see."

"What did you expect him to do! You've scared 'im to death! Put the bit down, William, and go back to the fields." Her husband stood before her, the strap clenched in his hand. "Put it down!" she repeated; this time she reached for his arm.

"Fine," he barked, but he jerked away and held the straps fast in his hand. "But you get 'im sorted out as long as he stays under my roof. I'll be damned if he don't work like the rest of us."

"Go, William. I won't have you here. I'll tend to your leg this evenin' after you cool down. You've done enough here."

"We'll see about that," he smirked. "He's as sorry as his father ever was. As far as I'm concerned, his crazy mother let one too many rats out of the trap. He ain't good for nuthin'!"

"Don't you talk like that, William! Don't you ever let me hear you say somethin' like that again! He's just a boy,

for God's sake! Go back to the field. Our sons are waitin'
for you. Remy'll be ready for work in the mornin'."

"He better be," he sneered.

"He will. Now go."

William pitched the bit at Remy's feet and stormed out
of the barn. Once he was out in the waning sun, he turned
back, pointing with a single finger, and stared at Remy.
"There's more where that came from, boy. If you eat, you
work. You quit when I tell ya, and not before!"

"Enough!" his aunt cried. William left. Helen Marie
knelt at Remy's side.

"Are ya hurt, Remy?" He was, but he could not bring
himself to answer her. His back stung so that he could not
speak. His shirt was cut open. He felt warm blood on swelling, numb skin. He couldn't keep from crying, and that
shamed him even more.

His aunt wiped the tears from his face. "What happened
this time?" she asked quietly. Her voice soothed him as his
mother's once had.

"One of the mules threw a shoe," he said, struggling. His
throat was so dry, it burned when he swallowed. "They
sent me here to fix it. I was 'posed to take it back, but I
figured it was too late."

She smiled at him. "Not that late, Remy."

He looked out the barn door. "I hate him," he said.

She held her finger to his trembling lips. "Ssshhh. Don't
talk like that, son. William's a good man and a good farmer.
You can learn much from him."

He squinted and bit his lip. His gut burned. "He only
teaches me one thing."

"Some of that's your fault, Remy. A farmer's life's not
easy, especially this time of year. All of our boys work just
as hard as William. He asks only the same from you."

"They're older."

"Maybe so. But when they were your age, they worked
just as hard as he's askin' you to now. Elijah's but two
years older than you, and he works all day. I'll see to it
that William does you no harm, but you must not provoke
him. And you must do as you're told if'n we're to have
peace."

Remy felt his chin drop to his chest. "I'll do it for you,

Aunt Helen," he told her. "But I hate that man, and I hate it here. As soon as I'm able, I'll move out to my own place." The beating reminded him of how much he wanted to be out from under his uncle's thumb. His parents' farm was the only way he saw to do it. It was his promised land.

"Good," she said. "Then you have a goal for yourself, a dream. You know I'll help you all I can, but ya gotta help me, too. I'm happy to have you here, but you kin see that it ain't easy for us. We had a bad crop last year. There's not much money. Your parents left you nuthin' but the farm, an' your daddy never tended it like he should. That don't matter much to me. I already think of you as my own. But, we've all got to do our share. I'll look to you to do yours. Agreed?"

He nodded slowly. She was right and he knew it. He understand that life meant work; he just should've realized before now that his uncle was a little more serious about it than his father had been. William never played with him like his father used to, and now he lived under William's roof. If nothing else he understood how powerless he was. He was an orphan, at the mercy of others.

"Good," she said with encouragement. "Now let's get some cool butter on your back. Then you kin help me get our supper ready. Get your book and let's go."

Remy stood and dusted himself off. His shirt stuck to his back. Blood was the adhesive. His aunt groaned at the sight of it, lifted his shirt clear, and wiped away the blood with the hem of her skirt.

"What's that you're reading, Remy?" she asked as she worked.

"An account of the frontier," he told her. The only thing available in their house was a dog-eared copy of the King James. It was not enough, not for him. It was she who cared enough to borrow books for him. This last she'd gotten herself from Reverend Thatcher. He picked it up and handed it to her. She thumbed through its pages briefly, and then handed it back.

"Such nonsense, Remy," she said. "I didn't know that was in this last bunch. You should read about history and politics. Study mathematics and agriculture."

"Maybe so," he admitted. But he loved the romance and

adventure of a pioneer caught up in the Indian Wars. It allowed him to think about something—something magnificent—beyond the fences of that lonely, grubby farm.

"Come." She extended her hand and Remy took it. When he rose, a single page fell from the book. Elizabeth picked it up and examined it. "What's this?"

"A map of the Spanish frontier. It was my pa's. He always kept it with 'im, and now I always keep it with me. I got it and the Gump rifle and nuthin' else. He always wanted to explore the West. I always wanted to go with 'im. He would've let me go this fall if she hadn't kilt 'im."

He saw the sadness sweep his aunt's face. "I'm sorry, Remy," she offered, and he knew she meant it. "So very sorry. I know it hurts. I hurt too. I loved my sister very much."

The sting of his back only made him think of the deeper pain. It never left him. Try as he might, he couldn't hold back his tears. Who, he wondered, could explain what had happened?

"Why'd she do it?"

His aunt pulled him to her chest and kissed his head. "I don't know, Remy," she said. Her voice soothed him as no salve ever could. "She was sick at heart, I figure. She didn't see no other way out. It made her crazy. But I know she didn't do it to hurt you."

"Well, she did," he spat. "I hate her as much as I do my uncle."

"Ssshhh. Don't talk like that, Remy. It's all right to be angry about what happened, to be afraid. Lord knows it was an awful thing for a boy to see. But hatred can ruin your life same as it did your folks'. You gotta understand that your mama was sick, Remy. I knew her real good. She weren't like that."

"It don't matter now," he said, and his gaze fell on the yellowed map she still held in her hand. Some day he'd cut his own path through the wild places scratched out on that paper. Some day he'd be free.

When Helen noticed his attention had turned to the map, she folded it and stuck it back in the closed book. "Best to think about the farm for the time bein', son. It'll save you a world of trouble."

He craned his neck to look at his back. The sting was gone, but he could feel the blood running to his waist. "I'm sorry, Aunt Helen."

"For what?"

He nodded toward the fields. "The trouble with my uncle."

"I know you are."

"I didn't mean to make 'im mad. I damn sure didn't mean to hurt 'im."

"He's all right," she said, "and don't use language like that aroun' my house. Will never meant to hurt you, either, Remy. That's just his way. Nobody ever gave 'im nuthin'. His methods are hard, but he's got your best interest at heart. He wants to make a man of ya the only way he knows how." She wiped the fresh blood from his back. "These'll soon heal," she said, "and we'll just go on. I'm proud of you, son. Not many could bounce back like you have. Not after what you saw. You've got a great spirit and a good mind. You'll make a fine and handsome man some day."

"That's if Uncle Will lets me live."

She laughed. "Where do you get such notions?"

"Where d'ya think?"

"I wonder 'bout you," she said, her eyes narrowing. "This farm may be a little small for you after all."

"Don't worry. There's another one waiting for me across the hollow. That first, and then maybe I'll push on west to trap in the winter like my father did."

"That's good, Remy. Your farm is rich, the top-soil deep and black. Land's all ya need to have a good life. And I don't wanna hear nuthin' 'bout this frontier business. That's your father's blood talkin'. You mustn't listen. I don't have to tell you that life's hard, Remy. It's like a storm. It washed your mother and father away from you. Don't let it happen again, do you hear? You go and work that land, let your roots dig deep into that soil and hold tight. There ain't no better way."

Remy nodded intently. There was nowhere else to turn for advice, and he wouldn't treat his aunt's cheaply. She reached out and drew his neck to her shoulder. There was peace and comfort in her embrace.

Together they walked out from the darkness of the barn. Her auburn hair glistened, like fresh honey, in the late afternoon glow. It was identical to his mother's, save the streaks of gray. Helen was younger than his mother, her body stronger, her complexion cleaner. At daylight, she'd throw those shutters open and sing those same sad songs. She was exactly what his mother had once been before the joy left her life, and Remy knew he could cling to Helen, do as his uncle bid, and know contentment in a mother's warmth again.

Chapter Four

Cold Knife had instructed him to stand still but proud before the shaman. This strange old man had a scar from his forehead to the center of his left cheek. His left eye was covered by a white, opaque film. His right was bugged out, as if to compensate. Grotesquely gaping, Three Bears went over every inch of Little Hand's body, as one did with a horse trade.

"How old's the boy?" he finally asked.

"This coming winter will make sixteen," Cold Knife answered.

"You should've brought him to me right after his hair came and his voice cracked." The medicine man turned from Little Hand and looked back at his grandfather. "He's late, in my opinion."

Little Hand just about swallowed his tongue. His grandfather crossed his arms across his chest. "My own son did not go out with the war parties until eighteen winters," Cold Knife said. "I think it's for the best. We don't get in so much of a hurry among our clan."

"You don't get much in the way of warriors either," the medicine man pronounced. "You spoil the child. He'll be the weaker for it."

Little Hand was about to tell this old fool to stick his bare ass on an ant mound when he felt his grandfather's thump in the back of his head. How well his grandfather knew his rebellious mind.

"He's spoiled, maybe, Three Bears," Cold Knife admitted. "Complain to his mother about that. He spends too much time with her, and what should a grandfather do about that? But he's not weak. He's a fine boy. I'm quite proud of his progress. He's an excellent bow-man and hunter. He knows the woods and the prairies, and no man rides like him. Help the boy find his medicine and he'll be fine."

The medicine man gawked at his dingy fingernails. "Ah, that's a big job," he said casually. "I'm quite busy these days. There's a fever in camp that puzzles me. Your problem comes at a bad time."

Cold Knife knew what to say next. "I'll pay you well," he offered. Three Bear's attention returned, and he grasped Little Hand by his jaw and pulled him closer. Little Hand thought that the old man's protruding eye looked right through him. His breath smelled awful. "Of course, I've got better things to do, but I like this boy well enough. He's got a special light to his eyes. I can help. Let's get started."

"First, let's fix the fee," his grandfather said cautiously. Little Hand remembered that his grandfather had warned that Three Bears was expensive. He also knew his grandfather was a skilled negotiator.

"Well," Three Bears began, "I normally ask for ten horses of my choosing for something like this. But you're in a hurry. Let's make it fifteen and be done with the squabbling. This boy's future's at stake. I can see the nervousness in his eyes. He has obvious misgivings." The medicine man reached for Little Hand's wrist, raising his arm. "See how his hands tremble? He fears." He let Little Hand's arm drop. "It'll take something a little special to find his animal spirit. That's hard work for an old man."

"I'll pay you twelve, and a full parfleche bag of freshly smoked antelope meat. The boy brought it to camp just last night."

"You're a lucky man, Cold Knife. You've caught me short of meat, and my stomach growls for freshly smoked antelope. The flesh is of good quality, properly prepared, I trust?"

"The best," Little Hand promised. "I did it myself."

"Then, that'll do, I suppose. Twelve horses of my choice

and a full parfleche bag." Cold Knife looked at Little Hand
and then nodded. "Let's get started," Three Bears said. "I
need a moment to myself."

Three Bears closed his eyes while Little Hand looked on
curiously. Then the medicine man began to chant quietly,
circling the boy in small, chopped steps. He produced a
talisman, a rattle, with the scalp of a Tonkawa brave dangling from it. This went on for some time, mesmerizing
Little Hand, until the old man suddenly stopped, breathed
deeply, and then spoke.

"This is how it must be," Three Bears told him. Little
Hand needed these things: a buffalo robe, a bone pipe,
tobacco and a flint and kindling for making fire. He should
take a knife, but not one of Spanish steel. It should be flint,
like the Nemenuh of old, before the time of the God Dog,
when they skulked in the north near the great mountains.
They were Shoshone once, Three Bears said. They share
their tongue, and their blood.

"Hear me, boy," Three Bears said, rocking back and
forth, his good eye closed. "Listen well." He said that Little
Hand's ancestors had once lived at the foot of the great
mountains far to the north, along the banks of the Snake
River, since the beginning of their time. The French came
and gave guns to their enemies, the Cheyenne, the Crows
and the Lakota, but withheld them from the People. They'd
lost many in the wars that followed. In search of peace,
they came to this place, where the God Dog was waiting
for them and the river of buffalo never ended. It was a
land of plenty and they'd won it by war.

He said then that Little Hand was the son of the Penateka band of the Nemenuh, the Honey-Eaters, the Wasps,
the Principal People. The Spanish, their enemies, called
them Comanche. They were allied to the Kiowa, the Wichi-
tas and the Kiowa-Apaches. They were the mortal enemies
of the Tonkawa, the Lipan Apaches, the Karankawa and
the Caddo. The People would depend upon him, as a warrior, to defend them and provide for their needs. There
was but one way for the Nemenuh man, and that was the
path of a warrior. All of this Little Hand understood. He'd
heard it since the time he could remember.

"Everything," Three Bears told him, "that you've been

taught was to prepare you for this day. To become a warrior and walk the straight path, you must find your animal spirit. If, after several attempts, you fail, you should not return, for you'll never be a warrior, and you'll have no place of respect among the people. If you do find it, your life will be changed forever. You'll take your place at the war councils and be quiet; for there are many more brave and experienced than you. You listen to the wisdom of your elders and follow their instructions." Here he paused. "Oh, and stop closing the smoke flap on the old men's lodge. We've got no time for such foolishness." He straightened. "Now, do you understand everything, boy?"

"Yes," Little Hand said, not really certain that he did.

"Good. You take the things I told you to take and nothing else. Leave camp alone. Speak to no one. Do not touch cookware or anything that contains grease. Wear only a breechcloth and moccasins, and head west for the buttes. My vision tells me to send you to the grave of Wolf Eyes, my great uncle and war chief of the Wasps. Do you know the place?"

He'd hunted there often. "I know it well," Little Hand said.

"That's too far," Cold Knife interjected. "He'll never make it back when he's weak from hunger."

Little Hand saw that strange eye turn from him to his grandfather. "And you say it was his mother who spoiled the boy?" Cold Knife bowed his head in deference and Three Bears continued, "No place's too far for this, and nothing's more important." Then he turned back to the boy. "You must go there, Little Hand. Wolf Eyes had great medicine, and it's my wish that he'll share it with you. Agreed?"

He nodded, fascinated. He wanted it to happen. He was ready.

"Stop exactly four times along the way, no more, no less. Each time you stop, you should smoke your pipe, pray and then continue. If you know the grave of Wolf Eyes, then you know it's located on the south slope near the top of the tallest butte. From there, you could look both east and west. At the break of day you should face the rising sun in order to receive the benefit of its strength. Drink no water, eat no food. Follow the position of the sun each day. When darkness falls, cover yourself from head to toe in the buffalo robe, again facing east. In this way you must wait four days and nights. Do not despair if no vision comes. We can try it again next month if necessary. It may take as long as a year for it to happen, but you mustn't give up. Have faith in yourself. If your heart is good, it'll come in time."

"What am I waiting for?" Little Hand asked.

"For whatever comes, boy," answered Three Bears. "For whatever comes."

Cold Knife managed a nervous smile as he patted him on the back. Little Hand could see that he was gravely concerned. "Go now," he said softly. "It's a long way. Be careful. If you don't return after five days, I'll come and look for you myself." Little Hand took a great deal of comfort from that.

"Remember well what I've told you, Little Hand," Three Bears said. Then Little Hand understood that his counseling was at an end, nodded, and walked away.

Little Hand arrived at the butte at sunset that same afternoon. The day had grown warm, and he was thirsty, but he was forbidden to drink. He did as he was instructed to do, and despite his anxiety, he was worn out and slept well. At first light, he arose and faced to the east. Nothing happened. When darkness fell on the second day, the wind shifted to the north. He shivered to keep himself warm, sleeping little. The third day was identical to the second, with the night air also very cold. Nothing.

The sun came up scowling like an angry old woman on the fourth day. Little Hand could no longer judge distance. The far hills seemed to sway in the breeze. Colors were brighter all around him; there was no longer a clear distinction between earth and sky. His stomach shrank against his ribs. There was a bitter taste in his mouth.

About the time that a sense of defeat had set in, Little

Hand heard the sound of approaching footsteps. He lay motionless, afraid, until at last he saw a coyote. He reached for his knife to protect himself. But the animal stood calmly, staring at him from a safe distance. Whether the beast actually spoke to him, Little Hand could not say. It never moved its mouth like a human being. But it was very clear to Little Hand that they understood one another. Despite his fatigue and hunger, Little Hand was both startled and fascinated by the sudden magic of his life.

"Ah, it's one of the Nemenuh," the coyote said, as if confident of his determination. "Which band?"

"Penateka," Little Hand answered, astonished.

The coyote looked across the expanse beneath them and then back at Little Hand. "Did you see a jackrabbit pass by here, my friend?"

Little Hand shook his head.

"Are you certain?"

"I've been in this miserable place for three days. I've seen nothing."

"Well, that confuses me, brother. I can smell his scent on the ground. I thought surely that I'd find him near here. If he's not just been here, he comes by often. I can tell you that much."

"I couldn't say," Little Hand said, watching.

"More than likely he's hiding under a bush around here somewhere. Your human smell overcomes that of his and buys him a little more time. I'll move upwind and see what I can turn up. Good day to you."

"Wait, brother," Little Hand called. As strange as it was, it wasn't much in the way of guidance. What did hunting jackrabbits have to do with his purpose? There must be more, he thought, and he felt the time had come to make inquiries. "Are you my animal spirit?"

"Me?" the coyote said as if entertained by his question. "No. I'm on the hunt, like I told you." But then he paused, and those sharp predator's eyes fixed on his. "But I know that it's coming."

Little Hand's hunger made him desperate. "What will it be?"

"That's none of my business. Out here we keep to ourselves. I only know that it comes."

"When?" he demanded.

"Soon, brother hunter. Give it time." And as Little Hand watched, the animal rushed off down the slope and out of his sight. He nestled in against the rock face, and soon fell asleep.

His eyes popped open at the sound of great beating wings. Little Hand saw that a red-tailed hawk had landed on the limbs of a scrub cedar. He was elated at his good fortune. Only the eagle had more power. Its black and beady eyes looked directly at him.

"What brings you to the grave of Wolf Eyes, young Nemenuh?" it asked.

"I've been waiting for you," he answered. He heard his voice crack from thirst.

"I've got nothing to do with you," the bird said. The hawk's head swiveled, its magnificent neck feathers wrinkled against those of its upper breast. "It's a little windy for me today. I've come here to rest. When the sun sets and the breeze grows still, I'll be able to find a fat mouse down there on the prairie. I'll be the better for it. It's been a lean couple of days for me."

"You're not my animal spirit?" Little Hand asked, confused.

"Not at all," the hawk answered as if bored. "I'm a fellow hunter, who, like you, is hungry."

"I've had enough," Little Hand said. "I'm going home."

The hawk blinked its great eyes. "That, brother, would be a grave mistake. You must stay a little while longer. It comes for you. I hear it whispered on the wind."

"I'm dying."

"Maybe so, but I don't weep for the Nemenuh. They are strong and life is hard. There's no time for pity out here. Whether you live or die, brother, is entirely up to you. I've got my own problems to attend to." Little Hand watched as the bird looked out over the vacant expanse below. "Do you see there?" it asked.

"I see nothing."

"There are two pack rats, both very fat for this time of year. I'll swoop down on them from the east where they'll not see my approaching shadow. One of those will surely die so that I may live. Watch me, brother, and learn. Life is hard. And for you, it gets harder. Watch what I do and learn something about hunting. I've got to go, as an opportunity presents itself, but you must wait."

The hawk spread its wings to test the wind, and then turned its head to face him once more. "Your guardian spirit knows you're waiting in this place. It comes for you. Patience, little brother. All is well." And the great bird flew from its perch.

Night soon fell. Little Hand could no longer sleep, he ached so from hunger. Even if he left now, he did not know if he possessed the strength to return to the river. His grandfather had been right. He was too young to undertake this. He was certainly about to fail; maybe he already had. Time passed slowly and nothing else came.

He wondered what had gone wrong. Though the experience had been strange and wondrous, none of it was intended for him. The animal spirits had all passed him by. Had even the cowardly turkey offered himself to him, he would have accepted gladly.

He had succumbed to his misery when he heard the distinct sound of human footsteps on the ground nearby. He sat up, startled, and wiped the dust from his eyes. He wrapped the buffalo robe tightly around his shoulders to kill the chill. He feared that their enemies, the Lipan Apaches, had tracked him down. Too weak to run, he sheltered himself against the little bluff to await his fate.

But what emerged instead out of the blankness was the form of a Nemenuh warrior in full regalia. As Little Hand watched, the large frame swept past him. Little Hand's entire body trembled; his knees knocked. Then the figure paused and turned to him.

"Don't be afraid, boy," the warrior said. His voice was deep, smooth, and soothing. "I'm here for you."

Little Hand struggled to focus on the image, rubbing his eyes. First talking animals and now this. "Pull out your tobacco," the image said. "Let's smoke together." He moved forward. "May I sit?"

"You're welcome to what little I have," Little Hand said. He didn't know whether to offer his hand or run like a jackrabbit for the nearest bush. He stuck out his palm with the tobacco nervously bunched in its center and the warrior took it from him. The warrior's fingertips felt cold.

"You've much more than you know," the man said calmly. He took an ember from the fire and lit his pipe. Little Hand could see him more clearly now in the orange glow of light. The man was clearly a war chief, but the skin of his face was pale, weathered and drawn. A shadow covered his eyes and nose, and Little Hand could see only his mouth move as he spoke. There was a hole in his shirt. Blood stained the hide all around it. There was dried blood on the corners of the warrior's mouth. Little Hand shuddered from the sight. He saw the man exhale the smoke and then study him in silence.

"Why do you tremble, boy?" he asked. "You were sent to Wolf Eyes' grave to wait for him. Why are you surprised to see Wolf Eyes?"

"I'm afraid of ghosts," he stammered.

"I've got no time to play with you, boy. I've traveled far so that we could visit. I've come for you. You've made it four nights in this place. Tomorrow you can go home, if you can. I'll tell you what you need to know. But you must not fear me. I died in battle against the Lipans, in my prime. I led the bravest of lives; the people still sing my name. I'm neither ashamed of my appearance, nor should you fear it. You, my friend, will see many more dead before your time is through. Get used to it."

Little Hand nodded his head, not really certain if he could.

"Now," the warrior said, crossing his legs, "who are you?"

"I'm Little Hand," he muttered, "son of Big Hand, grandson of Cold Knife."

"Ah, yes. I knew Cold Knife well. A very good man. Does he still live?"

Again he nodded.

"I'm glad to hear it," he said as he offered the pipe. "The prayers of Three Bears told me of your troubles. I think I can help. First, I bring gifts." He gave Little Hand a handful of sweet-grass, which he explained was for his protection; a bird's claw, which inspired skill and courage; two smooth stones from the foot of a glacier, which offered health and a long life, for stones never wear out; and the ball from a buffalo's stomach, which endowed strength and invincibility in battle to its possessor. "Keep them all together in this medicine bag," the ghost said, "and it should be with you always as long as you live—and you, my friend, will live a long time."

Wolf Eyes reached for the pipe and put it to his bloodied lips. The wind whisked the smoke from him in straight gray lines. "We'll talk awhile this evening," he said, "and then you must rest. Tomorrow, your world changes."

Little Hand's anxiety quickly gave way to anticipation. At last he would know exactly what to expect, what he was up against. "What can you tell me about tomorrow?" he asked.

"Nothing," Wolf Eyes answered instantly.

"Nothing?" He was confused. Why nothing? How could things be more of a mystery than they already were? "How about a hint or two?"

Wolf Eyes laughed. "You're still such a child. Tomorrow that'll change. I'm your companion, counselor, and friend. I'm happy to tell you what I can. But tomorrow is between you, your animal spirit, and whatever the Great One wills. My purpose is to prepare you."

Little Hand watched him in silence. For the first time, he saw his eyes. They were dark and shining, warm and clear. "I can tell you this," Wolf Eyes said. "I'm told that our way of life is at risk. Tomorrow I think you'll understand the nature of the threat."

Little Hand watched as Wolf Eyes lifted his gaze to the stars. The night breeze swept his hair. Then he looked over the hills and finally turned back to Little Hand. "We belong in this place," he told him. "Our mother, the earth, welcomes us and feeds us and keeps us warm. These hills are her bosom. It's the home we won for you. Our struggle now becomes yours."

Little Hand was puzzled as he listened to what Wolf Eyes said. The ghost continued.

"Your time is coming, Little Hand. Know that you're not alone. Your ancestors are watching. Our proud blood runs in your young veins, the strength of generations moves with each twitch of your muscles. You belong to the thread of our nation, into which we are all woven, whether living, dead, or waiting to be born. All of our hopes and dreams breathe within you, and we're proud of what we see. You're cherished and loved. Be proud to walk the earth as a Nemenuh."

He drew again on the pipe and then handed it to Little Hand. "In your hands lies the fate of all Human Beings. Tonight you can wonder. But tomorrow you'll understand. I envy you for this opportunity because in the end it will make you great. Yet I pity you for the hardships you must endure." He reached into his medicine bag and then offered his open palm to Little Hand. Little Hand saw a morsel that he couldn't identify. It appeared to be a small, shiny stone. "Here. Take this. Put it into your mouth and swallow it."

Little Hand shook his head. "I can't eat until I've received my animal spirit."

Wolf Eyes explained that what he was giving him was not food, but something to restore his energy. It would not betray his destiny, it would ensure it. He said that when the sun rose in the morning, Little Hand would surely meet his animal spirit and then proceed on the beast's terms. After that, Wolf Eyes said, his destiny would become clear.

The ghost said that Little Hand would come to be known by two very different names; one by those that loved him, the other by those who would seek his life. Wolf Eyes then warned him not to speak of his visions or the visitation to anyone because they would never understand. Their relationship was a private affair. The others would learn of Little Hand's power by his deeds and by his example, because there were no better teachers.

Wolf Eyes said that he, as a warrior spirit, once a great war chief, came to no man who was undeserving. But he was now at Little Hand's beck and call for life, because Little Hand was the savior of their people. No man among the living Nemenuh was more important than Little Hand. His was a greater purpose, one of blood, suffering, and struggle, but also one of honor, power, and joy. Wolf Eyes said he would help him manage the responsibility. "Ask for me when you are troubled," he told him, "and I will come."

A great sense of pride overcame Little Hand. Images of

his youth flashed across his excited brain. He could now see the natural progression of his past and that he now sat at the threshold of his future. Something great was going to happen to him. He could feel it.

"I'll do the best I can," Little Hand promised. "I give you my blood oath. I offer the People my life."

"That's all we ask," Wolf Eyes said, and he reached to fill Little Hand's pipe. "The bargain is accepted. Honor it."

When the pipe was lit, they sat facing each other and talked well into the night. Wolf Eyes spoke of the tribe's history, the power of their religion, the benevolence of the Great Spirit and his plan, the importance of family and the tribal traditions. Little Hand had many questions. Wolf Eyes answered them all.

Little Hand's fear was gone. He felt confident, worthy, assured. They talked until the crack of crimson light appeared in the east, and Wolf Eyes told him that it was time for him to go.

"Rest what little you can, Little Hand. Today your battle begins. When the sun rises go to the spring below and bathe. Let cold water cool hot blood." Wolf Eyes drew on the pipe one last time, exhaled, and then embraced him chest to chest. "It comes for you," he whispered in his ear. "Do not be afraid."

Little Hand turned away to check the coming of day. When he looked back, Wolf Eyes was gone. All he heard was the sound of the night wind rushing between the buttes and the distant howl of a lone coyote.

Three days later, Little Hand stumbled to the banks of the river where he immediately collapsed due to exhaustion and the loss of blood. He had nothing left from his animal spirit, save its hide and its claw mark on his chest. Relatives carried him semiconscious to his father's lodge. He asked them to send for Cold Knife, who promptly arrived, wringing his hands, to check on his grandson and then called for Three Bears to come and attend to him. The medicine man soon came and examined his body as Little Hand watched on.

"The wounds are deep," he heard him say, "but the bleeding has stopped." Three Bears called to Little Hand's mother. "Woman, bring your son some water and a little soup." Then he reached into his bag and pulled out some pulverized mad-stone, the leg-bone of the Great Cannibal Owl, a being that no longer walked the earth. The Nemenuh believed the powder had marvelous healing potential.

Little Hand watched as Three Bears sprinkled it over the gashes, four deep tears in his chest, and then reached for a piece of prickly pear cactus. Three Bears carefully burned off the spines with the coals of the cook fire, sliced it in halves with his knife, and laid it flat against his wounds. He wrapped his chest with deer hide which he fastened with sinew thread, and then waved the others out of the lodge.

Little Hand felt no pain, and said nothing. His mind was full of the images of the last few days—the mystery, the promises, the oaths, the challenge, and lastly his animal spirit's dying portent. The violence of their encounter had at first confused him. He knew of no other warrior whose animal spirit had come for his blood. He saw right away that it was his life or the beast's, and he'd reacted accordingly.

But now that he'd had time to reflect, the symbolism of their struggle was not lost on him. Little Hand was marked for war, the claw marks cut deeply into his chest a reminder for life. He resolved to heal himself and prepare.

"Of course he needs rest," he heard Three Bears say. "Give him water, as much as he'll take. In due time, he'll be fine."

"Do you think he had his vision, Three Bears?" asked his grandfather.

"What do you think?" Three Bears scoffed. "He's so full of medicine that I could barely touch him. His power is great! By all rights, you ought to give me a couple more horses. I did an excellent job for you, and very cheaply at that."

"Your payment was satisfactory to my mind, Three Bears. The boy'll bring you a horse from his first raid if he remains grateful for your work."

"I'll be around to see him again tomorrow, to change the dressing on his wounds. Send for me if he takes a turn for the worse, which I think is unlikely. You were right about that boy. He's very strong. He'll make a fine warrior. Pray to my great uncle, Wolf Eyes, and thank him for his interest in your relative."

"Gladly." A young boy ran up and gave Cold Knife the hide Little Hand had carried back to camp.

"He dropped it where he fell," the boy explained. Little Hand watched silently as Cold Knife unwrapped it while Three Bears looked on.

"What is it?" Cold Knife asked. He was clearly perplexed.

Three Bears studied it a moment before Little Hand saw the light come to his face. "Why it's a bear!" Three Bears shouted. "A white bear, the greatest of animal spirits! Who would've known it would be given to such a silly boy? Go and bring me four more horses, you old fool! What a bargain I've given you."

Cold Knife looked curiously at Little Hand, who managed to smile back. Little Hand saw the worry leave the old man's face, replaced by a beaming pride. He reached for his hand to say thank you, and the old man took it.

"I'll have the boy bring them to your lodge when he's up and around," he said. "It's worth it."

"That's no boy," Three Bears said. "That's Kills White Bear, a Penateka warrior. Little Hand is no more."

Cold Knife nodded. He put his free hand to Kills White Bear's brow. It was not hot. The old man re-wrapped the bear hide and placed it next to Kills White Bear's body.

"I take it that it's done, then?" his grandfather asked him.

Kills White Bear nodded. Yes, it was done, he thought, better than you could ever know. You'll be proud of me. And I'll always be grateful to you. There would never be another time when he realized how much he loved that old man.

"I'm happy for you," Cold Knife said. "What you've done is great."

Now there was other business to attend to. Kills White Bear could now see clearly how things must progress. "Do me a small favor, Cold Knife," he mumbled.

"Name it."

"I know that I should send a good friend to do this for me, but you and I've always been close. It's a delicate thing, but I think you can do it."

"Whatever it is can be done."

"Go to the lodge of Running Stream. Ask what he might take for his oldest daughter. She'll welcome your efforts. We've already talked of this."

Cold Knife scoffed. "A warrior one day, a husband the next?"

"I can't explain it to you right now. Will you do this thing for me?"

"It would be best to wait until your twenty-fifth winter or so before you think about marrying. There's much to do. You have no property of your own, nothing to trade for her."

"Find out what it'll take, and I'll soon get it. Others want Morning Song. She wants me." He had no idea how soon the trouble would begin. All he knew was that change was coming, and he had to take what he wanted while he could. He also knew he could not explain it to anyone else, not even Cold Knife. "Please," he said. "There's no time to wait."

"Talk to your father and mother of this plan, my son. Seek their advice."

"I know what I'm doing," he said. "Please do as I ask."

"All right, all right. I'll let you know tomorrow."

Before Cold Knife could depart, Kills White Bear's sister returned with water. She reached for the bear hide to move it out of the way, but Kills White Bear snatched her arm, causing her to drop the gourd.

"Never . . . ever . . . touch this!" he warned her angrily. He'd never spoken to her like that, but then he'd never owned something so important that was so easily defiled. "Do you hear me? Never!"

"Fine," she said. "Get your own water." Then she turned to her grandfather. "The boy has a vision and he thinks he's a chief."

When Kills White Bear awoke he had the sense that someone breathed the air of his father's lodge with him. He
opened his eyes, wiped the sleep away, and stretched his
aching limbs. His chest felt hot. There was the sense of
slight pressure. He made out the form of a man sitting next
to him. He blinked his eyes and squinted to focus. Only
then did he recognize the bald head of Maguara, the
Spirit Talker.

He was the *Par-riah-boh*, civil chief of Penateka, and
though Kills White Bear had watched him from a distance
since he was a boy, they'd never once spoken. Cold Knife
had told him that Maguara was a mystic warrior, a shaman,
whose wisdom enabled him to rise and to speak for all.
There was not a man in the nation who looked and acted
as strangely as Maguara, and there was no one Kills White
Bear respected more. Every move he made, each word he
spoke, reflected his stature among the people Kills White
Bear knew he loved. To see Maguara was to see the two
hands of power and benevolence clasped together in
prayer, one man who cared for thousands.

Now Maguara sat with his legs crossed before him, his
hand resting on the wounds of his chest, patiently waiting.
The honor of it stunned him.

Maguara smiled at him when he saw that he'd awakened.
He reached for the cup and handed it to him. Kills White
Bear felt the coolness of the water as it slipped down his
burning throat. Out of respect he attempted to rise regardless of the pain but Maguara gently pressed him down.

"It's all right, young warrior," the chief told him. "You
need your rest." He moved the cup away. "People are talking about you, Kills White Bear." His hand stroked the fur
of the white hide. "When I heard, I decided to come and
see for myself. As I touched you, your spirit shared your
vision with me." He closed his eyes. "I saw what you saw.

I know what you know. I heard the rumbling of the gathering storm that I always knew was coming. I've wondered for so long who would lead us through it. I've been waiting," he said quietly, "for you."

Then he reached over and put his hand across Kills White Bear's brow. "Speak of it to no one," he told him. "We'll talk again when you've healed."

There was a warming calm to his touch and with it came the deepest sleep.

Chapter Five

Remy moved quietly through the underbrush, the slick forearm of his father's Gump rifle across the crook of his elbow, its butt nestled under the pit of his arm. He knew this ridge well. His eyes scanned the canopy of oak branches overhead for a flash of fur or the twitch of a tail. All was still, save the sound of teeth grinding against the shell of last winter's acorn, but Remy could not place its source. His cousin Elijah tapped his shoulder and then pointed slowly to the west with the barrel of his shotgun.

Elijah Johnson was a big, sturdy boy, red-haired and fair-skinned, freckled from head to toe. Helen said that he looked like Remy's grandfather, a man Remy had never seen. Elijah lacked the seriousness of his two elder brothers, an asset as far as Remy was concerned. Remy admired him for his balance of good humor and sound judgment, but he also possessed two qualities that Remy valued above all others. He was as stubborn as the Scotch-Irish came and as rebellious as the best of them. Remy's older cousins stood by his uncle in their continuing feud, but Elijah had the guts to side with his mother on Remy's behalf. This hunt was a part of that. No matter how much fun they had, Remy knew his uncle would be waiting when they got back.

"There he is," his cousin said, "in the fork yonder." Remy looked, and the squirrel's auburn form emerged from the background of gray bark.

Remy cocked his rifle, shouldered it, and rested the barrel against the trunk of a sweet gum.

"What're ya doin'?" Elijah whispered.

"What does it look like I'm doin'?" he said, casting his eye down the barrel, through the dovetail sights, to the bushy tail fifty yards distant.

"He's too damn far. Let's just ease up on 'im."

"I'm fixin' to ease up on 'im right now," Remy said, and he squeezed the trigger.

The fifty caliber ball smacked dead center against the main mast of the great oak, sending pieces of limbs and bark everywhere. The squirrel scampered down the length of its largest limb, jumping to that of another tree beside it, and another still, until it disappeared into a hollow in an old snag.

Elijah just shook his head. "You don't listen to nobody, do ya?"

"I could've made that shot any day," Remy said. "The load must've been off."

"It's your head that's off, fella. You ain't ever gonna put a squirrel on the table like that. Like everythin' else you do, you're in too damn much of a hurry."

Remy apologized. This play blown, he suggested another spot, a better one. His cousin said there was no need.

"Come on," Elijah said, holding his finger to his lips. "It ain't over yet. Reload that smoke-pole an' I'll learn ya somethin'."

When Remy was ready, they descended the ridge. The forest floor was moist, dampened by a dawn rain. Their boots made no sound. Elijah hid Remy facing one side of the old snag. He took the other himself, and then he started barking, just like a male squirrel does in the spring. Although Elijah's rendition was surprisingly real, Remy didn't think for one minute that the old squirrel would be fooled. It'd heard that sharp clap of thunder on this sunny day. Accordingly, Remy lay his back against a trunk, the rifle across his lap, and waited for Elijah to give up.

Not twenty minutes later, the squirrel's head emerged from the darkness, looking for the male that had usurped his territory. He was cautious at first, then curious enough to crawl out completely and take a better look. When he crossed over out of Remy's view, Elijah shot him dead. The blast blew it back over the fork to fall at Remy's feet.

"Goddamn!" Remy exclaimed. "I never thought you'd do it."

"It's all about patience," Elijah said.

Remy reached to pick up the animal. Elijah snatched his arm. "Watch an old squirrel, now," he said, poking it with the barrel of his shotgun. "They're tougher than you think."

He showed Remy the scarred flesh of his hand between his thumb and forefinger. "I once picked one up just like that, and he bit the hell out of me." He cocked his eye toward Remy. "Ya learn to listen a little better, and it don't have to happen to you."

Remy examined the squirrel. It lay motionless, its eyes open, its head a bloody ball of matted fur. "This one's 'bout bit out," he said. "You peppered him good."

"Take 'im and let's go," Elijah said as he reloaded his shotgun. "We'll try that other place now. But no more of them wild-ass shots. We'll still hunt 'em together. They're out feedin' this mornin'. If we don't spook 'em too bad, we can work 'em good."

"Your pa's gonna wear us out," Remy said.

"Naw," Elijah told him, pointing at the dead squirrel. "We got somethin' to trade."

"All right," Remy said, and off they went.

When they came to the clearing, Remy stopped. Although the homestead was just a black spot burned into the earth, spotted with thistles, the barn and outbuildings still stood. Remy's heart leaped when he saw it. Regardless of what had happened there, it was still his.

He stepped forward, but Elijah paused. "Now why do you wanna go down there?"

"I just do," Remy told him. "And I want you to come with me."

"What fer?" Elijah asked, peering from the corners of his gray eyes. "It's still kinda spooky."

Remy waved him on. "There ain't nuthin' to be afraid of," he said, stooping to pick the beggar's lice from his britches.

"I don't see it that way. Pa's done told me what went on."

"You wanna work this place with me, don't ya?"

"Sure," Elijah said. "In about ten years. There ain't no hurry."

"Let's just go down an' see what's left," Remy said. "I wanna know what we've got to work with." He turned to go. This time, he heard Elijah follow.

Remy was supposed to spend his day sawing boards from the stubborn, knotted and weeping pine logs his uncle had hauled in with the oxen teams. They were building a bigger and better cabin, and the foundation was already laid. But the blade was dull and progress was slow, and he thought that maybe this time his uncle had asked too much of him. Those old twisty pines wouldn't give up straight planks without a fight, it seemed. Remy decided to file the blade sharp for a cleaner cut, and maybe remind his uncle that this was a job for two men. In the meantime, Elijah had come along with other ideas, and Remy had gone off with him into the woods.

Now they'd come back, guns in one hand, a half dozen bushy-tails apiece in the other. Remy saw his uncle waiting, the strap already curled in his hand.

Elijah held up his mess. "Got dinner, Pa." Remy saw that his uncle's expression never changed.

"Where you bin', boy?" William asked maliciously when they were close enough. He was addressing Remy alone.

"I went huntin'," Remy answered. "I needed the file to cut them logs."

His uncle snorted, mildly amused. He eyed the stack of uncut logs and then turned back to Remy. "So you up and decided to go off huntin', did ya?"

"We both went, Pa," Elijah told him. "It was my idea."

"You had the day off. But Remy had chores to do."

"I needed the file," Remy repeated. "That saw's too dull."

"I know what you need," his uncle sneered, "and it ain't the file. You know what you got comin', boy. Let's be done

with it, and then you'll spend your night sawin' them goddamn logs like I done told ya."

Remy recoiled at the very thought. His back had not
healed from the last time, and he knew Aunt Helen wasn't
there to save him. "Please, Uncle," he pleaded. "I'll do it."

"I know you'll do it, Remy," William answered. "I'll see
to that. But first your punishment and then the chore. It's
for your own good. You don't listen, boy."

Remy felt himself crumble beneath his uncle as he
slipped off his shirt. He stretched his arms against the side
of the barn and braced himself.

"I'll take his licks for 'im, Pa," Elijah said. "He can't
take no more."

There was a pause, a hesitation, as his uncle deliberated,
and then he cut his eyes. "Get your shirt off then, son. But
he'll get his for bein' lazy, and you'll get yours for bein' a
goddamn fool. Ya'll are two peas in a pod. You're both
gonna straighten out, or I'm gonna break ya each in half."

Elijah took his place beside Remy, all the while looking
at him. His father's shadow seemed to block out the sun.
Remy saw Elijah wince when the first lash fell across his
back. Remy shook his head to say "No, you ain't gotta do
this." But his cousin stood firm as blow followed blow until
Remy counted six. It was his turn after that.

Remy screamed when the whip, slick with Elijah's sweat
and now maybe a little bit of his blood, cut him again. He
opened his eyes, blurred with tears of pain and humiliation.
Elijah just stood there, still supported by the barn wall. Six
quick ones and it was done.

His uncle pointed to the log that lay waiting between
two pine sawhorses. "It don't need filin'," he said. "Jes' git
over there and git it done."

Remy worked the blade back in the groove he'd started
earlier and drew the handle to his chest. When he shoved
it forward again it went too easily. He looked below and
saw that Elijah had his hands on the opposite handle.

"Nice an' easy, cousin," Elijah told him. "We got all
night."

The first plank fell free, and Remy stacked it. Elijah
started the groove for the next, and they took their places
opposite one another. Remy pushed, and Elijah pulled.

"He's got to come up with somethin' that hurts a whole lot worse than that to keep us out of the woods, ain't he, Remy?" Elijah said, always cheerful, always resilient.

"Don't tempt 'im," Remy said. "He just might."

"Tell me them stories about the wild places again, Remy," Elijah said. "After we quit, I wouldn't mind takin' another look at that map, too."

Remy nodded that he'd certainly oblige him, and they worked on. By midnight they'd cut enough.

Chapter Six

During the moon when the white-tails dropped their fawns, Kills White Bear watched his grandfather lead the ten Lipan horses proudly through the camp to Running Stream's lodge, which stood at the brush's edge. The price had been fixed the moon before, and Kills White Bear joined the raiding parties until he'd met it. The cost had been a stab wound to his chest, but that was nothing to him.

His grandfather had told him how the transaction had gone. After some small talk, Cold Knife had come to the point and then had left without receiving an answer, as was proper. Morning Song had told him the rest.

Her father had had reservations, of course, all of which he expressed to her mother.

"A moon ago," her father had said, "I told that old fool that I would take ten horses for Morning Song's hand. I thought that would be the last I'd hear of that. Cold Knife tells me now that the boy's already got them. He's brought them to me and they're magnificent."

He'd looked at his daughter's face. "If I were a good father, I'd insist she marry a more established warrior, at least ten years older than that wild boy. By all rights, I should turn those horses loose back to Big Hand's herd. But I love Morning Song. I know that her heart belongs to this boy. And so with your blessing, Mother, I'll accept the horses."

Her mother had nodded in silence.

"It's done then," he'd announced, and Morning Song's

arms fell around him. "Put on your best dress, Daughter.
You're wed to Kills White Bear, for better or worse. Remind your husband that it's now his obligation to hunt for
his in-laws. Your widowed aunts alone are killing me. I
expect fresh meat at all times of the year."

And with that, Running Stream had led the horses out
to where his own horses were pastured. It was done.

Kills White Bear had been watching to see how it would
go. When he saw the destination of the horses, it struck
him that the dream of his youth had come true. He would
have the heart he'd always wanted. There was not a more
beautiful spirit in Maguara's camp. Morning Song would
live with him.

He returned to his own teepee, mounted his horse, and
rode to Running Stream's lodge to wait. In a moment
Morning Song's mother emerged with his bride. She placed
her hand in his, and he pulled her astride the horse with
him. Together, her back nestled against his chest, they rode
slowly back to his waiting lodge.

"This," he told her proudly, "belongs to us."

"I couldn't be happier," she told him, and he pulled her
down from the horse and carried her inside. Even with his
wounds and the weakness they caused she weighed nothing.

At the beginning of her ninth moon of pregnancy Morning
Song began to construct her own lodge. Not allowed to
help, Kills White Bear could only watch her do it. During
the day he hunted and tended to his weapons. Nights he
spent with her.

Under the mist of sleep he sensed something was wrong.
He sat up, rubbed his eyes, and saw immediately that his
wife had left his side. He heard the first moans and knew
the contractions must have begun. The child was coming!
In a panic he left to find the medicine woman.

Herded ahead of him, the old woman arrived carrying a
good supply of sage and hot coals. She was sleepy and

irritable, but Kills White Bear understood that old, fat women often were: All he cared about was his wife and baby, and he made this very clear when she started to complain of the hour.

"Go and heat some stones," she ordered him. He flinched at her harshly uttered words. His wife's agony troubled him. Certainly something so natural couldn't hurt so much. Something must be wrong. He reached out to soothe her brow, but the old woman shoved it away. "This is not your place," she snapped, and with that, the flap was snatched shut. Kills White Bear immediately went to Big Hand's lodge and awakened his mother.

"The child comes," he whispered to her. "Please come and care for my wife," and then he left to find smooth stones for his fire.

When he returned with the stones, he saw that Morning Song lay naked on a buffalo robe on her side, her skin flushed yet golden in the soft glow of the fire light. Both midwife and mother attended to her pain. There were two pits dug next to her; one he knew was for the afterbirth, the other for heating water and steaming. By the bed were two stakes driven into the ground, each about four feet long. The old woman massaged Morning Song's abdomen with her fingers, probing it. As many mysteries as Kills White Bear had been privy to this past year, this was the most mysterious yet. He rebuked the midwife for telling him to go away. He intended to stay.

"It is early yet, child," he heard the old woman tell his wife. "Try and walk a bit to ease the pain. When it comes more often, grasp the stakes and squat."

The midwife asked for the stones. They were so hot that Kills White Bear juggled them in his hands. The old woman asked for more stones, a ruse he was certain, but he left again to find them anyway. When he returned, he saw that she took one and laid it into the pit, where she sprinkled water over it. The other she used to massage the small of the Morning Song's back. Kills White Bear paced about the inside of the birthing lodge, poking at the fire with a green limb of mesquite.

"You should not be here," the old woman hissed. "It's bad luck."

"We make our own luck," he said and remained where he was. "See to your business and don't mind mine." He heard Cold Knife now standing quietly outside drawing on his pipe, waiting. Kills White Bear stepped out to see him and was greeted by the old man's shining eyes.

"Sit with me awhile," his grandfather told him. "It may take some time yet."

At the break of day, Kills White Bear awoke to the sound of his mother singing. Then he heard his baby's startled cry and poked his head back through the flap. He watched as the medicine woman cut the umbilical cord, coiled it in her arms, and then exited to hang it from the limb of a nearby hackberry tree, as all the old women did. The Nemenuh believed that if the cord were left undisturbed, the child was meant for a long life.

She returned to collect the afterbirth and took it to the running river, the purifier that nullifies black spirits. Kills White Bear's mother stepped past both men in silence, bathed the infant, wrapped it in soft rabbit skins that she had prepared, and then lashed it to a cradle-board. Cold Knife called to her, and she stepped out of the lodge with the baby in her arms. Kills White Bear was about to burst with unbounded pride.

"Well?" asked Cold Knife.

"It's your close friend," she said.

"I knew it all along!" Kills White Bear exclaimed, for his mother had just confirmed that it was a male child born to him. Kills White Bear let out a loud whoop in elation. His mother beseeched him to be quiet. Others were still sleeping.

The medicine woman returned from the river and addressed Cold Knife. She would not even look at Kills White Bear. "Tell your grandson that his wife is to remain in this lodge for ten days. He should not enter this place in the meantime. You make sure. The young fool won't listen to me. I'll be here to look after her. Tell him the baby is healthy, and the mother is fine."

"I've brought some soup," Kills White Bear's mother said. The midwife flicked through it with a long, knotted fingernail and saw that it had some venison mixed in.

"Not a single bite of red meat," she cautioned. "It makes

blood and may cause hemorrhage. Some broth will do for now."

While they were discussing the final arrangements, Kills White Bear reached for the baby.

"Let me hold my child," he said.

"The infant needs rest, my son," said the medicine woman.

"Nonsense. Like any Nemenuh, he's born restless. He needs to go for a ride." Kills White Bear snatched the cradle-board into his arms and mounted his horse. He led another horse behind his and walked quietly through the camp. He came to a man, a camp crier, who was just rising.

"You there," he called. "Good morning to you. This is my new friend. He would like for you to accept this horse, his father's favorite war-pony, as his gift to you, the first warrior he sees. When you wake the people this morning, tell them Kills White Bear has a son."

"Why, thank you," the man said, and Kills White Bear handed the bridle to him and continued on through the encampment. When he was just outside the camp, he sunk his heels in the horse's ribs and galloped across the plains. He climbed the familiar bluff that overlooked the San Sabá, the one on which he'd prepared for all of his successes, and rested the child across his chest. Daylight revealed the vast expanse of green and gold before them, and he could see the infant's dull, narrow eyes struggle to comprehend it.

"Do you see here, my son? All of this belongs to you. I introduce you to your friends, the rising sun and the morning breeze. You're fortunate. You're born a Human Being, a Penateka, a Wasp, the strongest of the Nemenuh blood clans. Someday you'll be the son of a great war chief. The Great Spirit blesses both you and me. For us, life is good."

The child locked his eyes, midnight black, on his father; his hand gripped his father's finger. To the east, the sun loomed large and red on the horizon. Kills White Bear felt its warmth bathe his face and turned the baby so that he would feel it also, lifting him proudly above his head.

"You are Red Sun," he told him, and then he thought the better. "If your mother agrees, of course. You'll soon learn that she has her own mind."

Not once did the infant cry.

In the course of that year everything promised to Kills White Bear consummated in the birth of his son. He had continued to raid to the south. Many young men were proud to ride with him, but his purpose was more to watch for the coming of the invaders than for the bounty he won. The albino bear's warning had been clear. Danger was out there somewhere. Nothing he saw threatened him, and he took that as a good sign.

Although the whites settling in the East best fit the description of his vision, he suspected that the threat lay elsewhere. He had heard talk that the Méxicanos were at war with their Spanish father, and the presidio forces near the *Nemenuh Socobí,* the land of the Nemenuh, were weakened as a direct result. This also was a good sign. He learned that what whites remained still clung to the river the Méxicanos called the Sabine, well out of their country. A threat by them, if any, remained distant. Where, then, he wondered, was the threat?

Wolf Eyes had told him that if a spirit made one knot for each generation in the great thread of the Nemenuh, there would be eight hundred. Kills White Bear had become a man, taken the woman he loved as his wife and fathered a beautiful child while the Nemenuh were largely at peace, unchallenged. This made eight hundred and one.

But with his marriage and the birth of his son, he chose to stay close and leave the raiding to others more hungry for prestige. He already had what he wanted. He awoke in the morning to the baby's cry, the smell of Morning Song's hair filling his nostrils and the warmth of her skin against his as she nursed the child. This was contentment in a way he'd never known it. His health was good, his heart strong, and his spirit indomitable. Everything was in place and as it should be. The boy who'd slain the white bear was now a man with a family. For him, the stakes were now higher and more personal. If war came, he'd be fighting not for honor but for those he loved. He knew there could be no greater incentive.

There was one thing more, however, that troubled him. On the fourth day after the birth of his son, he returned to the hackberry tree, and he saw that a raccoon had nibbled at the cord. There was no mistaking the tracks. Greatly disturbed by this evil omen, he took down what remained and buried it. He spoke of it to no one. When asked, he said that nothing had disturbed it. His son, he said, was truly meant for a long life. He was blessed, he said, and they all agreed, for no one could deny that Red Sun was a fine boy.

For weeks, however, Kills White Bear left his lodge after dark to kill whatever raccoons he found, hoping that he would ultimately punish the offender and rectify the wrong. This was what he considered to be making his own luck. The old men taunted him, unable to understand why a warrior on the rise would continue to pursue a boy's game. But Kills White Bear bore their ridicule in silence. He resolved to stay close and ensure that everything humanly possible was done to refute this evil portent. No harm would come to his son as long as Kills White Bear was alive. Wolf Eyes had told him that he was promised a long life, and this he truly believed. He'd said nothing, however, about his son.

BOOK TWO

———✦———

The Search

1826

Chapter One

Dr. Fisher emerged from the bedroom in silence. Remy saw that the physician was somber-faced, dark smudges under his drooping eyes. It was late July, the dog days of summer, and the night air hung moist and hot. Sweat dripped from the doctor's weary brow as his eyes met William's.

"How is she?" William asked in a voice feeble and desperate, his words guided by anxious eyes. His hand trembled as it brought a dingy handkerchief to mop his forehead.

"The fever rages, William," the doctor announced. His voice was authoritative, but not pompous. Remy could sense the man's compassion for his aunt. "I've done for her what I can. I dare not bleed her more. She's in God's hands now."

"Will she die, Doctor?" This was but a whisper.

The physician weighed the question. "I've seen worse cases make an abrupt turn for the better," he said. "She's stronger than most. There's an obvious will to live. That counts for something in my book. I've hope for her yet."

"What should I do?" William asked in a tone that assured Remy that nothing was too much.

"She needs rest. Don't allow your sons to pester her. Keep her warm, of course. Slip water past her lips whenever she'll take it. Boil it first. A little chicken broth to sustain her if she'll take it. You might fortify it with a little brandy to cool her fever."

His uncle's gaze dropped to the floor. "All we got's a little corn liquor."

"Very well, then. A drop or two," the doctor said. "Send

for me if anything should change. I'll pop 'round in a day or so just to look in on her. Many of your neighbors are down with the same malady. It's seasonal, of course, but it's worse than ever this year. It has something to do with such a wet spring, I think. Bad for the lungs, you know. A north wind would be a blessing."

"Can I see her now, Dr. Fisher?" William begged him.

"I don't see why not," he said. "She's asked to see both you and young Remy here. She's in and out, but I'm sure it'd be a comfort to her when she wakes to find you by her side."

"I'll be there," he said with conviction. Then he looked at Remy and corrected himself. "We'll be there."

"I'll be off, then, gentlemen," the doctor said as he slipped his felt hat back over his head. His stiff, oily hair jutted out at his ears. "I've got other patients in the area, as I said. God bless you all."

Remy spent a restless night on the porch, the buzz of mosquitoes in his ear. He heard his cousins rustle beside him. Just after sundown, clouds like blankets pushed in from the west, sealing in the heat of the day. There was not the first hint of a breeze. All was damp, still, and oppressive.

Remy, like his cousins, was distraught and could not sleep. It was a long, humid, and agonizing night, broken only by the sound of his uncle's nervous steps and his aunt's dull moans.

Without a word Remy rose and went in to sit with Helen. He found his Uncle Will, as promised, by his wife's side. He stared sadly at Remy, and then motioned that he was welcome to join them. As Remy took his place, he thought about how empty the house felt without his aunt's laughter, the humming of hymns as she worked, or the smell of her pies cooling on the windowsill. Whatever warmth he'd felt in that household emanated from her. He loved her more than he'd ever loved his own mother.

The sight of her suffering unnerved him. It seemed a struggle just for her to breathe. She groaned with each labored rise of her chest. Remy's hope for her vanished with the color of her cheeks.

His uncle gently stroked her forehead with his callused hand until she fell back asleep. To Remy she looked pitiful lying there. He said nothing until his uncle breached the uneasy silence.

"She looks bad, Remy. Real bad. I'm scared as hell."

"She'll be all right, Uncle," Remy said, but in his heart he knew better. Her skin appeared dry, clammy, with a yellowish tinge, as if someone had sprinkled her with sulfur. Her eyes were deeply set in drawn sockets, her mouth lay open when she slept, dry black lines etched deeply around it.

Every half hour or so Will attempted to give her a sip of water but she would not take it. The liquid rolled out of her parched lips onto the feather pillow, already soaked with her sweat. Will fell asleep in the rocker, her hand in his. Remy sat across the room by Helen's dresser and watched until he also drifted off.

At half past three, he was awakened by the subtle sounds of his aunt's now raspy voice. The sweetness of it was lost to his ears. Her eyes were open, staring blankly at the ceiling above as Remy's mother's had looked at him on the last night of her life. He knew Aunt Helen was pulling away.

"William," she called faintly. It was like a gasp. The sound of it in that dark, hot and musty room haunted him.

His uncle rocked forward in the chair and planted his elbows in the bed by her side. "I'm here, Helen."

"I think I'm dying."

His hand again stroked her cheek. "Don't talk such nonsense, woman. The doctor says the fever'll quickly pass. You'll be on your feet in two days tellin' us all what to do. You'll be as big a nuisance as ever."

She closed her eyes, attempting a faint smile, and then shook her head. "That's not true and you know it. The swamp fever's got me this time. I can feel it."

Remy closed his eyes when he heard the words. His chin collapsed to his chest. He knew then she'd surely die. He wasn't ready to lose her. Death had come for her so quickly. There was no time for him to prepare for it, just like before.

"I won't hear talk like that, Helen," his uncle barked, as if he could order fate around like a field hand. "You set your stubborn mind to heal yourself."

"I know you'll look after our boys, William," she said, ignoring her husband's plea to fight. "You're a fine man. I have a great faith in you. I'm sorry to leave you like this, with our work unfinished. There's so much to do." Remy watched as she shook her head, her eyes closed. "It's my wish," she continued, "that you stay here in this place if at all possible. We had a rough go of it, but you an' I've been happy here. In time, you'll be happy again. I'd never fault you if you remarry. Find yourself a good woman, somebody who'll be a good mother to my boys."

"Ssshhh, Helen," William whispered. "Quiet now. You must save your strength." He looked at Remy, his jaw muscles twitching, his eyes wild. "Get her some water or something, Remy. Please! Help her!"

Remy reached for the cup on the nightstand, but as he did so Helen shook her head again. "I don't want it, Husband. I don't have much time. We have to talk about Remy. Call 'im in here. I want him to hear this, too."

Remy looked at his uncle. Can she not see me? his expression asked. "I'm right here, Aunt Helen," he finally said.

She managed a weak smile that cracked the corners of her mouth. Then she turned back to her husband. "I know you two don't see eye to eye but you're all he has in the world now, Will. I want you to promise me that you'll look after 'im. I owe it to my poor dead sister," she gasped, "and now you, my husband, owe it to me."

"I don't know that I can do much of anythin' without you, Helen," Will said.

Her eyes narrowed. "Well, you're gonna do this. You hear? You do everythin' in your power to help him on his way. No more arguments, no more fights. Promise me you'll never raise a hand against him. He's a good boy, Will. What you give him'll come back to you. You'll see."

Every word Remy heard her speak was like a soft hand stroking his cheek. She knew she was dying and yet her last thoughts were of him. Though he'd never questioned that she loved him, he had no idea how much. He felt blessed and damned at the same time.

William spoke. "We've gotta talk 'bout that, Helen." He hesitated. The words came hard. "I . . ."

"Now you hush up, Will, and listen to me," she said. "You listen, too, Remy. Let there be no more bad blood between you two. That's my dyin' wish. Ya'll put your differences aside and help each other after I'm gone. I want ya'll's word on it."

"I'll do all I can from here out," William affirmed quietly. Remy believed he meant it. "I swear."

She turned to Remy. "Now you. Say it. Let me hear the words."

"I'll do the best I can, Aunt Helen. I give you my word."

"Good," she nodded. "I'll hold each of ya to it." She seemed satisfied, her gaze drifting to the rafters overhead. "I love you, William. I always have. I couldn't have asked for a better life."

"Yeah, you could have too," his voice tinted with the deepest remorse. They were poor and it shamed him, Remy knew. "You just didn't know no better."

"Hush, now. Just tell me you love me."

"You know I do, Helen. Always."

Her eyes looked back down her nose at Remy. "And you, my dark-eyed boy. So much goes on inside of that stubborn head. I've tried to love you like my very own. Forgive me if I failed. I did my best. Honest to God, I did."

Remy struggled to answer. The words were choked in his throat. "I never felt no different from the rest. I love you dearly, Aunt Helen. You've been more than a mother to me. I'll never forget all ya done."

She smiled once more. The light of the candle mirrored a single sparkling tear as it rolled down her ashen cheek. She closed her eyes the moment it crossed her lips. "We did it, Will," she whispered faintly. Remy caught just a glimmer of the old glow.

His uncle crouched closer to her until his lips rested at her ear. "Did what, my darlin'?"

"We made this wilderness our home. My father said we'd be back to him within a year's time. It's been twenty-two, and we never thought about givin' up. As rough as it's been I wouldn't change a thing. I got no regrets."

"I think I got only one," he said. Remy looked at him curiously. His uncle's expression revealed nothing.

"It's a fine time to bring that up now," she said, a little stronger. Her eyes opened again to study his face.

"It ain't got nuthin' to do with you," his uncle assured her. "Don't you fret, Helen. Remy and me'll work out this one little problem we've got. You heard us swear that we would. You rest now," he said, the tears streaming down his face. He wiped them with the heel of his hand. "Just rest. This'll pass. In the mornin' you'll be on your feet barkin' at everybody like always."

She shook her head. "I won't see the mornin', Will. I want you to write my mother. Tell her what's happened. Tell her I said that I loved her. Tell her I want our boys to come and visit after I'm gone. You tell her that I said it was important that she make arrangements for Remy to see his grandfather, too. The boy has the right. This nonsense can't go on. Tell her what a fine man he's become. Remy needs to know his family to heal his heart, give 'im a sense of where he comes from; who he is. The past must be repaired for me to rest easy. Tell her clearly that this was my last wish."

She reached into the empty air for Remy's hand and he gripped it. "You go see 'im, Remy," she said. "You hear me? He's stubborn, but he's a good man. Once he lays eyes on you he'll forget all about what's happened. He'll help you, just like William will. You go."

He nodded to please her, and yet the mention of his grandfather put a twist in his stomach.

"And lastly, boy," she told him, "you stick to that piece of land. After I'm gone, you'll come to understand that farm means everything. You promise me now. It's for your own good."

"I remember," Remy said, and he knew he always would. He had her to thank for that. He turned to his uncle just as Will's expression sunk a little deeper.

"I'll write the letter soon as I can," William promised, never looking at Remy. There was regret there somewhere, Remy thought, mixed with the agony.

Remy watched as she closed her eyes again; her breathing was slow, labored, erratic. His uncle climbed clumsily onto the squeaking bed to lie beside her. William held her hand, attempting to settle in, when Helen let out one deep, terrible gasp. Remy pressed forward to listen for the air to rush in again but his uncle held up his hand to stop him.

"It's no use, son," he said, defeated. "She's gone. May God bless her soul." As Remy watched, William kissed her on the lips and then rose from her.

William pulled the sheets over her head then returned to the rocker. His head collapsed in his hands, his chest jerked uncontrollably as he began to wail. Remy stood over his aunt's body, his hands crossed reverently below his waist, stunned. There was nothing to say, nothing to do. Already he felt a great ache in his heart. How he'd loved her. He'd only blinked his eyes and she was gone.

Chapter Two

Well after sunup the next morning, Remy, at his uncle's bidding, set out to dig the grave. When he'd finished, he and his cousins helped William wrap Helen's body in bed-sheets, and together they gently laid her to rest in what they believed was her best and favorite dress, a fine floral pattern made of English cloth bought in New Orleans, stitched by Helen herself. She'd worn it only to church on Sundays.

After they had all gone, William remained at the grave, alone.

Remy watched him for hours from the loft of the barn. At sundown, William turned away and walked toward him. He entered the stillness and called Remy's name. With some reluctance, he answered.

"Why is it I always find you here when I'm looking for ya?"

"It's quiet," Remy said, and then added, "an' I can slip out the back when I see you're in a dander." The humor of it was lost on his uncle, but then again it wasn't really all that funny to him either.

"Well, we gotta talk, Remy," he said. His tone was more official, more composed, now that Aunt Helen was dead and buried. "I gotta tell you somethin' you ain't gonna like."

Remy said that'd be mighty fine, go ahead. This was certainly part of what he'd mentioned to his aunt the night before. Remy had marked it well in that late hour, waiting suspiciously for the time when the truth be told. An expression like his uncle's typically meant some kind of beating was in store. What, he wondered, would this one be?

"I know you and I've never really gotten along," his uncle began, his face solemn, his manner uncharacteristically gracious. "I'm truly sorry about the way things have been, but I want you to know right off that you're welcome here. My place'll always be yours. I consider you a part of my family. Things'll change between us now that Helen's gone, just like I promised."

Remy thought for a moment. What was there not to like in that? The man spoke in earnest, he thought. Remy, better than anyone else, appreciated the effort it took for his uncle to be civil. Will was trying and Remy thought that maybe he should, too.

"You'll git no more trouble from me," he said. "I'm nineteen now, pretty much growed." He likewise had a decision he needed to share with his uncle, thinking it would come as no surprise. "While I thank you for your kind offer," he said, "I think it's time for me to move on out to my folks' place and begin to work it best I can."

The news seemed to startle his uncle, but for the life of him, Remy didn't know why. With Helen gone, Remy felt the time had come to heal old wounds and move on. That, he figured, was what this was all about. "Although we've had our problems," Remy explained, "I'm old enough now to see that some of it was my fault. I'm too damn skinny to carry much of a grudge. We'll just let it all go and start fresh. Fact is you've done more for me than you should have. I won't forget it. But it's time for me to go and work my own place. It's what Helen always wanted." He smiled, extending his hand. "Let's part on good terms."

Will wouldn't take it. His head just kind of sunk. "That's what I've got to tell ya, Remy." He hesitated and then raised his gaze to Remy's. "We had three years of drought here. You seen yourself what it done. Most of the cattle died off after the grass burned. The bank was sweatin' me for payment on the goddamn notes and I didn't have it."

When his uncle paused, Remy prodded him. "What's that got to do with me?"

Will looked away and sighed deeply. When he turned back, he was rubbing his chin. "The truth is, Remy, I had to sell Elizabeth's farm. I'm sorry to tell ya this now, when your aunt's just passed, but ya had to know."

"*What*!" Remy felt the rage begin to swell inside him. He couldn't hide it. He didn't try.

William crossed his arms across his chest, struggling for the words. "Remy, ya gotta understand, son! I had no choice! I had to keep this place at all costs. It was a roof over our heads, and yours, too. I'm sorry. I hope and pray you'll understand."

That would be some hope, some prayer. There was nothing to understand about that. "It weren't yours to sell," Remy snapped.

His uncle's gaze fell to the ground. "Helen Marie an' me was your legal guardians. I could dispose of your assets for your well-being if'n it came to that." He paused and looked up at Remy. "Well, it did."

His uncle raised a single finger, not as a threat but in explanation. "You lived here for several years free of room and board. I was glad to do it, regardless of how we got along. You're my kin. But when the time came to meet the note I had no other choice."

He lowered his finger, but Remy said nothing. "What I done—an' I ain't proud of it, Remy—was right in the eyes of the law. Judge Hargass hisself signed the papers."

Remy just stared.

"That land was useless to anyone, Remy; it'd have taken you better'n two years to make any kind of a crop. If I can't make a livin' farming this place, you damn sure couldn't have made one on Norbert's farm. Times is hard, son. I'm sorry."

"You're sorry," Remy said, shaking his head in disbelief. All his plans were shot. He was both confused and furious.

"You shoulda told me 'fore now!" he said, his voice low, vicious.

"You're probably right 'bout that," his uncle admitted. "It ain't no secret that you an' me didn't get along. It's true that spite had somethin' to do with the way I done it. And although what I done was right, I admit that I was wrong about not tellin' ya, or Helen Marie for that matter. She never knew." He sighed. "I gotta live with it. An' now, Remy, so do you."

Remy sensed a shift in his uncle's tone. The meanness was gone, if that meant anything now. Softer words, harder impact. Remy's mind was a storm.

"Listen to me now, Remy," his uncle urged. "Helen's passin' made a big difference in the way things'll be aroun' here from now on. You'll see. We kin work this thing out in due time, if'n you'll give me the chance. We gotta depend on each other. I ain't sayin' that I don't owe you, Remy. I wanna make things right jes' like I promised my wife. I got a bargain for ya if'n you'll hear me out."

Regardless of what his uncle had to offer, Remy knew it wouldn't be good enough. He was no longer willing to let go of eight years of torment. This last had clinched it. Will had wasted his past, and now he'd sold his future. What use were his uncle's concessions after he'd ruined the one dream that had carried Remy this far?

William proposed that Remy work his farm with him for the next three years, receiving a quarter of the harvest on the condition that the money, every cent, be banked each year in Remy's name. He said he'd sold Remy's farm to an attorney in New Orleans for two dollars an acre. That gave him three hundred and twenty dollars before taxes, commissions, and legal fees. After he paid off the loans, he had a hundred and thirty-seven dollars left which he deposited in an account bearing Remy's name. In spite of all appearances to the contrary, his uncle said, it had not been done with a total disregard for Remy's future. With that sum drawing interest, and three years of his percentage from the farm, he could easily buy his own place, cash, and he'd be but twenty-one years of age. That ain't so bad, his uncle told him; better than most.

Of course, he'd have a lot to learn, but with effort and

patience, in three years he could be more than ready for his own farm and, God willing, his own family. Nothing, William said, would please him more.

Remy considered none of it. No matter how sweet Will's offer sounded, it left a bitter taste in Remy's mouth. It was funny how the world turned, he thought. The night before he'd promised to forgive and forget, in honor of his aunt's dying wish, and go on. Now, he'd just learned that he had nowhere to go.

"Please stay and help me," his uncle pleaded. Like Remy, he said, he was an orphan. He said that he knew what it was like to be alone in the world. He just lost the only woman he'd ever loved, the person he felt closest to in his whole life. The loss, he said, he shared with Remy. "I need you. You need me. Let me do this for ya. Help me find peace."

Remy rubbed his hand over his face, finally shaking his head. "I won't spend another day around this goddamn place. It don't feel right. It never did."

"Think it over a couple of days, Remy. It's a big decision. I'll teach you everythin' I know."

Remy answered immediately. "No thank you, Uncle. You've done plenty for me." As far as he was concerned, his uncle had cheated him. Right was right, deathbed promises be damned. He'd have chewed off his own arm before he'd have let his uncle wriggle out from under the weight of his own guilt.

"As far as your teachin' goes," Remy told him, "only thing I learned from you I learned from the back of your hand. I watched my folks die in front of my face, and I *never* in nine years got a kind or encouraging word from you! I did twice the work as any of your own boys and caught twice the grief. You treated your dogs better than you treated me, an' I got the scars on my back to prove it! You sold my inheritance just like you sell that sour milk, without so much as a howdy-do. But that was what I should've expected from the likes of you." Remy spit. "No sir," he said, "I don't believe I *need* no more of you."

There, he thought. He'd done it. Now he'd walk away and let him fester awhile. There was only one other thing.

"I'll be needin' what's left of my money," he told him, "and then I'll be out of your hair."

Remy could see his uncle was devastated. "I don't have it on hand, son. It's at the Mercantile Bank in New Orleans."

"Then, you wouldn't mind drafting me a letter sayin' I could have it."

"No, dammit, you stubborn bastard." This was delivered in the old way. How easy that good will had been stripped away. "I don't mind."

Remy nodded toward the pasture. "And them sixteen head of cattle you bought this spring; they was bought with my money, were they not?"

"From the trust, Remy. It was all perfectly legal."

"I ain't talkin' about what's legal; I'm talkin' about what's right! I can't abide by that. Since you didn't have enough money to pay your own notes, I figure you bought them cattle with money that belonged to me, legal be damned."

"That's right," he said, and Remy heard the spite return. "I did."

"Then I figure you owe me a few as my stake. I'll take half of 'em. A cow and a calf'll bring ten dollars a pair. That ought to get me into somethin' somewhere if'n I look hard."

"Maybe. Where you plan on lookin'?"

"I got no idea," he said, wondering why his uncle cared. "Away from here, anyway. Maybe in the Arkansas country. Maybe to the west a little ways, I don't rightly know yet. Everythin's new today."

"Don't buy land from them Bowies, Remy, for God's sake. They say their titles ain't no good."

"I don't know nuthin' 'bout the Bowies. I'll leave in the mornin' first light. And I'll need my father's rifle, if'n you ain't sold that, too."

"It's yours to take. I just wish you'd cool off a little; think this thing through. I'm doin' for ya what I can, like I promised. I hate to see you go off in the world half-cocked and mad about it."

"As far as I can tell, that's the only way to go. I'd appreciate it, Uncle, if'n you'd get my letters wrote. I leave first light."

"Will you at least go and see your grandfather? You promised Helen."

Remy shook his head. "I never meant nuthin' to him when I was a boy. Now that I'm growed, he don't mean nuthin' to me. Aunt Helen's death ain't gonna change that. I kin live the way things are. That old man can die that way."

As Remy glared defiantly, his uncle backed down. Remy understood it. If he didn't keep his promise, his uncle could never honor his. Remy relished the thought. "I'm sorry, son," his uncle sobbed.

Remy felt strangely satisfied, like his mother must have felt when she burned her unhappy home to the ground. Now he understood his legacy, his crazy mother's last and only gift to him.

He measured the last eight years and where they'd brought him. He accepted their weight. In a way, he was glad his uncle had cut the final, frayed cord. He was free. There was one lesson from all of this, he thought, and one lesson only. Never again would he depend upon someone else to take care of him.

Chapter Three

At dawn, Remy baited the cattle to the barn with a bucket of his uncle's bad corn. A cool breeze kicked up just after daylight. The skies cleared. Fog settled into the lower areas out in pastures where it would soon disperse in the heat. He separated the animals he wanted from the small herd, figuring that it was pretty much his choice, all things considered. He pushed them in the holding pen next to the barn and went inside the house to get his things, which he'd packed the night before. Everything fit into one coarse cotton pillowcase, yellowed with sweat.

His uncle crept out of the house to check on his progress, an envelope in his hand. "Here's what ya need for the bank," he said with his customary stiffness. "Take care of it, son."

Remy snorted. "Take care of it," he thought. "It's pretty much been taken care of, best I figure."

William seemed to read the expression on Remy's face and went on around it. "You'll play hell keeping them together on foot, Remy."

"Looks like to me that I'm playin' hell just about any way I go," he said. "I'll make out."

"I believe you will," his uncle said. "Just the same, I'll send Elijah with ya on the mule. He'll keep ya square."

"Suit yourself. Elijah's welcome to travel with me if'n he wants." William turned and motioned for his son to saddle up. Remy welcomed his company.

"I'll need to pack a few things," Elijah said.

"You don't need to pack nuthin'. This ain't no goddamn holiday. It's just straight to the stockyard in Baton Rouge and straight back. Remy don't need ya to hold his hand after he sells them cattle. There's things for you to do here."

Elijah cut a piece of tobacco from a soggy square and shoved it into his mouth. "All right, Pa," his cousin said. "Don't get your knickers in a twist, I just thought I'd get a change of clothes or two. Maybe a little jerky, some coffee and some corn meal."

"That you can have. I'll get what ya'll need."

"You'll spare me the shotgun, won't ya, Pa? Might jump a quail or two."

"Take it. Give me a second, and I'll get ya'll some grub collected." William disappeared into the house and emerged later with a cotton sack of goods, handing it to Elijah. "Ya'll be careful, boys. Don't mix with strangers, and if ya do for Christ's sake, don't tell 'em you're packin' cash money. There's a lot of evil out in the world."

"And a little aroun' here, too," Remy said under his breath. Elijah grinned.

Remy started down the path, past Helen's grave, and Elijah followed on the mule. The sweet smell of fresh soil still hung in the air. One of the heifers turned back toward the barn. Her calf followed. Remy cracked her on the hip with a green hickory limb. She bawled but turned back around. Elijah turned to wave, but Remy did not look back once.

Remy watched as the clerk stamped the current application with a big red DENIED and then read his name off the next one in the stack.

"Fuqua," he called as if he didn't care if anyone answered. Remy emerged from the rear of the office where he had been waiting for his turn, passing by the spurned applicant. Elijah stepped up beside him.

"That'd be me," Remy said. "How yew gettin' along today?"

The clerk rested his scraggly chin in his hand. His wooden teeth clicked when he spoke, which Remy found distracting. "I'm fine, son. Real fine. What can the land office do for you today?"

"I'm figurin' to apply for a homestead," Remy said proudly. He patted the bulge in his pocket to indicate that he meant serious business.

"You an Uhmerican citeezen, ain't ye?"

"Born in Ouachita Parish, territory of Louisiana. Of course, it's a state now."

"That's what they tell me," the man said. "How old are ye?"

"Twenty-one," Remy lied.

"Married?"

"Lord no." Elijah winked.

"You can qualify for a hundred and sixty acres."

"I don't need that much. Not yet."

"That's the least I can sell ya."

"So be it. Can't argue with the goddamn government. Where's it at?"

The clerk turned and pointed to the shaded area on the curled map behind him. "Arkansas territory," he said, the upper Ouachita River Valley. Remy's father had known it well. It was big timber country, the redlands. "It'll need to be cleared," the clerk warned, "but that's all that's goin' these days aroun' here. It's mostly French settlin' up there, but lookin' at you I believe you'll fit in all right."

"It'll do. What're the terms?"

"By Gawd," he said, a little astonished, "ain't you full of spit and vinegar. A dollar an' two bits an acre. Cash."

Remy's enthusiasm drained. "Cash?"

"Cash." He screwed up his face and leaned closer. "That's a lot of money for a boy. You got it?"

Remy had the money, but he'd have to surrender every cent. How would he buy the tools he needed? The food while he cleared the land for crops? It might take two years to make new land pay. It might take four. He saw it was time to shuffle a little bit. "Listen, mister. I'll give you sixty dollars cash down today, sixty dollars every two years, the balance at the end of the third."

"More'n likely I'd never see ye again, son."

"I'll be farmin' that land you're sellin' me. That's where you can find me. I see you got a map. Draw me an x, and I'll be under it."

The clerk turned to eject a stream of tobacco into an unseen spittoon. Remy heard it land with a distinct plop. "I'm sorry, young Mr. Fuqua," he said, running his forearm across his lips. His cuff caught a splinter, and out came his teeth. He jostled them back in. Click. "It's gotta be cash," he said, arranging his jaw. "It's the law."

Remy was thinking a little sandpaper might fix all that. "I heard where the government was sellin' public land to homesteaders on credit terms," Remy said.

"Ye ain't heard nuthin' like that lately. There wuz a crash back in '19. The banks failed. If ye didn't live so far back in the woods, you'd know there wuz a depression on in this country. Money's scarce, and credit's like my grandpa's ghost. It might be out there somewheres but ain't nobody seen it. I'm sorry, Fuqua."

Remy rubbed his face with his hands. "Mister, I ain't got that kind of money."

"It's no shame that you don't at your age. Hire yourself out for a time. It wouldn't hurt ye to learn a trade or some such. With a little thrift, ye can save what ye need. Don't be so much in a hurry. You're just a kid. No way in hell you're twenty-one."

Remy leaned forward on the counter. What he needed

now was advice. "What would you do in my boots? I ain't got nowhere to go and farmin's all I know."

The clerk seemed to warm to him. "Well, seein' how ye say ye got cash in your pocket, ye might buy land from a private owner on workable terms. A land speculator could subdivide for ye what you can afford if'n they've got a mind to. It'll probably run you a little more per acre, but you can own it if'n you've got sixty dollars to put down. Ye do have that, don't ye?"

"I got it, Mister, sure as I'm standin' here. What're they likely to charge me?"

"The cheapest will be three, three and a half an acre, maybe. But, if'n you're lookin' for good farm land, it might run ye better'n ten dollars."

Remy peered at his cousin, whose expression offered no counsel. It was the stare of hopelessness. "I guess I'm done for," Remy sighed.

The clerk rummaged through some papers in his roll-top desk and handed one to Remy. It was a newspaper ad, crumpled and yellowed. "Ye might consider this here, then. It's all the rage in these parts. Most everybody's in the same boat. People these days is goin' where they gotta go."

Remy stared at the flyer. "What is it?"

"Why, it's Texas, son." He said that if Uncle Sam didn't have no place for him, the Mexicans might. They were allowing Americans to settle with the Colonization Act of 1825. People had been squatting across the Sabine for years but now they could do it legally. It was something to think about, he said.

This struck Remy's fancy. "What's the terms?"

"Favorable, but I'd read the small print if'n I were you. There's a lot of if's, and's an' but's with them Mexicans. It's risky business but a lot of folks say they're headin' out that way. If'n I was as young as ye, I'd give it a little thought. Like ye say, you've got nuthin' to lose."

Remy read the advertisement and then slapped it back on the counter. "I'm goin'," he said. "How do I get there?"

"Ye can go overland across the Sabine through Nacogdoches. But I wouldn't recommend that for a greenhorn. It's dangerous as hell. You'd have to pass through what they used to call the Neutral Ground. Ye know 'bout that?"

"Nope."

He said that there didn't used to be no agreed boundary between the U.S. and México, and so it became a sort of dumping ground for vermin avoiding the laws of both countries. The U.S. army took to flushing them out of there from time to time, but them bastards tended to settle back into the low ground shortly thereafter. A bull can swat at the flies with his tail all he wants, he said, but they still hang pretty near close to his ass.

"It's a bad bunch in there," he said. "I'm here to tell ye. Better to go by schooner from here in New Orleans. For a nominal fee, they'll drop ye off at the coast." He patted his hand on the flyer. "The man that run that ad's named Austin. There's others in the business but he's been there the longest. I'd recommend ye see him."

Details now, Remy thought. "Who do I see 'bout a boat?"

"Go down to the wharf and make inquiries. They'll set ye right."

"'Preciate it, Mister," Remy said. "You're all right with me."

"Good luck, boys. Fare ye well."

Remy watched him stamp his application DENIED and shove it aside.

Remy and Elijah pushed their way through the heart of New Orleans to an area called Sainte Marie. The docks, they were told, were not far. The houses in that part of the city were far different from any they'd known in Ouachita Parish. Most were red brick, some still wooden, and the state bank, of stone imported from the North they were told, was by far the most beautiful.

The city hummed with activity. Manufactured goods from the North coming in; cotton, flour, rice and other agricultural products flowing out. On the streets Remy heard French, Spanish, and English used by groups passing by.

Once they reached the wharves, Remy saw hundreds of ships—frigates, corvettes, barges—flying all flags. To Remy, everything was wondrous.

They found a schooner bound for Texas in only two days. After Elijah stabled the mule, they rented a cheap hotel room and kicked around New Orleans while they waited. Remy bought a bottle of whiskey but Elijah took it away.

"No you ain't, you damn fool," he told him, and he poured it into the chamber pot.

On the morning of the appointed day, Remy rose early, arranged his things, and asked Elijah to see him off at the dock. He loaded his things where the deck hand told him, and then he returned to the oak planks to say his farewells.

"Your pa'll kill you for stayin' with me so long."

"Prob'ly will," Elijah agreed. "But I couldn't let ya come down here yourself. You're just a kid, and a dumb one at that. Besides," he said, "I wanted to see this place, same as you."

Remy stared at his cousin. He knew Elijah better than anyone. He'd been reticent, a little cool maybe, ever since his mother passed, which was understandable, but Remy knew damn well his cousin remembered that day they were squirrel hunting and Remy had led him to his folks' burned-out farm. They'd talked of a future together and had made their plans. Had his uncle not sold the place, Remy was certain that Elijah would've moved out there with him, just like they'd always said. Remy didn't see now how a change of locale made any difference. But something did. And it looked to Remy like Elijah would just let him go.

Remy couldn't bear it, but couldn't say it either. He didn't know why. He hoped his expression conveyed his thoughts and he gave his slow cousin ample time to read it. It took a while.

"Ain't no way in hell," his cousin finally said.

"C'mon, Elijah."

"To Texas? No and hell no. I'm stayin' put. I'll inherit my pa's land after it's all said and done."

Remy knew where to dig. "That ain't much of an inheritance. Besides, you gotta split it with your brothers."

"We'll make out."

"Yeah, but just barely." Just as Remy thought, Elijah

never budged. "Suit yourself. I know I couldn't wait as long as you'll have to."

"Now that's for sure," Elijah said, nodding.

"Well, that's it, then. Thanks for seein' me through."

"My pleasure, Cousin. You be careful over there. Ya might have to work, ya know."

"I'll be rich some day. You wait. They're gonna sell me over four thousand acres of land for twelve and a half cents an acre. I'd think about that if'n I was you."

"Don't think that I ain't, Remy. I read the flyer, same as you. But I figure my place is with my pa. At least I think so."

Remy understood. Elijah had better prospects than he did where his uncle was concerned. "I'll miss ya, Cousin."

"In a pig's eye."

The captain boarded the vessel and instructed the hands to prepare to cast off. Remy shook his cousin's hand one last time and went on board. Elijah watched, waving when Remy looked back. Remy thought he ought to say something more, try one more time. Before he could speak, a man in a suit passed by. Elijah stopped him.

"How much ya give me for my mule, Mister?"

Remy slapped his hands together. "Hot damn!"

The man seemed puzzled. "What mule? I see no mule."

"The big, strong gray at Cavendish stables," Elijah said. "You can't miss it. It's the only one there."

"I'm not in the market for a mule, young man."

"You look like a man of means. You'd take advantage of a good opportunity if'n it slapped ya in the face. Give me fifteen dollars, and I'll scribble you a bill of sale. You can sell it to Cavendish for twenty easy."

He stroked his chin. "Is there a mule there, son?"

Elijah squinted his eyes. "There is. A fine one."

"Is it really worth twenty dollars?"

"Easy."

"And it belongs to you, does it?"

Remy saw his cousin falter. He answered for him. "It's his pa's, Mister. He can't take it back where he's goin'. Might as well sell it to you."

"All right," the man finally said. "It's risky business but I can see you're in a pinch. I don't mind assisting young people when I can, particularly if I can turn a little profit along the way. I'll give you ten Yankee dollars."

"Ten, hell! Gimme twelve and like it. You don't meet a fool in a hurry every day but a man's still gotta sleep at night. What d'ya say?"

"Done," the man said, and they shook hands. "Here's a pen and an envelope." Remy watched as the man shook the pen and then handed it to his cousin. Elijah wrote the man the document he needed to conclude his business with Cavendish. Remy's heart leaped. He had a companion, and a haggler at that.

Elijah ripped the envelope in half. "Along with the deal, I'd oblige you to mail this note to this address. It's to my pa. He'll be expectin' to hear from me. It'll worry him to tears if'n he don't. He'll get the idea about what's become of his mule too. Will you do that for me, Mister?"

"Indeed I will. You may rely on me."

"I believe I can. Thank you, sir. Now, good day and good luck with that mule."

Elijah took his cash and stuffed it into his pocket, shook hands with the stranger and leaped on board. Remy watched as the man glanced at the boy's scribbling. He appeared to pay closest attention to the bill of sale.

"What'd it say?" Remy asked him.

"It said: Dear Pa: G.T.T. with cousin Remy. Cheap land and plenty of it. Sold the mule for travel money. Sorry. Your son, Elijah." He paused to think about it for a moment. "That's good enough, ain't it?"

"It is for him," Remy said, and he settled into his place, the smell of salt and fish in his nose. He thanked God for his good fortune. He'd given him his only friend in Elijah.

Chapter Four

Kills White Bear returned to the encampment after having been on the raiding trail for nearly a week. A warrior of twenty-five winters on the rise, Kills White Bear was expected to bring honor to himself, and therefore to his people, and he did not disappoint. A personal herd of over five hundred horses accounted well enough for him, should one fail to note the dozen scalps that hung from his lance and bison-hide shield.

He was hungry and tired, having ridden most of the night to avoid being overtaken by the would-be avengers of his victims. He divvied up the horses amongst his companions as a tribute to their courage and rode for his lodge to greet Morning Song, who was now expecting their second child.

The heat of summer was upon them. Insects stung their skin; bull nettle and cockleburs pricked their bare ankles and calves. Already exhausted, the heat took from him what little he had left. His patience was gone. As he rode through camp he noticed the mules of Comanchero traders, the New Méxicanos, the people of the war chief de Anza.

In the time of his grandfather's father, de Anza had warred with the other bands, the Yamparika and Kotso-teka, as no other Spaniard had. In the words of the old men around the council fires, de Anza seemed to understand the nature of plains warfare and fought the Nemenuh like Nemenuh. He earned first their respect and then his peace, and the People agreed to trade with the New Méxicanos for as long as the rivers ran. The Penateka had never been defeated by de Anza, and so had never smoked with him, but they honored the agreement their cousins had made. The Comancheros were welcome.

Now they had come, and Kills White Bear accepted it, but then his gaze settled on a strange man among them. He had white skin, the very same the albino bear had warned him against ten winters before. Kills White Bear did not see how this intrusion was included in the old bargain. A group of Nemenuh were huddled around the traders, rummaging through the goods being offered.

One of the New Méxicanos was admiring a man's horse as Kills White Bear rode up.

"What would you take for it?" he heard the man ask in the tongue of the Spanish, which all southern Nemenuh understood. The trader grabbed its horse-hair bridle to examine its teeth.

The warrior shook his head. "This one's my favorite. I choose him in war and also for the buffalo hunt. He's the finest I've ever owned. He reads my mind better than any woman. Moreover, I love him. He's not for sale."

The trader nodded that he understood and did not pursue the matter further.

Kills White Bear had heard enough. His vision had told him, among other things, that Nemenuh things should remain Nemenuh. What they did not already have, they did not need. These men brought the unwanted outside world to his. The civil chiefs, Maguara included, accommodated the will of the People, who welcomed the convenience of the goods. But Kills White Bear, who was not a chief, could assert a warrior's more personal and militant position and, furthermore, he intended to do so.

He spurred his mount, his skin slick with sweat, bear grease and the grime of the trail, and headed for the center of the crowd, dispersing it. There were three traders with the group, one Méxicano and two white. He'd seen the latter before, but from a distance. Now up close he saw how truly ugly they were. They were dingy, full-bearded, and smelled like dogs. Kills White Bear looked at them with contempt, his teeth clenched, clearly revealing his disgust for their presence. One of the elders observed his apprehension and came forward to soothe him.

"Please, young warrior," he told him. "We're trading quietly with these men. They're known to us. There's nothing to worry about."

"They've nothing that we need," Kills White Bear snapped. "It's not a good idea for them to know the location of our main camp. Send them away from here and they won't be harmed."

"Look here," the man said. He held out a packet of a dozen metal arrowheads complete with a file to sharpen them. "They give us these in exchange for one buffalo robe. They're fools," he said, grinning. "Let us have our way with them."

Kills White Bear knocked them out of his hand. "If you need metal you need only come to those who raid. I myself could trade you metal enough to make a thousand."

"But these are all the same weight and size, and ready for use. It's easier this way and takes none of my time."

"You can fashion metal heads much quicker than the

flint ones of our fathers. That's easy enough. Your laziness weakens the nation and puts us all at risk from our enemies. The traders take much more than they give. No good can come from them. Tell them to go or I'll run one through with my lance. The others will run like rabbits."

Kills White Bear scowled at the traders. He saw that one of the whites in particular looked sickly. Beads of sweat had formed on his forehead and there were red bumps dotting his pale face, some of which were open and oozing; the rest were scabbed. He believed the man trembled from both fear and fever. Kills White Bear rode closer to him for a better view.

"It's a waste of time to kill this one," he said in his language. "He'll soon expire on his own." He turned to the others. "Look at these miserable people, my brothers. They're a sickly and disgusting race. What do they have that we need?" Then he faced the traders and spoke in theirs. *"¡Vayan ustedes! ¡Ahora!"*

The traders immediately began re-packing the mules as quickly as they could. The elder stepped forward and spoke to them. Kills White Bear loomed near.

"This young warrior hates outsiders. In particular, for some reason, his heart is black to the whites. He's a known hothead, full of power, very dangerous. I know you've come a long way but I fear for your safety. It's best that you go now, as he threatens you with harm. When the leaves fall, we'll send along our own sons to Béxar and call your name with many fine buffalo robes to trade. Let there be no evil between us for this thing. I'm sorry."

The traders led the mules out on the prairie, pack flaps flopping, to the south. Kills White Bear followed behind shouting just to hurry them along. Some of the other young men with whom he'd been raiding came with him because they, too, understood.

"This is the land of Human Beings," he yelled at them. "You're not welcome here. Never come again."

When they had disappeared, Kills White Bear withdrew and the others followed. He decided that he would bring up the issue of camp safety with the council the following moon. It was for their own good. It had to be this way. The old ways were best. Those that had needs could tell the raiders and they in turn would seek them out. In the end they would get what they wanted and there'd be no reason to trade—at least, not with the whites. It was the way the Great Spirit had always intended, and Kills White Bear's vision had told him that he was the protector of the Great Spirit's way. The rest of his tribe, he thought, would learn from his example. There was no better teacher.

Within ten days of the traders' visit, most of the camp had fallen ill to some degree. Kills White Bear succumbed to the illness as well and lay in his lodge burning sage grass while his fever raged. He also suffered from throbbing headaches, abdominal and back pains, and a general malaise. His legs were unsteady, his arms weak. Red Sun, now eight winters, grew desperately ill, and Morning Song did her best to care for both husband and child until she, too, fell with the fever. Continually nauseous, Kills White Bear vomited till there was nothing left. His tongue was thick and coated. He could eat nothing. Kills White Bear kept the fire burning, though it failed to warm his family. They shivered violently even under the best and warmest buffalo robes. Morning Song cradled her son in her arms to sleep next to Kills White Bear. Not an hour later, he awoke horrified to find the boy in frenzied convulsions.

"Husband!" his wife cried in terror. "What is this?"

"I don't know," he said, and he snatched the boy's flushed body to bathe it in the clear water of the stream in order to cool it. The convulsions soon ceased, giving way to hysterics, and Kills White Bear quickly carried the screaming child in his arms back to his lodge. Morning Song wrapped her son in her softest buckskins and cradled him to her chest. She sang until the child stopped crying. Soon he was asleep. Kills White Bear, who felt powerless, his gut burning with anger, watched on.

"I've sent word for the medicine man but he doesn't

come," he said. "Everyone's sick. Stay close to me. Death will not come to this lodge. This will soon pass."

And within three days it did. Slowly, Kills White Bear and the others resumed their normal activities. A few of their number, mainly the weak and aged, had died. Most had made an immediate recovery. There was now hope for those who languished. The mysterious fever had come and gone. The worst, Kills White Bear thought, was over.

Then the strange rash appeared, first about his mouth, face and head; then it spread to his torso, and finally to the external limbs, covering all. Once begun, the process took two to three anxious days. The red, sometimes purplish bumps, most of which were about the size of a tick, soon blistered and filled with a clear watery liquid, at which time they began to enlarge.

On the fifth day after their appearance, a depression formed in the center of each blister. The following day Kills White Bear noticed that the blisters formed pearl-colored, pus-filled points. These soon ruptured into oozing, open wounds. The fever now returned with greater fury than ever before. This was something new.

Kills White Bear went again to find Three Bears. He was stunned by what he saw as he picked his way through the stricken camp. Women sat weeping by untended fires, their children convulsing in their arms as Red Sun had done. The elderly staggered about the camp in a state of general delirium. People he'd known all his life didn't recognize him. The ones that did were too sick with diarrhea and nausea to speak. Their inflamed skin was like leather. He could grip them by the arm and then let go, and the impression of his hand would remain. They looked at him sadly with their sunken eyes and then slipped away in grim silence.

Death was everywhere. All normal activity had ceased. Kills White Bear didn't know what had done this, but he could see that the grip of the disease was universal and complete. He knew it had come for them all. Three Bears was not to be found.

Kills White Bear's lesions developed internally as well— deep into the nose, mouth, throat, and even the rectum and genitals—and became ulcerated. Breathing became labored and painful. His breath was putrid and offensive, and at a time when Kills White Bear wished to comfort his family members, they actually repulsed him with their stench.

As bad as it was among his own immediate family, he knew it was worse elsewhere. Kills White Bear saw that many developed lesions in the eye and could no longer see clearly or even at all. In some, blood appeared at every orifice, including the rectum and vagina, which added to his fear and foreboding for his stunned people. Even his fever-scorched mind realized that the more they gathered to care for their own inside the confines of their respective lodges, the more completely they succumbed to the disease.

One by one, they fell to this new evil, no record of which existed in the verbal history of their nation. As bad as it was, Kills White Bear sensed that the worst was yet to come. Yet, as a warrior, he could not express such a bleak opinion. The others, he knew, relied upon his strength. As sick as he was, he could not waver. But even his body was too weak to respond to his great will.

During the seventh night he watched Morning Song miscarry her female child. The little girl Kills White Bear had so desperately wanted would never draw a breath, never open her eyes. This was the worst kind of evil. The image of it pushed him down into the deepest despair. Weeping, distraught and confused, her fever burning, his wife buried the child in the soft earth not far from their lodge and then crawled back under her buffalo robe to grieve. Kills White Bear washed the blood from her thighs while she lay there, still and quiet. It hurt too much to speak the words that might console her.

Word came to him that most of the pregnant women of the tribe miscarried as well. Never had he known such misery. Under normal circumstances, the people would have gathered to mourn such a tragic event, to console the victims, to defend themselves as a group against such evil, and to encourage the young wives to try again as, in the face of such a disaster, it was now imperative that the People augment their declining numbers.

Instead, with the full onset of the disease hard upon them, they languished in their lodges just as he did, the skin between the pocks red and inflamed, their throats choked from the constant secretion of mucous and the drainage of pus, their eyelids, face, hands, and feet swollen and painful to the touch, their infected throats and lungs too diseased to afford wailing; they no longer possessed moisture in their bodies sufficient for tears. Those that survived, he knew, did not have the strength to gather and mourn. The disease reduced Kills White Bear and all he knew to their own private suffering, alone. There was nothing he could do but endure it.

The second week of his misery eclipsed the first. The pocks ruptured, their contents now dry, hardening into yellow or brown-tinged crusts. The areas of the skin most thickly studded with the lesions now became a mass of continuous, festering scabs. At this point the skin exhaled a truly offensive odor. Kills White Bear's own family literally nauseated him. His wife and child were mutilated before his very eyes.

He knew in his heart he could defeat this disease. He was promised a long life and he refused to be cheated. He attempted as best he could to relay this conviction to his family. He prayed for that moment when the worst would be over. As the days languished, it became clear to him that it had not yet come.

Weak from the days of fever and nausea, Kills White Bear was now susceptible to a host of infections he had seen before on the wounds of others. Normally they healed with simple care and herbs. But now they came when he was so weak that they secured their holds in the festering wounds—ideal sites for exponential growth—and then traveled from the limbs toward the torso until they overwhelmed the body's blood with their poisons.

Experience told Kills White Bear that such infections would ultimately kill. He set his mind to heal himself; he had to stem the tide. When he went in search of fresh water, he came across those suffering from severe headaches, violent convulsions, paralysis, blindness, delirium, as well as loss of bowel and bladder control. Many, he was told, had slipped into a deep sleep. Death soon followed. Some of the elders, those he respected most, were driven from delirium to absolute madness. Kills White Bear watched the wisest among them rot to death after they'd gone insane. When, he prayed, would the evil pass over? How much more must they endure?

The infections ran their course in the second week of the disease, and it was then that so many more perished. The coughing sickness that soon followed claimed that number again. Kills White Bear saw that there were not enough healthy people remaining to bury the dead, so corpses were dragged a short way from the encampment to decompose shamefully under the sun. The stench overwhelmed him. The sight of the dead and dying broke his spirit. He fell to his knees and wept.

On the thirteenth day Kills White Bear's fever finally broke. His wounds were scabbed over and healing. The infections were gone. The power slowly returned to his arms and legs, as did his appetite. His prayers must have been heard. Now he set himself to care for his family as best he could because now he knew that they too would live. He bathed their afflicted skin in clear spring water and kept the sage grass smoldering in the fire to overcome the stench. He sang to his son and poured broth down the child's ulcerated throat.

Two days later, from a sporadic moment of sleep, Kills White Bear awoke to find his wife's lifeless body. It crushed him so that he lay numb beside her, as lifeless as she. When day broke he went weeping to his mother to seek her help, but she was too ill to respond. Alone, Kills White Bear resolved to bury Morning Song.

He left his lethargic child in the care of his family and, carrying his dead wife in his trembling arms, he mounted his horse. He followed the river north until he found a canyon suited to his purpose. Then he traveled along the west bank until he came to the highest possible burial site. It was the place, he remembered, where he'd first told her that he loved her.

Kills White Bear bathed her one last time in a spring and clothed her in the garments she wore on the day he had brought her to his lodge. He painted her entire face with vermilion and sealed her eyes with red clay. He kissed her cracked lips, now grown cold, this final time and then carefully drew her legs up to her chest, her head down to her knees, and bound her with leather thongs. He wrapped her body in his best blanket, again binding it tightly with leather straps. Then he lowered her into a sharp crevice, taking care to position her where she would always face the rising sun. He sealed off all access as best he could with stones and dead limbs, the tears streaming down his pale and sunken cheeks. When it was done, he rode back to camp alone. The overcast skies opened up, and the rain poured. He thought of nothing else now but his son.

Chapter Five

Kills White Bear rode straight to Three Bears' lodge. He called to him, but the old medicine man did not answer. Kills White Bear entered the teepee and found Three Bears chanting over his daughter and grandson, the pocks on their faces protruding and inflamed. They lay motionless, their eyelids swollen shut.

"I need you to come and see to my son," he commanded.

"My own people are ill," Three Bears muttered. His stare was detached, distant, "As is most of the camp. I can't come."

For Kills White Bear the excuse was not good enough. "Listen to me, old man. I've lost my wife. My son's all that I have. You'll come and look after him." He paused a minute and then added, "Now."

Three Bears looked at him—the light of his only good eye was absent—and then shook his head. He wasn't going anywhere.

"What is this thing?" Kills White Bear asked him.

"I've no idea. I've never seen anything like it. Its power is too strong for my own. So many are dying. I can do nothing."

Kills White Bear was desperate. He'd do anything to see his boy live. "Fifty horses to look after my son. I'm a great hunter. I'll provide meat for your lodge as long as you breathe."

"Nothing works," the old man said, and then even he, an elder and a great shaman, began crying. Kills White Bear pitied him. "I've lost my wife and two children. I know these," he said, pointing to the two children that lay near his lap, "will die soon. My heart is broken. I can do nothing."

"You've got to try," he pleaded. But the old man closed his eyes and slowly shook his head. Then he raised his arm. Kills White Bear could see that it was black and rotten. The sight of it sickened him.

"In two days' time," the old man said, "Three Bears will be gone." And with that, Kills White Bear left him thinking that he would not live a day longer. He heard Three Bears begin to chant his death song before he remounted his waiting horse.

As he approached Big Hand's lodge, he heard the sound of his mother and sisters wailing. When he stepped inside, he saw that his mother had his son cradled in her arms, rocking him. The boy's body was pale and lifeless, straight and stiff. His head was round and swollen, his eyes were popped open and protruding in a ghastly expression. He was gone.

Kills White Bear collapsed to his knees and shrilled so loudly the horses in the pastures cried out. For him, the worst had finally come.

Kills White Bear hugged the boy in his arms. He ran his trembling fingers across the child's brow, closing his eyes. His mother reached to soothe him but he pushed her away. His older sister quietly fetched the hide of the white bear from his lodge and wrapped it around his shoulders. He snatched it away and flung it outside in the mud.

His reason for being, his hope for the future, lay still in his scarred arms. He felt hollow and empty, betrayed. In silence, he took the boy and returned to his home. For one whole day he held the boy close to him and mourned. He spoke to no one and no one dared speak to him.

Kills White Bear prepared Red Sun's body as he had done the boy's mother before him and carried him to the same place. He would allow no one to help him. He uncovered the grave and then lowered the boy into its darkness. Next to him, he laid the little bow they had built together, along with six crooked arrows the boy had made himself. Then he slit the throat of his son's favorite pony, and then ten horses more, allowing their blood to cover all.

When all this was done, Kills White Bear sat on top of the bluff and waited for his own time to come. His grief gripped him more completely than the illness ever had. No food or water passed his lips. He did not sleep. Over and over he chanted the song Wolf Eyes had taught him when he was just a boy. Only the raindrops falling on the bare limestone bluff marked the slow passage of time.

At dawn on the twentieth day of the plague, he heard the sound of hooves approaching, but he did not look up. He saw the white legs of a horse standing near and then he heard his name. He recognized the voice of his spirit guide, Wolf Eyes.

"I'm sorry for your loss," the ghost warrior said. "They were both beautiful people. You must be content with the happy time you shared together." Kills White Bear did not respond.

"The evil that took your family also came for you but you were too strong. It's decided to go and look for someone weaker. It'll never come again." What, Kills White

Bear thought, did that matter now? But Wolf Eyes would not let him be. "Mourn to your broken heart's content, young warrior. Then rise up and bathe yourself. Get something to eat and care for yourself as best you can. Your people need you now more than ever. Show them your courage."

These words meant nothing to him now. Bitter tears stained his cheek. Harsh words left his parched throat. "What people!" he cried. "Have you not seen? They're all dead or dying. Kills White Bear also wants to die."

"And you will," Wolf Eyes told him as he dismounted. He came and sat next to him, and put his arm around his shoulders. "But not today." Kills White Bear laid his head against Wolf Eyes' chest. Even the words of a spirit could not soothe him.

"You can't see it now," Wolf Eyes told him, "but the burden of your sorrow will make you stronger. For you the struggle continues. The price of greatness is high, but the White Bear has the strength to pay it—that promise is already spoken. The Nemenuh are your family now. You must look after them as you looked after Morning Song and your young son. I'm truly sorry for your suffering, but nothing can change what's happened. You have a great destiny, Kills White Bear. That also cannot be changed. Pick yourself up and go on. Your people are waiting."

Kills White Bear rose, stoop-shouldered, his head bent, his body convulsing as he wept. Wolf Eyes rose with him. Kills White Bear did not wish to hear of his destiny now—certainly not one without Morning Song and Red Sun.

Wolf Eyes put his finger to Kills White Bear's chin, lifting it. "Do you remember the traders, Kills White Bear? Especially the white man who appeared ill?"

He thought a moment and then nodded slowly. He felt his eyes narrow. His anger burned away the tears. "I do," he seethed.

"Were those marks on his face not the same as the ones on your wife and son, and all the others that are lost to us?"

The image of that sickly white man flashed in his brain. "They were," he finally said.

"The evil spirits that took your family from you rode on

his back to this camp. From his breath, they traveled the wind to find your wife and son, and took them as they've taken so many others. The spirits of the dead cry out for revenge. The whites must learn to fear the Nemenuh. To do so, they must fear Kills White Bear. They must not be allowed to set foot on Nemenuh land. Otherwise, this tragedy is but the first of many to come. Make an example of the ones that brought death to your lodge. Leave one alive to tell the others, but maim him so he will not forget and others will know not to risk his fate. Hold them back from this country, my son. Teach them what they've taught you. Trade blood for blood.''

Kills White Bear felt the strength return. It was, he knew, the power of rage. Ten years on the warpath had taught him how to use it well. "I'll go now."

"There's no hurry," Wolf Eyes cautioned. "I'll tell you where these men can be found when the time comes. First you must eat and care for yourself." Wolf Eyes reached into his medicine bag and pulled out a dark stone. "Let me paint your face for you, Kills White Bear," he said, and Kills White Bear felt the subtle pressure on his cheeks. "Having beaten the spirits, you're now made stronger. Everything within has changed."

Wolf Eyes explained that he was painting Kills White Bear's face black, a streak of red lightning on his left cheek, a white skull on his right. The flesh above his beating heart, he painted solid black. The spirit stepped back a minute, as if to admire his work. "In battle, paint your face this way. Your enemies will see it, recognize the warrior who has come for them, and they'll be afraid."

Kills White Bear stood over a puddle of rain water, staring at his image. How clearly it reflected his mood. Then he took his knife from its sheath, and drew the blade from his shoulder, across the claw scars of his chest, to the waist. The blood poured from the gash, but he did not cry out. "Where are they?" he growled, his voice cracked. "The rain has washed away their tracks."

"Not now, Kills White Bear. Your body needs rest, food, and water."

"This body needs only revenge. I'll rest when they're dead."

"Your *puha* is strong, but your body's weak. I can promise you revenge when the time is right, but you must wait."

Kills White Bear stared at him. Now he had a purpose again. Its execution could not be delayed. "Where?" he demanded. He would not be denied.

"So be it," Wolf Eyes said sadly. "The risk is yours. The men you seek went among the Mescaleros after they left here. They are returning to the old Spanish mission called Béxar. You'll find them just west of there, south of the clear water lake, following the river the Méxicanos know as the Medina."

Having told him that, he heard Wolf Eyes' attempt to caution him one last time. "It's not wise, Kills White Bear," he told him. "I fear for your life."

"Why should you?" Kills White Bear said as he swung his bare leg over his horse's back. "I'm already dead."

Chapter Six

It was the first day of August when Remy and his cousin set sail with fourteen other passengers and three crewmen. The weathered schooner drifted quietly across the muddy mouth of the Mississippi, past the sand bars and the oyster beds, out to the blue water of the Gulf.

It was crowded on deck and very hot. Remy could see that Elijah had second thoughts, but once out on big water they didn't seem to matter any more. For his part, he never thought twice. It had all happened so fast it made his head spin. He felt good about everything in a way he never expected. He was free.

"That fella don't know it yet," Remy finally said, "but he's bought hisself trouble on four hoofs with that goddamn mule."

"Old, too," Elijah added. "Price was right, I reckon." He wasn't smiling. "This better work out, goddammit," he finally said to Remy. "I'm a fool travelin' with a bigger one."

"Quit whinin'. I never had no place else to go, and neither did you, best I figure. You were just too ignorant to know it. It don't matter no more. 'Less you know how to swim pretty good, I wouldn't talk myself out of Texas just now. I kin just barely make out the coast."

Elijah looked a little pale. "Shut up, will ya, Remy. I'm gonna chuck."

The man who sold him the ticket told Remy that an average trip from New Orleans to the mouth of the Colorado normally took around seven days. Provisions, he learned later, were stored for ten. On the third day, the wind swung from out of the west and the little schooner's boiler could not compete. On the twelfth day they had not yet seen the island of Galveston. When the water ran low, the captain suggested that the passengers sustain themselves with sips of vinegar, sugar, and a little whiskey if they had it. Remy, along with the others, languished in the thick and humid air of the summer gulf sun.

Mid-morning on the fourteenth day, a pelican flew close to the boat. Remy had watched him for some time when Elijah promptly shot it out of the sky. One of the deckhands gaffed the bird and quickly prepared it for the pot. The captain graciously supplied some bruised and cracked potatoes for the soup they heated on the ship's boiler. Although the broth reeked of dark and greasy fish smelling flesh, they all ate it without complaint.

That afternoon the wind shifted to the southeast. Along with the favorable breeze came swells of three feet or more, violently rocking the westbound schooner. Most of the passengers became sick, but since they'd all been without water for so long they mostly dry-heaved. It was a miserable business.

Before sunset, they passed Galveston Island, which Remy knew was last populated by Lafitte, the buccaneer. Remy pleaded with the captain to drop anchor. He and Elijah both offered to search for fresh water and game. But the captain refused, citing the danger of sandbars and the unlikely presence of potable water that late in the Texas summer. He explained to them that they were already long overdue and must make haste. The wind was right, he told them, and he could not take the risk. In grim silence, they sailed on.

The water soon muddied with river silt. When the captain appeared convinced that he was near enough the mouth of the river, he dropped anchor, and began loading the skiff with wasted passengers and their scant belongings, three or four at a time.

Remy looked at the coastline, then back at his cousin with a broad smile. "Is that the mouth of the Brazos, Skipper?" he asked.

"Nope. It's the Lavaca."

Remy squinted his eyes. "That's the wrong one, ain't it?"

"Not if you're headed for DeWitt's Colony," the captain replied.

"Which we ain't. I believe we mentioned Stephen Austin's grant back in New Orleans, and several other places along the way."

"Maybe so," the captain admitted, "but I never did. All these other people told you that they was headed for DeWitt's Colony. This here's a one-stop operation."

"I wish you'd been a little more clear on that point, Captain. We're sorta new at this."

"It's clear enough to me. You boys said you wanted to go to Texas. That," he said, pointing to the deserted dunes, "is Texas. That's close enough for this line of work. Get your gear," he said gruffly. "You're next off."

Remy glanced at his cousin, who shrugged his shoulders. "How far to the mouth of the Brazos, Captain?" Remy asked.

"Seventy miles or so east," he answered. "But I wouldn't travel the coast, son. By Mexican law, there ain't supposed to be a settlement within twenty-five miles of the Gulf. That leaves it pretty much to the Karankawa. They eat human flesh when they can get it. You wouldn't be much more than a little snack to them, but I've known 'em to take 'em skinnier."

The captain guffawed at his own joke but Remy paid it no mind. He was thinking more about this last little detail the land office clerk had neglected to mention. "Well, ain't that a hitch!" he said. "You can't come overland from Louisiana without an army for the thieves and murderers; and you can't follow the coast for the damn Indians. How ya supposed to get into this Texas?"

"You best hook up with DeWitt's men," the captain grunted. "They'll be along directly. Buy yourself a horse and then bear to the northeast to Austin's Colony when you get some food in your belly and let your clothes dry. DeWitt's settlers can tell you the way."

Elijah reached for his cousin's arm. "Don't argue with 'im, Remy," he whispered. "He's liable to make us eat some more of that rotten bird if'n we stay. I'll take my chances anywhere off of this goddamn bathtub. Let's just git and be done with it."

Remy listened to what Elijah had to say and then said the hell with it. He was ready to get off as well. Things weren't going as planned, but when had they ever? They would just have to patch the pieces together as they found them.

"All right, Skipper," he said. "I guess we'll cut out from here. You skinned us good. We'll ask a few more questions next time out."

"Well, I'm here to please," the captain said before he yelled at one of his men. He turned back to Remy. "I've got supplies here for DeWitt. They know I'm comin'. They'll be down to see if we've made it in. Mexican troops patrol here lookin' after colonists. If nobody picks ya'll up after a day or two, I'd send your party north up the river. Fulcher and McHenry squat six to eight miles from the landin'. Ya can't miss 'em. They keep dugouts handy. They'll set ya right," he said and then added a qualification, "more or less."

The skiff pulled back alongside the schooner, and Elijah began placing Remy's meager belongings in the bow. Other than the shotgun, everything Elijah owned was on his back. The deckhands loaded a few barrels of flour and sacks of coffee and beans from below deck.

"You had all that handy and didn't give it to us!" Remy barked. "We was half-starved!"

"It weren't yours," the captain stated unfazed. "Them colonists need it worse than you. You'll see that for yourself soon enough." The skipper prodded him with a flick of his wrist. "Let's go, son. We got things to do on shore, as well. The tide'll be out soon. My little pop-gun cannon ain't workin' right. I don't want to be here after dark when them Karankawas get busy."

"I'm not sure we do either."

The captain laughed gruffly. "In for a penny, in for a pound," he said, and then he pointed a fat, bronzed finger north. "There's Texas, boys. Have at her."

Well into the afternoon Remy and Elijah waited with the others. They battled the heat, the horseflies, the mosquitoes, a burning thirst and an aching hunger. Around four o'clock, just as the captain had promised, Fulcher and McHenry appeared. They drifted in silently on the current, paddling one dugout canoe. Four others trailed behind them strung by a strand of twisted rawhide. Not one looked to Remy as though it should float. As he and the others watched, the men waded ashore, tugging the other canoes up the muddy bank beside their own.

"Welcome, folks," one man said. Remy noticed that his teeth, the ones that were left, were stained dark brown, near black at the edges and at the gums, from tobacco. They were rough-cut, sunburned and dirty-skinned backwoodsmen, their hands callused and their fingers stained and cracked. The buckskin they wore was slick from wear, weather, and human grease. Weapons of every sort hung from every available place. Remy thought that if Texas was a land of milk and honey, these two, the first Texicans he'd seen, hadn't learned where to look. It troubled him, and one look at his cousin's frowning face told him Elijah had concerns as well.

"We know ya'll are 'bout give out but we best be gettin' a move on," McHenry announced, noting the position of the sun. "DeWitt's ten miles up river past our own place. It'll take us a good while the way the river's runnin'. I've brought some fresh water and a little jerky for you all. Get yourselves a snip, pass it around, and let's load up."

Fulcher surveyed the supplies. "Hell, McHenry," he drawled. "We can't take all that today."

Remy watched as McHenry looked for himself and then said that it was true enough. He decided that it would be best to leave a couple of men out overnight to look after the goods. They'd be back in the morning first light, they said, and take the rest. The exhausted colonists looked briefly at each other, most of them soon fixing their gazes on Remy and his cousin.

"Looks like it's us," Elijah told him. Remy nodded that it probably was.

"That's good. Help us get these people movin', boys." They did as Fulcher asked. Just before the party cast off, McHenry threw a sack of venison jerky and a little coffee at Elijah's feet. "That ought to hold ya till we get back down here. If ya brew that coffee, do it 'fore dark. I wouldn't have nuthin' burnin' after sundown. The Karankawa know well enough that we use this place as a landin', but I wouldn't advertise the fact that we're usin' it today."

"What do ya suppose we ought to brew it in, Mister?" Remy asked. "Our hats?"

"Learn to make do, feller. That's all I can tell ya. Here's a blanket or two to keep the chill off," he said, and then quickly added, "I'll be needin' them back." And then they pushed off.

Remy propped himself on an appropriate pile of driftwood, settling his rear into the soft and shifting sand. It didn't take him long to find a configuration to suit. "How come nuthin' pans out accordin' to our plan, Elijah?"

"What plan, you goddamn idjit! Now, shut up and gimme some of that jerky."

"Help yourself," Remy said, tossing him the sack. "I've already tried it. It's hard as a rock. They smoked it too damn hot."

"Beats pelican, Cousin," Elijah grinned. "Pass it along. That's what these here grinders are for."

"That and wearin' me out with your idle chatter."

Remy watched his cousin's teeth clench down on the meat as he twisted and tore the rest away. "The way I see it," Elijah told him, "you got no call to complain 'bout the present company, Remy. This was your fine idea."

"I got a feelin' that ain't the last time I'll hear that," Remy said, and he fell back in the sand between two piles of rotten wood watching the great clouds drift overhead.

"Well, it just might. We're liable to get our throats cut

tonight guardin' somebody else's grub. I needed to get my licks in while I can." Elijah smacked away. An old heifer probably chewed her cud more quietly, and more attractively to boot. Less saliva dripping here and there, anyway. Remy turned his head away.

But when he turned back to Elijah, he saw that his cousin was looking east across the misty expanse of the Gulf. Remy clasped his cousin's jaw with gritty fingers, rotating his head around to the mainland that lay to the north. "From now on," he said, "you need to look this way."

Chapter Seven

As far as Remy could tell, he'd only been asleep for a moment or two when his cousin nudged him in the ribs. Remy felt Elijah's hand clamp his mouth. Remy's eyes popped open. Elijah bent toward him and whispered in his ear.

"Torches," he hissed. "At the landin'."

He sat up to see for himself. Sure enough, they were there. "You figure it's them yahoos from DeWitt's?"

"Not likely," Elijah said. "They said it'd be mornin' 'fore they'd be back."

"Who do you reckon it is, then?"

"Who do ya think?" Elijah said, his face like stone.

Remy thought for a moment. "Let's lay low. If them torches start for us, we'll know they come across our tracks."

About then, one by one, the torches went out. There was silence until Elijah spoke up. "Ah, hell, Remy! They're comin'," he moaned. "They want to see us 'fore we see them. It don't take an Indian to track a man in the sand, and I think them're Indians."

"Let's crawl back in the brush as deep as we can go. Make 'em flush us like rabbits."

"I'm froze up stiff, Remy," Elijah gasped. "I'm scared."

"You think I ain't? Let's go. We gotta move. Try not to leave any sign from here out."

Remy crawled on all fours toward the underbrush, managing the rifle as best he could. He looked behind him to check on Elijah's progress and then came to a stop. "Reckon you might have cause to bring that shotgun?" he whispered.

"What for?" Elijah answered. "It's loaded with bird shot."

Remy couldn't believe what he was hearing. "Bird shot! Why the hell's it loaded with bird shot?"

"Up till now I was only shootin' pelicans. It was the right load at the time."

"Go back and get it! You'll just have to let 'em get close up 'fore ya shoot."

"If'n they get that close, it ain't gonna matter what kind of load I got in that bore." Remy shot him a look. "All right, dammit. Jes' a minute."

"Hurry up."

Elijah crawled back with the shotgun and followed Remy deeper into the undergrowth. Considering the thickness of the brush, they crept in virtual silence. After they had traveled maybe two hundred yards from the earlier site, Remy came upon a nearly impenetrable pocket of thorny vines and slithered on his stomach underneath. Elijah soon came up in his wake, but in the darkness could not find his cousin.

"Remy?" he whispered. "Where ya at?"

"In here. Let's split up. Find yourself another place."

Elijah shook his head firmly. "Not likely. If they find you, they find me. Move your ass over."

Elijah muscled in close to Remy, nearly breathless with fear. Remy attempted to calm him. When he had done so, he set about calming himself. He listened carefully to the sounds of the Texas night, all of them strange and threatening. The wind played tricks. The brush clicked, the loose, dead leaves rattled to taunt them. Remy's heart skipped a beat at the sound of a twig falling to the ground or a limb scraping against the trunk of another tree. Several times he was certain that he heard the sound of footsteps approaching their thorny little hut, but no human form appeared.

He could see much better when the moon finally rose, but he cursed the unwelcome illumination. The skies above cleared, pressing the veil of fog close to the earth, and he was grateful for it. Dew formed on the cold steel barrels of their guns, their shirts felt heavy and damp, clinging to their now sweating backs.

"Did you hear that?" Elijah hissed.

"Ssshhh." Remy again cupped his hand over Elijah's mouth. His lips said, "Don't make a sound."

"I heard a man's voice," Elijah whispered through his fingers.

"Not a man. An Indian. Now shut up and cock the hammer on that thing."

Elijah screamed about the same time Remy heard a violent commotion in the brush behind them, but before his cousin could react, the warrior, who had somehow slipped through without a sound, clubbed Elijah in the head. Remy heard the wood fall solidly against his cousin's skull and then saw Elijah collapse, motionless, against the moist earth.

Before Remy could do much of anything else he felt a pair of strong, angry hands grab both his ankles. He jerked them free and scrambled just enough through the brush to sit up and aim his father's rifle. The warrior stood before him, fearless, and shouted his war cry. Remy pointed the rifle at the man's chest and yanked the trigger. The flint sparked well enough but the gun missed fire. The dew must have dampened the powder in the pan, he thought. The warrior cried once more and then hauled Remy from the briar until he could get a grip on the hair behind his head, dragging him out to his howling companions.

Remy was dragged by Elijah's motionless body. He looked dead. Blood ran from his ears and nose. Remy tried to struggle but he did not have it in him. He was exhausted from both hunger and fear. They were going to kill them both, he knew it. Remy could not control his awful trembling. He knew the Indian mind well enough to know that he shamed himself. He felt empty, defeated. It would soon be over, or at least he hoped so.

The six warriors had followed their tracks to the bush and then circled them. They were on them in a flash. What easy prey they'd made.

Remy assumed these were the skipper's Karankawa, the cannibals. Just to see them made him shudder. They towered above him, well over six feet in height, muscular of

build, skin slick, well-oiled and copper-red. They were
lighter than most of the Indians, the Choctaw or Chickasaw, whom he'd seen in Louisiana as a boy. They were
naked except for some sort of fiber thongs on their feet,
and a breechcloth whose tail fell below the knee. Each
warrior's body was decorated with animal teeth, strings of
strange seeds, and a shell or two from the beach. They
wore their hair, rust-colored in the moonlight, very long.
He thought it must have been bleached by hours spent each
day in the Texas sun. Their faces were painted half with
bright red ochre dyes, the other black as night, accentuating
the tattoos that adorned their cheeks and their chests. A
shaft of cane pierced the nose of each; another shaft ran
perpendicularly through the lower lip. To Remy, they
looked like demons drawn in the pages of an old book.

They carried bows as long as each man was tall that
appeared to be made of red cedar and were strung with
strands of what Remy recognized as twisted deer sinew.
One young warrior carried a lance tipped with rusted iron;
another gripped a club.

The Karankawa had dragged Elijah's body back to the
place where he and Elijah had originally slept. They shoved
Remy under a large limb of some kind of oak, motioning
for him to stand and place his hands above his head.
Remy's hesitation earned him a slap across the face. Another warrior observed his resulting scowl and clubbed him
solidly in the chest, knocking out his wind.

Remy crumpled to his knees, half coughing, half crying.
They yanked him up again by his hair and raised his arms
for him. The elder Karankawa bound his wrists together,
above the limb, with braided reeds that had the consistency
and feel of hemp. When it was done, he kicked Remy's
feet out from under him to make sure the knot would hold.
Then he dragged Elijah over and secured him in the same
fashion. His cousin's body hung still and limp; blood dripping from his nose formed a small, congealed pool on the
ground.

The Karankawa quickly raised a fire from the dead and
dry limbs lying about in a shallow pit they dug in the
ground. They took positions around the fire, casting a mali-

cious glance every now and then at Remy, who stared back. They talked amongst themselves in a guttural tongue that Remy could not understand.

Much to his surprise, they began acting somewhat like people, laughing and joking, slapping one another on the back. Remy had no idea what plans they had for him and Elijah but he hoped to God they weren't slated for dessert.

Before long the Karankawa finished their meal. By this time, Elijah was moaning but had not opened his eyes. Remy still glared, his wrists numb, his arms and ribs aching, awaiting his fate with what courage remained.

"Come on, you sons of bitches!" he yelled. "Kill us and get it over with!"

The elder glanced at Remy and then at the others. He rose and squared off to face him and jerked Remy's face to his by a fistful of tangled hair. He barked at him in that strange tongue. Remy felt the spray of his saliva on his cheek as he spat the words. Then he shook his hand free of Remy's head in disgust and walked off.

One by one, the warriors filed past with hard and hostile eyes. The last one stopped, smiled strangely at him, and then lunged forward, white teeth flashing, and took a large bite out of the meat of his upper arm. His teeth felt hard, warm, and sharp. Remy shrieked in pain as the warrior shook his head to tear the stubborn flesh free. When it was done, he stood before him and chewed it, the blood staining his gums and outlining the cracks between his teeth. He swallowed, his dark eyes locked on Remy's, who had no idea what would come next, and then disappeared into the brush.

They left as quietly as they'd come, but Remy could not trust them. He waited in agony for the burn of an arrow, or the crack of a wood club, or the feel of cold steel as it pinched against his throat before slicing into it. Perhaps they would return with more wood and just burn him alive.

But the time passed and nothing happened. The wind grew still, and there was only the sound of Elijah's infrequent moaning and the dripping of Remy's blood as it fell from his shoulder to the ground. They weren't going to kill him after all, he thought.

What in the world? Remy wondered. He'd read the flyer

well enough. It said that he was welcome. He came where they'd brought him, a little wide of the mark perhaps, but they had assured him that this was Texas. He and Elijah were as tired and worn as the other travelers yet they, in their youth, had willingly deferred to their elders at their guides' request. It seemed like the neighborly thing to do at the time. But no neighbor he'd ever had would've set him up like this. Where they were from, settlers looked out for one another. They'd fallen in with bastards with the first step they'd taken. It was the worst kind of luck.

And what had provoked these God-awful savages? Why the hatred in their eyes? The Spanish had held Texas for over three hundred years. That's what his history books said. Had the savages not accepted white men after all this time? Where he was from, they had no choice. Remy and Elijah weren't the first immigrants to come. They certainly wouldn't be the last. What kind of greeting was this?

Everything so far in Texas, from the mosquitoes on up the chain, wanted their blood, and Remy knew that there was definitely a limited supply of that. As the minutes turned to hours, Remy resolved that if it was blood they wanted, he would no longer make his so readily available.

Elijah had said it best. This Texas was a rough place, and if he was going to make it here, if he was to get what he came for, he knew he'd better smarten up. Next time Fate came for him, by God, he'd be bleeding for something he owned.

Chapter Eight

Hey," Remy heard a voice call in the distance. "Here ya go." It sounded to him like that McHenry fellow, who must've just cut their trail. Soon Remy saw them as they slipped through the brush, rifles cocked and borne forward, eyes looking everywhere. Fulcher reached Elijah's body first.

"This one's a little bloodied," he said, lifting his cousin's chin, "but he's still alive."

Remy's eyes followed McHenry as he stepped in front of him. "You all right, son?" he asked him. Remy just stared. McHenry pulled his knife from its scabbard and sliced the reed thongs. Remy collapsed legless to the sand, as did Elijah's body when Fulcher cut him free. Remy said nothing, rubbing his pale wrists and hands to get the circulation back. McHenry surveyed his wound.

"It's good that they let you live," he said. Remy didn't reply. "Austin says he's got a treaty with them Kronks but I guess they don't read too good. We've been havin' lots of trouble with 'em. From the looks of things," he said, nodding to Remy's shoulder, "it appears you had a little yourself. I'd say you're lucky, except for this here one little bite." McHenry brought his face so close to the wound that Remy felt the warmth of his breath. "I bet that hurt like hell," he said.

He began to search around the area. "Them bastards didn't make off with my blanket, now, did they?"

The blanket. All the fool was worried about was his goddamn blanket.

Remy scrambled to his feet and lunged for McHenry, tackling him. When he had him down on the ground, he began swinging wildly at his stomach and ribs.

"Easy, now, fella," he chuckled, as if Remy's blows had no effect. Remy aimed for his grizzled jaw and that appeared to be the end of his amusement. "Pull 'em off of me, will ya, Fulcher!" he hollered.

Remy felt Fulcher yank him by the back of his collar. He struggled on until Fulcher slapped him solidly across the face. Now both of his cheeks were warm and swollen. His aching head rang. "It's over!" Fulcher barked, his raw hand still tight against Remy's throat. He looked at Remy with a face about as mean as a man's gets and Remy's anger dissolved before it.

"You're alive! They're gone! An' now we're goin' too. Cut out yer bullshit an' get your gear stowed. That's the last time I'm goin' to tell ya. Them Kronks done a good job of welcomin' you here, and now you know you ain't wanted."

"They could've kilt us," Remy said.

"But they didn't, did they?" he growled. "But pretty soon somebody else is gonna try. I got no time for yer foolishness out here. I ain't your mama. I don't even know your name, and I don't wanna. You either buck up or you don't. It's nuthin' to me one way or the other." Remy stumbled when Fulcher released him. "I've seen your kind come an' go, boy," he said, shoving a wad of tobacco in his mouth. "An' I kin tell you that last night ain't gonna be yer worse." Fulcher gathered his things. "Let's go if'n you're goin'. I ain't waitin' no more."

And then he picked up his rifle and walked off for the landing. McHenry rose, dusted himself off, and followed. Remy sat there a moment, thought about it, and then stood. He picked up Elijah and slung him over his shoulder, and trudged off for the flat, where he laid his cousin on his back squarely in the center. McHenry returned with a flour sack and unceremoniously rolled Elijah to the edge. "The supplies go in the middle," he said matter-of-factly. "They can't git wet. Help us load the rest." He wasn't asking, he was telling and Remy acquiesced until they had it all aboard.

When they cast off, he sat down by his cousin to see if there was anything he could do. Maybe make him a little more comfortable. McHenry observed his activities and then said, "He's all right for now. Get yourself a pole, son. The current's fierce today."

Remy rose and picked up a spare pole. He watched Fulcher and McHenry for a time, then did as he saw them do. His wound ached, the flesh around it warm and swollen. Soon it began bleeding again.

"What's your name, son?" McHenry asked him without looking.

"Fuqua."

"French, ain't it?"

"That's right."

"What 'ja do?"

"How's that?"

"What did you do?"

"I don't follow."

"Are ya runnin' from the law, Fuqua?" he asked. "Did

ya leave them ol' nasty bad debts behind? Did ya get some young filly in a family way? Which is it?''

"Why, none." He was confused. He thought the reasons they came should be obvious; but since they weren't, he told them. "We came for the land," he said, "a new chance."

Both McHenry and Fulcher laughed, their eyes on the murky river passing by. Remy could see the glint of their teeth reflected in the water.

"Hey, same for us," McHenry said, and they laughed again.

The local trader, Anderson, had taken them in. Remy sat at a warped table sipping coffee when the man who called himself Green DeWitt stepped through the door. The cabin was windowless and had no floors. It smelled moldy, stale, and damp. Remy believed his uncle's cattle lived better than this man Anderson did. DeWitt introduced himself as a government-licensed empresario and took a seat opposite.

"Heard you fellers had a rough time of it last night."

Remy nodded. Elijah, whose appetite—if nothing else— had recovered, was busy shoveling in his grub.

"Well, you're out of harm's way here, I should think. I've got better'n four dozen families settled here, and more comin'. The folks that come in with you are already on the way to their homesteads. You get your rest, and we'll look aroun' for some place for you."

Remy already understood that empresario was a fancy Mexican term for a land speculator, a dirty word where he came from, the equivalent of scoundrel or thereabouts. They were principally promoters. Remy naturally assumed he and Elijah were being promoted. That told him to be suspicious of what he heard.

As for what he'd seen, he was not impressed. He'd already decided that he'd look elsewhere and planned to let DeWitt know as soon as he could get in a word. "We thank you for your kindness, Mr. DeWitt," he said, seizing the first opportunity, "but we had a notion to settle in Austin's Grant."

"You're a little wide of the mark, ain't ya, son?" DeWitt asked as his teeth sank deeply into a yellow onion Anderson had set out. He ate it like an apple. "He's up the Brazos."

"That's what they tell me."

"You're better off here, Mr. uh . . ."

"Fuqua. Remy Fuqua."

"You're better off here, Mr. Fuqua," he said, sprinkling a little salt on the onion. "Austin's colony is better established, that's true. But most of the good land is deeded out. He's already filled his original contract of three hundred families. He's movin' on north now. That puts him at odds with the Comanches and the Tonkawa. Them Indians'll give you a world of trouble up there."

Remy glanced at his arm. "They've already given us a little down here."

It occurred to Remy that DeWitt obviously had dealt with reservations in the past. He told Remy, who was listening, and Elijah, who Remy knew was not, that he was sorry about their misfortune, but that was merely a misinformed Karankawa war party. They didn't get along very well with the other Indian tribes in the area, let alone the whites. But their numbers were obviously dwindling as time passed, and as they were adapted to live along the coast, they weren't really the problem anymore. The Mexican empresario Martín de León, his neighbor to the south, had seen to that. While the Karankawa that remained were not openly friendly, as they may have seen, they were no threat. The Comanches, he said, were another story.

DeWitt said that he had originally founded a settlement called Gonzáles to the north. The Comanches stole all their stock, burned their crops, and pushed them back down here. When DeWitt's people caught their breath, why they'd run out the savages again and re-settle the area in greater numbers than they had before. Next time they went, they went for good. It was a minor setback. Austin, on the other hand, was settling his new arrivals much deeper north, in the heart of the *Comanchería*. If they thought last night was bad, he told them, let the Comanches get a hold of them.

He had Remy's attention. One bite had taught him to steer clear of that dog. Remy thought it wise to consider what this man had to say.

"You look like fine young men," DeWitt continued, "made for this country. I don't care what you done back home. I don't ask no questions."

Here it was again. Remy didn't like the insinuations that he had done something criminal. "We ain't done nuthin'," he protested.

DeWitt grinned and cocked his head. "Oh, I believe ya. Not a reason in the world not to," he said, adjusting his expression to its prior formality. "But the fact is, if you stick it out with me, I'll make it worth your while. I'll be a little more flexible with my empresario powers than you'll find Don Estévan Austin to be. He's a stickler for formality. I'm a lot easier to get alon' with. You work hard, mind your business well, why, you'll die wealthy men. You can't go wrong."

Maybe so, but it looked to Remy that Anderson certainly had. "Mister DeWitt," he said, "I'll just give it to ya straight. I was raised poor in Louisiana, but we were rich compared to what I see here. Bein' young and all, I think we'd better make our homestead in an area that's better established. We got a lot to learn. I hope you understand."

"It's up to you, son," DeWitt said. He pitched the rest of the onion out Anderson's door and leaned forward in his chair. "But you're makin' a mistake. You'll need to have the proper documents to settle with Austin. He goes by the letter of Mexican law. You got passports? Letters of recommendation? Slaves? Equipment? I don't see any of that stuff." His eyes glistened. "I'm willin' to give you a chance, son. Hell, an opportunity. Reach out and grab it, Mr. Fuqua. It's yours for the askin'."

Warm talk, but Remy's mind had cooled. They had a plan, sort of, and Remy decided to stick by it. "My cousin and I left out from New Orleans for Austin's colony. We've got our heart set on seein' it. I 'spect we'll be makin' for there when my cousin's able. We're happy to settle up with you for room and board until that time. Whatever's fair."

"Ah, don't think of it, Mr. Fuqua. We're a family here. You're welcome. You rest up and think about what I said. When you do, I know you'll stay."

Chapter Nine

The empresario surveyed the new applicants carefully. He was taller than Remy, wore his curly hair a little longer, was thinner but carried it well. His eyes looked to Remy as if they were too large to fit in that head. His nose was aristocratic, as was his manner. He appeared to be intelligent, educated, rigid—as tight as DeWitt was loose— yet Remy sensed that he was someone that might be trusted. It was just an air, an impression. Still, it would take more than that to convince Remy that he could rely on this strange man after what he'd seen so far.

"You've got nothing?" Austin finally asked. Elijah and Remy both shook their heads.

"We saw your bill in New Orleans," Remy explained, "and we just came."

Austin sighed and massaged his temples. "You're aware that it's too late in the season to do much now in the way of farming?"

"We grew up on a farm, mister," Remy said. "We know."

"Well, I shouldn't settle you here. If you read the advertisement like you say, then you also must have read the conditions that went with it. They're all strictly abided by here."

Remy responded immediately. "DeWitt said he'd settle us with what we got."

Obviously Austin was not impressed. "DeWitt will settle anybody. He's desperate to fill his contract. I'm not just puttin' people on land to make money. I'm building something here. I need men of character. I need men of commitment. You've brought me no evidence of either trait."

"We come this far with nuthin', mister," Remy told him. "That's evidence of both. And we've got cash American money to pay down for our grant. That's better than most, from what we've seen."

"That's something," Austin agreed, "I guess."

"Could ya tell us what the terms are?" Remy asked.

"You boys would live together?"

They both nodded.

"Two single men qualify for a married man's grant. I can allow you one hundred and seventy acres for farming. Farming means farming. It's not a base for hunting and trapping, whiskey brewing, gun running, tobacco smuggling, or any other frontier riff-raff. I want no leatherstockings here. The price is twelve and one half cents per acre. You can pay out the balance on time, in cash, trade, a percentage of your crops, what have you, over the next seven years."

He spread his arm to the north. "Where we stand is the high coastal plains. The soil's black and rich, the elevation protects us from the floods. By law, improvements must be made and made quickly. The land must be cleared, a homestead erected, pastures fenced. In short, we have to see that you're workin' your land productively." He looked at Remy as if to confirm that he understood all of this.

"We will. Sounds good to me," Remy said. Elijah agreed.

"Of course, I can allocate more land for ranching."

The cousins looked at each other. "Ranchin'?" Remy asked. "What's ranchin'?"

"It's a Spanish practice," Austin said. "This land is well suited for it. The Méxicanos to the south've done it successfully for over a hundred years here in Tejas. One allows cattle to roam free, proliferate, and then the animals are sold on the hoof for their meat and by-products."

"Well, we've done a little of that over the years," Remy said, looking at his cousin. Elijah nodded that, yeah, they'd fooled with plenty cattle all right.

"The Méxicano government authorizes four thousand four hundred twenty-eight acres for a ranching operation."

Remy looked at Elijah and grinned. "It's funny," he said, "but me and my cousin here was just talkin' 'bout maybe tryin' our luck at this ranchin'."

Austin's lips pressed into something that resembled a smile, Remy thought. "Careful," Austin warned. "You'll have to pay for it, of course. Same price as the rest. You don't want to get in over your heads." He stroked his chin. "What religion are you?"

Remy had to think about that a minute. "We're Presbyterians, I guess." He looked at his cousin, and Elijah nodded in such a way as to say, yeah, that was most likely what they were.

"We recognize only the Catholic faith here."

"Mister," Remy answered, "for twelve and a half cents an acre, we'd worship the devil hisself."

That earned Austin's grin. "Catholicism's not quite that bad," he said.

"It don't matter if'n it is or if'n it ain't," Remy said. "We'll do what we gotta do. We ain't goin' back. Give us the land, Mister. We'll work it hard, and we'll do ya right. You'll see."

Don Estévan tapped his finger against his lips for a moment, thinking. "All right," he said, "here's what I can do. Do you boys have a trade?"

"Like we said, we're farmers," Remy told him.

"You can't farm now. What else can you do?"

"Like what?"

"Such as carpentry or blacksmithing."

"We can do a little of both."

"We'll see. There's a man with a blacksmith shop on the edge of the settlement by the name of Noah Smithwick. He's a gunsmith by trade, but he can perform all manner of metal work. Report to him and see if you can be of any assistance. He's a busy man. If you display a certain industry, I'll settle you both together on a family grant after the new year." Elijah slapped Remy on the back. "But," Austin said, his tone shifting, "if you demonstrate other tendencies, if you choose to drink whiskey or are otherwise idle, I'll have you escorted out of the colony at the first opportunity. Is that fair enough?"

Remy nodded then winked at Elijah.

"It's up to you, now, is it not?" Austin said. "You have your chance."

"That's all we're askin' for," Elijah said.

"And that's all you'll get."

Events of late had taught Remy to be a little more cautious. "Now we got your word on that, ain't we, Mr. Austin?" he said, craning his neck forward.

"Don Estévan," he corrected him. "You do."

"You'll forgive me for making sure, Don. We've been disappointed a time or two lately." He looked at the chunk missing from his arm.

"Haven't we all?" Austin said, "And Don's not my name. It's just a title, like mister."

"All righty," Remy said. "Well, Mister Don . . ." Austin grimaced. "Did I say it wrong again?"

"Don Estévan." This was crisp, impatient.

"You got an awful lot of names for just one feller," Remy said.

"Damn if he don't," Elijah muttered, his nose wrinkling.

"Maybe I can just get you to write 'em all down so I can practice later," Remy said. "The fact is, we don't know ya. We don't know if we can trust you, that's all."

"Then you can see my problem," Austin told him.

Elijah elbowed him in the ribs, telling him to shut up, they'd got what they came for, but Remy went on. "It's just if we do this work—for nuthin', I reckon, 'cause I don't hear nuthin' 'bout no money—if we do this work and do it right, you'll give us our fair share of land?"

"That's right. Fair work for room and board. A deed to follow in the new year if I see for myself that you'll work it."

"And we've got your word on that?" Austin nodded once, lips pursed. "And you're a man of your word?"

"Well, yes," Austin said dryly, "but I suppose you'll just have to take my word on that." His eyes twinkled.

It seemed fair enough to Remy, sort of. He'd have to think about it, he said. Austin's clerk arrived and introduced himself as Williams. Remy heard him tell Austin that a group representing the settlers was here to see him. The empresario nodded his head to indicate that he would speak to them presently.

"Now, be off to see Smithwick, gentlemen," he told them. "I'm occupied for the moment but I'll be around to speak with him directly."

"Appreciate the opportunity, Mister . . . uh . . . well, you know," Remy said, losing his nerve.

"Gladly. Good luck, and good day to you both."

Austin stepped out onto the porch where six men were waiting for him. They looked disgruntled. Remy and Elijah hung nearby, out of interest, to hear what they had to say. Remy thought they just might learn something valuable.

"Good afternoon," Austin said. "What can I do for you?" One of them stepped forward.

"My name's Cox, Don Estévan."

Ah, Remy thought. That's it.

"I know you, Mr. Cox. You're in from South Carolina, are you not?"

"That's right," Cox said. "But a group of us from all over met last week. I agreed to come down and speak with you about our concerns."

"I'm happy to do so. Speak your mind freely. What troubles you?"

The man fumbled a moment searching for the words. Austin's authoritative presence, though quiet and unassuming, still seemed to intimidate him. Remy understood it. He'd felt the same way. It was those eyes, and the formality on which they silently insisted.

Cox looked at the others with him and they urged him to go ahead. "Well, what we don't understand is why we gotta pay you for our grants when the Mexican government allows you payment for your services in land, a lot more land than we're allowed to own. It seems to us that you get paid twice, and us bein' poor and all, we'd 'preciate it if'n you'd let us slide on the twelve and a half cents an acre fee."

"I think the terms are most generous," Don Estévan said calmly. "I ask you to recall that most of you've paid me nothing to date anyway."

"But we're supposed to," Cox argued. "An' when we do, you'll get rich."

"Rich, gentlemen?" he asked, surprised.

"All due respect, Don Estévan, but sixty-five thousand acres of land per two hundred families settled is proper payment. That's what the Mexicans give you, ain't it?"

Austin shook his head. "I don't know that anyone's giving me anything, Mr. Cox. It's what I earn."

"You've got near six hundred families settled. You're then quite wealthy already, whether you admit it to us or not."

"Do I appear to be wealthy to you? I wear homespun. This shanty here," he said, indicating his log cabin, "is my home as well as my office. It's not the property of a rich man. I can't eat my land, friends. My grants do not support me. For the time being, they have only paper value. You must be aware that little to no cash comes my way, and what does, I might add, is reinvested in the grant."

The men said nothing. Austin continued. "I ask you, Mr. Cox, is the land not worth the price?"

"We hope so, Don Estévan," Cox said, turning to the others. "It's early yet to know for sure. It appears to offer potential but we've had drought and other hardships. Of course, we're willin' to stick it out provided we can come to terms. But we're the ones takin' the risk."

Risk was something with which Austin said he was very familiar. He said his father took the risk when he traveled to San Antonio de Béxar to initiate the first communication with the Spanish. The journey, more or less, had claimed his life. It was his father's wish that he continue with the plan. At the time, Austin was a federal magistrate in the Territory of Arkansas. Other promising interests were nearby. He had forsaken everything for the colonization of Texas. He spent years in México City, at his own expense, hazarding both his life and health amongst the turmoil of revolutions, working first with this government and then again with that one, until he finally earned the right to settle this land. It was a slow, frustrating process. Risk, he said, he certainly understood.

Who, he asked them, would've undertaken such a thing without the hope of compensation? But even this was not the real issue. The fruits of his labor were sold very cheaply to all who were willing to work. Austin had created this opportunity for them, and by doing so he'd earned his fee. This is what he told them they had to realize.

Remy saw that they were not yet convinced, and so Austin pressed on. He said that he understood their fears. But they all had to realize that this was not a matter of exploitation. He, as empresario, had to think of the future, their future together, and he needed their payment to ensure its success. He was involved in things of which they had no knowledge, yet in the end it would directly benefit them all. He was soliciting a market for their products. He'd personally borrowed money to finance the machinery they needed. He was bringing tradesmen to the colonies to build gins, ports, factories, and schools. This, he explained, was where all the money went.

Without the development of commercial enterprise to link them well beyond their borders, the colony would flounder as did the other neighboring empresario grants. Someone had to think beyond the crops and the cattle, and that someone happened to be him.

He asked them to consider the improvements that have taken place in just one year; most people believed they would have taken four or five. The rate of growth was funded at the rate of twelve and a half cents per acre, one-tenth the price they paid for less fertile land in the states. "Look around you, gentlemen," he said, spreading his arms like Moses. "We're thriving. And you all thrive with it."

He then said that he knew that many of his immigrants considered him principally a land speculator. It brought with it an element of natural distrust, which he understood. But in the Méxicano wilderness, he told them, he was also their guardian and benefactor. They should consider the advantages that they received from his labors and ask themselves if his motives were pure. Despite all gossip to the contrary he remained, he said, a poor man with a rich dream which he very much intended to share.

Remy could see the man was still not satisfied. "You've got land, Austin," Cox said. "Lots of it."

Now Remy could see that Austin was clearly frustrated. "I've explained things the best I could. I can't for the life of me please you all, nor shall I try to. I'll satisfy myself by doing justice to all. In short, gentlemen, you must trust me; and you must pay me the fee."

"Well," said Cox, "we figured you'd see things that way. Accordingly we intend to take it up with Saucedo at San Antonio de Béxar."

"You're free men. Do as you please."

"You'll be hearin' from us."

"I welcome it."

"They'll be no further payment until this's worked out."

"I'll accept the decision of the government, gentlemen. Good day."

Don Estévan offered his hand but Cox would not take it. He retreated back among the others and they walked away, muttering to each other. Austin's clerk watched his employer's expression carefully. Remy continued to watch them both.

"Don't concern yourself," the clerk said. "In time they'll understand."

Austin sighed and smacked his lips. It was to be expected, he told him. It was innate in an American to suspect and abuse a public officer whether he deserved it or not. On the Méxicano frontier, he said, the empresario was the law. It was human nature, he said, that some of his colonists would challenge his absolute authority.

He said that considering the licentiousness and turbulence of the settlers, he hadn't fared so badly. Certainly much better than the other empresarios. This country's settlement demanded a strong and rugged nature in the colonials if the grant was to be successful. Such people were always hard to manage. Missouri and Arkansas had taught him that at an early age. He knew the frontier and the people that survived it. All of the settlers who were coming were once Americans, and for the most part were either ignorant or had been badly burned at least once before. No one had ever given them anything in the past, so when it happened as it was happening here, they were naturally suspicious. For them, independence meant resistance and obstinacy, right or wrong. This was particularly true of frontiersmen. And only they could endure the hardships of Texas.

Nevertheless, he said, he was working to earn their trust, and so they'd just have to wait and see. The future was easy to predict. "It will either get better," Austin said, "or very much worse."

All of this set Remy back. He'd questioned this man about his word! Back home a man in his position would've stuck a shotgun up Cox's nose and told him to scat if he wanted to keep it. This man Austin reasoned with him as an equal. Remy realized how rare such a man was anywhere he'd been.

Chapter Ten

Kills White Bear found a fresh set of tracks. He knew right away that they belonged to the traders. By sunset, he'd run them down, making camp near a little arroyo that joined the river the Méxicanos called the Medina. A small plume of smoke rose in the sky. Béxar was not more than a day's travel to the east. Another sun more would've been one too many.

It was clear to Kills White Bear that they'd been out for some time. Their pack animals were most likely loaded with buffalo and deer hides, and also maybe a little silver for which they had traded with the Lipan and Mescalero Apaches. The mules were overloaded and therefore worn and irritable, and for this reason progress had been slow. It was fitting, Kills White Bear thought, that the greed of these men had allowed him to catch them so easily.

There was nothing to think about, no strategy. He would sweep down on them like a north wind—sudden, cold and powerful—exactly the same way that the disease had come. He slipped his ankle in the noose that hung from his saddle, snapped the horse's bridle against its neck and then bore down on his quarry. The sharp-eyed New Méxicano saw him first and yelled a warning to the others. They immediately scrambled for their guns.

Kills White Bear screamed his war cry, spurred his horse, and raced for them. When their rifle barrels came up, he slipped down along the flank of the horse in the manner he'd practiced so many times as a boy, preparing to shoot his bow from under its foaming neck.

As he provided no target, they shot for his horse. The New Méxicano fired and missed, as did the other white man. Kills White Bear heard both balls whistle overhead. But the third trader was more patient and less rattled. He must have led the animal a little, for Kills White Bear felt the shudder of his horse's shoulder as the lead passed through its lungs. The animal collapsed instantly with a deep, prolonged groan, its stomach skidding hard against the rocky earth, its useless legs dragged beneath its own weight.

Kills White Bear separated from the horse as it fell, rolled two or three times on the ground, regained his feet, and raced for the traders, who were now frantically reloading their rifles, the butts of their stocks in the dust. When it became clear to them that there would not be time, the two closest to him reached for their knives and braced for Kills White Bear's attack.

His first arrow buried itself to the fletching in one of the trader's chest. He fell to his knees, paused a moment, and then fell forward into the dirt. The weight of his dying body snapped the arrow shaft in two. Kills White Bear dropped his bow and charged the other white man with his tomahawk. The trader lunged for him with his knife, but Kills White Bear struck him first in the arm, breaking it, and then buried the weapon to its handle between his eyes. He screamed horribly and fell. Kills White Bear anchored his bare foot on the man's throat and jerked the weapon free.

When he looked up, he saw the New Méxicano scrambling to reload his rifle. When he had, he threw the rod down at his feet and brought the rifle to bear as Kills White Bear turned toward him. In his terror he fired and missed, and Kills White Bear knocked him to the ground with the flat edge of the bloody tomahawk. He struggled to stand but Kills White Bear was on top of him, striking the other side of his beaten head with the weapon.

He straddled his victim and held his knife blade close against his throat. "Look at this face, *diablo*!" he grunted in Spanish. "Hear its words; for you'll hear no more. You brought death to my people, and I bring it back to you in return. It's an even trade, the first of its kind for you. Never set foot on the land of the People. The fate of these," he said, pointing to the dead men, "awaits any who dare."

With quick, precise strokes, he sliced off both of the man's ears and stuffed them in his mouth to muffle his screams. Then he rose from his victim and struck him once more with the flat of his tomahawk, knocking him unconscious. He waited to ensure that he would not choke. This one must live, he thought, as Wolf Eyes had instructed. When he was certain that he would, he scalped the other two and mounted the best of their fresh horses. With his war cry, he disappeared across the plains as quickly as he had come.

H

He found himself alone and exhausted in the rolling hills near Wolf Eyes' grave. He rode up to the stream that ran below it, the one in which he'd fought the great albino bear for its spirit, and fell from his horse into the cool water. He already knew by then that Wolf Eyes had been right. He had been too weak to wage that little war. He could not feed himself. He could not make it back. He crawled to the bank and whispered the words of his death chant, clutching his medicine bag in his right hand.

Then he heard movement in the bushes. He opened his eyes to focus on a single buffalo, a yearling bull, standing there proudly before him. He understood its thought, as he had the beasts on his vision quest ten winters before. He cocked his head to listen carefully as the miracle unfolded. "Take me," it said.

"Go on," Kills White Bear groaned. "Leave me." But the bull would not go.

"I'm here for you," it said.

Kills White Bear told him that he was grateful for such a sacrifice but he would not trade his life for the young bull's. He had nothing, he explained, to live for. His family was dead while the buffalo's must still live. Kills White Bear said the little bull should leave that place and return to the prairie where the deep grass grew.

This, the buffalo said, it could not do. The plains would be lost to both of them forever, and to all of their kind, if Kills White Bear allowed himself to die; it was surrendering its blood of its own free will for a greater good.

It said that the buffalo, all of them, loved life no matter how hard it was; and it was this respect and devotion that made this sacrifice so easy. The Great Spirit had told him to offer himself to the Nemenuh called Kills White Bear and no other, and the Great Spirit must be obeyed. In the end, he said, he was glad to do it. The land was everything to the buffalo, and it was well known that Kills White Bear would defend the land. It was, it said, their common heritage, their shared bond. His little life, then, was worth Kills White Bear's. "Now come and take it," it urged him. "I beg you."

Kills White Bear thought a moment. He didn't want to do it, of course. At least not like this. But the buffalo's words intrigued him. Wolf Eyes had told him as a boy of the promise he later thought the sickness had taken away. Now this buffalo reaffirmed those old, still unfulfilled words. If they were true—if great things were still to come after so much misery—then the struggle must continue regardless of the cost. He reminded himself that ten winters before he'd sworn to accept it. In order to honor his part of the bargain he would have to take the young bull's life.

He rose from the stream's bank, took his knife from the sheath and staggered toward the beast. It showed no sign of fear or apprehension. Yet Kills White Bear still hesitated.

"Do it while you still can," it said. "I'm ready."

"Stand still," Kills White Bear told him. "I'll make it quick." First he hung his head in prayer to thank the spirits for their gift and then, in one quick motion, he slit the animal's throat until its blood covered his hands. He cupped them beneath the flow while the bull stood still for him. When his hands were full he brought them to his lips and drank deeply.

Slowly the great animal collapsed, front legs first, then the rear. Its head rested on the soft green grass until the last long breath left its mouth. It grew still. Kills White Bear rolled it over as tears streamed down his face. He slit its belly from the pelvis to the ribcage, and cut its viscera free from the sheets of white membrane that held them, careful to leave its heart firmly in place out of respect. He found the liver and ate it raw. The salty gallbladder fol-

lowed. With the food in his stomach he collapsed, exhausted, against the warmth of the carcass and fell asleep.

The following morning he rose, stiff, sore, and famished,
and built a small fire. Then he peeled back the bull's hide,
and worked free the identical slabs of rich meat that lined
its spine. He smoked them well into mid-day and then ate
them as well. He rested one more day, gathered his things,
prayed to the Great Spirit to thank him for the bravery of
the young bull and to reassure him that his life, what was
left of it, belonged to his people. Then he caught his pony
and rode for the San Sabá.

The disease that took his family never left his thoughts
on that lonely trail home. The memory of his mangled wife
and child, the elders who had gone mad, that smell—the
smell of death—haunted him. But, there was much to do.
Kills White Bear would sit with the council, those that remained, and devise a strategy for the Wasps' survival. They
would take many child captives, he thought—Indian, Méxicano, and whites, too—and weave them into the Nemenuh
blanket in order to compensate for the dead. The raiding
would continue; the old ways would be taught. The Nemenuh must endure.

But as time passed he knew that the plague had left its
mark on the living. Not one family survived intact. Kills
White Bear watched the scabs of those who lived heal over
time as his had. Their hearts, however, were another matter. He learned later that it would take months for their
voices to return to normal. Until then they sat around fires
together and said nothing as if ashamed. In most cases the
lesions left scars that would ultimately disappear over the
course of that difficult year. Kills White Bear knew that his
own were deep enough to remain for life. Pock marks pitted his once smooth face, as rust did steel; the fever had
boiled the youth right out of his soul like sap from green
wood in a hot fire. And yet he sensed it was as Wolf Eyes
promised. He was maimed, yes, but he was also stronger.
The weak among his people clung to his muscled arms and
he welcomed them.

Something else was new. The blood he'd taken on the
Medina had served its initial purpose, but he soon learned
that it had done much more. Word had come to him that

the Méxicanos wanted to avenge the death of the traders. They wanted to make an example of any who defied their authority. Presidio soldiers were searching for a young Comanche warrior, he was told, known to them as Black Heart. The trader he let live had misunderstood who he was that day he'd chased him from the village. That pleased him as no other recent news had. Wolf Eyes' omen had come true. Surely the rest would soon follow. It was a matter of time and preparation. Both he endured alone.

But he knew that those happy family years were gone forever. No longer would he hear the sound of his son's laughter; never again would he lay beside that beautiful woman and stroke her hair, or feel the heat of her soft skin against his. On cold nights, his hatred for outsiders would warm him; Wolf Eyes had said that what took his family from him was a white disease.

Months would pass before he would even learn its name: the Comancheros called it smallpox.

Chapter Eleven

Remy awoke to the sound of a rider approaching. He rolled out of his bunk, shook Elijah, and then slipped his feet in his awaiting boots. His muscles were sore from the work. Smithwick had kept them busy from sunup to sundown for nearly four months.

A man called to him. Remy recognized the voice as Josiah Bell's, Austin's second in command, and emerged from his loft above the blacksmith shop with a lantern in his hand.

"What's the word, Bell?" he asked.

"Tonkawa raid at Sylvanus Castleman's place. They got off with his entire caballada, about thirty head of horses, give or take."

"What the hell do you want us to do about it?"

"Austin's called up the militia. That means you two fellers. Saddle up a couple of Smithwick's horses, get your smoke-poles, plenty of powder and balls, a little grub maybe, and come with me."

Soon Remy and Elijah were mounted and off for Austin's office at full gallop. They found Don Estévan ready, standing beside his horse, waiting for his men to arrive. He spoke with Josiah Bell. Remy remained at Bell's side.

"Confound it, man!" Austin declared, and Remy knew that was the absolute depths of his swearing. "My own horses were out there at Castleman's."

"Let's git after 'em, Don Estévan," Bell said. "We've got enough men on the hoof."

"It's too dark. Are you certain it was the Tonkawa?"

"No doubt in Castleman's mind. His man got a good look. No mistakin' them scrawny, thievin' Tonks."

Austin rubbed his face a moment, thinking. "Karankawas harass us along the coast, and the Tonkawas dig at us from the north. I've had it with this sort of thing. We'll take care of them one at a time." He turned to Bell. "Take the news to Lieutenant Morrison. Tell him to assemble his company of rangers at Castleman's at dawn. Do the same for Robinson and the others. Mr. Fuqua and Mr. Johnson will alert the Kuykendall brothers as well. We'll have fifty men in the field at first light and then put this business to an end."

"I'll spread the word," Remy heard Bell say. Then they spurred their horses and rode on.

Lieutenant Moses Morrison knelt at the banks of the Colorado at mid-morning. He looked up at Austin. Remy stood just behind him. "They crossed here," Morrison said slowly, "and then headed east."

"How many?" Austin asked.

"Eight or so," the tracker replied. "It's hard to tell since they were runnin' with loose horses."

"If they're bearing north they must be of Sandia's band. Are they not?"

"Most likely, Don Estévan." He spit out a stream of tobacco. "Most likely."

"Let's push on."

At a quarter after two that afternoon Austin rode at the head of his column into Sandia's encampment. The women and children were startled from their lodges, where their fires still burned to ward off mosquitoes despite the heat of the day, and ran into the brush. Sandia's warriors stood fast until the chief emerged to calm them.

This was Remy's first look at the Tonkawa. Glass beads adorned the lobes of the chief's ears, a necklace of these same beads alternating with shells wrapped around his thick neck. Tattooed rows of finely ground charcoal formed vertical lines on his brow, another set on his chin. On his dark chest Remy saw white lines that he guessed marked his stature among his people. The skull of a small animal was tied in his long, black hair; silver rings adorned several of his fingers. In his hand, he clutched a hand-carved limestone pipe, dyed red with vermilion; its ayume leaves, which Remy was told the Indians used as tobacco, still smoldered.

Sandia greeted Austin in Spanish, and the empresario answered in that same tongue. Remy, who had learned French as a boy, discovered that he had a facility for Spanish. He had made it a point to learn from whatever Méxicanos were available at San Felipe. He followed the conversation as best he could.

"¿Me conoces, Sandia?" Don Estévan asked.

"I've been at your lodge, Austin," Sandia replied gravely. "I do know you."

"Then you also know of my land and my people."

"I know your strange people. I know nothing of your land. No man owns the earth. It belongs to all."

It was the old argument, Remy knew. Austin brushed it off and got to the point. "Last night horses were stolen from my brother, Castleman. We followed the tracks to this place. We want the horses returned and we want the men who took them."

Remy saw that Sandia thought well before answering. He knew he was weighing options. "What will you do with those men who you say stole your horses?"

"Austin will punish them under the law of the Méxicano father," the empresario answered, using the third person as Remy was told was the Indian way.

The old man paused a moment. Remy could see that

he was worried. "Is it Austin's wish to hang them?" he finally asked.

"No," he said. "Not this time."

Sandia thought a moment, and then surveyed the riders with the empresario. "These men have anger in their eyes, Austin. They're here for blood, I think."

"It's true that they're angry. No food has passed their lips all day. The theft of the horses is a crime under our law. We won't tolerate this sort of thing, Sandia. Not anymore. If you don't give us the horses, we'll take them. We are many. The Tonkawa are few. Your warriors will die today if that's your wish."

The old chief puffed on his pipe as he surveyed the white men before him. *"Un momento,"* he said. "Let me talk to my people."

Austin nodded sternly. "Do so quickly. Remain where we can see you. We're waiting."

Remy and the others watched as the chief spoke with his men. The discussion was heated. Some of the younger warriors argued bitterly, stamping their feet, fingering their weapons. One young warrior in particular was furious with Sandia.

Remy sensed trouble, and instinctively cocked the hammer on his rifle as silently as he drew breath. He watched a moment more and then pulled the set trigger. Only a slight touch more and that rifle would fire. Austin had seen him, and he reached over and patted the hand that rested on the rifle's breech.

"Easy," he said quietly, "let's not make it worse." Then he turned away.

In an instant the young warrior broke from the band, a tomahawk in his hand. He dashed straight for Austin with the weapon poised over his head. Without thinking, Remy popped his Gump rifle—seven and one half pounds of flamed maple, English lock and Damascus steel—to his shoulder, where it fit as naturally as a third arm. His right eye fell down the sights, found the warrior's sweating chest, followed it as he ran, and then Remy cleanly jerked the second and last trigger. Smithwick had set it to less than a pound's pull. There was that instant when the hammer's flint snapped against the battery carrying the spark to the

pan, the pause between the ignition of the primer charge
and the powder packed behind the patch in the bore—the
hang-fire—when Remy regretted pulling the trigger. There
was an angry young man lined up in those cold, iron sights.

Beneath the cloud of drifting white smoke he saw the
impact of the ball as it struck the Tonkawa squarely in the
chest. The force blew him backwards. He screamed in
agony, blood bubbling from his nose and mouth, but none
of Sandia's band moved to comfort him. In a moment, all
movement ceased.

Remy was wild-eyed and breathless as the Gump slid
from his shoulder. He did not mean to kill this man. It just
happened. He could feel all eyes present, both Indian and
white, upon him. He tried to save face, to look manly, as if
this is what he'd chosen to do. He hadn't. There wasn't time
to consider consequences. His heart sank as he looked upon
the still, bloody body of the Tonkawa warrior. He'd killed
someone who appeared to be his own age. He looked at
Elijah, his face flush, cheeks puffing. His cousin's startled
expression asked, "What have you done?"

Sandia walked calmly over to Austin. "That was one of
the raiders," he said. "The other six are coming with the
horses."

Austin remained mounted, waiting. Remy was beside
himself. His breathing escalated, his hands shook. He did
not dare try and reload his rifle. He wished Elijah would
come up and comfort him but his cousin stayed clear.

Soon the stolen horses were brought before Austin's men
but the Tonkawa took them by the reins, and held them
back. Six Tonkawa warriors emerged and stood unarmed
before Don Estévan. He signaled for Morrison's men to
take them. Remy noted that none of the militia men had
to be told what to do. They just seemed to know. The
rangers tied each brave to a live oak, ripping the buckskin
shirt from each of their backs. Then they took their knives
and shaved each warrior's head. The cherished braid, which
Remy knew was the sign of manhood, was the first to fall
to the dirt. Then, one by one, Morrison whipped them with
a lash. Not one warrior cried out. Tears of pain streamed
down the faces of the youngest ones. The others showed
no trace of the agony Remy knew they must be feeling.

He looked at the expressions of Austin and the others. They were like stone. No one cared for the others. It was war. Remy grimaced at the sound of each stroke, the crack of leather against bare skin. Horses by the thousands supposedly ran free in Texas. As far as Remy was concerned, this punishment was far worse than the crime.

When it was finished the rangers returned silently to their horses. They looked confident, vindicated, relieved. Sandia signaled for his men to release the thieves. When they were free, they stood with the rest of their people, staring at the white men with eyes of hatred. Most of them were focused on Remy. He knew that in their minds he was the worst of them all. Sandia approached Don Estévan once more. "These are the horses you seek, Austin?"

"I recognize my own among them, but there're forty head of horses here. Only thirty-two were taken from us."

"Sandia brings eight of his own as his gift of peace."

"The gift is accepted with much gratitude. In exchange, I offer you tobacco if you like."

"*Sí,*" he answered.

"I don't use it, but the men have plenty to give." At his suggestion, several offered their pouches to Sandia, who distributed them amongst his men, those that weren't bleeding. This was all very strange, Remy thought.

"Understand me, Austin," Sandia began. "Raiding's a way of life for the Tonkawa. It makes warriors of young men. These you have humiliated before their fathers are but boys. None of your people were killed, but I have one son to bury. My warriors meant you no harm. It's our way."

Austin leaned forward in his saddle and spoke. "There are plenty of wild mustangs on the prairie, Sandia. They belong to no one. If the Tonkawa must steal to become men, the Comanche have many fine horses, as do the Lipans."

"Those Indians steal from the Tonkawa. Like Austin's people, they are many and the Tonkawa are few. We're between two fires." Remy understood that well enough.

"We have a treaty with Carita's Tonkawa," Austin told him. "They do not enter the colony and they do not steal from us. In exchange, they're not interfered with and can

live as they please. Carita's warriors raid whomever they
like. But they can't raid us. We offer you the same terms,
Sandia."

"So be it, Austin," Sandia agreed. Then he said that the
empresario could take his horses and his men and go; make
their scars in the earth until their teeth fell out; cut down
the trees until the wind blows their silly clothes off their
backs; look after those stupid beasts that ate the prairie
grass down to the roots so that the rivers ran black after
the slightest rain. Their meat, he said, was tough and
tasteless. The Tonkawa had no need of them. They were
like white men with fur—big, dumb, ugly, and everywhere he looked. When the rains came in the spring,
maybe all the whites would be washed away in the muddy
rivers because their beasts had stolen the Great Spirit's
grass. Everything they touched soon died. For all Sandia
cared, they could live in peace with their sickly women.
They'd gotten what they came for, and more. Sandia said
he wanted nothing more to do with any of them. "Where
did you all come from anyway?" he asked. "When I was a
young warrior, one never saw a white man. Nowadays
that's all there is in the world."

"We'll meet under better circumstances next time, Chief
Sandia," Austin told him.

"I don't think so," the old man said.

"If your people are hungry, Sandia, come to Austin and
he'll feed them. If they're cold, he'll clothe them. If the
Tonkawa need powder and lead to hunt game, he'll trade
you fairly for it. There need be no war between us. But if
your people steal from Austin there'll be more bloodshed.
Tonkawa women will weep for their men. Hear these
words, Sandia. What Austin says is true."

"I hear you, Austin. The Tonkawa want nothing from
the whites but to be left alone."

"Then we are both the same," he said. "Good day to
you, Sandia."

Austin wheeled his mount around and rode through the
column. After they re-crossed the Colorado, he leaned over
and spoke to Remy.

"Are you all right, Fuqua? You look pale."

"Did it have to be like that?" Remy asked.

Austin did not look at him. "I abhor violence," he finally said. "But violence is the only thing those people understand. I've tried everything. Nothing else works. The more we give them, the more they steal. If it'd been your property they took, you'd feel differently."

"The horses weren't worth that boy's life."

"In Texas, they are."

"Somebody else should've shot that man. It shouldn't have been me. Nobody else moved. I *had* to do it."

Austin's eyes steadied him. "It was my life or his, Fuqua. I'd like to think you did the right thing. I can see you're shaken but you must adapt to the frontier. The rules you learned in your mother's house don't apply here."

"The hell they don't," Remy said.

Austin looked at him curiously. "I know it's not easy, Mr. Fuqua; but you have to understand. First the savages must fear us. Then we'll earn their respect, and only then will we have peace. We can't live together as things are. I hope they'll change, I sincerely do. Otherwise, should they continue to get in our way, they'll die. It's as simple as that." Remy said nothing. "I know it takes a little getting used to. We make hard choices here. We make them everyday."

Hard choices, Remy thought. The words made him think again of his mother and of the one she'd made. He could see her lips on that shotgun just before she pulled the trigger, the blood's distorted path as it dripped from those cheap window panes, the flames that engulfed his father's house as he ran through those dark woods to a place that was even worse. He could still feel the sting of his uncle's leather straps on his back. He knew what those young Tonkawas felt: the numbness of their blistered skin, the blood drying on wounds that would never really heal, the despair of submission, the humiliation of defeat. He thought he'd left all of that pain behind him the day he left his uncle's farm. He had no idea that what he'd run from in Louisiana was waiting for him here. New faces, same ruthless game. The price of land in Texas was twelve and a half cents an acre, plus the blood of those you took it from. It wasn't so cheap after all. Where was that place on earth, he wondered, where you could pay your money, own your land,

and live in peace? He had to ask himself, how much further would he have to go? Now he'd taken another man's life, and his was changed forever.

What troubled him most, however, was that he knew he could do it again if he had to. The next time, he believed, it wouldn't bother him half as much. He'd discovered something about himself that day. Something horrible. He'd inherited the ugly instinct. At his core he was every bit the killer that his mother was.

1827

Chapter Twelve

Remy and Elijah were busy repairing a plow, their hands grimy with a mixture of rust and axle grease. Its owner arrived to check on their progress and seemed satisfied. He paid Smithwick for the work with three bushels of fresh corn and a gourd of liquor.

"Where ya headed, Gibbs?" the smith asked, his hand already fumbling with the cork.

"Out to the plains," the man Gibbs huffed. He was a square-headed barrel-chested man, rough and vigorous. "I'm in need of horses, and maybe a beeve or two."

Up went the gourd. Its contents nearly choked Smithwick. "Augh!" he grunted, his face skewed, eyes misty. "That's mighty good." He wiped his lips with the burnt sleeve of his shirt. Remy wondered what would happen if he drank the really bad stuff. "Need company?"

"I'm not opposed to it, Smithwick," Gibbs roared, as if Smithwick were deaf. "I'll be out some time, I think. Prepare accordingly. Course there won't be time for any tobacky smugglin' or some such." Remy had heard that Smithwick was a smuggler. Apparently Gibbs had too.

"I'm not thinking of me, Mr. Gibbs." He turned and

pointed to Remy and his cousin. "These fellers here are plannin' on farmin' after the new year if Don Estévan gets off his stiff arse and gives 'em their grant. They could use horses, and cattle as well. I'll vouch for 'em. They're good boys."

Elhanan Gibbs looked closely at the two prospects and then smiled and shook his head. "They're a little too smooth in the chin for my likin', Smithwick. They couldn't keep up."

Remy had heard much talk of the wild horses. He didn't know much about them but he knew he wanted some. He stepped forward to state his case. "We'll tag along with ya, Mister, if'n you'll let us. If we give out, you leave us where we fall." He nodded toward Elijah. "My cousin and me'll go at our own risk. We ain't your problem if we can't pull our own weight."

"Well, now, Smithwick," Gibbs huffed. "Your man is spicy." He turned back to Remy. "Fair enough. You're free to come alon' on those same terms. We'll leave at dawn."

Noah Smithwick smiled at Remy. "Let's work them guns over this evenin', boys," he said. "I'll outfit ya both the best I can, but I don't have horses to spare for that length of time. Mind you don't forget where you got this stuff."

Up went the gourd. "Augh!"

At first light, Remy and Elijah met Gibbs at the appointed place. From there, the party moved southwest. Gibbs was mounted, Remy and Elijah on foot. They crossed the Colorado River, then the Navidad and the La Vaca, and clipped the southeast corner of DeWitt's Grant. By sundown the following day, they had forded the Guadalupe River and entered Martín de León's survey.

Gibbs said that he knew de León well, having traded horses to him in the past. He explained to the cousins that de León had settled his grant mostly with Mexican colonists; many were his own lieutenants, vaqueros or ranch hands and peons. Green DeWitt had told Remy that he found Martín de León to be a quarrelsome neighbor, but Gibbs thought otherwise. They arrived at de León's hacienda around three in the afternoon on the third day, and Remy was surprised to see that the ranch, which was magnificent, was also nearly devoid of activity. The two things just didn't seem to match up in his mind.

"Siesta," Gibbs explained. "The Mexicans know better'n to work in the heat. Draw some water from the well and take a load off. Somebody'll show up directly." Remy found some shade and lay down to rest. Elijah reclined next to him.

After six, de León surfaced from the great limestone *casa mayore*, the big house. Shortly thereafter, several of his vaqueros appeared as well. Gibbs approached and shook the empresario's hand.

"Ah, Don Martín," he said in Spanish. "It's good to see you."

"Señor Gibbs, your visit pleases me. What brings you here this hot afternoon?"

"I'm out after mustangs."

He nodded toward Remy and his cousin. "With these two boys?"

"I'm afraid so."

"Are they *sin pies*?" he asked, meaning horseless.

"I'm afraid they are."

"Oh, I couldn't bear that in this heat," he exclaimed. "Let's find them a nag, shall we?" Don Martín ordered his foreman to have his caballada driven in so that they could choose. Soon the herd came running in a thunder of hooves and a cloud of fine dust. Never before had Remy seen such fine stock, nor had he witnessed such excellent horsemanship, effortless as breath, as by Don Martín's vaqueros.

He and Elijah, deeply impressed, were surveying the lot when a young woman caught his eye. All interest in the horses vanished. She stood quietly, in vaquero dress, a finely embroidered cloth coat, handworked leather chaparreras wrapped tightly around her legs, boots to the knee, silver spurs at her heels. Her hair, like black satin, flashing silver when the sun caught it right, was tied back in a ponytail, which she wore draped across one shoulder. When she finally moved, Remy noted her caution, reserve, grace, and dignity. The only thing Remy could think of in comparison was a deer. No woman he'd ever seen had carried herself like that.

Another man in fine dress observed the object of Remy's attentions and stepped into the line of sight between Remy and the woman, staring him down coldly. Remy'd forgotten he was a foreigner until he was treated like one. Intimidated, he returned his gaze to what Gibbs called the *corral de leña,* a working pen of mesquite post corners, solidly fenced with wood. Remy tried to focus on the business at hand, but he could not keep from stealing glimpses whenever he had a clear shot. He stepped back and forth several times to get around the man he assumed to be her father, who kept adjusting his position as well, to thwart him. Every now and then, Remy'd catch her looking at him through dark, narrow eyes. Whether it was out of a general curiosity or a genuine interest in him personally, he couldn't say. He didn't propose to understand women. Yet he assumed that if it was the oddity that intrigued her, she would've naturally focused on Elijah, whose big nose, buckteeth, awkward mannerisms, and bristly red hair, like a razorback boar on fire, stood out in any crowd. But on that one occasion when her eyes caught his and she smiled warmly back at him, he felt he had his confirmation. Remy nearly melted right out of his clothes.

That was the end of it. Her father had seen what Remy had, wrapped his arm around her shoulder, and escorted her to the far side of several men.

Gibbs left Don Martín's side and walked up to the corral.

"Choose one, boys, and let's be off," he said, and when Remy didn't respond as Gibbs thought he should, he elbowed him in the ribs. "Mind your business, dammit. You're burnin' my daylight."

"What's he askin'?" Elijah inquired.

"It's a gift."

"He must want somethin'," Remy said.

"It's yours if you can ride it. Don Martín's a generous man."

"In that case I'll take that one," Remy said, pointing to a large, muscular bay stallion in the center of the bunch.

"That one appears a little spirited for a tenderfoot, son. Understand these is just off the range and ain't saddlebroke. I'd take the old gray mare if'n I were you. All you need is a sway back for your ass and four feet. She's got 'em."

"I'll stick with my first choice," Remy insisted. As he watched, a vaquero cut the designated stallion from out of the nervous herd, slipped a horsehair bridle over its head and a bit between its teeth, and then held it securely while he waited for Remy to approach.

Remy saw the horse's eyes were wild and frantic, its breath snorting through flared nostrils. He'd never fooled with a horse like this. Every chiseled muscle on that animal twitched with nervous power. Remy mounted the horse precariously, struggling to place his awkward feet in the huge Mexican stirrups. As soon as the vaquero let loose, the horse's head went down and his rear shot up. With its first bolt, Remy found himself laying on his back in the dust. He tried a second time, with the same result.

All the vaqueros roared with laughter, joking among themselves, mimicking his awkward movements, slapping each other on the back. Remy couldn't stand it. He intended to ride that goddamn horse.

"¿Otra vez, jinete?" one of them asked, calling him "horse breaker." Remy ignored the insult, picked up his hat, slapped it across his thighs to knock off the dust, and then pulled it down tightly over his head.

"Sí, hombre," he said, before he spit out the grit. *"Otra vez."*

Gibbs and de León stood with one foot each up on the corral posts. Remy could hear them talking.

"I should mention that we have burros available also," Don Martín said. Gibbs was likewise amused, but only briefly. He kept looking at the position of the sun then back at Remy with an expression that said there just wasn't going to be a whole lot more time.

Remy waved the holder away and mounted, his teeth clenched, a third time. Before he could position himself the horse began to spin. Remy stuck with the beast for awhile until it threw him through the top posts of the corral. They snapped and fell beside him. Elijah went to help him to his feet but Remy rose of his own accord to the tumult of the vaqueros' laughter, defeated.

"You try," Remy said to Elijah.

"Like hell. That goddamn mare looks mean enough. We didn't have horses like these in Louisiana. These here ain't never been rid, an' I don't expect they're ever gonna be." Remy looked around, observing that all eyes were upon him. Worst of all, the girl was watching too. He might as well've been out there in his knickers with a lollipop in his mouth. He was certainly used to people hoping he'd fail. That's all his uncle had ever done. He just wasn't used to them enjoying it so much. Remy decided he wouldn't give them the satisfaction.

"I ain't licked yet," he declared, biting his lip, and at his request the horse was led back to him for yet a fourth attempt. In one hand he gripped the reins white knuckled; in the other he held a fistful of the horse's mane, equally tight. Another vaquero, apparently more sympathetic to Remy's plight, held his sweat-stained sombrero over the horse's eyes, speaking to it in calm, smooth words, allowing Remy the time he needed to get secure in the saddle.

"*¿Está listo, joven?*" the man asked.

Remy exhaled and nodded his head. "Yeah, I'm ready," he said, and the Mexican released the animal. The horse reared twice but Remy held on. Then its head dropped, and it began spinning. Remy's back fell against the horse's hip but he remained firmly in the center. When that failed, it raced for the corral fence at full speed, locking all four legs just inches away from the wooden border. Remy slid up from the saddle over the horse's head. He desperately clenched its neck with both arms and legs and would not let go. Then the horse wheeled for the opposite corner. Remy could not get back in the saddle. This time when it stopped the horse threw him clear of the fence, flipping him head over heels, where he landed on a small prickly-pear cactus. Elijah ran over to help him up.

"You all right?" he asked.

"I'm licked," Remy said. "I can't ride that son of a bitch, Elijah. He'll kill me first."

That was all it seemed that Elijah needed to hear. Remy

saw him turn to Gibbs. "If'n you don't mind, Mr. Gibbs, I believe we'd prefer to walk for a time."

Gibbs reported the conversation to de León, who laughed along with his men, but bowed to acknowledge how hard Remy'd tried.

"I understand your concerns," the Tejano told him. "Another time, perhaps, when your backsides are better callused and there aren't so many cacti around." Then he turned to Gibbs, "Tejas is a hard place, and these are Tejas horses. They're not the best mounts for beginners."

Gibbs quite agreed. Somewhere out there in the Wild Horse Desert, he said, was an old mare for them to ride. He hoped for their sakes that they came across it. "Well, I guess that we'll be off, Don Martín," Gibbs said.

"So soon, Señor Gibbs?"

"I've crops to look after."

"A good harvest is expected, I trust."

"If we get some rain maybe. In Texas, ya never know."

"Best of luck to you," the empresario said. "My regards to Colonel Austin. Have those boys return to me when they get some hair on their chests. My offer remains open. I'll mount them well, one horse each."

"I'll pass that along," Gibbs replied with a wink of a sparkling eye.

Remy rose and knocked the dust from his pants. He attempted to walk with what was left of his dignity but could not do it. The needles stung him with each choppy step. He picked out what ones he could reach, but he could not get them all. He asked that Elijah remove the rest. Elijah couldn't reach the tough ones with Remy standing, so he bent over with some reluctance. The vaqueros howled.

"Is that it?" Elijah asked.

Remy took a step or two. "Naw," he moaned, "more yet."

"Drop 'em," Elijah said.

"Like hell," Remy argued.

"Suits me," his cousin said. "But if'n you want 'em out, ya gotta drop your drawers."

With the deepest remorse, he let his pants drop to his knees and bent over, his bare ass exposed to the sun. Most of the vaqueros fell off the fence in hysterics. There was little for Remy to do but stick it out, get it over with, and get the hell out. At least the girl wasn't around anymore to witness his humiliation.

As he looked around his gaze fell on a little Tejano boy sitting calmly with his back to the barn. He was dressed the same as the other vaqueros, only in miniature, like a doll.

"Somethin' like this ever happen to you?" Remy asked in Spanish.

The child shook his head, and then said, "My mother won't allow me to talk to Anglos." Remy laughed, and told Elijah what he'd said.

"Well," Elijah smirked, "you're talkin' to one now, ain't ya, ya little greaser."

Remy straightened and popped his cousin on the shoulder. "You don't talk to a kid like that. What's wrong with you?"

"Why the hell not? He don't know what I'm sayin'."

"It don't matter if'n he does or don't. It ain't right. Your mama'd be ashamed."

"Well you oughta know," Elijah snapped.

"What's that supposed to mean?"

Elijah didn't answer, not to that. "What I'm ashamed of," he said, "is havin' to spend my afternoon pickin' needles out of your ass in front of God and all these Mexicans. It's damn embarrassin'."

"Shut up, and keep a-pickin'," Remy said as he bent back over, certain that Elijah shoved the next one in a little deeper before he yanked it out. "Ouch!" he cried. "You just wait. Your time's comin'." Remy turned back to the boy. "I wonder why your mother told you that?" he asked him.

"She says white men are the sons of the devil."

"Well," Remy said, "if she meant my cousin here, she'd be dead on; but I'm all right." The boy stared at him for a moment, nodded, and then agreed that Remy looked all right. "What's your name?"

"Cristóbal Picosa," the child answered.

"Well, Cristóbal," Remy said, "you look like a man that knows a lot about horses."

"I know everything about horses, señor."

"Is that a fact?"

"It's a fact, señor."

"What am I doin' wrong, then?"

Remy was damned if the kid didn't have some ideas. The more intently Remy listened, the more the boy's chest puffed with pride. Cristóbal told him that Remy should've stroked the horse, maybe tried to feed it a little fresh hay or sugar, let it get used to his scent before he flopped his rear on its back. His father, he said, was a firm believer in placing his mouth over an animal's nose and blowing into its nostrils several times before ever attempting to break it. All of these things were generally good to know, the kid said. But they were of no use to Remy for that particular horse. He was never going to ride it.

"Why's that?" Remy asked.

"Because he just didn't like you," the boy said.

"You can tell that?"

"Oh, yes. Always," he said, and then he explained exactly how. Remy listened to every word, turning back every now and then to wink at Elijah, until Cristóbal's mother called him to come for his supper. They shook hands as they parted.

"That sounds like mighty good advice," Remy said, grinning. "I'm gonna get a chance to try out some of it here pretty soon. I'll be sure and let you know how it turns out."

"If you do," the boy said, "the next time I see you, you'll be mounted on a fine mustang. I promise."

Remy combed his fingers through the boy's fine hair, soft like black corn silk. "You made a friend today, little Cristóbal."

"So did you," the boy said, and he drifted away toward the sound of his mother's voice.

Remy watched the boy until his attention was drawn to the thud of a boot heel and the accompanying chink of spurs somewhere in the barn. Through the cracks in the boards he clearly saw the line of her embroidered collar; then the creased knee of those long, shiny, golden brown chaps; a glossy curl of that raven-black hair; and lastly a brief glimpse at her cheek—smooth, the tint of his aunt's summer roses—as she turned back to see if he'd heard her, before she passed under the doorway and disappeared into the shadows that lay between the barn and the big, white stone house beyond.

Chapter Thirteen

Remy lay prone between Gibbs and Elijah on a bluff overlooking a water hole. The arroyo that fed it had long since dried, but the pool was cut deep in limestone and the water was clear.

"It's hot as hell out here," Elijah said.

"That's why we're waitin'," Gibbs told him. "Them mustangs'll come to the water directly."

"I wouldn't mind a little splash myself," Remy said.

"You sit tight, son," Gibbs barked. "I'm here for horses." Remy studied him a moment.

"How exactly you plan to catch 'em from up here?" he asked.

"Why, I'm goin' to crease 'em," Gibbs explained. He never looked at him.

"What?"

"You watch. Look yonder out on the flat. There they be."

In the haze of the afternoon sun, the horses almost appeared to be sailing on a cloud of dust as they swept toward the water hole. Remy counted over thirty head in this band. Most he judged to be mares of various ages; half a dozen were colts and as many were young stallions, all driven by the dominant male, a magnificent black-legged bay.

Such a grouping, Gibbs told him, the Mexicans called a *manada*. Remy was stunned by their majestic beauty, their coats glistening in the late afternoon sun. From where Remy watched, they looked to be a little smaller than de León's stock.

All the way out to the desert, Gibbs had talked of the horses. They weren't really called mustangs, he'd said, which was a frontier corruption of the Spanish word *mesteña*, or feral, but the name had stuck anyway. Gibbs said that maybe as many as one million head roamed free on the open grass, rivaling the buffalo herds of the southern plains. The horses, he said, were of Spanish descent, and therefore Arabian and North African, mixed with other European blood lines. They had evolved in the arid climate of Spanish Andalusia, so they naturally thrived in the similar environment of the Mexican frontier.

Gibbs had explained that breeding among the horses was intensely competitive, as much as with any truly wild beast, and only the most powerful males proliferated their line. Any weakness in the bloodline, therefore, lay with the mares because the strongest stallions bred them all. Unlike truly wild animals, Gibbs said the horses had no specific mating season that he knew of, so the dominant males bred with their manada mares throughout the year, which explained in part why their numbers escalated rapidly in this place where they had few natural predators.

Gibbs pointed a chapped finger at a wrinkled map, to an area marked the "Wild Horse Desert," a triangle below San Antonio de Béxar and points west, extending all the way south to the Río Bravo. It was the land of the mustangs, he'd said, the negligent by-product of Spanish colonization, and the herds owned the southern range by right of sheer overwhelming numbers. They adapted to the land and then controlled it. Tough, smart, and aggressive, nothing native, Gibbs had said, could stand in their way. There was most likely a lesson in that, Remy thought. In this new land, nature seemed to favor the unnatural. Whatever problems the horses' presence might pose, he could not deny that what he saw before him was truly magnificent. They charmed him as nothing else had, short of that woman, as he watched them emerge from the badlands, swatting at the cloud of gnats with their uncut tails. Already, he loved this place called Tejas.

This particular manada, Remy observed, circled downwind from the pool, testing the air. At last a cautious young stallion—clearly not the manada's dominant male as far as Gibbs, who hung back with his mares, driving rather than leading them, could tell—walked slowly to the bank, his head back probing, his restless eyes watching all. In time, he was satisfied and lowered his head to drink. The others in the band stood in the distance, nervous eyes all on him.

"That one there'll do for starters," Gibbs said with a squint. "We'll work up the others later. That big bay stallion yonder runs that bunch. He'll keep 'em together after the shot." He slid his rifle forward, resting the forearm on a limestone rock. Taking careful aim, he squeezed the trigger, and the hammer fell. The young horse immediately collapsed, its front legs twitching, on the muddy bank.

"What did 'ja do that fer, Gibbs?" Elijah asked, a little miffed.

"Now don't you fret, boy," Gibbs said. "He's just stunned. Let's go get a rope around him 'fore he regains his senses."

Gibbs was off down the draw like a shot, slowing only as he neared the fallen animal, at which time he carefully tossed his braided rawhide lariat around the animal's neck. He pulled it tight, made three or four wraps around the trunk of a scrub oak and prepared for the inevitable fight. "Get back, boys. He'll give us hell here in a minute or two."

They waited. But the horse just lay there, motionless. Not too long afterwards, Elijah stood and walked over to the prostrate animal. He bent over to examine it more closely. Then he rose and kicked it squarely in the nose. Nothing.

"This one here's caught good," he said. Gibbs released his grip and moved toward the animal himself.

"Guess the shot fell a little low," Gibbs explained, shaking his head humbly. He examined his rifle, as if he thought something might be wrong with it.

"What do'ya say we try and catch one alive?" suggested Remy, deeply disappointed.

"I've creased these mustangs a hundred times," Gibbs stated defensively. "It works good."

"I kin see that," Elijah said, kicking the horse again.

"Well, hell," Gibbs said, scratching his oily head. "I guess this one we'll skin out and eat. Then we'll move out deeper to the south. I'll get the ol' barrel warmed up here directly. Wild horses are thicker'n fleas on a mule's ass out here."

Remy glanced at Elijah and he knew right off that his cousin didn't place any more faith in Gibbs's shooting than he did. It'd been a long, hot walk. They needed horses. He looked around to see how the land lay, reflected a minute about how they'd trapped his uncle's hogs in the Quachita River bottom, and then he knew he had a better way.

"We're new at this, Gibbs," he said. "But maybe you could push 'em yonder into that little draw. They can't jump that bluff there and it's nearly in the shape of a skinny horseshoe. Sooner or later, they'll figure they got to get out the way they come in. Me an' Elijah'll wait at the neck with them ropes you got. We oughta sag off and let 'em drink their fill. I ain't no expert, but I know an animal can't run as fast with a full belly as with an empty one. If they're as thirsty as they look, they'll drink plenty. If'n you can get 'em in there we'll more'n likely catch us a few, still kickin', too."

Gibbs scratched his head. When his fingers left it, the hair still stood. "That's how the Comanche do it, I suppose. I prefer to crease 'em, though. It ain't so damn dangerous."

"It is for the horse," Remy said.

"For the horse, that's right. But that lassoing ain't as easy as them Mexicans make it look."

Remy's experience with de León's stock told him that Gibbs was probably right. Nothing those vaqueros did was as easy as it looked. But his idea might still work with a little adjustment. He could still see the horses grazing out there in the flat. They hadn't run far. They must need water badly. He certainly did. God Almighty, what heat! If he and Elijah were careful, and lucky, maybe the herd would come back in to drink.

"Me and Elijah'll see 'bout closing off a part of the canyon with brush and sticks and what not," he told Gibbs. "If we can't rope 'em, we can maybe pen 'em in."

Gibbs thought about that. "I'm game to give it a try, fellers. But your brush wall gots to be thick to fool 'em. If they see

it for what it is, they'll bust right through it. It'll take us a
little time to get something to make do." He squinted his
eyes to look over the layout. "But this damn canyon's narrow
and the water here's good. Them horses ain't goin' nowhere,
I'll wager ya that. I'll help get the trap set up. We'll practice
a bit with the ropes too, I reckon. 'Fore it's all over they'll
have to be roped. Watch you don't get run over. A broken
leg out here'll do ya in. I can't pack ya."

The thought of injury had never crossed Remy's mind.
Now it just kind of stuck there. He shook it off. "We'll
worry about that, Gibbs," he told him. "Head 'em this a
way when the time's right. We'll be ready. I'm gonna catch
me one of them horses 'cause I ain't walkin' back."

"Me, neither," Elijah said. "It's either the horse or me."

"It'll take us a day or so to make ready, boys," Gibbs
allowed. "The wind's all wrong, too. We need to work with
the breeze. Otherwise, they'll smell the both of ya and
they'll never set hoof in that canyon."

"It might be days 'fore the wind changes," Elijah said.

"Maybe so," Gibbs agreed. "The thing to do is hang with
'em at a safe distance; let 'em get used to our scent so they
don't spook so goddamn bad. At the same time, we'll keep
'em away from the water, rather'n give 'em some. We'll
stay close enough to keep 'em nervous where they won't
sleep. But we gotta keep after 'em. A wild horse don't need
but four hours a day to stay sharp. We'll take shifts to see
that they don't get it for the next couple of days. That'll
throw 'em off kilter enough so maybe they'll be fool
enough to get pushed into that canyon. The other two'll
get the brush line set up. If it works, we'll catch mustangs.
If it don't, you boys got a long walk ahead of ya. I can't
stay out here forever."

"Neither can we," Remy said. Elijah nodded.

At dawn the next day, Remy rode in cold and thirsty. Gibbs
was up first, brewing that awful coffee. They ate dried horse

meat and corn bread, which Gibbs had milled from his own grain, and then went back to work before the day grew too warm.

By mid-morning, the wind was back up, blowing hot and dusty. It chapped their lips and cracked the skin on their hands. They worked throughout that day and the next, each taking a turn to watch the mustangs.

Toward afternoon, the horses drifted toward the water hole. Remy watched as Gibbs let them get close enough that they could taste it on the wind, and then as he rode slowly between them and what they came for, they just stood and stared at the mounted rider, too tired or too thirsty to run. Gibbs didn't hoop or holler or move too close. He did nothing to agitate them. He just stood there watching as they watched him.

Meanwhile, the brush wall grew taller and more stout. By midday the following day, the breeze swung around from out of the west. Remy knew that a cross wind was good enough. He watched as Gibbs traipsed up and down the line, shaking limbs and kicking at stones. Finally he smiled at his partners and announced that all was ready.

"Course, it'd be better to have a proper picketed corral, I reckon," he allowed with unwelcome reservation. "That's how the real mustangers do it, but we ain't got the man-power or the materials. I gen'ly crease me a couple and go on about my bizness. Just the same, this might work. Them yonder," he said, meaning the mustangs, "is 'bout give out. I know I ain't thinkin' right in this heat and don't 'spect they are neither. I don't think they'll get out if'n we can get 'em in. It's all or nuthin', boys. Ya'll game?"

"Goddamn right," Elijah said. Remy agreed. He planned to ride something home even if it was his cousin's back.

"All righty then," Gibbs said. "Let's catch us a horse." He gathered his things and mounted. "When they come in for the water this afternoon," Gibbs said, "I'll approach from the south. You fellers get ready and say your prayers. I count thirty-two head and there ain't a nag in the bunch. We want 'em all."

"You just get 'em here," Remy said. "We'll do the rest."

"Mind you stay clear of that stallion. He kin easily kill the both of ya and he's liable to try. He's tired and he's thirsty, but he's a long way from whipped. He's a damn fine animal, well worth the time. But, he's gonna give us hell. I grant ya that."

"We gotta catch him first," Remy said.

"And we're agonna. I'll be back directly."

Remy sat in the shade of the skinny mesquites to rest until the time came. His cousin soon joined him.

"I'm run down worse than a dollar watch," Elijah said.

"You best wind yourself back up. We gotta catch them horses or we're done for."

"I don't know 'bout this Texas, Remy."

Why would this come to his cousin's mind now, Remy wondered? This was the best time Remy had ever had in his life. Would Elijah prefer hoeing weeds in Will's sorry cotton fields to laying under the stars dreaming of wild horses? Just the same, he knew what was coming next.

"Don't say it, goddammit."

"What?" Elijah asked, his face blank.

"You know what."

"Well, it was your idea, weren't it?"

"Just don't say it." Remy tossed out what remained of his coffee and set the tin cup upside down on Gibbs's rock. Then he went to check their corral one last time.

Remy had drifted off when he was awakened by a rumble in the distance, the sound of horses on the run. He jumped up and nudged Elijah in the ribs with his booted foot. Remy saw then that Gibbs had them all galloping toward the mouth of the canyon. He hung back, zig-zagging across to cut off any attempt to rise out of the narrowing draw. Once they were a couple of hundred yards from the mouth of the V, Remy's heart raced. He knew they had them.

Now Gibbs pressed the horses, bellowing as loudly as he could. In they went. Gibbs herded them past Remy and Elijah, who hid behind the trunks of the weepy mesquites, waiting with long limbs that would seal off the only remaining opening in the makeshift pen. Gibbs raced up, leaped from his horse, and frantically helped them seal the flimsy barrier between the horses and freedom. Remy forgot all about his exhaustion, the ache in his muscles, the sting of sweat in his eyes, because the mustangs, all thirty-two of them, now belonged to them.

"If that ain't luck I don't know what is," Gibbs said, breathless. "Usually they bait the stallion in with a tame mare and the others follow. I just kind of walked 'em in here like we was in a parade in New Orleans. Who'd have figured? It'll never happen again in my lifetime, I can tell ya that."

"What now, Gibbs?" Elijah asked.

"We gotta break that stallion and the most rowdy mares. When that's done, ya'll kin ride 'em back. The rest'll follow wherever they go."

"How ya gonna do that?" Remy asked. Gibbs studied him a minute before he answered. Then a smile came to his dingy, tobacco-stained teeth.

"I ain't," he said.

Once he had him trapped in the pen, Gibbs never let the stallion alone. Remy watched as he constantly stalked him, beseeching him in deep, smooth tones, getting as close as he could without upsetting the nervous horse. Gibbs made a point of remaining upwind so the animal could get even more accustomed to their scent, just like Cristóbal had suggested. He would not allow anyone to bathe. "Nuthin' can change," he said, and nothing did.

The stallion, who Remy thought must've been exhausted, still paced relentlessly about the length of the brush bank, prodding it with his snout, pawing with his hoof, searching for a way out. At times he reared up on his muscular hind legs, coal black from the knees down, and just kicked at the brush bank. But much to Remy's satisfaction, it held.

Even though the horse feared the men on foot, it must have gotten somewhat used to their scent in time, or else it hated them enough that it stood his ground in defiance. Remy couldn't tell which. The other horses hung next to the walls of the little bluff, as if they feared their leader's wrath, because this horse's every breath was fire and rage. They'd confined the horse, but they hadn't captured it.

When he thought it was time, Gibbs took out his braided horsehair rope, which he said wouldn't spook the animal near as bad as one of any other making, and carried it coiled in his hand. At times, from a safe distance, he would gently cast it across the stallion's back, as if to tickle it, continuing to talk to him calmly and evenly. After a couple of hours of this, he finally tied one end to the trunk of a mesquite and formed a loop in the other end. He slipped up behind the horse and tossed the loop over its head. When he was certain that he had him, Gibbs snatched it tight.

The horse, stunned at its first sense of constraint, bolted immediately. It raced for the rear of the canyon until the slack gave out, violently snatching its head around. The stallion lost its feet, crashing to the dusty and rocky earth with a solid thud. The horse screamed in anger, struggling to stand; and when it finally did, it ran again with the same result. It scrambled to its feet again, this time confronting Gibbs as it shook the dust from its coat, its wild eyes red with a most wicked rage.

Then the mustang charged him, its black tail stuck straight out at forty-five degrees as it reared on its hind legs, tearing at him with hooves sharp as worked flint, and then it was Gibbs's turn to run. He scrambled back through the barrier.

Remy and Elijah nervously replaced the limbs as quickly as they could and then stood back. They watched in wonder as the neck muscles of the great horse pulsated, black mane and tail tossing in the afternoon breeze. The ears were pricked, the mouth open and foamy, the teeth bared. The stallion gnashed sometimes at the rope and sometimes at the men hiding behind the wood and stone, it did not seem to matter which. Remy could hear its teeth clicking between vain attempts to break and run.

In time, already fatigued and aching from thirst, the animal stood still, panting, sweat darkening its blood-red coat, nostrils flared, flanks shuddering, eyes locked instantly on any man's slightest move. This went on until nearly sunset when at last Gibbs announced that it was time. When Gibbs strapped the skinny saddle to its back the horse never moved.

"All right," Gibbs announced. "I done my part. You do yours." He was looking at Remy. Remy immediately looked at his cousin.

"That'd be a good horse for you," Remy said. "I give 'im to you."

"Like hell. I don't want 'im; never did. I've always been fond of a good mare, like that old, fat one over yonder, there."

Remy rolled his eyes. More of the same from Cousin Elijah, he thought. Breaking a horse like that was worth arguing over, at issue broken bones or worse, and Remy and his cousin probably could've argued into the new year if Gibbs hadn't grown impatient.

"Enough of your whinin', boys. One of ya mount up." Gibbs looked from one to the other. Elijah just turned away.

"All right, dammit," Remy snapped. "You just remember what you said out here when we go to divvy up the brood."

"He's burned down, Fuqua," Gibbs offered with encouragement. "I think he can be rid."

"That's what you said back at de León's. You was wrong."

"Those were fresh. This one's half dead."

"What d'ya say we take 'im on down to an even three quarters? He looks like he's got plenty of fight left in 'im to me."

Gibbs set his jaw. "Quit your bellyachin' and slip them green, bony legs over his back, son. I've got no time for this. Look at 'im. He can barely stand."

Remy couldn't help himself. His knees knocked. "He's gonna buck me off against them rocks. Them other horses'll trample me good.

"No, they ain't," Gibbs said.

"How d'ya figure?"

"'Cause I'm gonna open this pen, that's why. You're gonna run him on the open range until he's broke." Remy looked again at Elijah.

"Sounds right," Elijah said. "All ya gotta do is hang on."

"If its so damn easy, why don't you do it?"

"Mares. I like mares."

"You mean, *now* you do," Remy said, "you gutless bastard."

"That's right," Elijah said. "Uh huh. This was your god-damn idea. I was plenty happy back at San Felipe."

Remy shrugged his shoulders and spat. "All right. Let's do it."

Gibbs gave him some last-minute advice. "Boy, you listen to me. You hang on to whatever you can get ahold of—the rope, its mane, the neck, whatever. All you gotta do is stay on. He ain't got much left; and don't you even think about lettin' 'im go. I want that horse."

"How 'bout a bigger saddle maybe," Remy said, his mouth dry. "Maybe a better bridle."

"He won't stand for that now."

"What d'ya say we give that creasin' another try?"

Gibbs shook his head. "Get on 'im," he said slowly. It was like a threat. Remy could see that he was tired of fooling around.

"All right, dammit. I guess my bones'll mend."

"A little crooked maybe," Elijah said, "but they'll mend sure enough."

"It's mares for you from now on, you son of a bitch."

"That's right," Elijah said. "An' I'm proud of it."

"It's time, Fuqua," Gibbs said. "We'll have to wait a whole 'nother day to burn him down like this. I wouldn't put ya on 'im if'n I didn't think he was ready. You kin do it, son. Just move toward 'im real slow like. Talk to 'im like he was that pretty Meskin girl you bin oglin'. He'll let ya get on, I think."

"You think so, huh?" Remy inhaled deeply, preparing himself. "All right," he finally said. "You hold him tight."

Gibbs grabbed the rope and eased toward the panting animal. The horse would not allow him to touch it, but he got pretty close. Gibbs waved Remy forward and he came, walking in slow, deliberate steps, as instructed. "Easy, boy," Gibbs moaned. "Fuqua ain't gonna hurt ya."

Elijah prepared to open the barrier just enough for the horse's escape. Gibbs held the rope tight as Remy slid his legs over its back. Gibbs let go and allowed the horse to pull against it. He could not go left or right, but backed against it. Remy held tight; his knuckles were white, his face felt flushed. He stared at the neck of the animal, attempting to anticipate which way it would go first. Gibbs stepped back over to Elijah and waited until the horse settled down. It took a while. Remy held fast. Soon he could feel that the stallion accepted the weight on his back. It had no choice.

Remy looked at Gibbs and nodded that he was ready. Gibbs walked toward the rest of the manada, and the horses pushed in close against one another at the far end of the corral. When that was done, Gibbs signalled to Elijah to open the wall, and the great horse dashed for it, again stumbling when the slack gave out. By some miracle Remy held on and rose with the animal in a cloud of dust.

"Are ya hurt, son?" Gibbs hollered.

"No, I ain't!" Remy panted. "Set 'im free!"

"Ya sure now?"

Remy nodded and said, "Hell, no, I ain't sure; but I'm willin', I think," his stare fixed on the back of the stallion's neck. Gibbs pulled out his knife and, when Remy was ready, tossed it up to him.

"Cut it, Fuqua," he said. "Leave yourself a little slack, now."

"There ain't no tellin' where he's gonna take me."

"Sure there is," Gibbs said. "The Rocky Mountains is out there somewheres. Water all aroun' if he busts through."

"That's it then," Remy said, and he took a deep breath and sawed through the rope until the loose end fell to the earth. Remy gripped the other end tightly.

The horse staggered a little with the sudden loss of the restraint, gathered himself, turned his head as if to see what manner of beast was on his back. Then, his ears taut and pointed, his wild eyes red and rolling, the horse reared his front legs. Remy tossed the knife away, leaned in toward the horse's neck for balance and held tight. The horse spun once, twice, three times. When the stallion failed to lose him, he simply stopped and stood there, motionless. Remy could feel the stallion's chest swell and quickly collapse with each panting breath between his cramped legs. When the stallion turned his head to the open ground beyond and blew loudly, Remy knew the pause was only a brief respite and braced himself for what was coming. A moment was all it took. In an instant the stallion raced up the canyon, banking hard to the west once it cleared the little bluff.

"Run, you son of a bitch, run!" Remy hollered. "I ain't lettin' go!"

Chapter Fourteen

Kills White Bear sat alone in his lodge, the flap open, picking the last of some freshly smoked venison meat from the bone. The sun hung just above the low hills. When he heard the crier's warning, he reached for his bow and ran out into the camp.

"What is it?" he asked.

"White riders," a young warrior replied. "Coming this way from the east."

"How many?"

"I don't know."

Kills White Bear's instincts answered for him as he gathered the best of the scrambling young men. "Remember first the women and children. Six of you take them to the brush up the canyon. Never let them out of your sight. Take the horses with you and see that everyone is mounted and ready. If we are overrun, you take them up to Crow's camp. Do you understand?"

"Yes, brother," one of the warriors said, and they were off to see about the others.

Kills White Bear whistled loudly. His horse appeared. Kills White Bear mounted, slung his quiver over his back, and raced out to meet the whites. Behind him followed a dozen other warriors. Kills White Bear was directing them to the high ground east of the camp when he heard the sound of hooves approaching. He knew then that there was no time to take the fight away from the camp.

"You three come with me," he ordered. "You others take cover. We'll lead them to you."

Kills White Bear stood ready. He nocked an arrow to his bowstring just as the first white rider appeared. The man bounced wildly on the saddle. There was no halter, no bridle. He held only a single rope in his hand. He had no rifle that Kills White Bear could see, no long knife, nothing. At the sight of the Indians, the man did not attempt to turn the horse but allowed it to race directly for the center of the camp. Kills White Bear's suspicions immediately turned to the open ground beyond. This one was bait, he thought. The others were circling.

He raced off to the north, where a narrow brush draw would allow a concealed advance to the encampment. But he heard nothing. Saw nothing. There was but this one strange man who had run straight past him.

Kills White Bear rode back to the warriors who waited in ambush. "Did you kill him?" he asked.

"We didn't get a chance," one complained. "He was here and gone in the blink of an eye. Even an arrow could not catch him."

Kills White Bear was puzzled. Almost a dozen winters on the warpath and he'd never before come across anything quite like this. He ran through a list of scenarios in his mind. None made sense. It was just like Wolf Eyes had told him. The whites were mad.

There was nothing to do now, he thought, but be cautious. "Mount up and ride the prairie in a big circle around the camp. One group east; one west. See that no one else lies in wait. When you're certain there's no threat, we'll send for the others to come back."

"What was that all about?" a young brave asked, equally puzzled.

Kills White Bear looked to the west, the way the man had gone. The dust had not yet settled. He shook his head in confusion. "I have no idea," he said.

Chapter Fifteen

Remy awoke, the bright sun burning his eyes, startled by the sound of a rider's approach. Stiff as a board, he just lay on his side and closed his eyes again. He didn't care who it was. In his hand he still gripped the end of the rope that had been around the stallion's neck. Somewhere along the way he'd tied the free end around his waist. The longer it took, the more committed he became. Where that stallion went, Remy'd vowed to go also. He'd just never imagined it'd be quite like that. He heard Elijah's voice call to him but he did not answer. A moment later he heard it again.

"Remy?" his cousin said quietly. Remy opened his eyes first, and then his mouth, moving his jaw from side to side to see if it were still attached. He checked all arms and limbs, and then tugged lightly at the rope. The deepest disappointment swelled within him when it came free.

Elijah knelt at his side and studied him. "You all right, Remy?"

"Is there a horse on the other end of this rope?" he asked coarsely; his parched throat had to be coaxed to voice the words.

"There was," Elijah answered.

"I know there was, idjit! I'm talkin' 'bout now!"

He saw his cousin look just to make sure. "He's here, Remy. I cut the rope so he wouldn't run off with ya again; but he's still layin' here, as give out as you."

"That's good," he muttered and he closed his eyes again. "You're sure now?" he mumbled.

"Yep. You sure you're all right?"

"Yeah, I'm all right."

"Damn. I didn't know if I was ever gonna see you again."

Remy sat up to see for himself. The horse was there. His excitement returned, as well as his caution. "Get another rope on 'im, just in case. Tie it to Gibbs's saddle horn." Elijah did so, quickly and quietly, while Remy lay still on his back.

"Where'd he take you?" Elijah asked.

"God only knows," he said, his lips so chapped he could feel the skin crack as he spoke. "It was some ride. I think I saw mountains. I know damn well he rode right through some Indian camp. They couldn't do nuthin' about it, and neither could I. They was just runnin' to get out of the way, and it was all I could do just to hang on. Its all a blur."

He rubbed his throbbing forehead, looking twice through his fingers just to make sure the horse was there. "I ain't never seen a horse go like that one," he told his cousin. "I kept thinkin' he'd run himself to death any time and I'd be miles from nowhere, but he never did. Finally, he just stopped where we're at and fell over. I fell with 'im and was damn glad to do it; I figured he'd whipped me and deserved to be free. But he just laid there. And you see how it is this mornin'." The horse lay so still, it concerned him. "He is alive, ain't he?"

"Yep. He's layin' there like a slab of beef, but he's breathin' all right." Elijah shoved a chunk of tobacco in his mouth. He looked a little overwhelmed by the whole thing. "I don't know what to think about it, Cousin," he said.

"I do," Remy quipped. "I think I got myself a horse."

For three more days they worked the mustangs. Remy spent most of his time bringing the stallion along under Gibbs's direction. Slowly they worked a spare bit into his mouth. The horse bitched like hell but finally accepted it. Remy rode for hours each day, using only a blanket for a saddle until the raw spots on the stallion's back healed. He did everything Cristóbal told him that he could remember, delighted to see the promised bond grow. The more he cared for the horse, the more it seemed to care for him. Unaccustomed to such unqualified reciprocation, Remy cherished it.

Elijah broke the younger stallions much more quickly than Remy had broken his. The mares, crazy for food and water, were more or less acquiescent. A couple featured Spanish brands and must have been cut loose by Indians or have wandered off from the rancher's herds. They had no way of knowing for sure. Either way, by Mexican law, the horses were theirs now.

By the morning of the fourth day they were ready to ride out. It had taken eleven days in all and Gibbs in particular was anxious to get back to his fields. He'd seen clouds building to the southeast, a sure sign that the sorely needed rain had fallen near the coast in his absence.

Gibbs tied three mares together and led them out of the corral. The others naturally followed just as he'd said they would. Remy and Elijah brought up the rear, mounted on their stallions, watching for stragglers. They watered the entire herd for the first time at the hole and pushed on. They re-crossed the skinny Nueces at a gravel bar and headed northeast.

"What ya gonna name that horse?" Gibbs asked Remy as he pulled up alongside.

"He's already got a name," Remy said, stroking the stallion's neck.

"What is it?"

"I don't know," Remy said. "He won't say."

They reached de León's spread just before sundown. Gibbs asked Don Martín's permission to corral the mustangs, which was granted. The empresario seemed anxious to inspect what they'd captured. Remy sat confidently, shoulders a little hunched in imitation of the Mexican riders to indicate his newfound comfort, as he drove the animals into the little corral. One look at de León's face told Remy that he was impressed with the catch.

"They're all very fine horses, my friend," Don Martín remarked in Spanish. Remy nodded in thanks. "You've done very well for yourself. You learn more quickly than the other gringos I've seen."

Remy watched those dark eyes study his stallion. "That one in particular," Don Martín said, "is magnificent. It appears that you no longer need me to give you a horse since I have none that could compare, but you might accept a saddle."

Remy felt proud. De León and the others had made fun of him when he left. Now he honored him. The horse had done all that. How quickly the stallion had changed every-

thing. Remy sat tall on its back, his shoulders square. He'd
seen and admired those Mexican saddles, the look of finely
tanned leather, the craft of the silver and brass fittings, the
grace of the styling. He knew damn well he wanted one.
Nothing he'd seen in the East could compare. "I'll trade
you three out of my share of horses for it," he told him.
"Your pick."

Don Martín responded with a nonchalant flick of his
wrist.

"The saddle's a gift," Gibbs explained.

"Much obliged, sir," Remy said, and one of de León's
vaqueros appeared with a saddle on his shoulders. He
dropped it at Remy's feet and withdrew without a word.
"I thank you, and my sore ass thanks you," Remy said.
Don Martín laughed and offered the use of one of his bunk-
houses for the night. "Let's get something to eat, Señor
Gibbs. Rest with me as my guest."

Remy was standing there, basking in the warmth of success, when he saw the boy admiring the stallion. Immediately, he went to him.

"Is it truly yours, señor?" Cristóbal asked, enchanted.

"It is," Remy said, "thanks to you."

"I did not teach you to catch a horse like this," he said.

"Oh, yes you did," Remy told him, and he reached into
his pocket for the last silver dollar he owned and flipped it
to the boy. "For you," Remy said, "from the devil."

Gibbs, Remy and Elijah took turns bathing in a large tub
at the bunkhouse. Campensina women brought in buckets
of steaming water and pale, wax-like wedges of tallow soap.
Remy shaved the whiskers from his chin and the fuzz from
his cheeks, slipped into clean clothes that their host had set
out for them, and then joined de León's men with Elijah
and Gibbs for their supper.

He watched intently for the girl but did not see her. He
recognized her father though and tried to speak to him.

The man made small talk and nothing more, as if Remy wasn't worth the time. They exchanged cool glances as they took their places over mesquite-grilled *cabrito,* young goat, a welcome change from the poorly creased mustang. Remy had never tasted such fine meat, almost sweet, slick with grease, its taste of smoke and strange spices bathing the lips like a woman's kiss. Just one bite, and he forgot all about the Mexican's arrogance. Elijah nearly inhaled his portion, to the astonishment of all. Remy sampled the relish next, or what looked like relish—diced tomatoes mixed with onion, little flecks of something else green. It looked so fresh, so delightful. *Whoa!*

He gulped his water, swishing it around loudly in his mouth. When that didn't do it, he reached for Elijah's; Gibbs's was next, and that was the last of his countrymen's. That left the Mexicans' glasses—full, half full, sitting on the table, or resting in their hands; it didn't matter. He took them all amid de León's riotous laughter, most Tejanos just offering their glasses up in amusement when their turn came. Pretty soon he came to that man's, and snatched it. "I'm sorry," Remy gasped. "I'm dyin'."

The Mexican held fast, twisting it out of his grasp until it popped free. Some of the water sloshed out on the man's jacket, which made him even less happy. "There is a well outside, señor," he told Remy calmly, controlled, his eyes fixed on the fresh spots of his lapels. "I suggest you use it."

Only when the doors closed behind him did the howling laughter subside.

Remy was too embarrassed to go back in. He drifted out instead to the corral to check on the horses. Elijah and Gibbs soon followed.

"They want you to come back in for drinks," Gibbs told him. "It's the custom."

"I don't think so," Remy said. "I drank enough."

"Suit yourself," Gibbs said, chuckling. "I'll explain." He turned to Elijah, who said that he would stay with the horses as well. Together they approached the stallion to admire him but the animal was nervous, snorting, stomping his hooves.

"Now see there, goddammit," Gibbs said. "It's like I said. He don't know ya if ya don't stink. You stay with 'im out here for as long as you can stand it and let 'im get familiar with your fancy smell. We ain't got time to start over. You don't wash again till we part company. He's your problem after that."

Gibbs said good night and slipped back into the dinner hall. Remy and Elijah leaned against the corral, upwind of the horse. Remy talked to it.

"It's me. Remy. The same guy you like to kilt the other night. We're friends now." The horse faced him and snorted, his eyes blinking as if to see if Remy was truly this same man. Remy found a bucket of oats and fed the stallion across the fence. He told him that he was the first horse he'd ever owned and he'd never imagined owning one finer. No amount of money could buy an animal of such spirit. He promised he would always treat him well, like a brother. Remy said that while he knew nothing could replace life in the wild, they still faced a great future together. He'd always care for him, he said, as he cared for himself.

Don Martín arrived, the stems of three glasses threaded through his fingers. "I knew that I'd find you men here," he said. "I'd consider it an insult if you refuse to drink with your host."

"In that case, we'd be much obliged," Elijah said, and he took his offered goblet before Remy took his. Badly burned once, Remy sniffed it cautiously. Don Martín threw his down his throat like water. Elijah followed his lead, his eyes rolling back in his head, little beads of sweat forming on his brow. Remy hesitated.

"What is it?" he asked.

"Añejo tequila," Don Martín said. "Very smooth. Very fine." He urged Remy to sample his. Remy exhaled and tossed it back as the others had done. As soon as it had passed his lips his guts started wrenching. He tried to smile but the moisture had evaporated from his mouth, his tongue felt scorched and swollen, the consistency of an old boot sole. Uncontrollable gagging followed, but Remy fought it as best he could until the sensation passed. When he'd regained control, he handed the goblet back to his host, his fingers trembling, and said, "That really hit the spot. Thank ya, kindly."

"Since you both like it," Don Martín said with a wry smile, "I'll have more brought out." He turned to do just that when Remy reached out and grabbed him by the elbow.

"Can I speak frankly with you, sir?" Remy asked.

"By all means, señor. We're friends."

"I'd like some advice," Remy said, struggling to speak more politely than he'd ever tried before. "Do you know the young woman who was at the corral the other day?"

"Very well," Don Martín said. Remy couldn't help but noticing that some of the earlier warmth had left his voice. "She is Beatriz, the daughter of Don Carlos Amarante de la Cruz, my good friend and business associate, the man currently wearing a very wet coat."

"Well," Remy said, "I was wondering if you could tell me the proper way I could arrange to call on her."

"The proper way, you ask?"

"Yes, sir."

"There is no proper way. Not for you."

Remy was confused. "Why not? I clean up pretty good."

"It doesn't matter, Señor Fuqua. You have to understand. Don Carlos is a powerful, well-connected ranchero. He will insist that his daughter mix only with her own rank and kind. I'm already quite fond of you, as I hope you realize, but I'm sure you understand that you qualify as neither. In a year or two, Don Carlos will send her to school in Mexico City, at which time she'll be properly introduced to society. After that, most likely, her marriage will be arranged."

Remy's chest deflated. "Oh," he said.

"I'm sorry," Don Martín continued, "but what you ask is quite impossible."

"Well, I was just wonderin'," Remy said.

"Wonder about someone else," Don Martín advised, the warmth returning, "and save yourself some trouble."

"I will," Remy said. "Thank you." They spoke of horses after that.

Then the young woman approached from out of the darkness, walking silently, assured. She'd traded her vaquero gear for a flowing, cotton dress. She smiled first in greeting to Don Martín, her black eyes sparkling, then to

Elijah, and lastly to Remy before she turned to admire the horse. "Uh oh," Don Martín quietly moaned. The stallion's majesty yielded before hers.

"I like him, too," Remy said in Spanish, never taking his eyes away from her. He was stunned; Elijah was speechless.

The woman climbed the fence as easily as any man, but with more grace, and approached the stallion. Remy stepped forward to stop her, but she indicated that he was not to worry. She spoke to it in Spanish and in a moment was stroking its forehead with her long, bronze fingers.

"Look at that, will ya?" Remy sighed.

"He likes her," Elijah said.

"He's a smart horse."

She walked back over to the fence next to Remy, propping a boot on the lower pole. He had never seen a woman more elegant, mysterious and confident. Every movement, every sound she made, enchanted him. She spoke only to Don Martín.

"I was wondering," she began, "if it would be all right for me to sit near the cemetery tonight for a while."

"Of course, Beatriz. Go where you like."

"I was meaning, of course, the one south of the barn, behind the oak grove. You can't see it from here."

"Yes, I know," Don Martín told her. "It's the only one we have."

"If one follows that stone path," she pointed, "will it not lead directly to it?"

"Very truly, Beatriz," Don Martín sighed, "it will."

"And the little pavilion with the stone benches? Does it not still stand on the northwest corner?"

"Yes . . . yes . . . yes, Beatriz. I'm quite certain that it does."

"Very well," she said. "I'll be sitting there for a time, if it pleases you. Alone."

"Are you sure you know your way, my child?" Don Martín asked, his eyes narrowed.

"I think so," she said, and she drifted away. Remy and his cousin watched her go and then turned to look at one another.

"Shall we return to our friends, gentlemen?" Don Martín asked.

"I'm sure my cousin would like to go," Remy offered, "but, if it's all the same to you, I'd prefer to stay out a time and visit with my horse." He winked at Elijah, and then added, "Gibbs told me to."

"Well, we wouldn't want to disappoint Señor Gibbs, would we?" Don Martín asked. Remy shook his head. "Come, Señor Johnson."

"Gibbs told me to stay, too," Elijah shot back.

"Like hell!" Remy snapped. "Don't act like the bumpkin you are. Git in there and do right."

"I ain't goin' nowhere, Remy. Nowhere! You hear?"

"You're gonna hear your bell ringin' in a minute, you son of a bitch!" They squared off, Don Martín stepping between them.

"Please, boys. She's only agreed, sort of, to your company for a brief time, and nothing more. I've already told you what will happen, and I hope you listened carefully to what I said. Talk to her if you wish, but the two of you together is better for you both, and Beatriz, as well." Don Martín turned to leave. *"Buenas noches."*

"You won't say nuthin' to her pa, will ya, Don Martín?" Remy asked out of caution.

"How can I speak of something I know nothing about?" the empresario said, turning the goblets upside down as he walked away.

Remy stood with his cousin in silence, each, it seemed, waiting for the other's move. Remy turned his gaze north, opposite the direction of the cemetery. "Uh oh," he gasped. "Look yonder! A Comanche sneakin' in!" Elijah swung his head to look, and Remy dashed off down the path.

"I ain't so easily fooled," Elijah said when he caught him.

"No," Remy agreed, "but you're damn easy to trip," he said as he shoved his cousin into the thick bushes and ran on.

It went better than he ever dreamed it would. Of course, it would have been perfect if his gawky cousin hadn't arrived, bowing to her with all those leaves tangled in his red hair, like a damn fool. But they talked, her voice smooth like spun honey, and she was kind to them both, interested in who they were, why they'd come, and what they had planned for their futures.

Remy sat on the bench with her. Instinct told him to inch closer as time went by, and nothing she did told him he shouldn't. Another two feet and he thought he might be close enough to peck her on the cheek and see how the wind blew. A little more time, a little more talk, a little more sense shown by his ugly cousin so he'd just give up and get the hell away and Remy'd be right there, close enough to feel the warmth of her breath on his cheek.

He'd scooted to within about a foot when he felt the rope drop over his shoulders and immediately draw tight. As he struggled he saw another fall over Elijah as well. He turned to see the vaqueros quickly loop the rope ends around their saddle horns and spur their horses. Both he and Elijah left their feet instantly and were dragged several yards backwards from the cemetery, away from Beatriz, all the way back up to the corral. When they reached it, the ropes, still fastened to the saddle horns, went slack.

That man, Don Carlos, Beatriz's father, rode between Remy and Elijah. Beatriz dashed up the path, pleading with her father not to embarrass her like this.

"¡Véte a la casa!" he barked. *"¡Ahora!"*

Despite his anger, she argued with him, saying that nothing was happening, but her father cut her off. *"¡Véte!"* he yelled again, accompanied by a stare that would ice a water glass. She bitterly relented, kicking at the dust with her boot.

Remy was wondering what was going to happen next, when his attention was drawn to his stallion. It'd become nervous, snorting, prancing back and forth along the fence, with its ears stuck back. Don Carlos dismounted and approached Remy and his cousin, still roped and lying on the ground. The Mexican's eyes were dark and focused. He wore only a white cotton shirt now, unbuttoned below his muscular neck. His leather boots squeaked with each angry step as he marched toward them. He rubbed his moustache

with his index finger and then spoke. His English was refined, authoritative, perfect.

"Stay clear of my daughter, gringo," he said. "She's not
for you."

Remy realized he really wasn't in a position to argue,
but he did anyway. "All you had to do was say so," he
told him.

"It was clear enough, I think," Don Carlos answered.

"You git these ropes off of us, and we'll talk about it,"
Remy said.

"There's nothing to talk about, señor. You've insulted me,
as all you people eventually do, and now you're leaving."

Remy's anger had the best of him now. He was not intimidated. "The Constitution of 1824 says that this is a free
country, Mister. I've got a Mexican passport. I'll sit with
your daughter or anybody else I please if they've got a
mind to. It's got nuthin' to do with you."

"*Nothing*?" he said with a look that Remy could only
explain as disbelief. Then he turned to his men and said,
"Ah, these people." He shook his head, while the others
laughed. Then he stared back at Remy and the laughter
stopped. "So be it," he said, "I'll make my point another
way." And he slapped Remy soundly across the face with
his gloved hand as hard as the Karankawa warrior had
done the year before. Remy heard the same dull tone ringing in his ears.

Remy charged at the Mexican until the slack ran out of
his rope. He kicked wildly with his fist at Don Carlos's
face, but he was out of range. Don Carlos motioned for his
men to drag the captives further into the brush. "It's clear
that you can't stay here. I'll inform Gibbs that he can find
you on the trail ten leagues to the east. My vaqueros will
see that you do not come to further harm."

Remy heard the snap of splintering wood. He jerked his
head in time to see his stallion, who had shattered the top
two poles of the corral with his front legs, easily leap over
the lower poles that remained. He thundered for the vaqueros' horses. Rearing from his hind legs, the stallion kicked
at the mounted riders who held Remy and Elijah and bit
viciously at their necks with his bared teeth. The riders
lashed at him with their whips, but they could not control

their own horses, who were immediately afraid of the mustang's wrath. The animals fled, taking their riders with them, leaving Remy and Elijah where they sat. The stallion paced back and forth between the vaqueros and his owner and would not let them approach.

Remy stood and removed the lariat from around his body, tossing it to the ground. He reached for his horse, and slid his legs over its bare back. The animal instinctively knew what was next and squared off with Don Carlos, the Mexican's horse nervous at the encounter. The man struggled to control it, but it feared the mustang as the others did, giving Remy the advantage he desperately needed.

"It's my turn to talk. I mean you and your daughter no harm. I like her. But I won't be treated like that. Not by you; not by anybody."

The man was angry. His horse tried to increase the distance between himself and the mustang but its rider kept jerking its reins to face Remy's horse. "You're in México, my friend! You'll be treated exactly how you deserve!"

"We'll see about that," Remy spat. "I ain't done nuthin' to you."

Don Carlos's face nearly glowed red. "Boy, your rudeness appalls me! Under no circumstances are you qualified to even speak to my daughter, never mind spending time alone with her! If it weren't for that wild demon of a horse, I'd have you tied to the nearest pole and lashed to teach you a lesson. But," he said grimly, "I'm sure there's another way."

"What ya gonna do, mister?" Remy snapped. "Shoot me?"

"Not you," he said, and with that he drew his pistol from the long leather holster on his side, cocked the hammer and aimed with a dark, determined eye at the mustang's head. Remy leaped from the saddle and stood between his horse and the man who threatened to kill it.

"Don't you do it, Mister!" he screamed. "You do and you'll soon regret it. I promise you that." Remy's face was hot with rage. He faced the Tejano for what seemed an eternity. Some of the other vaqueros drew their own weapons and cocked them. Remy saw clearly that they intended to reinforce their don. The closest one to Don Carlos, an older man, leaned over from his saddle and spoke slowly and calmly to him. Remy heard every word.

"Let him be, Don Carlos," he counseled. "What harm has he done? This is not your ranch. He's a guest of Don Martín, as we are. Don't do this thing."

"He's nothing like we are, Diego!" Don Carlos sneered. "He's just another ass with a passport. They're everywhere I look."

Remy had clenched his fist and had stepped forward to teach this man a lesson when he felt Elijah's hand on his shoulder. "C'mon, Remy," his cousin beseeched him. "Ain't nuthin' gonna happen here. Just step back."

Remy stood his ground. Don Carlos seemed to consider the situation a moment more and then cooled. He uncocked the hammer of his pistol and returned it to its holster. The man called Diego looked at him and nodded slowly in approval.

"God damn these gringos!" Don Carlos said. "These *pelegrinos*!", or blacksheep, a term Remy'd heard often in San Felipe. As far as he was concerned it was just like "nigger." "Who let these bastardos in here?"

Remy remounted and then turned back to Don Carlos. "The Mexican government. And we're here to stay."

"No you're not. Not with that kind of arrogance. The future for men like you in Tejas is dark indeed." Then Don Carlos turned to his men and ordered them to disperse. He looked back once more at Remy. "A word to the wise, señor. Next time you'll not catch me in such a good mood. The girl is not for you, and that's the last time I'll tell you so kindly. *Buenas noches.*"

With that, he wheeled his horse around and cantered off, never looking back. Remy rode the mustang back to the corral, easily jumped the fence, and dismounted. He and Elijah were repairing the damage as best they could when Gibbs arrived with two of de Leon's vaqueros. Once they had seen the situation, they left, returning with freshly cut mesquite poles and rawhide ties, which made quick work of the repairs.

"Want to tell me about what happened?" Gibbs asked.

"Nope," Remy said.

"It's the girl, ain't it? Her daddy don't like you."

1828

Chapter Sixteen

By the first week of January, they were ready to leave. Austin had honored his promise only the week before. Remy and Elijah, fresh grant in hand, packed their belongings into a borrowed wagon, already full of borrowed tools, and left San Felipe. They traveled northwest, following their map, hugging the Colorado River, until they'd entered the mysterious enclave of slow-rolling, red-clay hills thick with big woods pine, a scattering of strange oaks, towering cottonwoods, and pecans with trunks as wide as the wagon at their base. For Remy, the land had the look of the only home he'd ever known. It was right, he thought, that Austin had sent them here, to his "Little Colony." They passed Wood's Fort, still under construction, and headed for the new country beyond.

Remy brought the team up to where Elijah had dismounted. His cousin stood over a white pine stake, still sticky with sap; hand-painted, blood-red, dripping letters spelled JOHNSON-FUQUA.

Elijah, his face beaming, studied the map intently. "This here," he said, "marks the southeast boundary. Our grant runs due west to the river, an' north for better'n a mile an' a half." He rolled up the map, and stuffed it into his knapsack, and then looked up to mark the position of the sun. Remy judged it to be around ten o'clock on that crisp, clear January day.

They traveled the perimeter to each of the boundary markers, and then crossed the land from one corner to the other. By then, in the early afternoon, they knew where the cabin should stand.

First they constructed a corral for the horses, attaching

a small shed for temporary accommodations. They lived with a great draft exposed to the late Texas winter as work on the cabin began. In the mornings they cleared their fields to make way for spring crops of corn, for consumption, and cotton, for sale. The sad and disgruntled team of borrowed oxen ripped the stubborn stumps free from the rocky and clay-based earth. Each afternoon, they returned to work on the homestead. They quit only when they could no longer see, inhaled fresh venison or salt pork over coffee, and collapsed, with splinters in their fingers and swollen thumbs, side by side to keep each other warm. By first light they were at it again, seven days a week.

Elijah laid out their cabin the only way Remy had ever seen it done: two large, separate rooms partitioned by an open airway, running north and south, designed to catch the southern summer breeze. In the winter, it was closed off. Remy called the structure what his father had—a dog run. The walls were made from rough-hewn logs of cedar, readily available in the brakes above the river, laid horizontally and fitted together at the ends by axe and chisel notches. The inevitable spaces between the cedar logs were filled by river-bottom clay mixed with Spanish moss and prairie grass and a little lime if they had it. Hand-riven "shakes" or shingles, split from the heart of blackjack oak, scaled the roof of cottonwood rafters to seal the interior from the Texas winter rains. Elijah fashioned a porch on the front and an extended eaves on the back. The gables featured an overhang of better than two feet. Before Remy had even caught his breath, Elijah had laid out the foundations of the outbuildings, sheds, and root cellars. The work seemed to go on forever.

Short of cash, they traded horses for materials they could not harvest or manufacture themselves. They bartered for a pair of father and son masons to come and fashion a fireplace of native limestone, rather than one of clay and grass lined with flat stones like most folks had. Remy understood how lucky they were just to be able to afford nails. Most homesteads he'd seen in Texas were built without them.

Although Elijah was the better carpenter, Remy, who'd spent much of his boyhood years with his aunt, had a better idea about how the inside should look. He fit the windows with hinges of rawhide, which worked as well as a metal counterpart if he got the crease just right, at least for a while. He trimmed the vaulted ceilings of exposed rafters with fresh oak planks and constructed lofts on which to sleep in the opposite gables. In the corner of each loft he crafted "one leg beds," with long straps of rawhide to support their canvas mattresses stuffed full with dried prairie grass. They were soft enough. In colder weather, they'd take them down and sleep side by side near the hearth.

Remy decided that it was best to spend the time laying a wooden floor for his home rather than deal with the continual dust, so he and Elijah split similar sized oak puncheons, wide side up, which were set in place with long wooden pegs to keep them from warping as they cured. The smell of the green wood permeated the house. Remy breathed deeply, reveling in the aroma. The interior windows and door frames were trimmed with split and hand-polished cedar.

Remy had no time or patience for the construction of cabinets; shelves and wooden pegs driven into the walls sufficed to hang clothing or to store what few goods they kept on hand. A low shelf near the door supported a store-bought water pail; several gourds for that same purpose hung nearby. Next to them swung a quarter of smoked beef or venison, whatever they had, and next to that stood the firearms, rifles and a shotgun loaded with buckshot, forever ready.

Remy fashioned homemade tables, benches, and chairs of Spanish oak with rawhide bottoms laced in for support. He traded two young mares to a merchant in San Felipe for glass panes, which were hard to find, but the glass allowed them the luxury of leaving the shutters open during even the coldest days, providing light.

At night, of course, the exterior wooden shutters were fastened closed and the leather latchstring to the door was pulled inside; a bolt of rough-hewn oak was shoved across the girth of each—especially on the cycle of the full moon when they learned that the Indians came.

Remy watched as Elijah reached across the table over his outstretched legs for the coffee pot. On the way back, he knocked Remy's booted feet from the table. It was just after dawn. He looked out the window at the pastures, still shrouded in early morning fog. He turned back to face Remy, who hypnotically watched the steam rise from Elijah's cup.

"How many horses you figure we got there?" he asked him.

Remy was gnawing on a piece of smoked venison which he dipped in a pot of honey. It'd taken him three days to follow the bees, their legs burdened with yellow pollen, to the hive. On the afternoon of the third day, he'd smoked them out and packed his profit home in a deer-hide pouch. "I don't know," he answered. "Twenty or so. Maybe more."

"No. I meant today."

Remy understood what that meant. He popped up from his chair and looked for himself. He saw maybe a dozen.

"Goddamn Indians! Let's go after 'em."

"Now?"

"Right now."

Remy dressed, gathered a few provisions and snatched the Gump rifle from its rack above the door. Elijah followed with the rifle he'd bought from Smithwick. They caught and saddled their horses and took several ropes with them in case they found the missing horses. They came across the Indian tracks soon enough. The ground was soft, the impressions deep and crisp. Elijah dismounted and put a finger where a man had stood maybe two hours before. He wasn't sure how long exactly, he told Remy, unless he saw the fellow standing in them. But they were damn fresh, he told Remy, he knew that.

"Comanche?" Remy asked, unamused.

"Nope. If'n it were Comanche, me an' you'd both be bleedin', the cabin burnt down, and all the stock gone. These here more'n likely Tawakona or Waco. Thieves more than murderers. Somebody like that." He looked up at Remy. "They didn't want blood. They just wanted the horses."

"Well," Remy said, "I want 'em back."

They followed the tracks into the woods until they came

to a little clearing. Here they found two freshly butchered carcasses and two hides, the ground between them soaked in blood. Remy looked at it a moment, and then at his cousin.

"Hell, they ate 'em!"

"No doubt about it, Fuqua. You can read sign." Without a word, he turned his horse's head to the direction from which they'd come.

"Where ya goin'?" Remy demanded.

"Home."

"What for?"

"They need 'em worse than we do. In the spring things'll loosen up a little. In the meantime, the thing to do is corral 'em at night."

"That ain't worth a shit," Remy said. They'd taken these. They'd soon take some more.

Elijah never skipped a beat. "What d'ya wanna do, Remy? Run them Injuns down and kill 'em? Maybe get kilt! I don't wanna shoot nobody over a horse I got for free." He paused a moment and then said, "Maybe you an' me's different in that regard." Remy recognized the dig over the Tonkawa. The killing haunted him and Elijah knew it. "If so," his cousin added, "you go alone. I got work to do."

Remy turned his horse and thought a moment. He still felt the guilt keenly enough. Austin was wrong. The fact that he owned the horses had made no difference. He didn't want to kill anyone else over property. Stolen horses could be replaced easily enough, it seemed, with the exception of one. "You're right, Elijah," he admitted. "Let's go. I'll do somethun' else."

Remy had stopped to wipe the sweat from his brow, when he heard the angry crack of a whip. Elijah had spent most of the afternoon with two head of oxen chained to a cottonwood stump. After an agonizing struggle, he stomped off to hitch up two horses beside the oxen. Elijah beat them furiously but still the stump would not give.

"I wouldn't leave no marks on them oxen, Elijah," Remy warned. "They's borrowed."

"It's either them or me," Elijah said.

Spring would be there soon, and the fields were far from ready for planting. With the cabin built and the best of the horses secured, their thoughts naturally turned to their first crop. Corn was everything out there and they knew it. They burned off what canebrakes they had, but Remy knew it was not enough land. A good June flood besides, and they were done for. That meant they had to clear the wooded lots: higher ground, better soil. Clearing was slow, tedious, backbreaking work, and that particular stump seemed rooted to hell itself.

Remy went over to help him until the chain broke. He and Elijah collapsed to the earth, exhausted. The oxen, still harnessed, stared at them both. The horses, never keen on the idea anyway, had broken their braces and vanished together over the hill.

"We gotta burn this one," Remy said. Even in the cool air, sweat soaked through his shirt. The breeze chilled him whenever he stood still.

"Can't. It's green. Won't burn." Elijah sighed, and then added, "Not this year."

"Plant aroun' it, then."

"May have to."

The thought crossed his mind as it had daily since the work began. "We need slaves, Elijah."

"Okay," he said flatly. "Go get us some."

This was a joke and Remy knew it, but he set his mind to think about where they might be found and how he could buy one. Austin had told him that he hoped to build his colony on cotton. And cotton, as had been firmly established back home in Louisiana and the rest of the American southeast, was grown with slaves. Austin had told him once that he had assured the Méxicanos as a condition of his empresario grant that his settlers would tame the frontier with cotton, but had also advised that to grow it, they must be allowed to bring their slaves along with their farm implements. It was, he'd argued, the only way.

Slavery, to be sure, was clearly against Méxicano law. Yet Remy had already come to understand that the Méxicano government desperately wanted the Tejas frontier settled. It was, Remy was told, the final solution to Indian depredations and American encroachment. As distasteful as it was, Méxicano officials begrudgingly looked the other way while over a thousand miserable souls walked barefoot into Tejas. Remy knew that Jared Groce, one of Austin's oldest, richest, and most irascible settlers, owned over a hundred slaves.

Now, looking over the fields where three dozen more equally stubborn stumps waited, Remy would have settled for just one slave. He told his cousin he'd be back soon.

Elijah just stood there looking at him, scratching his head. "Slaves ain't just sittin' on the shelves in San Felipe like a jar of pickles," he told him. "And even if they were, we couldn't afford one anyway. I can't sit out here on my thumbs and wait while you go to town to find all that out. Your time's better spent repairing this chain an' helpin' me git this damn stump out."

"I'll be the judge as to how I spend my time," Remy said, and left the field, washed up, and mounted.

Remy returned the following day with a man and a big smile on his face. Elijah seemed shocked, perhaps by Remy's rapid success, but most likely because the slave he come back with was not a Negro.

"Who's that?" he asked, leaning over the back of one of the oxen, swatting the gnats from his face.

"This here's Quelepe Ortiz," Remy said proudly. "Our new, uh, helper."

Elijah stared blankly, apparently more confused by Remy's return than by his departure. "Looks like to me that he's about helped out. He's gotta be seventy years old."

"A sprightly sixty-two," Remy stated. "Or so he claims."

Elijah was obviously not convinced. "An' skinny to boot." He shook his head. "How much?"

Mr. Ortiz looked at Remy strangely. "Why nuthin'," Remy said.

"Well, price was right, I reckon." Then he brought his face so close to Remy's that he felt his tobacco-tainted breath. "Can I talk to you a minute, cousin?"

Remy politely excused himself and stepped aside. Elijah's first words came quickly. "Have ya lost yo' goddamn mind?"

Remy said that he certainly had not. This man was the best he could do on short notice. They wanted close to a thousand dollars for a black and that was if they could find one. They didn't have the money, and Lafitte, he said, was long gone. They could put their order in with smugglers near the coast and wait, he supposed, but time was short.

He explained that Señor Ortiz had lost his family to a cholera epidemic, was alone in the world, and for lack of anything better to do, he agreed to accompany Remy back to their grant. Although Remy admitted that such a skinny man could not solve their labor problems, he could keep the home fires burning and manage most of domestic chores. Those things alone would prove useful. It did not appear, Remy said, that he ate all that much either.

Elijah didn't seemed convinced of the benefits. He was explaining his conception of slavery when Remy observed Quelepe taking an interest in the stump at issue. The old man dug a little here, pried a little there, and picked around in between. He cut one smaller, longer root with an axe, kicked another with his booted foot, whispered into the twitching ears of the waiting oxen, repositioned the chain, motioned once with his finger and the earth gently yielded the stump of one of its most magnificent plants. Elijah was telling Remy exactly where his Mexican could spend the rest of eternity for all he cared when Remy motioned for him to turn around. When he did, the sight struck him dumb.

"You're hired, old man," he said, "or whatever." And that was it.

Chapter Seventeen

Remy took his place at his table across from Elijah. The cabin was neat. A hot meal of corn fritters, honeyed yams, and bobwhite quail lay before them; a bed of coals pulsed under fresh wood in the hearth.

"Now we're gettin' somewhere," Remy said, as he slid

his plate toward him and dug in. Quelepe sat at the far end of the table in silence, watching them gulp his fare.

When he'd finished, Remy rose from the table and belched loudly. Elijah never budged. Remy stepped out in the crisp spring air, shed his soiled clothes, waded into the shallows of the Colorado, and washed himself clean. He walked naked, save his boots, back to the homestead where Quelepe had laid out a fresh set of buckskins, dyed tan with the bark of a huisache tree, across the railing of the porch. Remy slid his arms and legs through the supple garments, the bitter scent of new leather in his nose, and admired the cut and fit. He fancied himself more adventurer than homesteader in those duds.

Then he stepped back through the door, the river water still dripping from his midnight-black curls, and pulled his stool by the fireplace to dry himself. He slid up another stool, patting his hand on the smooth oak until he had the old Méxicano's attention.

Elijah just looked at him and shook his head. "Again?"

"Damn right," Remy answered.

"Just keep it a little quieter than you done last night, goddamn ya. A man needs his sleep. I was up all hours listenin' to ya'll's prattle."

"You were snorin' not two minutes after you laid down yer ugly head," Remy told him, motioning for Quelepe to come and get started. The Méxicano did as Remy bid him.

"What do you want to hear tonight?" he asked him. "More of the conquistadores? Or maybe the Comanche wars?"

"All about you, now," Remy said. "Start from the beginning."

"All right," Quelepe sighed, poking at the coals. "I suppose that I'm a product of the Spanish mission reduction policy. The Spanish had hoped to stabilize Indian tribes around a mission-presidio complex, ultimately bringing us into Méxicano society, although as Indians my ancestors were welcomed at the lowest social level. They were treated like dogs."

"Yeah," Remy said. "They'll let ya in but they start you at the bottom. Same damn thing everywhere, I reckon."

"That's probably true," the old man said, the flame of

the fire mirrored in his eyes. Catholicism, he explained, supposedly provided the spiritual catalyst in the process to mold a Spanish subject from a savage. Reduction worked well enough, he said, with the more stable or stationary Indian populations, such as the Pueblos to the west and the Caddos to the east, as well as many of the coastal tribes, but it was clear enough to Quelepe's mind that with the nomadic horse Indians it was another matter. The Lipan Apaches, though vastly depleted in numbers after three hundred years, and particularly the elusive and fierce Comanche, had never bent their knees to Spanish domination. The Karankawas, of course, wanted nothing to do with anyone whatsoever and also resisted. However, the rest of the coastal Texas tribes, as far as Quelepe could tell, were systematically annihilated, his own among them.

"I thought things was pretty bloody now," Remy told him, his mind fixed on the violence he'd seen. "But they must've been far worse back then."

"I have no doubt," Quelepe said. He explained that he was the illegitimate product of a presidio soldier and a Coahulitecan mother. As such, Quelepe knew a little about alienation. This fact alone drew him immediately closer to Remy's heart. The Coahulitecans, he said, like most of the "reduced" tribes, were gone. Surviving remnants of the band had either joined other Indian tribes or had moved south across the Río Grande into the Méxicano desert. What had become of them Quelepe did not know, but it was clear that all Quelepe's ties to his Indian ancestry were abruptly severed. Quelepe claimed that he was not an Indian, but he was also not a Spaniard. He was a hybrid product of both, a new race for the New World.

Quelepe said that the Spanish, sticklers for organization, had placed his kind near the bottom of the *gente de razon's* thirty-two racial categories of their New World subjects. He was mestizo: a mixture of Spanish and Indian blood. Experience told Remy that most Anglo colonists would naturally assume that he had inherited the worst characteristics of both races. But Remy could take one look at his face, sense its wisdom and warmth, and know that he possessed the best of each. In his heart, Remy hoped the same were true for himself.

As Quelepe went on, Remy leaned back in his chair, listening with his eyes closed in fascination. Quelepe represented the link with the magic and mystique of ancient Tejas in a way that only the adventurer Cabeza de Vaca had seen it. Tejas, as presented to Remy, was a series of burnt fragments. Quelepe knew how to weave them all together into one long piece. How quickly Remy's desire to conquer the land gave way to the most intense desire to belong to it.

But even that wasn't the extent of Quelepe's influence. Remy also learned that the old Méxicano knew something of herbal remedies and the powers of the *curandero*, and he functioned as their doctor. While Remy and Elijah were out working, Quelepe established a *huerta* in which he cultivated an odd assortment of strange plants such as hierba buena, manzanilla, albahaca, ruda, estafiate, muicle, camphor, rhubarb, melons and beans, and many other plants brought with him from his gardens at Béxar.

The old man also knew how to unlock the secrets of wild native vegetation. Tea brewed from the leaves and branches of the cenizo worked as a remedy for Elijah's hacking cough, as did a syrup derived from the fruit of the nacahuite tree. Hierba amarilla promoted the healing of sores, while the split leaf of the sabila, or aloe, reduced inflammation and soothed any type of burn to the skin, all of which Remy and Elijah seemed to incur daily.

With Quelepe around, the wilderness no longer threatened Remy the way it once had. The old man whispered its secrets into his ear. The wind told Quelepe of the coming weather, the rain crow forecast precipitation, the behavior of wild animals warned him when danger was near, the moon told him when it was time to plant crops, and the stars guided him home on the darkest nights. The signs had been there since the dawn of time, but now Quelepe taught Remy how to read them. Such an education, Remy knew, was invaluable.

Quelepe also further instructed Remy in the Spanish tongue, frontier slang and nuance. Soon enough Remy spoke like a Comanchero trader. The little man also understood the Indian mind well enough to manage the savages' strained visits to their grant as delicately and diplomatically as possible, a skill Remy absorbed. This, more than the chain, led to the end of the horse raids. Gifts were exchanged, food when they had it, and, most importantly, the warriors saved face. In time, Quelepe told him that, although the raiders didn't like the idea of Remy and his cousin living there, they had accepted them. The Indians kept their dignity, and Remy kept his stock, and no blood was drawn. Remy knew of others who weren't so lucky.

Lastly, and most miraculous to Remy, Quelepe was a seer. He never claimed to see the whole picture, but he was frequently offered a glimpse of an image. At first, Remy disregarded Quelepe's notions as nonsense. But as time passed he came to realize how accurate Quelepe's prognostications were when the old man foretold the coming of a storm or a stranger's appearance. The truth was there to be strained out somehow and Remy learned to consider the old man's visions carefully.

He thought of these things as Quelepe spoke of his lost past. Remy saw soon enough that Quelepe was indispensable. He had to provide an incentive for him to stay.

"What are your plans now?" Remy interrupted him.

"To stay until things are settled with you boys," he said. "I've grown quite fond of you both."

"Let's make it permanent like," Remy said. "You pull your weight around here. Would you stay on if we gave you a stake in the place, a percentage of the crops, say?"

"All I want is a home again, Remy. A place I could call my own."

"This is it," Remy answered, "an' it pays ten percent of our crops, which ain't nuthin' to get all that excited about." And then he added, "For now."

"You don't have to pay me anything, Remy. You asked and I came."

"I didn't ask for what I got," he said. "Right's right and our place is yours." He thumbed toward Elijah, snoring overhead. "I'll break the news to Red in the mornin'."

Remy rose from his seat, stretched, yawned, and dashed out the rest of his coffee on the coals. A white cloud of steam rose up the chimney. "That's all I can handle this evenin'," he said. "Tomorrow night, I want to talk to you about a little problem I've got."

"What would that be?" Quelepe asked.

"A woman. I want to know how to get her."

"Who?"

"A Méxicano girl, Beatriz Amarante de la Cruz."

"The daughter of Don Carlos?" Quelepe asked, astonished.

"That's the one. I need to know how to court her, what to say, what to do. I expect I've already made a mess of things."

"That's a tall order," Quelepe said. "A peasant like me doesn't profess to understand the workings of a *hacendado* family."

"Well, it can't get no worse," Remy said. "We'll just do our best and see how it goes," Remy said, and he drifted off to his bed. The last thing he did was yank Elijah's hair to stop him from snoring. It worked for a while.

Chapter Eighteen

Elhanan Gibbs swung Don Martín's gate open with the toe of his boot. Whistling, slapping his coiled rope against the flank of his stallion, Remy drove the mustangs into the corral.

"I'm glad that's over," Gibbs sighed. "I'm wore smooth out."

Remy spit the grit out of his mouth. "Are ya kiddin', Gibbs?" he said. "Catchin' horses is like a holiday for me. Elijah's workin' me to death out there at our place."

"I'm sorry he couldn't make it," Gibbs said. "I miss that boy's company."

"So do I," Remy answered, "like a headache."

Gibbs turned his head to admire the catch. "Well," he said, "we done all right anyway."

And they had. This made Remy's fifth time out on the southern plains. Whenever Gibbs called him, Remy made the same excuses and then he went. The best of the mustangs he and Elijah kept for brood stock, the rest they traded for the things that they couldn't make themselves: a decent plow; tack, harness, and halter for their own two oxen; store-bought shovels, picks, and axes; a cask of bear

oil for their new glass lamps; and a little whiskey for the
cooler nights. This last time Elijah had argued that they
had what they needed, but Remy didn't agree. For him,
there was always a better reason to visit Don Martín's, and
he never missed an opportunity to go, all too happy to
weather his cousin's curses.

Twice, Beatriz had not been there, to Remy's deepest
disappointment, but the time she was had been magnificent,
the stuff of dreams. Her father was not there to shoot him,
so they just sat and talked without Remy having to look
over his shoulder all the time. They rode together for
hours, Don Martín insisting that three of his vaqueros escort them. They were as cool to Remy as they were obse-
quious to her, but they kept their distance well enough.

It was then, Remy thought, that his infatuation evolved
into love. It wasn't just the way the sunlight brushed her
golden skin or the way she let her hair blow wildly with
the breeze, the glint of white teeth behind rose-colored lips,
the warmth and mystery of her dark, pure-blood Spanish
criollo eyes. It was the way she carried herself—pride
mixed with compassion—that endeared her to him. It was
not only what she said which awed him, it was how she
said it. It was not what she looked like, but what she did
and the way she did it: her soothing voice, her effortless
movement, her calming grace. Every time he saw her, he
felt the deepest ache in his chest.

Had it been any other woman, he was certain that he
would've already asked her for her hand. Yet, he waited,
partly because there was the very real problem of her father, and he'd marked Don Martín's warning very well, but
mainly because he didn't know the proper Spanish words.
If he had, he would've said them to her on that very same
afternoon, just as the sun set, the three vaqueros be
damned, and taken his chances. But that opportunity had
passed all too quickly. He came to his senses soon after
that, knowing he must proceed more delicately if he were
ever to overcome the twin obstacles of culture and a father
who liked to wave pistols. But he had hope, and he had
time, and he resolved to manage both to his best advantage.

As always, Don Martín arrived to inspect the latest catch.

His experienced eye studied two of Remy's mares. He consulted with his vaqueros, who nodded just as he had done.

"What would you take for the pair?" Don Martín asked him. "I have just the sire in mind."

"Just your hand," Remy said, and he offered his own. Don Martín grinned and grasped it. "They're yours, Don Martín, for your kindness. I don't run across many like you."

"Nor I you," Don Martín said. "I can only accept if you'll agree to dine with me."

"Done," Remy said, "just have plenty of water handy."

Don Martín laughed. Remy slipped his saddle off the stallion's back and led the horse to a lone corral. As he turned back, the vaqueros were cutting the mares out from the other mustangs. Remy looked around for the girl but didn't see her.

"I don't expect Beatriz is here with you?" he asked.

Remy noted that Don Martín stiffened a little. "She is," he answered, "for a little while."

"Her pa?"

Don Martín nodded.

"Where might I find her?"

"She's already seen you come in, Señor Fuqua. You can find her in the cemetery. I'm sure you know the way."

Remy felt like running down that stone path but he gathered himself. "I'd like to bathe before dinner," he told him.

"There's no time, señor," Don Martín said. "I'd suggest you go as you are. It won't matter to her."

Just the same, Remy went to the horse trough and washed the dust from his face. He raked his wet fingers through his hair, staring at his reflection in the calming waters. Good enough, he thought, and he went to find her. She was sitting on the bench beneath the pavilion, arms at her sides, palms stretched out flat against the stone, shoulders hunched, her dress pressed so tightly against her back that he could see the straight line of her spine. She sat quietly, staring into the distance, a touch of sadness in her face. It pleased him that she brightened when he arrived. She brushed the hair from across her eyes and invited him to sit.

They began, as they always did, with small talk, which

quickly gave way to a strained silence. Remy had consulted with Quelepe in preparation for just such an event. He reached for her hand and waited for her gaze to meet his. And then he said, "Your eyes are like flowers on a summer day."

She took her hand from his, brought it to her face, and bent over. Soon, she was convulsing, and Remy was certain that the tenderness of his words had moved her to tears. He was delighted, thinking of how he would break the news to Quelepe of this miraculous success, when he realized that she was actually choking with laughter. His exuberance drained when he saw that his plan had missed fire.

"What flowers are those, Remy?" she asked him, her teeth biting her bottom lip, when she'd finally caught her breath. "My eyes are brown."

"Hell, I don't know," Remy said, thinking he was going to strangle that old fool first chance he got. "Dandelions, maybe?"

She howled. "They're yellow, I think."

"The center's kinda brown, ain't it?" he said. "To tell ya the truth, I ain't never really looked." This time when she buckled over, he broke down with her. "Well, you get the general idea anyway, don't ya?"

It went much better after that. They just talked, and they laughed, just as Remy felt they should do. When a lull came again, Remy didn't rely on Quelepe's foolish teachings.

"I don't know how you feel about this, Beatriz," he told her, "but I think it's time I tried again with your pa. I don't want to sneak aroun' no more just to talk to ya. I think, if we saw him together, that he might think twice about tryin' to hang me and let us carry on normal-like." He paused, trying to read her. She looked almost grim. "That's of course, if you feel the same way. All you gotta do is say. I'll understand."

She turned away. "I can't, Remy," she said.

His confidence snapped. "All right," he said, and he rose to leave. He wouldn't eat. He'd just mount up, take his share of the stock, and go. "That's all I needed to know. I'm sorry that I embarrassed you like this."

She reached out and grabbed his arm. "It's not what you think."

"What is it, then?"

"He's sending me away," she said softly, "to México City."

At first, he was glad to hear that it wasn't about him. But when he thought about it more, when it truly sank in, he panicked. His plans for patience were shot. "When?"

"Next month. This is my last visit to Don Martín's."

Remy brought his hand to the bridge of his nose and squeezed it. "Damn," he said, and then he heard the twang of the dinner bell above them. "I guess that's it, then," he said in resignation.

"I'm sorry, Remy. If things were different, if I thought there was a chance he'd change his mind, I'd go to him with you just as you say. But it's no use. You know how he feels."

Remy recalled the words of Don Martín, Gibbs and Quelepe—all of whom had warned him of this very moment. Now that it'd come, he saw no other course than to accept it with the same kind of grace that Beatriz had shown him. "Well, I'll tell ya somethin', Beatriz," he said. "This might sound a little strange comin' from a white devil an' all, but I'm sure you can do a whole lot better than me."

She slapped him gently on the shoulder. "Don't talk about yourself like that. You're a wonderful man."

"Just not such a wonderful race, I guess," he said, scuffing the ground with the toe of his boot. "But that ain't really the point." He turned to her. "I would've given anything to have a man, a father, care for me the way Don Carlos cares for you. If I had, I'd do whatever he asked." He shoved his hands into his pockets. "It just ain't somethin' you can take lightly. I know it's hard, at least it is for me, but it's probably best that you do like he says." He turned away. "I won't trouble you no more."

She rose to stand opposite him, her hand swept his cheek. "You were never any trouble, Remy," she said. He felt her fingers creep tentatively behind his neck and then press his face to hers. She kissed him briefly and then let him go, as the dinner bell rang angrily again.

"I really wish you hadn't have done that," he moaned, and she smiled. Then she slipped a necklace, a crucifix, from over her head, the chain tangling in her hair as she worked it free with long, nimble fingers. She draped it over his neck, lifting his curls from under the chain.

"For you," she said, "to think of me. We were friends."

"Friends," Remy repeated, and then they walked up the path together.

Chapter Nineteen

It was just before sundown when Remy quit the fields and came in to wash. The breeze had grown still and cool. The smell of green mesquite smoke hung in the air. He was slipping into his newest set of buckskins when Elijah rode up, covered with the grime of black clay, sawdust, and sweat.

"You must think farmin's some kind of government job," Elijah said. Remy didn't answer. "Ain't you got somethin' smart to say, Remy? All you've done since you come home with them mustangs is sit and brood like a hen that can't lay."

"How 'bout this?" Remy sneered, shooting him a look. "Shut up."

"That's a start," Elijah said. He pulled his shirt over his head and flung it on the porch. He stepped out of his pants, so stiff they nearly stood on their own, and poured the bucket of water, always waiting, over his body. Without another word, he stepped naked into the cabin. Remy followed the wet prints of Elijah's big feet.

"Ah, Quelepe," Elijah said, lifting his big nose high in the air, "that sure smells good. What cha' got for us?"

"Turkey, my child," the old man answered.

As Remy looked on, Elijah inspected the bird. He saw the wrinkles come to his cousin's puckered face. "It looks like it was run over by a wagon and then burned."

"I buried it in a pit to smother with coals," Quelepe explained. "That's the best way."

"With the goddamn feathers on?"

Quelepe never looked at him. "With a little patience," he said, "the feathers come off."

"I'm so goddamn hungry it don't really matter. Pull me off a drumstick and I'll take my chances."

"Why not dress first, my son, and I'll serve you a plate," Quelepe told him. "The gobbler might yet run for it if he sees you like that." He winked at Remy. "I know it was my first thought."

As Elijah waddled off to slip into fresh clothes, Quelepe peeled the skin from the turkey's breast. Remy, too full to leave the table, watched as Quelepe picked at the meat with his bony fingers like a praying mantis does a fly. The feathers came off with the bird's hide. The pink meat was moist and tender; its steamy, mesquite aroma filled his nose. Remy reached for yet another taste when Quelepe slapped his fingers. No problem. He'd had plenty. As Elijah sunk into his chair, Remy rose from his. He primed his rifle and slipped into his winter coat.

"Where ya headed, Cousin?" Elijah asked between smacks.

"I'm goin' to get her," he announced calmly.

"Get who?"

"Beatriz."

"Now?" he asked with a twisted face. The grease made his lips shine in the fire's light. "It's dark out there, boy."

"Best to travel at night," Remy said. He continued gathering his things. He checked his possibles bag to see that it was full of good dry powder, patches, and bear-greased balls. "I'll sleep in the woods during the day," he finally said.

"You'll sleep a lot longer than that if them Indians catch ya off by yourself."

"Which they won't. I know the way to de León's pretty good. I don't think they do. I'll stay off the trails."

Elijah's gaze remained fixed on his plate. "I know it don't matter if'n I tell ya you're wastin' your sweat," he said. "You're too damn stubborn to listen anyways. But I will say that this ain't the time to go, Remy. We got work to do."

"Not for a couple of more weeks, we don't."

"Wait till after we get that new field plowed, dammit. We got time yet to plant it and make a crop. After that I'll go with ya. Maybe Gibbs'll go along too, or one of the others from the settlement. You can't go out alone."

"You watch me." Remy went to the fireplace and pulled out a piece of charcoal and ground it to a point against one of the rougher hearth stones. He paced across the floor of the east wall and then drew a line. "While I'm gone, build me a wall here, a thick one, with a door, of course. Even if she don't come back with me, at least I won't have to listen to you bastards snore all night."

Elijah's jaw dropped. He looked at Quelepe, who was looking at him. "Yes, sir, your majesty," he said, his teeth back on that bone. "Maybe I kin plaster it for ya while I'm at it. I'll fix a little flower box outside your winder there."

"Now you're thinkin'. An' you'll need to move the outhouse fifty yards to the north. It's a little too close for good health."

"That'll make night shits a little risky, don't ya think?"

"Not as risky as day shits are now." Remy could see that Elijah was irritated with him. He always was.

"I don't care to travel that far in a bind," he said. "No tellin' what's out there at night."

"I'll guess you'll just have to hold it till mornin' then."

"Apparently Quelepe's cookin' ain't had the same effect on you it's had on me."

Remy looked at his cousin and smiled. "Look. Woman or no woman, the fact is your shit stinks, Elijah. I know you don't believe it, but it does. We need a little more breeze movin' between here and there. It's for your own good. And dig the new pit deeper this time, dammit, you lazy bastard. If you're worried about Indians, go to San Felipe and get us a mean dog. I'll be back in a week or so. I want this place clean. And learn to say somethin' without cussin', goddammit. There's liable be a woman aroun' here soon." He turned for the door. "I'll see ya when I see ya."

With that he mounted his saddled horse and put his Méxicano rowels to its flank. The sound of its hooves on the pastures grew silent, lost in the humid air of the late spring night.

Don Martín, apparently having been alerted of a stranger's approach, was waiting on his porch when Remy rode up.

"Buenos días, Jefe," Remy said. He took his hat off and beat the dust from his new buckskins. Last night's rain had shrunk them to beat hell. Once supple, they now had the consistency of an eggshell. The hem of his pants had risen above his ankle, gripping so tightly his toes tingled. The inside of his thighs where he rubbed against both horse and saddle had worn dark and smooth. Quelepe was a wizard when it came to tailoring, but Remy was damned if the old buzzard didn't understand the weather's startling effect on his materials. Remy knew he walked ridiculously straight and stiff, like a hired pallbearer. He could barely raise his arm to shake the empresario's hand.

"Buenos días," Don Martín replied, settling his big frame into a squeaking chair. "You've come alone for the mustangs so soon?"

"No, sir."

"The girl, then?" he said with an uncharacteristic gloom. Of course he knew. Remy nodded. He'd planned to confide in Don Martín, get whatever advice he'd give him about this thing and then go and see her wherever she was. "I'm afraid she's already gone," he told him.

"Where?" he asked, far from dissuaded.

"She went home to Béxar one week ago to see her relatives. She's probably on her way to México City by now." He looked to the south. "Somewhere on the Camino Real."

"Damn," he said, working a crease in the elbow so he could scratch his itchy head. "Who's with her?"

"Her father, of course. Several of his vaqueros. He also hired some soldiers to ride along for protection. They have two dozen men, or so. Any of which," he added, "would not be pleased at the sight of you."

That was a given. "Where kin I pick up the Camino Real?"

De León shook his head. "You must cross the Nueces and travel west," he said with a sigh. "It connects Béxar with Laredo, to Saltillo from there, and then on to the interior and México City." That explained, his tone shifted. "But, it's no use, Fuqua. Why not stay with us and rest?

Then return to your own *sitio*. I'll send some of my men with you for your own protection. It was foolish to come alone."

Remy didn't really have a plan other than wanting to see Beatriz. He considered the empresario's advice, which he had anticipated, and then he said, "Thank you kindly, Don Martín, but I'll be headed southwest."

The old Méxicano leaned forward, resting his forearms on his knees. "It's ill advised, my young friend; and all for naught, I'm afraid. In México, one cannot go against the father's wishes. Don Carlos is my dear friend and business associate. I must support his decision in this regard. The girl is not for you."

"I'd just like to hear it from her, I guess," Remy said.

"And get yourself killed in the process?" He leaned back grunting, and crossed his leg over his knee. "*Escuchas bien, hombre.* I know young men get lonely, but I wouldn't be in such a hurry if I were you. *Las mujeres saben màs que el diablo,*" he told him. Women know more than the devil. "Especially *las Tejanas.* They're a breed apart, and proud of it! I'm especially fond of Beatriz, as you know. But what a temper! You've sampled the sugar but not the spice. She gives her poor papa fits. Give the matter a little more thought, *mi amigo.*"

Remy laughed at the flavor of the old man's warning. Beatriz's spirit attracted him to her. It was what he admired most. She, he thought, was like him, sort of. "Thanks for the advice, Don Martín, but I got to see her. At least, one more time. I'll take my chances."

Remy looked into the empresario's dark eyes. He studied Remy for what felt like an eternity. Remy did not speak. Finally Don Martín slapped his hands on his thighs, and rose from his chair. "Ah," he said, shaking his head. "I can't help you, Fuqua."

"I didn't ask you to. You've done what you said you'd do. The rest is up to me. Good day to you."

Before he turned away, Don Martín spoke. "Don Carlos Amarante de la Cruz does not wish to harm you. Beneath that hard exterior is a very fine man. But, if provoked he can be dangerous. I'd not expect him to be pleased with your appearance on the trail. And that's if you make one.

Los Comanches, as always, are out on the prairie. You make an easy target for them. Either way, you may lose your life, I'm afraid. I'd hate to see you come to harm. Stay with me, Fuqua, as I've suggested."

"My mind's made up. I've got to see her."

He sighed. "As you wish. *Vaya con Diós, mi amigo.* I wash my hands of the whole affair."

"I'd be much obliged if I could borrow a sack of oats for my horse. The prairie grass ain't come back. What's out there don't seem to do 'im much good."

Remy saw Don Martín's eyes move down the flank of his horse. The empresario agreed that the stallion looked tired. He begged Remy to let him loose in the pasture for a day or two to restore its spirit. Remy answered that there was no time. Beatriz's party would soon cross the Río Bravo if they hadn't already. Don Martín threw his head back, breathed deeply, and then told Remy to take what he needed and go, along with two horses more from his own *caballada,* may God help him. They'd provide fresh mounts for Remy, he said, when he must run from the Comanches or Don Carlos, or perhaps the two combined. De León winked, and then called for his vaqueros. "Enrique will show you which two to take," he said. "Cut them loose if Don Carlos overtakes you. He knows my brand well. I wouldn't like him to know that I've given you horses."

"I'll repay your generosity with two of my own in the spring. The best I have."

Don Martín shook his head. "I'm not giving them to you, foolish gringo," he said, his cheeks blustering. "Please note that they are merely loaned. If they are lost, you owe me replacements of equal value."

Remy smiled. "I understand," he said. "Don Carlos won't like it that you've helped me."

He threw up his hands. "That goes without saying. Don Carlos is in the way of providence, I think. I won't be. You want your answer, go and get it." Don Martín knocked the bucket into his well. "There's one thing more," he said, working the crank.

"What's that?"

"If I were going to ask a beautiful woman to spend her

life with me, I don't know if I'd wear those pants. They are, quite frankly, absurd."

Remy looked at his clothes. "Damned if I can do anythin' about it. I gotta go with what I got."

Don Martín dipped his ladle in the bucket and drew it to his lips. "They could not have been tighter when they were still on the deer," he said, offering Remy the handle.

"Prob'ly fit him better though." Remy shrugged his shoulders to work his arm loose. The sleeve hung on his elbow. He could barely breathe. "They was quite dandy when I cut out," taking his first sip. "A couple of rivers and one good shower and, well, you see what we got."

Don Martín chuckled. "Get your horses and your grain. I'll go and see what's available. Anything is better."

Chapter Twenty

With his horses fed and watered, Remy struck off south by southwest with Don Martín's stallions in tow. They'd practically had to skin him out of his clothes, kind of like a dead squirrel. He made excellent time, often switching horses, and he looked a lot better doing it in a pair of finely stitched Méxicano pants. Silver buckles lined the seams. He crossed the white soil, where strange and hostile plants grew that only Quelepe could name. Buzzards sailed the thermals overhead.

By nightfall he came across the wagon wheel ruts that marked the King's Highway. As Quelepe had told him, the Camino Real was an old trade route that wandered through the open and higher ground. It naturally discouraged ambush. The road was well-traveled for that time of year. Several parties had recently traveled south, but only one or two were moving north for Béxar, at least since the last good rain. Although he could not be certain whether or not Beatriz's party had already passed this point, he decided to move on south toward Laredo. He reasoned that if he did not overtake them, he would make inquiries at the town to determine whether or not they had passed. If not, he could pick his own place on the Camino Real and wait for her.

Remy found himself a deep draw, shrouded with scrub mesquites maybe a half-mile from the road. He hobbled both of de León's horses, tying off his own just to be absolutely certain he'd at least have one handy in the morning, and then fell asleep.

He awoke at first light, saddled his horse, gathered the other mounts, and rode hard to the south, parallel to the Camino Real. He came across two different parties of travelers, each stating that they had not seen Amarante's group. By sunset, he spotted a third party in the distance. He circled west to a ridge and watched carefully, while remaining out of sight. There were two carriages and maybe forty riders, one of which appeared to be Don Carlos. Next to him rode a woman on a sorrel mare. He felt certain that this was Beatriz. He would get his chance to see her after all. What would come of it, he could not say. He had been warned.

Remy waited until it was dark. The southern skies were overcast, and his form did not leave the slightest shadow on the dusty ground. Cook fires flickered in the distance. Sentries were surely posted in all directions. He chose to approach from the south, which featured the most cover, and perhaps would be the least likely direction of ambush. Three times he mounted his horse, thought about it for a moment, and then dismounted to wait a little while longer. At some point exhaustion overtook him and he nodded off.

A coyote's howl awakened him. It must have been around three or so judging by the crescent moon. The fires were burned down to a slightly pulsating glow. The evening breeze came out of the north, but was almost still now. In a couple of hours dawn would break. He knew he had to go now if he were going. He mounted for a fourth time, rubbed the sleep from his eyes and prepared himself.

Three hundred yards or so from the encampment, Remy dismounted and tied his horse's reins to the trunk of a mesquite. He shed his boots and socks, and tread, unarmed, across the ground that lay between himself and the sleeping Beatriz. He smelled the smoke of a *soldado's* cigarette about the time the first mesquite thorn stung his heel and he crept, cringing, well out of his way. Elijah was right, he thought. He'd lost his goddamn mind.

Remy drifted toward the center of the camp, dimly illuminated by the glowing coals. His fingers and toes were numb with cold. The horses, tied in rows with lariats, intently watched him but made no sound, most likely because Remy smelled more like a horse than a man. Not a soul stirred. The soldiers and Don Carlos's vaqueros tossed in their sleep beneath woolen blankets; some of them were snoring. There were two tents struck near one of the wagons, which displeased him as he pressed forward. He folded back the canvas door of one, startled to find Don Carlos's whiskered face. Remy's eyes widened, and he quickly and silently closed the flap, damning the bad luck. The other tent must be the one.

He slid back the door to this one, and waited for his eyes to adjust. In time, he made the form of Beatriz, lying curled under a blanket. Dropping to all fours, he allowed the canvas to swing closed, cracked a little to allow the firelight's unfaithful illumination. He crept beside her, and then shot out his arm to cover her mouth.

"Beatriz?" he whispered, his mouth to her ear. "It's me. Remy." The woman sprang out of her bedroll, the whites of her eyes glistening in fear, her arms swinging wildly at the figure that held her. With one hand, Remy reached for the back of her neck, the other he held fast to her mouth. "It's Remy!" he whispered. He could see her eyes focus on his. Her breathing decelerated. "Remy," he said once more, and a smile came to his face, then to hers. He released her, and her arms quickly surrounded him and pressed him so close he could feel her heart beat.

"¿Que estás haciendo?" she gasped, pulling away.

"Te quiero, Beatriz." He said it with conviction.

"Yo te quiero también; pero mi padre . . ." He put his finger to her lips and said he wasn't there to talk about her father.

"¿Quieres casàrte conmigo?" There, he thought. He'd done it. He'd asked this woman to be his wife. His eyes waited.

"¿Ahora?"

What did she think? That they'd talk it over in the morning with a cup of coffee? *"Sí. Ahora mismo,"* he insisted.

"Why do you always speak to me in Spanish?" she asked him.

He cocked his head. "It's your language."

"I speak English perfectly."

He rolled his eyes. "Well, this is a fine time to tell me. Marry me, Beatriz. Come with me and be my wife."

"My father will kill us both."

"Me, maybe," he said grinning, "but never you. Just the same, I don't intend to make that easy for him. If you say yes, we'll be long gone before they wake up. In two days, we'll be back at San Felipe."

"I don't know . . ." Her words drained him. "I didn't expect this."

He scrambled for a response. "Hell, I didn't expect this either, believe me. But, I'm here and I'm askin'. If ya need time to think about it, ya gotta go with me now just the same. I'll take ya back to a safe place and you can tell me when you're ready. If you don't want me, I'll see to it that you're returned safely to your family." He gripped her hands in his. "Ya gotta trust me, Beatriz, and you've got to come with me. But if ya go on to México City, I'll never see ya again. I know it. I had to come." He paused and then added, "I love you."

She thought a moment, and then nodded stiffly. "All right," she said.

He wasn't sure what all right meant. "You'll marry me?"

"Maybe."

"Maybe?"

"Yes."

"Yes, you mean yes you'll marry me, or maybe yes you might, or yes, you'll go and think about it maybe."

She looked confused. "I don't speak English that well. What are you talking about? Speak plainly."

"Will you marry me?"

"I said yes. Maybe. Probably. *Vàmos*."

His face flushed with pride as she spoke, and he reached for her. She pushed him away and reached for her boots.

"Not now. Let's leave this place. You have no idea how angry my father will be about this."

"I've got some idea. That's why I snuck in here in the dead of night barefooted. Speaks for itself, I'd say."

"I had a dream that you'd come for me."

"I've thought of nuthin' else."

She pulled him to her one last time and kissed his cheek.
He could smell her. He closed his eyes and inhaled deeply.
Then he released her and peeked out of the tent flap. When
he turned to her to tell her it was clear, she asked him
about his pants. He said it was a long story and would have
to wait. When he was certain that no one stirred, he slid
through the opening, and she quickly followed. In an instant, they had slipped from the flickering light of the dying
coals into the dark cloak of the brush.

Before daybreak they cut the Nueces, Remy deciding to
travel the shallow river east for a time, hoping the running
water would cover their tracks. After a half mile or so of
that, Remy threaded his horse up through the thickest
brush of the bank, holding the limbs back so that Beatriz
could follow, and then they bore hard north for the Frio,
where it forked with the Atascosa, and thereby cross two
rivers at one time.

Always he looked after Beatriz, but she was always there,
at his horse's tail. "After we make this next crossin'," he
assured her, "I'll find us a spot to rest on some high ground.
I'll watch over you while you sleep."

"No need, Remy," she said. "I know my father and the
men with him. He'll overtake us with no difficulty if we
stop now."

"Then we'll go on," he said, "but you tell me when
you're tired, an' I'll find a place."

She nodded that she would and they rode on. When they
came to the fork between rivers, Remy feared the current.
The water looked too deep to him. "Let's try upriver," he
told her, but before he'd even finished saying the words,
she'd turned her mount south. A quarter of a mile distant
she splashed into the river.

"We cross here," she said. He swallowed hard and followed her. The water came only to the horses' knees.

"I'll be damned," he said, racing past her up the bank to head back north.

By noon, they forded the San Antonio and entered the low hills. He crested the tallest and dismounted. "I can see for better'n two miles from here," he said. "Why don't you rest?"

She rode right past him. "Not yet."

In the late afternoon, unusually still and hot for a spring day, they cut Ecleto Creek. For the last hour, she'd worn her cotton shirt unbuttoned, revealing the dark cleavage and the start of the two smooth mounds of her breasts. It was hard to pick the trail watching them rise, round like ripe peaches. She must've known it, since she rode past and picked the trail for him. That suited him better anyway, as it afforded him the opportunity to watch her hips, cocked on that saddle, sway back and forth on creaking leather. Remy was thinking that he'd soon be hearing a similar creak on their marital bed, providing he could afford to honeymoon on one that actually had springs. Watching her, he decided that he'd sell all the horses, the grant, Elijah and Quelepe if necessary, just to borrow one for their first night.

Remy knew his imagination was a little too vivid. He was adjusting his seating for the fourth time when they crossed the Ecleto and Beatriz looked back to judge his progress. Remy feared she'd spot that extra saddle horn, so he slid from the stallion's back into the stream and lay on the bottom until he'd cooled. When he came up for air, she was dismounted, poised at the bank, her skirt drawn up past her knees, drinking water from her cupped hands. He followed the line of her legs up to where the shadow began, imagining his hand making that exact journey. She looked at him, smiled, and said, "Let's go." He sunk to the bottom to wait a little bit longer for the throbbing to subside.

"Aren't you worn out, Beatriz?" he asked her when he resurfaced. "Let's rest a while on the bank." But she had already mounted her horse, turning its head, whipping its flank, knowing that it was time to turn due east.

Remy startled awake, not remembering where he was. His head lay on something soft; he felt fingers combing through his hair. He looked up, and there she was. The dream was real. She'd come with him.

He reached up to stroke her cheek, illuminated by the moonlight. The cadence of crickets marked the late hour. The sound of running water filled his ears.

"Better now, Remy?" she cooed.

"Yeah. Thanks. I'm sorry. I haven't slept well lately."

"It's all right," she said. "They're not following us. They must not have thought we'd come this way."

"I'm thirsty," he said, and she pointed to the creek below. He went down, slid the shirt off his back, and waded into the water. It was clear and clean, a little chilly, and he knelt down until it ran into his parched mouth. He turned to look back up at her, and she smiled warmly. He left the water, draping his shirt over his arm, and returned to her side.

He kissed her. She opened to him. He moved in closely until he felt the warmth of her against him. He slid back her shirt, and cupped her breast, and she moaned softly in his ear. He dropped his hand to the inside of her thigh, and stroked it. She breathed deeply, and he went on. When he reached the part where her legs ended, he spread his fingers and felt softness, warm and moist, on his fingertips.

She reached for his forearm and took his hand away. "Don't, Remy," she whispered. "I'm Catholic."

"That's a coincidence," Remy panted, "so am I." He made the sign of the cross over his chest, certain that he had it all wrong, and then started again where he'd left off.

This time when he snatched his hand, she stared firmly into his eyes. "I'm impulsive, Remy. But not a fool."

"There ain't nuthin' foolish about this," he said.

"First the vows," she said.

Remy drew back, seeing how the muscles of her jaw tightened, and thought that it was best not to press his luck. This lovemaking was, most likely, like hunting in some respects. Patience was a virtue. "When you're ready then," he told her, the corner of his lip curled.

Then she reached around his back to hold him, which was better anyway. How he relished her touch. He began purring like a kitten. Then he felt her fingers rub across the numb scars and stop cold.

She jerked away, and turned his back around to her.

"My God!" she gasped. "What happened?"

"Nuthin'," he said, and he reached for her again.

"*Nothing*?" she said, her expression pained, a stiff arm now between his body and hers. "Have you committed some crime, Remy?"

He closed his eyes, and sighed loudly. "No, Beatriz," he moaned. "I ain't a crook, an' I ain't a scoundrel; an' I'm damn tired of everybody—particularly you—thinkin' that I am."

"Who did this, then?"

"My uncle. We didn't always see eye to eye. He settled things with a whip."

"Noooo," she said, incredulous.

"Oh, yes."

"I can't believe it."

"There were plenty of times when I couldn't either," he explained, but her expression remained blank. There wasn't anything he could do but stop and tell her all about it. He started with his parents, and what happened afterwards, and continued all the way up until he saw her the first time at Don Martín's. She nodded quietly and listened to the gritty details he'd left out in earlier conversations, sometimes stopping to ask him questions.

"Such cruelty, Remy," she said, her gaze falling to her lap. "I don't see how you have so much kindness left."

"Well, I do," he assured her. "I've never told anybody about all that stuff. There was never anybody who wanted to know."

"I do, Remy," she said. "I want to know everything about you."

"That's the worst of it, Beatriz, an' it's all behind me now. I made a new start in Tejas, and you're the biggest part of it."

The sorrow in her face made him wonder if she had new

doubts. Shocked by the scars on his skin, she might be
afraid of the ones that he'd just admitted lay much deeper.
"I want you to know somethin' else," he said, his voice
steady, his fingers lifting her chin. "I'm nuthin' like any of
my kin. It doesn't matter what's happened, what I've seen,
where I've been; not anymore. I could never hurt you, Beatriz. I'll never raise my hand. I swear it."

"If I thought for one moment that you would," she told
him, "I'd never have come."

He exhaled loudly and drew her again to his chest. This
time, as her fingers crossed his scars, they stroked them
gently. The two of them fell beside one another, his face
to hers, and talked on. The more he told her, the tighter
she held him.

When daybreak came, the first thing he did after he'd
covered her with his jacket was pick the grass from her
hair. He was so careful not to wake her.

Chapter Twenty-One

Kills White Bear closed his ears to his warriors' com-
plaints. Having been out for a week, they were tired
of the long, midnight rides of the raiding trail and longed to
return to the encampment where they could rest in peace.

"We have what we came for," one of the youngest said,
"why do we not go?"

"Because we don't have what I came for," Kills White
Bear told him, and he held his eastern course.

"What is it that you want?"

"Knowledge." And when they argued that he didn't need
them for that, he bid them do as they pleased, and rode
on. He heard their horses' hooves stumble on the loose
stones as they left him and turned northwest. It was just as
well, he thought. What he wanted to know, what he wanted
to be certain of, was for him alone, as the dying bear had
willed.

He forded the river the Méxicanos called the Colorado
and followed its course south. One by one, he came to
those silly wooden shelters. The smell of wood smoke

mixed in the air with the scent of the fresh dirt. These new people had skinned the hide from the land as far as his eye could see under the guise of planting their crops like Tonkawa women, as if they were unaware that Mother Earth would provide.

At first they'd come as a trickle, their numbers swelling slowly. They came in floods now, the traders told him, a fact made obvious by the patches of bare earth he saw everywhere around him.

Four winters ago, Maguara had smoked the pipe with the man called Austin. In exchange for trade goods and an alliance that meant nothing, the Penateka were sworn to stand back and watch these white men defile the earth with big iron teeth and with spiritless beasts so lazy they refused to migrate even when the grass was gone and often lay in their own filth. Thirteen winters before, Maguara had said that he saw what Kills White Bear had seen when he, then a boy, fought the albino bear for its spirit. It was clear enough to Kills White Bear that these men best fit the dying beast's description. If so, why had Maguara ignored its warning? The civil chief moved often enough among these white men. Maguara was older and wiser than he, two reasons why Kills White Bear had deferred to his judgment. But now he desired to see with his own eyes. His journey east was a part of that.

When he'd seen all that he thought he needed to see, he crossed the river again and climbed the tallest bluff. There he dismounted and tethered his horse, and sat down to remember the bear's warning.

The day after his time with Wolf Eyes, the fourth of his spirit quest, he had awoken anxious as the morning sun fell on his face. He was still called Little Hand then. Whenever he thought of his boyhood, he used his boyhood name. He had methodically undressed, carrying only his medicine bag and the knife, as Wolf Eyes had instructed, and had picked his way silently through the brush and the loose rock until he found the gurgling spring below. He no longer felt tired or cold.

Four buffalo bulls, the symbol of his people, followed him shoulder to shoulder in silence. They kept their distance. Their interest in the coming events enhanced his own and he knew then that his spirit animal was coming. He waded into the depths of the stream to bathe and submerged his head, but he did not drink the water. Just the same, he was renewed and ready from the miracle he'd witnessed the night before. When he arose, his copper skin blushed from the chill of the air, he found an immense grizzly bear hunched on the bank, waiting. Its shimmering coat was as white as the great drifting clouds of summer. Its every move meant power. Little Hand greeted it, as he had the animals before, but the beast answered in a loud and angry growl.

"What're you doing in this place?" the bear demanded.

Little Hand did not answer at first. He thought about how he should respond, and finally said, "I'm here, where I should be." The words didn't come out with the confidence that he'd hoped for.

"This is my land," the beast bellowed deeply and clearly. "I offer you one last chance to leave it."

Little Hand was confused by the bear's belligerent tone. "Why do you treat me like this? Are you not here for me? I was sent to learn from you, not to argue. This land belongs to the Nemenuh. We share it with you and all the others in the world."

"The white bear shares with no man. Defend it, or die trying." At that, the animal raised itself on its powerful hind legs, growled ferociously, and lunged at Little Hand. Its claw raked the front of his trembling chest. Little Hand watched his skin part and he shrieked in pain. The water around him turned red with his own blood. Now he understood the terms. If he were to have this spirit, he must fight for it. The bear waited for his reaction as if it felt that this one blow was enough.

Little Hand was shocked and terrified, yet he understood then that he could not run from his fate. He reached for his knife, gathered himself, and lashed desperately and de-

cisively at the animal. A quick slash of the throat might do
it. But the bear must've anticipated his decision and rushed
forward again to meet him. Its arms pulled him helplessly
to its chest. Little Hand felt its cold teeth gnashing at his
throat.

Overpowered and exposed, Little Hand went limp and
slipped beneath the water out of the bear's grasp. The animal's great head plunged below the surface to search for
him, but Little Hand swam behind it and emerged, his knife
poised and ready. He swung his arms around it and clung
desperately to the bear's back, choking the beast with his
left arm while plunging the blade deep into its chest with
his right. With one frantic swing of its arm, the bear
knocked Little Hand clear, almost to the rocky bank. The
knife slipped from his grip.

The bear turned and charged him again, squeezing him
to its chest so tightly that Little Hand smelled the stench
of its breath. Little Hand bit down hard on the bear's snout
and clawed at his fiery eyes with his fingers. The bear
screamed in agony and flung him away a second time.

Little Hand found himself again on the bank. He picked
up a large rock and, with both hands above his head,
dashed it against the bear's forehead. The animal was
stunned and furious. Its roar shook the leaves. Little Hand
saw the knife in the sand in shallow, still water and lunged
for it. When he held it, he turned and faced the bear. Although his instincts were to flee, he gripped the knife and
darted for deeper water where the bear's size lost its advantage. It followed him without fear into water up to its neck,
its arms poised above its head. Little Hand settled to the
bottom, squatting on a flat rock, and then shoved forward
with all his strength for the white mass of his attacker. He
sank the knife deep into the thick of the animal's exposed
chest, twisting the blade one way and then the next until
he felt it cut hard into rib. He was certain that he'd punc-
tured its lung.

He shoved himself away and sprang to the surface for
air. The bear moved the opposite direction, until it stood
in water up to its waist. Blood poured from all of its
wounds but most freely from the last one. Patches of red
covered the wet, white, matted fur. The bear collapsed

backwards, floating, breathing deeply, struggling for air
when there was nothing but water. Little Hand saw that it
made no more effort to injure him, and the battle, he knew,
was won.

He swam behind the bear. He touched its hide. Nothing.
He nudged it. No response. At last he thumped it with his
knife handle and the beast mumbled, "Enough." It was truly
over. Little Hand dragged its body toward the bank until he
could pull it no further. With great effort, he rolled it on its
back in the shallow water. The bear coughed; its bloody chest
labored for breath. The bear's black eyes frantically searched
for him. When they found him, the bear grew still.

"See how my blood runs, young Nemenuh?" it grumbled.
"I won't live long like this. You fought well. I didn't expect
it from such a skinny human being."

Little Hand stood over him, the blood running from his
own deep wounds, his chest rising and falling in a hectic
rhythm, every muscle of his body twitching, the veins protruding from his neck, his knife gripped in the white knuckles of his own hands that shook from anger. Tears of rage
welled up in his eyes. "We could've shared this place if
you'd have considered it! It didn't have to be like this! It
should not have been! Few warriors must kill an animal to
possess its spirit. I needed your strength, not your life."

The bear's speech was slurred and sloppy. Its blood
choked its throat. "It was out of the question," it said.
"This was bear land or Nemenuh land but never both.
Predators do not share. We take what we want and are
prepared to fight for it. When two strong forces meet claim-
ing the same earth, only one can remain. It was important
for you to know how vicious the battle must be. From the
very beginning, it was either you or I, with no compromise
possible. Our battle was inevitable. And so it'll be in your
battles to come."

Little Hand listened in despair, confused. The bear went
on. "Know that I would have killed you if I could," it told
him. "You wanted what I must have. But the issue has
been decided. I yield this place to you to keep as long as
you can hold it, for there are other white bears that want
it, and the same rules apply."

Little Hand tossed the bloody knife on the bank and

sank to his knees. He was exhausted. The tears of frustration came again. "Something's wrong!" he cried. "It shouldn't have been like this. I was cheated."

"*You* were cheated?" the bear asked. "The Great Spirit promised me this place as *my* home. A boy has taken it from me, and the promise is broken. To be cheated, someone must take it from you." The bear groaned in agony, and then added, "And I promise you that they will try."

This last caught his attention and Little Hand wiped the tears from his eyes. "*Who* will try?"

"Thousand of white bears—no kin to me and no friend to you. Men apart from the Great Spirit. Hunters with full bellies, warriors without a tribe, strangers who, not knowing what they want, take everything. The trees fall in their wake of destruction and blood covers the earth where they've been." He paused, and then said, "They are coming for you."

Little Hand stared at the bear. All of this was not as it should have been. In his agony, he kicked the bear's side. "What're you talking about? Tell me!"

The bear lay still. "See how my blood runs, young warrior?" it mumbled. "My body grows cold. My time's finished, but yours just begins. This place is now yours. Keep it if you can."

"No one will ever take it from me! I swear it!"

"Maybe they will, and maybe they won't. The only thing that's certain is that they'll try."

By now, the blood bubbled from the bear's snout. Its speech was strained; its eyes looked wild. "Now you must listen to me," it told him quietly. "When I die, take my hide from my back and place it in your lodge. It will protect you. Your name's no longer Little Hand but Kills White Bear, for I have marked this name on your chest in blood forever." It motioned to him with a single paw.

"Come close to me, now. Put your mouth on mine. Catch my spirit as it leaves this body, for by all rights it now belongs to you. Breathe in deeply and it will never leave you. My death is life to you; my struggle is now yours. Come now. Do as I say."

Little Hand did so, and when the bear breathed its last breath, Little Hand inhaled it, its thick blood on his lips, the taste of salt in his mouth, and held it deep within his lungs until he thought they might burst. His mind cleared as does the air after a spring rain. He was no longer angry. He was no longer confused. His vision, regardless of its complexities, was complete. He knew he would rise to the challenge of the bear.

He rose from the beast's body and gave a great cry. The voice he heard was that of a man. Its strength and clarity surprised even him as the echo returned it to his ears. He heard the turkeys gobble, as they do out of respect when the coyote howls, and the squirrels scurry across sprouting pecan limbs for the dark, protective knotholes of burr oaks. He'd earned that voice.

He quickly skinned out the hide from the beast, rolled it up in his arms, and from there he ran home without stopping. He was not hungry; fatigue never touched him. He felt alive, connected, and vibrant. He'd won his *puha*, power, and no man he knew had conquered and then absorbed the spirit of the great bear.

As he ran, Wolf Eyes' words mixed with those of the bear he had beaten. There was a dark omen there that tarnished even this great and shining victory. He was proud to be chosen to defend his people and their land against any and all, yet he'd been warned that his struggle would be hard. His battle was but the first taste of that, a tinge of bitter mixed with the sweet. He could not have been happier and, at the same time, more troubled. Who was coming? And when?

And now, years later, when he was certain the portent had come true, he was bound by honor to watch his enemies' twisted roots take hold in his country. Maguara, in his blindness, had made it so, and Kills White Bear could do nothing.

Chapter Twenty-Two

The morning of the third day Remy and Beatriz rode into San Felipe. They made straight for Austin's house, stopping in front of the horse trough. The heads of their mounts immediately pressed against the surface of the water. Remy and Beatriz pushed in between them, splashing the dust from their faces.

Remy heard boot heels on the pine planks of the porch. When he looked up, Don Estévan stood before them, looking down his sharp nose.

"Good morning, Mr. Fuqua," he said crisply. His expression, always flat, always grave, today begged an explanation.

"Mornin', Don Estévan," Remy said, and left it at that.

Austin looked curiously at Beatriz, who stood before him in silence, nodding. *"Buenos días, señorita,"* he said. Then he turned back to Remy. "What brings you to the settlement? You ought not be done with your planting, I should think."

"This here's Beatriz Amarante de la Cruz," Remy declared, his shoulders square, his chest full, "my fiancée."

"Your what?" Austin's eyes widened in shock. "What in heaven's name have you done now, Fuqua?"

"What comes natural," Remy said. "We wanna get married."

Austin squinted as he addressed Beatriz in Spanish. "Señorita, are you the daughter of Don Carlos Amarante de la Cruz of Béxar?"

"Sí," Colonel Austin." She wasn't the least bit intimidated. Remy loved it.

"My heavens, Fuqua," he said, his brow furrowed. "She's quite a catch."

"You don't know the half of it," he said.

Austin thought a moment. "Should I take it then that we do not have the approval of Don Carlos for this union?"

"Not exactly," Remy said. Beatriz said nothing. Austin again turned to her.

"In that case, I'd suggest that you return to your father's house—under my protection, of course. Mr. Fuqua could then make arrangements in the customary fashion. That's the best way to proceed. Otherwise, we'll have trouble."

Remy had expected this sort of thing. Austin ran the grant, but he didn't run Remy's private life. He stepped forward. "With all due respect, Don Estévan, that ain't gonna happen. I been that route already and it didn't work out to my satisfaction. I want her, she wants me, and that's

all anybody needs to know. All we need now is a priest."
He looked at her and smiled. "An' I mean quick-like."

Don Estévan stuck his hands in his woolen pockets and
dragged the toe of his brogan shoe across a worn plank.
"Well, we haven't got one."

"What?"

"There's no priest."

"You're a Catholic," Remy stated, and Austin nodded.
"She's a Catholic. I'm supposed to be a Catholic. All of
Tejas is Catholic and you tell me that we ain't got a Catho-
lic priest?"

"That's right," Austin said, as if nothing were amiss.
"The Méxicano government waived all taxation from the
colonists for ten years. Taxes would support the clergy. As
it now stands, the central government can't afford to give
us one and we can't afford one ourselves. And so we simply, as you say, ain't got one."

Remy slapped his thigh. "Well, if that don't beat all.
How do folks get married aroun' here?"

Austin stroked his chin. "Some marry under Protestant
oaths. We get a discreet, traveling minister coming through
from time to time. Others are just common law, waiting for
a priest to come up. Under the circumstances, I couldn't
suggest either of those options for you two." He paused, his
lips pursed. "I'm sure you realize that yours is a particularly
delicate situation."

Remy looked helplessly at Beatriz. She didn't have any
answers either. "What do we do then?" he asked.

"As I said, I'd return her to her father's house and give
the matter further thought. You're young, Fuqua. There's
no hurry."

"Everybody keeps tellin' me that."

"On occasion, everybody's right." Then Austin turned to
Beatriz. "Do you want this man as your husband?" Remy
grew anxious. This was all he needed, his own empresario
attempting to talk Beatriz out of it. If anybody could do it,
he knew Austin could.

"Yes," she said calmly.

"Are you sure? He's poor, as are we all. Life will not be
easy with him."

"Where is life easy in Tejas, señor? It doesn't matter. I love this man. I've agreed to be his wife."

"Will you go with me to seek your father's approval for the marriage?"

She shook her head. "He'll never give it."

"He might."

"He won't, I assure you. But once it's done, he will adjust. I'm his only child. He loves me. And I love Remy. In time, my father will also." She reached for Remy's hand. "All will be well, Colonel Austin. Please help us."

Remy looked at Austin and smiled. "Satisfied?"

"Yes," Don Estévan said, his hand out, palm up. "They hoped we'd intermarry with Tejanos when they allowed us to settle here. I don't think they counted on this particular marriage, but in general it's what they wanted. It'll be unpopular among the more conservative Méxicanos but perfectly legal. That's the only issue of concern for an empresario. Regardless, it's certainly not for me to object if this is what you both want. I'll send to Béxar for a priest. He'll be more likely to accept our invitation if he knows the bride is the daughter of Don Carlos. In the meantime, I'd suggest that you stay as a guest with the Hamiltons here in San Felipe. Miss Anna would be pleased."

"I want to stay with Remy," Beatriz insisted.

Austin immediately shook his head. "Oh, that's just not a good idea. We must conduct ourselves properly, above all reproach. We don't need any scandal attached to this thing."

"How long?" Remy asked.

"I couldn't say. I'll need a few pesos to encourage the priest to come quickly."

"I haven't got any," Remy said, ashamed. "I'll give four mustangs."

"Cash is better. I could scratch a little up. You can owe me." Beatriz reached into her pocket, producing a leather pouch. She pulled a single coin from it, and handed it to Don Estévan. Remy saw it flash golden in his palm.

"This should do," she said calmly.

Austin looked first at the coin, then at Remy, all the while jiggling its weight in his hand. Remy had never seen real gold before, and it appeared as if it'd been some time since Don Estévan had come across any. Best of all, Beatriz acted as if it meant nothing to her except the means to an agreed end. Remy couldn't have been prouder of the way she'd handled the transaction.

"I believe it should," the empresario finally said. "All will be arranged. Do not fear. Should I notify any of your relatives, Señorita de la Cruz?"

She shook her head.

"As you wish," he said and then turned to Remy. "Make ready for your wife, Fuqua. I'll send for you. We'll soon have a wedding in San Felipe, may God help us."

Chapter Twenty-Three

Before they'd even finished their plates, Beatriz was staring at him again, her ivory teeth nibbling lackadaisically at a chicken bone, her pinkie flicking a curl from her cheek. It was the look, Remy knew, of hunger, and what a surprising appetite that skinny little girl had. It was the third time that same day he'd seen that same twinkle, and his reaction was always the same. Remy swept his wife into his arms amid the clatter of plates, cups, and steel flatware, kicked open the door to their bedroom, passed over the threshold, and then kicked the door closed.

Remy had promised Elijah that the work would resume with a new fury after the wedding and in a way it did, but not the work Elijah had expected. Just as soon as the priest, soused on wild grape wine and bust-head whiskey, had slurred the last of their vows, Beatriz made no more excuses, considered no theological arguments, and conjured no further reasons for delay. No sooner had Remy snatched the certificate from Austin's hand, the ink of the empresario's signature not yet dry, than she whispered scandalous notions in his ear. Shocked to hear any woman—let alone his young, sweet, well-born bride—speak in such a manner, he quickly shook off his astonishment, keen to discover exactly what her suggestions meant. Though it was clear enough to him that they'd both be learning, Beatriz promised not to disappoint, and Remy had no call to doubt her. She was damn motivated. That was clear enough to him.

For the wedding, Austin had planned a grand celebration, which Remy chose to ignore. He and Beatriz mounted his horse, leaving in their wake a host of bewildered and bemused guests, and rode north. They'd ridden no more than a mile when she slipped from the stallion's back, shed her wedding dress as quickly as the husk is peeled from a fresh ear of corn, and stood naked before him. He got down beside her and cast his own garments onto the nearest bush. Then she led him down to the river to a bed of lush, green moss. Against that velvety backdrop, under the waxing summer moon, her body glowed golden.

Remy lay beside her, stroking the creamy skin of her stomach and breasts. With the slightest touch, goose-bumps erupted, her nipples stood erect. She pulled him on top of her, locking her muscled legs around his buttocks. He didn't know exactly what to do. Impatience got the best of his imperfect instincts, and he thrust two or three times without success.

"Easy, *mi amor*," she moaned to calm him, "there's no hurry." It certainly felt like there was to him. He had swollen as if a bumblebee had stung him, stiff and knotty like a pine spike, throbbing so hard that it hurt. He felt her fingers grip it and lead the way, as he had already learned was her habit whenever he faltered, reassured that her instincts were better than his whenever they entered new country together. He slipped into her, warm and wet, like a finger into a hot glove stitched especially for him. It wasn't clear to him who howled the loudest. But he was certain, when it was over and they lay breathless, beads of sweat running down the crease of his back, her heart beating against his, that he'd never loved anybody more.

They stopped three more times on that long ride home. The fourth time, the best, they didn't stop at all. The stallion just stood in confusion, craning its long head back to see what all the commotion was about, as if it didn't understand why its load would never balance. Remy slapped his free hand on the animal's flank, his other locked on Beatriz's hip, and the horse walked on.

Their passion had gone on like that to this very day. At

lunch and dinner, they had no time for Elijah's plans and
Quelepe's stories. They rarely sat at the table long enough
for the first fly to show. Disappearing into the bedroom,
they would make love and then, maybe an hour later,
Remy would appear alone, a foolish grin on his face, he
knew, ready for work, or so he claimed.

Sometimes, much to Remy's outward embarrassment and
secret delight, Beatriz couldn't wait for a dinner break. She
came to the fields, under the guise of bringing water. One
thing led to another, and, soon enough, Remy abandoned
his cousin, leaning his freckled, sunburnt arm on the handle
of his hoe, his eyes rolling as Remy and Beatriz rode off.
Worst of all, they took the water with them. Remy might
be gone an hour, depending on what she had in mind, or
he might be gone two if he came up with his own ideas.

So Remy assumed that it must've been no surprise to
Elijah and Quelepe that yet another meal had ended this
way. The door slammed shut, and he and his wife, wrapped
in each other's arms, fell naked into bed. Despite the thickness of the new walls, Remy knew the sound of their passion filled the cabin and, most likely, kept both bachelors
awake. He regretted it deeply. Sure he did.

Chapter Twenty-Four

After their breakfast, Remy and Beatriz saddled their
horses and rode out to look over the pastures. Elijah
was keen to know how the summer grass was holding and
all he had to do was mention his interest. Remy and Beatriz
instantly volunteered.

At mid-morning, they lay on the bank of the river to rest
in the shade of a great cottonwood. With her head in his
lap, he gently stroked her black, silken hair. It was now
late May, and the river valley echoed with the sound of
gobbling turkeys still looking for mates.

They were startled from their reverie by the sound of
galloping hooves. Elijah raced toward them, his horse lathered, its chest heaving deeply.

"Mount up! We got trouble!"

In an instant, both husband and wife were mounted and ready. Remy pulled his rifle from its scabbard. Beatriz did the same. He winked at her. She was not afraid.

"What's wrong?" he asked.

"Armed riders comin' this way! A couple of dozen at least!"

"Indians?"

"Nope. Mexicans, I think. I ain't sure. They don't look like they're comin' for lunch, though. Let's get to the house. They'll play hell gettin' us out of there. If we stay out here, they'll overrun us."

Remy and Beatriz followed Elijah as he dashed over the hill and through the middle of the little draw that led to the homestead. Once close to the house, Remy sagged off to get a glimpse of the approaching riders but could not make them out clearly. Elijah called to him, and he dismounted and slapped the flank of his horse, which trotted off to the pasture with the saddle flopping on its back.

Once Remy had passed over the threshold, Elijah dropped the oak planks that barred the door. Quelepe had already secured each of the window shutters. Each of the inhabitants picked one of the cross-shaped portholes and watched, rifles in hand.

Remy saw the riders again as they cleared the ridge, surrounded by a cloud of dust. When they were within about a hundred yards, they stopped. Elijah licked his thumb, slid the barrel out of the porthole, nestled the stock to his shoulder and looked through the sights.

"I'll drop that fat bastard in his tracks if they make one move."

"Hold on, Elijah," Remy warned. "Let's see what gives." One of the riders noted Elijah's rifle and in their excitement, the riders drew their own weapons. Elijah pulled the set trigger, aimed a little over the leader's head, and then pulled the second one. Although that rider and one other remained mounted, the rest disappeared from their saddles and fell prone to the ground.

"That's close enough, goddammit!" Elijah bellowed. "State your business and be quick about it!"

The smoke from Elijah's rifle hung above the porch for a second before the summer breeze began to carry it off.

When the smoke had cleared, Remy squinted his eyes to focus on what he believed was the figure of Don Carlos Amarante de la Cruz. He'd finally come. Beatriz had been with him for almost two months now. That was more than enough to win her, he thought. There was nothing her father could do to pry her away from him now. Best to go ahead and get it over with; that is providing Don Carlos just wanted to talk.

"It's your pa, Beatriz," he said flatly. She looked down the breech of her rifle and confirmed it and then looked back at her husband. "Hold your fire, Elijah," Remy said. "It's just our kin."

"That's one mean lookin' bunch of in-laws, I'm here to tell ya'll. I'd sooner spend Christmas in a rattlesnake den." He pulled his ramrod from the bore and shouldered the rifle. "I'm gonna part that fat one's hair permanent-like if he blinks a way I don't like."

"Don't shoot now, dammit," Remy said. "We knew he'd be comin'. Let's just see what he's got to say."

Remy watched on as the other mounted rider, a man in a large-brimmed straw hat, conferred briefly with Don Carlos. Then he approached, both his hands open in the air. When he came closer, Remy saw that it was Don Estévan. Don Carlos must have come to him, and now Austin brought him here.

"Gentlemen," he called stiffly. "A word if you don't mind. These men mean you no harm."

"They don't look what they mean, I guess," Remy answered through the porthole.

"Put your rifles away, Fuqua. The man wants to see his daughter. He's come a long way."

Remy looked at his wife. She knew best, and she quickly shook her head. That was all he needed to know. Then he turned to yell out the window again. "Tell 'em we're not prepared to entertain visitors just now. My wife ain't ready yet. The place is a mess. Tell 'em to come back in a year."

Don Estévan kept walking. "Nonsense. Step out a moment and let's talk about this."

"He ain't takin' her," Remy barked. "She wants to stay with me. I'll fight for her if I have to. She'll fight with me."

Austin looked exasperated. "No one's taking anybody,"

he sighed, "and no one's here to fight. He knows you're legally married. There's nothing he can do about that anymore. He's just here to talk. I told him you'd be happy to see him. Please don't make me out a liar." He paused, clearly expecting compliance. When Remy hesitated, he started again. "Step out if you don't mind and let's discuss this problem like reasonable men. There's no sense in violence. Let's not make things any worse." Austin craned his neck. His eyebrows arched above glaring sockets. "This might be a good time to remind you that yours is a provisional grant," he said.

Remy again looked to his wife. This time she nodded. He retracted the barrel of his rifle and then called, "All right, dammit. We're comin' out. Don Carlos can come. But them others best keep their distance." Austin said he'd arrange it. Remy put his rifle down and turned to Elijah. "Keep us covered. Quelepe, you take my place. I'll signal ya'll if somethin' happens I don't like. Don't shoot Beatriz's daddy, for God's sake."

"How 'bout I just wing 'em?" Elijah said.

Beatriz looked at Remy. "He's just jokin'. You *are* just jokin', ain't ya, Elijah?"

"Yeah," he said in a way that worried Remy. "Just give me the word and I'll clear 'em out."

Remy stared at his cousin. "Don't shoot nobody. You hear me?" When he was certain he had a clear understanding with Elijah, Remy opened the door and Beatriz and he stepped out on the porch. Austin was standing there tapping his toe, waiting.

"I had the opportunity to speak with your father in San Felipe, Mrs. Fuqua. He just wants to talk. I hope the both of you will listen." With that, he waved Don Carlos forward. When he turned to face them again, he noticed that the barrel of Elijah's rifle was still pointed at the Mexicans. He pushed it to the side slowly with his hand. "Do you mind, Mr. Johnson?"

"Sorry," Elijah said, and he slid the barrel back into the darkness, replacing it with a wild, staring eye.

Don Carlos dismounted and tethered his mount to the post. He nodded curtly to Colonel Austin and then even more curtly to Remy. He focused on Beatriz, who looked at her father and smiled.

"You've done well, Mr. Fuqua," Austin said. "Let's have a closer look at your fields."

Remy wasn't going anywhere. "You can see 'em well enough from here. I'd like to stay close by for the time bein' if'n you don't mind."

"Let's give them a little room, Mr. Fuqua," Austin insisted, his hand on Remy's shoulder. "Step back with me here."

Remy did so, but not so far that he couldn't hear what was being said. Once he stepped clear, Don Carlos approached his daughter.

"Hola, Beatriz," he said. His words were more gentle than any Remy had heard from him before. *"¿Cómo estás?"*

"Bien, Papá. ¿Y tú?"

"Your mother misses you dearly."

"She would have missed me just the same had I gone to school in México City." Remy smiled. She was good.

"It's not the same, Beatriz. There you'd have been in civilization, among cultured people." He seemed to catch himself. "But that doesn't matter anymore. It's not safe for you out here. Your mother and I are sick with worry." Remy figured that wasn't the only thing that made them a little nauseated here lately.

"I'm fine," Beatriz said. "I'm happy here."

"It would appear so, but only God knows how. Your face is so pale. Are you well, Beatriz?"

"I believe I'm with child," she said unashamed, and her face brightened just as it had when she told Remy. Remy watched her father's head sink into his hands.

"Saints preserve us," he moaned. "Little Anglo ruffians running around my hacienda. Why does God play such mean tricks on me in my old age?"

"Not tricks, *Abuelito.* He bestows blessings."

Don Carlos reached for his daughter and pulled her to his chest. Engulfed in his embrace, after a moment's hesitation, she reached for him. A tear ran down Don Carlos's cheek and crossed his smiling lips. It touched Remy. He felt sorry that it had happened like it did. He could see he had caused much pain. He had thought much of Beatriz's parents, knowing they were disappointed, but then again the way it'd happened wasn't his fault. He'd tried to do it right.

"I've missed you so, Beatriz," her father said.

"I've missed you."

"You could have had your pick among the finest *norteño* families. Why would you choose this . . . ?" Remy didn't care much for this line. He wondered what he should do about it. Beatriz handled it to his satisfaction.

"Chist . . ." she hissed, pressing her finger to his lips. "This is what I wanted," she told him. "No one ever asked me until Remy did. I love the country, Papá. I would've been miserable in México City."

Don Carlos's eyes never left his daughter. "Is he good to you?"

"Better than I'd ever hoped. He's a good man, a very hard worker." She'd not told Remy this. He was proud to hear her say it.

"So is a mule," Don Carlos answered, "but at least a mule is not so stubborn. I've heard bad things about how these Anglos treat their women. I'll hang him if he ever lays a hand on you. I swear it." He looked angrily at Remy, who did nothing. He figured Don Carlos had the right to complain. Nothing he could say would change anything.

"He would never do so," she said confidently. "He's an orphan, Papá. Besides his cousin, I'm all he has in the world. The bond between us grows stronger each day. I've chosen well. He's industrious, Papá. Like you. Look around you. He and his cousin have built all of this in less than one year."

Don Carlos only managed a cursory glance. "It's all right for chickens," he said, "but where do you stay?"

"Insults are not the way," she warned him.

Don Carlos sighed. "I suppose you could stay here if you insist, but your mother and I want you and your uh," his hands went out flat, as if he could find no other words, "goddamn gringo, to return with me to our hacienda for obvious reasons. If you say no, I'll still post some of my men here for your protection." He raised one finger. "I won't argue with you about this. I'll foot the cost. You're all I have in this world. No harm must come to you, or my little gringo grandchildren, may God help them. However, I beg you to return to the protection of my house. I'll make things right between us. You have my word."

"If you can accept my husband, we'll consider it."

"Ah," he sighed, "the thorn beneath the rose petal. What can I say but yes, Beatriz? He can stay in the stable with the other asses until he learns to conduct himself properly. I fear it will take some time."

"No jokes, Father. He's very sensitive. He has his pride."

"Sensitive?" he scoffed. "Like a mud turtle's shell."

"*Chist* . . . He also speaks Spanish very well."

"Good. Then he understands the sacrifice I'm making." He turned to Remy, curling his index finger. "Come here, señor. It's time for us to talk."

Beatriz called quietly to Remy when he hesitated. Slowly he made his way to stand beside her.

"My father wishes for us to return with him to live."

He'd heard; and he'd already decided on what to say. "Thank you but we have our own place to worry about, honey. This here's our home."

Don Carlos spoke. His eyes were nervous and intense. Yet Remy sensed an assurance that Don Carlos felt things would go his way.

"My friend," he began confidently, "I own fifty square leagues of the finest ranch land in Tejas. Beatriz is my only heir. It's best that you spend some amount of time learning to manage such an estate. It's no easy thing. I see you've done well here but it simply does not compare. I offer you a place in my hacienda, as my—forgive me, but these words are still hard for me to say—son-in-law. There." He gratuitously grinned. "I've done it. With full rights and privileges as a citizen of México, you're entitled to a few leagues of land of your own. That fact alone should interest an immigrant. What I'm offering you bears some serious consideration."

Austin nodded his head in agreement. "What he says is true, Mr. Fuqua."

Don Carlos continued. "My wife and I want our daughter near. As her husband, you're welcome also. Beatriz tells me that she's . . . pregnant." The Méxicano bit his lip, grimacing as he said it. "She'll need care that you cannot possibly provide. I see no doctors here, no women who know about these things. For the sake of your children, please give the matter some thought."

There was something to that, Remy thought. He didn't know the first thing about babies. He'd talked to Quelepe about it and Quelepe said that he'd delivered many, but he'd also said he knew how to make a fine-fitting set of clothes and what should be said to a young woman. "This comes as a surprise," Remy said. "I'd need a little time to think about it and discuss it with my wife."

"We've all had a few surprises here lately," Don Carlos agreed between clenched teeth. "But I know my daughter's mind. At least, up until recently. I would think, all things considered, she'd prefer to be with her family, would you not?"

As Remy watched, his wife nodded. "If my husband agrees," she said.

"Is this what you want, Beatriz?" Remy asked. She looked at him and smiled.

"Our hacienda is beautiful," she told him, and he knew what that meant. She was only a visitor in his world.

Maybe it was time to give a little, he thought. Perhaps it could work. "Let's give it a try, then," he said, and she flung her arms around him. "At least until the baby comes. I've got an interest in this land, as well. I'm happy to do what's expected of me at your place but I'll have to divide my time between the two. Come harvest time, my place is with my cousin. I'm committed to 'im."

"That is not a problem," Don Carlos said. "I'll send whatever workers your cousin requires."

"It requires me, I think, Don Carlos."

"As you wish. It's done then. Pack your things. We'll return with a carriage in two days' time." He hugged his daughter one last time, shook hands firmly with Remy, and ordered his men to prepare for departure.

Austin said his goodbyes but hung back from the Méxicano contingent. Remy stood beside him as they watched them ride off. Beatriz went back into the house to get out of the sun. Austin wanted something. Remy knew it.

Remy studied him carefully until the empresario's eyes gripped his. "What?" he asked.

"You, my friend, are a very lucky, very wealthy man."

Remy didn't quite see it that way. Lucky, yes. But wealthy? He'd never even dreamed of what that would be like. "I'm the same man that walked into San Felipe a year ago, dead broke and hungry," he said.

"No, sir," Austin said, shaking his head slowly, his eyes glistening. "You are not. You're the acknowledged son-in-law of Don Carlos Amarante de la Cruz. I can't believe your good fortune." He smiled, the first time Remy'd ever seen him express true delight, and clapped his hands together. "Who would've believed it?" he exclaimed, his eyes to the heavens.

Remy didn't like the way that sounded. "Are you sayin' I ain't good enough for them?"

Austin brushed him off. "Not at all, Fuqua. I see now that you're very good indeed." He nodded very slowly as he said it. Remy didn't understand.

"Don't you see?" Austin asked, his head cocked.

"I guess not," Remy said. "I love her. She loves me. We got married." He shrugged his shoulders.

"That's right." Austin grinned. "But with you goes the future of Tejas. You think about that over these next few months. The American settlers cling to their ways, the Tejanos to theirs. A country so divided cannot thrive. We must adjust to each other as rapidly as possible. You can help us."

"How?" Remy asked him.

"You must consider your position and bring honor to it. I expect great things from you, Fuqua. Mingle in Don Carlos's society. Few whites have seen it and none are welcome. I'm accepted by the Méxicanos but alien to them. They trust me, I suppose—at least I hope so—but don't understand my ways. In one fell swoop, you've attached yourself to one of the most powerful families in Béxar."

He slapped Remy on the back. His words came fast. Never had Remy seen him be so invigorated. "Now listen to me, Fuqua," he urged. "Good manners are everything among the Tejanos. You must, for a time, keep your place. Earn their trust. I know you'll work hard. Demonstrate the

best qualities of our people. Please . . . please . . . please,"
he said, his face pained, "try as best you can to avoid that
god-awful slang. You're a smart man. I know you read
books, you're always borrowing mine. They come back wet,
but read, I think. Display your intelligence and rise with
this opportunity, Fuqua. You can do it. Despite your youth
and poverty, you've somehow been taught well somewhere
along the line. You're not nearly the bumpkin you profess
to be. The Tejanos will come to accept you, I think . . ."
He paused. "If you'll just shut your mouth and listen."

Remy grew suspicious. He sensed a tinge of manipulation
in the lecture. "What've you got in mind, Don Estévan?"

His gaze was steady. "Peace, Fuqua. I want peace."

Chapter Twenty-Five

Remy packed the last of his things in leather pouches
fastened over the hips of the mules that Don Carlos's
men had provided. Elijah sat crouched in the shade of the
porch, a weed stem wedged in the gap between his teeth,
poking at the planks with a stick, watching. Quelepe sat
across from him in silence. Remy didn't own enough things
to fill the pouches, but he made sure a little something
went in each for the sake of appearance. Remy buckled
the last of the straps and looked over the back of the mule
at his cousin.

"You through moanin'?" Remy asked him, tightening
the mule's cinch.

"I expect I got quite a bit of moanin' comin' 'fore I've
had my due," Elijah answered, looking away.

"It'll have to be good and loud for me to hear it." Elijah grinned.

"I'll be back 'fore harvest time," Remy assured him,
"like I promised."

"I 'preciate that," Elijah said, spitting out the weed, "but
I kin already see it ain't gonna work like this. This here's
a two-man and one broke-down old man operation. Always
has been. Quelepe'll do his part best he can but he ain't
gonna take up your slack."

They'd already been through all of this. Remy wasn't going back today. "I'm sorry you got a rock in your craw 'bout this deal, Elijah. I cain't help it. I never planned things to work out like this."

"That's the problem, Remy. You never plan nuthin'. You just go."

"Yeah," he said, "an' I'm goin' now." He didn't blame Elijah for being unhappy with him but he wasn't going to listen to it. Remy'd made his decision. Now he was going to mount his horse and go to Beatriz. She'd only been gone two days but it seemed like thirty. "You take care now, Cousin," he said, mounting. "Get yourself a wife. It'll take your mind off your troubles." Then he smiled. "Might save ya a little money, too."

"Where might I find a wife in this country?" Elijah sneered.

"Wherever you can. Just go and fetch one somewheres, I reckon. It worked for me." He winked and sat atop the horse, waiting.

Elijah looked at him. "What?" he finally said.

"Ain't ya gonna say it? You're not likely to see me for a while. Better get your licks in while you can."

Elijah looked back at the ground. "Naw, I ain't gonna say it. You don't give a rat's ass no way."

"Go ahead," Remy told him. "It'll make ya feel better."

Then he said it without a trace of emotion. "This was your idea." Elijah didn't mean it anymore.

"That's right," Remy snapped. "And it was a damn good one at that, come what may. Good day to you, cousin Elijah Johnson." Remy tipped his hat. *"Adiós!"*

"Good day, Señor Fuqua. Cuss words on your cheap tombstone, you no-workin', bastard half-blood, Creole, lucky son of a bitch."

Remy smiled at his cousin and waited. Elijah just lay back on the porch, his hands behind his head. "Well, come here," Remy said. Elijah rose with a groan, stepped over to the side of Remy's horse, offering his extended hand. Instead, Remy swung down and embraced him. After a moment's hesitation, Remy finally felt his cousin's arms tighten.

"I love ya, Elijah," Remy said. The words came hard.

His breath blew the hair on the back of his cousin's neck. "You're the best friend I ever had."

"And you're the worst."

"Be careful. Keep your powder dry. Watch your back. Keep that corn watered. We gotta note payment due at the end of the year. I'll see ya in the fall."

Elijah let go and stepped back from the horse. "Okay to move the shithouse back?"

Remy smiled and nodded his head. "Do what you gotta do."

"See ya, kid," Elijah said. "Watch your backtrail." His gray eyes finally warmed. Remy had expected him to give him a much harder time. He knew Elijah didn't have it in him to do it. Here, at the very end, Remy sensed acceptance.

He turned lastly to the old man. "Take care of my fool cousin, Quelepe. Tell 'em what you've told me. He'll listen now. *Hasta luego, señor.*"

"*Adiós, joven. Buena suerte.*"

Remy let the reins fall loose and spurred his mount, heading west in a trot, the mules tied behind him. He left one partially conquered world behind him; another, more complex, and even more foreign, lay just ahead. What life would hold for him now, he could not say.

In just a year's time, he had achieved the wildest dreams of his troubled and lonely youth. In the span of a week, he'd let it all go. What he was doing, he told himself, he was doing for his wife. But with so much land and wealth at stake, it seemed an easy sacrifice. He knew he loved Beatriz. But as much as he loved her, he knew that he'd come to love Elijah almost as much. Remy was going his own way, and in doing so must abandon his cousin, leaving both very much alone among strangers.

It was probably true, as Don Carlos said, that he would one day inherit an empire. It might also be true, as Austin wished, that the decision to leave the grant would somehow signify the future union between Tejano and Anglo Tejas. As Austin had said, it was a first step. These were both, in themselves, grand schemes for an orphaned northeastern Louisiana homesteader. He could not deny that the future appeared to offer much, and he knew he had to seize it and hold on. Who, he wondered, would fault him?

But regardless of what Elijah thought, his decision was not without the deepest remorse. With so much ahead of him he still found himself looking back on the trail after all. He'd given his word to his cousin, and he knew, despite his best intentions, that sooner or later he would have to break it. He felt hollow, empty. There was the ring of failure to it somehow. The way he left did not feel good; it did not feel right.

As he rode quietly across the rolling hills, his father's Christian Gump rifle, well-oiled, loaded and freshly primed, lying across his thighs, the distance between his grant and the new life beyond growing greater with each step of his horse, Remy knew that the distance between him and Elijah would also grow.

In essence there was no romance to his decision. But there was a coldness to it that chilled him at his core. He felt ashamed. He'd asked Elijah to come with him and he had come. Beatriz asked Remy to leave him and he did. The two people he loved most tore him in opposite directions. He never thought he'd end up going with one over the other. Beatriz was his future; he knew that now. But Elijah was his only link to his past. Remy never saw these crossroads coming. He never knew to look.

He knew he'd get over it. He had a knack for that. Just the same, it still worried him to think that he could. The road southwest to San Antonio de Béxar was lonelier than he'd ever expected. After awhile he couldn't bear to look back anymore.

BOOK THREE

———◆———

The Encounter

1829

Chapter One

Those first awkward months in San Antonio de Béxar
passed quickly. To Remy, living in the de la Cruz man-
sion was almost like living in a church or courthouse, and
just as uncomfortable. A homesteader from birth, he preferred the solitude and fresh air of the open places to the
bustle of Béxar, a city of nearly four thousand traders, merchants, smiths, soldiers, and government officials. Beatriz
did her best to help him acclimate, but the only time he
felt truly content was when he was alone with her.

Comanche raiders had come with the full moon of August. Some even rode through the streets of Béxar, terroriz-
ing its inhabitants. Remy shot at one wearing a great cape
of white fur—the sign of a chief, Remy thought—as he
passed beneath the balcony of the de la Cruz home. He
missed. What stuck most in his mind after the attack was
the image of his mother-in-law, sitting on a sofa Remy
knew had been brought up from Laredo, fanning the white
smoke that filled the room from her face while she coughed
like a consumptive. From then on, at her request, he did
most of his shooting out of doors.

When September came Remy honored his promise to his
cousin. He left his wife's side and rode back east to harvest
the corn. He and Elijah cribbed what grain they needed
for feed and dry-stored what they had to have to plant
again in the spring. The rest they sold or traded for supplies. Austin was paid for the year. The year following,
Elijah told him, they'd plant cotton.

Despite Elijah's every attempt to shame him into staying
longer, Remy returned to his wife as soon as he could.
Elijah and Quelepe had gone on without him and he sup-

posed he should be glad that they had. Just the same he felt almost as awkward there as he did at his mother-in-law's house in Béxar. That was the price he had paid. Living in two homes, he felt he truly belonged to neither. He felt he had no center anymore.

Winter passed in Béxar without event. The following spring Don Carlos informed him that it was time to go to the ranch. And Remy, keen to leave the city but not his wife, reluctantly followed.

A̲s̲

Don Carlos pulled the reins on the large gray and surveyed the expanse of deep grass before them. "What do you know about ranching, Remy?"

Remy rubbed the neck of his stallion. "I've got a vague notion, Don Carlos," he said.

"Umph. *Los gringos* are vague on most things in my experience." Remy rolled his eyes. All winter long, his father-in-law had never missed an opportunity to vent his low opinion of Remy's kind. Without Beatriz around to temper her father's comments, they were starting to chafe Remy's ears.

"Listen carefully," Don Carlos said, turning his head so quickly that he nearly caught Remy's disenchanted expression. "I'll start from the beginning."

Cattle ranching, he said, settling back on his saddle, was a Spanish institution. It had begun in the tierras of Zamora and Salamanca, in the province of León, and perhaps in Segovia and Avila in Old Castile. In the Middle Ages, the cattle raisers had moved their stock to the arid and unpopulated plains of Andalusia, a rocky land with thin soil. Of little use to farmers, Andalusia, like Tejas, had good grass. Other countries raised cattle, it was true, but it was the Spanish who had devised methods to produce them on such a grand scale, methods which evolved into the art they now practice in northern México.

On his second voyage, Don Carlos explained, Columbus

had brought with him horses and cattle to breed in Hispaniola. These were the first ranches in the New World. Cortéz had brought the descendants of Columbus's horses with him to México when he conquered the Aztecs, but six months before conquistadores captured México City, Gregoria de Villalobos had already established the first cattle ranch in México near Tampico.

Villalobos imported hundreds of animals from the West Indies, all of Andalusian stock. Most were the Barrenda, or piebald, a white-bodied animal with black markings on the neck and ears; the Retinto, of a reddish hue with a long, narrow head; and the Ganado Prieto, which was known as the Andalusian fighting bull. This was important to remember, Don Carlos said, because these animals interbred over the centuries that followed.

What Remy saw before him, Don Carlos explained, was the breed that naturally emerged. As the sons of Spain born in the New World, they were called *criollos*. They were long-legged, which allowed them to traverse the brush with ease. Their horns were wide and long, and their instincts were to use them. Their temperament as well was suited to conditions on the frontier. Don Carlos's father's brand on their ass meant next to nothing, he said. They were wild beasts and dangerous.

Nothing in nature, Don Carlos said, was a match for a criollo bull. The savages feared them as they feared no other beast. Their milk was of little use and their meat was tough and stringy. One could not plow with them, and they were useless in the wagon teams. There was no reason, therefore, to corral them. They were allowed to roam wherever the grass grew until the fall of the year, when the time came for the rodeo or corrida. Then the cattle were gathered and Don Carlos took what he needed.

Don Carlos then said that what Villalobos had begun on this continent had not yet ended. The climate and environment of the New World was well suited to the needs of cattle, as well as horses, and the herds continued to thrive. In 1540, Coronado had no difficulty in rounding up five hundred head for his expedition into the north. These were the first cattle in Tejas, but they were not the ancestors of the beasts Remy saw before him, as some people said.

The mines discovered in the north of New Spain established a market for cattle, and ranching moved north to
meet that industry's needs. Wherever the Spanish went,
with them went their horses and cattle. The further north
the Spanish traveled, the better the grass they found. The
herds continued to flourish. Meanwhile, other hacendados
pushed north beyond José de Escandón's settlements,
northward across the Río Bravo. Don José Vásquez de
Borrego, one of Escandón's settlers, was the first to cross
the Río Grande, staking claim to one hundred square
leagues of land, or 440,000 acres to Remy's Anglo mind.
Others of that same spirit followed. In 1762, Blas María de
la Garza Falcón established the first ranch on the Nueces
River. In all, two hundred or so land grants were commis-
sioned in Tejas by the Spanish crown in the last twenty-
five years of their rule, Don Carlos's family's among them.

Most of the early cattle operations in this area, he explained, were conducted by the missions. But the first secu-
lar ranches were established by descendants of soldiers
from Nuevo León and Nueva Estremadura who came to
this place with the early *entradas*, or expeditions; many
came with Alarcon when he founded the villa of San Antonio de Béxar in 1718.

Because of the threat of the savages, Don Carlos explained, soldiering and ranching had always been two sides
of the same coin. The sons of these soldiers bore names
such as Crabajal, Hernández, Ximenez, Urrutia, Barrera,
Guerra, Castro, Menchaca, Flores, Galván, Maldanado, and
they lived on in the ranching community. These were Don
Carlos's people.

In 1731, fifteen Canary Island families—farmers, fish-
ermen, and laborers, mostly—and also some families of Andalusian descent were brought to San Antonio de Béxar
with the token title of *hidalgo*, or "sons of something" Don
Carlos explained with a smile, a title which provided social
standing that they had not enjoyed before. The islanders
received land and free seed stock from the Spanish crown.
Beatriz's mother's people were among these. Their names
were Delgado, Rodríguez, Arocha, Leal, Santos, and Tra-
vieso, among others. They soon learned the ways of the

land and joined the descendants of Alcarón's expedition and other soldier-ranchers of the criollo herds.

By this time, the *orejanos,* "eared" or unmarked wild cattle, numbered in the thousands, having escaped from the ranches south of the Río Grande and the missions of Tejas, or been driven off by Indians, free for the taking by those of spirit. That brought him to his own land.

It was Andrés Hernández who settled the first ranch in El Rincón, the Corner, in 1753, the land between the San Antonio River and Cíbolo Creek, the finest and richest ranch land in all of Tejas. Don Carlos and the other rancheros called it La Jolla, the jewel. The de la Cruz holdings bordered Hernández's original grant. Other families had other land, all laid out in porciones adjoining the river so that all had access to good water. Remy, Don Carlos said, would meet all these people in due course. The ranchers of El Rincón were, for the most part, all related to one another—by blood or by necessity, either bond equally strong. They quarreled among themselves from time to time, Don Carlos said, but they stuck together against any outside threat. They had braved the wilderness together, endured depredations by the Apaches and Comanches, fought with the missions and the Spanish for the right to gather the wild herds, and then again for the cause of Méxicano independence. Now they reaped the bounty of the land as one.

"Unlike the Anglos," Don Carlos said, "who seem to move on with each generation looking for anything better, especially something they can steal, *los Tejanos* stay put. We paid for the land with our blood; our fathers and grandfathers are buried in this soil." There was no mistaking the pride in his voice.

Don Carlos said that he himself had ridden with the rebel Miguel Menchaca in defense of his family's land against the Spanish General Arrendondo at the Battle of Medina back in 1813. The rebels were defeated and young Menchaca, the bravest of the brave, fell. Many died in the harsh Royalist retaliation that followed, virtually depopulating Béxar.

But after independence was won in 1821, those who survived the revolution came back to claim what had always been theirs. Through drought, plague, revolution, and continual Indian warfare, they had all endured. They would never leave. Their roots, Don Carlos said, had grown strong and deep. If Remy was really meant for this life, he'd soon grow his own.

Don Carlos said that as the power of the Spanish crown waned, the hacendados inherited the responsibility of establishing order on the frontier. The ranchers soon succeeded where the Spanish *encomiendas* and the missions had failed. In the end, it was the ranchers who settled the wilderness. As far as he was concerned Austin's Anglos had only followed in their wake. Accordingly, the patrónes and hacendados had become lords and masters over their respective domains. They did not rely on the government or the church to feed or clothe their people. Their welfare, as well as the future of Tejas, depended upon the rancheros' continued success.

Remy listened carefully. Quelepe had already shared his mestizo peasant's point of view; now he understood how the Méxicano dons looked at it. Of course, they varied. Where Quelepe saw the destruction of cultures centuries old, Don Carlos saw progress. Quelepe saw oppression, Don Carlos only opportunity. And it went on from there. It was, as Remy quickly understood it, the traditional American discrepancy. He'd just never realized that America was larger than the United States.

None of that mattered much to him at the moment. He was an immigrant and an in-law, both positions equally unstable and powerless. He could not concern himself with the clash of nations and the besieged native cultures between them. What concerned him now was where he should take his place in this new life. His focus returned to this one specific issue.

"What do you want me to do?" he said. He hoped that Don Carlos marked the ring of commitment.

Don Carlos seemed pleased by his tone. "In order to facilitate your acclimation to this place, I intend for you to spend much of your time out here. Keep your beady gringo eyes open and your mouth shut. Learn the ways of my vaqueros, but keep your distance. You're the son-in-law of *el patrón*. You must earn their respect. I'll have my *mayordomo,* the foreman, keep an eye on you. Your task is to learn this ranch inside and out. The business end will come later." He leaned back in his saddle. "Any questions?"

Remy had just one. "Can I call you pa?" It was a joke but his father-in-law's acerbic sense of humor clearly failed to extend to him. Remy already knew that where he was concerned, Don Carlos saw nothing funny.

Don Carlos squinted and shook his head. "Absolutely not," he snapped. "All of that history, and this is what comes to your mind? I really don't understand you people. You'll continue to call me Don Carlos, as is proper."

Don Carlos had answered many questions but the most important to Remy had not been addressed. "I'm happy to stay here and do my part, but what about my wife?"

Don Carlos's response was immediate and definite. "She'll stay with her mother in Béxar. It's not entirely safe for women here."

"I've seen women around." He'd meant to state this as fact not as an argument. Don Carlos didn't see it that way.

"Those are *peónes,*" he answered, clearly irritated, "wives of vaqueros and laborers. They're here by necessity as well as by choice. *Los Comanches* are relentless. I choose to keep my family safe in Béxar. You'll be back and forth enough to see Beatriz. For the time being, your place is here. There's much to do."

And despite this one significant setback, Remy was glad to do it. He was more than ready to carve his own niche. "Let's get after it, then. What's first?"

"Not so fast. You gringos are always in so much of a hurry. It's a beautiful morning. The spring air's still fresh and cool. Let's ride and enjoy the day. Work'll begin soon enough. For now come and see the beauty of what God has given us."

"Suits me. I'm right behind you."

Don Carlos galloped off into the morning mist rising above the San Antonio River. Remy followed. Earth met sky on a horizon that Don Carlos claimed as his own, and Remy found himself somewhere wondrously in between with the wind in his hair. The more he saw, the more he realized that he'd never seen anywhere quite as beautiful as El Rincón. Someday, he couldn't help from thinking, it would all belong to him and Beatriz.

Chapter Two

Remy woke instinctively an hour before dawn. Don Carlos, who'd left the previous afternoon, had seen to it that his son-in-law was installed in the casa mayor, the house of el patrón. To Remy's eye, it was nothing short of spectacular. Don Carlos was clearly proud of it and took the time to explain its construction to his son-in-law.

Its walls, Don Carlos had told him, were of thick carved limestone, abundant in the Balcones escarpment to the north, skillfully laid by Béxareno masons. The structure was rectangular, three stories high, with high flat ceilings and a roof of *chipichil,* a mortar-like substance of lime, sand and gravel, covering layers of cypress planks and a mixture of clay and grass for insulation, all supported by thick-hewn beams of cypress from the river banks.

Indian attacks were a frequent occurrence and had been for a hundred years. Don Carlos explained to him that the casas mayores were built so that they could not be burned. They stood as small citadels, reminiscent of defensive Andalusian structures built in the time of the Moors. The walls extended three feet or so above the roof as parapets, so that a rifleman could be protected as he fired upon the houses' assailants. Rain run-off traveled along the *canales,* or gutters, that jutted out from the exterior walls, emptied into barrels, and was stored for consumption. There were no windows on the first floor, other than the *troneras,* or gun ports, and none large enough for a child to pass through anywhere throughout the other floors. Thick oak doors, hung with iron rings set in the stone, opened to the north and south to provide for ventilation when needed. The interior walls were plastered and whitewashed. The floors were of smooth limestone covered with deer, bear, and coyote skins. The furniture was spartan yet elegant and as far as Remy's experience was concerned, entirely functional.

Remy could see that the house was an impregnable fortress, perfectly suited to the frontier. During his time in

Tejas, Remy had seen no comparable Anglo structure. He and Elijah had cut down hundred-year-old trees, hoping their cabin might last a decade, withstanding dry rot and termites. The Tejanos built with stone—cool in summer, warm in winter—for the ages.

Don Carlos had suggested a bedroom on the third floor. Remy was exhausted after riding from sunup to sundown on his first day on the ranch. He opened the thin oak planks which covered the windows to allow for the cool evening breeze. He slept well that night but awoke to the smell of mesquite smoke and the sound of a woman's singing.

He dressed and walked downstairs to find a gray-haired elderly *peóna*, apparently of Indian blood, grinding corn on the worn stone metate. The *horno,* or oven, elevated so that she could cook while standing, had been laced with mesquite coals brought in a smudged clay pot. A copper pan of stewed meat gurgled, steam rising around the woman's face. Its aroma filled the room like a mother's embrace.

"Buenos días, patrón," the woman said.

"Buenos días, señora," he responded. *"Me llamo Remy."*

"¿Quieres cafe, Don Remy?"

"Sí. Con mucho gusto." He slipped his legs under the long oak table and rubbed his hand over its smooth grain. She brought the coffee. He sipped it as he stared at his bare feet.

"¿Ha visto mis botas, señora? No los puedo encontrar."

"Sí. El mayordomo sent a boy around for them this morning. He wanted to clean and condition them for you before you began today's work."

"Well, that's mighty kind," he said. She brought the freshly made corn tortillas and meat stew for him to eat and filled his coffee cup. One taste and Quelepe's cooking was like a bad dream. While he ate, she stepped out the front door and yelled into the darkness. In a moment a skinny, bright-eyed, rosy-cheeked boy appeared carrying Remy's boots. Remy recognized him as Cristóbal, his little teacher, but before Remy could call to him, the boy handed the boots to the woman, an impish grin on his face, and dashed off.

"Aquí están sus botas, Don Remy." She placed them at

his feet. "The boy tells me that the vaqueros are mounted outside, ready for the day's work."

"Guess I cain't keep 'em waitin'," he said, and he gulped down the last of his *guisada*. He reached for his boots, slipping the left one over his bare foot. When he reached for the right, he heard a strange noise. He shook it a second time, and then jerked it away from his ear, and turned it upside down. A skinny diamondback rattlesnake, maybe thirty inches in length, fell out on the floor. He kicked it away with his booted foot, noticing that its jaws had been sewn together with coarse thread into a grotesque frown. He grabbed it behind the base of its head, its body writhing wildly, and held it before him. He gently flicked its mouth with his middle finger. The snake could not bite. The woman saw it and immediately became angry.

"*¡Dios mío!* Was that in your boot?"

"Yep."

"I'll pin that child's ears back. You just wait."

"Don't worry yourself about it," Remy said. "Boys will be boys." He knew how he should handle it.

Remy tied the snake in a square knot around his neck, like a bandanna, its loose ends squirming, its head popping at his chin to no avail, and rose from the table. The woman was shocked and swung clear of his path. He stepped outside to face the waiting vaqueros. They were snickering as he passed from the shadow of the casa mayor. When he entered the dawn's light, he knew they saw the snake. Their eyes popped open at the sight of the struggling snake. Remy did his best to pay it no mind.

"Mornin', boys. Sleep well?"

One of the vaqueros slapped his neighbor on the back. "*¡Viva patrón!*" he yelled. "*¡Que bravo!*"

Remy's horse was saddled and ready. He stuck his foot in the stirrup and swung his leg over the horse. He trotted over to a large, heavy man at the front of the vaqueros.

"You the mayordomo?" Remy asked, aware that he'd seen this man also at de León's. He was more thickly set than Don Carlos, with darker skin, and rougher, more deeply chiseled features. His face was shadowed by a two-day growth, yet appeared to be illuminated by intelligent eyes. He sat his horse like a man confident of his abilities. One look and Remy liked him.

"*Sí,*" he said. *"Me llamo Diego Picosa."*

"Remy Fuqua," he said, extending his hand. Picosa took it. "I'm ready to work if ya'll are."

"*Bueno.* We're a little late today." Picosa turned to the others and motioned for them to follow. He faced his horse to the south and took off. Remy fell in. The others followed behind them. At the end of the procession rumbled two old wagons, one full of empty oak barrels.

Remy pulled up alongside Picosa. "You like my tie?" he asked.

Picosa maintained his gaze on the country ahead but the edges of his coarse mouth cracked into a smile. "It's very nice," he finally said without looking.

"Maybe I can get you one sometime. Nicer than this. Bigger, maybe."

"Don't trouble yourself on my account," Picosa told him. "I'm only a worker here."

"It's no trouble," Remy assured him. Then he added, "I ain't much of a tailor, though. Sometimes my stitches don't hold like they should."

Picosa turned and studied Remy's expression. It took a minute. He'd probably not practiced on a white man before. "I'll have my son teach you," he decided. "Very soon."

"Might be wise," Remy said, and he sensed that Picosa probably liked him as well. They rode on.

Remy unwrapped the snake from his neck, holding it firmly behind its head. He then pulled his knife from its sheath and carefully slit the threads that held the snake's mouth shut. He dropped it on the trail and turned, one arm riding on the stallion's hip, to watch it. The other vaqueros rode to one side or the other, observing its struggle. The rattler looked stunned, seemingly unaware that it was now free. Soon it gathered itself and slithered off into the deep grass. Remy turned forward and rode on.

The morning air was crisp and clean. He heard nothing but the sound of quail chirping in the distance, the squeaking leather of the Méxicano saddles, the jingle of fine Méxicano tack, and the cadence of the bulky wagons as they bumped along behind. Everything was again new.

Picosa sat back on his saddle, watching a herd of criollos grazing in the distance. Remy rode up beside him.

"What'cha got in mind today, Señor Picosa?" Remy asked.

"In one month's time Don Carlos expects a ship from Spain to land at Matagorda," Picosa said. His dark narrow eyes glistened in the morning sun. "He's arranged, along with some of the other ranchers of El Rincón, to sell some products. We're to get them ready." He lit his hand-rolled cigarillo. "This is dangerous work, *joven.* You hang back and watch the vaqueros carefully. When you understand how it is done, it'll be your turn."

Remy nodded and stood fast as Picosa motioned for his men to circle downwind of the herd. He explained briefly to Remy that *los criollos* had every instinct of the wild animal, particularly the sense of smell. Warned of a man's approach, they could disappear into the thickets and the brush more rapidly than any deer.

Then Picosa selected four men to follow him along the arroyo that lay east of the pasture. They remained in the cover of the mesquite and live oaks, circling the cattle until they were between the animals and the open pasture. The vaqueros slipped their *desjarretaderas,* or half-moon shaped hocking knifes, from their saddlebags. Remy heard a chink as steel brushed hard leather. Those wicked blades were held by steady, confident hands.

Remy had heard of these instruments but had never seen one used. He'd been told by Don Carlos that they were outlawed as vicious and inhumane by the Spanish a century before. But frontiersmen, as usual, did as they pleased, and Picosa made no bones about it when he told Remy that the blades were used almost daily in Tejas.

Together, on Picosa's signal, the vaqueros rode slowly

out from the brush. Remy saw that the movement of the
approaching riders disrupted the calm of the morning,
frightening the cattle, and at once they dashed instinctively
for the closest brush. Other vaqueros raced across the
plains to turn them, and the herd wheeled back across the
open flats for the more distant *encinales,* the oak groves.

"¡Vámanos!" Picosa grunted, and the vaqueros put their
spurs to the horses' flanks and galloped in pursuit of their
prey. The others moved out after them at a trot, Remy
among them.

The advance riders sought out the older animals, easily
run down in the open by the swift and sweating horses.
When near a *criollo,* the vaqueros would lean over with
the blade in one hand, the reins in the other, and hamstring
the animal in one quick, precise, and ruthless motion. The
beast tumbled to the ground, unable to rise. Once they
were certain the animal was down, the vaqueros pushed on
after others. Remy had never seen such magnificent horsemanship. Man and beast moved as one.

Remy's group rode up to the fallen criollos, struggling in
the dust, trying to rise on their front legs, a wake of blood-
drenched soil and bent grass behind them. These riders also
possessed the curved blades, and they carefully approached
the wounded animals from behind. In one motion, a vaquero slashed the muscled neck of the bellowing animal
at the base of its skull, severing its spinal cord, causing
instantaneous death.

A skilled hand could skin the bulls out in less than five
minutes. Remy watched as one skinner removed the firm
deposits of yellowish fat, the tallow, almost as quickly, then
wrapped them in the hide until the wagon units could come
forward to collect them in the waiting barrels. Picosa called
it the *matanza,* the killing. Remy thought there was no
better name. He stared at the white ribs of that bloody
carcass until the sound of the vaqueros leaving tore him
away. With the spring wind in his hair, Remy followed them
to the next fallen criollo.

"Don Carlos said that ya'll did this in the fall," Remy
said to one worker.

The vaquero kept his eyes on his work. "He does it
whenever the ships come, *patrón,*" he said.

"What about the meat?" Remy asked. They never touched it.

"There's no money in the meat, *patrón*," he said, and he was again mounted and gone.

The wagons bobbled along at the end of the procession. They collected the waxen tallow, now grown slick and shiny in the late morning heat, into the oaken barrels and then staked out the hides—after they had scraped them clean of all flesh, fat and tissue—to dry in the sun. In the afternoon, Remy understood that they would come and collect them to be tanned back at the hacienda. They took half an hour for a lunch of tortillas and frijoles under the shade of a large cypress on the banks of the river, drinking its cool water to quench their thirst.

By midafternoon it was too hot to continue and their horses were exhausted anyway. They walked their mounts back to the hacienda to see about the tanning of the hides the boys had collected. They'd taken over thirty animals in one day by Remy's count. Tomorrow, Picosa told him, they would do it again. When they had collected two hundred, he told Remy, they would have enough.

Chapter Three

After two weeks, the killing was over. Attention was now turned to the preparation of the hides with the tannin the vaqueros had obtained by stripping the bark from live oaks and distilling it, as well as the customary maintenance work to be done at the Hacienda de la Cruz. There was always plenty to do.

Picosa saw to it that Remy was provided with the clothing and equipment of the vaquero. His worn felt hat was replaced by a sombrero of woven palm fiber. Around his neck, he wore a cotton bandanna, much more convenient and utilitarian than a rattlesnake. He shed his buckskin shirt for one of long-sleeved cotton. It soaked up his sweat and then cooled him in the breeze. He was issued a set of *chaparreras*, protective leather coverings for his legs, and a new set of proper Méxicano spurs with rowels six inches in diameter. He was instructed in the making of *la reata,* the lariat, out of either braided rawhide or horsehair. Picosa taught him that, originally, the vaqueros had attached the noose end to a lance and simply slipped it over the head of an animal. Over time, they had learned to throw the reata at a full gallop, a feat of considerable skill, and the lance had been long since discarded.

One look at the vaqueros' skill with the rope and Remy knew he had to learn. He practiced for hours on end, first with mesquite fence posts, then with chickens and pigs, and every now and then with small *peónes* children willing to contribute to his proficiency. The saddle Don Martín had given him the previous year was admired by all. Picosa explained that such a marvelous example was the natural evolution of the *jineta* saddle, adopted, he'd been taught, by the Spanish from the Moors, and the stock saddle, developed in the West Indies by early rancheros. Most significant were the large and heavy iron stirrups, a compromise, he said, between the enormous stirrups of the *conquistadores,* weighing fifty pounds or more each, and the English saddles used by the Americans of Remy's world, made of wood almost weightless by comparison. Remy soon learned by experience that such stirrups provided a rider with greater balance and comfort for long hours on horseback, and their leather covering protected the feet from hide-peeling brush. They secured stock with a quick turn or two of the reata around the saddle horn. The vaqueros called this technique *da la vuelta,* an expression corrupted by novice Anglo ranchers in the empresario grants, who mispronounced it "dally." Remy'd heard Gibbs refer to it in this way. Now he knew the right pronunciation. Remy readily adopted all of these tools necessary for the conquest of El Rincón.

Picosa authorized the construction of two new *jacales* for the housing of his laborers. Pairs of mesquite corner posts—cut only in the afternoon in the cycle of the full moon on Picosa's firm order, which he explained made them more resistant to rot—were set to each of the four corners. Between each pair of posts, smaller diameter mesquite limbs were laid horizontally, one atop the other, forming the walls. Whatever gaps remained were filled in with smaller branches, grass, and river mud. The interiors were then plastered with limed clay. Ridgepoles and rafters of mesquite were spaced along the structure as supports for smaller limbs. These, in turn, were tied together with strips of agave leaves brought in from the brush country. The roof was then thatched with bundled sacahuiste, or saw grass, again fastened with agave leaves. The doors and windows were of carrizo, reeds picked in the river bottoms, woven together with strands of hemp.

The floors were dirt, mopped with a wet broom and then pounded with a heavy square block of green oak. A table was made of cypress; stools of thick, naturally fashioned roots were the only chairs. For beds, they used sheepskins with the leather side up in the summer, fleece side up in winter. The horno, or oven, was constructed of clay and grass and was outside, separate from the jacale because of its heat. It was protected from the elements by an arbor, from whose rafters hung an earthen pot called an *olla,* the water container for the home. In colder weather, coals from the horno would be brought inside to warm the inhabitants.

Most important, however, was the installation of an *altarcito,* boasting a wooden statue of a favorite saint illuminated by candles of tallow, and found in every Tejano structure. It was here that Remy observed firsthand the *peóna matron* instructing her children in the Catholic faith and the traditions of the mestizo class. Remy watched it all, worked as hard as any and, in the process, learned much more. It was strange yet enchanting. In a very short time he felt certain he could make a place for himself here.

In the heat of the afternoon, they rested. As the sun began to set, Remy watched them emerge from their separate homes to celebrate the end of another day at Rancho de la Cruz. To honor the completion of the new jacales, the homes of two newly married vaqueros, Picosa authorized the slaying of three young goats. They were broiled over mesquite coals while the men sharpened their knives and whittled, talking about the weather. Men skilled in leather-work constructed new saddles or mended old ones, hand-rolled cigarillos dangling from their lips as they told absurd, bawdy jokes. Dark-haired, bright-eyed, and white-toothed children played naked in the river while their mothers and older sisters beat the cotton laundry clean on large, smooth stones. Other women pulled weeds from their family *huertas* or hauled fresh water back to the villa in clay urns to fill their ollas.

When darkness fell, they pulled the sizzling *cabrito* from the coals and feasted together. Pots of beans, stewed with onions, peppers, and animal fat, were brought out along with stacks of freshly grilled corn tortillas. Later in the summer, Picosa told Remy, they would have melons available, which they cooled in the waters of the San Antonio River. Remy ate his fill and sat with his back to a mesquite post, content to watch the merriment all around him. There was none of the isolation he'd known on his uncle's farm. This ranch was a community, its inhabitants understanding the importance of work in life while never neglecting its joy. Already he loved it, just as Beatriz had hoped he would.

With Remy's day so full, sleep came easy.

When he dreamed, he dreamed in Spanish.

The celebrations were greatest when the matanza was finally over one week later. Remy ate a great dinner and then sat to watch the delight all around him. When the moon rose on that dark night, two of the younger vaqueros led his horse to him, saddled and ready. His lariat hung coiled, tied to its side. *"Venga, Don Remy,"* one said, and he rose without question and mounted the stallion, joining six other young riders.

They rode for some time until they came to the matanza pastures where the criollo carcasses lay rotting. As Remy watched, the young vaqueros roped the black bears that had come to feast under the cover of darkness. The best among them lassoed half a dozen in twenty minutes, first around the head, then the legs, until the frightened and confused bears were at their mercy, sprawled on the ground, helpless. When it was done, they let them all go, save two of the fattest, which they killed for their prized hides, pork-like meat, and fat. They knew how to use everything and to obtain it seemed only a sport.

When they returned to the celebration Remy saw that the people were still out around the fires, singing and dancing. He dismounted, unsaddled his horse, and sent it out to pasture. He took a place near a group of vaqueros who were gambling at a card game they called *monte*. He was listening to them argue over the last hand and then over the results of a cock fight a week earlier, when a young, pretty woman asked him to dance. He told her he did not know how and she answered that she had anticipated this. She would teach him, she said. Awkwardly, he learned the steps of the *fandango,* as an old man strummed the ancient cords of the *bolero* on his guitar, accompanied by another old man on violin. The music resounded throughout the river valley.

Remy had plunged into the ebb and flow of their life. They worked like dogs, rested like cats, feasted like kings, and played like children around the glow of the fire. The magic built steadily until at last they were dancing. Remy's newfound confidence with the strange steps, embellished with a small cup of mescal, allowed him to take the initiative—when suddenly it all stopped cold.

Everyone froze as the sound of the music faded into the hills. There remained only the sound of the wind cutting through the stick walls of the jacales and the crackle of the fire. Remy looked around to see all eyes turned east. Slowly he turned his head in the same direction.

Don Carlos, escorted by a dozen men, rode solemnly into the villa. Without a word the *campesinos,* eyes cast to the ground, filtered into the shadows, leaving only Picosa and Remy remaining. Remy could not see clearly as his eyes were accustomed to the light of the fire, but soon he made out the form of Beatriz mounted beside her father. He went immediately to her side and reached for her. It'd been three months since he'd last seen her. She looked tired and pale.

"You shouldn't have come," he told her.

"I wanted to see you," she said quietly, and she stroked his hair. He put his hand on her stomach, protruding now in her eighth month of pregnancy. She smiled strangely at him, as if it required effort, and then brushed his hand away.

"I've missed you," he told her. She looked at him almost sadly, said nothing, and then nodded her head.

While he stood there, Don Carlos made inquiries of Picosa. The mayordomo told him that all had gone well with the shipment of hides. They expected the return of the travelers to the coast any day now. Don Carlos nodded without a word and then gave orders for the care of his horses. He told Picosa to see that the casa mayor was prepared for them. While Remy listened, Picosa told him that all would be ready as soon as possible, but it would take a little time since that they had not expected the *patrón*. Don Carlos told him very precisely that he should always be expected. Then he turned and studied Remy coldly.

"Only the gringos," he said, over his shoulder to his guests, "aspire to become peons."

Remy smiled but, when he looked at the others, Beatriz included, he could see that they did not see the humor. Don Carlos summoned others to take his horses and dismounted. First, he came to Beatriz, and helped her down from her horse.

"Are you coming inside with us," he asked Remy, "or do you plan to sleep in the jacales with your new friends?"

Remy was embarrassed, his cheeks flushed and warm. "My place is with my wife," he answered, but he knew he hadn't said these words with the proper authority. His confidence had deserted him the moment he had sensed that something was wrong.

"Good," Don Carlos said with all the arrogance of their first meeting at de León's. "You do remember your place after all. I wasn't sure." And then he wrapped his arm around his daughter and led her into the big house where lamps were now being lit and the fire stoked. He heard scrambling, anxious, sandled feet flee before the slow, authoritative cadence of fine Méxicano boots.

Remy remained where he was, stunned that his wife had not defended him the way she always had. He watched as Don Carlos and Beatriz picked their way to the house. As they walked up the steps, she looked back at him, clearly saw his confusion, he was certain, and then turned away to pass under the threshold into the isolated warmth of the great, cold, stone house. The oak door swung shut and he was left in silence.

Remy closed his eyes. His wife was tired, he told himself. She was also very pregnant. Why had Don Carlos brought her here? And why had she looked at him that way? That haughty, aloof expression certainly was most unusual. He'd never seen it before on her face.

That Beatriz loved him, he had no doubt. She'd risked everything for him; and he'd forsaken all for her. Their first magic months together on his homestead had been the culmination of his dream. In a very short period of time, he had grown closer to her than to any other person in this world. He loved her as he loved no other.

But then there was that curious look, that instant that was frozen in his mind. He saw it a dozen times in an attempt to analyze what it meant. Try as he might to interpret it differently, he knew her well enough to know that what she had seen had somehow disappointed her. That look, he realized, was the first inkling of regret. She'd seen a side of him that was unexpected and not welcomed. He was being himself, and she clearly disapproved.

The problem was that he didn't know how to be anything else. Don Carlos had ordered him to acclimate, and that is what he'd done. No other distinctions were made; no further instructions provided. Absolutely uncertain of himself, he thought he'd done as well as could be expected. Throughout this transition, the one thing Remy knew he could depend upon was the support and understanding of his wife. Beatriz was the catalyst that would mold him to the Tejano ways of the *familia de la Cruz*.

But with that one piercing and distant look, he felt that his ties to her had somehow frayed. Don Carlos had suggested that they remain apart in these early months, and Don Carlos must have been pleased at this disconcerting result.

Remy felt a sickness inside. What had he done that was so wrong? He already loved these people, and he thought that they were in the process of embracing him. He'd worked hard beside them to earn their acceptance. What else could the de la Cruz name expect of him? Then he remembered what Don Carlos had already told him. They expected him to keep his place—to maintain a barrier between himself and the peónes, a precarious and absolutely alien position to a Louisiana farm boy. He was to work these people, not live with them. He was to learn what they had to teach him and then use it to Don Carlos's advantage. That was how this game was played, its rules unwritten yet strictly observed. He'd breached the invisible line between patrón and peon, and even Beatriz had never warned him that it was there.

Before now, Remy had thought of himself and his wife as equals. Different, certainly, but the same. They shared a spirit and a dream, and that knowledge allowed him to take his place at her side with confidence. Now he was certain that she felt he had slipped an essential notch below her as a result of this first crucial test. That was what that look was all about. He'd seen Beatriz's expression at that precise moment in time when she realized that she'd married beneath her. He'd made one mistake, and now he thought she believed that she'd made one as well—Beatriz's, very clearly, the worst and most irreparable of the two. There was no hiding that on that beautiful face. The image of it crushed him.

Diego Picosa passed by him on his way out of the house. Other servants came and went, all trotting. "Go inside, Don Remy," he said. "They're waiting for you."

"I'll just bet they are," he seethed and marched toward the house. When he entered, he found Don Carlos, his leg propped up on the fireplace, a glass of French brandy between his long, dark fingers, telling stories. His associates from Béxar were around him, laughing.

"Ah, Remy," he said. His rigidity had vanished, he was smiling now. "Show us some of those steps you've learned." Remy watched as Don Carlos's free hand fell across his stomach and he started to shake his ass.

Remy felt his face flush as he struggled to control his temper. His hair bristled on the back of his neck. His fingers trembled. Don Carlos saw it. The others must've seen it, too. "I'd like a word, Don Carlos," he said, struggling to hide any crudeness of Anglo inflection. His father-in-law motioned for him to speak. They were among friends, he told him.

"In private," Remy demanded. Don Carlos walked out of the *sala* after apologizing to his guests. His warmth and gaiety vanished as soon as the door closed behind him.

"Well?" he asked; it was almost a growl.

Remy's hands rested on his hips. "Why'd you bring her here?"

"She wanted to see you," he said. There was something malignant in that stare. He sipped his brandy and then added, "I wanted her to see you as well." Remy interpreted his father-in-law's callous tone. The scene was premeditated, just as he'd thought.

"I don't want you takin' chances with my wife and child," Remy snapped.

Don Carlos's eyes glistened. "It was she who took the chance! If I've learned anything this past year, it's that my daughter has her own mind. She does what she wants, when she wants. She gets that from her mother. If it has been a mistake to come, she'll have to see it for herself. There's nothing I can do."

Remy never moved back. "I'd say you've done enough."

"Don't blame me for any problems between you and your wife."

"I blame you for all of 'em."

"Calm yourself, señor," Don Carlos cautioned, though Remy sensed it was not for his benefit. "None of this is my fault. When two worlds collide, the middle ground is always rocky." His eyes narrowed. "I always knew there would be trouble. Now you both know it also. Don't involve me in your marital problems. Go and talk to your wife."

Don Carlos stared intently at Remy; Remy returned his stare. He didn't know what to do, but he knew he'd never outtalk this man. "If you'll excuse me," Don Carlos told him, "I've guests to entertain. Hopefully, you'll soon learn that good manners are everything among our people." He turned to leave, but Remy grabbed him by the collar and shoved his back against the wall. He couldn't help it. It just happened.

Don Carlos's eyes flashed. "Get your hands off me!" he snarled, but Remy held him fast.

"This is between you and me. We're gonna settle this thing. Right now."

"No, señor," he said. "Again you are mistaken. It's between you and our world. It's a question of whether or not you belong. But this problem you have is yours alone. You came to us uninvited. We did not come looking for you."

"That's a lie!" Remy cracked. "You asked me here!"

Don Carlos stared at him coldly and then shook his head. "That was after you'd invited yourself. It became a matter of repairing damage, not of my making, that was already done." He looked down at Remy's hand. "Now, you must excuse me. This discussion can wait."

Don Carlos shoved Remy's hand away, straightened his collar, and opened the door. Remy saw all eyes fall on him. The rebuff rankled him. He'd heard Don Carlos say what he'd always sensed about him. He also knew what he was going to do about it.

It all happened so quickly, like the snapping of a twig. Before Don Carlos passed through the door, Remy spun him back around and slugged him squarely in the jaw. Remy felt a great release of his anger. After that, he stood ready to receive its consequences. He had the immediate sense that the cost would be dear. But his regret came too late, and his anger had little trouble suppressing it.

Don Carlos tumbled into the *sala*, where he fell face down. Remy was in an unthinking rage and stood in the doorway, his chest heaving, waiting for whatever came. All was then silent.

He saw the shock on the faces of Don Carlos's guests. One in particular, however, whom Remy judged to be only a few years older than himself, pulled his pistol from his holster, cocked it, and aimed it squarely at Remy's chest. Remy froze.

"*¿Qué deseas, Don Carlos?*" the man asked. His words were cool and lethal, his eyes locked on Remy's. Don Carlos sat up and worked his jaw with his hand to see that it remained in place. Then he looked around to reassess the situation at hand, clearly alarmed.

"Put it away, Don Enrique," he mumbled. "That's perhaps the best solution but not the right one. It would make my daughter most unhappy."

"He has insulted you in your own home," the man snapped. "As your guest, with your permission, I'd be happy to set things right. The weapons are his choice."

Remy turned to face this man when Don Carlos held up his hand. "Please, calm yourself, my friends. Enough harm's been done. This quarrel is all within my strange family. When one brings a wild bull into his home, he should expect that some things will soon be broken." He managed an artificial smile. "Of course, I'd always hoped it wouldn't be my jaw, but we're all getting used to disappointment around here. He's acted like I always knew he would. We hope to breed this trait out in coming generations."

Don Carlos regained his unsteady feet. He stretched his arm out to his son-in-law. Remy was confused. He stood still. "Come here, Remy," Don Carlos said with a pleading, beseeching tone. "Take my hand. I forgive you. We can quarrel if we must but we can never fight. Nothing's as bad as you think. It just takes time. I'm sorry that I angered you. I truly regret what I said." Then he looked to see that his friend had put his pistol away. When he did, Don Carlos thanked him. He then waited for Remy to take his hand. "Come," he repeated.

Remy had no idea how to respond. This man had humiliated him, taunted him, driven a wedge between him and his wife. He had deliberately provoked him, and now that Remy had struck him in his own lair, when Don Carlos had the clear advantage of place and numbers, he was letting it all go. In his whole life, he'd seen nothing like it. What had he done? Now that he'd drawn first blood, Don Carlos's reaction was to offer his hand and welcome him back into the fold. He couldn't take it. His anger dissipated into the deepest shame. The very walls around him seemed hostile, closing in.

"I'll be goin'," he finally said; he felt his eyes drop to the floor. The other men present heard his words, shook their heads, and waited to see what Don Carlos would do.

"Going where, Remy? It's late."

"To my place."

"This is your place," he insisted.

Remy shook his head. "No it ain't," he said with his

natural drawl. He'd just proven how ignorant he was. "Not after what I just done. I'm sorry, Don Carlos. I gotta go."

Don Carlos's tone shifted. "And what of your wife?"

"If she wants me, she can come."

Don Carlos's displeasure wrinkled his face. "She can't travel to that country, Remy. The baby's due soon. Let this go. Don't do something else you'll regret. Enough is enough."

"I can't stay, Don Carlos." Already he felt himself backing away. "Not now."

Remy passed by Don Carlos and the others on the way out of the front door. Without turning back, he removed the Gump from the rack. Then he went to the stable and saddled his horse. He walked the stallion slowly out of the courtyard when he looked up at his bedroom window. He could see the silhouettes of his wife and her father. Clearly they were arguing. As he watched, Beatriz snatched open the shutter and looked down at him. He stared at her for a moment but couldn't read her expression, at least not as well as he read the one before, and then turned the horse's head northeast, the steel of its bridle cold and clinking, and rode out alone.

The cabin was absolutely dark when Remy arrived. "Elijah Johnson!" Remy called out, his voice echoing in the crisp night.

He heard clattering within: a chair knocked over, a toe stubbed, an old Méxicano cursed, a rifle cocked. Soon the door opened and out stepped his cousin, naked to the waist. He squinted, holding a lantern in front of him, the rifle under his arm.

"Remy?" he asked drowsily. "That you?"

"Yep."

"What gives?"

"I'm whipped. Ya gotta extra bunk in that shack?"

"Depends on how many's stayin'?"

"Just one."

Elijah scratched his upper arm with the rifle barrel.
"Yeah, come on," he said as he started to turn away.
"What've you done now?"

Remy hung his head. "I made a mess of things, Elijah."

"Well, sooner or later you always do. Get in here. Quelepe's burned some damn good meat. I'll scratch a little up
for ya. You better hope it don't scratch back."

Chapter Four

Kills White Bear was eating his evening meal in Running
Stream's lodge. He had remained close to his father-
in-law all these years since Morning Song's death, still hunting for her immediate family, though it was no longer his
obligation. It was their company he cherished. Running
Stream's wife had died of smallpox as well, but he'd taken
another one, Sleek. They were sitting there together when
a boy came to tell Kills White Bear that the council wished
to see him.

Kills White Bear knew what they wanted. Long Knife,
the war chief of White Bear's branch of the Penateka, had
grown old. The council talked of naming a successor. No
other war leader possessed his honors, so Kills White Bear
knew that he was the most likely candidate.

At twenty-nine winters, White Bear was considered
nearly middle-aged, in his prime. The older men trusted his
judgment and consulted him not only in matters of war but
also about their family problems, disputes, and politics.
That was another good sign.

Despite hardships, the years had nurtured Kills White
Bear. Time had balanced him. He cared deeply for his people, their land, their ways. His physical prowess and deeds
of war naturally evolved into a sense of personal power.
Yet he never used his gifts to enhance or decorate his warrior image, always allowing his bounty to pass from his
strong arms to the empty hands of others. All that he had,
he gave his cherished people. His own possessions, save his
horse herd, which flourished, remained few. While there

were any number of young warriors who would follow him
on the raiding trail at a moment's notice, Kills White Bear
genuinely preferred to stay near the camp, visit the sick,
feed the poor, and teach the young warriors the ancient
and precious Nemenuh ways. He no longer had anything
to prove but he had much to protect. None of this, he
knew, had escaped Maguara's watchful eyes, and now it
was Maguara who called him.

Kills White Bear had already planned his speech. Even
though he'd set aside the dreams and warrior ambitions of
his youth to look after the People, his vision from that
happy time had never faded. He diligently monitored the
progress of the white bears. The further west and north
they settled, the more troubled he became. At these times,
he was given to moodiness and brooding. Many preferred
to raid the Méxicano ranches. Some had traveled so far
south as to return with parrots and other strange objects.
But Kills White Bear almost always concentrated on the
settlements of the whites unprotected by Maguara's treaty
with the man called Austin. Dozens of their scalps hung
from his rawhide bison shield, others from his lance, more
still were fastened to the white bear's cape. He fully intended to add several more.

His policy was unpopular with the older men. Instead of
facilitating the war against the settlers, Maguara discouraged it. Kills White Bear expected this policy to change
with his ascension. He held a different view, an extension
of his vision, and once he was named war chief, Maguara
would have no choice but to yield to it. His time had come,
as Wolf Eyes had promised.

Kills White Bear dressed himself in his finest regalia:
buckskins Morning Song had stitched for him, their texture
supple, chewed by her own teeth; bone and beaded breastplate across his scarred chest; a brass medallion, a bear's
claw engraved on its front, hung from his neck; silver rings
on his fingers and dangling from both ears; a single eagle
feather woven into his long braid, slick with fresh bear
grease. He draped his white bear hide proudly across his
shoulder and left to meet the council.

He entered the lodge gracefully, stood erect, and pulled
the flap closed behind him. All eyes of his elders turned to

him. They were seated in a circle around a small fire. At
the far end sat balding Maguara, the *Par-riah-boh,* civil
chief of the Penateka.

"You called, my uncles?" Kills White Bear asked. He
spoke softly out of reverence. He admired almost all of
these men. Maguara nodded and motioned for him to sit.
He accepted the pipe, which he smoked slowly and deliberately, allowing the plume to engulf his head.

"My son," Maguara began, "in the moon when the flowers of the prairie bloom, we will go to speak with the Méxicano Father in Béxar. He says that his people are weary of
war. He's sent word to us that he wishes to talk peace. This
thing is good."

Kills White Bear nodded.

"He makes one condition, however. In exchange for the
talks, he wants the man who killed the two traders and cut
the ears from the third." Maguara paused a moment. Kills
White Bear said nothing. "The man he seeks is you, is
it not?"

He again nodded. "Those men killed my people and
yours. Revenge was my right."

"It was," the chief agreed. "But, this act is an obstacle
to something greater than a warrior's revenge. We must
give the Méxicano Father the man he calls Black Heart. In
exchange, we'll ask him to draw a line on the land. He will
stay on his side, the Nemenuh on theirs. That way, things
can go on as they have."

Kills White Bear knew better and said so. "He won't do
it. He never has."

"There have been disappointments in the past," Maguara
said, "but we must try again." The others nodded.

The sight of them, the wisest among them, agreeing to
such foolishness set him back. He'd never dreamed the reception for which he'd waited a lifetime would begin with
a compromise. He chose the words for his response carefully. "My uncles," he began, "Kills White Bear's willing
to do what's asked of him, for the good of our people. As
a boy he pledged his life to them. But he won't trade it for
a lie."

He handed the pipe back across the fire. Maguara took
it from him and waited for him to continue. "You must ask

yourselves why we now find the Cherokee, the Delaware, the Kickapoo, and other strange people from the east hunting on our land. The People war with these men, when we should be learning from them. Ask them why they came here and they'll tell you that they also drew a line with the Great Father. But the line was not honored and they fled for their lives with their women and children."

Maguara nodded his head, the light of the fire in his eyes. "That is probably true," he said, "but these Indians put their mark on the paper in the American Father's crooked fingers. The whites in our country look to the Méxicano Father as their chief. They must do as he says. His heart is open to us. He wants peace, as we do."

Kills White Bear listened to what Maguara said. Then the weight of Maguara's words fell on his shoulders. He understood what they wanted. The price for the talks was him. "Is it your wish, then," he muttered quietly, "that Kills White Bear give himself to the soldiers at Béxar?" Before they answered, he felt the power surge within him. He spoke like a man, undaunted. "If so, he won't do it. They'll surely put the rope to his neck and his spirit will never be free." Now his words held them. "But, Kills White Bear will go to them alone in arms, kill as many as he can before they kill him. He'll paint a black heart on his chest so the Méxicanos think they have who they want and fight until they put a bullet through it. Kills White Bear will die as he's lived—as a warrior, with his pride. He offers you this, and this only."

At once all of the elders began to grumble. Maguara motioned for them to be quiet.

"No," the old chief said. "That's not what I have in mind. We'll take one of the Waco captives, the ugliest one, dress his wretched body as best we can as a Nemenuh, give him the name of Black Heart and trade him to the Méxicano Father for peace. When he tells them differently, Maguara will say that he's a coward and a liar, and that's why he killed those men. These words the Méxicanos will hear."

Kills White Bear felt relieved. He knew that Maguara's animal spirit was the coyote, the trickster. Now he knew why. He smiled, but he quickly saw that the old chief was not smiling with him.

"We do ask one favor, however," Maguara added, his eyes like slits.

"Name it."

"You, honored Kills White Bear, must travel north with the Nokonis for a time. All raiding against the Méxicanos and whites must cease, at least until this thing is done. If it comes to pass, we must leave the Méxicanos and the whites in peace, as Maguara will have given his word."

Maguara's decision struck him speechless. The old man puffed on his stone pipe and then leveled his glance at him. "Your heart is black to the whites. You hate them above all of our enemies . . ."

Kills White Bear cut him off. "And you should, too."

Maguara ordered him to be quiet with a chop of his arm and a cold stare, both daring the young warrior to defy him. "The young men look up to you," Maguara said quietly. "They're wild and thoughtless and will ask you to take them south to raid the rancheros. If you're not here, Long Knife and I can control them better. That is why we must ask you to go."

Kills White Bear knew there was nothing more to say. The decision had been made. Any warrior could disagree with the council's wishes. All a dissenter had to do was leave peaceably. Since this was what they were asking him to do anyway, his protest was mute. "Before the dawn breaks," Kills White Bear obliged, "this warrior will be gone."

Maguara nodded, the others following his lead. "Use this time wisely, brother. Go and see the great mountains to the north. Learn the ways of other Nemenuh. Go with them in raids against our ancient enemies, the Utes, the Cheyenne, and the Lakota. They're as evil as any. Your talents will not be wasted. You'll continue to grow. When the time is right, I'll send for you. Don't forget that you are the valued son of the southern Penateka. We'll welcome your return with open arms again. Your place is with us. Some day you will sit at my side as Long Knife does now, as War Chief. But for now, you must go."

Kills White Bear was shaken but did not wish for the others to sense it. He rose to leave; then he felt Maguara's hand grasp his wrist.

"One last thing," Maguara said. Kills White Bear remained standing. "We know you've mourned these past three winters for your young wife and child. We all lost many to the great sickness, but we've gone on as best we could. You, however, have chosen to remain rooted in the past. While you do many fine things for our people, your heart is choked with your own bitterness. I can see it in your eyes. To be brave is one thing, to be sick is another. While you are among the Nokonis, why not take another wife? Father more children? The love of a woman and the laughter of children in your lodge will heal your heart and make you whole again."

Kills White Bear resented Maguara's intrusion into his personal life. His reply was caustic. "Kills White Bear appreciates your concern for his welfare. Maguara thinks of one man's happiness at the cost of the nation's." The civil chief was stung by his words. "But his chief asks and Kills White Bear will answer," he continued. "Kills White Bear has seen no woman that can replace the one he's lost. Each day he thinks of her. We played as children. We loved as adults. There's no room in his heart for another."

Maguara let his insult pass. It was, Kills White Bear knew, what made him great. "Room can be found if you make it so. You must bury the pain of the past as you buried Morning Song. Otherwise, it will destroy you. Enough time has been wasted already. Peace will come to the Nemenuh when the line is drawn. This is what Maguara sees, and his eyes look for a nation."

This, Kills White Bear knew, was the response to his slight. "But peace will come to Kills White Bear only when he loves again. Maguara sees this also and so it is spoken for the wise to hear. It takes two to make one. Only a good woman can make Kills White Bear a whole man." Maguara pointed to the north, the direction he must go. "Think of what I've said while you are amongst the Nokonis." Then the old chief motioned toward the flap and fell silent.

Kills White Bear left the lodge for his own to gather his things. He had expected honor. What he'd received was banishment. He was to live with the Nokonis, the wanderers, because he was in the way of peace. It was a mistake and he knew it. The Méxicano Father might intend to keep his word, but the whites would not obey him. Had Maguara not seen the trees falling in the east? The whites would keep coming, especially if the raiding ceased. They would clear the ground and make their scars in the earth. Their presence would spook the game. Their beasts would devour the grass until mud choked the rivers. They were a plague much worse than the one that had taken his family. Was he the only one that understood this? Had Maguara not said that he shared his vision? Why were those old eyes so blind?

But Kills White Bear knew that he must accept the decision. Sooner or later, he thought, the treaty would be broken and, as Maguara had said, his time would come. It was promised. The question that remained, however, was, what would be lost in the meantime?

Chapter Five

Remy lay in his bed asleep when the sound of riders reached his ears. He heard Elijah take his shotgun from the rack, go out and talk to them in his god-awful Spanish. There was no argument. They just talked. Then there was a thud, the sound of a body hitting the ground, and then many footsteps scrambling inside the house. Before he could do much of anything, there were many hands on his body. In the darkness, he still recognized Diego Picosa and the others. They tied him up from head to toe and dragged him out of the homestead to where a black mule was waiting. They slung him across its back, feet to one side, head and shoulders to the other. From that awkward position, he saw Elijah lying in the dust. They'd stiffed him and were laughing about it.

"You'd better not've hurt him, goddammit, Diego!"

"*¡Cállete, cabron!*" Picosa barked. The mayordomo gave the word and they rode off.

When they arrived, Picosa led the mule to the front of the great house. He loosened the straps that held Remy and let him fall to the ground. Then Picosa walked up to the door, knocked, and stepped away into the shadows. Don Carlos appeared in the doorway.

"Thank you for coming," he said. "I have something to show you." And then he disappeared back into the house. When he returned, he cradled a dark-haired, dark-eyed infant. He held the child in front of Remy. "This," he said proudly, "belongs to you."

He ordered Picosa to untie the ropes and Remy stood, working the circulation back into his cold, cramped limbs. Don Carlos handed him the infant, wrapped in soft cloth.

"What is it?" he asked quietly. His wrists were numb from the ropes, but he no longer minded.

"It's a son, Remy. Your son." Remy looked at the child as if it were a miracle. "In your regrettable absence," Don Carlos told him, "if you approve, I took the liberty of suggesting to your wife in the strongest terms available that we name the child Carlos Amarante de la Cruz . . ." He paused. ". . . Fuqua, of course, goes at the end." Don Carlos focused on the child. "We call him Carlito. He's already very spoiled."

"Is Beatriz all right?" he asked, his eyes never leaving the baby.

"She is. The birth went well. She's waiting for you inside."

Don Carlos saw to it that the child was properly covered. Remy held him awkwardly, afraid to squeeze too tightly. The infant's dark eyes locked on his. On such a cool night, it brought him indescribable warmth. These past two months he'd thought of nothing but this moment. It'd been a torment to stay away.

"He's beautiful," he finally breathed, like a benediction.

"Yes," Don Carlos agreed, "and not too white either." He then looked at Remy and smiled. "I'm sorry," he said. "I hope all is forgiven. A child changes everything, does it not?"

Remy nodded his head that indeed it did.

"Come, Remy," Don Carlos said. "Take your place in our home." Remy smiled when Don Carlos worked his jaw.

"No harm's been done. This past week I could chew meat again."

Remy felt awkward and hesitated.

"Come," Don Carlos urged. "You're wanted here."

"You had one hell of a way of showin' it."

"Beatriz obviously could not come. I myself could not part from this precious child. I had to send Picosa; and Picosa, as you know, is not a delicate man." He reached for the baby and Remy let him go. "Please, come and see your wife," Don Carlos said. His faced beamed at the sight of his grandson. "Of course, he looks just like me," he said proudly.

Remy smiled and looked lovingly at his son, excused himself and slipped past his father-in-law. He first went and bathed in the icy river. Don Carlos sent him clean clothes and cologne. Remy entered the house invigorated, checked briefly on the child, and then went upstairs to their bedroom. He cracked the door open to find Beatriz sitting on the bed combing her hair.

"Beatriz?" he called to her softly. *"¿Estás bien?"*

"Yes, Remy!" she answered turning to face him. Her eyes sparkled in the lamplight. "I'm fine." She motioned for her husband to come and sit beside her.

He moved slowly at first, uncertain. "I'm sorry," he whispered. "I lost my goddamn head."

"You've done nothing," she said. He took the comb from her hand. "I've missed you so very badly." Those words were sweet.

"I know what you want," he told her, stroking her cheek. "I didn't understand. Now, I do. I can be that man." He waited. He saw a tear begin to roll down her cheek.

"It's not your fault, Remy. I listened to my father. I shouldn't have. He lied to me. We got all that worked out while you were gone. Things will change. I was miserable that you weren't here for the birth, but I didn't blame you. Don Carlos has learned his lesson and I've learned mine. I don't care what you do here as long as we're happy. If you want to go back to Elijah's, I'll go. Tomorrow. I swear it."

"No," he said. "It's better here. Believe me." He felt he should explain more about what had happened, or at least try to. "I had a rough time growin' up, Beatriz. Nobody ever gave me nuthin'. I don't know what it's like to be part of a real family. I didn't handle it good." He rubbed his brow. "And my temper—my goddamn temper. I get out of hand so easy. I can't help it."

Beatriz said she understood. Yet he could see there was pain in her eyes. He asked her to tell him about it. "I'm sorry that I was cold to you," she offered. "It meant nothing."

Remy pulled her to him, her smell filled his head and comforted him.

"I'll learn," he whispered to her. "I swear I will."

"It doesn't matter," she said. "I love you."

"I'm so sorry, Beatriz. I made such a mess of things. I wasn't even here when you needed me."

"Chist," she whispered. "Don Carlos was the author of all that. I should've seen it coming. It was as much my fault as it was yours. Let's forget it and go on. We have a child to think of now."

He rose from the bed, blew out the lamp, disrobed and stood naked before her. The river water still dripped from his hair to the floor. She drew the covers back from the bed and motioned for him to lie beside her. When it was warm, when he felt his skin against hers, he forgot all about that look.

1830

Chapter Six

With the arrival of the spring rains and the renewal of the prairie grass, Don Carlos ordered the seasonal *corrida,* the gathering of the stock, and work began in earnest. The yearlings were branded and released. Many of the young bulls and older heifers were kept in the *corral de lena,* waiting. When Remy asked why, he was told that some of these animals were to be driven east to Louisiana to sell.

Remy knew, as he thought everyone did, that trade of any kind with the United States was forbidden by Méxicano law. When he mentioned the restriction to Don Carlos, his father-in-law casually replied, *"Recibidas, obedicidas, y no cumplidas,"* which Remy loosely translated as "received, obeyed, and not carried out." The phrase, he learned, was as old as the Spanish missions. He understood then that his in-laws, like most frontiersmen, obeyed the laws of convenience and practicality above and beyond those legislated in distant capitals.

Don Carlos explained that it was next to impossible to raise cash money in Tejas. This Remy understood well enough. Austin himself had once told him that propertied people in his colony often did not handle five dollars cash in a year's time. In Remy's experience, goods were assigned a cash value and exchanged as legal tender. A cow and a calf, for instance, were worth five American dollars.

Now Don Carlos had assembled just over three hundred head of bulls and older heifers for sale. He'd traded cattle to a man in Natchitoches, Louisiana, whom he'd met and trusted during his years in exile after the battle of Medina back in 1813. He was tired of waiting to export hides and tallow to Spain whenever a ship was available on the portless Tejas coast, tired of the futility of shipping these same products south to saturated Méxicano markets. In New Orleans, Tejano cattle were in demand for a fair price and that was the only law that caught Don Carlos's attention. "The politicians be damned," he told Remy. "We need the money."

And so Remy and the others gathered the criollos from the distant pastures and corralled the most incorrigible. The rest were herded night and day by young vaqueros on good grass near the river. The bulls, on average, were around four to six years old, some weighing half a ton or more, a good weight, Don Carlos said, for them to have carried over the winter.

Other than the few black cattle, the Ganado Prieto, that remained nearly pure blood, the muscled and brush-scarred hides of the criollos were generally dull and earth-like, much like a deer's. Some were brindles, or blues; others grullas, the color of the sand hill crane, an ash gray; sabinas, which were peppered red and white; duns; and all hues of yellow and brown. Remy recognized nature's mark of wildness in the discolored, coarse-haired stripe that ran the length of their backs, sometimes in the form of a cross over the shoulders.

He learned that, like the Spanish before him, Don Carlos did not castrate bulls; however, he and Picosa carefully selected the bulls which were left on the range to breed. The others were butchered for their hides and tallow. A few, apparently, were sold in defiance of Méxicano law.

Remy understood that whatever European strains were introduced among *los criollos* were quickly absorbed into general herd characteristics. While they all looked different, they were in their essence the same. For whatever reason, possibly the selection of the breeding bulls, the infusion of English blood from the old ranchos of Florida and Louisiana, the quality of the Tejas range, the minerals in the soil, the temperate climate of the North, or the combination of all of these and others unknown to Remy, Don Carlos told him that the Tejano cattle were larger, tougher, longer, and more heavily horned than those south of the Río Grande.

Remy knew that the pure bloods, like the black Ganado Prieto, the Andalusian fighting bulls, were called "Spanish" cattle by the Anglos. These were rare. *Los criollos*, the mongrels, were usually termed "Méxicano," although some of the immigrants began to refer to them by their most impressive and striking trait—their long horns.

Like many other Anglos born and raised on farms, Remy had moved cattle from place to place. He'd herded his own with Elijah to Baton Rouge to sell. However, those were docile, short-legged and portly—domesticated English breeds. *Los criollos* were fiercely wild and more numerous, and they were to be driven hundreds of miles across the open range. Such an expedition, like most things he'd encountered in Texas, was something new and alien. He did not see how a dozen men could control three hundred head of cattle.

Diego Picosa, on the other hand, showed no sign of concern. He ordered his vaqueros to make ready and walked calmly from corral to corral observing his herd. He saw that the wagons, carefully caulked with pitch and straw for the river crossings to come, were properly provisioned with food and equipment. This journey, he told Remy, is one that he'd made two dozen times. There was nothing to worry about, he said.

Don Carlos had thought it important for his son-in-law to make the drive, learn more about handling the stock, meet his business associates, enhance his experience as a rancher and, thus, prepare for that day when he would control all. And Remy was keen to do so despite his reservations. "Get some sleep, Don Remy," Picosa told him just before midnight. "We go at dawn."

Before first light Remy felt Don Carlos's hand on his shoulder. Remy kissed his wife's cheek and slipped quietly from her side. He leaned over the crib to kiss his sleeping baby, then gathered his things and walked out into the light.

Downstairs, the señora had some breakfast ready as well as tortillas packed for his lunch. Remy had a cup of coffee with Don Carlos, who offered some last minute advice as Remy slipped on his boots, chaparreras, and leather jacket. Don Carlos brought him one of his own carbines, which he explained would be better on the trail than his long rifle, as well as two fancy pistols. Remy holstered them both, draped his goatskin *armas de agua,* his protection from rain, over his shoulder, and walked outside in the crisp morning air to saddle his horse. He found droopy-eyed Picosa, who'd apparently been up all night in final preparation, already mounted and ready. Several of his vaqueros had also stayed up to mix with the cattle so that the beasts could not rest. They would begin their journey exhausted.

When all was ready, Picosa quietly signaled for the corrals to be opened, and the exhausted criollos filtered out; slowly at first, in a steady stream, then more rapidly once they saw the open plains unfold ahead, behind the oxen that led the way northwest. Remy, at Picosa's suggestion, stayed back with the manada of spare saddle horses. When all the cattle had passed before him, he fell in behind and walked on.

The vaqueros were quiet and solemn. Remy could hear only the sound of the hooves on the damp ground, the turkey gobblers celebrating the arrival of spring as they perched on their river bottom roosts, and the occasional bawling of the anxious and confused cattle as they left their home range.

The first day passed without event. They crossed the Cíbolo at midmorning, coming to the Guadalupe at dusk. Picosa paused for a moment to examine the water's flow. He drew Remy's attention to the spume floating on top. A sure sign, he explained, that the river would soon rise. It had been raining, he said, in the hills to the north. Even Remy knew that one did not wait to cross any river at the end of the day. Such was the uncertainty of Tejas. Picosa ordered his men to drive the cattle across and make camp on the east bank. When the lead bulls balked, Picosa unharnessed the oxen and sent them across first, followed by a half-dozen of the tamer cattle. The criollos soon followed. Picosa led them to a flat a mile east and made his camp.

Where to bed the cattle, Picosa explained, was a delicate business. It would be foolish to select a narrow valley where the cattle would be haunted by their own echoes, or rocky ground that sounded hollow underfoot which would unnerve them. It must be a flat area with good grass, a bedding ground that they themselves might choose. This was the art of a cattle drive and Remy absorbed every morsel of information.

Picosa allowed the stock to water themselves fully in the Guadalupe before they moved on to the rich pastures, where they grazed for the first time until content. With their bellies full, they were more likely to bed in this strange place. Picosa had sent one rider ahead to flush any wild ducks that might be rafting in the lower areas that held water. Nothing, he told Remy, should be left to chance. When that was done, he moved the herd slowly forward to the chosen ground. He ordered his vaqueros to keep the restless young bulls moving in a circle around those that bedded. The others settled around the wagons waiting for their dinner. Picosa advised Remy to get some sleep, as soon it would be his watch. Picosa splashed the contents of his coffee tin on the ground and mounted. "If

we can keep them quiet for two weeks," he told him,
"they'll settle into the trail."

"What're you worried about?" Remy asked. "They look
reasonable enough to me."

"*La estampida,* Don Remy," he answered gravely.

"Sounds mighty bad," Remy said. "What the hell is it?"

"If the weather curses us, you'll see soon enough." He
looked skyward and studied the heavens. Then he turned
back to Remy. "Now you listen carefully, Don Remy. If
they run, you stay with the herd. If it's nighttime, let go of
your reins and let your horse guide you. He sees much
better than you do in the dark. Whatever happens, you stay
with the herd, do you hear me, Don Remy? Don't be
afraid. *Los criollos* will not hurt you. They won't run you
down."

"What sets 'em off?" Remy asked.

"Anything, *joven*. Lightning and thunder usually. The
sound of a lobo, a gunshot, certainly, a shout from a man,
quick movements by a thoughtless boy, the snapping of a
twig under your horse's hoof, even the blink of a nervous
eye. Move slowly and quietly as you see the others doing.
I don't have to tell you that these cattle are not like your
American breeds. They do not rise pausing on their knees
to pray. The wilderness has taught them to spring to their
feet like a cat. It's one jump from their bed, the next jump
to hell." He looked toward the bedded herd. "When they
run, and sooner or later they will try, you stay with them,
all night long if that's what it takes. In the morning we'll
gather them, calm them down and move on. *¿Entiendes?*"

Remy nodded that he understood and Picosa rode off
into the darkness. Remy wrapped himself in his blanket
next to other vaqueros who were already sleeping. His
horse, still saddled, was tied to an iron stake he'd driven
in the ground with a log of green mesquite. He fell asleep
to the sound of the herders singing to the cattle in the
distance. The night air was warm for the season, still and
humid. The sky was clear. All was quiet.

"¡Depiértense, muchachos!" At first, the words interrupted a quiet dream and Remy pondered their significance. Then he heard them again and he snapped awake. Remy jumped to his feet and immediately swung his leg over the horse and was mounted before he'd wiped the sleep from his burning eyes. A north wind had kicked up; its cool breeze swept his face. He shuddered, flipped his collar up around his neck, and waited for his eyes to adjust.

In the distance, he could see the northern horizon flash against the vast starry void above. The cloud bank that hung there was thick and low, its dull thunder rumbling in a low growl. There was the clean smell of rain in the air. Picosa's weathered face flickered in the gray light and then vanished. His voice was calm, assured.

"We'll need everybody out tonight" he told them. "Ride the edges and keep them circling tight. Turn back the stragglers. It's just a spring shower, not enough to make them run. It'll pass."

Remy was among the first of the sleepers to reach the herd. To his surprise, given the storm that threatened, most remained bedded. The heifers bawled for their young; the bulls turned their heads in unison to the north, watching.

Within a half hour's time, the front sailed overhead. Remy watched as a band of low, thin, white-tipped clouds drifted just above him. Behind them, only darkness. Distinct branches of lightning pierced the hills to the north. The thunder was sharper now, more immediate, threatening. Remy called to the cattle in a low, soothing voice. "Easy, now," he begged them. "Easy."

He heard other vaqueros do the same. *"Tranquilos, diablos. Tranquilos."*

The air was strangely dry, the sky discolored, the hue of a musket ball, surreal. The lead bull stretched out his swollen neck from his bed, looking first south, then east, even back west toward the river. Without being told, Remy knew he was choosing his direction. Remy was walking his horse over to stand in front of him when the light blinded his eyes. Before he could blink, there was that sharp, stifling crack. The percussion nearly knocked him from his horse; his hat was blown off onto the prairie. The air smelled bitter, like burnt sulfur. The trunk of a Spanish oak, not thirty feet away, split at its center, each half falling in opposite directions. Before it hit the ground, the entire herd popped to its feet as if on cue. Silence.

Remy gathered himself and rode to cut off the lead bull, who was now pacing from side to side. Then Remy saw something strange amid the cattle and squinted his eyes in the darkness in order to discern what it was. There were balls of dull, phosphorescent light balanced on the tips of the cattle's horns and occasional flickers of electricity connecting the spine of one bull to the other just for an instant, and then moving on to other animals in other parts of the unsettled mass. He'd heard of it before but never expected to see it. Remy's people called it "fox fire"; the Tejanos called it "St. Elmo's."

The mysterious halos confused the cattle as much as they did Remy. They shook their heads as if to throw off the lights; horn clanked against nervous horn among the three hundred. The lead bull jerked out of the darkness, moving in a circular motion to his right. The herd followed almost magnetically, the sparks of electricity shooting across their muscled, quivering backs. Then one final blue-white jolt from above netted the entire prairie around them, the boom of the thunder followed immediately, and that was all it took. In one instant, in one mass, they ran. And Remy, leaning low against the horse's neck, raced with them—bone, muscle, hide, horn, and hoof—into the dark, woolen night.

The rain splattered to the earth so loudly that it drowned the rumbles of a thousand frantic hooves. In the flickers of lightning, Remy saw the rain fall in a straight line, like crystal shafts of straw woven tightly in a single mat, almost like a cage. Its volume choked him. He raised one hand to his nose to keep from inhaling it, the other held fast to the saddle horn. He'd let the reins go long ago.

Although it was impossible to tell for sure, Remy thought that the cattle had turned back east, and then finally north, into the storm. The rain slacked off to some degree and Remy sat back up in the saddle in order to spot a landmark. A cedar branch across his face told him that they'd left the *llano* behind, and he crouched again against the horse's back lest the next one fracture his skull.

The herd raced on for what seemed like an hour. Then everything stopped but the wind and driving rain. The darkness wrapped around his head like a blanket. The cattle made no sound. Remy could make out the asses of frozen bulls ahead of him, flanks of cattle to his side; others bumped in behind him. He felt each successive jolt.

"This is it, huh, you sons of bitches?" Remy said, and he decided to move forward in search of the lead bull. He reached for the ears of the cattle around him to feel for the one that Picosa had notched deeply. This, he immediately recognized, was futile, and he decided to spur his horse forward to the head of the column, where the bull would most surely be. He reached for the loose reins, slick with water, and flicked them against the horse's neck. The animal refused to move. Remy removed a boot from the stirrup, and kicked at the side of the animal nearest, hoping to make a path. The beast would not move. Next Remy raked his spurs up the horse's flank, whipping its hip with the wet reins. Nothing. Frustrated, Remy then shoved his spurs deeply into the horse's flesh. "Git up now!" Remy yelled. The stallion groaned in pain, stepped twice forward as if to please him and then stopped again.

"Now what the hell's wrong with you?" Remy asked. The next flicker of lightning answered his question. The entire herd was poised on the edge of a canyon. How deep it was, Remy could not say. The lightning could not find its bottom.

"Back up, now," Remy moaned. "Back up." He tugged the reins gently to his chest. His horse attempted to step backwards but immediately came up against another cow. They could not move any further. Remembering what Picosa had told him, Remy dismounted, flipped the reins over the horse's head, and picked his way against the barrier of hides. At times, he pressed his full weight against a cow's ribs, his boots slipping in the black clay mud, in order to clear a path. He could see nothing but, wherever he found cattle standing, he knew he had firm ground.

As best he could, he moved directly opposite from where the bluff stood. In his wake, the bulls turned and followed. Their horns clashed loudly. Soon, they spearheaded their own path through the herd. When Remy felt them rush

past him, he remounted. Before he could do much of anything, the herd wheeled in mass following the bulls and
they were off again, Remy and his horse swept off with the
others. After that, Remy cared nothing about staying with
the herd. What he had in mind was staying with his horse,
the herd be damned. That cliff had spooked him and he
didn't want to find another one the same way. A blink of
lightning revealed that other vaqueros were now with them,
all running with the wild bulls, waiting for the thunder to
cease or the break of dawn, whichever came first.

Remy awoke with clear, cobalt blue skies overhead. Not a
cloud remained. He found himself at the feet of his horse,
several criollo heifers laying beside him, calmly chewing
their cud. A pile of fresh, shiny dung was near his head.
He rose, stiff-legged and sore, the feel of dried blood on
his cheek, to find all of the cattle bedded for the first time.
Picosa and the others milled about the edge of the herd,
smoking cigarillos and drinking tin cups of warm coffee.
Remy could smell both amid the stench of wet saddle
leather and soaked cattle. He slowly led his horse out of
the herd until he reached Picosa. The mayordomo watched
as Remy advanced, a big smile pasted on his face.

"That, Don Remy," he offered wryly, "was *la estampida*.
Much excitement, no?"

"Much excitement, yes," Remy answered. He failed to
see the humor. "Where's the goddamn bull that started
all that?"

"He lays to the east of the herd." Remy searched the
sky to get oriented. The sun was already high. He had no
idea until Picosa pointed. "Over there," he said.

"Reckon a gunshot would spook 'em?" Remy asked
grimly, looking in the bull's direction.

"Nothing will spook them today," Picosa said. "They're
exhausted. They need rest."

"And that bull's gonna get plenty," Remy said, and he

pulled the pistol from his holster and cocked the hammer, walking straight for where the beast lay. Picosa pitched his coffee and rode over to stop him.

"No, Don Remy," Picosa protested. "That animal's valuable."

"So am I," Remy sneered. "That son of a bitch nearly run me an' everythin' else in God's earth off a cliff last night. I'm gonna kill 'im for it." And he staggered forward through the herd.

Out of the corner of his eye, Remy saw Picosa signal to other vaqueros who were near, and they immediately rode toward him. Remy pressed on. People killed cattle for their hides in Tejas, Remy couldn't see why he shouldn't do this one in for attempted murder. Just as he put the muzzle to the base of the bull's skull, the first of two lariats fell over his shoulders and tightened. The young vaquero gave the rope *la vuelta* around the horn and turned his horse from the bull.

"Let me go, God damn ya!" Remy yelled. "I'm doin' us all a favor."

Picosa rode up beside Remy and held out his hand. *"Dáme la pistola, Don Remy,"* he pleaded. "For all his faults, the bull is a born leader. The others look up to him."

Remy was unfazed. "Well, they can look down on 'im from now on," he said, and then he swung back to Picosa to explain his reasons for what he was about to do. "I don't ever, as long as I live, wanna spend another night like that." Then Remy turned to the young men that held him. "If you boys like your job," he spat, "you best turn me loose. *¡Ahora mismo!*"

Both men looked immediately to Picosa. Remy felt the flash of his anger. It gripped him in an instant. "Don't look at him!" he shouted. He saw it got their attention. "You listen to me! Git these goddamn ropes off me or find yourselves another hacienda."

They still looked to Picosa, which angered Remy more, and the mayordomo nodded solemnly. It was only then that the vaqueros worked the lariats free. Remy walked straight to the bedded animal, his arm extended, the pistol cocked in his angry hand, and stopped it two inches from the base of the bull's skull. Then he pulled the trigger.

Blood spewed from the bull's head like milk from a
pitcher's spout as the great animal rolled over, all four legs
kicking violently. In a moment, all movement ceased, except for some of the other cattle that popped up at the
sound of the gunshot. They did not run. Then Remy flipped
the pistol around so that he held the warm muzzle in his
hand. He handed the butt end to Picosa.

"Load it for me," he ordered. Picosa took the pistol from
him, all the while shaking his head.

"That was not wise, patrón," the mayordomo said. At
the same time, he ordered the others to rope the dead bull,
and drag him downwind so that the herd would no longer
smell its blood. He sent word to the cook to come and
butcher it. Remy watched all this and waited. When the
others had gone, he spoke to Picosa.

"Let's get one thing straight," he said. "You could've
talked me out of shootin' that bull. I'll listen to reason. But
you don't order any of these men to rope me, or get in
my way, or anythin' of the sort again. I've had enough of
that. *¿Entiendes?*"

Picosa said nothing.

"Answer me, old man!" Remy thundered. "You hear me
talkin' to you!" Remy saw that the other vaqueros were
watching now. He knew they didn't like what they saw and
it didn't matter.

"I like you, Diego," he said. "You know that. But the
days of you doin' as you please where I'm concerned are
over. You see somethin' I do that you don't like, you come
and whisper in my ear, same as you do Don Carlos. We
can git alon' all right like that. But don't you ever shame
me in front of the other men; don't you never order them
different than I do, and don't let me hear you say a word
against me. *¿Entiendes?*"

Picosa's gaze was fixed on a cactus at his horse's feet.
"Sí, patrón," he answered.

Remy's temper had the best of him now. While he had
Picosa's attention, he decided to set him straight. "For the
last two to three years, every time somebody ropes me, or
handles me like a sack of flour, you've had a hand in it.
It's gettin' to be a habit for some of these half-breed bastards. It's gonna end. You tell these men—you make damn

sure—that they comprende that the next son of a bitch throws a noose my way's gonna get shot! Dead as a god-damn hammer! Understand?"

"Sí," he said flatly.

"All right," Remy announced, cooling now that he'd vented. Already he felt badly about what he'd said. The mayordomo had deserved the browbeating, he thought, but Remy hadn't expected him to cower before him quite like that. Remy had drawn the line between them as Don Carlos had advised him to do but there was no pleasure in it for him. Now he figured he should repair their relationship as best he could. They had a long way to go together.

"I've got a great deal of respect for you, Diego," he said, speaking more calmly now. "There's no reason for any of that to change. We just had a little problem to talk over. I was rode hard and laid up wet. I got a headache and my stomach's plastered against my ribs. I woke up with my nose in cow shit and so maybe this weren't the best time. I'm sorry. I'm not in a good mood, but I am the patrón. I wanna be treated like one." He paused. The vision of Picosa defeated filled him with instant remorse. "Now I've had my say. You can have yours."

Picosa said nothing but tapped the powder horn to sift the charge into the pistol's pan.

"Go on. Git if off your chest. What's eatin' ya?"

Picosa, as usual, had only the task at hand on his mind. He snapped the battery down and blew to check its seal. "What shall we do for a lead bull today, patrón?" he asked, matter-of-factly, yet he stressed the last word for emphasis.

"What'd ya have in mind? It's your call. You wanna let 'em rest, or push 'em on east?"

"We should move on," he said flatly, as if no option looked promising.

"All right. Git 'em up and git 'em movin'. Whichever idiot moves to the front is your new lead bull."

Picosa began rolling a new cigarillo. "Everything's so simple these days now that the gringos have come," he said, as he slid it between his chapped lips.

"Don't get smart."

"Why should I? What use would that have around you, Don Remy?" He exhaled the smoke. "But, I'll tell you this," he said. Remy implicitly understood he was being warned. "Last night taught these cattle that they can run. Most likely they'll wait until dark before they try it again. Storm or no storm. Like us, they're creatures of habit. I hope we won't lose our lead bull each time. If so, we won't have three sorry cows to sell before it's all over. Your father-in-law may be disappointed."

He handed the loaded pistol back to Remy.

"It's yours," Remy said. Now he wished he hadn't shot the bull or succumbed to the outburst. The consequences of both would certainly linger. He'd drawn the line, but he'd stepped a good way over it. "I won't need it again." And then Remy walked over and took the reins of his horse and headed for the wagon. He saw that Picosa gathered the vaqueros, no doubt explaining the new rules, and then they circulated around the herd whistling and whooping, stealing cool glances at him. The cattle rose drowsily to their sore feet.

Remy intended to eat a little and then saddle up and follow. Picosa had already motioned for the cook to pull his wagon to the lead. Remy scooped the last of the guisada from a warm pot and told him that it was all right to go. He helped him load the fresh and bloody quarters of the dead bull, drenched in salt, onto a piece of clean hide. Before he turned around, his horse bolted. Then he saw the lion emerge, its chiseled coat shining in the sun, from the cedar breaks to the north. The great cat tested the breeze, obviously smelling the blood first, which must have overcome the scent of the men.

Once the lion had seen the criollos, it crouched on its front paws, licking its long, ivory teeth, silently watching them all.

Remy moved slowly to his horse to slip the carbine from its scabbard. The horse bolted again and ran before he could get his fingers around the stock. Remy cursed it. He'd never seen it afraid before, but prey intuitively recognized predator, and Remy understood. Then the lion screamed, a haunting cry like an injured child. The cattle, all at once, froze. The bulls closest to it instinctively formed a ring, horns out. The lion easily ran around them, first starting for the wagon and the bloody flesh inside, but then distracted, it picked one of the younger heifers, plunging straight for the heart of the terrified herd.

Some of the vaqueros tried to shoot the lion, but it was running very rapidly through the prairie grass. Cattle were darting in and out of their sights. Three shots rang out. Not one, Remy knew, drew blood. The cattle, who must've smelled the beast, wheeled together and ran. Remy stood directly in their path. The oxen were already running. The wagon was gone with them, rumbling over stone and stump. There was nothing for him to do but stand there, waiting. He braced himself as the herd approached. He knew they'd crush him. There was nowhere for him to go.

All at once, they parted around him and ran on. Remy turned as they swept past him. Picosa and the others ran with the herd—the horses drawn behind them—and the estampida was on again. Remy was left behind. He heard the thunder of hooves and the shouts of men long after they'd disappeared.

"Damn," Remy said to himself, "if that ain't some bad luck." They would be back for him soon enough. Surely they would. He waited all that day and the next. Nothing. They must've run to Georgia, he thought. At dawn the following day he decided to follow whatever wagon ruts the storm had left back west toward home. When Picosa sent someone back for him, maybe they'd see his tracks and come after him. Maybe. After two days, he didn't have much hope.

Chapter Seven

The Nokonis followed Kills White Bear south. He had been lonely and bored among his strange cousins. He could not deny that they were a happy, vigorous people. Yet instead of immersing himself in the joy of the Nokonis, as Maguara had advised, he spent his time brooding about the Penateka's future. The days seemed to pass more slowly on the northern plains. When the four young Nokoni warriors had asked to join him at his fire, Kills White Bear had welcomed them. A late snow had fallen and the warriors complained of the bitter cold. They had plans to ride south, where it would be warmer, to raid the Méxicanos. But they'd never been, and they had asked Kills White Bear which trace he thought best.

"The one behind my horse's tail," he'd answered slyly, and they all smiled as Kills White Bear dashed the fire with water, gathered his weapons, and stepped out into the wind.

They rode into the great Palo Duro Canyon, where they visited their cousins, the Quahadis, the Antelopes, in their early spring camp. They traded for fresh meat and horses and rode on. Six Antelope warriors chose to ride with them as they slipped through the great pass of the high plains the Spanish called the Llano Estacado, the stockade plains. From there Kills White Bear led his band south along the east bank of the river the Méxicanos called the Colorado, which would take them to Tonkawa country. His own people would be in the San Sabá Valley, and Kills White Bear thought it would be best to swing wide of them lest Maguara learn of his defiance. He would not allow any of the warriors to raid until they were well south of the Penateka encampments, below the Río Grande. If the Tonkawa wanted trouble, they would find it. Otherwise, Kills White Bear intended to ride through their land peaceably and then bear south by southwest.

They rode mostly at night once they reached the scattered white settlements, sleeping well into the afternoon in great thickets of cedar. It felt good to travel in his own country again. The Nokonis expressed a desire to view San Antonio de Béxar from afar, of which they'd heard much. Kills White Bear saw no reason not to oblige them. After that, he would lead them across the great river for the Méxicano desert and the raiding would begin. By the time word reached Maguara's ear of what he would consider Nokoni activities, Kills White Bear will have returned north to the great mountains. No one would ever know that he had led a war party against the Méxicanos.

But east of Béxar, on the coastal plains, Kills White Bear's horse came up lame. He knew well of the ranches that lay between the Cíbolo and the San Antonio River and that there a replacement could easily be found for his animal. Some of the others expressed a desire for fresh mounts as well. Others wanted to take books from the great houses to stuff their pages into their bison-hide shields or use them to smoke tobacco. This meant raiding the big houses, which Kills White Bear staunchly refused. They had traveled far, the young warriors complained, without taking the first scalp. They would travel further still if they wanted to ride with Kills White Bear, he told them, knowing how easily word of such a raid would reach Maguara's long ears. The young warriors dared not defy him, the Wasp who wore the great white hide, two dozen scalps tied to it, across his broad and war-scarred shoulders.

When darkness fell, Kills White Bear led his band along the banks of the San Antonio. In time, they came to a great white house with several smaller buildings beside it. Everything in the world was circular, he thought, yet these people insisted on building their lodges square. Such inconsistency was testament to their ignorance. West of there was a large stone and wood building where he knew they would keep the best horses. They'd found none on the prairie, at least none that they could catch. It had now been dark for several hours. Lights were on inside the big house, the smaller structures were dark and silent. Kills White Bear dismounted and signaled for one other man to do the same.

"Remember," he warned the rest, having already explained that there was a reason why that house had stood for a hundred winters against the Nemenuh raids, "the horses and nothing else. We'll take only what we need," he said, snapping his fingers, "and go."

Kills White Bear and his chosen Quahadi silently entered the barn from the west. There were several fine Méxicano saddle horses available, as he knew there would be. When the stallions caught the first scent of the Nemenuh, they grew uneasy. One in particular neighed loudly in alarm. Kills White Bear moved at once to soothe it, whispering in its ear. As he stroked the animal's chest, he saw the lamp light approaching. He signaled to the other warrior to intercept the watchman and crept back into the shadows.

When the door creaked opened, the warrior pounced. He slit the Méxicano's throat in one lethal movement. The victim, a boy about fourteen, shrieked until his vocal cords

were cut and then collapsed to the ground. He dropped the
lantern that quickly fired the dry hay. Kills White Bear let
go of the stallion so that he could stamp out the flames.
The other warrior kept anxious watch out the door. Kills
White Bear then heard the barking of angry dogs and yelling of frightened men. The entire village came alive under
the light of the roaring fire.

When Kills White Bear realized that the flames were out
of control, he called to his accomplices to take what horses
they could and get out. Fire quickly blocked the way they
had come. The front doors were the only safe escape.

When they stepped out, eyes burning from the smoke,
Kills White Bear saw that a line of men with rifles, *viejos*
and boys, had formed. Behind them, women and children
were scrambling for the security of the big house. A man,
an older Méxicano, was herding them in as quickly as he
could. Then the men fired at them. A bullet caught the
young Quahadi square in the forehead and he fell to the
earth without crying, dead. Kills White Bear was stunned.

He stayed behind his horse for protection, waiting for his
eyes to readjust to the darkness after the blinding flash of
light from the guns. At the sound of the rifles, the other
warriors dashed into the courtyard and bore down on the
scrambling Méxicano defenders. They killed them all in a
hail of arrows just as the big doors, quickly studded with
shafts, were sealed shut. Kills White Bear called to them
to get out of the light as a voice boomed from atop the
stone house.

"¿Qué quieren?" it demanded.

Kills White Bear was in the process of answering *"Un
caballo, nada más,"* when one of the young warriors answered for him.

"Sus vidas," he yelled angrily in Spanish. Before they
could release the next volley of arrows, several shots rang
out from the rooftop. Most of the Nokonis and Quahadis
fell where they stood. The Méxicanos began frantically reloading their rifles. Kills White Bear, knowing that he
could never leave his wounded behind to be hanged, rode
bareback, one hand holding the horse's mane, into the
courtyard.

Two of his men moaned for help. He reached for them,

instructing them to lay across his horse's back. Then he looked up again to the roof to see how much time he had. There was a woman, a beautiful woman with long black hair, dressed in a long cotton gown whose tail blew in the breeze. She shouldered a large rifle and aimed it directly at him. He loaded the wounded on his horse and scrambled for the shadows.

His ear rang from the roar of her rifle. He felt the sharp, piercing pain in his upper back. Then warm blood, his blood, flowed across his bear claw scars, his breechcloth, and onto the white back of the horse. He looked briefly at his chest and saw the terrible wound she'd made.

He rode on the best he could. The Méxicanos, he thought, would not dare pursue them until daylight. They had no way of knowing the Nemenuh raiders were so few. When he was far enough away, he dismounted. One of the young braves was already dead. The other was nearly so. His own bleeding had not yet stopped. The horses had scattered in the commotion. He instructed the one remaining warrior to wait where he was, and Kills White Bear would return with a horse for him to ride. When he did, the man was leaning against a tree, dead. In his bloody hand was the page-less bison-hide shield. A bullet hole had pierced its center. He'd spent his last moments coughing up his own blood.

Kills White Bear took what he needed and mounted the dead man's horse. He headed east for the Cibilo, growing fainter by the minute. He knew he would have to stop soon and rest. Otherwise, he would bleed to death. He took some herb grass that every Nemenuh warrior carried, stuffed it gently into the wound, and rode on.

In his mind burned the image of a raid gone bad and the faces of the dead and dying warriors who'd followed him. It should've been so easy, he thought, done without a care. And then his thoughts turned to the repercussions of disaster. When word got out, it would be the first smudge on his name. There would first be the stigma to overcome, then the shame. The families of the dead would curse him forever. Their anger would follow him like a shadow. He must go to their families and tell them that their sons and husbands lay dead from Méxicano bullets. He must tell them that he'd left their bodies behind, that they were not buried properly, and admit to them that because of him their spirits would roam the earth forever. The thought of it chilled him more than the loss of his blood.

He saw also the unmistakable face of that determined Méxicano woman. In all the chaos he'd focused on her beauty and not the flash of her angry eyes. It was a deception that caught him off guard, causing him to pause just long enough to make an easy target for her. He marked that face well, burning its image into his tormented brain. He would remember. And he would come back and trade pain for pain.

Chapter Eight

By mid-morning on that fourth day, Remy arrived at the Cíbolo, the eastern-most boundary of El Rincón. There were supposed to be rancheros all over this part of the country, but he was damned if he could find one. No matter now. He was within a day or so of Rancho de la Cruz and home. He'd stick it out. He had no other choice.

His gut ached from hunger. He'd shivered most of the night from the cold, but at least he could do something about his thirst. He knelt at the bank of the stream, where the water formed a still pool, and drank water from his cupped hand like one of Gideon's chosen. His father had taught him that all predators hunted a water hole. Remy remembered that now.

The water was clear and fresh. It bathed his parched throat. When the rippling on the stream settled, Remy saw the reflection of a man, his face dried and weathered, the crowfoot lines around his dark eyes etched deeply, the first gray hair prematurely lining his temples as he remembered they'd lined his father's before him.

In a way it shocked him, the first signs of the years taking their toll. He was but twenty-four, yet he looked forty and felt older. The sun had done some of this, and the hunger. But his temper, he thought, was burning his hide right off his bones. Certainly it was wearing a hole in the sole of his boots. His feet ached; his heels burned from the blisters. All of these things, he felt, were a warning.

When, he wondered, would he learn to think things through before he shot off his own foot? How much more misery would he cause? Some day, he thought, his anger would get him killed. And now, he had so much to live for. It was a matter of control and he knew he didn't have it. He understood then how strongly his past ruled him, guiding every misspent deed. He felt damned.

He scattered that troubling image in the water with his chapped fingers and continued drinking. The water dripped between his fingers, spotting his chapparreras. When he had had his fill, he fell backwards into the soft grass and watched the clouds drift overhead until at last sleep came.

His eyes popped open when he felt a cold muzzle pressed against his nose. Before him stood the fuzzy image of an Indian. He placed one foot on Remy's chest. Remy struggled briefly but found that he could not move. This was it! he thought. At least it would come quickly. He watched in terror as the warrior cocked the hammer, then hesitated, wavering in the sun. The savage's eyes rolled back into his head and then he collapsed. Remy immediately snatched the rifle from his would-be killer's hands. The grip of the stock was sticky with fresh blood.

It was mid-afternoon before the warrior's eyes opened. Remy had never been so close to what he assumed was a Lipan Apache before. The man was well built and muscular, rather stocky in appearance, standing perhaps five foot eight or so, it was hard to tell. His skin, pitted by smallpox, was deep bronze. All facial hair, including eyebrows, had been removed. His thick black hair was shoulder length, tossing gently in the breeze, with the exception of the thick braid, wrapped in fur, that lay matted in blood across his chest, next to that awful wound. The part in his scalp was painted red, and a single Eagle feather, as decoration, flickered in the breeze. In his pierced ears he wore rings of silver. His face was painted half white, half black, with a lightning bolt on the darker side and a man's skull on the other. Despite his malicious intent, Remy thought he was magnificent.

The savage's black eyes, set widely in his almost oriental face, peered intensely at Remy as he hovered over a fresh spit. The man did not seem afraid. Remy had the Indian's rifle resting across his knee.

"Easy, fella," Remy said. "I ain't gonna hurt ya." When the man did not respond Remy asked him if he talked American. Nothing. Then he asked, *"¿Háblas Español?"* in his strange accent. The Indian answered, almost guttural, in an accent stranger still.

"Sí," he said.

"¿Puedes comer?" Remy asked, and he pointed at the freshly smoked venison. Remy had been lucky enough to stumble across a bedded whitetail doe at midday. The Indian shook his head no. Remy went to the creek and filled his hat. He handed it to the warrior, who drank ravenously as Remy watched on. Then he asked, "What tribe are you? *Los Lipanes?"* The man shook his head and moved his open hand and forearm in a wavering motion, like the letter "s." Quelepe had taught him long ago that this was the Indian sign for the Comanche. Maybe, he thought, just maybe, he should kill him. But that notion passed quickly. "What band?" he asked, because he'd heard there were several.

"Penateka."

Southern Comanche, Remy thought. The ones the settlers hated most. "We know them well," Remy said. *"¿Cómo te llamas?"*

"Mata Oso Blanco. ¿Y tú?"

"Fuqua," Remy replied, and then he extended his hand. Kills White Bear took it. Then Remy pointed to the man's chest. *"¿Qué pasó, hombre?"*

"Los Lipanes," he explained.

Remy looked more closely at the wound. "That shoulda kilt ya," he said. The Comanche shook his head as if, somehow, that wasn't possible.

Kills White Bear studied him a moment. He looked puzzled. "What kind of man are you?"

Remy laughed. "I was just askin' myself the same damn question when you poked that rifle up my nose."

"You dress like a Méxicano yet you look and speak like a white."

"Well now there ya go. I am a Méxicano but I'm also white. I'm half-blood French and Scottish, if that means anythin' to you."

Kills White Bear nodded his head. "Our fathers traded with the French." The way he'd said it made Remy think that for once he was acceptable. Kills White Bear paused a moment and then asked, "Where do you come from?"

"El Rincón. 'Bout a day's ride from here. West."

"You were born in that place?"

"Nope. I was born in America. Louisiana."

Kills White Bear nodded. Then his tone abruptly changed. "Will you kill me, Fuqua?"

Remy looked up at the sky, then back at the Comanche. "I thought about it," he said finally, "an' I ought to since you tried to kill me. But I don't think so. The reason I'm in this predicament now is 'cause I killed somethin' I shouldn't have." Then he added, "Course you might die just the same."

"The soldiers?"

"The wound, hombre," Remy said, pointing to his chest. "It's bound to have nipped the lung."

The Comanche never looked away. "What will you do with me?" he asked.

"Whatever you want. I don't have a horse. You don't have a rifle. Not anymore. But I'll take you where you want to go. Within reason, of course. You're southern Comanche. Your people aren't far, I expect."

"They're camped at the *Tsoko-ka-ahi-humo* River."

"That's a new one on me."

Kills White Bear searched for the words. "The Méxicanos call it Río San Sabá."

"Now that one I know," Remy said. "I bin up there, Kills White Bear. I know the country. I could take you." Remy explained that his family did not live far away. He would borrow White Bear's horse and go for fresh mounts, food, and maybe an escort. It was, as Remy put it, a matter of trust. He had given his word that he'd return. He intended to keep it.

Kills White Bear told Remy that it was not wise to travel west. The Lipans were out there somewhere, searching for him. Kills White Bear, he told him, was a great warrior among his people and therefore a great prize. They would surely kill Remy, recognize the horse, and backtrack to him. "Besides," he told him, "if I do not get back to the medicine man soon, I'll die." If Remy truly wished to help him, Kills White Bear said, it must be now. Remy said he understood and then asked him what should be done first.

Kills White Bear explained how to fashion a travois. They used the green hide of the doe Remy had killed, along with his chaps and a couple of sturdy cedar posts Remy clipped with White Bear's tomahawk. He lashed the travois to the Indian pony and helped Kills White Bear situate himself on top of it. He covered him in his bear hide. It was then that Remy saw the scalps hanging from it. Some of them, he was certain, were white.

"Don't be gettin' no ideas, now," he said. "I'd like to keep my hair for the wintertime. An' no tricks, Kills White Bear. I'll kill ya if'n ya try." He meant it.

Kills White Bear managed a smile despite his obvious agony. "You'll be safe," he assured him.

Remy briefly checked that all was secure and then said, "But will you? We've got to swing wide of Béxar. The garrison'll hang you on general principles. They finally hanged Black Heart last year." He swung his leg over the horse, settling into the strange Indian saddle. Black Heart was also said to be Penateka. "Did you know 'im?" Remy asked.

"Well," Kills White Bear answered. They rode on.

Chapter Nine

Remy crossed the Cíbolo near its Santa Clara Creek fork. Next came the steep, shady-banked Guadalupe, and from there he bore west northwest. Remy paused when Kills White Bear's wound began to seep. He removed the grass, washed the pink flesh with clear, spring water, and then rewrapped it, under Kills White Bear's instructions, with the last of the Indian herb. He ground some of the smoked venison with a stone and the Comanche ate a little. Three times that first day, Kills White Bear had called to him to stop. He'd seen a plant or a root they could use, and Remy dug them up. Sometimes they ate them raw. Some were to be boiled into strange teas. Others he plastered to the wound.

At night the Indian's fever burned. Remy was up caring for him, pouring water down his parched throat, wrapping him in what clothing he had, stoking the fire to warm him. At dawn the following day, with the bleeding again stopped, they rode on.

Before noon, Remy came across riders herding a drove of mustangs east. The Comanche suggested that they avoid them, but it was already too late. They had been seen. When the riders came closer, Remy saw that he did not recognize any of them. They were rough, hard-eyed, and dirty. Their buckskins were worn smooth with wear and human sweat; dirt was ground into their coarse skin like tattoos. They were the kind of men Austin hated to see in this country. Remy hated to see them, in particular, right now.

"Mornin'," Remy said as the riders closed the distance between them. He looked over their catch. "Looks like ya'll done all right."

"Fair," one answered, spitting a stream of tobacco juice onto a flat rock. He squinted. "Where yew headed out here all alone?"

Remy motioned to the travois. "My guide got hurt. I'm takin' 'im home."

The man's eyes shifted from him to Kills White Bear. "Is that a fact? What kind of injun is yo 'guide,' friend?"

Remy wasn't quite ready for that. "Caddo," he lied after a moment's hesitation, knowing that his expression didn't look quite right.

"Caddo?" The man said as if startled, and then gawked at his partners with a tight-lipped smile. "You're goin' the wrong way, ain't ya?" he said. The others laughed. "Only Comanche," he said, waving his arm west across the hills, "live yonder way."

Remy grew apprehensive. "I'm just goin' where he tells me," he said, and he left it at that.

"Let's just have a look-see," the man said. Remy heard him click his jaw twice, and then his horse walked around to the travois to afford the rider a better view. When he had it, he dismounted and started looking all around.

Remy smelled trouble. "What're you doin', Mister?" he asked.

"I'm lookin' for a tree big enough to hang this son of a bitch. He's Comanche and you know it." He untied the lariat that hung from his pommel.

"Leave 'im be, Mister," Remy snapped. "He ain't done nuthin'."

The man never stopped his preparations. "Oh, he's done sumthin', kid. Ain't he boys?" The others nodded. They remained mounted. Cheap, dirty rifles rested across the pommels of their saddles.

Remy said the only thing that came to mind. "I'm Remy Fuqua. Son-in-law of Don Carlos Amarante de la Cruz. That Indian's mine."

The man paused a moment, squinting in the eastern sun at Remy. "Well hell, if you're related to the Meskins, maybe we're supposed to bow or sumthin', huh?" He did so, and motioned for the others to do the same. "Now we'll hang 'im."

Remy popped the rifle up from his lap, cocked the hammer, and brought it to bear on the man on foot. "Is his life worth yours, Mister? 'Cause that's what it's gonna cost ya."

The man looked more puzzled than afraid. He motioned to the others not to do anything rash. Then he turned back to Remy, who was checking to see that his second pistol was available. "What the hell you doin', man! He's just a greasy, dirty-assed Comanche. Ain't yew seen them goddamn scalps? They're *white*! Yew shoot me over him and them others'll kill you dead." He snapped his fingers. "Just like that."

Remy's eyes slipped across to the others. They all looked ready enough, but also slow, liquored-up, and stupid. The man to kill first was the one who did the talking. With the others, he might have a chance. He wouldn't surrender the Comanche. Just the same, he moved his finger out of the trigger guard as a show of good faith. "I don't want no trouble," he told the man, "but he's mine. You

let us ride on, there won't be any." He pointed the barrel
of the Comanche's rifle to their stock. "Ya'll got some fine
horses there, worth good money. Jes' take 'em and go."

Remy used what time they gave him to put a little distance between himself and them. He put his spurs to the
horse and walked on slowly at an angle. His eyes never left
them as they rattled among themselves. He stopped on the
high ground above them, where the roots of oak trees caressed lichen-spotted limestone, a place he thought he
could defend if it came to that, and waited.

Soon they moved on and he did also, in the opposite
direction. They did not follow. Once they were out of sight,
he bore hard east, riding parallel to them, the one direction
he thought they would not think he'd travel in case they
doubled back.

ℏ

Despite his delirium, Kills White Bear's directions were distinct and accurate as they picked their way through the low
hills over the next two days. They crested a long rise and
Remy made out maybe three hundred teepees in the distance. As they approached camp, Remy was accosted by a
pack of skinny dogs, then he heard the war whoops of
the warriors who dashed out to threaten him. When they
observed that it was Kills White Bear that he carried, they
took Remy's rifle from him, led his horse into the village
and sent word ahead.

The crowd assembled around Kills White Bear parted
when the old, bald-headed man arrived. He appeared
angry. He stripped the hide from Kills White Bear's body
and inspected the wound personally. He had harsh words
for his warrior, who was clearly apologetic for someone so
close to death. Then, in the arms of boys, Kills White Bear
was carried away.

The chief turned and looked at Remy, studying him.
Remy had never seen a stranger Indian. The old man spoke
to him in Spanish, thanking him for bringing Kills White

Bear home. He said that he was called Maguara. He asked
if Remy was hungry and Remy said he was. Maguara called
for others to take his horse when Remy dismounted. He
was led to a large lodge in the center. Food and drink were
brought and laid at his feet, as was his rifle. He was told
to rest.

It was dark when he awakened. He startled at first, for
he'd forgotten where he was. He had the sense that others
were with him. When he opened his eyes, Maguara and
others sat cross-legged before him, passing a pipe back and
forth in silence, waiting.

"You are called Fooh-quay?" Maguara asked quietly.
Remy nodded. "Did I say it correctly?" and Remy replied
that he had. They passed him a buffalo horn full of clear
water from the river and he drank it all. When he dropped
the horn from his lips, he saw that Maguara was staring at
him through a veil of smoke.

"What do you want in trade for the warrior you captured?" he asked.

Remy answered immediately. "Nuthin'. I didn't capture
him, I just found him."

Maguara looked at the others as if to say "I told you
so." Then he excused them all. When they had gone, the
old chief began to speak.

"Kills White Bear tells me that you're some sort of a
Méxicano white man. What is that?"

"I'm an American," Remy explained. "But I live with
the Méxicano Father now. I took one of his daughters as
a wife."

Maguara nodded. "You're a captive then?" he asked.

Remy smiled. "Sort of." Then Maguara reached out and
took his hand. Closing his eyes, he hummed a strange song
to himself and, when he finished, he sat in silence. Then he
opened his eyes, which glistened in the light of the crackling coals.

"Your heart is good," the old man told him, "but there
has been much pain in your life. Your parents are dead, as
is the mother who raised you. You're alone in the world,
afraid."

Remy was dumbfounded. "Who you bin talkin' to?"

Maguara said that Remy's spirit spoke truly to him. It

said that Fuqua was of a warrior nation in some strange, unhappy place, across the great water, where the winters are long and the people go hungry. Remy's soul is ancient, he said, older even than his own. It had seen much. It cried to him of white man against white man, tribe against tribe, wars that lasted the lives of a hundred men. One tribe consumed another and then was consumed by another still, again and again. Remy listened to all of this, fascinated.

Maguara continued. "Your soul passed from old man to new—a new language, a new way—but always the same spirit." Then he paused a moment. "You, Fuqua," he continued, "are the child of war; the blood of many lost nations, whose language is lost on the tongues of men, runs mixed in your veins." He paused as if to ponder what he'd said. "I had no idea," he continued, "that this was so of white men."

Maguara put his fingers to his temples and massaged them, closing his eyes again. "Where is this place you come from? I can see it clearly. But it's strange to me."

"It ain't Louisiana, I don't think," Remy said.

"Across the water and the air. Some other place. Some other planet maybe."

"Sounds like Europe maybe. Same planet."

Maguara looked at him and smiled. "It's not possible," he told him calmly. He'd seen most of his world but he'd never seen a place like this. It was truly alien, he said, his eyes wandering. Then he focused again on Remy and asked, "Tell me about the whites, Fuqua."

"Which whites we talkin' 'bout now?" Remy asked. "You've got me thinkin'."

"The whites that have come to our country. I want to hear all."

Remy did his best to rise to the challenge, picking up where he felt perhaps his spirit had left off. He relied on Robertson's writing, and also the writings of David Hume, Edward Gibbon and even Sir Walter Scott, whose works he adored. He began by explaining that he knew his own people best, but that his story was only one of millions. Maguara replied that any true information would be useful to him because the whites remained an enigma to him.

Remy began by telling the chief of the many nations of

the world, that millions of people, of all races, shared this planet with them. If he bored a hole in the ground like a gopher and drilled straight through, Remy told him, he would find several great nations. In other lands lived other great people. The Comanchería, Remy explained, was not a world unto itself, an open expanse of infinite grass, but rather an enclave on a spinning ball, surrounded by millions of people much like the Comanche, all of whom were closing in from all directions.

"Why don't we see them," Maguara asked, "if there are so many?"

"You soon will," Remy said. It was inevitable, the way of a populous world, Remy assured him. This, Maguara clearly could not believe. Yet Remy could see that the old chief did not think he was lying, but rather that he had been misinformed somewhere along the way.

Remy scratched the continents into the dust and the great oceans that lay between them. These barriers of water, he explained, were why white men and red had lived apart for so long. He drew an X on France, the country of his father's ancestors; and Scotland, that of his mother's. "We came from here," he explained, and Maguara nodded.

Then Remy spoke of Columbus and the Spanish, the discovery of the New World, the race among European powers to claim vast holdings in the West—the Comanchería "belonging" to the Spanish. He spoke of the wars in Europe that had decided the fate of America, of the Industrial Revolution and the rise of the middle class from serfdom. And then of the Reformation and religious struggles, the breach between old and new that forced so many to western shores. "Suffice it to say," Remy told him, "that the old world coveted the new for many different reasons."

"But who are you?" Maguara asked.

Remy answered that his blood was mixed. Of his French half, Maguara probably already knew much. The old chief expressed the opinion that, of the white races, the French understood the Comanche mind much best. Although the French had forced the Nemenuh's own migration by trading guns to their enemies, it turned out for the best, and the Nemenuh held no grudge. Remy agreed that Maguara's thoughts about the French were probably true, since they

were primarily interested in profitable coexistence with the
Indian nations. Remy explained that his father's family had
been exiled from what was then known as Acadia, now
called Nova Scotia, by the English King George II. Many
of the refugees had resettled in Louisiana. Remy's own father had been a trapper and trader and had known many
of the eastern nations, the Choctaw, Creek and Chickasaw.
More than that, Remy could not say. He explained that
he'd not known his father well and, as his spirit had told
Maguara, his father had died when Remy was but a boy.
Maguara said that he was sorry for his loss.

Remy then said that it was his mother's people, the
Scotch-Irish, that had shaped his life. He spoke of the
warlike Scottish border tribes, or clans—a mixture of
Dane, Gael, and Saxon, if one believed William Robertson. Of this hybrid race, his spirit had already spoken. Like
the Spanish and the French, the Scots had warred with the
English for generations. Ultimately they came to follow the
religious teachings of a man called Knox who taught them
that Catholicism, the religion of Spain and all of Europe,
was gaudy, stale, and selfish; that aristocrat and beggar
alike were both useless; and that industry—work—was everything. A man was not who he was but what he did.
Maguara agreed entirely but then asked him to explain
work. Remy did his best, but knew that he could never do
it to a Comanche's satisfaction.

Just the same, Remy said, the Scots' acceptance of a new
religion guaranteed that they no longer had a place in a
European world. Cromwell, who had beheaded the English
King, had exiled thousands of highlanders to Northern Ire-
land in order to kill two rebellious birds with one stone.
From then on, the clansmen were known as "Scotch-Irish."
On the Emerald Isle, Remy said, most of them found no
home. In search of another, they soon left for the wilds of
America. When Cromwell died and the English Crown was
restored, thousands more, fearing reprisals, also set sail.
Maguara said this was often the case when an old chief's
spirit left this world.

The clans were broken forever one hundred winters later,
Remy said, when Bonnie Prince Charlie was defeated at
Culloden Muir and hundreds of Scots were slaughtered as

they fell upon companies of English riflemen, with only clubs in their hands. Those that survived were banished forever, wandering. That, Remy said, was most likely why his spirit complained of restlessness.

The reasons the Scots left Scotland were all different, but the reasons they came to the New World were all the same. They wanted out from under the thumbs of kings, it was true, but most of all they wanted land.

Once in America, Remy explained, the Scotch-Irish had pushed straight through the cities and settlements away from order, structure, and taxes—in the hated image of Europe—heading instinctively for the frontier. They crossed one border and settled on another. Unlike the French and Spanish, who had come to make their fortunes and return, the Scotch-Irish exiles had come to stay. Yet they escaped from conflict only to find greater conflict still, and they welcomed it. The land suited them, and the price was never too high.

They settled first in the valleys of the Alleghenies and Appalachians, cleared the forests, burned out the stumps, warred with the Indians, and then planted Indian crops.

Against the backbone of the great mountains of the East, ethnic lines, which Remy called tribal, blurred. Those who found themselves on the frontier, whether English, Dutch, German, or otherwise, for the most part subscribed to the Scotch-Irish way of life. They were isolated and alone by choice yet curiously disciplined and of one mind. They were coming west. Remy said that the American Father did not encourage their migration, he just tried to keep up with them. The closer he came, the further west they went. To them, like the Comanche, freedom was everything.

The restless, rootless, and armed followed Boone through the Cumberland Gap into Kentucky and Tennessee and to the shores of the Father of Waters, and then on across into Missouri and Arkansas. This, Remy could tell, Maguara already knew.

Finally he spoke of Stephen Austin, the man of vision, who Maguara knew, and of the enticement of cheap Méxicano land to Scotch-Irish farmers in their perpetual search for rich black dirt. It was the one thing forever withheld from them in Europe and, when they'd finally claimed it for their own in America, they had not used it wisely. When the soil was exhausted, they were forced to move on.

"Why use it in such a foolish way at all?" Maguara asked him. "Like locusts."

"Because they know of no other way," Remy said, and he saw Maguara's expression grow heavy.

"It's what I hate most about them," the old chief scowled.

"I understand," Remy said, explaining that land to the whites was a tool, a commodity, as he understood the Comanche used the buffalo, and the Scotch-Irish found it just as plentiful.

"The buffalo multiply," Maguara said stiffly. "The land does not."

When Remy fell silent, Maguara urged him to go on. "What do you want to know now?" Remy asked him.

"Will the Méxicano and American Fathers war against each other?"

"Most likely," Remy said. It was no rare opinion. Most people he knew predicted conflict of one kind or another between the two. Remy said that the War of 1812 had removed the British threat from the struggling American nation. The Méxicanos had thrown off their Spanish masters about the same time. Both fathers had the taste of blood in their mouths, and liked it. They were now glaring at one another with Texas between them. It was considered only a matter of time before they were at each others' throats.

Maguara nodded as if pleased and then reminded Remy that, as the child of both nations, he would also find himself torn between the two. "Which world do you want, Fuqua?" the old man asked. "You know you can't have both."

Remy thought about this, as he often did. "I don't know," he said. He explained that he thought of himself as yet another mixture, a true Méxicano-American, but that his loyalty was not to some king or government but to the people he knew and loved and the land they owned together. Whatever happened, Remy said, would happen, and when it was over Remy and his family would carry on as they had.

Maguara said that he thought this was what he would do

as well, that he hoped for war between the whites and the Méxicanos, in which he would take no side. When it was over, regardless of who won or lost, the Comanche would still be standing in this place, defiant.

Remy then spoke more generally of the white villages where millions lived in stone houses, of factories, of the steam engine and the trains and boats it powered, the cotton gin and other machines that did the work of fifty, great ships where a thousand could live, machines of war and inventions of peace. At times, he drew figures on the walls of the teepee with a charred stick so that the old chief could see more clearly what he described. Maguara quietly listened, quite fascinated, to all this and more.

When Remy saw that the dawn was breaking, Maguara slapped him on his thigh and said, "Wondrous! Wondrous! What great things the whites can do!" Then he relit his pipe, yawned, and said calmly, "They are hopelessly lost. If they live like locusts, they'll die like locusts. A short plague to be endured, and it's done. The Great Spirit will destroy them if they don't destroy themselves first. They won't come again in my lifetime."

Chapter Ten

When the sun was up, Penateka women brought Remy his breakfast of boiled corn and pounded venison mixed with juniper berries. When he finished eating he stepped out into the daylight to mix with the Comanche in a way he knew that few white men had ever done.

The women, with their infants strapped to their backs on cradle boards, worked at their chores: preparing food, tanning hides with the brains of the buffalo or deer—Remy wasn't sure which—or patiently stitching buffalo hides together with deer sinew for new lodges. They wore dresses of carefully sewn buckskin, richly ornamented with fringe, beads, little bits of iron, tin and silver, no two alike. They wore their thick raven hair shorter than the men; often it was draped down over their shoulders, partly daubed with dyes. Their bronze faces were painted, their eyes accentu-

ated with red or yellow lines above and below the lids,
sometimes crossing at the corners. The insides of their ears
were painted red, and both cheeks typically featured a solid
red-orange circle or triangle. Their faces were wide, much
more so than the eastern Indians Remy had seen as a boy,
with thin-lipped, wide mouths. They had a rugged, almost
chiseled appearance, as if sculpted by nature herself to
adorn those barren hills.

Remy watched as an elderly woman lay several garments
next to an ant hill. When he asked her what she was doing,
she explained that the lice were a favorite food of the ants,
and after she walked away, Remy removed his own leather
jacket and spread it out next to the other skins.

The men were not nearly as active as the women. They
idled away the morning hours talking among themselves,
young boys sitting quietly at their feet, nibbling a candy
they said was made of bone marrow and mesquite beans.
Grimly Remy tasted it when they offered. It wasn't bad
at all.

Others tended to their weapons, fashioning bows out of
Osage orange, called *bois d'arc* by the French; strings were
made of deer sinew. Nearby bundles of wooden shafts, dogwood or mulberry, waited to be crafted into arrows. Piles
of owl feathers lay nearby. When Remy asked why they
did not use the feathers of the eagle or hawk, as he'd been
told they did, an old man said that such feathers, although
beautiful and born of hunters like themselves, were easily
ruined with blood.

On the plains above the village, the horse herd grazed.
Remy estimated perhaps more than a few thousand head.
Mounted teenage boys rode among them, watching. Others
raced about on horseback, practicing the arts of war. They
slipped gracefully to the animals' flanks, their bodies suspended by their ankles, which were bound to their saddles
by a rawhide noose, firing arrow after arrow at stumps.
Young children, perhaps only three years of age or so,
raced about effortlessly on the bare backs of mustangs.
Some of them spent all day mounted. Remy had never
seen such skill, not even among the best of Don Carlos's
young vaqueros.

Most of the young children went about naked. Older

boys wore breechcloths, leggings, and moccasins like Kills White Bear had worn. The chill of the morning air remained, so some of the older men wore full-length buffalo robes. Beneath them they wore hunting shirts of buckskin. The veil of woodsmoke from a hundred cook fires hung heavily over the San Sabá Valley; underneath it was the barking of dogs, the neighing of horses, the laughter of children, and the songs of busy women. Men calmly brushed their hair with brushes of porcupine quills. They seemed especially fond of the cracked mirrors they held in their hands. Everywhere the camp buzzed with activity.

And Remy had the privilege of seeing it all.

Remy had intended to spend a few days, at most, with the Penateka. He stayed more than a month. He worried about his family and missed them even more, but his boyish fascination anchored him in those golden hills. He did not believe that Picosa could've returned from Louisiana by now to report him missing. That thought alone gave him the peace of mind to stay.

His days were filled with mingling among the Indians, observing their normal activities, eating strange foods, learning Comanche words. On occasion, he looked in on Kills White Bear, who remained uncommunicative under the care of the medicine man. His fever had broken; the wound was healing, and his cough was gone. And yet he never spoke to Remy, turning his head away whenever he came. Concerned, Remy sought out Maguara to ask him of Kills White Bear's behavior.

"He's a mystic warrior," Maguara explained. "Very powerful, very special, but very strange. His vision requires him to keep to himself for some reason," he said. "But know that he remains grateful for your help."

Twice Remy was awakened before dawn to ride with a hunting party in search of buffalo. Maguara had explained that they took only what was needed for food this time of year. The great communal hunts took place late in the summer, when the bulls had grown fat from grazing on the prairie grass and no longer carried their winter coats, or late in the fall, when their hides were in their prime.

Nights he spent with Maguara, and other elders, talking. They called him *Chemakacho*, "the good white man." From them Remy learned that the name Comanche derived from the Ute word for enemy, *Komantica*. They called themselves Nemenuh, which Remy understood meant something like "human beings" or "the people."

Maguara explained tribal history, which fascinated Remy. They had followed the great buffalo, the symbol of their people, the gift of life, to the Texas plains, where the God Dog, the horse, was waiting for them. They'd been driven by their enemies to this place and embraced it. The God Dog, they told him, changed everything. First they had mastered the horse, then they had mastered the plains. They had fought the Lipan Apaches among others, the Spanish included, for possession of this land, and had defeated them all. After that, they had thrived in such a way as their Shoshone ancestors had never imagined. Families had grown into clans, and then clans into bands. The bands had formed a nation. The Nemenuh were wealthy beyond their wildest dreams. A Lakota chief might have fifty horses, Maguara said. A common Nemenuh warrior should have at least three hundred. The Nemenuh tongue, Shoshone, was the language of trade on the plains. If one wanted horses, he must come to the Nemenuh and speak Nemenuh words.

Maguara said that they lived by raiding, the privilege of a powerful and gifted people. It was, they said, a right given them by the Great Spirit. They no longer skulked in the mountains scratching a meal from the hard earth. They did not raise corn, beans, or melons, as did the Caddo or the Tonkawa and other "lesser" nations. This was beneath the warrior class. This, more than anything, told them that the farmer whites were weak at heart and could be defeated. Remy laughed when he heard this, but he quickly grew quiet when he noticed that none laughed with him. The look on the old chief's face told him it was time for more serious talk, and Remy waited.

"Will the whites come north?" Maguara finally asked him. His tone was solemn.

"I won't," Remy answered.

"And the others?"

"I don't speak for the others."

Maguara's eyes sharpened. "What would you guess?"

"They might," he said quietly. "They just might."

And when he heard those words, Maguara grew angry. It was as he expected, he said. He described his great frustration over the Méxicano refusal to draw the line. The Nemenuh would draw their own boundary, Maguara said, marked in Anglo blood.

The chief said the God Dog was the gift of the Great Spirit. The white man was his curse. If such a change was coming, it was unnatural and not welcomed. The God Dog made the Nemenuh strong; the whites made them weak. The disease they brought to his people—and he knew it came from them—had killed thousands. The Nemenuh had not forgotten, especially, he said strangely, his eyes glowing, the great warrior whose life Fuqua had saved.

Then the chief said that, after speaking with Fuqua, he could not think of the whites as men. Remy suggested that the opposite was also true, and this would certainly lead to tragedy. Remy said that the frontier had hardened the white's vision; it had made their blood run cold. When they had returned home to see their crops burned and heard their children cry for food, or when they had found their family, friends, and neighbors tortured and mutilated, it had aroused a hatred of Indians in them that the Comanche had never before faced. Such anger made them all the more dangerous.

These men would not fight the Indians as the Spanish and English had, Remy explained. They were not fools in red coats that marched in lines or who hid in presidios like rabbits under a log. They would fight them like evil brothers, tomahawk against tomahawk, blood against blood, an eye for an eye. The Nemenuh could kill a thousand, and a thousand more would soon take their place while a thousand waited for the chance.

Remy said he knew these people well. They could track a man like the Nemenuh wearing the same moccasins the

Nemenuh wore, eat off the land while on the warpath. Like the Nemenuh, they lived in one place and raided in another. They, too, had the God Dog, the great American horse, larger and faster than the Indian pony, and able to range greater distances. They also had the Kentucky rifle that could shoot one day and kill the next.

Remy reminded them that all the eastern nations that had warred against the whites were soon broken. Those nations, too, had once enjoyed the confidence of the Nemenuh. Their thread had been broken, and many no longer walked the face of Mother Earth.

These are things, Remy offered, that should be kept in mind in the years to come. It was not, he told them, an enemy's threat. It was only a friend's warning. Maguara had told him he had a warrior's spirit. That was news to Remy, and he did not wish to rely on it. He, like Austin, continued to hope for peace, and there were many others who felt the same. A way to live together must be found. Maguara thanked him, saying that peace could only come as it always had—through strength—and then he promised to kill the very next white man he saw, Remy, he assured him, excluded.

Remy finally asked if it were not true that the Nemenuh had taken the Comanchería from other weaker nations. Maguara agreed that it was, but that it was a natural process, the will of the Great Spirit. "Then," Remy said, "the Nemenuh, above all others, should understand when still stronger nations would try and take it from them. Would that not also be natural?" Remy asked.

Maguara responded by clutching a handful of dust in his swollen fingers.

"Let them try," he snapped angrily. Those who do not live with the Great Spirit, he said, will die by it. The Nemenuh were his children; their hands clutched his knife. The whites had been allowed to come west only to meet their fate. In the end, it would come quickly. He only hoped he lived long enough to see it happen.

Then he got up, allowing the dust to filter through his fingers, and left.

Chapter Eleven

Remy's wife and child were always on his mind. By now it was certainly possible that Picosa had returned from Louisiana. If so, Beatriz would be distraught. He explained this concern to Maguara and told him that as much as he'd like to stay, he must go. Maguara said that he understood, and arranged an escort of twenty warriors to see that *Chemakacho* arrived safely in Béxar. He gave him three of his best horses; strapped to the back of one of them was a parfleche bag filled with Spanish gold. Remy looked in on Kills White Bear one final time. It was then that the warrior gripped his hand in silent thanks. Remy left and mounted his horse.

By nightfall, they came to the Pedernales River. Without speaking to him, the warriors made his bed. They cooked their meat over open fires. A coyote howled in the distance. All movement ceased. Twenty ears turned in one direction. Then the coyote yelped a second time, and they went on about their business. Remy was glad to see that even the Comanche had to listen carefully to know whether it was actually a coyote or a Lipan war party.

The Comanche escort left him just north of Béxar. From there, Remy traveled without event to Rancho de la Cruz. The reunion with his family was cheerful. He sat with his arm around Beatriz, his young son squirming in his lap. As enlightening as his time with the Comanches had been, nothing could take the place of his family.

The entire hacienda was abuzz with the news of the raid. Some of the women were still dressed in black, mourning their dead. Remy was stunned by the violence that had come so close. He'd not believed the ranchero was vulnerable to such attacks when there were so many others not so easily defended. He began to wonder what tribe had taken the chance.

First they upbraided him for being gone so long. Then they embraced him in relief. He listened to Don Carlos boast of Beatriz's calm under fire, that she had killed two warriors and shot another, obviously their chief, who wore a white robe, but was never found.

Remy was shaken by these last details. When Don Carlos handed him an arrow taken from one of the dead Remy felt the hair bristle on the back of his neck. He studied it, and then snapped it in two. It was the same as those he'd seen being made in Maguara's camp.

Remy stitched the details together: the location where he'd found the wounded Comanche, Kills White Bear's reluctance to allow Remy to go for fresh horses, Maguara's anger when they first arrived at his camp. The savage had deceived him from the very beginning. All the mystery and enchantment of those past weeks evaporated before his deep regret that he hadn't killed the man who'd killed his people. He shuddered at the thought of how close Beatriz had come to harm, but he said nothing.

Kills White Bear had lied, and Remy wouldn't forget it. The next chance he had, he'd even the score.

Chapter Twelve

Maguara entered Kills White Bear's lodge and immediately waved the attendants out. He pressed the back of his hand against Kills White Bear's brow and then removed the hides to inspect his wound.

"I'm no longer angry with you, my son," he said calmly. "From talking with the man Fuqua, I think it's best that the raiding resume. Our treaty with the man Austin must hold, but I've spoken no such words with other white men. It's best that they fear us, I think, so that they'll someday come to us wanting to draw the line. You may stay with us and live as you have."

Kills White Bear thanked him. All was not lost if Maguara's eyes were now opened.

"This morning I was talking to my cousins, the crows," Maguara said, his casual tone piquing Kills White Bear's curiosity. Maguara might speak of foolish things, but he was not a fool. This was going somewhere. "You know they're such horrible gossips. They say Fuqua knew the people you raided. And knew them well. In particular, he knew the woman who shot you."

Kills White Bear looked at him blankly, knowing that Maguara knew, and yet he'd told no one.

"It was a woman, wasn't it?" Maguara asked.

"I was only looking for a horse," Kills White Bear lamented.

"And what you found instead was fate," Maguara said flatly. "The crows say that Fuqua plays heavily in your future, as well as ours. It was good that you brought him here to meet us; Maguara has learned much. But whether the meeting will come to good or evil, the crows did not say." His eyes narrowed. "You know how they are about their secrets."

Kills White Bear wasn't listening anymore. He resumed his brooding about the raid. Never had he known such failure. Or such pain. His wound was healing, but his agony was deep. Soon he would travel north and tell the warriors' families of their fate. This must be first, he thought.

Secondly, he remembered the face of that woman. Certainly he knew where she could be found. One day he would return. He promised himself that. Perhaps he owed Fuqua, but he owed no other. That Fuqua knew these people meant nothing to him. The same mistakes would not be repeated. He would not come to raid. He would come for revenge. The scars that were certainly forming on his chest and back would make two sides of this same oath.

He felt diminished by allowing a white man to save his life. It shamed him. Maguara's visit, he thought, was a part of that. The old buzzard had rubbed salt into a wound that was already burning. "My spirit guide warned me not to befriend a white man," he reminded his chief. "In my weakness, I disobeyed him. Had I been true to my vision, I should've killed Fuqua."

"That's funny," Maguara said as he turned to leave. "The crows say he should've killed you."

1832

Chapter Thirteen

Remy saw it coming. Anglo settlers now outnumbered Tejanos ten to one, and no one understood the resulting danger better than the Méxicano government. Remy sensed the ill winds gathering when General Mier y Terán decided at last that México must occupy Tejas militarily or lose it forever to Andrew Jackson, whose election to president in 1829 virtually assured an American policy of aggressive westward expansion.

Terán quickly reinforced the garrisons at San Antonio de Béxar, Goliad, or La Bahía, and Nacogdoches, and established new posts on the Brazos River, Galveston Bay, and another near the mouth of the Nueces. In an effort to further Mexicanize the province, Terán gave these new outposts Aztec names: Tenoxtitlan, Anahuac and Lipantitlan, respectively. General Terán explained that the military buildup was a measure of protection for the colonists, but Remy knew better.

Article 11 of Terán's new law of August 6, 1830, strictly forbade future immigration from the United States. It also enforced tariffs on imported goods, banned the further importation of slaves, and encouraged counter-colonization by Méxicano and European settlers. The Méxicano government, it seemed to Remy, had decided at last to slam the door on their restless white children.

Don Carlos and the other Tejanos, now a minority in their own land, welcomed the new law, and Remy couldn't blame them. They were tired of being overrun by foreigners. But the stunned Anglos, Remy knew, would have a different interpretation. A policy of benign neglect was being replaced by strict regulation of immigration and taxation, as well as the promise of armed enforcement of both, a situation American colonists had faced before under British rule.

Don Estévan quietly worked through diplomatic channels to earn an exemption from Terán's law for his and Green DeWitt's colonies. The articulate empresario successfully argued that the phenomenal growth of his colony was in accordance with the guidelines of Méxicano law and, therefore, should not be constricted in any way. Loyal Méxicanos—and his Anglo colonists were—should not be hampered in their efforts to settle the Méxicano frontier, he'd said. Terán admired and trusted Austin, and ultimately agreed with his arguments. Legal immigration resumed on a regulated basis. Slaves came with the immigrants as they always had, wisely presented to Méxicano officials as indentured servants. General Terán somehow endured it.

These concessions, Remy knew, calmed most of the older settlers, who felt cut off from their families and friends in the East. Yet illegal immigration continued. Hundreds of American "wetbacks" crossed the Sabine to squat on Méxicano soil. If there was to be bloodshed, Remy was certain that it would begin well beyond Don Estévan's influence, in East Texas.

General Mier y Terán erred in judgment when he appointed Captain John Bradburn to head the new and volatile post at Anahuac. Bradburn's reputation for arrogance had preceded him. In a very short amount of time, the native of Kentucky had alienated Anglo and Mexican alike. The state government of Coahuila y Tejas, in an effort to defuse the potential for conflict among its disenfranchised settlers, sent along surveyors and officials to grant land titles to proper applicants in troubled East Texas.

In response, General Terán angrily dispatched Colonel Bradburn to the scene. Bradburn promptly arrested the state officials, abolished the recently established municipality of Liberty, and arbitrarily redistributed the land grants as he saw fit. The conflict, as Remy understood it, was a matter of states' rights, guaranteed under the Méxicano Constitution of 1824, being usurped by an armed federal authority. Remy watched as panic gripped all of Anglo Tejas.

In May of 1832, Bradburn took control one step further. He declared ten leagues of the Tejas coast under martial law, and arrested several civilians whom he considered militant. One in particular was an attorney by the name of William Barret Travis. Remy knew Travis well from San Felipe.

Remy thought Travis was particularly obnoxious and, most likely, had provoked the commandant. Bradburn was probably wise to jail him, he thought, even without specific charges. Remy realized that Bradburn had nevertheless managed to make a number of enemies in Tejas, several of whom showed up in the ex-town of Liberty, rifles in hand.

Violence was avoided by Colonel José de la Piedras, the commandant of Nacogdoches. He demonstrated considerable diplomacy where Bradburn had shown none. Federal concessions followed, as did Bradburn's forced resignation.

However, a splinter group of about a hundred and sixty Anglos, unaware that Piedras had found a bloodless solution, attacked the garrison at Velasco at the mouth of the Brazos, ultimately defeating it. The surviving Méxicano troops marched back to Matamoros about the time the victorious Texians learned that the fire, much to their chagrin, had already been extinguished. The Anahuac War was over.

Unwanted and outnumbered, Colonel Piedras later abandoned Nacogdoches. The commandant of Tenoxtitlan on the upper Brazos did the same. The garrison of Anahuac was recalled in response to disturbances in the interior of México, where the civil war raged, and Velasco had been defeated. The ring around the Anglos dissolved. But Méxicano blood had been spilled in the process, and Remy braced for the government's retaliation.

What came instead was an invitation to a party.

Don Carlos read it with a look of disbelief and then tossed it on the sofa next to Remy.

"The Anglos," he said as if it pained him, "are slipperiest when wet. Colonel Mexía comes to put a rope around their necks and they ask him to dance." He sipped his brandy, thought a moment, and then said that both Remy and Beatriz should probably go. "If nothing else," Don Carlos said, "it will be interesting."

Remy read the invitation and smiled. It was, he knew, Don Estévan's work.

Remy, Beatriz, and Don Carlos then discussed events in México. Slippery alliances were the order of the day down there. Gómez Pedranza had been elected to the presidency in 1828. The loser, Vicente Guerrero, a mestizo, had organized a military coup. In 1829, Guerrero was forcibly removed by his vice-president, Anastasio Bustamante. It was Bustamante who had dispatched General Terán to Tejas. In 1832, Antonio López de Santa Anna Perez de Lebron, the pure-blood criollo responsible for repulsing the Spanish invasion of México in 1829, revolted with the *grito* of liberalism, and the young Republic was again engulfed in civil war.

Colonel Mexía, the *Santanista,* was in the middle of a campaign against the Bustamante supporter, Colonel Guerra, in Matamoros. When news of the Anahuac War reached his ears, Mexía immediately suggested the two opposing factions put their differences aside for the moment, join forces, and crush the Anglo revolt in Tejas as a matter of national interest. Guerra promptly agreed, and four hundred men marched together for the Brazos.

Don Carlos, who claimed he was not a political man, welcomed Mexía's arrival. The law in México began at the top and filtered downwards, not the opposite direction, as he said the Anglos would soon learn. The clergy, landowners, and criollo elite battled regional factions and each other for power in México. It was a game, Don Carlos said, that the Anglos had not yet been invited to play. Colonel Mexía would give these mischievous children a good spanking, and Don Carlos thought it was about time.

Remy knew that Stephen Austin was in Saltillo, the capital of the state of Coahuila y Tejas, at the time Mexía organized his campaign. He rushed to Matamoros, met with the colonel, and then sent word ahead to organize a grand reception. For reasons obvious enough to Don Carlos, Austin had seen to it that Remy, among many others throughout the state, was invited.

"Are you sayin' that he wants to use me?" Remy asked his father-in-law.

"Of course," Don Carlos answered wryly. "And I'm grateful that *somebody* has at last found a way."

Remy and Beatriz rode to the sound of the thunderous cannonade. It led them to Brazoria, where hundreds had already gathered to honor Colonel Mexía and his army. The sound of the fiddles hung in the humid, coastal air of midsummer. Remy tethered the horses and then waded together with his wife through the crowd. They passed under the banner that said "Santa Anna Dinner and Ball" and caught Don Estévan's eye. He waved them forward and introduced them to the guest of honor.

Don Estévan told Colonel Mexía that this particular marriage signified the hope he had for Tejas's future. The Colonel said that he was pleased to meet them both, that Don Carlos, though not a close friend, was indeed an acquaintance and a man of excellent reputation. He rose from his chair, excused himself, and asked Beatriz and Remy to join him.

Out of Don Estévan's earshot, Colonel Mexía said he was interested in Beatriz's opinion as to recent events. Don Estévan, he told them, had assured him that the rebellion was solely against Bradburn, Mier y Terán, and their president, Bustamante. They'd all pledged their allegiance both to the Méxicano Constitution of 1824 and the man that promised to restore and honor it, General Santa Anna. What, he asked, did Beatriz think of all this?

Beatriz looked at Remy before she answered. His nudge encouraged her to speak her mind even though he sensed that he wouldn't like it. Beatriz, like all of the Tejanos, understood the problem very well.

"Certainly," she began, "Bustamante's efforts to control Anglo immigration had precipitated the revolt. If Santa Anna and his federalists were to gain control of the government and stabilize it, much of the immediate danger of revolt would be gone." Here she paused. "But the real problem goes much deeper," she added, and she left it at that.

Remy rolled his eyes. Mexía asked her to explain.

She began by saying that she had an Anglo husband and loved him dearly. But he had acclimated himself to the Tejano way of life, and in doing so, was the exception. Most of her people, she said, meaning Tejanos, believed that General Terán's course was the correct one to follow. His plan was not tied to his political connection to Busta-mante, but to the greater interests of the Méxicano nation.

"After a decade in Tejas, the Anglos," she continued, "are not Méxicanos. Most do not even speak Spanish. They take oaths of Catholicism but practice the Protestant faiths. In short, they carry on as Americans in México, and, if nothing else, the revolt has demonstrated how they would react when forced to change." She caught her breath as Remy caught his.

"I know I should make an example of some of these people," Colonel Mexía said, twirling his moustache. "At the very least, I should jail the leaders. But it's hard to do when they've thrown me such a nice party."

Her dark hair glistened silver in the sun, the breeze tossed it gently across her face as she swept it back. "The party will soon be over," she said quietly.

Colonel Mexía then asked her what she thought should be done. Beatriz said that her father and the other ranche-ros had always questioned why the Anglos had been al-lowed to immigrate in such waves. If the government had wished to build a wall against American encroachment, they'd clearly used the wrong materials. General Terán was right to insist that future colonization, if needed, should be by Europeans or southern Méxicanos.

She said that the argument that the Anglos created a buffer against Indian attacks was ludicrous. Austin had made a treaty with the Comanches for his colonies. The savages simply by-passed white settlements and raided the rancheros as they always had, hers included. The horses and mules they stole were traded in America for guns and whiskey. In short, she said, the Americans, though industri-ous, created far more problems than they solved. Despite the appearance of such a nice party, trouble waited for the government—any government—in Tejas.

Remy knew that Beatriz was worried about offending him. Instead, he could not have been prouder of his wife.

She spoke her mind and that of her people. He put his arm around her and pulled her close. Finally, a thin smile emerged on her lips.

Colonel Mexía said all of this was well known, but for the moment there was little to be done, with the government in shambles. He must return to the interior soon to take his part in the federalist revolution. For now, he said, Tejas appears calm. They had declared themselves loyal to Santa Anna and the constitution and that was what he had come to see. But Santa Anna would be back, and the Tejas problem would be addressed.

"Please tell your neighbors this," he asked her. "Tell them to be patient. They are not forgotten."

After Colonel Mexía had left them, Beatriz told Remy that she didn't feel comfortable around so many Anglos. Remy said that he didn't feel comfortable at parties in general, so he agreed to take her back to de León's for a short visit and rest and then home from there.

Austin had a number of questions for him, some of which Mexía had asked them; but more about what the Tejanos in Béxar thought about state reforms. Remy said that just about everyone agreed that Tejas should separate from Coahuila. It wasn't just the 800 leagues of distance between them. It was the difference in the land, the way of life, different people and different problems. Most of the Tejanos thought that the federal government should establish a court system, schools, better roads, provide priests—those sorts of things. This would all most likely come, he said, when the whites quit shooting at tax collectors, because the money had to be raised somewhere.

"They paid taxes back home," Remy said, "and sooner or later they'll have to pay 'em here."

Austin said that with peace restored, the time had perhaps come for representatives throughout the state to meet and organize. They should prepare a strategy for the federal government to draft and approve a state constitution.

Remy knew the answer to that. He said that most of the Tejanos would be reluctant to attend any organized initiative. To make demands on the government the day after an armed revolt was perhaps, at best, a little premature. Don Carlos and the others wanted change, certainly, but they would never force the issue by attacking the garrisons as the white settlers had. They were more patient than that.

Austin said that from here on, all would be dead calm in Tejas. But the problems the state faced must be addressed if further violence were to be avoided. Still, he admitted that events of late had caused him much worry. After years of detachment from Méxicano politics, circumstances had forced him to take sides in the civil war. He was deeply concerned about the consequences, especially if Santa Anna should meet with defeat.

"I would think you would be, Don Estévan," Remy told him. "You've committed yourself."

He nodded toward his wife. "We," he said proudly, "have sympathies." Beatriz squeezed his hand because he was speaking of himself at last as a Tejano. "But in México alliances are always dangerous. You learn you're on the wrong side when they slip a rope aroun' your neck. Don Carlos says that on the frontier it's best to allow political storms to blow over and just try to keep your roots in the soil. There's a lesson in that for all of us, I think. Immigrants ain't runnin' the show aroun' here."

Austin ground his teeth; his jaw set. Remy could see that he'd struck a nerve.

"It was not my wish to declare for Santa Anna, Fuqua. I'm not by nature a political animal. I was forced into this."

"Let's just hope," Remy said, "that it don't force you out. Santa Anna looks like a safe bet. You might get lucky."

"If so, it would be the first time," Austin said.

At breakfast, Don Carlos arrived at the table to find Remy and Beatriz cuddled up like doves in the spring. He glanced at Remy as his coffee was poured and rolled his eyes.

Remy beamed. Don Carlos looked at him as if he were out of his mind. "What is it now?"

"Beatriz has news," Remy said.

"And what could that be?" he asked. "You two are off to storm the capital?"

"I'm pregnant, Papá," she said.

Don Carlos stared first at Remy, then at his daughter. A smile grew on his lips. "*¡Dios mío!* And I thought you two were fighting up there."

"Don't be silly, Papá," Beatriz told him. "I'm a month along, at least."

Señora Vásquez must have heard it all, and hugged Beatriz, a chicken egg in her hand. A moment later, with Beatriz's approval, she rubbed the egg on her bare abdomen whispering Catholic prayers mixed with Indian chants. Then she broke it in a bowl, blew in it, and brought it in front of a peering eye. "It's a girl," she announced, her face glowing. "Most certainly."

Don Carlos clasped his hands in elation. "*¡Brava, Beatriz!* At last! Someone sweet to comfort me in my old age." He clutched his daughter to his chest, reaching around her back to shake hands with Remy. Then Don Carlos turned to the Señora Vásquez, and asked, "Where did you learn how to do that anyway, you evil woman? I'll be keeping a close eye on you from now on."

A letter arrived for Remy after Christmas that year. It was from Jim Bowie, the husband of Vice-Governor Veramendi's daughter. Remy read it and then handed it to Don Carlos.

"Señor Jim wants me to come to Béxar," Remy said.

"What on earth for?"

"He's got a friend that wants to meet Maguara. He wants me to take him."

Don Carlos's eyes scanned the letter; then he handed it back. "Don't do it, Remy."

"Why not? I'm welcome at Maguara's camp. Bowie knows that nobody else is."

"Do you not see the name of his friend, for God's sake. It's the American, Sam Houston."

"Never heard of him."

Don Carlos rolled his eyes. "Think about it," he said. "What business do the Americans have with the Comanche? It's trouble, Remy."

"It damn sure is," Remy agreed, tossing another log on the fire. "Especially if I meet up with my old friend, Kills White Bear."

He started up the stairs to tell Beatriz that he'd be gone a month to the San Sabá country.

1834

Chapter Fourteen

Remy monitored developments within the Méxicano government closely. He had questions for everyone. He learned that the usurper Bustamante's centralist coalition had eroded before the liberal onslaught of Antonio López de Santa Anna. In a move that astounded Remy and everyone else, Santa Anna returned Gómez Pedraza to the presidency from which he'd once fled, in order to complete his rightful constitutional term. Santa Anna was hailed as a national hero of the liberal cause, which struck Remy as especially ironic, since it was Santa Anna who'd run Pedraza out of office in the first place. Don Carlos looked at it this way: in Méxicano politics, short memories were the most convenient.

Santa Anna rode a wave of national popularity, Tejas included, that swept the presidential election of 1833. As his running mate he selected Gómez Farías, a man of impeccable credentials who was committed to populist reform. The Méxicano masses had their champions at last.

However, Santa Anna, citing reasons of health, retired

to his estate at Jalapa, leaving Vice-President Farías to implement the drastic reforms. Many hailed the chief executive's selflessness when it came to government, yet Don Carlos smelled a rat. He recognized that Farías had to contest the influence of the landowners, the church, and the military for his program to be successful. Farías, it seemed, dreamed of a true republic.

To achieve it, Don Carlos knew Farías had to step on the toes of the powerful elite of México, toes that had quietly prodded Santa Anna along the bumpy road to office. No one knew this better than their president, whose retirement was more likely a matter of convenience than illness. Santa Anna had scooted off the hot seat to wait. Farías, Don Carlos predicted, was about to be sacrificed on the bloody altar of the Méxicano Republic.

Don Estévan had moved swiftly, confident of a liberal victory. Disaster had been avoided with Colonel Mexía, and Santa Anna, the states' rights federalist, had come to power. Now the time was ripe to address the problems of Tejas.

A convention was called in 1832, another the year following. A list of reforms, and the reasons they were necessary, was prepared. When it came time to present the finished product to the President of México, Austin was selected, along with respected Tejano rancher Juan Seguín. In the end, Austin went alone in April of 1833.

Don Estévan met with a succession of frustrating delays. Vice-President Farías was far too busy with national reorganization to focus on the problems of a remote northern state. The fledgling government was already engulfed in chaos when a cholera epidemic crippled the capital city. Remy received news that Austin's impatience had eventually alienated the bookish Vice-President Farías. Austin had warned Farías that Tejas would not submit to further delays. Farías considered this, as any politician would, as a threat. Austin's future efforts were then coolly directed to President Santa Anna. These two got along well enough when they finally met in November of 1833.

Santa Anna sanctioned most of the Tejas reforms. He approved the repeal of Terán's hated immigration law of 1830 and promised improved mail service, reform, and lib-

eralization of the tariffs, and even agreed to consider trial
by jury. Separation from Coahuila, however, was impossible
at this time because the constitution of 1824 clearly required a territory to have eighty thousand residents before
it became a state, and Tejas—not counting savages, and
who could—was still some fifty thousand short. President
Santa Anna, he assured Austin, was a constitutional man.

While Santa Anna was glad to institute much needed
changes, he was also glad to send four thousand Méxicano
troops to Tejas to ensure that they were carried out. The
measure assured Don Carlos that Santa Anna did not trust
the Anglos any more than previous administrations had.

It seemed to Don Carlos that Don Estévan was uncharacteristically aggressive in his mission to México. While he
was there, apparently in a state of frustration, he'd written
a letter to the San Antonio de Béxar ayuntamiento, the
town council, detailing his disappointment in their failure
to take an active part in the conventions. The note, which
Don Carlos himself had seen, said very plainly that with
the national government so engulfed in turmoil, Tejas
should be prepared to act on its own.

Don Carlos explained the council's position well enough.
In México, he said, the initiative and referendum so charac-
teristic of the American frontier had another name. It was
called plot and intrigue. One could court the government
for favor, Don Carlos said, but not insist on it. It was folly,
the *ayuntamiento* had written Austin, to follow one revolution with another. It was additionally unwise, Don Carlos
said, to provoke the national government, regardless of its
personnel, at any given time. Patience, as always, was the
key, and the accursed Anglos would just have to find
some somewhere.

Nevertheless, it was regrettable, Don Carlos said, that
the Béxar *ayuntamiento* had forwarded a copy of Austin's
letter to the state authorities. From there it went on to
México City, until at last it reached Farías's hands. Austin's
statement was, plain enough, treason. Farías was outraged,
ordering the empresario's immediate arrest. On January 3,
1834, as Austin, en route to Tejas, walked into the office of
the commandant general in Saltillo, the order was executed.

Chapter Fifteen

Remy leaned against the corral fence watching Carlito's progress with the pony. Don Carlos was at his side yelling encouragement as Picosa finally let loose of the long reins. Carlito gracefully raced the animal around the corral, leaping well above the little jumps. "Bravo, Carlito," Don Carlos said. Remy said nothing.

"What troubles you, Remy?" Don Carlos asked.

"The same that ought to be troublin' you." He kept his eyes on his son.

"Austin's arrest?"

"That's just the beginning," Remy said. The rest was the rise of the War Dog party. There had always been a faction among the Anglos who wanted Tejas separation—not as a separate Méxicano state, as most desired, but as an American one. Possibly even a separate nation. The older, better-established immigrants, loyal to Austin, and as such, loyal to México, kept quiet, as Don Estévan himself had advised. But the War Dogs, in the empresario's absence, had the excuse they needed to openly organize an armed revolt. Their greatest obstacle languished in a thirteen by sixteen windowless cell.

Remy grew anxious in the weeks that followed the news of Austin's troubles. Don Estévan had gone to México City to prevent a revolution. His arrest, Remy believed, guaranteed one. Where would Carlito's place be, as a half-breed, when the changes came? Try as he might, he could not help but worry.

"They'll reach an understanding, Remy," Don Carlos assured him. "Then they'll let him go. Troops are coming to keep order in the meantime. Little will change."

"You don't see what I see," Remy said. "You don't know what I know."

Don Carlos looked at him and then said, "And who would want to?"

This was a typical response, Remy thought. It frustrated him, as did so many things Don Carlos and the other Tej-

309

anos did. They were oblivious. War was coming. He saw it
clear enough. Soon they'd be worried, too.

Don Carlos changed the subject. "The boy rides well,
eh?"

"Well enough. He's ready for a horse, don't you think?"

"It's too soon, Remy. He's only four."

"We'll see," Remy said, and he ordered Picosa to saddle
a mare, an older one, for the boy. Then he waved to Carlito, who rode over to the corral.

"You want to ride a big horse, like your pa?" he asked
him.

The boy smiled. The sweat on his temples wet the dark
curling hair of his head. He was beaming. *"Sí, Papá,"* he
said. Picosa led the mare to the center of the corral and
waited.

Don Carlos pressed forward. "Ride your pony for now,
Carlito. Abuelito will pick you a fine horse for your next
birthday."

Remy shot him an angry glance and then turned back to
his son. "Till then we'll ride this one, all right?"

Remy picked up the boy and set him on his shoulders.
Then he walked over to the horse and placed him astride
the saddle. It pained Remy that Carlito looked apprehensive. "You want to do this?" he asked him, and the boy,
whose expression had gone a little pale, slowly nodded his
head. Then Remy told Picosa, who held the reins, to begin.
Remy returned to his place beside his father-in-law. All
went well. Remy never looked at Don Carlos.

After ten minutes, the boy's assurance returned. Remy
told Picosa to hand the boy the reins, and out of the corner
of his eyes he saw Don Carlos shake his head. Picosa
balked. "Do it!" Remy said, and Carlito rode the mare
around the corral.

Remy smiled at his son's success. When he finally looked
at Don Carlos, he saw him smiling as well.

"He does have a way with them, doesn't he?" Don Carlos admitted.

Then Remy opened the gate and said, "Let's see how
much." That was the end of Don Carlos's smile.

The horse moved instinctively toward the open pastures.
Remy let it pass. Carlito did well enough, until the horse

moved into a trot of its own accord. Carlito's little body bobbled in the saddle. Out of fear he let the reins fall and gripped the horn. The reins tangled with the front feet of the horse, and tripped her. She buckled one knee, and Carlito flew over her neck, flipped in the air, and landed on his back. The boy screamed.

"Happy now?" Don Carlos said.

Picosa and Don Carlos ran over to the boy. Remy walked. He'd seen it well enough. Carlito had landed safely in a thick mat of grass. He wasn't hurt. It'd just scared him. When he got there, Don Carlos held the boy in his arms. Tears streamed down his dusty cheeks. Remy ran his fingers through his son's dark hair, pulling it back out of his eyes.

"You ain't hurt," he said. His son looked at him, then back to Don Carlos. Remy reached for his jaw and turned his face back to his. "I'll tell ya when you're hurt, Carlito. You ain't hurt." And then Remy looked at Don Carlos. "Put 'im down," he instructed quietly. Don Carlos reluctantly did so. "You wanna ride that horse some more?"

"No." His son's response was definite.

"That horse ain't gonna hurt you, Son. You just can't let go of the reins. Now, do you wanna ride her?"

"No!" He was crying now.

"Well you gotta ride her back to the barn. There's no way aroun' that."

"You do it, Papá," he pleaded. The words came between gasps.

"I didn't ride it out here," Remy said quietly. "You gotta ride it back."

Don Carlos was angry. "Remy, please. What good would it do? The child's frightened."

Remy's words were short. "We're all scared. He's gonna learn he can do somethin' about it. It can't end like this."

Then he picked up the boy once again, dusted him off, and climbed with him onto the back of the mare. Carlito turned to look at him, but Remy did nothing. "You gotta do it," he said, handing the boy the reins. Carlito turned the mare's head and walked her slowly toward the barn. "That's the way, Carlito. She's all yours now. Don't let them reins go again." Then he slid from the horse and told

Picosa to follow the boy back. This left Remy alone with Don Carlos.

"The boy loves you, Don Carlos," Remy said. "It's good. But you ought not get between me and him on somethin' like this."

"I won't see the child hurt, Remy."

"And neither will I," he said. He had to make Don Carlos understand. "But there's a world of pain out there for a half-breed. He's gotta be ready for it."

His father-in-law was not convinced. "Let's not bring the evil of the world to his home. He's just a boy, for God's sake."

"That's just it," Remy said. "It'll be here soon enough of its own accord. Babyin' him ain't gonna help."

"Certainly not like breaking his neck would."

Don Carlos wasn't getting it. "You want to help 'im, don't you, Don Carlos?"

"You know I do. I'd do anything for that child."

"Then don't help him. Let 'im learn to do for himself. It hurts. Lord knows I know. But ya gotta let 'im get those bumps and bruises. They'll be worse ones on down the line. You and I ain't gonna be here for those."

Don Carlos turned from him to study the sky. At last, he exhaled. "You people," he sighed, "are such mercenaries. Even with your own children." Then he looked back at Remy. "Life will harden Carlito," he said. "I know it. But I don't have to have a hand in it. Love is all I have to offer my grandson. I'm sorry that God has made me so weak."

Remy listened, and then smiled. "You ain't weak, Don Carlos. If the boy turns out to be half the man that you are, I'll be proud. But think about what made you what you are. Nobody gave it to ya. You earned it. It'll be the same for him as long as I have a say. I just want him prepared, that's all."

"Well," Don Carlos quipped, "let's go bathe him in cactus, then, and slap him dry."

"I'd just like to go inside and get a cool glass of water."

By then Carlito was running toward them. "Did you see me, Papá!" he cried. He leaped into his father's waiting arms.

"I'm proud of you, Son. I knew you could do it." He held him so tightly that he was not certain the child could breathe. The smell of him, like a puppy, filled Remy's nostrils. The greatest contentment came with the grip of that child's skinny arms around Remy's neck.

For a moment, he forgot all about the trouble in Tejas. Every fiber in him, every thought, every breath, was devoted to his son and the rest of his family. The more he gave, the more he got. Their love had healed him and had made him strong. He understood that now and, in doing so, he also understood Don Carlos's politically reserved position. It was a matter of keeping what was most important to him. In attempting to teach Don Carlos, he realized that Don Carlos had taught him.

Carlito popped his head up from Remy's shoulders. His eyes sparkled not from tears, but from joy. "Can I ride her again tomorrow?"

Remy could not mask his pride in this little victory. "Sure you can. Don Carlos'll take you. I got my hands full with that little girl and whatever the next one is." He looked at Don Carlos. "Won't you, Abuelito?"

"Yes," he said. It was a capitulation. "Of course. May God help me." Then Don Carlos thought a moment. "What do you mean whatever the next one is?"

"Beatriz is pregnant."

"Nnnnoooo. Again?"

"Yep. We think so."

"My God man! There're jackrabbits in the pastures with fewer children than you. Carlito! Run to your mother and tell her we're coming. I'll go and find that strange woman. I've got to know."

Don Carlos dropped on the sofa with a basket of chicken eggs in his lap. Beatriz drifted downstairs looking a little pale, Remy thought. Her father motioned for her to sit beside him. She handed the baby, Elena Marie, to Remy, who remained standing. Then Don Carlos called for Señora Vásquez to come. He held the basket up to her when she arrived.

"Pick any one you like," he told her. "We need another boy. If you don't see one the first time, I'd like you to try again. Take your time."

"*Chist*, Papá," Beatriz said. "It doesn't matter."

"Of course not," Don Carlos said turning to Señora Vásquez. Remy saw him mouth the words, "a boy," nodding his head once for emphasis. Then out loud, "Go ahead. Pick one." He smiled at Remy.

Remy watched as the señora began her ritual. Her dried, bony fingers rolled the egg against the smoothness of his wife's olive stomach. Don Carlos, insufferable with his foolish grin, hovered above them both.

The señora then broke the egg into a small bowl and blew. She stared at it, and turned away, briefly closing her eyes. Then turned back to look at it again. The smile vanished from her face. "It's a boy," she said quietly and moved away. Don Carlos snatched her arm.

"What's wrong, woman?" he asked her.

"I can say nothing more," she answered curtly, and then she bowed her head, turned, and drifted toward the kitchen. Remy heard her begin to sob.

Remy watched Beatriz's mood sink. Don Carlos put his arm around her in an effort to console her.

"I'm sorry, Beatriz. It was just a joke. I meant no harm. That woman's just an ignorant peasant. It means nothing."

Beatriz reached for Remy's hand. She managed a brave smile and he returned one. Then she reached for the baby. Remy handed her gently to his wife. He watched as Beatriz clutched the child in her arms. A single tear ran down her pale cheek. He wiped it with his thumb.

"It means nothing," Don Carlos insisted. "Nothing."

BOOK FOUR

———— ◆ ————

La Matanza

(The Killing)

1835

Chapter One

Elijah had come alone. Señora Vásquez led him into the sala, where Remy lay on the floor playing with the baby. Elena Marie, now a pudgy two-year-old, rode on his back, fistfuls of his hair in each hand. Remy pulled free and shook his head so that his hair would fan Elena Marie's face, delighting her. Her laughter filled the room.

"What brings ya to these parts, Cousin?" he asked without looking at him. Out of the corner of his eye, Remy saw Beatriz rise from the sofa to hug Elijah. She offered him a glass of cool water. Remy took his first glance. Elijah looked tired, certainly, but Remy thought it was entirely possible that the toad might have something on his mind.

"Take them nasty boots off outside dammit," Remy said. "You ain't got the sense God give a gopher. They got nice rugs in here."

"Sorry," Elijah said, skulking toward the front door. When he came back, he stood unashamed in his bare, knobby feet.

"I don't know which is worse," Remy said as Elena Marie snatched his hair again. "Ouch!"

"Damn. You're covered up with 'em, ain't ya, Remy?"

"Yep. Yep. They're all aroun' buzzin' in my ears like skeeters. I love 'em all." He broke free from Elena Marie and handed her back to her mother as soon as Beatriz had given the cup to Elijah. She returned to the sofa and placed the baby, facing her, in her lap. The child immediately reached for her earrings.

"What's on your mind?" Remy asked. In the five years since they'd parted, his cousin had never visited. Elijah's call had a purpose.

"I need some help, Remy."

"With what?"

He hesitated. "The land," he finally said. "It's harvest time."

"I know it's harvest time, idjit. What d'ya need me for?"

"Weeds."

"Weeds?" Remy cringed. What in God's name, he wondered, could he do about the goddamn weeds?

"Weeds," Elijah repeated with newfound confidence. "We got weeds. Gotta git 'em off." Remy thought his cousin's demeanor was exceptionally strange, even for him. One glance at his wife, and he knew she sensed the same thing.

Remy leaned back and crossed his arms. "This ain't about the land, is it, Elijah?" Elijah's foolish expression told Remy he was searching for an answer. Remy knew his cousin would have to look hard, but Remy already suspected what the visit was about. How could he not? The trouble had started.

The tariff exemption had run out. In January of that year, Antonio López de Santa Anna, who by then had dismissed congress and assumed full control of the government, had sent troops to reoccupy the customs houses of Anahuac and Velasco. Revolt had begun again in the same chickenshit way it had in 1832 as far as Remy was concerned. Except that Don Estévan, who remained in a Méxicano jail, was not around to defuse it.

Austin's imprisonment gave a certain leverage to the War Party—recent immigrants, merchants, lawyers, and land speculators—who anticipated the inevitable pinch of governmental control and planned to resist it. Shots were again fired. The troops were forced to withdraw. This time, however, Remy knew a dinner party was not the answer.

Everyone knew that General Cós, the brother-in-law of El Presidente himself, was crushing a revolt in nearby Coahuila when the news of civil disturbances in Tejas had reached his ears. He sent a dispatch to Captain Tenorio at Anahuac of his intention to occupy Tejas just as soon as he'd pacified Coahuila. Tenorio's instructions were to hold on in the meantime. Don Carlos said that Cós could only chain one barking dog at a time. The communiqué was intercepted at San Felipe by the War Dogs, and they had their confirmation of the government's intent. For most of them, Remy knew, it was what they wanted to hear.

In June of that year, Remy heard that a force of some two dozen men under the "command" of William Barret "Buck" Travis, the very loud lawyer, had attacked Anahuac, and had forced the surrender of Captain Tenorio.

Most of the farmers, planters, and ranchers in the area, Remy included, were incensed at this episode. Travis was universally denounced as a half-cocked traitor and fool, the blind Samson who was bringing the temple down on himself and everyone in it. Seven separate Tejas communities had organized a formal statement to the government that said, in effect, that Travis and the War Dogs' actions did not speak for them. Despite all appearances to the contrary, the rank and file colonists—the farmers—remained loyal to the government, and they had decided to dispatch harried messengers to General Cós to advise him of their position.

Remy had been asked to go, but Don Carlos suggested that he not lend his face to revolution, even to stop it, lest it be remembered at some inopportune future date. Remy sat at home that summer playing with his children and going for long rides with his wife.

Cós, at the head of an army of thousands accustomed to quashing civil disturbances, had a number of demands to be met by the Texian emissaries before he would even begin to discuss a solution. He asked for a list of insurgents, and the list, however reluctantly, was provided. Travis's name, among others, was on it. The Anglos had informed on their own, and they quietly endured their shame.

But that was not enough for General Cós. He ordered the colonists to arrest these same men and turn them over for prosecution. In México, Remy knew, this meant that, despite all formality, sooner or later they'd be shot. Even the most fervent loyalists among the Anglos could never take such an action. This was all General Cós needed to know.

As the representative of the "Supreme Government," he then demanded the surrender of agitators and unconditional compliance with Méxicano laws. The colonists were not to assemble, consult, or otherwise unlawfully organize themselves. Just to make damn sure, Cós told them he intended to occupy San Antonio, and, in time, points east. When order was restored, he said, he would then break up foreign settlements in Tejas. The Anglos could submit or fight, he told them. He did not care which. The time for parties had long passed.

Remy understood that without Austin, the Peace Party, the moderates, had no center. They were desperate for one calm voice; instead they heard hundreds of frantic shouts. They should've been in their fields, harvesting their grain. But the War Dogs had turned their plowshares into swords. Panic, Remy knew, was everywhere.

On September 16, the day before his cousin came to visit, word came to Remy that General Cós had entered San Antonio de Béxar. With him he'd brought 800 pairs of iron hobbles.

And now his cousin had arrived.

"This ain't about the land. Is it, Elijah?" Remy repeated.

Elijah looked first at him, then at Beatriz. Then he said, "Yeah, it is, if you wanna keep it."

"Godammit, Elijah," he moaned, disappointed. "Don't get sucked into this mess. It was Travis, Miller, Johnson, Three-legged Willie and all them other War Dog bastards that brought this on. You got crops to get in, and everybody else does, too. Let Cós run 'em out, and all this'll blow over."

"That's the way I saw it, Remy," Elijah said. "Till Austin got back. He's been down there nearly two years. He's seen the picture close up."

Remy knew that was true enough. Santa Anna had simply let him go. He was not acquitted, vindicated, or cleared. They just let him go. Remy had wondered how he'd react. Maybe Elijah could tell him.

"What's he say?"

"He says we gotta fight or run. You tell me which the others'll do." He pulled a crumpled flyer from his pocket. Remy read it. It said, in part: "War is our only resource. There is no other remedy. We must defend our rights, our-

selves, and our country by force of arms." It was signed by
Stephen Austin. Don Estévan was no more.

He handed the paper back to Elijah. "It ain't just the
goddamn War Dogs no more," Elijah said. "It's everybody,
from the old Three Hundred and up, Austin included this
time. He sent me to get you."

Remy rubbed his face, looked at Beatriz, who said nothing. It was what he'd expected. War was coming, and his
people came to him for an answer. He gave Elijah the one
he knew he must make. "I can't go," he finally said. "I
promised my wife I'd stay out of it." His answer irritated
Elijah as he had always known it would.

"You can't stay out of it! And neither can they," Elijah
said, pointing to Beatriz. The rest was for her benefit. "It
ain't against the Mexicans, Beatriz. It's against Santa Anna.
He's a dictator. We can't abide by that. We'll whip 'em."

"And if you don't?" she asked calmly.

"Then we won't be here no more. Don Carlos and the
others can do what they like to smooth things over. Cós
wants Zavala, Navarro, and maybe Seguín, but the rest of
the Tejanos can ride it out maybe; same as always." He
was pleading now. "But Remy's got to go with me. Today.
He hedges your bet. Ya'll can walk both sides of the fence
and who'd blame you? I'd do the same if'n I were you. But
if Remy don't come, and we win this fight, there's no tellin'
what'll happen. Change is comin' either way." Then Elijah
said something Remy wasn't expecting. "I'll look after 'im,
Beatriz. He'll be safe."

Remy didn't know what to do. There were so many immigrants loose in Tejas now. Young, wild-eyed, hungry, and
armed Americans, spoiling for a fight. This, he knew, was
the War Dogs' work. They'd spread the news throughout
the American South that a revolt was in the works. In war,
everything was up for grabs, particularly land. They smelled
the blood and were immediately drawn to it. What if he
left with Elijah, and these bastards stumbled on this place
and found only Mexicans, neutral Mexicans? Hell, they'd
burn it down. He had to stay and show a white face. That
was best. The situation for him was different than for the
others. Austin would understand.

"I can't go," he finally said. He thought his wife would be pleased with his decision. She wasn't.

"What Elijah says is true," she said. It was a matter of states' rights and defense of the Méxicano Constitution of 1824. Austin's participation confirmed it. Tejas had finally been sucked into the Méxicano Civil War. That was how everyone—Tejano as well as white—must look at it. If the revolt were left to the War Party, ruin would come to them all. But loyal Méxicanos had sympathizers everywhere in the nation. Zacatecas, Yucatan, and Coahuila, among others, all continued to resist Santa Anna. It was not unreasonable, she thought, that Tejas—all of Tejas—would as well. Santa Anna had many enemies among his own people. Remy could safely show his face among these. She would send for him if trouble came near. Picosa and the other vaqueros had fought Indians for years. They were good men. Rancho de la Cruz was well fortified. Don Carlos would take measures to see that it was even more so. She and the children would be safe.

"You get your things and go with your cousin," she finally said.

"What about Don Carlos?" Remy asked. After all, he'd given her father his word.

"I'll explain," she said. "You go."

His wife's blessing was all he needed. His American heart had always reacted angrily to the thought of dictatorship, an unmentionable impulse around the moderate Don Carlos, but Beatriz had finally spoken to that. Remy was what he was.

He scrambled around the house for his gear, saddled his horse, and led it to the front of the house, where Beatriz and the children waited.

The afternoon sun caught the first wrinkles etched into that beautiful face. Streaks of gray tinted that dark, glistening hair. He embraced her, promised to be careful. She was not to worry. Remy would stick close to Austin, and in doing so, would have the exposure they needed to survive. "The things we do for property," he said, but she did not see the humor in it.

"Cuidado, mi amor," she whispered. Elijah slid his boots back on his feet and mounted. Remy kissed both of his

children goodbye. Carlito was with his grandfather out on the range. It pained Remy that he could not see his oldest boy before he rode off for God knew how long. When Elena Marie saw that he was going, she burst into tears.

"Your papa'll be back soon, honey," he told her. "I promise." He looked at them all one last time, then flipped the reins of his stallion. Elijah moved up beside him.

"Weeds, my ass," Remy smirked. Elijah said nothing, and they rode on.

At nightfall Remy watched the clouds roll in from the south. They were thick, heavy, and oppressive, choking out all light. The woods seemed to close in. Alternative trails and short-cuts well known to Remy seemed to evaporate in the solid blank. More than once he backtracked to find an ax-blazed trunk or a pile of rocks on the side of the road. Trails crisscrossed everywhere, yet he couldn't find one familiar to him in this chunk of darkness. The ones he did find he did not recognize. This was an unsettling surprise to his experienced eye. Nothing looked the same. It confused him to the point that he dragged up and let Elijah lead.

The southern wind swept them along the main road east. Somewhere out there, Remy thought, a war was waiting.

Chapter Two

It was October 1 when they finally reached Gonzáles, De-Witt's capital. The settlement was buzzing with revolutionary fervor. The women and children had already been led away. The ferry that crossed the Guadalupe had been removed and hidden in a bayou. All other boats were already gone. Remy heard that the Méxicano army lay west of the river, calmly waiting for their answer.

They had asked for their cannon. Why exactly, Remy couldn't say. It was a sorry six pounder, with a long history and a short barrel. Captured from the freebooter Magee back in 1813, the Spanish had once spiked it to ensure that it never again be pointed in their direction. A blacksmith later removed the obstruction, but left a touch-hole the size

of a man's thumb which Remy thought must've seriously
debilitated its operation. He knew it had seen service at
the Alamo before it was finally loaned to DeWitt to ward
off Indian attacks, more with its thunder than anything else.
Now, in order to defuse growing colonial resistance, the
Méxicanos sought to confiscate all ordnance, the little cannon included. Eighteen Gonzáles men refused and buried
it in a peach orchard. A plow covered their hasty tracks.

Remy and Elijah stumbled through the mass of Texians
that had responded to Gonzáles's plight. They were a rough
bunch: hard-eyed, barrel-chested, tobacco-chewing. Remy
knew a few of them. Much to his surprise, Elijah knew
most all. This army was about as ragtag as you could get,
Remy thought. Some had newly outfitted buckskins; the
rest, mostly old-timers, wore old buckskins, conditioned by
rain and human grime, slick, black, wretched, and usually
too damn small. Some wore Mexican sombreros, others tall
"beegum" hats or coonskin caps. Some had military-
looking headgear from God knows where. Store-bought
coats stood next to mangy buffalo robes. They wore plain
brogans, or handmade moccasins. Not everyone was armed.
Some had shotguns. Some had Kentucky long rifles, many
so sorry Remy wouldn't use them to pry a stump. But
Remy certainly had his, and he kept it close, well-oiled and
shiny, by his side.

Remy was more disturbed by the disparate goals of this
group than by its appearance. Some had come, as he had,
to defend the Constitution of 1824. Others wanted Texian
independence and made no bones about it. He sensed that
the wildest leather-stockings among them all didn't care
one way or the other. They'd just come for a fight.

Remy remembered what Maguara had said during his
visit to the Comanche camp all those years ago. These last
were warriors who stumbled across a battle and naturally
lit on it, like flies on a rotten peach. Somehow the principle
that had thrown them all together was lost. In the absence
of an ideal, however, instinct alone served as the common
bond. Whites gathered to kill non-whites. The reasons for
this specific altercation, Remy knew, were not important.

This was exactly why Remy had been reluctant to take part.
These people, he realized, were no longer his.

Chapter Three

Colonel John Moore had ordered the silly cannon to be unearthed, cleaned, oiled and then mounted to a wagon. Suddenly it was known as the "flying artillery." Other militiamen cut cane in the bottoms and fixed iron points at the end. They cleaned their guns and ground razor edges on their "Arkansas toothpicks." That very evening, Moore had decided, they would attack the Mexican cavalry of some one hundred men. Remy half-heartedly did what they wanted him to do, thinking the whole time that while the world had certainly trapped him, it might also take his life.

At around seven o'clock, Remy and the others secretly crossed the river on the Guadalupe ferry. He watched as the current swept them along. Once across, they wandered about in the foggy river bottom, climbing toward the high ground, until they bumped into the Mexican pickets about three o'clock in the morning. Both forces seemed equally surprised. The sound of a barking dog and the roar of a Mexican carbine broke the silence.

Realizing that his men could not see to fight, Colonel Moore ordered a withdrawal. Remy and the other soldiers bided their time, feasting on ripe watermelons they found in some unlucky farmer's field. Remy spit his seeds on Elijah.

When the fog lifted the next morning, Remy saw that the two armies faced each other on an open plain. Moore ordered the cannon fired. They had no balls for it. It was loaded with scrap iron and shot. It did nothing but bring forth a single rider yelling, "Don't shoot! Don't shoot! I have a message."

A Gonzáles local crouching next to Remy recognized the voice of Dr. Lancelot Smither. The Mexicans, the doctor told them when he was close enough, wanted to talk. Moore looked around for someone who spoke "good Mexican." Elijah, black seeds still stuck in his red hair, shoved Remy forward. Together with Moore and Dr. Smither, he rode out to meet the Mexican commander. At least they were talking, Remy thought. It was a good sign.

Remy heard Captain Casteneda's opening remarks and was immediately taken aback by them.

"What's he say?" Moore asked.

"He wants to know why the hell you're shootin' at him. He says somebody's gonna get hurt."

Moore looked equally confused. "He wants to know why?"

"Yep. For some reason he don't know."

Moore reached for an answer. " Cause it's war," Moore said, and Remy translated.

"He says what war?" Remy said, turning back to Moore. "His orders were to come only for the cannon. He says that he knows it's useless. Just hand it over and he'll go. He ain't lookin' for a fight."

Moore answered immediately. "My answer is on that flag wavin' yonder." Remy translated Moore's response and pointed at the flag. Black, hand-painted letters daubed on Mrs. DeWitt's white cotton skirt said "Come and Take It."

Remy shook his head. "He don't understand what that means. No Mexican would."

"All right," Moore said, confused. "All right. We'll start from square one." Remy listened as Moore launched into that sort of political babble for which American frontiersmen were famous. These days he heard it most everywhere he went. It was nothing unusual. "Tell him that cannon yonder was given to the Texians for the defense of themselves and the constitution and the laws of the country, while this feller here's actin' under the orders of the tyrant Santa Anna, who has broken and trampled underfoot all state and federal constitutions of Mexico, except that of Texas, which this army will defend. Tell him that."

"That's a mouthful," Remy sneered, "but I'll take a run at it." Captain Castaneda listened patiently as Remy explained and then answered that he knew all about that. He himself was a Republican, he said, as were two-thirds of the Mexican nation, but he was also a professional officer of the government, and he, as well as the Texians, were bound to submit to its orders—which were simply to ask for the cannon. If refused, he was to take a position nearby

and wait for further directives. In short, there was no need
for violence. At least not today.

Remy told Moore all of this.

"All he wants is an answer, huh?" Moore said, his eye
cocked.

"That's right."

"Well, hell, I would've thought that little cannon yonder
had already spoke for us, don't ya reckon?"

Remy ground the palm of his hand into his eye socket.
"He's just doin' what he's told. He wants to save face. Just
give 'im an official no and back off. He'll leave."

Moore had different plans. "If he's a Republican, like he
says, ask him to join us."

"He won't do it, Moore."

"You ask 'im; and that's *Colonel* Moore. I won the goddamn election, son."

Captain Castaneda appeared somewhat shocked by
Moore's request. His reply was that while he had his sympathies, he also had his orders, and it was the latter that
must be obeyed.

Remy knew the talking was over. Each commander rejoined his troops, but the Mexicans did not withdraw. Remy
believed Castaneda was thinking that soon the rebels would
come to their senses and avoid conflict. Remy knew better.

Moments later the Anglos advanced. When they were
close enough, Colonel Moore yelled, "Charge 'em, boys
and give 'em hell!" It was a standard.

Remy did so, and so did the others. But before the
little cannon could be fired again, Castaneda and his
forces quit the field. This, the Anglos believed, was an
example of Mexican cowardice. But Remy knew the captain was outnumbered and outgunned, and, as he'd said,
he had his orders. They did not include attacking the
colonists. Mexicans, he knew, were like that. In spite of
what was happening in their political arena, the rank and
file did not enjoy killing their own citizens. They also
weren't particularly enthusiastic about being shot by
them. As far as Remy was concerned, Castaneda had
done the right thing. He was cutting his losses and giving
peace another chance.

Texian casualties consisted of one man knocked to the

ground by a spooked horse. His nose was bloodied. The Mexicans had not been so lucky. They lost one, maybe two. The first shots had been fired from scrubby Anglo rifles. The War Dogs had their war.

Chapter Four

Kills White Bear found Maguara alone on a bluff. He was naked to the waist, his head back, silently watching the skies. The night was dark, and the stars sparkled.

"You sent for me, my uncle?" Kills White Bear asked. He watched as Maguara pointed one long arm to the west.

"Do you see that, Kills White Bear?"

Kills White Bear looked. He saw a large white star burning a wide path across the sky. Its tail drifted behind for what seemed like an eternity. "What is it?" he asked.

"A sign," the old chief said, and his glance fell from the sky to Kills White Bear. "It begins."

Kills White Bear did not understand. "What begins?"

"The whites make war on the Méxicano father. Everything will now change."

"In what way?"

"That star is not interested in the affairs of human beings, one way or the other. It came in the time of my grandfather; now it returns in mine. It tells me nothing except that the season of fire has come again to cleanse the Mother Earth." His eyes looked briefly at the comet. "It's what I've been waiting for," he said strangely. Then he turned to Kills White Bear. "And you."

The chief's hand rested on his shoulder. "Patience, White Bear. They may kill each other after all. You ride south with the young men, and see what can be learned. Then bring the news to the ears of Maguara. Attack no one; choose no side. Just let them know the Nemenuh are watching from a distance. Once we know more, we can decide what the People should do."

Chapter Five

In the long, hot autumn days that followed, Austin rode up from San Felipe. The scrambling provisional government had asked him to command their army, now totaling about three hundred and growing each day. Bowie had come with his men, and Fannin with more. But Remy was happiest to see that Alcalde Benavides of Victoria had arrived with thirty Tejano ranchers, as well as the young and fiery Juan Seguín, who rode at the head of citizens from Béxar. Suddenly the revolt had Tejano allies. Remy knew then that his own participation would have the approval of Don Carlos. Beatriz had been wise to send him. He found his comfort in legitimacy.

With the initial victory in hand, Remy didn't have to ask what was next. San Antonio de Béxar was the key to Tejas. "General" Austin was glad to see Remy, quickly informing him that he was now a lieutenant of this awkward volunteer army, with no specific terms of enlistment and no oath. Men came and went at will, sometimes withdrawing in squads when their orders didn't suit them. It was the biggest mess Remy'd ever seen, and now, much to Elijah's vexation, he was an officer of it. Austin simply pointed the mass toward San Antonio, and much to Remy's surprise, most of them went.

They ran short of ammunition, blankets, shoes, clothing, and medicines. When the provisional government sent cannon, they arrived without proper munitions. This, Remy knew, was only the beginning. It seemed to him, as it had occurred to others, Sam Houston included, that prudence dictated they not march until both the government and the army were better organized. At this point it appeared some very uncommon people shared some sort of amorphous common goal, but it did not go further than that. Austin would not hear of it. He intended to strike while his iron was hot, suggesting that the Mexicans were equally confused. Remy could not imagine that this was so. One look around at his comrades confirmed it. Nevertheless, the army pushed on as Austin willed.

Remy's general sent for him.

"Fuqua," he said. The words were spoken with fatigue and desperation. "Go and see them at San Felipe. Tell them what we need." "Them," Remy assumed, referred to the government, whatever that was. He would ride to San Felipe, distribute Austin's orders, and hope like hell somebody—anybody—would respond. He would try Houston (he had a lot to say these days), maybe the Wharton brothers (who always did), Henry Smith would be around, David Burnet, whoever. He knew there would be no shortage of chest-thumping authorities. It was the institution that would be hard to find. Just to go and see "them" was a mighty diffuse directive. He told Austin that he was glad to go and do his best just the same.

"And in the name of almighty God," Austin groaned, "see that they send no more ardent spirits to this camp! If any are on the way, turn them back, or have their heads knocked out."

Remy sensed the frustration in his voice. "You should leave the army to someone else, Don Estévan . . ."

"I am Stephen," he said, "when we're alone. General Austin at all other times."

"Right," Remy apologized. Titles came and went in a hurry these days. "But your place is with the government."

"I thought the same. I offered command to General Houston. He declined."

"For what reason, d'ya think?" This was rhetorical. Remy felt he already knew.

"Not because I'm the most qualified, I can assure you. He doesn't agree on our tactics. He wants to hold from the Guadalupe east. He doesn't think we can meet Cós in the field and prevail." Then he pointed to the men. "Let Houston tell them that. I think we can take Béxar in twenty days."

Remy spoke his mind. "It's because they don't want you in the way while they form the government."

Austin's expression told him that his insight struck home. "We won't need a government if this army fails. We'll need an undertaker. Besides I'm not popular these days. I'm supposed to be a moderate, a Mexican sympathizer. I'm warring with our masters, but I'm a moderate."

"Without you there'd be no war. They know that. They'll use you like they're usin' me. I don't mind so much, but your place is in San Felipe."

Austin shook his head. "I can't leave these men, Fuqua. But when you go for supplies, reiterate my request for a replacement. As soon as I'm able, I'll go and help form the government. Texas does not belong to me. It never did. But I won't let it belong to them. They won't shove me out of the way as easily as they think." He straightened, looking south. "But now's not the time for conflict between us. We must act as one. Béxar's not five miles away."

Remy rode out watching the army roll over the smooth, round hills toward San Antonio de Béxar.

Events in San Felipe were not as chaotic as he'd suspected. Some very good people were doing some very remarkable things. They were sacrificing their own money and property to support their army in the field. San Felipe was, and always had been, the seat of Anglo reason in Tejas. The efforts of these people, the oldest and best established settlers, would make or break the revolt. Remy knew these people placed a great faith in Austin. If he wanted to take Béxar, they'd do all in their power to support him. When Remy saw firsthand their commitment to the initiative, he felt more comfortable about his own part in it. If Texas stood unprepared, at least it was united. This was all that concerned him. As loose as the revolt appeared, it was somehow stitched together tightly enough.

They gave him all that was available and a little more. They gave him their hope.

When Remy returned, he requested to ride with Bowie's command, as he and Bowie had already discussed. One of very few Anglos that moved confidently in Don Carlos's tight circle, Señor Jim was a friend. They both hailed from poor Louisiana families of Scotch-Irish stock. Remy's, of course, much poorer. Bowie leaned toward upward social mobility through charm and bravado, relying on a series of schemes, shams, and nefarious enterprises to finance the trip. These, Remy knew, included fraudulent land titles and illegal slave trade. Remy had spent most of his youth clad in homespun, strapped to a mule's ass. Bowie had traveled extensively throughout the American South and México. Remy'd walked the length of his uncle's fields a thousand times with a hoe in his hand, and then had scrambled for the cover of Tejas. However, they'd both come to México to hide and begin anew; and each, in turn, embraced it. Jim Bowie was famous, or infamous, depending on your slant. Remy had been another face among thousands. Their very different and entangling paths had soon crossed.

Bowie had washed through the Anglo settlements straight for San Antonio de Béxar. Remy's arrival had been a slower process. However, they'd both spent much time in that city in the early days, and both had been fortunate enough to take prominent Tejano wives. Jim Bowie's charm had endeared him to the conservative Béxarenos, who quickly accepted him. He was an example to Remy, who had faced the same challenge. Bowie had taught him the value of grace and good manners, and Remy had done his best to move confidently yet quietly among the Tejanos as he had observed Bowie do. At that juncture, however, their paths sharply diverged. Remy had chosen to adapt entirely to the Tejano way of life; Bowie continued to hack out his own way.

Jim Bowie, Remy believed, would probably wish one to think of him as an entrepreneur and adventurer. By hook or crook, he'd come to quickly control vast amounts of land. He was part owner of a textile mill in Saltillo, no doubt financed, Remy believed, by his father-in-law, Vice-Governor Veramendi. When he wasn't out looking for silver mines, he'd been traveling to Louisiana to oversee his business interests there. But Don Carlos had told Remy that Bowie's flamboyant style, despite all public assurances to the contrary, was subsidized by his wife's family. Remy thought it hypocritical to fault him for that. He still lived in Don Carlos's house.

Bowie was hot-tempered and violent, it was true. It was a weakness that Remy knew they both shared from their hardscrabble past. But Bowie was also loyal, kind, and generous. Between these extremes, Remy thought, was a good man. Remy knew that Bowie's youth had left him hungry. On the frontier, that hunger had naturally evolved into greed. This was a common illness of the times, and Remy understood it.

Then Bowie had lost his wife and children to cholera in 1833, the same epidemic that had taken Beatriz's beloved mother. He'd drowned his grief in debauchery and alcohol. Remy was exposed to his harder edge after that. He became cantankerous, irritable, and mean. It was then that the political storms of the time had swept up his restless, tumultuous spirit.

But there was something about Jim Bowie that Remy liked and admired. It overcame all Remy's doubts. Despite Bowie's shortcomings, he was a good, loyal and generous friend through the good times, and now through the bad. He had never asked for or demanded Remy's respect, he'd earned it. He was also a natural, fearless leader of men. Though somewhat wild-natured, with a gambler's instincts, Remy thought his judgment was rock solid. If Remy could choose his place in battle, it would be next to Jim Bowie.

Elijah, on the other hand, perhaps a little disgruntled by Remy's officer's commission, had stuck with his neighbors against Remy's advice.

Bowie's command was composed of companies led by Fannin, Briscoe, Coleman, and Goheen. Closing in on Béxar, Austin had sent them ahead in search of a defensible position from which to lay siege to the city. Juan Seguín was with them also, along with eighty-nine other Anglo and Tejano men, old-timers all, so Remy felt he was among good and seasoned friends. At nightfall, after looking at two other sites, Bowie found the place he wanted—the Mission of Purisima Concepción.

Austin had ordered Bowie to keep in close contact. The general did not want the army to remain separated for long. Bowie was to reconnoiter and return as early as possible, no longer than one day. Instead, owing to the late hour and his fear that a Mexican garrison could also fortify and defend that same ground, he had dug in.

Remy knew that Austin would not be happy that it had taken all day to find a place and that when Bowie had done so, he deliberately disobeyed orders. But that was Bowie. In order to mitigate Austin's certain anxiety, Remy rode alone through the darkness to let him know that they were waiting for him at Concepción. He reached Austin's camp at nine o'clock that evening and told him how the day had gone. Austin was uncharacteristically enraged.

"This is just the situation I wanted to avoid, Fuqua!" he said angrily. "I told Bowie I wanted to reunite before dark. I've been worried sick all afternoon, and now that I've heard what he's done, I'm beside myself. If we're attacked now, they'll defeat us piecemeal."

Remy didn't know what to say. "Best to get alon' then, General," he said, for they were among others. "Soon as you can."

While Remy waited, Austin summoned his officers, advising them to prepare to move on Bowie's position at dawn. Then Remy picked his way through the oaks and mesquites back to Concepción.

But Cós must've been aware and he acted. Probably one of the Concepción priests had told him what he needed to know. Remy was startled by a shot in the darkness before dawn. The sentries returned in a huff, one with his powder horn shot off. Remy felt the hair bristle on the back of his neck. The Mexicans knew the value of this place. If Remy and the others were to hold it, they'd have to fight. Bowie kept his cool.

"Keep under cover, boys, and reserve your fire. We haven't a man to lose." Remy huddled with the others as the dragoons approached from out of the low fog. An army could defend Concepción, but could they?

"If they flank us, we're whipped," he told Bowie in the grip of sudden anxiety. "We've got that river at our rear. The water's a good eight feet. They'll cut us down when we cross it."

"We ain't crossin' no river, little brother," Bowie assured him. "At least, not that one," he added with a sly smile. "Keep yo' head down, and yo' eyes on them sights."

Much to Remy's surprise the initial skirmish came to nothing. The Mexicans withdrew, and all again grew quiet. Then, around eight o'clock that morning, three hundred Mexican dragoons and one hundred infantry began to move. Bowie's scouts confirmed all quiet on both flanks, and Remy lost all fear of being swept from the hill. It appeared to him that Cós intended to butt head against head.

Bowie must've already understood this. When he was certain that the Mexicans were committed to a frontal assault, Bowie ordered his previously angular forces in one consolidated mass to meet the Mexicans, all entrenched on high ground and in good cover.

The Mexicans rolled out two cannons and put them to immediate and continuous use. Grapeshot and canister ripped through the trees overhead, showering pecans on Remy and the rest of Mission Concepción's defenders. Remy watched as the others broke the pecans open with their knife handles. He nibbled on one or two himself, his eyes watching.

When the Mexicans were close enough, Remy and the others opened fire. The Mexicans seemed to have too much or too little in the way of ordnance. Their cannon fire flew over Remy's head, the rounds from their Brown Bess muskets fell short, bouncing into the thicket. Remy's rifle, however, and those of his compatriots, were just the ticket from the cover of brush. Remy shot slowly and deliberately, as he heard the others do, and soldiers fell in droves before his eyes on the plains.

But even with their diminishing ranks the Mexicans continued to come. Remy heard the screams of terrified horses and wounded men. Sometimes he heard the dull thud of a rifle ball pound into a man's chest; other times it was the sound of limbs cracking or maybe bones shattering. Through the confusion of it all Remy kept shooting. *Fire, ram, powder, patch, ball, ram, splash the flash pan, aim, fire!* Remy and the others cut them to pieces.

Fannin's line held. Coleman's swung around opposite and flanked the soldiers. The Mexicans were now in a crossfire.

A lull in fighting allowed the smoke to clear just enough for Remy to have a better view of things. Some of the Mexicans were now in retreat. Bowie must've seen it as well and ordered his men to swoop down on the cannon positions. Remy went with them, reaching the cannons first. Together with two others he turned one and peppered the fleeing Mexicans with their own grapeshot.

If things weren't going badly enough for the Mexicans,

Remy saw that Austin's advance cavalry had arrived, commanded by, of all people, that maniac Travis. His orders, as Remy later learned, were to stay on the defensive and delay any attack. Like everyone else he disobeyed his orders and charged the Mexicans as they scurried back into Béxar. Travis was too late, Remy thought. The Mexicans were already beaten. Remy's first real battle was over.

Remy returned to the river and drank deeply, the sound of the rifle fire and cannon ringing in his ears. In his reflection, he saw the powder burns on his cheek, but also the sparkle in his eyes. Today was his first real test, he thought, and he was proud of his performance. He was anxious, yes, uncertain. War was still new to him. But he had not been afraid of it when the time came, and the killing had not unnerved him. He was certain that his own rifle had taken a half-dozen lives. That fact didn't haunt him as he had anticipated it would.

The chaos and confusion that had marked the campaign ceased to trouble him. It never should have anyway. Chaos and confusion had marked all of his days. He should have been used to it by then. Regardless of the government it represented, or lack thereof, "The Army of the People" was a coalition now, a regional, factionless force in a struggle for what he now perceived as a just cause. The blood of those men lying dead at Mission Concepción was on Santa Anna's hands. Remy, like all the others, he thought, was fighting for his kind, his country, his land, in a civil war. All doubt had evaporated with the first white clouds of gunsmoke from the plain that surrounded Concepción. He was consumed.

But he recognized that some other force was at work here, one from within and not without. Something mysterious, primeval, innate, and unspeakable had marked that ruthless hour. He became the killer he himself had predicted on that day he took the Tonkawa's life, but this time he felt no shame, no remorse. Perhaps before the sun was down he would kill again, with that same indifference. The ability appeared unasked when needed. Violence, it seemed, took him as naturally as sleep. Maguara had been right. Remy was born a warrior. Beatriz had told him before he left that blood now called to blood. And Remy understood that his own had answered.

Chapter Six

Within a half hour, General Austin arrived. Remy knew he'd ridden most of the morning just waiting to bitch at Bowie. What he'd feared would happen had happened. It was the results that he'd figured all wrong. So advised, Austin could not mask his excitement.

"How many enemy casualties, Colonel Bowie?" he asked.

"We count seventy-six killed or wounded."

"And your men?"

"One badly wounded. Richard Andrews. He won't make it, I don't expect."

Austin shuddered with excitement. Remy had never seen him quite like this. The plains before Béxar, though littered with enemy dead, were wide open. "The army must follow them right into town," the general said.

Bowie looked first at Austin, then to Fannin and Briscoe, and finally Remy. "Not without cannon, we don't," he said, turning back to Austin. "Béxar's well fortified, easily defended. If we enter those streets, what just happened to them'll happen to us. We ain't goin'. Not until we're ready."

Remy watched the General's face. Austin had just given what sounded like an order. Bowie had responded with what had the ring of refusal. Most of the best men, Remy included, stood next to him as he said it, nodding their heads. It was clear to Remy that if God himself commanded it, Bowie wasn't going to take his men into Béxar. Remy knew Stephen Austin well enough to know that he was sorting through alternatives in an effort to find one that might work in this uncomfortable situation. It would not take long.

"Very well then," he said, unfazed by what looked pretty much like insubordination. "Let's put our heads together and come up with something else then, shall we?"

That seemed to placate all dissension. Then he looked at his errant cavalry commander. Now here was a man, Remy thought, who could use a little discipline. Austin apparently felt the same. "Travis," he began. "A word. . . ." Remy knew that tone.

Remy believed it was fortunate that he was accustomed to chaos. It ruled the weeks that followed the chance victory of Concepción. Others apparently had no such experience with it. Besieged Béxar had neither fallen, nor had it even been attacked.

Those with horses scoured the prairies for signs of Mexicans, good grass, or supplies. Travis occupied himself by burning the range south of Béxar, his own private scorched-earth policy. The rest languished in camp. Austin could neither keep their spirits up, nor keep the liquor out. Drunks staggered through the camp at night, firing their rifles like fools. The farmers, with spring on their mind, had volunteered to come, and then, reporting to no one, quietly volunteered to go. For them, their fields came first.

Winter had come. Most did not have sufficient clothes. Supplies, as always, were short, but not as short as the tempers of the remaining volunteers. The officers bickered among themselves. Drunken brawls were common. Austin, weak from two years' incarceration, grew ill. Bowie was gone. He had argued with General Austin over strategy and had decided to quit the campaign. This time Remy could not go with him.

Béxar, the fortress, loomed before them. Remy knew that Cós awaited reinforcements. Still stinging from the humiliating defeat at Concepción, he refused to show his face.

The twenty days that Austin had said he needed to take San Antonio de Béxar had come and gone long ago.

Remy received word that General Austin wanted to see him. Since Bowie's departure he had rejoined Elijah under Burleson's command. Remy had not seen his commander in a day or two. Austin looked pale, sickly. His cough was deep, rattling in his chest.

"You all right, Don Estévan?" he asked. "Sorry. I meant General Austin."

"Oh, I don't care, Fuqua. Come in here and look at this."

Remy took a seat as Austin handed him a paper. It was from the government in San Felipe. He was relieved of his command, and had been appointed a commissioner to the United States.

Remy returned the paper. "That's a better deal, ain't it?"

"Yes," he answered, "and I'll take it, but not yet. Some prudence will be necessary to keep this army together should I leave at once." Remy watched as he collapsed in his chair. "I'm really so worn out, Remy. But I want Béxar. We're suffering, yes, but Cós suffers too. I'll see it fall before I go. I promise you."

"I'll attack Béxar with you, General," Remy said, not really sure if he would.

"Yes, but how many of the others will?"

"Now that's a good question. I can't say."

"We'll soon see," he said, and he fell into a fit of coughing. Remy left him with a sense of pity.

Three days later, on November 21, Austin issued the order to prepare for the siege. Unlike other times, he did not ask for permission or advice. He simply gave the order like a general should. But it was too late for that. His army refused to participate.

The great man was crushed before Remy's very eyes. This, Remy knew, was Houston's doing. The government had appointed him commander in chief of an army that didn't exist. For whatever reason, most likely because Houston had never favored the assault of Béxar, he had sought to undermine Austin's leaky initiative. He'd quietly enlisted Bowie, Fannin, and the others to his cause. The rest of the volunteer army had long ago lost faith in Austin, and no one, Remy knew, understood that better than the retiring general himself.

On November 24, Austin asked that his army parade one last time before him. At that time, he asked how many would be willing to continue the siege. Four hundred and five responded that they would, providing they elected a leader of their choosing. The next day, Austin left the siege for San Felipe. He was, at long last, out of the way.

Chapter Seven

Edward Burleson was elected in Austin's place. Remy didn't think he could control the army any better, and events soon confirmed this impression. Some were for the siege; some opposed it. Much to Remy's surprise, Burleson handled the dissension in the same way his predecessor had. He called for a vote. The overwhelming sentiment was clear enough. Burleson called for the army's retreat. They'd failed.

On the morning of December 4, Remy and Elijah were packing their gear to leave. It had been nearly four months since he'd left his wife and children. As much as he wanted to see Béxar fall, he wanted to see them more. He was content to let it go.

He heard voices arguing. Nothing new about that. This time, however, was different. They stepped out to see what was happening. Many others had done the same. Colonel Frank Johnson and Ben Milam, the empresario, emerged from Burleson's tent.

Milam looked determined. "Who will follow old Ben Milam into San Antonio?" he yelled. His voice was rich, full of frontier vigor, the way Remy remembered his father's was. He saw that the response to it among those who remained was immediate.

"I will," one said, stepping forth. Then another. Several more. And then Elijah Johnson said, "I will, too." Remy stepped up beside him. Before it was done, Remy counted three hundred and one committed to storm Béxar.

In darkness the following morning, Remy and Elijah assembled with the others just outside of the city. The north wind chilled them as they huddled there in silence. The only sound they heard was the sentries' periodic cry, *"Centinela alerta."* All's well.

Around five o'clock the nervous calm was broken by the abrupt and thunderous roar of Neill's cannon in the distance. While Remy and the others approached the city, Neill had rolled his artillery across the San Antonio river within range of the Alamo. It was, of course, a diversion. Before they committed themselves, Remy and his men waited to confirm the Mexicans' response.

Remy heard the sound of Mexican drums and bugles, the summons cry of the officers, the shuffle of frantic hooves as horses were hitched to the groaning axles of the Mexican artillery, the clanging of a thousand arms being readied amid the clacking of two thousand boot heels on stone— all moving toward the Alamo garrison. The diversion had worked.

Remy watched as his commander, Johnson, waved them into the city. They came within sight of Mexican sentries sitting around the glow of a fire to warm themselves on that cold morning. Some men prepared to fire on them. Jesus Cuellar, a Mexican officer but a native of Béxar and staunch federalist who had recently deserted, convinced them otherwise.

"First we get in," he said. "Then we fire." They agreed and snuck past without shooting once. After so long, they slipped into the city unopposed. Remy thought it was like a dream.

Johnson's objective was to take the Veramendi Palace. Remy knew exactly where it was. They raced down Soledad Street, almost within sight of it, when the first shot was fired by a Mexican sentinel. Remy dove for cover, Elijah next to him, as Deaf Smith shot the man dead. Remy knew they could not be more than two hundred yards from the central plaza.

But the shooting must've alerted the Mexican defenders. In an instant their cannons roared, sending metal screeching down the narrow streets. Remy ducked into a doorway and yanked Elijah next to him. There was nowhere to go. Remy turned and kicked in the door behind him. Huddled there on the floor, in their nightclothes, was a family of Béxarenos. They were terrified.

"Tranquilo!" Remy said. "We won't hurt you." Just the same, they dashed out into the streets and ran for their lives.

"I don't expect they was convinced, Cousin," Elijah said.

"Who'd blame 'em?" He shoved open the window, took aim, and fired. Elijah loaded the house with stragglers. Remy saw other rebels storm other houses. They were in. Thick walls of adobe protected them. They frantically reinforced windows and doors with whatever they had.

The Mexicans could not easily dislodge them. But for the city to fall, they had to stay on the offensive. The men who climbed to fight from the roofs were gunned down by Cós's snipers. Contrary to what Remy had been told, these men shot their English Baker rifles well. The roofs were not safe. If they were to move, he knew, it would have to be house by house. The streets exposed them to cannon fire. That left one alternative.

Remy and three soldiers pulled a rafter free from the ceiling and began ramming the walls. The adobe crumbled before him. When the hole opened up wide enough they looked through it. If noncombatants were there, they shooed them out. If they spied alarmed, dusty soldiers, they poked the barrels of their rifles through the gash and fired repeatedly until the screaming stopped. Then they took that house and began on the next.

Every now and then, Remy and the others would stumble across a well-fortified house. They would send for Milam's cannon, and it soon came. After they had sufficiently pummeled the enemy position they attacked it man to man. Remy's hair was singed by Mexican rifle fire, and yet he pushed on. The others did the same.

It went on like that, more or less, for three days.

The nights were quiet, with messengers moving back and forth between Milam's company and Johnson's, each attempting to keep the other advised of his comrade's progress. Inch by inch, house by house, the rebels took Béxar.

On the morning of December 9, Remy saw that the flag of the Mexican eagle had been replaced by a solid white banner. A single Mexican officer, a lieutenant colonel by his braids, stepped from behind the breastworks, through the rubble and the fallen bodies, under the flag of truce. As this man passed by, a Mexican colonel grabbed him by the arm. They were so close Remy could hear them speak.

"You will not go," the Colonel said. "The Morelos Battalion has never surrendered, and we won't now."

"General Cós has sent me," the other said. "Enough is enough. Let me pass." As Remy watched, the colonel's hand fell, and the peace messenger went on.

Béxar had fallen.

It took Burleson hours to hammer out an acceptable arrangement. The Mexicans presented a number of difficult conditions. In the end, Remy thought it wise for Burleson to acquiesce. The Mexicans were not beaten, and they had not laid down their arms. But they would surrender if the terms were right. They were tired and hungry. Their impressed convicts had given them more trouble than the insurgents. They were as ready for the conflict to be over as Remy was.

Burleson conceded what they had to have: all soldiers kept their personal arms and ten rounds; they could all rest in Béxar for a period of six days, after which they would withdraw south; the sick and the wounded would stay on

under a surgeon's care; Cós would be permitted to take a
small cannon in his defense; the Texians were to provide
food and provisions as best they could. In exchange, General Cós agreed to march to the interior, and pledged never
to oppose the re-establishment of the Constitution of 1824.
That, Remy thought, was fair enough. The Mexicans had
their honor; the Texians held Béxar.

Though the terms were favorable to the Mexicans, the
treatment they received was not. Burleson had not controlled his men before the campaign, and he didn't fare
much better after it was over. The Mexican officers—well-
educated, refined, courteous—found themselves surrounded
by rows of rough, jeering, and boastful frontiersmen; some
of whom wore the silver spurs and other accouterments of
their fallen comrades, which they proudly displayed to
taunt them. The Mexicans found tobacco spit on their
leather boots. Their horsehair plumes were snipped from
their polished helmets, and they heard harsh words spoken
from between rotten teeth. There was no honor in
humiliation.

Remy could feel the hatred that seethed from their still-
defiant eyes. They had all suffered, each army, in the
months preceding that early morning hour when the paper
was signed. It was an uneasy peace.

When they did at last retreat, Remy and the others
watched them go. Once they crossed the Río Bravo, there
would no longer be Mexican troops on Tejas soil. For
Remy, that meant the war was over. Others had apparently
arrived at the same conclusion long before he had and were
already gone. And Remy wanted to go, too.

The storming of Béxar had sated whatever instinctual
appetite he had for war. The ringing in his ear from the
rifle and cannon fire soon subsided; the screams of the dead
and dying never did. The assault held none of the magic
of the Battle of Concepción. The difference, of course, was
distance. Concepción had been a turkey shoot. The attack
on Béxar had been hand to bloody hand.

He'd now seen several, Méxicano and Texian alike, die.
He had been so close, he could see the terror in their eyes.
He'd watched them struggle up until the last breath. It
haunted him. Ben Milam had been shot through the head

by a Mexican sniper and died on the spot. After that, Remy had a healthy respect for Mexican riflemen. They were, after all, as good as any. He saw the faces of terrified women and children running through the streets as their homes were demolished before their very eyes. They were less afraid of shrapnel and grapeshot than they were of him. He never wanted to frighten innocent people like that again, nor expose them to that kind of risk. He'd seen one man lose an arm, another lose an eye, and another still lose his leg. Remy found him with his back against a wall, delirious. His blood had formed a viscous pool around him while he screamed for help that would never come.

Whatever propensity he had for war had to be suppressed from here on. There was no glory in war, nothing to be personally gained. The Texians had tarnished their victory by their shameful behavior.

He'd told himself that he was fighting for his land. Nothing else, other than his family, had ever mattered, but he'd never expected for it to cost so many lives, each of them innocent by a matter of degrees. This was Santa Anna's and the War Dogs' argument. And neither of them had fought and died in the streets of Béxar. Austin must've known it would end so bitterly. Don Carlos, the veteran of the *encinal* of Medina, also knew. Now Remy did, too.

1836

━━━━━◆━━━━━

Spring

Chapter Eight

It was, without a doubt, the coldest winter Kills White Bear could remember. Maguara had sent them south, to the land of Coahuiltecans, a people now long gone. It lay buried in snow between the icy Nueces and the Río Bravo.

The wind piled drifts as high as his horse's knees. He shook the crusted flakes from his bear cape and drew it tightly around his neck.

One moon before, the Méxicano soldiers had passed this way. Kills White Bear had sent a young warrior racing back to Maguara with the news. The Méxicanos had been defeated at Béxar. Kills White Bear hurried his party north in order to take his place at the council fire and hear the elders' words. The Nemenuh and their allies now stood alone against the whites.

Kills White Bear had heard that the Texians, although victorious, remained in disarray. They would be at their weakest. The Wasps had to sting quickly as one. Kills White Bear knew he could help with that.

His party had not yet reached the Pedernales when they came across Comanchero traders with news from Saltillo. Another Méxicano army was moving north. Kills White Bear turned his party back south to see if it were true.

In no time at all he found them. Five times as many came as had gone the moon before. The war between the Méxicanos and whites was not yet over. Maguara, he thought, would be pleased.

In his absence other bands of Nemenuh had raided the hapless Méxicano army. In such a harsh winter, the buffalo migrated further south than normal. The five bands had come with them and had quickly encountered isolated pockets of the weary Méxicano soldiers waiting well ahead of the main army with supplies and fresh horses. They made easy prey.

The warriors took food, blankets, guns, ammunition, and horses whenever they could, distributed them with pride among their people, and then returned to take more. The Méxicanos had sent horsemen to punish them more than once, but the Nemenuh easily ambushed them on the open plains, and Kills White Bear saw their frozen scalps hanging stiffly from the warriors' lances and shields.

Kills White Bear sought out the war parties. There were so many loose in that country. One by one he met with their leaders, pleading with them not to molest the Méxicanos. At least, not this year. The Great Spirit had beseeched the Méxicanos to return and kill the whites, he told them. They must be allowed to pass. There was a greater value, he said, in allowing them to reach their destination than in what their supplies could bring in trade. The security of the Nemenuh nation was more important than blankets and guns.

They said that they were glad to yield to Kills White Bear's wisdom as a great warrior among their cousins, the Wasps, which pleased him. If they did not know him, they'd certainly heard of him. They assured him that future efforts, if any, would be directed against the Lipans. Others simply agreed to return home to warm lodges and fat wives. The buffalo, as always, would see them through this winter of other men's war.

Chapter Nine

There was nothing but silence in the house, save Señora Vásquez's humming in the kitchen and the sound of Don Carlos every so often flipping a page of his book. The children were already asleep in their feather beds. Sitting in the sala before the roar of a fire with Beatriz and his father-in-law, Remy remembered how he had longed for calm moments just like these when he was on campaign against Cós at Béxar. Now that he had them once again, they were especially sweet.

Picosa entered and slammed the door on the storm behind him. In a brief glimpse, Remy saw that yet another wet snow blanketed the ranch. Picosa knocked the ice from his boots and then his gaze met Remy's. It was obvious that the mayordomo had come for him. He whispered in Remy's ear that Elijah had arrived.

"Well, tell 'im to come in, dammit. I sure as hell ain't goin' out."

Then he turned to Beatriz. They'd already discussed the likelihood of Elijah's visit and a decision had been made. Remy patted his wife's leg to assure her that he had not forgotten.

Elijah Johnson stepped over the threshold. "Evenin', all," he said. He removed his buffalo-hide jacket, which engulfed him, and shook off the ice. Quelepe had, of course, made it much too large. He hung it on the wall and stepped toward the fire. "Warm in here," he said, but before he could take another step, Remy cleared his throat. When Elijah looked, Remy pointed at his dripping boots.

"Oh, yeah," he said, and slipped them from his feet. Then he stood in front of the fire, rubbing his hands. Remy watched Don Carlos stare at Elijah's bare, white, and callused feet before he turned to him with a look of disbelief.

"No trouble with weeds this time of year, I trust, Señor Johnson," Don Carlos said. The open book never left his lap.

Elijah turned to face him. "Oh, no sir. Weeds ain't the problem now." He was smiling. Remy wasn't. "I guess ya'll heard," he said.

They'd heard. Remy, Don Carlos, and several men had gone to Béxar to salvage what they could from their home. At that time, rumors abounded. Santa Anna was on the march. Remy and the others took what they wanted and quickly left. Anyone who had any sense was doing the same.

Nobody really expected the Mexicans to retaliate so swiftly. The earliest Remy thought they could field an army in Texas was in the spring, when the grass returned to sustain the troops' horses and oxen, and that was if they came at all. Much of México remained in revolt. At the time Béxar had been under siege, Santa Anna's army had been occupied in a violent campaign against the wealthy mining state of Zacatecas. (Other fires of revolution burned in other areas.) It was simply a matter of which Santa Anna would choose to extinguish next. Remy did not think that distant Texas would be a top priority.

As it turned out, Santa Anna had quickly crushed the revolt in Zacatecas and had started on his way to relieve his brother-in-law, General Cós, even before Béxar had fallen in December. On February 23, the first of his men arrived. Rumor had it that before long, six battalions of seasoned Mexican regulars would tighten the noose around the city.

"We know they're here," Remy finally said.

"If you hurry, you can still get in the Alamo." Elijah

spoke these words as a matter of course, as if all this mattered to Remy. It didn't. "Colonel Travis sent me to find you and several others. I'm on my way to Goliad to get Fannin."

"*Colonel* Travis?" Remy scoffed. Those two words did not seem to go together. "I'd sooner serve under a skunk."

"Bowie's still there commanding the volunteers."

This was no improvement. "And he's blind drunk. He's been drunk ever since Concepción. He's out of his goddamn mind."

Elijah's tone shifted. "They need help, Remy." He paused. "They need you."

"Like hell," Remy said. He knew the Texians needed much more than that. They needed disturbances in the interior to keep Santa Anna occupied and out of Texas. These hadn't occurred, at least not sufficiently to distract El Presidente. They needed a government. They didn't have one. Governor Smith had dismissed the council. The council, in turn, had impeached Governor Smith. And it had gone downhill from there. How such people could rebel against the government of México because of its instability was a source of great wonder to Remy.

They still needed a regular army. They had one on paper, but they didn't have one in the field. Remy knew that the volunteer army was out cavorting somewhere. In order to focus things a little, Governor Smith had named Sam Houston commander in chief. The Council, on the other hand, appointed James Fannin and Frank Johnson as co-commanders in chief. Nevertheless, the consensus was to march with anyone who would go to Matamoros and carry the war to the Mexicans.

Houston didn't seem interested, but as the Smith-appointed commander in chief, he thought maybe he ought to tag along just the same. When he arrived, a man by the name of Dr. James Grant, a disenfranchised owner of a sizeable estate below the Río Grande, and clearly a man with an incentive to expand the war southward, informed Houston that he was the acting commander in chief. By Remy's count, this made four.

At this time Houston somehow convinced Bowie to peel off and assist J.C. Neill at the Alamo. With what exactly, only God might know, but Remy believed Houston must have been content to convince anybody of anything. The Alamo had been wrecked in the siege of Béxar, and Dr. Grant had taken whatever he could carry for the Matamoros expedition. Neill, along with a few die-hard volunteers, had worked day and night to refortify the Alamo with what little Grant had left them. Remy had seen it. Neill's efforts were impressive. But if Cós's thousand couldn't hold it against three hundred leather-stockings, Neill could never hold it with a hundred men against Santa Anna. But they were still there and still working, at least when they weren't rollicking drunk.

Remy knew Houston had marched with Grant's army in an effort to talk them out of the Matamoros expedition, until the Council deposed Governor Smith and ousted Houston from the position he hadn't truly held anyway. Colonel Fannin, God bless him, was now in charge of the Matamoros expedition. Whether they were actually going or not was beyond Remy's scope. But Frank Johnson brought news that Houston had gone to see Smith, who, despite some hard evidence to the contrary, still considered himself the governor of Texas. At least he had the state archives in his possession, as well as the official seal, and threatened to shoot any son of a bitch that tried to take either. Smith, probably with his pistols in hand, had ordered Houston to negotiate with the Cherokee Indians, for what exactly Remy couldn't begin to guess, and Houston rode off for East Texas. No doubt, with an ample supply of whiskey stored in his saddle bags.

As if things could possibly be worse, the garrison at Goliad, foreigners all with not one month in Texas, could not grasp the centralist and federalist struggle in México. They'd taken sides in it, but they really didn't know what it was all about. In order to simplify matters—and Americans, Remy knew, were good at that sort of thing—these boys simply issued a proclamation of their very own for Texas independence. This they did without consulting any known authorities, which Remy felt certain they could never have found had they tried. It was an effort to reduce the revolt to an "us," meaning white, versus "them," meaning Mexicans.

That, they apparently felt, made things much easier for all involved.

The Tejanos, many of whom had fought at Gonzáles, Concepción, and Béxar, were understandably outraged. It confirmed for them what Remy knew the Anglos had always thought anyway. The government, or some faction representing the government, or perhaps some men with clothes still clean enough to appear reasonably governmental—Remy couldn't say—quickly moved to slap the Goliad garrison's white wrists. They were here to do the fighting and not the "proclamating."

The Tejanos, however, were not convinced, and rightly so. With the exception of Juan Seguín and a few other diehard rancheros, the Tejanos distanced themselves from the Tejas revolt. Whatever problems the dictator Santa Anna posed for them, he did not hate Mexicans in general, which made him a little more attractive than the rebels, who clearly did. Don Carlos, his clansmen, associates, and every other Tejano who was not deaf and blind had decided to take their chances with Santa Anna. What Elijah did not know was that Remy had too.

Sam Houston, the commander in chief of nothing, had said it best in San Felipe. Every new state was infested, more or less, by a class of noisy, second-rate men, who were always in favor of rash and extreme measures. But Texas, he'd said, was absolutely overrun by them. It was true enough in Remy's experience. And these same men had just cut each other's throats. For Remy it became a matter of survival once Santa Anna crossed the Río Bravo in force. Remy had every reason to believe the anarchy would get much worse now that all of Texas was under Santa Anna's gun. The revolt, Remy was certain, would unravel. That brought him finally to Don Carlos's quiet camp. He knew the cause was lost.

Those who intended to keep their land had best keep their heads down and familiarize themselves with a *centralista* oath. The rest, certainly the War Dogs, and any other high-profile, part-time revolutionary, had best be headed for the Sabine. Santa Anna would certainly sweep Texas clean.

Remy knew that Santa Anna had seen it done before.

Don Carlos bore witness. El Presidente, then a young officer, was with General Arredondo back in 1813 when he
did it. Thousands—armed Anglo insurgents, their Tejano
confederates, and civilians alike—were murdered in the reprisals that followed Arredondo's victory at the encinal de
Medina. If a person, any person of any race, was suspected
of Republican sympathies, that person died. As savage as
it was, Santa Anna must have seen that it bought the Spanish, and the Mexicans that followed them, two and a half
decades of peace in Texas. The precedent was set. The
methods, Remy knew, would be the very same.

Now it was time to make all of this clear to his thick-
headed, frostbit cousin. "I'm stayin' out of it from here on,
Elijah," Remy informed him, his fingers still laced between
Beatriz's, his stare fixed on the rising flames. "I ain't risking
my life for them sons of a bitches no more, and I damn
sure ain't goin' to the Alamo."

Elijah bunched up the freckles on his flushed cheeks.
"*What*?"

"I ain't goin'," Remy repeated.

"You think you ain't already in it up to your neck? Them
Mexicans'll pull you out of your bed and hang ya."

"We've talked about that," Remy said, rising from the
sofa. "Don Carlos is clean. He ain't raised his hand against
the government. I'm his son-in-law. I'll stay close to him."
He paused a moment. "And I want you to stay here with
us."

He placed his hand on Elijah's shoulder. Elijah pulled
away.

"Ain't no way in hell, Remy!" he said, slowly shaking
his head in disbelief. "I'm gonna fight, and I'm ashamed
that you, my own flesh and blood, ain't goin' with me.
Those men in the Alamo are gonna die!"

"That's right," Remy snapped back. "They are. And I've
got too much at stake here to die with 'em." He caught his
breath. "Understand me, Elijah. I got a wife and kids to
think about now. And I'm thinkin' about you, too."

"No sir!" he declared. "Not Elijah Johnson! I won't let
them bastards run all over me."

"You've got no choice."

"Well," he huffed. "I never figured you for no coward."

Remy felt stung. "You know damn well I ain't no coward. I fought at Concepción and Béxar. Most of the time you were behind me. But I ain't no fool, either. I'm keepin' what's mine."

"Well, that's just the problem, ain't it, Remy?" Elijah sneered. "It ain't yours! It's his!" He pointed at Don Carlos, whose palms came up to ask that he be left out of all of this. "All you have is what this man give ya. You can cling to the Mexicans like a rabbit if you want. The rest of us have to fight for our land." He moved from the fireplace toward the door. "I'll be goin', Remy," he said. "There's men out there dependin' on me."

Remy moved with him. "At least let me loan ya a pair of socks, for Christ's sakes. You'll catch your death."

Elijah shoved his arms through the sleeves of the great coat. "I believe I've already caught it," he said. He turned to Don Carlos and Beatriz and said good night. He said he held no grudge against them. He understood. It was Remy that had disappointed him.

"Step outside with me a minute, Remy," he said. He wasn't asking. "I wanna have a word."

Remy followed, and they stood together on the porch, the cold wind washing flurries between them. "I want you to know somethin', Remy," Elijah said, as he flipped the collar of his coat around his neck. "You spent your whole life feelin' sorry for yourself, and I felt sorry for ya, too." Out came his finger. "But I'm here to tell ya once and for all that you never had it no worse than anybody else. When my Pa beat you, he usually beat me harder 'cause I stuck up for ya. You went cryin' to my ma; but I had nowhere to go. You took the shoulder that I should've leaned on. She was too busy wipin' your tears to wipe mine. It was always Remy first, then Elijah. Always."

Elijah had never expressed any personal feelings before. Remy never thought him capable. And now, when he did, this is what came out. Elijah was punishing him. And he was doing a very good job.

"I'm sorry you feel that way, Elijah," he said quietly. He didn't know what else to say.

"I don't feel it! I know!"

Remy shuddered from the cold. "She knew I didn't have nobody, Elijah. You don't know what that's like."

"The hell I don't!" his cousin roared back. "Even when she was dyin', man, she called for you and not me. You think about how I felt, and my brothers, too. She was our ma."

Remy felt those old wounds tear open. That sense of helplessness, the fear of being alone. Elijah was pulling away. Remy realized that with so much deeply rooted anger, they'd never really been as close as he'd thought. He'd reached out to Elijah, but Elijah had not reached back. This unseen barrier, more bitter than the winter cold, had always been between them.

"I never asked her for nothing, Elijah," Remy said calmly. "She just gave it to me. And I loved her for it. That's all I can say."

"Well, I wish she could see you now, sittin' in that big, Mexican house while other people are fightin' your goddamn war!"

"This ain't my war!" Remy said. "This is a bunch of idjits that can't agree that the sky's blue. And if they could, which they can't, they'd wouldn't want Mexicans under it with 'em anyhow." He squared off, arms open, with his cousin. "I'm a Méxicano, Elijah! Beatriz's a Méxicano. My children are all goddamn Méxicanos. I won't fight to help those bastards shut out my family. And I know they'll do it, and so do you. You've heard the talk." His tone grew quiet. "They've gone too far, Elijah. My wife and children mean more to me than this war."

"You think I don't want a wife?" Elijah said, his voice was cracking now.

"What's that got to do with anything?"

"Everything, goddamn ya!" Elijah's eyes glistened, reflecting an anguish Remy'd never seen before. "You think I don't want a woman lookin' at me the way Beatriz looks at you? A little kid at my side thinkin' I hung the goddamn moon?" Elijah shook his head. "I wanted all that, Remy! I wanted everythin' you ever had. It all came so easy for you." Elijah's gaze fell to his feet. "And it hid from me, just as easy."

"Boy, you sure don't remember things the way I do."

Elijah lifted his head and stared. "I remember, Remy. I

remember good. I remember we came to Texas together. We got ourselves a place, and we worked it—just me an' you. You met her and off you went."

"We was farmin' together, Elijah. We wasn't married. I can't help it if I found a good woman. It just happened."

"And I can't help it if I found a good war. It just happened, too."

Remy snorted. "You ain't found all that good of a war,"

"You're prob'ly right," Elijah admitted. "But it's the only one doin'. Santa Anna's gonna run me out if he don't kill me." He looked pained. "I got no choice. An' I'm askin' you, as your blood kin and the only white man that still likes ya, to come and fight with me and the rest of your kind." He paused, shuffling his feet. "I wanna be together again, Remy. Like we were."

There it was. Elijah had laid it out for him once again. Blood calls to blood. But Remy couldn't hear it anymore. "We can never be like we were, Elijah," he said. "But we can be together if you stay here. My kind's on this ranch, and we intend to keep it. Santa Anna'll wash right through here, and then wash right back out. We'll go on as we were." He pointed inside the house. "Don Carlos knows what he's doin'. I'd listen to him 'fore I'd listen to any of them other bastards."

"I don't believe that," he answered. "I don't see how you can."

This gave Remy pause. He had to think about that a moment. The response came soon enough. " 'Cause I got to, that's why. I just hope like hell and hang on. I don't know what else to do."

"There's nuthin' for me to hang on to, Remy," Elijah said, his chin dropping. "I'm a loser either way. I think maybe you are, too."

"Well, we're both damned, then," Remy said.

"Same as always."

Elijah seemed to hang nearer now but fell silent. Remy guessed he'd said what he wanted to say. It'd probably killed him, but he'd done it. For thirty years worth, it wasn't much. Now that he'd finished, there wasn't a trace of anger on that freckled face. Unlike Remy, Elijah didn't have it in him to stay mad for long.

"You won't stay?" Remy finally asked his cousin.

Elijah shook his head. "Can't. I gave Travis my word. I gotta find Fannin and tell 'im to carry his ass to the Alamo."

"Listen to me, Elijah," he told him. "You do what you gotta do, but you don't go into that Alamo. If they send you there, you tell 'em you didn't understand your orders—they'll believe that, I guarantee—or else you get lost on the way. Anywhere else, you got a fightin' chance. And you can always desert with honor from a Texian army. Hell, they all do it an' you've already done your part." He felt his eyes steady. "But if you go in there, you'll die."

"Well," Elijah answered, "I'll keep that in mind."

"You do that. And if there's anythin' you need, anythin' at all, you come to me. I'll vouch for ya. I'll swear for ya. I'll hide ya. I'll fight for ya if I have to. I hope you know that. It's them other bastards I won't have nuthin' to do with. Not anymore."

For the first time Elijah seemed to warm to him. Remy could not have been more pleased. A woman, a few children, a piece of land, maybe these things could keep them apart. This war couldn't.

"Now that you mention it," Elijah said, "there's one thing, you half-breed son of a bitch."

"You name it."

"How's about goin' back in yonder and fetchin' me them socks?" He grinned. "They wool, ain't they?"

"Yeah," Remy said smiling. "They're wool."

"They'll do for starters. My dogs is froze up stiff."

When Remy returned with six pairs, Elijah was already mounted, waiting. Remy handed him one pair and stuffed the rest in his cousin's saddlebags. His fingers felt cold glass. He took out a vial and studied it. It was half full of some heavy, viscous, silver liquid. Mercury.

"What's this?" Remy asked, holding up the container. Elijah looked and then soberly turned away.

"Quicksilver," he finally said.

"I know that, idjit," Remy snapped. "What's it for?"

Elijah flipped his calf across the saddle and pulled off the first boot. "I reckon I bin with the pay women one too many times," he said.

"Ah, Elijah," Remy moaned, returning the bottle to the

saddlebag. Elijah said nothing. He just slipped on the socks, his jaw set. When he'd finished, he stuck the toe of his boots back in their stirrups and cocked an eye at Remy.

"They'll be Mexican officers recollect you from Béxar," he said. "You know damn well they will."

"Like hell," Remy answered. "I'm gonna grow a moustache."

"Ah," Elijah huffed, flipping the reins against his mule's neck. The beast grunted and walked on into the white blank. "You still ain't man enough to grow no hair," Elijah called over his shoulder. "You'll have better luck wearin' a dress."

Chapter Ten

Three times each day Remy heard the defiant solitary thunder of the Alamo's eighteen-pound cannon. It had begun the day after Elijah left. The daily blasts were a reminder to Santa Anna, and practically the rest of Texas, that the Alamo still held.

On Sunday, March 6, Remy awoke in the pre-dawn blackness to the sound of distant rumbling and continuous thunder. Yet another late winter front, he thought. Spring would never come this year. He pulled the blankets over both him and Beatriz and fell back to sleep, the warmth of her body against his.

All that day he listened for Travis's cannon. All he heard was the north wind whistling through the bare limbs of winter trees.

The very next morning Remy was saddling his horse when Don Carlos appeared.

"Where to?" his father-in-law asked. Remy sensed he already knew.

"I gotta go see, Don Carlos," he said. "I gotta know about my cousin."

"That would not be wise."

Remy kept on as if he hadn't heard him. The leather creaked as he tightened it, the brass buckles chinked. Remy leaned under the horse's belly to check the cinch. When he did, he saw the toe of Don Carlos's boot slip into the stirrup. In one quick motion, his father-in-law was mounted.

"I'll go," he said quietly. Remy didn't see the use in arguing. Don Carlos rode out. Instinctively, Picosa and a few others followed him in silence.

It was well after dark when they returned. Remy had waited anxiously all day. When Remy found them they were quietly putting away their tack. Their faces were pale and grim. Remy waited.

"The Alamo fell yesterday," Don Carlos began. He kept his attention to Remy's saddle. Not once did he look at him. "They say it took a little longer than an hour."

"How many survived?" Remy asked. It was the first thing that popped into his mind.

Don Carlos did not answer. Picosa's eyes fell on Remy, as did the others'.

"How many?" he demanded, looking from one blank face to another.

"None," Don Carlos finally said, "save the women and a Negro slave."

"Bowie?"

"Dead."

"Travis?"

"Dead."

"What about . . ."

"All dead, Remy," Don Carlos said impatiently, as if he were annoyed. "They're all dead."

Remy felt himself sink. "Elijah?" he asked.

"I saw every single body," Don Carlos said, "a hundred and eighty-three by my count. Elijah's was not among them."

Remy drew a deep breath when he heard that news. All was not lost as long as his cousin was alive. Elijah must still be with Fannin, and Fannin, Remy knew, still held the fort at Goliad. He then thought of his sad friend Bowie and the others he knew. Béxar was in disarray. Their families were certainly scattered if not dead. Remy said that he would go with Picosa and the others to see that they were properly buried. It was the least he could do.

"There's no need," Don Carlos told him, his voice grave. "They've burned them all, together."

Remy felt confused. "That ain't possible," he muttered.
Don Carlos stared at him.

"I've seen it. I smelled it. There's nothing to bury, and
nothing to do."

"Them sons of bitches!" Remy said angrily, and he
moved to stop Don Carlos from unsaddling his horse. "I'm
gonna see for myself."

"There's nothing left to see," Don Carlos said stiffly.
"And you," he snapped, clutching Remy's collar, "aren't
going anywhere."

Remy was in agony in the days that followed. He
wouldn't eat. He couldn't sleep. He spent his days brooding; at night, he paced the floors. Everything else grew still
at Rancho de la Cruz. Despite their gloom, the campesinos
went on as best they could.

Vaqueros he did not know brought news to Don Carlos.
Santa Anna waited at Béxar. He'd ordered his forces split
for the march east. The Anglo settlers were already scrambling for Louisiana. Remy heard that Gonzáles had been
burned to the ground. Houston had recently withdrawn
from that same locality with a force of some four hundred
men. He obviously hoped to merge with General Fannin
and perhaps make a stand at the Colorado, or somewhere.
It wouldn't matter anyway.

The Mexican contingent under General Urrea was sweep-
ing the Texas coast. Another hurled itself at San Felipe.
Another still subdued points north along the Camino Real.
They would meet, Remy knew, at the Sabine.

Rancho de la Cruz was a hornets' nest of rumor. Fannin
was stymied at Goliad. Houston's force had deserted. Tejano ranches to the south were being attacked by enraged
whites. The Comanches were active to the north. Don Carlos prepared to meet any and all threats. He fortified his
casa mayor and waited for new rumors. And Remy, as hard
as it was, waited with him.

A Tejano rider appeared one Saturday afternoon in late March. He bore a letter for Don Remy Fuqua. It was from Elijah, writing from Goliad. Remy squinted to discern his cousin's scratchy hand. It read:

Dear Cousin:

A note to tell you I'm well. For better or worse, I'm with Fannin. We was captured by General Urrea during our retreat, and we voted to surrender. A number of mistakes were made by our commander, but none of that matters except that I made one myself in not staying with you and Beatriz. We're now prisoners in our own sorry fort. Rumor has it that we're to ship out for New Orleans in a day or two. I'll soon be with my Pa and God help me. Sure I'll get an ear full. Probably make me pay for that mule to boot. Write and tell me when all's clear. I'll return to Texas when all's settled and start again just like we said. I know you'll help me.

Look after my place and Quelepe as best you can. Buy it back from the Mexicans if they'll let you. Maybe Beatriz can do it if a white man can't. And like it or not, you're still a white man, and you're still my cousin. You know it's good land. We both worked hard for it. The price should be right after the war. I'm good for it, you cheap bastard! I done better than I'd ever admit to you. Whatever you do, don't let my land go.

I'm sorry about what I said there at your place. I didn't mean none of it. I had a burr up my ass, and so I pissed in your boot while I had it handy. You done good, Remy. Real good. Your ma and mine would both be proud. I was jealous and who could blame me? You done the right thing in stayin' out of this mess, too. If I had what you had, I'd have done the same damn thing. I want you to know that. I don't fault you. Not one bit.

This fool's war's lost. I knew it. Fannin knew it. And I reckon you knew it too. As soon as Houston and them other square headed lawyers know it and quit this country, we can go back to work. I'd be proud that you were strong enough to say no. Otherwise, you'd be chained next to me about now.

See you when I see you. Love to Beatriz and all my

little second cousins. Don't worry about me. Urrea's a fair and honest man they tell me. He whipped us fair and square.

Elijah Johnson

P.S.: This note set me back 10 pesos. It better get there.

P.S.: They sent me to the Alamo. You better believe I got lost.

Chapter Eleven

Remy escorted Beatriz to the dinner table. Before they'd come down his wife had laid out a Tejano wardrobe on their bed. The shirt she'd borrowed belonged to Don Carlos, which was fitting, Remy thought. He looked just like him.

"Shut up and wear them, husband," Beatriz had told him. Even if she'd said nothing, he probably would've picked them anyway. What did it matter now? Might as well look like what he was, he thought.

All of the officers were standing when they arrived. As a precaution, Don Carlos had Remy peek through a crack in the door to make sure none of them present had been at Béxar. Remy, reminded of his cousin's warning, looked carefully. He did not recognize any of them. That done, he and Beatriz entered the sala together.

Don Carlos had brought out a case of French cognac and Méxicano red wine. They toasted Santa Anna, who urged them all to sit as he took his place naturally at the head of Don Carlos's table.

The sight of Santa Anna in Remy's own house brought immediate inner turmoil. The most powerful man in all of México was sitting at his family's table. Remy felt humbled, or at least intimidated. *El Presidente* exhibited the grace, manner, and cool aloofness of absolute authority. Nevertheless, within himself Remy suppressed a sense of disdain and smoldering anger. Their dinner guest had caused the deaths of several men whom he'd known and respected. If there was one man responsible for the ruin of Tejas, it was the one within arm's reach.

Despite his best efforts, Remy moved rigidly, nervously, his stomach in knots. A cold sweat broke out on his brow. He heard the strain in his own voice as he nervously exchanged pleasantries with the guests. He thought he'd rather be with Elijah in chains than in this room with the man who'd put him there.

Santa Anna had come to Rancho de la Cruz as he had come to Tejas—uninvited, but in force. He'd asked for nothing but a little food for his troops and absolute submission. The food had been the easiest to supply.

Remy had ridden with Picosa to the distant pastures until Don Carlos had sent for him. It was then that he'd caught his first close look at Santa Anna's troops. They looked exhausted, emaciated, and cold. Some were clearly Indians, most likely from the tropical South. They had not been given clothes for the Texas winter. Some of them were even barefoot. Their mood had been solemn and grim. In the face of victory, none could even manage a smile. They had collapsed where they stood, miserable. A hundred fires had quickly sparkled on the greening pastures under a thick mat of low, gray clouds.

Behind them all had come the *soldaderas,* their wives, women, and children. They fanned out among the rows of tents to look for their own.

Remy saw that Don Carlos's *campesina* women circulated with pots of warm corn, stew, and fresh tortillas. One of the women told him that every horno on Rancho de la Cruz had been fired; every metate was covered with grain and busy hands. Cattle and hogs had been brought in and butchered. A dozen men had walked about carrying slabs of meat in their bloody arms, headed for the spits. Seasoned mesquite had been quickly split and fired into crackling coals. Boys slowly turned them as dozens of hungry soldiers looked on. Remy saw some cut strips away with their bayonets and then tear at them furiously with white and shiny teeth. Cook smoke formed a dull veil between damp earth and gray sky.

The perimeter of the bivouac, Don Carlos explained later, was filled by conscripts, hence their wretched state. They had come against their will, possibly because of criminal activity, but most likely because they had fallen out of favor with their local *jefes políticos,* the village political chiefs. When Santa Anna demanded men, these were apparently shoved forward. They were mostly hollowed-eyed old men and skinny boys, all of whom looked ragged and worn. Remy pitied them. They were clearly not the monsters, the mercenaries, the War Dogs had claimed. They were people, like Remy, caught in a bad storm.

Remy had noticed that the quality and mood of Santa Anna's soldiers seemed to improve in those camped nearest the casa mayor. These men appeared to be seasoned veterans, well-equipped and in good health despite the rigors of the Tejas campaign. They had pitched their tents, stacked their weapons in order, and sat about cleaning their Brown Bess rifles or sharpening bayonets until it was time to eat. These too, however, rested in silence.

The siege of the Alamo, Remy thought, must have taken its toll. Don Carlos had told him that it was a bloody business. These men must have seen their friends and comrades die. They, too, appeared to long for hostilities to be over, as if the revolt was a disease to be endured as it ran its course. For whatever reason, morale was low. Everyone, it seemed to him, was suffering. Now, with dinner about to be served, it was Remy's turn.

He knew that Don Carlos expected him to sacrifice his honor for the sake of his family, as all of Tejas would have to do in time. But Remy had never really anticipated that it would be quite like this: polite, quiet humiliation that struck him numb. Beatriz gracefully guided him to his chair and he sat in it, not really knowing where to look or what to do. Three places down sat the dictator of México.

Campesinas served platters of whole grilled chickens, honeyed yams, and stewed potatoes, along with loafs of buttered bread, still warm from the oven. When Remy hesitated, his wife spooned food on his plate. He reached for his fork and stabbed at a potato. He brought it to his mouth and began chewing. At that time he looked to the head of the table at Santa Anna. Santa Anna was staring at him. Daunted, Remy returned his attention to his plate.

Somehow he was smaller than Remy had thought he would be. He was a handsome man with dark, energetic, penetrating and almost nervous eyes. His skin was olive, similar to Beatriz's, yet had a yellowish tinge that hinted of swamp fever. He was well dressed and well attended. He couldn't get a bite in without someone asking him if he needed something else. He waved them all away and chewed rapidly, one arm remaining in his lap.

Santa Anna's eyes, Remy sensed, never left him. He felt suspicion where possibly there was no reason for it. Just the same he was unnerved. He was, after all, an Anglo in a Méxicano house. All was quiet, except for the chinking of silverware against good china and the filling of silver goblets.

"I'm glad to see you at this table," Santa Anna finally said. And he'd clearly said it to Remy. "It's important for my officers to see that not all Anglos are up in arms against us. It gives me hope for the future."

Remy nearly choked. *"Muchos gracias, Presidente,"* he spat out. His lips felt greasy. He nervously started to wipe them with the sleeve of his coat when he felt Beatriz's napkin against his face.

"Tell me, Señor . . ." Santa Anna twirled his wrist.

". . . Fuqua," Don Carlos politely interjected. "He's French." A suddenly convenient nationality, Remy knew.

"Is he?" Santa Anna said, sipping his wine. "He looks very American."

"He was born in Louisiana, Your Excellency," Don Carlos explained with a strained smile. "But he's a Méxicano now."

"Ah," Santa Anna said, a single finger tapping the lip of his goblet. It was immediately refilled. "Tell me, Señor Fuqua. You must know some of the rebels."

Remy slowly nodded that he did.

"And they must have asked you to join them. How were you able to avoid the hostilities?"

This was a loaded question and one that unnerved him since he knew his forehead still bore the powder burn scars of Béxar. Don Carlos froze, as did Beatriz. "By not showin' up, I reckon, sir," he said as casually as he could. Santa Anna laughed first, then his officers gratuitously joined him.

"A wise reckoning," he said. "You've walked a fine line, have you not?"

"We all did," Remy answered. He didn't like the laughter. "Not everybody," he said, "favored the war." Don Carlos shot him a look that said *"cáyate, cabrón,"* but Remy felt an elaboration was expected and due. "Most of them runnin' now were against it from the very start. They wanted to work things out with your government. I was one of them. I didn't make any enemies, I don't think."

"Really?" Santa Anna sat the fork down on the edge of his plate and leaned back. His words were calculated and reserved. "And what did they favor?" Remy searched for a response. Don Carlos warned him with another sharp glance.

"They just wanted to get along, I guess, the best they could."

"He doesn't speak well for himself," Don Carlos interjected. "He means that many of the colonists, the ones he knew best, were not political animals. They were misguided by a small minority of militants, troublemakers, recent immigrants all. Not that any of this matters anymore."

Santa Anna listened politely but turned back to Remy. "Tell me more," he said.

"I don't know more . . . with all due respect."

"They objected to me, didn't they? Isn't that what all this is about?"

Remy scrambled for an answer. "In all truth, Your Excellency, I don't believe they ever really did know what it was all about. Had they known, things would've been different."

"Well," Santa Anna snapped, tossing his napkin onto his plate, "they do now."

And Remy nodded his head. "Yes, sir. They do now."

Remy fidgeted in his seat, tugging at his shirt collar until Beatriz took his hand away and laced her fingers between his, as Santa Anna told them what they already knew. He talked about how the United States coveted Tejas. How the American colonists had never really adapted. What a mistake it was to have allowed them to settle here in the first place. He said he was aware that several borderline Anglo loyalists resented his usurpation of the Constitution of 1824, but that it had never been for them to say one way or the other.

Nevertheless, he explained, his course was largely misunderstood. Not only in Tejas, but in most of México as well. What he'd done, he said, he did as a patriot. México, he said, despite its best intentions and greatest hopes, was not yet ready for democracy. Nor would it be in his lifetime. A decade and a half of civil war had taught him that. He'd simply stepped forward in a time of crisis to protect his beloved nation, as Cromwell had once done in England. And Cromwell, it should be remembered, had crushed all opposition to his authority in the interest of peace and stability. It was the same, he said gravely, with him. His destiny was México's, and México's his. This, more than anything, was the concept the Anglos had failed to grasp. In the end, he was sad to say, it would cost them everything.

Of course, he said, the rebellion in Tejas differed greatly from that in other Méxicano states. The revolt could not be truly defined as a civil war because it was led by foreign-sponsored mercenaries and pirates who fought under no internationally recognized flag. It was for that reason, he explained, that he'd flown the red banner of no quarter from the church steeple at Béxar. No insurgent, taken in arms, could expect mercy, he said. They would all be shot as invaders of México in accordance with international law. These were harsh measures, he knew, but the Méxicano people willed it as the just response to a grave and stinging insult, this so-called "Tejas Revolt," to their national pride. He was, he said, their sword.

Nevertheless, it grieved him to wage war as he had. The timing was all wrong. The weather could not have been worse. He understood the Tejanos, in particular, were sympathetic with the rebels. He knew they had lived together for many years. Many felt a certain allegiance to the Anglos, as was natural.

"But, you must all understand that this war we have here," he said, "is not between brothers but between competing nations." He had not come as a Méxicano to kill Méxicanos. Sadly, there had already been enough of that.

He had come, rather, to defend Mexicans against Americans who had come as thieves to steal their land. Houston, he said he knew well, was Jackson's dog. The bumpkin Andrew Jackson, he knew, had stolen Florida from Spain, and when that was done, he had cast his greedy eyes on Tejas. Once in power, he explained, Jackson had made ridiculous claims to Tejas as if it was magically included in the Louisiana Purchase. This had no historical basis in fact whatsoever. The French had never owned Tejas. La Salle's expedition was an abysmal failure. It was the Spanish alone who owned Tejas, and México had won it from them.

When the Méxicanos would not concede Tejas to Jackson, he tried to buy it. When that failed, he insulted officials with offers of bribery. "Now he's decided to steal it with spies and murderers posing as farmers and clerks," Santa Anna said. "He's done everything in his power but win it outright. This," Santa Anna vowed, "he'll never do."

The American president did not have the courage to face Santa Anna on the field of battle. The Alamo, he said, was but a warning of what would happen if he did. The time for sympathies had come and gone. *Los Tejanos* must choose one side or the other, and let the pieces fall where they will. Don Carlos, he said, had chosen wisely. And it looked as if his "French" friend Señor Fuqua had as well.

As for the insurgents, Santa Anna said, they were beaten now. The Alamo had fallen. Goliad had fallen. The blood of the vanquished was on Jackson's hands. The rest, as Señor Fuqua had already said, were on the run, and that rascal Houston was running with them. Santa Anna vowed to sweep the state clean of Anglos until he'd extinguished the strange light in their gray, killer's eyes. It was, he said, the only way to be certain.

Those who came before him, who submitted absolutely to his authority, would be issued amnesty. The rest, he said, could swim swiftly or die. With the American threat crushed, he intended to garrison the border, and Tejas would be forever Méxicano, as God intended.

Remy knew most all of what Santa Anna had claimed. The colonists, Austin included, had stuck out their necks. Santa Anna had legally sliced them off. Yet, it pained him to think about it. Good people—Anglo and Méxicano alike—were suffering. But he thought that if he were in Santa Anna's place, he probably would've done the exact same thing. He'd already accepted it. Those that stayed would have to as well.

Remy was glad to hear that amnesty was still possible. There were several good and industrious citizens among the Anglos who would certainly take him up on it. In fact, he knew many already had.

Remy then told the general that it was very wise for him to have paroled the garrison at Goliad. Once back in New Orleans, they would spread the news that the Texians had left them high and dry to fend for themselves and that once they had been forced to surrender the Méxicano government had turned the other cheek and treated them honorably.

Santa Anna looked strangely at him. "Parole? What parole?"

"For Fannin's men," Remy said.

"There was no parole," he replied. "They were foreigners all, taken in arms. The same rules of war applied. They were executed to the man on Palm Sunday." He pointed nonchalantly once again to his empty chalice. "I gave the order myself."

Chapter Twelve

Remy was upstairs fumbling in his drawer. Where, he wondered, was his goddamn pistol? Out came fuzzy socks, faded bandannas, folded shirts he hadn't worn in two years, all tossed to the floor with cold fingers. His mind was cluttered much worse than his chest of drawers. But a single purpose, one last plan, emerged.

"Remy?" Beatriz whispered behind him.

He kept digging.

"Remy!" This was a bark.

He found the pistol. He checked it. It was loaded and primed. He would get close, smile at him, maybe bring him another glass of cognac. Then he'd put the barrel to that bastard's head and blow his brains out.

He would not answer his wife. He had to do this. No

one could stop him. He suppressed everything—the consequences be damned. He wanted revenge.

He took one step past his wife for the door when he felt the blow to his head. There was a bitter, metallic taste in his mouth. The room grew dark and grainy. The planks of the floor seem to rise up and slap him on the nose.

Remy heard the sound of running water. A stream. He opened his eyes, squinting at the bright light. The air was cool and clean. Trees everywhere. Heavy brush. Thick vines. He heard cattle bawling in the distance. He smelled tobacco burning. He turned. Diego Picosa sat, a cigarillo dangling from his lips, with his back to a tree.

"*Buenos días,* Don Remy," he said. "You slept well, I trust."

"I'm cold," he said. His teeth chattered from the chill.

"Come closer to the fire, *tonto.*"

Remy tried to move. He couldn't. His hands and feet would not obey him. He looked and saw that they were tied.

"Oh," Picosa muttered. "I forgot." Then he stood with great effort, his bones cracking, until he reached his full length. He stretched casually and finally got around to dragging Remy's body by the ankles next to the flames. "*¿Estás bien?*"

"Untie me," Remy mumbled, but he still intended it as an order.

"Oh, I will," Picosa vowed obsequiously, "when Don Carlos tells me." He exhaled the smoke. "But it won't be today. And it may not be tomorrow. I've taken you to a doctor in Béxar. You had delusions of murdering the president of México up until you passed out from fever." He moved the palm of his hand behind his head and pivoted his wrist. "Much pain to the *cabeza* with this fever, no?" He grinned.

"Much pain, yes." His skull was throbbing like it was about to burst.

"Of course, I've seen these symptoms before on our little cattle drives, but they were an unpleasant surprise for your wife and father-in-law." He tested the ropes. "They found them most objectionable." Then he offered Remy a cigarillo. Remy turned his head away.

"He killed my cousin, Picosa." That one sentence above all others kept echoing in his head.

"And for him," Picosa said, stroking his chin, "this man you can't bring back, you would also kill your own wife and children, Don Remy? Bring ruin to Don Carlos and us all? What sort of thinking is this?" He sat back down in the grass. "No wonder Tejas burns."

"Untie me, Diego." He tried pleading next. "They've gone by now."

"Oh," he answered. He seemed amused. "It's Diego when I'm your captor. But always Picosa the *campesino cabrón* when I'm in the fields. We're *amigos* now, are we?"

"Just do it, goddamn ya!"

"Hungry?" Picosa asked, and he rolled up a tortilla and shoved it into Remy's mouth. His coarse palm pressed against Remy's face smelled of horse leather, tobacco, fresh earth, and, of course, grilled corn meal. There was nothing to do but chew.

Don Carlos sent Carlito out to set Remy free. His father-in-law made a habit of allowing those closest to Remy to observe his various predicaments. Remy explained to his six-year-old son that his papa had been ill, and this had been part of the cure. Carlito said it was strange, and Remy said that before it was all over he'd see stranger things still.

Before he left—and he was leaving—he tried to smooth things over with Beatriz. As angry as she was about what had happened, she raged when he told her what he was about to do. Remy never once turned his back on her. One bump on his throbbing head was plenty. But soon enough she calmed herself, as always, attempting to reason with him. It was no use. He wasn't about to ride the fence any longer, he told her. Santa Anna had pushed him off to the Anglo side.

Remy armed himself with his father's Christian Gump rifle and two Spanish pistols, one his, the other borrowed from Don Carlos. Then he took his father-in-law's doubled-barreled shotgun, sawed off nearly a foot of its length, and filed the tip of the bore smooth. He loaded them all. Then he filled his powder horn with fresh Double Dupont and placed both it and his hunting bag, a sheathed patch knife attached to its strap, and a full load of shot and ball in his saddlebags. He worked an edge on his larger bone-handled hunting knife, its blade shaped as Bowie's had been, with an Arkansas stone. A vent pick and brush hung from his belt. A loading block of white oak, with twelve full slots of patched and greased balls, dangled next to them. Everything was made ready.

He chose his handmade boots for the journey, as well as his leather *chaparreras*. The rest of his Tejano wardrobe he discarded, opting for his linsey-woolsey hunting shirt, and the fringed buckskin jacket Quelepe had made for him so many years before. The hat he chose was his oldest, a broad-brimmed faded felt that had weathered softly to the shape of his head. He stepped in front of the mirror and was pleased with the image. He would join the Anglos dressed as one of them.

He turned first northeast, out of the wake of Santa Anna's army. Once across the Colorado, he would bear south for San Felipe and circle them. This was the last place he'd heard Houston's army occupied.

Once across the river, the sight of the settlements and the surrounding farms shocked him. What was not burned was abandoned. Shop doors banged back and forth in the spring breeze, some of the goods still sitting on the shelves. There were no horses to be seen, no oxen, no wagons. But dogs, cattle, hogs, chickens, and cats meandered about loose, without a care in the world. The hens had flown their coops and left eggs at every fence post where the grass was high enough to hide them. The farmers' cribs were full of last fall's harvest; flocks of crows picked at the hard kernels through warped, narrow, sun-bleached pickets. The smokehouses hung with well-cured hams, beef quarters, and bacon slabs all left for the flies. The settlers' homes were left standing open to the four winds, the beds unmade, clothes still hanging on the pegs, the remains of a last hurried meal still sitting on the table next to a pan of curdling milk. They were there one minute and gone the next, running east with what they could carry. The rest, what he knew they valued most, they left behind.

Remy had pitied the Méxicano conscripts, but the sight of this once bustling land between the Brazos and the Colorado, the cradle of his kind, wrenched his heart. The symbols of Anglo industry—their homes, barns, stores, fences, and fields, representing years of risk, sweat, blood and backbreaking labor—smoldered all around him; white-gray ashes flurried, then fell, scattered to the cold earth.

But within him he felt no chill. His anger grew molten, hotter with each step of his stallion's hooves. There were many responsible, he knew, both Méxicano and white. He reasoned that the revolt was much more complex than it appeared; he'd sorted through its multiple causes many times. He'd lived through most of them. But his soul told him there was only one person directly responsible for the death of Elijah Johnson, and it was on this man, and on any other who would keep Remy from him, whom he vowed to vent a most violent and murderous rage. Revenge ruled his every thought, corrupted every image, tainted every smell; it consumed him as no other thing, blessed or damned, ever had. He had no further need of food or water, no requirement for sleep. He craved blood, and blood only.

When the horse grew tired, he walked ahead of it and went on. Cold rain warmed him; he was consoled by the blackest night. Time, it seemed, stood still.

The night wind called Elijah's name.

He rode to Gonzáles. Burned. Burnham's Ferry. Burned. San Bernard. Burned. San Felipe. Burned. On to the Brazos bottoms. Empty, save the coons and other scavengers that groveled in the sour muck left by a frantic army on the run.

The spring rains continued to fall. A harsh winter followed by a wet spring boded ill, as if Remy needed any natural signs. The muddy roads east were choked with exhausted women and crying children, who pushed wagons mired to their axles, or pulled makeshift, ungreased, and wobbly-wheeled carts with their blistered hands and bleeding fingers. Their men, Remy knew, were either dead or soon to be. Pots, pans, and furniture littered the countryside behind them; feathers from gouged mattresses crested the ruts in the mud like yet another unseasonable snow.

There was nothing much he could do but mitigate the refugees' worry. There was no immediate danger, he told them, at least not from the direction he had come. They thanked him as they cursed others, and he went on.

He came across three white men. They had the only empty wagon on the roads. With so many valuables handy, he saw they were keen to fill it. Scavengers. They figured him for a loner and offered him a share, his pick, if he'd help them load the heavy stuff. A mile or so back, they said, there was a piano. He countered with lead balls to the brains of two of them. They fell dead in the mud, ghastly eyes open, and stayed there. The third he hung, screaming, with his own dirty rope as a warning to others so lowly inclined. Before the man died, Remy rode across his swinging shadow and never looked back. It would be like this, he thought, from now on.

He headed for Groce's plantation. It lay twenty miles north of the cold embers that had once been San Felipe. Rumor on the road was that Houston's army was now hiding there.

Chapter Thirteen

Kills White Bear and his small band of warriors never slid from the backs of their horses. His interest lay in the whites' response to the Méxicanos' threat. He'd followed the Méxicano army north and then passed them by before they crossed the Colorado. And what he saw there thrilled him. Maguara's sign had proved true. If the lodges of the whites were not already burning when Kills White Bear arrived, they soon were.

Méxicano emissaries had traveled among all the nations. They wanted allies for their war. In exchange they offered to remove the whites and draw the line. Maguara had agreed, as Kills White Bear knew others had, but no Comanche warriors rode with the Mexican soldiers. Theirs was a personal agenda. As much as it must have frustrated the Méxicanos, the Comanches chose another, more certain way.

War parties representing the various bands were scattered and active along the river the Méxicanos had named the Colorado. Such a show of force, he knew, was all the incentive the whites needed to release their slipping grip from the land. Kills White Bear, the eyes and ears of the waiting Penateka, their unofficial war chief in the field, sought them out for news. A carving on the trunk of a tree, or a design etched into the sun-bleached scapula of a long-dead buffalo, told him who rode with what parties, where they'd been, what had happened there, and where they'd gone.

Kills White Bear came upon Eagle Claw's party. He was chagrined to see that there were wounded among them. He asked what had happened.

Eagle Claw said they had raided a small wagon party headed east. It had seemed easy enough, and it was. They'd killed two men, and taken one woman and three children hostage. They'd made camp on the stream the whites called Walnut Creek to rest. At dawn the following morning, they'd been surprised to learn that not all the whites were warring with the Méxicanos. The woman captive had escaped in the night. Rangers, in return, had tracked them to their camp like coyotes. Eagle Claw recognized Tumlinson as their leader, a man Kills White Bear respected. He had with him, Eagle Claw thought, about thirty angry men. He lost two good warriors in the fight that soon followed. Three others lay wounded. Eagle Claw swore revenge. Together, Eagle Claw said, they could rout them. He knew where they'd gone.

"Now is not the time," Kills White Bear told him, "to

put your young warriors at risk. Let the settlers running east pass. When they are gone the rangers, most likely, will ride south to fight the Méxicanos, and the Méxicanos, in turn, will make short work of them. All they need is a little more time. When it's done, it's only the ones who remain in our country that the Nemenuh must kill. And they," he assured him, "will be few."

Chapter Fourteen

Remy reached Groce's Plantation on the eleventh of April. He'd fully expected to find the same sort of confused rabble he'd experienced the fall before. Instead, they were drilling. He couldn't believe his eyes.

At noon, the respective companies were dismissed for their lunch. Jared Groce had graciously thrown his ample stores open in aid of the famished army. They were served plates of boiled corn, cornbread, and beef. Fresh water was drawn from Groce's deep wells. For the first time in days, Remy ate.

When he had had his fill, Remy milled around greeting his comrades. Most of these men he knew. For the most part foreigners—young boys from Louisiana, Mississippi, Kentucky and Tennessee—had fought and died with Travis at the Alamo and with Fannin at Goliad. He was encouraged. These men here with Houston were Texians, all with much at stake. It was their homes that were burning and their families out alone on the roads. They'd all lost friends or relatives to Santa Anna somewhere along the way to Groce's. Up until that time Remy believed that he was alone in his fury. But he saw right away that the same fever that burned in him burned in them all.

He saw Juan Seguín was there with his men. The Tejanos still fought; the revolt remained an alliance. Remy knew this was good for everyone, but particularly comforting to him.

"Buenos días, Don Juan," Remy said to the young ranchero. Remy felt that they had become friends long before they were comrades. They were roughly the same age; both

shared some percentage of French blood. Remy was proud of Juan Seguín's leadership and valor, as were all of the Tejanos. He'd proven himself a fighter long ago.

"It's good to see you, Don Remy." Despite the recent rest, Seguín looked worn and tired. "All is well with your family?"

"They have concerns," Remy admitted flatly.

"Don't we all," Seguín answered.

Remy pointed to the Anglo soldiers who had resumed their drills. "Things look better," he said.

"They could not look worse. They've learned how to march, it's true, but they've not forgotten how to argue. Houston can't control them. It's their hatred for Santa Anna that loosely binds them together."

"It's what brought me here," Remy said. "Where's the general?"

"Who knows? He keeps to himself."

"I'll go hunt him up, see what he's got in mind."

Those dark, intense, almost desperate eyes fixed on his. "If he tells you something, Don Remy, anything, you'll share it with your friends, no?"

"Count on it," he said. *"No se rinden, muchachos."*

"No surrender," Seguín repeated. *"Víva la revolución."* He did not seem enthused.

Remy found General Houston in Groce's blacksmith's shop. He was tinkering with a soldier's broken rifle lock, a crumpled map spread before him. He looked for a while at one, and then turned to the other. Remy didn't see where much progress was being made at either.

Remy stepped in quietly. Houston had not heard him. "Hello, Sam," he finally said.

That was exactly how he should say it, he thought. He had practiced several versions before the time actually came. He knew the man. He'd taken Houston to visit the Comanches back in '33, just as his friend Bowie had asked.

Houston had been impressed with his relationship with Maguara. He and Houston had spent weeks together in open and wild country until Houston's old war wound reopened and he was forced to return to the States. Their time together had been sufficient for their friendship to bond.

They'd seldom seen each other since. Houston was an East Texas War Dog, had been before he had ever legally immigrated. That fact alone distanced him from Remy. He was, furthermore, the most cunning of them all and therefore the most dangerous. Santa Anna had focused on the right man all along.

When Houston had undermined Austin's authority at Béxar, Remy had fully intended to sever all ties. Bowie had deserted Austin as well, of course, but Bowie was a Texian and a Béxareno with a Tejano wife. He and Remy had much in common and much at stake. Houston, the foreigner, had no such investment. Remy knew him well enough to suspect that what Houston did, he did for himself. This he had never forgotten when the bickering and intrigue had started.

It was well known by now that Houston had slipped, both personally and politically, from the underbelly of Jackson's administration, and settled in Tejas. Why exactly, no one knew, but they were all suspicious. Houston had opened a law office in Nacogdoches, received a grant from Austin and another one from someone else, and went about making a living as they all had to do. He financed his activities, Remy knew, with money from eastern land speculators. His hands were dirty from the very beginning.

He immediately linked himself to the War Dog element and spent much time whispering in the back rooms of saloons. If that wasn't bad enough, he was also vain, boastful, loud, and ambitious—a double-dealing land speculator and lawyer to boot; certainly a drunk, and certainly slippery. Remy could never bring himself to trust such a man, but he couldn't help liking him.

Houston turned to him. "Why Don Remy! A pleasant surprise, I assure you. I took you for a Tory."

"Shut up, General," Remy said, "and give me my orders."

Houston straightened at his tone. "I'm encouraged—more or less. Not many are asking for them lately."

"I'm here to fight," Remy said. "Find me a place."

Houston turned to his map. "You come at a good time, Fuqua. I'm looking for one now." He took a small vial from his vest pocket, poured a few grains of its contents on the back of his hand between the thumb and index finger, brought it to his nose and sniffed deeply. "Salt of hartshorn," he explained. "Restores the spirit. I'm drinking very little these days."

Remy hoped to God it was true. He couldn't really be sure.

The general looked at him warmly. "It's good to have a friend with me," he said, and Remy felt circumstances alone merited that whatever politics lay between them should best be set aside. He felt, perhaps, too easily won. He chalked the defeat up to Houston's charm. You either loved or hated him. With Houston he had realized long ago that there was no middle ground.

"It's good to see you, Sam," he admitted. They shook hands firmly. Remy's was lost in that big paw. "You look well."

"You, sir, are a damned liar, and not a very good one at that." He began tinkering again with the rifle. "I miss Jim Bowie," he said quietly.

"I do, too." Remy'd thought about him ever since he'd heard the news.

"He didn't listen to me, Fuqua. If he had, he'd be here with us right now. Travis didn't listen. Fannin didn't listen. *Nobody* is listening!" His voice built to a tense crescendo. Remy sensed its frustration and despair.

"Well, Sam," Remy said, "why don't you tell me what you've got to say. Maybe I'll listen."

"Maybe, you say," Houston grunted. "A qualification. Typical. I've got a thousand maybe's under my command." He pointed out the door. "Everybody's keen to fight, but they don't want to plan a strategy. And they're sick to death of mine. It's madness! We might just as well slice our own throats."

"What'd you expect?" Remy asked. "You told 'em you'd hold at Gonzáles. You didn't. You told 'em you'd fight at the Colorado. You didn't. You said the Mexicans would never cross the Brazos. They did."

Houston pursed his lips. "I was waiting for Fannin!" he growled. "He never came. I lost half my force at Goliad in one day. We couldn't stand against the Mexicans with what we had left. I've done what was best."

"They," Remy said, meaning the army, "don't see it that way. I can tell ya that for sure."

"They don't see at all," he said grimly. "Austin's gone. We don't hold elections in this army anymore. It's war, not politics. It becomes a matter of confidence, Fuqua—in me!"

Remy felt his stare deaden. Confidence was something you earned. Neither one of Houston's two faces merited the investment, not by men who were risking everything. Houston's past had finally caught up with him. "I know those men out there," Remy told him. "An' most all of 'em know me. You earn my trust, and I'll see if I kin help you earn theirs." It was a promise he intended to keep if he was satisfied that Houston was good for his word.

Houston thought for a moment, and then a smile broke across that big face. He held the gun up to him. "A private brought this to me," he explained, glancing at the dingy walls around him, "and, given my current surroundings, ordered me to repair it for him. It's a sad state of affairs when soldiers don't recognize their commanding officer. I'd say it speaks for itself, wouldn't you?"

Remy nodded.

Houston returned his stare to the rifle. "It's in a sorry state, I think."

Remy looked at it and agreed. "Near ruint."

"The irony," Houston continued, "is that I think I can fix it. In fact, I know I can. I told that boy to come round in an hour or so. At that time, this rifle will fire. And that young, ignorant soldier will learn that, despite his confusion, despite his blunder, he came to the right place after all. His faith in me, regardless of the fact that it was initially misplaced, will be rewarded nonetheless." He cocked his head and winked. "Do you catch my drift, Fuqua?"

"Yep," Remy answered. "I believe I do."

"I've got a decision to make here," he stated. "These men want blood. I promised them they could have it, but my heart tells me this isn't the time. Not now. I think they've got one good battle left in 'em. If it comes at the wrong time, they'll all die."

Remy was encouraged by what he'd seen. He thought maybe Houston would be as well. "I've seen the Mexican army close up, Sam. Santa Anna's pushed 'em hard. They're wore thin."

"And they'll get worse. Their supply lines are already stretched to the breaking point. He's split his forces without knowing where we are. He doesn't respect us, I know. But I respect him. I continue to favor the withdrawal east. But if I say so outright, the men'll mutiny. I know they will."

Remy thought it best to speak frankly. "And I prob'ly would, too."

Houston frowned. "That disappoints me. You're smarter than that, Fuqua. You'd know better if you understood the larger view. Somebody's got to look beyond the next battle. It's a big game we're playin' here."

"Tell me about it."

Remy could see Houston was weighing options. Finally, his gaze turned back to Remy. "It can go no further. Spies are everywhere. There's one on my staff somewhere. The government knows what I know before I know it." He paused a moment, his eyes sparkling. "But you, Fuqua, I trust. And like I said, it's good to have a friend with me. I'm hungry for counsel. I'd welcome yours."

He had to think about that before committing himself. Houston, after all, was very sly. "You got my word," he said, hoping like hell that he'd not regret giving it.

"That's enough for me," Houston said, and he closed the doors.

Then Houston told him what Remy knew immediately was the truth. Houston and Andrew Jackson had plotted the Texas revolt back in '32. There was no proof of it to be found anywhere. Jackson's notes and memos would, in fact, state the direct opposite. But they had a firm understanding, and Remy would just have to accept his word on that.

Jackson had always hoped for an internal rebellion. There could never be aggression on the part of the United States, lest England, Spain, and France intervene. They were all looking for a new toehold in America. An invasion of Mexico would provide the excuse they needed. Jackson was bound by treaty as well. If he took what he wanted, it would ruin him.

Much to their mutual surprise, he explained, the Mexicans themselves had opened the door to Texas. Houston had immigrated as Jackson's eyes. He had soon advised the President that an internal rebellion against Mexico was entirely possible. No foreign nation, the United States included, could intervene in a family quarrel, at least not without reprisal. The Texians would throw off their Mexican masters and then come to Jackson for admission into the American union. If the Europeans intervened at that time, Jackson would invade as a matter of national interest. He was a winner either way, and the United States would control the continent from the Atlantic to the Pacific. That, he said, was the dream.

But when hostilities began, they both knew they'd come too soon. They needed two more years and another ten thousand American immigrants. The Texas revolt had caught them unprepared.

Houston admitted that he'd overestimated Austin's loyalist hold on the settlers, and likewise underestimated Santa Anna's meteoric rise to power and his immediate response to the Anglo revolt. Events, he said, had thrown him and Jackson both off balance. Things appeared gloomy indeed for their schemes. It would not be as easy as they'd once thought.

They had talked, however, of the need for contingencies in this very case. Jackson knew of only one. The Americans and the Spanish had quarreled for years over the exact boundaries of the Louisiana Purchase. Jefferson himself believed the French had had a legitimate claim to Texas, or parts thereof. The previous administration had settled the question, or at least thought they had, with the Adams-Onis Treaty of 1819. They intended the Sabine River as the international boundary.

But Jackson had the treaty reinterpreted by the highest authorities in whom he trusted to tell him exactly what he wanted to hear. Due to a number of legal ambiguities and elastic phrases, as well as their commitment to reach an appropriate end, Jackson's commission concluded the true boundary was the Neches River, several miles west. Jackson was still looking for a delicate way to convey this more recent interpretation of the treaty to the Mexicans when war broke out in Texas. It was never publicized. Jackson intended to wield this paper weapon at the most opportune time. It hadn't yet come.

That issue aside, Houston continued, there was another provision of the Adams-Onis Treaty of interest. The United States had the undisputed right to cross the Sabine to pursue hostile Indians when they threatened American settlers. Everyone knew the Mexicans had beseeched the Comanches to embrace their cause, but they'd also come to the Caddo and Cherokee and others in East Texas. In doing so, Houston assured him, they'd wrought their own destruction.

Across the Sabine sat General Edmund Gaines. He was, Houston said, Jackson's man. One Caddo arrow aimed at an American settler anywhere close to the boundary, and Gaines had the excuse required by international law. He would ford the Sabine with army regulars and state militia. He had, Houston was told, thousands under his command.

Gaines would come under strict written orders to retain American neutrality. But, if fired upon—be it hostile Caddos or others—Gaines would fire back. If it happened that an unfortunate misunderstanding occurred between American and Mexican forces stumbling around out there in the gray areas, so be it. The distance between Washington and the frontier was great. It would be weeks before Jackson could even issue an apology for such an embarrassing incident. Jackson would, of course, disavow Gaines's regrettable actions, but the damage would have already been done. Santa Anna would be crushed by fresh troops at the tail end of a long, exhausting campaign; the Americans would withdraw in accordance with the treaty, and Texas would be left to the Anglos.

"So you see, Fuqua," Houston said wryly, "I'm quite the gunsmith after all."

Remy was dumbfounded. He knew a certain amount of plotting and intrigue was required to start a revolution, but this was simply beyond his scope. He'd been peeking at the war through a knothole in a warped board when Houston kicked down the whole damn wall. The sudden brilliance of it hurt his eyes. Santa Anna had known all along. The revolt was not between brothers after all. It was a game between nations in which brothers bled. He couldn't believe it, and said so.

Houston rose and motioned for him to follow. They stepped together out the door. Houston pointed to a section of uniformed men in the middle of the camp.

"You see them?" he asked. Remy followed the length of his arm, squinting at the end of it. "Who's that?"

"Soldiers."

"What kind, you fool?"

"Look like American, maybe. Hard to say at this distance."

"Gaines's men," he said. "Deserters." He winked. "When the war's over, you see if they don't desert back." Houston ushered him back into the little shop. The sun shone through the little cracks forming shafts of dusty light. "Help me get these men east, Fuqua. Victory waits for us there."

Houston must've thought the sight would console him. It didn't. Houston had lied to the Tejanos, to the War Dogs, even to the soldiers he led. The war belonged to none of them.

"I don't know whether I should hug you or shoot you dead."

Houston seemed startled by Remy's reaction. He was quiet for a while, and then said, "Either would be appreciated at this point." He reached for Remy. Two big hands fell on his shoulders and squared his chest to Houston's. There was no place for Remy to look but at those steely blue eyes. "I know it's easy to make a villain out of me, Remy. Thousands in two nations already have. But if it wasn't me, it was goin' to be somebody else. That's what you've got to grasp now. War with the Mexicans was inevitable."

"Like hell," Remy said. "You picked a fight you couldn't win."

"I did not, sir!" he thundered, stung. "I told you we planned to wait. Travis and those other half-cocked fools brought this on." He leaned forward, his tone shifting. "But it's up to you and me and the rest of those men out there to see it through. There's no other option. We've got one chance, I tell you, and that's to draw Santa Anna east into General Gaines's domain." He released him. "Help me, Remy," he said quietly.

Remy didn't like it, not one bit. It all could've been avoided. He thought maybe he should've stayed with Don Carlos and Beatriz after all. He knew Houston could not be trusted, like him or not. He silently cursed both him and Jackson for the misery they'd caused. But he still hated Santa Anna for what had happened to Elijah. There was no way back from that, and there was no way back from this goddamn war.

He would fight with these men come what may. He would help this son of a bitch Houston because it suited his plans for Elijah's revenge. That aside, it remained a good idea to watch the revolt closely. It was the only way to ensure that his family was protected. He would play Houston's game in the attempt to win it for himself.

"I'll try," he finally told him. "It'd help if you let 'em know about Gaines."

"That I can't do. It'd blow the lid off the whole deal. And you can't either. Jackson's hand is well concealed. I'm considered a highly unstable individual in Washington. To implicate Jackson beforehand would make a liar out of us both."

"I don't know if'n I feel a little better knowin' or a whole lot worse."

"Then you understand my position," Houston told him. "And I want you, as a friend, to know one thing more. I came here for the right reasons. I believe that. But I'm truly sorry for the suffering it's caused." He picked the rifle back up and started to reassemble it.

"I was a broken man when I came to Texas," Houston said sadly. "My marriage had failed. There was a vicious scandal. My political career was ruined. For three years I lived with the Cherokee and did little else but drink and plot a revolt. It hardened me, made me a little mean, I guess." He reached for a screwdriver. "But time and Texas has changed all of that. I love this country, and I love these people. The revolt isn't about me anymore, Fuqua. I want you to know that. I'd die for those men out there. And I will, if I have to. Texas is my home, just like it's yours. You've got to believe me when I tell you we're fightin' for the same thing."

Chapter Fifteen

Remy, now a troop-less captain, presided, more or less, over the Brazos crossing. They employed a steamship and an old scow. It took two days. Houston then marched his army due east. Remy spread what cheer he could without elaborating on its basis. He told them they'd soon get the fight they wanted and left it at that. There was little for them to do but walk on, bitching at every step.

Word had it that Santa Anna had descended on the temporary capital, Harrisburg, to the southeast. He'd burned the town, or at least what the Texians had not already burned, to the ground.

Remy knew the road ahead forked. To the north lay Nacogdoches, the Neches River, and General Gaines; to the south, Harrisburg and Santa Anna.

Remy knew well enough which way Houston wanted to go. But something had changed. They'd recently intercepted Mexican couriers with information on Santa Anna's whereabouts and, more importantly, the force of his army. They estimated he had perhaps five hundred men. He was moving swiftly now because he felt that Houston's army would never attack. The bulk of Santa Anna's army remained scattered behind him, maybe forty miles distant.

Houston conferred with his officers and they made their views clear. If Houston turned north, they told him, he would go alone. Remy wanted to tell them Nacogdoches virtually guaranteed victory. But, of course, he did not.

Houston rode toward the rear of the column as the advance guard reached the Which Way Tree. Mr. Roberts, the owner of the land that bordered the road, stood at his gate. A group of rebel officers asked him to point out clearly the way to Harrisburg. It was for Houston's benefit.

"That right-hand road will carry you to Harrisburg just as straight as a compass," Roberts said.

There was no hesitation when they reached it. They turned right. How it happened exactly, Remy didn't know. He couldn't see Houston's face when they'd turned, and he certainly didn't know his mind. It could be that Houston had remained undecided and let his army choose for him. Either way, the choice was made.

Texas would go it alone, without Gaines and Jackson. The men shouted in triumph, and Remy shouted with them. They were going to try and do it clean. For the first time since he'd learned of Elijah's death, Remy felt good about what was happening.

Despite the perpetual rains, they rolled into Harrisburg on April 18. They had covered fifty-five miles in two and a half days. When the cannon had bogged down in the mud, Houston himself had jumped down from his horse and put his shoulder to the wheel.

That same day Deaf Smith and Henry Karnes had intercepted another Mexican courier. He carried dispatches in deerskin saddlebags marked "William Barret Travis." Houston walked among his troops with the bags over his head. He'd done it to revive their spirits, but Remy didn't see how it was necessary. They all knew what had happened to Travis, and they all knew further what might happen to them. They were ready to fight.

But what was more important was the documents they contained. In his haste to finish off Houston, Santa Anna had temporarily cut himself off from his main army.

At dawn the following day, Houston addressed his troops. The morning breeze blew the mane of Remy's horse. "The army will cross Buffalo Bayou, and we will meet the enemy," he began. His voice was steady and deliberate. "Some of us may be killed and must be killed. Victory is certain! Trust in God and fear not!" He paused, and then continued. "But, soldiers . . ." his voice was building now, "remember the Alamo! . . . The Alamo! . . . The Alamo!"

His exhortation was short and cryptic. Well short of the eloquence of which Houston was capable. But then again, that army didn't require much in the way of speeches. They required revenge. They latched onto Houston's words as they latched onto their rifles.

Hundreds of long bores erupted in the moist calm of morning. Houston was stunned that they'd do this when the enemy was so close. But Remy knew the coastal humidity required daily charges of fresh, dry powder, and also that they didn't care a lick if Santa Anna knew they'd taken up his trail.

Chapter Sixteen

Houston had sent Remy for Seguín. When they returned together the general politely informed Don Juan that he could not guarantee the safety of his Tejanos. The inevitable battle, he told him, could become indiscriminate. Remy understood that this was a delicate way of suggesting that Houston's men might turn against any and all Mexicans in a blind rage. Houston then ordered Seguín and his men to guard supplies in Harrisburg.

"Not all of my men are with me," Seguín reminded his commander with the reserved dignity of his kind and class. Had Houston better understood the Tejano mind, he would have known, as Remy did, that despite his polite tone Don Juan was deeply offended. "Many died with Travis at the Alamo."

Houston was sympathetic but undeterred. "These men hate Mexicans, Captain Seguín—all Mexicans, I'm afraid. If you ride in battle, it may not be a Santanista bullet that finds you."

"That is the chance we must take," Seguín said. "We are—all of us—Béxarenos. Our homes are lost unless Santa Anna is driven out of Tejas. We therefore have as much reason as any man here, if not more, to hate that man."

Don Juan glanced at Remy, who nodded, then turned back to Houston. "We respectfully insist on front-line duty for the duration of the campaign, come what may. The blood of our fallen comrades has earned our place."

Seguín stood back as Houston deliberated. Remy noticed the change in Houston's expression. He understood. "Spoken like a man," he finally said. "And I agree. However, we must take precautions."

It was then decided that Seguín and his remaining nineteen Tejanos would mark themselves with cardboard insignias in their hat bands. When the battle came, Houston promised Don Juan that he could ride to the sound of Santa Anna's guns. Seguín bowed his head slightly and drifted away into the night.

They arrived at the junction of Buffalo Bayou and the San Jacinto River midafternoon of April 20. Santa Anna's troops were in sight. There were immediate skirmishes, a hasty exchange of cannon fire, and an ill-conceived cavalry charge by the Texians who were supposedly on reconnaissance. There were casualties on both sides, but nothing much more came of any of that.

Nor did much materialize in the way of war the following morning. Houston slept in while his men grumbled. He used a coil of rope as his pillow. By midmorning Santa Anna was reinforced by over five hundred men.

The Texian camp exploded with rage at what they perceived as a lost opportunity. Colonel John Wharton circulated among the men. "Boys," he said, "there's no other word today but fight! Fight! Now's the time!" Remy knew that Houston had heard him. They had another of those "animated" conversations. Obviously, they failed to reach an understanding, as Remy saw Houston turn away, sneering, "Fight and be damned!"

By noon the dissent was organized and their leaders de-

manded to see Houston. Or Houston may have sent for
them. One never knew.

For two hours, Houston's officers harangued the general
while he sat coldly rigid. Scouts reported that Santa Anna
now had approximately twelve hundred men. The Texian
force numbered about nine hundred. The numerical advantage, they complained bitterly, was lost. Other Mexican di-
visions were most certainly closing on their position; as bad
as things were, they would soon get much worse. They must
attack. Houston said next to nothing, but asked for a vote.
Should they leave the oak groves and attack, or should they
dig in and defend them?

Remy suspected that Houston was weighing a defensive
strategy against an all-out offensive. A defensive strategy
had worked well for Bowie at Concepción, and there was
plenty of cover at Buffalo Bayou from which Kentucky
rifles could pick off attacking Mexican units. But Houston
no longer confided in anyone.

A little over an hour later, Remy heard a commotion in
the camp. The separate companies were gathering. Houston
had called his troops to battle, quickly assembling them
into two parallel lines, ready to advance. The two six-pound
cannons, the "twin sisters," a gift from the people of Cin-
cinnati, were rolled dead center. Colonel Sherman commanded the left flank, followed in line by Burleson,
Hockley, and finally Millard on the right. Mirabeau Buonaparte Lamar, the Georgian, a private yesterday but a colonel today, led the Texian Cavalry. Houston rode a white
horse in front of them all. Remy hastily gathered his weapons and rode beside him.

After the commotion had subsided, Houston drew his
sword and advanced. His face looked tense yet committed.
His horse stepped forward and nine hundred men moved
behind it.

The smiles vanished from their faces as they set themselves to the grim task at hand. The Mexican army was not
three-quarters of a mile away.

Deaf Smith, the scout, raced in from the east. He rode
up and down the line with an axe in his hand yelling to all

that Vince's Bridge was down. This meant that Santa Anna's reinforcements could not easily reach him. But it also meant that Houston's army could not retreat. It was do or die.

Remy set his mind to its dark purpose. He would now get what he came for. The troops' quickstep rapidly escalated into a trot. Previously distinct lines merged into one swarming mass.

At about two hundred yards, Houston ordered the cannons spun around and fired. He heard the Mexican bugles answer in the distance. Remy and the others had already gotten remarkably close before the Mexicans reacted. Somehow, they'd surprised them. There were no sentries. No soldiers watching from the line. Their horses were unsaddled. Their rifles stood stacked. It was a miracle. Their first notice that the attack was under way was when grapeshot tore into the bodies of napping men.

When they were close enough to see the Mexican soldiers scrambling before them, Houston organized his men as best he could into one line of fire. He shouted the order and the entire field erupted in a staccato roar and plumes of white smoke. Houston ordered his men to stand and reload. They paid him no mind. Instead they threw themselves against the enemy line with indiscriminate fire.

"God damn you!" Houston shouted, enraged. "Hold your fire!" But Sherman's line broke forward. The rest followed. The secretary of war, Thomas Jefferson Rusk, screamed "If we stop now, we're cut to pieces! Don't stop!—Go ahead!—Give 'em hell!"

Those who hesitated now ran behind those who never had. Houston and Remy were quickly overrun by their own men, shouting *"Remember Goliad! Remember the Alamo!"* as they passed. Remy heard others scream *"You killed Isaac Baker!", "You killed Wash Cottle!"* and *"You killed Jesse McCoy!"*

Inspired, Remy yelled, *"You killed Elijah Johnson!"* and cut loose from Houston, his father's rifle strapped to his back, Don Carlos's pistol in one hand and his knife in the other, the reins between his clenched teeth.

The Mexican breastworks of packs, baggage, feedsacks, sticks, logs and dirt, were not seventy yards away. They bustled with confused soldiers who were scrambling to defend themselves. It appeared to Remy that the Mexicans never believed the Texians would attack. And Remy himself never knew it would be quite like this. There was no longer a main body of Texians to ward off. They'd broken into targetless shock troops—a general *mélée* of wild and whooping angry men. They fell viciously on the bewildered Mexicans like coyotes on a dying steer. Aiming from horseback, Remy was yet to have a clear shot.

Despite their confusion, a number of Mexicans rallied. They fired their cannon five times. Remy heard the whine of grapeshot and canister as it buzzed around him. The twin sisters answered with blasts of scrap iron and minced horseshoes into their position. Mexicans fell in droves as a section of their makeshift wall was leveled before them, the last barrier between them and the rushing hordes. Remy leaned low against the stallion's neck and dashed through the crumbling gap. A Mexican soldier took his aim as Remy shot him clean through the chest with Don Carlos's pistol.

It was then that he saw Houston fall, blood staining the white flank of his stallion. Mexican grapeshot had nearly gutted it. Remy wheeled his horse with his knees and found his commander another loose mount. Houston leaped on and followed after his men while Remy reloaded.

The Texians were already scrambling over the enemy's breastworks. The battle now escalated into hand-to-hand combat. No longer bothering to reload, the Anglos swung their rifles like clubs, or wielded tomahawks and Bowie knives. Remy heard the thud of steel gouged deeply into flesh and bone. He heard the screams of enraged men and the cries of their victims as they fell bleeding at their feet. The frantic Mexican horses would not allow Santa Anna's cavalry to mount. Shouting Anglos poured through the shattered breastworks. The Mexicans were defeated. When Remy shot now, he was shooting at their fleeing backs.

Remy turned to see Houston shot in the lower leg. Blood poured from the general's ankle as his horse collapsed dead. Remy dismounted, offering Houston his horse. Houston took it and waved Remy on.

Remy fell in with Seguín's men as they scrambled toward

the now fleeing Mexicans. Bodies were strewn everywhere. A Mexican general manned the cannon alone. He sat down, his arms crossed, and waited, refusing to run. Rusk, apparently admiring the Mexican general's bravery, cried "Don't shoot him! Don't shoot him!" and he angrily shoved several aimed barrels away from that officer. But he couldn't get them all. Remy watched as the general fell, riddled by Texian rifle fire. That was the last of the resistance. The battle had taken less than twenty minutes.

Routed, the Mexican army fled for the marshes and the bayous. Most had thrown down their arms. The fight was over and the killing should've ended. But the Texians, who now gripped their guns by the end of their hot barrels, ran the Mexicans down.

Don Carlos's second cousin, Antonio Menchaca, who, along with the others, was shouting *"¡Recuerden el Alamo!"* as he chased after stragglers, came upon a Mexican officer who recognized him.

"Spare me, brother Méxicano," Remy heard him plead.

"No, damn you!" Menchaca seethed. "My brothers died in the Alamo. I'm no longer a Méxicano. I'm an American." As Remy watched, Menchaca turned to the others and said coldly, "Shoot him." That was all it took. Menchaca didn't have to do it. There were a dozen Anglos nearby more than ready.

Everywhere Remy looked, Mexicans were attempting to surrender. It was no use. The precedent for prisoners, he knew, had been set by Santa Anna. One by one, they were shot, stabbed, or bludgeoned to death. Those who fell to the wild men, the backwoodsmen, were scalped.

His rage spent, Remy was now sickened by the horror of what was happening. He wanted no part of the carnage.

He saw a boy, a drummer. Both of his legs were broken and horribly mangled. The boy clung to the legs of one of Colonel Sherman's Kentucky mercenaries, crying, *"¡Ave María purissima! ¡Por Dios, salva mi vida!"*

Remy ran to him. "Let him go! He's just a boy!"

"He's a Mexican boy," the soldier sneered. Remy stepped forward to intercede. The soldier reached for his pistol and for a moment threatened them both. Remy had no choice but to back away. He looked on in horror as the man put the barrel to the boy's head and fired. His body crumpled to the bloody ground. Stunned, Remy watched as the soldier ran into the fray to find another.

Houston rode up and snatched him from his trance. "Fuqua! Catch a horse! Let's stop this madness! A hundred steady men could rout us!"

Remy snagged the bridle of a Mexican horse, mounted, and followed his commander.

"Gentlemen!" Houston's voice boomed. "Gentlemen! Gentlemen! Gentlemen! I applaud your bravery but damn your manners! Parade! Parade!" But the Texians ignored Houston. It seemed nothing would stop the killing.

Unnerved, Remy split from Houston. Why exactly, he couldn't say. He came to the marsh around Peggy Lake. Unarmed Méxicanos shouted *"Me no Alamo! Me no Goliad!"* On the bank, Texian riflemen cut them down whenever they came up for air. The water, full of scrambling horses and frantic men, ran red.

The army surgeon, Dr. Labadie, was pulling a Méxicano officer from the bog when several infantry men approached. Their intent was clear. "Don't shoot! Don't shoot!" cried the surgeon. "I've taken him prisoner!" The doctor's arm still held the Méxicano when the ball, fired at point blank range, crashed into his forehead. Brains and blood splattered Dr. Labadie. He collapsed to his knees in the bloody mud, speechless.

"Stop it, goddammit!" Remy shouted. "Stop it now! You are ordered to take them prisoner!"

One frontiersman allowed he knew how to take prisoners just like the Mexicans did. You just bashed their brains out with the butt of your rifle. And Remy's, he added coolly, would bash just as easy. "You don't like it, Fuqua, you just git!" he bawled, and he yanked the hickory rod from the barrel of his rifle and brought it to his shoulder.

The others watched to see what Remy would do. He knew he should kill that man on the spot, make an example of him. His fingers twitched on the trigger of his gun, but he hesitated. Before he even got close, the others would shoot him dead.

He wheeled his borrowed horse with the sad understanding that he could not make anybody do anything on the plains of San Jacinto. Like him, the Texians had come for revenge. They would continue the killing until their rage was spent. Soon darkness and fatigue would blind the rebels as blood did now.

West of Peggy Lake, Remy came across a Méxicano officer who retained command of several men.

"Do you surrender?" he demanded in Spanish. He recognized the man, a captain, as one who had sat at Don Carlos's table. He answered in perfect English.

"Yes, I'd like to." He was frantic. He could see what was happening to those that already had.

"Do you wanna live?" Remy asked.

"If my men can," he answered. "Otherwise, we fight on."

"Don't do it!" Remy cautioned. "Throw down your arms and make for that thicket yonder." He pointed it out just to make damn sure the Méxicano understood. "I'll come with a group of officers as soon as I can. It's far enough away that those on foot can't reach ya. But if those men come, you huddle together and do nothing to provoke them. If you want your life, you lay down on the ground and beg for it. Sooner or later, they're bound to cool off. I'll be back as soon as I can. You understand me!"

The man nodded. "What's your name?" he asked.

"Captain Remy Fuqua, Army of the Republic of Texas," he heard himself say without pride. "And yours?"

"Colonel Juan Nepomuceno Almonte."

He was Santa Anna's aide, inspector of Tejas. "I know the name well," Remy said. "You'll be safe."

"I don't think so," Almonte said, and Remy, already riding for help, didn't really think so either.

He found Colonel Rusk first. Under him he held a handful of steady men. Remy thanked God. They rode back to Almonte, forming a barrier against the hordes until the sun had set and passions cooled.

When darkness fell, they led the prisoners back to Houston's camp. Almonte had gathered about four hundred soldiers. Early reports confirmed that six hundred and fifty more lay slain on the San Jacinto plains.

Chapter Seventeen

Remy rode ahead of the column when he found Houston lying at the foot of an oak tree, calmly nursing his shattered ankle. Remy saw soon enough that Houston's serenity did not derive from victory but from the opium his physician had liberally administered.

"All is lost!" he shouted. "My God, all is lost!"

Remy looked over his shoulder to see if Houston saw something he didn't. It was only Rusk with Almonte's men.

"Those are prisoners, General," Remy informed him.

"Thank Almighty God," the general sighed, but with his next breath his anxiety returned. "Is Santa Anna among them?" He was told that he was not. "He must be found. All we captured were fools and raw recruits. General Urrea's out there somewhere with thousands. Filisola, too. They won't make the same mistakes. If they catch us in this condition on this plain, they'll do to us what they did to Fannin." He wiped the sweat from his forehead. "Certainly," he said, waving his arm over his own troops, "I can't take those men against anybody." He looked around hazily at his officers. "You can all stop your gloating, gentlemen," he said, the sound of authority returning to his voice. "We've won nothing without Santa Anna. Nothing!"

"We'll find him," Remy said.

"Keep looking, Fuqua" he said, and then he turned to the others. "All of you keep looking! If he's not already dead, God help us, he's not far. Find him!"

It was late when Remy's party returned with three more stragglers. He saw that the other prisoners sat around a blazing fire in the deep woods. They were surrounded by young men with a brace of pistols tucked into their hunting coats, candles cupped in their hands.

Remy greeted them, and released his prisoners to mingle with the rest. There was no place close to the fire for them. Then Remy found himself a place to sleep, and collapsed.

The next morning Remy arose sore, to the smell of woodsmoke. He ate quietly and then looked in on Houston. The general remained delirious from the drugs and the loss of blood.

About then Joel Robison came in with more prisoners. As they drew near most of the other Méxicanos bowed. The officers rose and saluted. The words "El Presidente" were whispered on the cool spring breeze.

Chapter Eighteen

Sam Houston's mood improved when Santa Anna, wearing a common soldier's uniform with the exception of his red worsted slippers and a silk shirt buttoned with diamond studs, was led before him. Houston skirted up against the trunk of his tree. A Mexican blanket lay beneath him. His face, despite the opium, contorted in pain.

"I am General Antonio López de Santa Anna," the prisoner announced. "President of México, commander in chief of the Army of Operations. And I put myself at the disposition of the brave General Houston. I wish to be treated as a general should be when a prisoner of war." Despite the haughty language, Remy noticed the man's hands trembling.

Houston looked sleepy-eyed and drugged. "General Santa Anna!" he slurred. "Ah, indeed! Take a seat, General. I'm glad to see you. Take a seat!" Houston tapped his hand on a black box. It was the only seat available. Lorenzo de Zavala stepped up at Houston's request to act as interpreter. Santa Anna recognized him well enough, calling him friend. Zavala bowed coolly.

Santa Anna pointed to Houston. "That man may consider himself born to no common destiny who has conquered the Napoleon of the West; and now it remains for him to be generous to the vanquished."

Houston waited for Zavala's translation of all of this, turning at last to reply. "You should've remembered that at the Alamo," he told him. Wild-eyed men, Remy among them, pressed forward. Santa Anna then understood. Nervous, he asked for a piece of opium.

Santa Anna, soon steady, inquired if they should set about forming the inevitable treaty. Houston told him it was not for the army to do. How about an armistice, then? That was sufficient. Would Urrea and Filisola surrender, Houston asked? Unlikely, Santa Anna said. But they might withdraw if ordered. Good enough, all things considered, and soon agreed. Santa Anna wrote the orders in his own hand. Deaf Smith packed the papers in his worn saddlebags and rode off. The immediate danger was over. Texas was won.

Now Remy surged forward, lariat in his hand. This was the one he'd come for. This was the one he would have.

"Remember me," he spat in Spanish. Santa Anna said that he did. His regards to his father-in-law. "You can swing by an' tell 'im yourself," Remy said, "on your way to hell." He started to flip the rope over Santa Anna's head when he was wrestled to the ground on Houston's order.

"Not you, Fuqua," Houston mumbled as Remy lay there struggling. "For God's sake, not you."

Remy spent that long night chained to a tree not a hundred yards from where Santa Anna rested under a heavy guard. Every time he was about to do something rash and heroic, somebody roped him, clubbed him, or otherwise restrained him. He was thinking that maybe it was good that they did. He had watched as Santa Anna's tent and personal belongings were brought up and pitched next to Houston's.

The general would never let his bird get far away. He'd vowed to use his prize wisely.

Rusk, Wharton, and Hockley all came by to see if Remy had cooled. He cursed them all and they slipped quietly away.

But Remy had cooled. He thought now about his family. He wondered how they would fare now that Texas had changed hands. It was good that Seguín had fought. That guaranteed a place in the future for the Tejanos. Perhaps they could go on as they had. He thought the new government would never disallow the Mexican land grants. Most people, white and Tejano alike, would lose their land if they did. He thought Rancho de la Cruz would be safe.

They would form a republic now, he knew. It was a formality. Soon they would apply for admission into the American union. For better than ten years, Remy had struggled to adapt to his new world. In only eighteen minutes, he guaranteed that his old one would now be stamped across it. For the first time in history, white men ruled Texas.

Settlers would flock to the land before the smoke cleared. He knew it was Beatriz now who must adapt. Remy would help her as she'd helped him, and they'd go on, governments be damned as they always were. Houston and his upstarts could have at it.

He couldn't wait to see her and the children, to swap the smell of dirty men for the fragrance of his beautiful wife, to trade the hard, pine cone-laden swamp for the soft warmth of their bed. He wanted to feel her skin next to his. He was eager to explain what happened in the quiet of a warm house and be soothed by that calm and certain voice, to explain this miraculous victory, and share his burden of shame. They would make their plans for a changing future, a future that still promised much for them both. He couldn't wait to go. As soon as he quit cussing them, they would unchain him from that oak. And when they did, he would leave all that pain behind him and go home.

1836

Summer/Fall

Chapter Nineteen

Kills White Bear had come to Enchanted Rock with a heavy heart. On summer nights the great mountain was the mouth of Mother Earth herself, speaking in some ancient tongue forgotten by all men. Kills White Bear scaled its granite peak and faced the setting sun in silent prayer. When night came, he sparked a brilliant fire and offered the spirit of the whitetail deer he had slain to its hungry flames. In exchange, he begged to understand the great rock's wails of wisdom. "Tell me, Mother," he whispered, "what you know."

Soon, he heard haunting groans and creaks from deep within her stone bosom, but they meant nothing to him. As the fire died so died his hopes for answers. She would not share with him. Deeply disappointed, he curled up beside the glowing coals, his skin warmed against the cool evening breeze, and fell asleep.

He dreamed that hundreds of Méxicano soldiers lay dead and bloated, rotting in the intermittent April sun. White men stood over them with grim smiles on their dirty faces. Where, he wondered, was this place?

It was strange country. Spanish moss hung from the twisted limbs of oaks. He saw tall pines in the mist. Mosquitoes and flies buzzed about the bodies. The ground was moist and boggy, the grass high and choked with cane. The water ran black.

He recognized that place. It lay in the east, near the coast of the great water, the land of the strange Attakapan, where he'd seen the Méxicano army go.

Through the smoke and the fog and the dead walked Wolf Eyes. His gaze was fixed on the destruction all around him until at last he turned to Kills White Bear. "Now is the time," he said, and then he vanished into the haze.

Kills White Bear awoke anxious, yet remembered to thank the Earth Mother for the vision she had shared. Although he already knew the dream was true, he decided it also must be confirmed with his own eyes. He descended the mountain to find his warriors waiting, and divided them at once in two. Some he sent northwest back to Maguara to tell him that something had gone wrong and to wait for news. The rest rode with him in search of the Méxicano army.

Two days later his eyes saw what his heart already knew. Thousands of demoralized Méxicanos were pulling back south, stumbling with heavy steps as if exhausted. Some no longer carried guns. Their wounded followed behind in wagons that sank deeply in the mud. They were beaten.

That so many could be defeated by so few bewildered him. What had gone wrong? If the whites had not already crossed the Sabine, they were on their way. The Méxicanos had nearly fulfilled the white bear's vision for him. Was it not the will of the Great Spirit? What had caused this bloodless victory to slip from the Nemenuh's grasp?

Treachery. The black magic and black hearts of the whites had overcome the will of the angry Méxicano Father. Kills White Bear knew that the Méxicanos could be beaten. The Nemenuh had defeated them since the grandfather of his grandfather first met them on the grassy plains. But he never expected that they could be beaten by the whites. What sort of power could such grubby men possess?

It was now one tribe against the other as it should be, he thought. The Nemenuh and their allies stood alone just as the white bear had predicted when he was a boy. A task of honor was left for his children, and they would certainly rise to it. This, he was sure, was what the Enchanted Rock had whispered in that woeful language no living man could understand. She had spoken the promise of blood.

Kills White Bear rallied his warriors and rode north to Maguara. He wanted to hear the Spirit Talker's words before the five bands together took the war trail against what was left of the whites. He would tell Maguara as Wolf Eyes had told him. Now was the time.

They followed the San Antonio River away from Goliad, where they'd last seen the soldiers, into the ranchland of the Tejanos. Kills White Bear was keen to meet with Maguara and then spearhead an offensive east, but his men were tired and hungry. The skies poured rain that same night. Their horses were thin, and they were anxious for the honors of war.

There were no whites in that area, at least none that he knew of, but if it was blood and fresh horses they wanted he knew where they could be found. He rubbed the scar the Méxicano bullet had made in his chest. The flesh there was raised, strange-looking, webbed like a fungus on a rotten log. It smudged the claw mark of the white bear, his badge of honor. It felt numb and cold, apart from him. He remembered now. In the absence of whites to kill, he could at least settle an old score.

His warriors became quarrelsome when he bypassed so many ranchos. He explained repeatedly that there was one in particular that he sought. Their patience, he told them, would soon be rewarded. Then he reminded them of what had occurred six winters before. Those who had not listened to Kills White Bear died. There would be food, guns, and blankets, he told them, and many fine horses. There would also be women and children to take as slaves and hostages.

But such fine possessions would be defended. There was only one way to take them, and that would be up to him. He knew these men with him were young, hotheaded, and impressionable. But unlike the time before, they were his own people. He felt they understood each other, and he knew they respected him. When the time came to act they would act as one.

By mid-afternoon they'd reached the big house that sat

on the high ground at a bend in the river. They crouched
in the brush downwind from the noses of the dogs, horses,
and cattle, and waited for the sun to fall. Kills White Bear
watched and made his plans accordingly.

A heavy dew fell with the darkness. The cry of a nighthawk soaring overhead told him it was time for the hunt
to begin. He ordered his warriors to leave their rifles behind and bring only their bows. "The Méxicanos can fire
one time," he told them. "We can fire twelve." Tomahawks
and knives of honed Spanish steel hung from their slender
waists. The youngest was told to stay with the horses and
to circle the rancho while they assaulted it. They would
meet northwest of the river and would reach the Comanchería that very night. After the plan was discussed and
understood, Kills White Bear crept forward.

He saw the shadows of four armed men cross in the light.
The Méxicanos expected trouble, he thought, unlike the
time before. With handsignals he assigned each to a warrior, and in time he heard the rustle of their clothes as their
bodies were laid out on the moist earth, their throats cut
in silence. In the little huts he heard the sound of voices
of men and women, and the laughter of children. Woodsmoke filled the air. Firelight glowed golden through slender cracks in the mud walls. He motioned for his warriors
to bypass them all. There may have been a hundred people
in that village—thirty or so women—but he wanted only
one, and he knew she did not live in the mesquite and
mud jacales.

A dog began barking. He knew they must hurry now.
He sent two men to the corral to free the horses. They
were to mount and herd the rest in front of the stone house.
Kills White Bear raced up the steps to the door. It would
not open. He put his shoulder against it, but it would not
budge. Inside, he heard the sound of feet scrambling amid
hurried whispers. He thought also that he heard the cock
of a gun.

All hope of surprise gone, he ran across the open area
to a corral. He mounted a horse bareback, and then rode
it against and then through the gate of the corral next to
it. It held young bulls. They would do.

By then, the Méxicanos had emerged from their huts.

The other warriors fired at them as best they could, holding them at bay. Shots rang out, he heard the whizzing of bullets near his head, but the arrows of his comrades found their mark. Some of the Mexicans knelt clutching arrows in their chests; others ran back for the cover of their huts as Nemenuh arrows chased them. Warriors set fire to the wooden fences and shacks that lay between them and the Méxicanos. The flames spread quickly, forming a barrier of heat and smoke. It gave Kills White Bear the time he needed.

The bulls ran free and Kills White Bear turned them toward the main house. The beasts shot up the steps, yet they balked at the front door. Some wheeled and slipped away to the side. Kills White Bear shouted and drove the rest back against the door until it crashed inward in one hulking mass.

Muffled shots were fired from the darkness. A bull collapsed to the floor. Kills White Bear motioned for his men to follow and guided his horse into the house. It hopped over the fallen bull, its hooves clicking on the wooden floors. Inside, an older Mexican in fine dress stood frantically reloading his rifle. Kills White Bear sent an arrow his way and watched the fletching pass through his chest. The shaft smacked into the wooden wall behind him. The Méxicano cried out as he sank to his knees.

By now, two other warriors had entered the house. They found an elderly woman who begged for her life. One well-placed tomahawk blade to the head and that life was over. They went room to room, but found no more people. Kills White Bear told them to take what they wanted but keep a watch posted outside. They would go as soon as he checked above. She was here somewhere. He knew it.

Smoke now filled the house. As they kicked at each other, the bulls splintered chairs and tables. Their frantic hooves cut half-moons in the hides that lined the floors.

Kills White Bear dismounted and raced up the wooden steps. He moved through each room but found nothing. He came across another set of steps and flew up them. Every door he came to was closed until he kicked it open. The third revealed what he'd come for.

She clutched a baby in one arm, a pistol in the other.

Two more crying children, a boy and a girl, crouched behind her. There was rage in her eyes when there should've been fear.

She raised the pistol at him as he advanced. Wolf Eyes had told him no bullet would kill him and he believed it. He felt nothing when she fired. The flash of it blinded him briefly, but he felt no pain. Powder sprinkled from a hole in the adobe wall behind him.

She laid the baby down and attacked. He felt her fingernails dig into the skin of his cheek and claw deeply. He snatched her by the back of her hair and yanked her, struggling, down. She fought on, teeth clenched, feet kicking. Such strength in this woman!

He hit her twice with his fists until her eyes rolled back in her head. Then he slung her over his shoulder, snatched the baby from the floor, and kicked the others from the corner of the room. They fled before him. Another warrior grabbed them both. The other was busy setting fire to all that would burn. As Kills White Bear rummaged through the destruction, he toppled a basket of eggs that sat atop a three-legged table. For some reason, he steadied it. One small egg fell to the floor and burst.

A voice shouted out that there was no more time. Kills White Bear emerged from the smoke of the house where a horse awaited him. He handed the woman to a mounted rider and slipped his legs over his own mount, the screaming baby clutched to his chest. They gathered what horses they could and sprinted for the thickets. They paused briefly to organize when they met up with their own waiting mounts. They distributed their bounty for the long ride as Kills White Bear switched to his own stallion. One of his warriors told him riders would be coming, maybe two dozen or more. Once they'd caught their horses, the Méxicanos would ride around the fire, and then backtrack to them. It did not matter, Kills White Bear thought. His party would not stop until the sun was up. By then they would be deep in their own country.

Chapter Twenty

Dawn was breaking when they rendezvoused. Their horses trotted quietly on the dew-wet earth. Yet he could still hear the Méxicanos coming. These men were good. Much better than he'd expected. His warriors had ridden all night. They were not tired, but they were weary of the pursuit, irritable and anxious. It was at such times, Kills White Bear knew, that mistakes were made. The Méxicanos were not afraid to enter the Comanchería. He hadn't anticipated that. It was time to change tactics, he thought, while the night still hid them.

They entered the foothills of the Balcones Escarpment. There were a thousand springs cradled in a thousand canyons to hide them, and Kills White Bear knew them all. Their exhausted horses would no longer leave such clean tracks on the rocky earth. He would choose one deep draw, where the cedar grew thickest and the bluffs were steep, and attempt to lose the Méxicanos there. If not, such a place might be defended. Just the same, he no longer had a choice. The Wasps had run as far as they could. If the Méxicanos passed, he would turn back west when it was safe and then start north for Maguara's camp. Should the Méxicanos backtrack and follow him there, they would die.

He wove his party uphill into the brush like a sinew threaded through a coarse, dark blanket. He sent one warrior ahead with most of the stolen horses. He found a place that was still and quiet, where he would have plenty of notice should anyone approach. There he laid his horse down, and instructed the other warriors to do the same.

He saw that the woman was awake now. She was bound and gagged with leather thongs. Warriors held her older children; one arm around their chests, the free hand across their frightened mouths. The baby's face was crimson. It would not stop crying.

Kills White Bear rocked it, hugged it, covered it in his bear hide, slung it to his shoulder and patted its back. Nothing worked. He took it to its mother and sliced her arms free with his knife. He set it in her lap, and ordered her in Spanish to feed and comfort it. When she balked, he ripped the dress from her chest to expose her bosom. She shrieked and he slapped her. But with the child, he remained gentle, silently demanding that its mother soothe it. He tried to convey the alternative to her with his desperate eyes. She seemed to understand, and she held the child to her chest, and whispered in its ears, all to no avail.

Kills White Bear cocked his ear to the draw below. Riders. He took the child from its mother, and wrapped it tightly in his bear hide, head and all. Now it screamed. He was thinking of what to try next when one of the warriors rose and walked swiftly to him.

"Give me the child, brother," he hissed. "I'll quiet it."

Kills White Bear pulled away. "No," he said. "It'll stop in a moment."

"Not soon enough," the warrior said and he reached for it. Again Kills White Bear pulled away. The man looked at him as if he questioned his judgment. "It's either him or us."

Kills White Bear felt himself sink as the man extracted the baby from his reluctant arms. There was nothing he could do. The warrior was right. Either this one must die or they all would. The young brave held it by his pudgy legs until he came to a large live oak. With one swing, he crashed the baby's head against its trunk. It made a sound like a green gourd crushed under foot, followed by the most ghastly silence.

Kills White Bear glanced at its mother. Her face was locked in horror, her wide eyes white and wild. She scrambled for her baby on wobbly legs. One of the others looked sternly at Kills White Bear and he nodded his head. The man slapped her hard with the flat edge of his tomahawk and she fell still.

Kills White Bear heard the quiet steps of the warrior as he carried the baby off into the brush. He heard its body fall gently on the crisp leaves and mulch and then watched as the man returned. They sat quietly to listen as the Méxicanos drew near.

Kills White Bear felt sick inside. It gripped him like poison. He had been a father, and he had watched his own children die more miserably than this one had. But that fact alone could not console him. He was beside himself with grief. The Nemenuh needed that child.

The People often killed the sickly or the deformed. It was their way. They lived close to nature and nature was hard. But this baby was fat and healthy, a perfect replacement for the many they had lost. It would have thrived among the Wasps.

Kills White Bear knew that such a strong-willed woman would never forgive him for what had happened. Her grief would cripple his attempts to assimilate her into the tribe. Normally, a captive began as a slave. Time would tell if she'd remain one. Some took to the Nemenuh ways; others were traded away for goods or if sickly, timid, or unbroken, they were killed. This woman's chances for adaptation no longer looked good. She would hate them all for what had happened, but in particular she would hate him. It was not at all the result he'd hoped for.

He was sorry now that he'd taken his party to that place. Sorry that he'd taken these people to placate his personal grudge. How could things have gone so badly a second time? The raid was swift and controlled. The mistakes he'd made before were not repeated. The Méxicanos had followed more closely than he'd anticipated. Certainly, they'd pressed him hard. But he never once thought it would come to this. He never thought they'd have to kill a child.

He looked over his men. To someone who did not know them better, it would seem that the baby's death had no more effect on them than that of any game animal. Kills White Bear knew better. They were as sick about it as he was. The Nemenuh didn't fear death, but they certainly respected it. This one, however brought only shame.

As the Méxicanos approached, Kills White Bear's warriors would not look at him or each other. He did not care if they were found or not. It was left to the will of the Great Spirit whether they lived or died.

When he heard the Méxicanos pass, he did not feel relieved. When he was certain that they'd taken the bait, he motioned for his horse to rise and mounted it. The others followed without a word. The woman, blood dripping from

her nose, was tied across the back of a spare mount. They
rode on in grim silence.

They reached Maguara's camp at noon on the fourth day.
The camp buzzed with news of the Texas war. There were
other raids and other captives. Kills White Bear heard that
the Quahadis had attacked Parker's Fort to the northeast
and had taken several women and children. Others from
his own band had routed a group of settlers they'd caught
alone on the southern plains near the settlement the whites
called San Patricio. They were running from the Mexicans
or the Texians, he didn't know which. They had claimed
they were English or Irish or some such, but the distinction
was lost on him. They were whites, and warriors of the
People killed the men and captured the women and children—the fate of any whites found in their land.

There must've been twenty or so captives bound and
huddled together in the center of the camp, sitting in the
rain, afraid. Old, mean-spirited, and toothless women and
young, callous boys circled them, keeping watch. They
shouted insults at the whites, blaming them for all their
misfortunes, whipping them with quirts if they didn't like
the expression on their hollow faces.

Kills White Bear divvied up the horses among his warriors as tribute for their skill and courage, and in consolation for the horror they'd witnessed. Then he led the
remaining three captives, which he now claimed, where the
others were being held.

The woman, in particular, moved like a ghost. Her gaze
was distant, there was no light in her eyes. Her hair was
matted with dried blood from her head wound. Her cheeks
were bruised, the skin around her eyes puffy and purple.
As soon as he'd untied her, she reached for her two surviving children and drew them near. They were crying. She
was not. Her heart was broken, but her spirit was intact.
He admired her. She was both beautiful and strong and

therefore rare. Her children, he thought, would share the same qualities.

He ordered one of the old women to bring them food and water. She refused. None of the captives would receive nourishment of any kind, she told him, at least not yet. He angrily rebuked her on his warrior's authority. "These," he told her, "have suffered enough." He warned her that if she did not care for them as he instructed, she would soon fare much worse. His stare must've convinced her. When he saw that it was done, he left to find Maguara. They had much to discuss.

As

That night the Wasps celebrated the success of the raids and the coming of war. The whole tribe had gathered. Kills White Bear sat with Maguara and the elders, a place of honor, and watched the young men dance. A great fire roared in the center, the captives sat bound beside it. The dancers moved in circles around them. They passed the fool's water between them, a product they now knew to look for whenever they raided. Wolf Eyes had instructed Kills White Bear never to touch it, but he watched as Maguara and the others put the white man's jug to their lips.

The young warriors grew more frenzied as time passed. The flames of the fire danced in their wild eyes. They slapped the backs and thighs of the captives with the ends of their bows, and sometimes touched their bare skin with the tips of glowing embers until they cried out. They cut the hair from the women's heads and tried to weave it in with their own. It was, Kills White Bear knew, the first step in breaking them down, but he had never enjoyed the process. It was the end result that interested him. War and disease had taken so many. They would incorporate the strongest among these and make them Nemenuh. The dance would tell them which ones to keep and which ones to trade.

Finally the warriors began ripping away what remained

of the captives' clothing. They screamed in terror, naked before the fire. If they ran from the circle, they were savagely beaten. Most clung to their children and each other as their tears glistened in the fire's light.

He watched as the younger women were snatched from the mass. They were thrown face down to the ground and held there while the first of several warriors mounted them. Their screams and wailing were lost amid the war whoops of the warriors and the taunts of the watching tribe. When they finished with one, they dragged her by the hair back close to the fire where the captive would draw up her legs and rock with her head against her knees. Then the warriors reached for another. In the morning the Nemenuh would begin to rebuild on what was left.

Kills White Bear watched and waited. His woman, though burned and beaten, had not yet been raped. She clutched her children to her bare chest. He'd observed her body carefully when they'd stripped her. She was taller than Nemenuh women, certainly a little skinnier than he'd like. But her shoulders were strong and square, her waist slender, and her hips round and smooth. She had a certain poise, even under such adversity. He hadn't seen a woman so beautiful since Morning Song.

He rose when they pulled her away from her children. She did not yell out; she did not cry. He could tell that she'd already resolved to get it over with and live. He could see that her eyes remained defiant, yet there was an acceptance there, he thought. Already he had admired her. Now she was earning his respect.

He almost let her meet the same fate as the others before her. He wanted her to feel callused hands on her body, feel hot breath on the back of her neck, feel a Nemenuh penis, lubricated with blood and semen, poke against the inside of her thigh—all the while helpless, with her ear forced to the dust. When a young warrior was close to entering her, Kills White Bear rushed out and yanked him clear. She never looked to see what happened. She didn't seem to care.

"This one," he said, "belongs to me."

Kills White Bear stepped between the warrior and his woman. He could see the man was drunk, otherwise the fool would never have challenged him. The man stood, embarrassed. He heard the laughter and became enraged.

"I'll have her like I've had the rest," he declared. "She's mine until she bleeds."

Kills White Bear stared into the man's cloudy eyes. "You take one step toward Kills White Bear, little brother, and you'll do some bleeding of your own." The people around them howled with laughter. Kills White Bear stood firm. He had no weapons. He didn't need them. One good blow and this boy would crumble to his knees. "This woman," he repeated, "is mine."

The young warrior scanned the taunting crowd and then turned back to Kills White Bear. He hesitated, then moved away and began dancing.

Kills White Bear took the naked woman in his arms and hustled her away to his lodge. He had his grandmother bring her clothes, blankets, and medicine for her wounds.

"Care for her as you would for me," he asked her. She looked curiously at him but nodded that she would. He then posted two men he trusted outside his lodge with instructions that, at the first sign of trouble, they should send for him.

Kills White Bear reentered the lodge and saw that his grandmother was nursing her wounds. He wanted the Méxicano woman to understand clearly that whatever benevolence she received came directly from him. He knew she understood how close she'd come to being ravaged. Despite all that had happened, all the bitterness that was between them, she had to understand that only he could protect her now. He hoped her will to live would guide her from there.

Then he went back for the children. He would keep them separate from their mother from now on. He himself would clothe and feed them both in the hope that they would soon respond. They were young and supple, the boy having seen no more than six winters, the girl maybe three. A little kindness, a little care, and the process would begin. He was confident that the People could win their hearts as they had countless others since time began.

But their mother, he knew, was another story. How well he'd marked the hatred in her eyes, and how well he knew he deserved it.

Chapter Twenty-One

Remy crossed the Guadalupe River well south of Gonzáles. He rode west, through the Tonkawa nation, paying his respects to Chief Placido. He slept under the stars at the headwaters of Ecleto Creek. He was, he thought, in the eastern corner of Rancho Flores. He rose before dawn, his clothes soft from the dew. Anxious to reach Beatriz and the children, he neither rekindled the fire nor ate breakfast. He saddled the stallion and rode out.

With daylight, the sanguine skies broke clear. A southerly breeze bathed him in sun-heated and humid gulf air. Spring had finally come. He forded the Cíbolo around ten o'clock, the Marcelina at noon. By then clouds were building. He rode due west until he came to the San Antonio River and followed its east bank home. Above him, the lower edges of the now solid banks had turned dark gray and black. He could expect showers when the sun went down and the air cooled. It'd rained nearly every day for the past two months. With the rays of the sun shut out, the wind blew cold. He looked forward to a long, hot bath, and a night of rest in his own bed next to the warm and soft skin of Beatriz. How he'd missed her.

His pace quickened as he approached his home. He first sensed that something was wrong when he saw the burned jacales and corrals. Campesina women wept over fresh graves on which they had piled white stones. Not one of the carved oak planks read "Amarante de la Cruz." He called to them desperately to tell him what had happened. When they turned to Remy, they only wailed louder. In a panic, he wheeled the horse and raced for the casa mayor.

His heart sunk at the sight of it. The door rumbled beneath his boots as he stepped across it. His steps echoed against the blackened walls of an empty house. Flies buzzed about a dead bull, and the stench of rotten flesh nauseated him. He couldn't determine whether the pools of cracked, dried blood on the floor were from man or beast. He found an arrow shot in the wall, yanked it free, and examined it carefully. Comanche.

His hands shook. His head throbbed. His eyes grew wild. He threw back his head and screamed for his wife. Nothing. He ran upstairs to search room to room. Nothing was burned, there was no sign of struggle. He then reached his room, and the disarray he found there told its own story.

. He wanted to fall to his knees and cry because he knew that his family had been murdered. Instinct demanded he run—run for his life—to his aunt's house, as he had as a boy all those terrible years ago. But Helen Marie was dead. Elijah Johnson was dead. The rest, he realized, were only missing; but in his panicked heart, where there were no lies, he knew they were also dead. What he'd run from in Louisiana truly had waited for him here. What he'd left at San Jacinto he found at his own home. It was a cruel joke to think that he could ever escape his fate. The misery of his youth had been but a prologue.

He struggled there a moment to push back the impulse to give up, to succumb to his despair, to weep for weeks as he had when he finally accepted that his mother and father were truly gone. But he had been only a child then. He was a man now. As much as he'd realized years later he'd loved his parents, he loved Beatriz and the children so much more.

One blood feud had ended on the plains of San Jacinto, and another had just begun. It would start, as it had when he learned of Elijah's death, when the shock subsided. He turned and walked quietly down the steps. He heard the cool rain begin to fall on the roof.

A boy waited for him. It was Cristóbal, Diego Picosa's oldest boy. He stood quietly, his eyes to the blackened and charred floor.

"¿Qué pasó, Cristóbal?" he asked quietly. His own voice failed him.

"Los Comanches," the boy answered, tears in his eyes. "They killed nine men and two women. They let the bulls run wild, and they stole the horses. They wounded Don Carlos, and took Doña Beatriz and your children captive."

Captive! His heart leaped. That thought had escaped him. Now he remembered. He'd seen both Méxicano and white women in Maguara's camp all those years ago, and children, too. They may not have killed them after all. There was hope.

"How do you know they were Comanche, Cristóbal?" He'd seen the arrow himself, but he wanted to make damn sure.

"My father told me so. He tracked them all night, even with an arrow in his chest, deep into the hill country. He recognized them well enough."

"Where's your father now?"

"In Béxar, with Don Carlos. We took them to the Alamo to see a doctor."

Remy began to plan. "How many vaqueros are left?"

"A dozen, maybe." There was more. "Angry white men came with papers. They want to take Don Carlos's land."

"What?"

"They said Don Carlos aided the enemy. They said they would come back, and when they did, they would hang any Méxicano they found here. Many have already left."

Remy had anticipated this. It was easily fixed by his presence, but he couldn't supply that right now. He tore a blank page from one of Don Carlos's books and wrote that since 1830, he, Captain Remy Fuqua, Army of the Republic of Texas, had legally owned the land originally granted to Carlos Amarante de la Cruz. Any son of a bitch that thought otherwise could take up the matter personally with him upon his return. Until that time, no inhabitant or employee of that same land should be harmed under penalty of Texas law. Whatever that was, he thought. He nailed the note and his officer's commission written in Houston's own hand to the threshold of the door with the butt of his pistol. He told Cristóbal to tell the others not to worry, gathered his things, saddled a fresh horse, and rode out with his stallion and another horse in tow for San Antonio de Béxar.

They were alive! The land would just have to wait.

The Alamo was in ruins. Most of its buildings were either gouged by cannon fire, or completely destroyed. Those that

remained standing housed hundreds of wounded Méxicano
soldiers. As Remy walked among them, he heard their
cries, their moans, their gasps for breath. Bloodied bandages had gone unchanged. There were few doctors, few
supplies, and no medicine. He did not find Don Carlos and
Picosa among these wretched men.

He rode across the river into town, toward the main
plaza. He stepped into Don Carlos's house, and was
stunned to see it also full of wounded Méxicano soldiers.
He went from body to body, looking for Don Carlos. Bodies were everywhere, in beds, on sofas and tables, and on
the floors. He checked the main bedroom. Three officers
lay there: one with no arm, one with his leg amputated just
above the knee, the last was gut shot. The stench of death
hung in the thick, stale air. He checked Beatriz's room and
found more wounded and dying men. He turned to look
elsewhere, when he heard Picosa call out his name.

Remy knelt beside him.

"*¿Diego?*" he whispered. "*¿Estás bien?*"

Picosa coughed. "I'm sorry I failed you, Don Remy," he
muttered. "They're in the San Sabá Valley, I think. They'll
soon go north."

"I'll worry about that, Diego. Are ya bein' cared for?"

He shook his head. "Cared for would not be the word,"
he said. "Tolerated, maybe." He reached out and snatched
Remy's arm. "Take me back to the rancho, Don Remy,
and let me die there. I want to see the land again. I want
to hear los criollos bawling in the pastures."

"Hush up, now," Remy said, pulling the blanket up over his
chest. "You ain't gonna die, Picosa. I know you better'n that.
You'll say any goddamn thing to git outta work. When you git
done lazin' aroun' here, I'm gonna hook your ass up good."

This last bit brought the hint of a smile to Picosa's rough
face. Remy saw a pitcher of water on the table. He got it
and poured a little in his cupped hand. He raised Picosa's
head and slipped some between his parched lips. He let his
fingers drip on his forehead to cool him.

"Where's Don Carlos?" he asked. Picosa pointed to a
lump under a blanket next to him. Remy knelt beside him
and pulled the blanket back slowly. His heart sank when
he realized that the wound to his chest, just above his heart,

was deep and seeping clear fluid. The blood had been wiped away, leaving black smudges. The flesh around it was first white, then red and swollen. There was no bandage and no salve. It smelled almost sweet.

Don Carlos looked thin and emaciated. His pale, chalky skin felt cool. His white cotton shirt had been torn away. His face was drawn and unshaven. He looked as if he'd aged ten years. Remy called to him, but Don Carlos did not answer.

"Damn!" Remy said, and he gently pulled the blanket back over him and turned back to Picosa. "Have ya'll seen a doctor?"

"Not lately," Picosa answered him.

"I'll be back," Remy said, and he angrily left to find one.

He found a group of soldiers occupying the Veramendi Palace. They sat around a table with two men dressed in dirty, crumpled suits, playing cards. He knew the soldiers from the siege.

"Fuqua," one said. "What brings you to town?"

"I need a doctor." As soon as he'd said it, he saw the two civilians look at one another but never at him. There were two black bags on the table and next to them, two near empty bottles of Kentucky whiskey. A third full one waited. "Either one of ya'll a doctor?"

"We are," one said flatly.

Remy pointed across the street. "My father-in-law's up there with his shoulder rottin' off. I want you to go and see 'im."

"I've been in there," the man said. "I saw no white men."

Fuqua felt his anger rise. "That's right. But you saw my father-in-law just the same. You come with me and have a look. Right now."

"I'd like to help, son. Fact is, I've got no medicine, no supplies. I can do nothing."

"He's dyin'!"

"They're *all* dyin'," he said. "I can't help it."

"Well, you're gonna try. Let's go."

Remy watched as the man sighed and then attempted to rise. His fingers fumbled for the worn leather handles of the bag. He staggered forward. Remy shoved him back in his chair.

"You're drunk, ain't ya?" Remy growled.

"That's right," the man admitted with an impish grin. "And you'd be too if you had my job."

Remy leaned forward and snatched him by the collar. "You see that house over yonder?" The man nodded, his glazed eyes blinked slowly. "You set one foot in there, and I'll saw your ears off with a dull knife and shove 'em up your ass. *"¡Comprende!"*

"Very well," he said, waving him away. "It's all the same to me."

The officer reached for his arm. "Let him be, Fuqua. You have no idea what he's been through."

"It ain't him I'm worried about," he said, and then he left. He grabbed an oil lamp on his way out and headed for the barrio. Dogs barked at him as he made his way down the narrow streets until he came to the house he wanted. He pounded his fists on the door. An elderly man cracked it open.

"¿Qué quiere, señor?"

"¿Está Señora Escajeda aquí?" Remy asked.

"Un momento."

He waited until the old curandera appeared in his lamplight. "Do you know me?" he asked. She said she did. He was the gringo son-in-law of Don Carlos Amarante. He told her Don Carlos lay wounded in his own house. The Anglo doctors were drunk and miserable. That, she said, she already knew. He reached into his pocket and pulled out two shiny coins, his share of Santa Anna's San Jacinto gold. It was the equivalent of eleven Yankee dollars, and she could have it all if she came. The streets were no longer safe, she said. They were, he promised, if she walked with him. She agreed, gathered her things, and joined him. Together they walked briskly down the quiet streets.

He boiled water and clean bandages for her while she mixed her potions. She poured thick, viscous syrups down her patients' throats and cleansed their festering wounds with hot water. She dressed them with powders and leaves of herbs and wrapped them in clean new bandages. They needed some place quiet, she said, some place clean. Remy said he could help with that.

He rose and ripped the sheets from the Méxicano soldiers who lay on Beatriz's bed. He saw no wound sufficient to impress him, and he picked up one edge of the mattress and dumped them out of it. He dragged them out of the room one at a time, and then came for the others. The rest, apparently sensing the time had come for a change, crawled out of their own accord. He found clean but dusty sheets still sitting on the shelves in the cupboards in the rooms below. He popped them open in the breeze out an open window and then carefully remade the bed. The window he left open to allow the stale room to vent. Then he went for fresh water and warm soup. He snatched stale bread from the doctors' table and whiskey from their lips and brought it all to Don Carlos and Picosa.

Don Carlos lay in Beatriz's bed. Picosa said that he preferred the floor. He'd never shared a bed with a man, and certainly didn't want to do so now with his employer. People, he said, would talk. So Remy made Picosa a pallet as Aunt Helen had once done for him.

Remy then asked Señora Escajeda what she thought. She said that both wounds were badly infected but that she'd done what she could. She would pray to God for them now. She would stay with them this night and the next, and then look in on them daily after that. She told Remy that she could not guarantee that the blood poisoning would not take them both, but she'd seen worse cases than theirs make a turn for the better. She remained optimistic, she said. He hugged her and kissed her forehead. Both of these men, he told her, meant the world to him. She said she already seen that in his eyes.

Remy knelt at his father-in-law's side. Already Don Carlos looked a little better, but then again he could not have looked worse. He held his hand and talked to him. "You get well, old man," Remy said. "The world ain't right without your bitchin'." When he finished, Don Carlos's eyes popped opened and he squeezed Remy's hand.

"She's alive, Remy!" he gasped. "I saw her in a dream as clearly as if she stood with us in this room. She is alive, and Carlito and Elena Marie as well! She's with a tribe that has a bald man as chief, as you once described. The man who took her from us now protects her."

"I know she's alive, Don Carlos," Remy said, stroking the old man's brow. "You rest easy. I'll go and get her."

Don Carlos shook his pale head beneath Remy's fingers. "Not you, Remy! That man hates you as he hates no other.

You've shamed him in some way I don't understand. You should not go yourself but send someone to trade for her. Send them guns, blankets, the best of my horses—anything they want. There's gold back at the rancho. I'll tell you where it's hidden."

Remy wiped the beads of sweat with the palm of his hand. "I'll take care of it, Don Carlos. You look after yourself."

He thought about what Don Carlos had said of his dream. He saw Beatriz and the two older children. But what of the baby? "Did you see little Remy?" he wondered.

"Did no one tell you?" Don Carlos asked. He closed his eyes and began to sob.

"Tell me what?"

"Please tell him, Picosa. I can't."

Remy swung to Diego. Diego would not look at him. "Tell me *what*!" he repeated.

"We found the child dead, Don Remy. I won't say how."

He jumped to his feet. Dead? Murdered! He knew then he'd soon trade with the Comanches, but it would not be merchandise. Don Carlos looked around the room and asked what had happened to the soldiers. Picosa answered that Don Remy had thrown them all out.

"Please, Remy. Those men were miserable. Enough pain."

"It's just beginning," he said, and he made his last arrangements with Señora Escajeda and left for Rancho de la Cruz.

Chapter Twenty-Two

The altercation had been short but bloody. Kills White Bear's cousin, She Denies It, had angrily ordered the Méxicana woman to gather wood. She soon did but only one stick. As soon as his cousin had turned her back, the Méxicana had clubbed her soundly over the head.

She Denies It had come to Kills White Bear for justice. When he refused, she went to Maguara. The Spirit Talker simply advised his cousin not to be so stupid in the future and left it at that. She Denies It huffed away.

Kills White Bear watched her until she'd disappeared; all the while he felt Maguara's eyes on him.

"What are you doing?" the civil chief asked calmly.

"How do you mean?"

"That woman," Maguara said, nodding toward Kills White Bear's lodge. "What plans do you have for her?"

"None."

"None?" he scoffed, a thin smile on his lips. "You lie, Kills White Bear. You don't treat her like a captive. You treat her like a wife. She's touched you in some way, and now you think you can touch her."

Kills White Bear shook his head. "I don't know what I think."

Maguara smiled. "The sign of true madness, I'm sure. I always knew something like this would happen if you did not take another wife."

"What would happen?"

"That you would destroy yourself, my friend, with your own hunger." He paused to deliberate. "Do you think, Kills White Bear, that if you were to rip off my arm, beat me with it, and then cast it off somewhere to rot, that I'd want to hug you with the one I have left? Is that the likely result?"

"No," he said quietly.

"Then why do you expect it of her? Do you really think that woman can come to see you as we do? Will she see the compassion of your spirit? The goodness in your heart?" To answer his own questions, Maguara slowly shook his head. "She is your enemy, Kills White Bear. And in my experience enemies make poor wives. If you want that woman, take her. You won her. Pleasure is your right. Even she expects it. But to expect love from her, after all that's happened, is foolishness. She's as dead to you as Morning Song."

"I won't do it like that."

"Then you'll never do it at all." He placed his hand on Kills White Bear's shoulder. "Take a wife from the People, little brother, as I've advised so many times. Open your eyes. No woman can forgive the man that took her children from her. You turn your back on her, and you won't be as lucky as She Denies It. The Méxicana will kill you the first chance she gets."

Kills White Bear listened but said nothing.

"Why not consider a trade, Kills White Bear?" Maguara suggested. "That is the easiest and most honorable way out. Continue to protect her and her children and then let them all go. We have other things to worry about, you and I."

Kills White Bear bit his lip and kicked the dust. He'd not taken these people to trade. These were replacements, for the Nemenuh and for him. He was convinced that the children would be easily molded. And although Maguara was probably right about the woman's poor prospects for making a similar adjustment, Maguara underestimated the power of Kills White Bear's hope. He had overcome so many obstacles; he could not help but believe he could overcome this one. He had taken the Méxicana to punish her, but now, just as Maguara had sensed, he had other plans.

No one knew the risk he was taking with his heart better than he. But no one knew of its longing, of its pain so intense that it compelled him to defy all odds. Regardless of the circumstances, that woman *had* touched him. He was certain that her spirit was a match for his and hopeful that with patience, he could win it. Nevertheless, until he knew for sure what would come of his efforts, he intended to keep her. "It's too soon to trade," he finally said.

"Or too late," Maguara answered. "The Méxicanos have a pitiful life, I know, but they love it. You also took that from her, and so you are doubly damned. There's no way around this thing, even for a warrior of your power. What began so badly, must also end that way. It bodes ill."

"It bodes as I make it," Kills White Bear said, his jaw set.

"Very well," Maguara said, disappointed. "If you will not listen to reason, perhaps a warning will suffice. The crows have been chattering about all of this. They won't leave me alone. They know that the woman's stout heart belongs to another. And the crows say this man is coming for her."

Not the crows again, Kills White Bear thought. He hated the crows. "Let him come," he said.

Maguara studied him, as if amused. "You know this man, my little black friends say. They warn that the trouble he brings is not worth the prize you've won. Not to you, and not to us. When this white man comes, and he is white they say, make peace with him as best you can. You owe him a life. Give him three, and express great sorrow for the one you cannot replace."

"White man!" Kills White Bear snapped. "I know no white man."

Maguara turned away from him, passing beneath the lodge's flap. "You know this one," he said and was gone.

Chapter Twenty-Three

Remy spent less than one day at Rancho de la Cruz. He found the gold where Don Carlos told him it would be, provisioned himself, and rode out. The men who had threatened to take the land had not returned. It had been a bold and ruthless effort against the helpless Méxicanos, attempted everywhere, Remy knew. But now that the scoundrels knew that this place was owned by a white man and an officer of the Republic as well, he didn't think they'd have the nerve to see their ploy through.

He needed men, and he dared not take what remained of the vaqueros in case trouble returned to the ranch. He followed the Cíbolo north to the Camino Real and followed it northeast and then again north from there to Webber's Prairie and Hornsby's Fort. The Comanche, he was told, were everywhere. These men would not leave with him to go looking for what had already come. He rode on to Tumlinson's Blockhouse and the same answer awaited him there. Everyone was on the defensive. The offensive, they told him, would come in time. Disheartened, Remy rode south.

There were no great men on hand to advise him. Houston was in New Orleans recuperating. Austin had gone on a diplomatic mission to the United States. The command of the Texas army, now stationed at Goliad, had fallen to Thomas Jefferson Rusk, Remy's comrade from San Jacinto. Remy poured his heart out to him, but Rusk had troubles of his own.

The army, now swollen by two thousand recently arrived immigrants, had not been paid. There was nothing to pay them with except land, and even if they wanted it, there was no system in place to dole it out. The Méxicano army had halted at the Río Grande, Rusk said, and these men wanted to go after them. When the Texas government told them no, they decided to go after the government. Patriotism, as always, was lost on the new immigrants. Whether or not he deserved it, the one man they respected was Sam Houston, and Sam Houston was gone. The tried and true Texian veterans of San Jacinto had long ago returned to their farms and families to pick up the pieces. What was left was trouble.

Remy asked for rangers, but Rusk told him rangers would not come. The frontier was ablaze. Wherever the rangers were, they were needed there. Then Remy asked for regular troops. They would have to do. Rusk looked at him and said, "Take your pick. Please. Take them all if you want."

"Could be dangerous," Remy frankly warned.

"Oh, I hope so," Rusk sighed.

It did not take Remy long to assemble fifty men. He passed over polished volunteers from Georgia, Mississippi, and the Carolinas. Sons of planters and the well-to-do, though eager, would never do. He chose those from Kentucky, Tennessee, and Arkansas, hungry frontiersmen who had a natural hatred of Indians—any Indians. He explained what had happened and what he planned to do. They were loud, rowdy, obnoxious, but the Texas campaign had taught him how to handle such men. When they asked why they should come, he simply said, "They can't pay ya. I can." And he took a leather pouch from his saddle bags and threw it on the ground. It burst open at the seams, revealing a number of shiny Méxicano gold coins. Fifty men stepped forward to accept, and fifty more said they'd go if these boys didn't. Remy had his army. The oldest man was five years younger than he. And Remy passed his thirtieth birthday on the back of his horse searching for his wife and children.

Remy wove his plan, stitched together with Don Carlos's gold. His only uncertainty lay in his personnel. They were

keen to fight, but they were also poor and ignorant. Remy
prepared them as best he could. Those who did not have
good rifles quickly received them. They were issued good
leather boots, cotton shirts, good socks and broad-brimmed
hats if they wanted them. He provisioned two good wagons
with supplies and rolled them north. Fresh water was everywhere that year. Two parties of three hunted the thickets
along the way for fresh venison and wild cattle. The buffalo
had already gone north for the summer. When they found
them, they'd find Maguara's Penateka.

Remy knew the country, but he didn't know it like the
Comanche did. He rode to Chief Placido's Tonkawa camp,
enemies of the Comanche, and offered them the opportunity to draw Comanche blood. Many leaped at the chance.
Remy smoked the pipe of war with four, gave Placido two
horses with the promise of two dozen more when the deed
was done, and he had his scouts for the duration.

Remy took his army to Rancho de la Cruz where they
passed a week. During that time, the vaqueros gathered
horses and mules for Remy's troops. He treated the men
well, fed them better, and paid them half of what was due.
Other than that, he remained aloof, as Houston had. He
tested them for obedience and was pleased to see that
every order was obeyed. The vaqueros taught them to ride
on the prairies and Remy taught them what he knew about
the Comanches. He was confident that they were born
knowing how to fight. All he had to do was make his quarrel theirs.

He followed the Cíbolo north to where the Paso de Payaya
cut through the hills. He forded the Guadalupe River just
west of El Monte de Diablo, skirted the Blanco, and then
crossed the Pedernales, the Llano, and the San Sabá at its
northern fork. The hills were bare of Comanche. The Tonkawa scouts assured him that they could be found west of

the Concho, where the grass grew deep, and Remy pushed on.

Remy asked a warrior how he would find the camp. He was told they would search for buzzards swirling above the carrion produced by any tribe of such numbers. It was, Remy thought, a fitting sign.

This was new country. Rolling hills cradled clear creeks. Tall grass blew like the hair of a woman in a gentle breeze. The buffalo were there, and the antelope, the elk, and the deer. At night the stars glistened like a baby's eyes out of the expanse of infinite dark, yet in daylight the earth before them seemed the greater. It should've cheered him to be a part of such a world.

But his mind was darker than the midnight sky. Remy's world had been ripped apart. Nature could not console him any more when he knew he shared this earth with the men that had stolen his family and killed his child. He took no pleasure in God's gifts. At night he sat listening to the coyotes howl, and he understood loneliness, too. It was the one thing all predators shared.

They made great, roaring fires at night, which made the Tonkawa nervous. Each morning, fifty rifles fired to clear their bores of moist powder. They made no secret of their coming. Remy wanted the Comanche to know. They kept their ranks tight, eight sentries up each night. But they saw no Indians. The tribes seemed to part for the thickets ahead of their angry advance.

Late one afternoon, the Tonkawa scouts rushed in to announce that they'd seen a Comanche raiding party make camp nearby. The raiders must have recently returned to their country, and not knowing that the white soldiers had come, must have believed they were safe in the bosom of the Comanchería. They were tired and careless and would make easy prey.

"What band?" Remy asked. One of the braves made the sign of the stinging wasp, and a smile spread across Remy's cracked lips. The Tonkawa said they thirsted for Comanche blood, and Remy promised they would have it. Some of it. The bulk belonged to him.

When it was dark, Remy rode out with a party of hand-picked men. They were to kill who they must but capture who they could. Remy needed warriors to trade, knowing the Comanche valued nothing more. The Tonkawa threaded through the brush like ghosts. Remy ordered his men to watch them and learn. This, he explained, was a different kind of war.

When he saw that the Comanche had failed to post sentries, Remy circled his men close to where they slept. When the men were ready, they crept in without a sound. Four Tonkawa slit four throats. Pistol fire killed two more. The rest were clubbed with rifle stocks and led away. The Tonkawa scalped their Comanche victims with rawhide lariats taut around their necks. Not once did the prisoners cry out or beg for mercy.

"Hell, they ain't the least bit scared," a man from Kentucky said.

"No, they ain't," Remy said. "But they should be."

Remy's party crested a bluff where the Tonkawa scouts waited. One pointed his finger northwest to where camp smoke rose in two dozen columns to the sky. Buzzards circled over the camp. Remy motioned for one of the prisoners to be brought forward.

"Maguara's camp?" he asked in Spanish. The warrior looked, said nothing, and then turned away. Remy reached for a fistful of hair and yanked the warrior's head around. "Maguara's camp?" he repeated. The warrior would not speak. Remy cut off his braid and tossed it to the ground. Then he spread the fingers of the warrior's right hand across the withers of the horse's back and held it there. He reached for his knife, and poised the blade above the warrior's hand. "Maguara's camp?" Nothing. He sliced off the little finger so deeply that the blade cut the horse's hide. The next, he indicated, would be the index finger, the one he knew the man needed to pull his bow. "And now?" he asked.

"That is Maguara's camp," he said. "Go to it, and die."

"Appreciate it," Remy said.

Once he'd picked his ground, Remy instructed his two lieutenants to rest the horses and be ready to move. Half the men should sleep; the other half must be on guard, Remy ordered. They would alternate on four hour shifts. Those awake should fill their canteens and water the horses. He told them that although the Comanche might try anything, they would not risk a frontal assault. The Comanche could not burn them from the hill with the grass so green, and under no circumstances should his men quit that position. Fifty good riflemen could hold off ten times their number, and Maguara did not have near that many. If they came to talk, talk. But they should face the Comanche as one faced a bad dog. Both smelled the opportunity of fear. Remy would go to Maguara's camp alone.

"What if you don't make it back?" Lieutenant Gibson asked.

"I'll make it back. I've got an open invitation at Maguara's camp. He'll honor it."

"And if you don't?" the lieutenant asked, his voice uncertain.

"Give me one full day. If'n I don't make it back, you're free to do what you think's best."

"Should we attack?"

"I wouldn't if'n I were you. I'd turn that column aroun' and head back south. If'n I don't make it back, there's nuthin' you can do for me. The Comanche won't fool with ya. And you needn't fool with them. Ya'll go on home and fight Mexicans."

"All right, Captain," he said, and he offered his hand. "Good luck."

Remy rode quietly into the camp, the Gump's barrel resting across his thighs. The people parted before him as he rode toward Maguara. He was pleased to see that there were few warriors around him. Far less than what he'd seen when he came the first time. He would be negotiating from a position of strength as he'd planned all along. It gave him confidence.

"Ah, *Chemakacho*," the bald-headed chief said. "Your visit pleases the Spirit Talker. Two moons ago Maguara saw that you were coming. Let your horse graze with our ponies and rest with us. You're safe here."

He reached for Remy's hand. When Remy extended it he saw Maguara's eyes close in reverie. This he'd seen before. He knew how accurate this strange man could be. When he snatched his hands away, Maguara's eyes shot open.

"It's all right, Fuqua," he told him. "I've seen enough. Come in Maguara's lodge. We have much to discuss."

Maguara called for food and water and then led Remy into his lodge where old men sat smoking. Remy settled into the open place, directly across from Maguara. He was handed a gourd of cool water and he drank it all.

"Maguara knows why you are here," the old chief began. Remy nodded. "And you are brave to come. He does not find fault in your anger. Know that the raid was a mistake, Fuqua, and my brother, Kills White Bear, does not make many."

"What's done is done," Remy said grimly, his eyes locked on Maguara's.

"True enough, Fuqua. But what becomes twisted can sometimes be untwisted. There are always knots and frayed ends, but the rope is still good in a wise man's hand."

None of this comforted Remy. He'd come for his family, not a sermon. He got to the point. "Where are my wife and children?"

"You know the infant is dead," Maguara answered gravely, "but your wife and two children are safe. Kills White Bear's eyes have never left them. When you go, they'll go with you."

"Why was my baby killed?"

"They did not know it was yours, Fuqua. They took its life to save others. That is the reason but not an excuse. Find what solace you can in these cold words. You came to Maguara years ago with an open heart. He sees that this same heart is now closed to him because of what's happened, and this saddens the Spirit Talker. But there's war between our people and we both suffer." Maguara drew on his pipe. "Fuqua has lost one child; Maguara has lost hundreds. And yet each morning Maguara awakes and faces the rising sun. Its rays still warm his old and scarred body. The earth remains solid beneath his feet. The rivers still run and the wind still blows. Maguara lives on with his loss; and Fuqua must live on also. Think not of what you've lost, but what you still have. Your family is safe, Fuqua. When the time comes, you may go with them in peace."

Remy breathed deeply, and closed his eyes. "It's best that I go soon," he said, opening them. He knew those men on the hill. They would not leave him. If he didn't return, they would attack. If Maguara delivered his family, there was no reason for them to do so.

"What's the hurry, Fuqua? You've come far."

"I didn't come alone."

"Oh," Maguara sighed, his head tilted. "Who's come with you?"

Remy did not like the look on Maguara's face. "You know damn well that soldiers ride with Fuqua."

The old chief looked at the others as if he were surprised that Remy would admit that he'd come prepared for violence. Then he changed the subject.

"Tell me about the war with the Méxicanos, Fuqua."

"We whipped 'em. They're gone, at least for now."

"And the Texians? What will they do?"

"What they've always done, I reckon."

"Will they draw the line with the Nemenuh as we've asked?"

Remy felt his safety was guaranteed and breathed easy. Maguara would not go back on his word and he knew it. It gave him a certain confidence. He used it to strike back. "Why do the Nemenuh ask for the line? The Méxicanos did not come into your country. It was you who came to theirs and murdered them. You've come to Fuqua's own lodge, now a war chief of his people. Now you ask Fuqua to draw a line for you to cross and kill his own as they lay asleep. What good would it do now that you've angered so many? Fuqua warned the Spirit Talker about this years ago. Maguara closed his ears."

Maguara told the others in Spanish, for Remy's benefit, that a good man had gone bad. Then he turned back to Remy and said, "Will more whites come to this country now that the Méxicanos are gone?"

"They're already coming, Maguara," he assured him. It

was a dig. The immigration of the whites to their country, he knew, remained their greatest fear. Remy's bitterness would enhance it. He'd been sick with worry for weeks. Now it was their turn to sweat. "The whites are like the buffalo," he continued. "They go wherever the land is good without asking. And like the buffalo, it's their right. You can't stop them any more than you can stop the wind from blowing. They'll blow the Nemenuh from this land like dust."

The others began mumbling. He saw that now Maguara grew angry. "And these soldiers," he said, "these very young soldiers, that you've brought to Maguara's camp to kill him. These boys fight the Texians' wars?"

"They do," Remy sneered. "They whipped six thousand Mexicans. They can whip whoever comes next."

He watched as Maguara whispered in the ear of the warrior next to him. He rose and left without a word. Then Maguara looked at him coldly. "The wind on the prairie," he said, "gusts many ways."

"What's that supposed to mean?"

Maguara did not acknowledge his question. "Do you know what time of year it is?" he asked.

"Yeah," Remy said crisply. "I know."

Maguara's eyes swept the plains around him. "The buffalo grow fat on the summer grass. With all the rain this spring, they did not travel far north this year. For the first time since Maguara was a boy all of the bands have gathered to hunt them. The Nokonis, Quahadi, the Yamparika, the Kotsoteka, the Tanima and Tenawa are all here with their cousins, the Penateka, for the summer kill. We are but the first camp you came to. The others are not a day's ride away." Then he turned back to Remy. "I don't think your man-eating Tonkawa scouts told you that," he said wryly. "This year we were very lucky, Fuqua. The hunting's been very good. And today it's gotten better."

Remy felt the first shudder down his spine. He knew Maguara was about to attack his men. He had had no idea there were so many Comanche gathered. His men could fend for themselves, but the losses would certainly be heavy. "Don't do this, Maguara," he begged. He felt his confidence dissipate. "I came in peace. I'll go in peace."

"And you will," he assured him as his eyes narrowed. "But the others must die."

"And your warriors with them," Remy added in desperation. "Their women will weep for them. There's no need."

"The Nemenuh will not rely on their warriors today," he said. "The Great Spirit will do this thing for us."

What this meant, he had no idea. Perhaps they were going to curse them, or something mystical like that. Harmless. Then Remy heard thunder in the distance. A storm had come out of the west. But how? The skies were clear. Then he heard the war whoops of men. Maguara stepped out of the lodge and motioned for Remy to follow.

His eyes focused on the hills above them. He saw the buffalo, thousands of them, being driven by warriors in one frantic mass over the rise where he'd positioned his men. On the bluff above, he saw squads of warriors confer with one in a white cape who directed it all. Kills White Bear sent some one way, and others the opposite, all converging on that one knoll. Remy knew the high ground would be useless against the frenzied tide of muscle, hide, and hoof. He'd seen what wild cattle could do. The buffalo would certainly be worse.

Soon he heard the sharp crack of long rifles, but he didn't hear them long.

Chapter Twenty-Four

Remy awoke just as day was breaking. Under cover of darkness Maguara had ordered him staked naked to the ground. He saw forms in the red morning light. First he recognized the horses. Then he saw the men. They lay in grotesque configurations, broken, stripped bare and scalped, their horrible eyes still open, their bloody faces frozen in contorted screams.

The Tonkawa scouts must have escaped the initial stampede. They must have mounted and run for their lives, but they had been captured and staked to the ground. Remy had heard their cries. With the light of day, he saw their fate clearly. The Comanches had peeled the flesh from their chests and abdomen, allowing packs of coyotes to rake their viscera with claws and teeth. The Tonkawa spent the night screaming until they died.

In the morning some of the predators remained. They licked the dried blood where bones protruded from torn skin. Each bloating body hummed from the work of hundreds of busy black flies. Already the buzzards sailed the thermals overhead, circling tighter and tighter. They would feast next.

Remy was sick with thirst and grief. It was worse than San Jacinto. The sight of it, the stench, the horror. What made it all so much worse was that this time it had been his fault. There was no one else to blame. Maguara had let them ride into the Comanchería not because the Comanche feared them, as he'd anticipated, but because it was what he'd wanted them to do. Don Carlos had warned him not to come, and Don Carlos had been right.

He wished Maguara would betray him. That he'd go back on his word and kill him dead, and Beatriz and the children, too. There was no way back from this. Even if they lived through it, life would never be the same. Little Remy lay dead. Beatriz had been captured and raped; he had no doubt of that. His remaining two children would never recover from the shock of what had happened. And fifty-four men lay dead and decomposing on the plains because he wouldn't listen. His little army lay in ruins around him, and Remy knew his life was ruined, too. All of it, forever. Texas had finally destroyed him. Texas and himself.

Chapter Twenty-Five

Kills White Bear sat again at Maguara's side as the tribe celebrated its greatest victory against the whites. This time there were no captives. He watched as the young warriors danced around the roaring flames, firing new weapons, with fresh, bloody scalps hanging from their lances.

Despite his success—it had been his idea to herd the buffalo over the whites—Kills White Bear brooded. Maguara had already told him of his promise to Fuqua. Kills

White Bear was angry that he had not been consulted, that Maguara had usurped a warrior's right of property. But his anger was also tempered by a growing sense of loss.

This time, when the fool's water passed his way, he drank it. Before he'd swallowed his first sip, he heard the lone howl of the red wolf. It was Wolf Eyes' warning, he knew. But if that burning liquid could ease his pain, he would drink it until he felt nothing.

But that was not what happened. He felt the warmth of it—the lightheadedness, yes—but the pain itself only intensified. There was a mean edge to the fool's water, and it cut him deeply. He stared in the fire and it hypnotized him. He thought of Morning Song and the child they'd had together in those happy times, the times before the whites had come to their land. Then he saw their fever burn in those flames, the oozing, stinking sores, the convulsions, how they'd postured straight and stiff as they died. Their bitter image was still fresh in his mind.

There was no woman or child on earth that could replace them, but over a very short period of time these captives had come close. Did the White Bear not deserve the chance for happiness again? Had he not sacrificed enough for his people? Was his misery the will of the Great Spirit? Certainly his captives did not belong to Maguara, and Maguara had no right to give them away.

He rose awkwardly. His own legs were not steady. His vision was blurred. Why would anyone want this? The dancers parted before him as he approached the fire. He threw his arms out, and the dancing stopped. He felt all eyes on him. He would throw his heart out to his people and let them decide.

"There is a white man staked out on the hill above us," he began. "He came to take from Kills White Bear what Kills White Bear took from him. Two men want one thing. I ask you to decide who should have it." His eyes scanned the crowd. "Kills White Bear will tell you all you must know."

And then he recounted his earlier marriage and the child it produced. They all knew what had happened, how horribly they'd died, and what Kills White Bear had resolved to do about it. For ten winters, he said, he'd avenged their deaths many times over. In doing so, he said, he'd found a purpose—not only for him but also for his beloved people. He cherished them more than he cherished his own life. Some day he knew he would lay it down for them.

But success in war had never soothed the ache in his heart. At least up until this last accidental raid, when fate had tricked him.

He acknowledged that he owed the white man on the hill one life. Kills White Bear had not intended to raid his rancho and to take his wife and children into the bosom of the Nemenuh. Kills White Bear had never meant to harm that man. But that changed nothing. They were here and they were his and his heart said to keep them.

Now wise Maguara had spoken words to the white man that Kills White Bear would never speak. Kills White Bear said he understood obligation and honor, that the Nemenuh were known as people of their word. Kills White Bear was in that man's debt. But he was spared the fate of his soldiers, and as far as Kills White Bear was concerned the debt had been paid. He asked them to consider what would have happened had this man come at some other time when the tribes were not gathered. Who would have killed whom? Fate, he said, had played tricks on them both.

He then repeated his plans for the captives and what they meant to him. But, he said, he could not decide what was right. He valued their opinion and would abide by their decision. What, he asked, should Kills White Bear do?

He heard the camp buzz in whispers until a white-haired woman, Maguara's wife, stepped forward into the fire's light. She said that she sympathized with Kills White Bear, but the woman he wanted would never be his. It was foolish to think otherwise, and in doing so Kills White Bear spared himself no grief. The Méxicana was strong and clever. She might someday lie beside Kills White Bear as his wife, but always she would be his enemy. The blood between them was too great. Some night she would slit his throat to avenge her dead son and lost children, and the Penateka would lose one of its greatest warriors. The woman would be hunted down and killed. This, she said, was not the way.

The Méxicana should be returned to her husband, as Maguara wished, and her female child as well. The boy, however, he should keep to replace the one lost. In that way, neither man could have everything he wanted, but they could each have a part. And that part would provide both with hope for the future and Kills White Bear will have paid his debt—not by war but by honor. And in doing so, he would continue to rise in the eyes of the People. If Kills White Bear wants a woman, he should find one among them. But the half-breed child should remain his.

Then she withdrew from the fire's light and took her place with the elder women.

Kills White Bear thought about what she said. It was good enough. Then he turned and faced Maguara, who was waiting.

"This," he said, "Kills White Bear will abide. In two days' time, you can have the woman and her child." The old chief nodded stiffly, and Kills White Bear left. Before he'd taken ten steps, he heard the Spirit Talker's taunting.

"CAAAW! CAAAW!"

He paid it no mind. Time was now short. The Méxicana didn't know her husband had come for her. He wouldn't tell her that soon she would leave with him. The fool's water filled his brain, confusing emotions that were already in conflict. He felt passionate about everything that crossed his mind, and so much did. But mostly he remembered what Maguara had told him weeks ago. *If you want her, take her,* he'd said.

And that is exactly what he decided to do.

Chapter Twenty-Six

They'd kept him alive to torment him with the overwhelming stench. At night, Comanche women had come with food and water. Even they had fed him with one hand over their noses. Much to his surprise, Remy had been able to eat. He was unable to starve himself; he was unable to die. Those days naked under the bare sun had revealed yet another weakness.

Now, oddly, a single woman came at dawn. As she approached, Remy saw that it was not a woman at all, but a short-haired man, dressed in a loin cloth and leather leggings. He held a knife in his clenched hand.

Then Remy saw his face clearly. It was the man he'd tortured to identify Maguara's camp. The warrior spoke to him in the Comanche tongue and knelt beside him. It sounded almost guttural, at times his tongue clicked in the roof of his mouth to make the strangest sounds. His face remained solemn. When he'd finished his prayer, or his oath, he held the blade against Remy's face, obviously taunting him with its sharpness, its chill. Remy cringed, anticipating the moment when steel would slice the arteries on his neck. Instead, the warrior sawed the little finger from Remy's bound right hand. Remy felt nothing but pressure. When he'd cut it free, he flipped the bloody digit onto Remy's stomach. Then the warrior cut him loose and simply walked away.

Other warriors rode up on horseback. With them was Beatriz, and two smaller riders entirely wrapped in buckskin—the larger held the smaller. His own horse, saddled and ready, was set free. It stepped immediately toward Remy, and, as if the stallion understood what he'd been through, it knelt down for him to mount. He slipped his burned leg over its back, clamping his thumb and index finger against the stub of his finger to stop the bleeding, and rose naked with the horse. A warrior tossed his clothes to him, and he slipped his arms through the sleeves of the shirt and pulled the hat over his brow until the sun was shaded from his eyes. That effort alone fatigued him. His pants and boots would have to wait.

His eyes turned to his wife. She looked well, all things considered. How his children looked and why they were hidden from him, he had no idea. He heard hooves to the east and turned. A single rider had come and paused directly beneath the rising sun. He could not see his face, but he recognized the voice well enough.

"You have what I want, Fuqua," Kills White Bear told him in Spanish. "And I have what you want. All is even. The debt is paid. You came once as a friend; you leave now as an enemy." He turned his horse's head. "Come no more," he said and rode off.

Three warriors escorted him and his family south. He

was kept from Beatriz and the two hooded riders. They would not allow him to touch or even speak to her. When she herself tried, they warned her. When she tried again, they whipped her with quirts. He looked at her to tell her to bide her time. All would soon be well. After that, they all rode in silence.

The heat distorted even the simplest of images. Nothing looked as it should to Remy. He wondered how life would change with Beatriz and the children. What would be the damage? Were Don Carlos and Picosa alive to help them stitch their lives back together? And what had that bastard Kills White Bear meant? He'd wanted Beatriz and his children and now Maguara had given them back. That is what Remy had that Kills White Bear wanted. That he understood. But what did Kills White Bear have that he was supposed to want? It made no sense. None at all.

He was allowed to bathe for the first time south of the San Sabá at the springs the Indians called *Waw-ban-see*. Two warriors sat on the rocky bank watching him. The water was fresh and cool for this time of summer. It went well with the smoked and juniper-berry pemmican they gave him. He ate and drank his fill. Beatriz forded upstream, watched by only one, and bathed in her torn dress. The children he did not see, and that continued to bother him. *"Te amo, Beatriz,"* he called before they struck him, but she heard him well enough and managed a brief smile. How she had aged! He would take her back to the ranch and care for her. He would send for Quelepe and maybe Señora Escajeda, too. They would restore her broken spirit. He was certain of that now.

He washed his clothes as best he could. The Indians threw a parfleche bag that held some sort of ointment for him. It smelled like bear grease maybe, he wasn't sure. It was mixed with mashed leaves and powders he couldn't identify. But as bad as it smelled it soothed his sunburned

skin and the rope burns on his arms and ankles. He dabbed
a little where his finger used to be. For the first time he
felt himself healing.

When he had dressed in his wet clothes, he remounted.
They again lashed his wrists, both of them, to his sad-
dlehorn, and they rode on. At mid-afternoon they rested
in the shade. At sunset, they mounted and rode until well
after midnight. They rose again at dawn. This went on for
three more days. Not once did he hear his wife and children
utter a word. They endured in silence.

At noon on the fourth day, they crossed the Guadalupe
and stopped. As Remy watched, the warriors cut Beatriz
free and left the knife in her hands. Then they took the
children and recrossed the river. Beatriz cut him free and
he embraced her. They both turned toward the children.

"Let them go!" Remy shouted, and they answered that
they soon would. "I need my guns! There's wild animals out
here!" And he watched as they laid them all down on the
bank—rifle, shotgun and two pistols, powder horn and shot
bag, all his accouterments—for him to retrieve after they'd
gone. Next to them they placed the smaller bundle and ripped
the buckskin away. It was Elena Marie. When she saw her
parents across the river and the Comanche still with her, she
screamed as if they were killing her. The second child tore
his own away as he remained mounted on his horse. It was
a boy, yes, but a Comanche. Maguara had tricked him.

Remy angrily cursed the retreating warriors, but Beatriz
had already forded the river to get the child they'd been
given. Remy followed her as quickly as he could. He
slipped on the smooth, moss-covered river stones, bruising
his feet and his knees. Beatriz reached Elena Marie first
and embraced her. Remy wrapped his arms around them
both. His chest convulsed as he sobbed like he never had
before. The dark, empty canyon that cradled the river
echoed with Remy's wailing. The three of them collapsed
together on the bank of that quiet river.

Remy found a cave, checked it for scorpions, bats, and
rattlesnakes, and then led in his wife and child. They were
too tired and depleted to go on. He brought them water
and told them he would go in search of food. They would
stay the night there, and then go on in the morning. Beatriz
protested. They'd been without food before; they could do
it now. But Remy could not bear to see them hungry, he
said, and he left the cave, carefully covering his tracks as
Quelepe had taught him years ago.

He tied the horses in an opposite canyon and gathered
a little grass for Beatriz and Elena Marie to chew while he
was gone. Then he returned to his guns, fired them all, and
loaded them with fresh powder and ball. He mounted his
stallion, and followed the Comanche tracks north. Despite
all the times his anger had failed him, it sustained his efforts
now. He had one last message for Kills White Bear.

The Comanche were sloppy. But then again they'd probably never expected Remy to come after them. When he
caught up with them he knew exactly what to do. He galloped through a draw that lay east of the Indians and circled back. He found the perfect spot, tethered his stallion,
ran up a little hill where the cedars hid him and waited.
Never had he been so sure of himself.

When they were close enough, he emptied both barrels
of the shotgun and two warriors fell. The third dashed
straight for him, but Remy brought his rifle to bear and
unseated him from the back of the horse. He was gut-shot.
As the Comanche rolled over in agony on the grass, Remy
saw a portion of his entrails protruding from his back like
some kind of worm. He wasn't going anywhere. The boy
raced on, and Remy mounted and ran after him. This one
he roped, brought back to where the others lay, worked a
noose up until it choked his neck, and threw the loose end
over a limb. The wounded warrior he slung screaming back
on his horse, and brought him next to the boy.

"Don't hang me, Fuqua!" the man pleaded. "My spirit
will not be free! Shoot me! I beg you!"

"You kin rot in hell, you murderin' son of a bitch!" and
Remy slapped the flank of the horse and the man swung
in the hot wind as blood bubbled from that awful wound.
Fuqua watched him die.

The boy was next. His eyes were wild with terror. Remy didn't feel a thing for him, not one tinge of pity. He whipped the horse and the lariat creaked as it took the boy's weight. He gagged and struggled while Remy watched. When he grew still, Remy cut him free and he collapsed like a sack of flour on the ground. Remy splashed water on his face from his canteen, and the boy gasped for breath. Remy snatched the hair on the back of his head and yanked him to his feet. Slowly he turned his head to the man suspended above him. Blood dripped on his cheek.

"You tell Kills White Bear this is far from over, you hear me. I want my boy! Tell him to bring him to Béxar before the moon turns full. I'll trade 'im fair. Whatever he wants. Otherwise, I'll kill 'im. Fuqua swears on the bodies of the slain. ¡Comprende!"

The boy nodded that he did, and Remy set him free. Before the wind had dispersed his dust, Remy rummaged for the Comanche's food and rode back to where his wife and child waited. They ate their fill, and Remy said they had to go on. Not once did Beatriz ask where that meat came from. Remy was pretty sure she already knew.

Chapter Twenty-Seven

Kills White Bear saw the boy return to camp alone and knew immediately that something had gone seriously wrong. The boy was telling Maguara what had happened when Kills White Bear reached them. He was speaking so rapidly that Kills White Bear did not understand everything he said. But he caught the worst of it.

He felt a sadness for the loss of three good men. He'd underestimated Fuqua. He admitted that. He himself would go and tell their families of their fate. He'd done so several times by now, but it never got any easier.

"I hope we did the right thing," Maguara said. "If I'd have listened to you and killed him, none of this would've happened." He was concerned that Fuqua would raise another army to ride against them. It would be a source of worry, Maguara said, as they prepared their meat for the winter.

While Kills White Bear likewise expressed remorse for the decision—that Maguara listened to crows when he should've listened to him—he was certain that its consequences were now over. He pointed to the hill where the dead soldiers still lay.

"Who," he asked calmly, "would follow Fuqua?"

Chapter Twenty-Eight

Rancho de la Cruz lay in ruins. Béxar was worse. Remy didn't know if Quelepe was alive or dead. He decided to take what remained of his family to the rancho of Don Carlos's second cousin, Felix Menchaca. It lay northeast of Rancho de la Cruz, near Holy Cross Springs.

The Menchaca rancho was untouched by the war. It bustled with activity as Don Carlos's once had. The Menchacas were more than happy to look after their cousins. They were all welcome there, but what would Remy do about what had happened to their land? Rancho de la Cruz had been seized by gringos. Other Tejanos had also lost their holdings under various false and nefarious pretenses. Don Juan Seguín and Jose Antonio Navarro were fighting to protect the rights of those who had opposed Santa Anna. As for the rest, Don Carlos included, may God help them.

To Remy, it was but another blow in a year in which he'd been bludgeoned. The first thing to do, he decided, was to gather his family as best he could. He would bring Don Carlos, Picosa, and whatever of the campesinos he could find to the Menchacas'. Then he would go to the government and regain what rightfully belonged to them. It was a mistake, he was confident, and one that he could clear up in time. And he wasn't about to go riding into Rancho de la Cruz and get hanged. Houston would help him, and Houston's name was on the ballot for President that fall. And he also had to go and find Rusk, or whoever had succeeded him if they'd lynched him by now. He had to report the loss of his entire command. He was still, more

or less, in the Texas Army, and he had a lot of explaining
to do. One fire, he thought, at a time.

What he needed first was rest. He spent that first night
with Beatriz. Her first thought was of him and their surviving daughter. The Menchacas bathed and clothed them, and
put them in their own clean room with servants to attend
them.

Remy slipped his wife and daughter between white
sheets. The drapes danced in the summer breeze as the
three of them clung desperately to each other. He stroked
their foreheads until sleep finally found them. The only
peace he'd known in months was the sound of their deep
breathing behind the safety of Menchaca walls.

He wondered if he himself could sleep, and if so, would
he ever dream again. Even as his body lay still in the security of a fortified ranch, he felt it being tugged in a dozen
different directions. None of them, he knew, was any good.
His peeling skin covered a sack of dried bones, most of
them gnawed to some degree. He felt empty, almost detached from the ruin of his world, although he could see
himself sitting in its smoldering center. Everything was
burned or bloody.

He needed a month's rest. He could have one day. In
the morning he had to gather what was left and go. What
he had to do could not wait. He had a life to rebuild,
obligations as head of his bleeding family, but he knew that
his heart would not be in it anymore, not after the loss of
his two sons. He stared out that lonely window. The night
was as dark as any he'd ever seen.

Remy knew it was useless to go to Columbia for help. President Burnet's crumbling government was besieged with
problems of its own, most of which Burnet himself had
caused. Remy went instead to Sam Houston, who he'd
heard was dividing his time between the homes of friends
and supporters at Nacogdoches and San Augustine in far

East Texas. Houston had "reluctantly" agreed to run for president. "The crisis demands it," was his explanation, but Remy thought it more than likely was his ego that had given the order. San Jacinto had already made him a legend, and Sam Houston knew how to use it better than most. Remy hoped he could use it a little too. It was now late August, and the election was two weeks away.

Remy tracked Houston down at the home of Adolphus Sterne. Remy dismounted and tramped on the pine planks of the painted porch in his Mexican vaquero boots. He pressed his hands and face against the windowpane and could see Houston well through the glass. He was sitting down to the dinner table, laughing, a glass of wine in his hand, when he caught sight of Remy.

He excused himself from the table, and asked Remy to come in. Remy politely refused. He said he was hot and dirty and would make poor company. His general told him where a place to rest could be found, a stable that doubled as a bar and hotel, and Remy went there to wait.

Remy was asleep, his head against his saddle, when Houston's voice called his name. Remy climbed to his feet and shook hands with him.

"I didn't know if I'd ever see you again, Fuqua," Houston said. "I heard you met with difficulty on the plains."

Remy nodded and pointed to Houston's ankle. "How's the leg?"

"Tolerable. They say I nearly lost it to gangrene. The doctors in New Orleans operated several times. I can waddle well enough with what they left me, but it still swells and seeps. All of my wounds heal slowly it seems, if at all."

"I know the feelin'," Remy answered. Then he got to the point. "They say you're about to become president of this country. I need help."

"With what, exactly?"

And Remy told him all that had happened. Don Carlos had been labeled a Mexican sympathizer which, more or less, was true. But he hadn't aided Santa Anna. Santa Anna had simply forced himself upon him, taken what he wanted, and left.

The speculators hadn't really taken Don Carlos's land by force, however. They'd run him down in Béxar shortly before he died of wounds the Comanche had inflicted, and pressed him to sell. Remy had lost two children, recovered his hollow wife and daughter, but had nowhere to take them. The war had taken him, the Indians his family, the land speculators his land. What, he wondered, could Houston do about any of this?

"Do you know these men?" he asked. Remy could tell he was sympathetic.

"Nope."

"They've got a deed?"

"They do."

"Why did he sell?"

"He thought my wife and me was dead. He was dyin'. Mexican ranchers were leaving San Antonio de Béxar in droves. They feared the whites more than the centralistas. My father-in-law was in no condition to argue. I don't know what he did with the money."

"What can I do to help?"

"Intercede on my behalf. I'll buy it back for what they give for it. That land's been in my wife's family for over a hundred years."

"But he sold it, Fuqua."

"Yeah, he sold it," Remy agreed, irritated that Houston was able to consider the opposing view, "with a pistol to his head. There's laws against that kind of shit, ain't they?"

"None that apply to the Mexicans, I'm afraid."

"Look," Remy said angrily. "I fought for Texas. I'm owed land. I only want mine back."

"The government owes you, Fuqua, but it doesn't owe you a hacienda. Even if I was to intercede on your behalf, it wouldn't look right. You can sue them under a claim of duress in the courts, as soon as we have some, and let a judge decide your claim."

"Sam, I ain't got the time or the patience for the law. What's right is right."

"Look, you're a smart man, Fuqua. I could use you in the government."

"I've been used all I care to be," Remy said, his eyes narrowing. "I don't want to be in the goddamn government, Sam. I want my land."

"You've got money, Fuqua. Go and buy some and be done with it."

"I can't near afford what I lost."

"Then you must buy what you can," Houston advised him. There were problems everywhere. New ones. The news from Washington was not good. Texas had not even been recognized by the United States, much less considered for annexation. The war had left the infant government over a million dollars in debt. The North feared war with Mexico and the expansion of slavery. Jackson's hands were tied. The army was in rebellion. Burnet's government was in chaos. The Comanche were raiding the entire frontier, but all of the tribes were active. Santa Anna was still in Texas, and Mexican troops were poised south of the Río Grande. Rumor had it they had already crossed it three different times. All false, he admitted, but the threat was very real. Such an agenda, he said, would consume his energies. Remy's personal problems would have to wait. "All things considered, Fuqua," Houston ended, "I'd say you're lucky to be alive."

"Lucky just ain't the word," Remy fumed.

"Look at it how you want," Houston told him sternly, "but we're all startin' from scratch aroun' here. Ride the trouble out, although painful, and profit. There's fortunes to made in this country now. You do what you must, but you're still in the service of the government. If nothing else, I'm sure you're available for Ranger duty. You've had a great setback in that regard, and I know better than anyone how failure can haunt a man. I'm truly sorry for your troubles, Remy. But, I'd chalk up your losses to bad luck and nothing else, and move on."

"That's just what I'll do," he said, accepting the futility of arguing further. He yanked his saddle from the dirt floor and moved for the door.

"You will remember to vote, I trust," Houston reminded him.

"Oh, I'll vote," he said. "For Austin."

Houston smiled and spoke to him as a father does a ridiculously rebellious child. "Ah, Fuqua. That's a bad choice."

"I've made 'em before," he said, and he walked out and

saddled his horse. If Houston would not help him get his land back, there was no man or government that would. Before he'd ridden another mile, he'd accepted it. What he needed was advice about what to do now that Rancho de la Cruz was lost, and there was only one man he trusted to give that advice. Austin had returned to Texas.

Chapter Twenty-Nine

Don Estévan was in a rundown, rented shack when Remy found him. It was an outrage, Remy thought, that such a man should be reduced to living in such a place. Austin had not fared any better in the war than Remy had.

They had not seen one another in nearly a year, not since the siege of Béxar. Remy was shocked by his appearance. Racked by malaria, he was thin, drawn, and jaundiced. He sat working at a wobbly writing desk when Remy entered. Always working. Austin shoved his papers and inkwell aside to make room for him. He apologized for his state, which he said he knew appeared rancid, but there was much to do as always. Remy noticed the tremble in his hands.

"I've often thought of you," Austin told him, and when he said it those great dark eyes still sparkled in his pale head. "You and your cousin Johnson were among my favorites. I'm especially proud of you, Fuqua. You've made quite a name for yourself. Rusk told me what you did at San Jacinto."

"Did Rusk tell you that I lost fifty young men up on the Concho?"

Austin looked at him sadly and shook his head. Once again, Remy told all that had happened. So much of it, he said, could not be undone, but that was not the worst of it. He had failed both himself and the one person he held dearest—his wife. The result was that he now doubted himself, his judgment, his ability, his will to carry on. He no longer knew what to do or where to go. That was the reason, he said, that he'd come here.

When he was younger, Remy said, it all came so easily.

Fortune had shone on him for over ten years. In the length of just one, he'd lost almost everything. "This time the year last, I was ridin' to Gonzáles with my cousin to win the world. A year later, I've got half a family and no home." Remy straightened, placing his elbows on the table. "I've come to you as I always have in times of trouble. I need advice, Stephen. Just plain, good advice. And this time I swear I'll listen."

Remy watched as Austin steadied his forehead with one trembling hand. "I'm sick, Fuqua. I'll not win the election, I know, and I don't care. I'll soon see my forty-third birthday, but I don't think I'll see many more. I've got personal problems of my own to manage. Like yours, they loom large. I don't find the strength anymore. But, as always, I think of Texas first."

Things would go better from now on, he thought. Santa Anna should be sent to the United States and offer Jackson the opportunity to mediate the Texas-Mexico dispute. Santa Anna's return to Mexico would once again plunge that government into chaos, and attention would be withdrawn from Texas. California, Yucatan, Sonora, and even besieged Zacatecas were on the verge of revolt, and Mexico must let Texas go.

The Americans balk now, he said, but Texas will be annexed in time. The Republic must seek recognition from the Europeans if the Americans will not oblige. Such an act would certainly grease the skids toward union. Immigrants were already coming in droves. Houston would be an able first president. As dark as the present looked, the future still was bright.

Much had been destroyed, he said. Much blood had been shed. Remy's own wounds, he told him, were certainly deep. But, he said, Remy could not and must not blame himself for the war. It was like a storm, and storms are inevitable. The raid that took his children was also none of his fault. Had he been there, he would have died with Don Carlos, and then what would his family have done?

He agreed that Remy's expedition on the Concho was unfortunate, but Austin himself would've reacted as Remy had. He'd dealt with the Tonkawa and the Karankawa in that very same manner, as Remy knew. Remy's decision and planning and execution were sound enough. It was bad timing, and nothing else, and who among them knew how the Comanche lived? They would be the next to fall, and Remy would be a part of it.

"But you must remember," Austin said, elevating his gaze, "when we—you and I—first came to this wild and beautiful country. Remember how you reveled when you first saw this land. Think of what you and Johnson have accomplished. You and Beatriz can do it again."

Remy shook his head, eyes cast to the floor. "You haven't seen her, Stephen." He paused. "She's different."

"I don't have to see her," Austin said, his eyes returning to Remy's. "I know the strength of your wife's heart and spirit. You're very lucky, Fuqua. There's no other woman in Texas better suited to conquer it." He opened the door and peered out. "These people think they've won the war. It's just beginning. Boundaries have shifted, one race replaces another, but the battle for the land still rages, Fuqua. Wars do not build nations; farmers do."

He turned back to Remy. "You ask me what you and Beatriz should do? You should go and farm. It's what you came for, isn't it? And it's what you already know. San Felipe was burned. Does it bother me? Yes, it was my capital. But does it mean anything?" He shook his head. "No," he said. "One stalk of corn shoving through the soil where a thicket once grew means more to me than any building. Go and plant corn."

"I don't know," Remy sighed. "I don't have the hunger no more."

"Of course you do," Austin said. "You were born for this land, Fuqua, and no war, no politician, no storm, no drought, can ever burn that out of your stubborn soul. Go and plant something, Fuqua. Plant something and live. I no longer have the strength, but you do. This is your country. Make Texas's future yours."

Austin's encouragement moved him. His mind considered options. There was one that was particularly attractive. "Do you think I still could arrange title to Elijah's grant? It was once half mine."

"Johnson's dead?" Austin asked, his lips pursed.

Remy nodded solemnly. "He was with Fannin at Goliad."

Austin rubbed his temple as his gaze fell to the floor. "My God," he moaned. "We've lost so many of our best." He looked back up at him. "I'm so sorry, Remy. He was a very fine man." He paused, thinking. "But that changes everything," he finally said.

Remy was puzzled. "In what way?" he asked.

"You'll soon see," and he began rummaging through dusty crates of maps, deeds, grants, and loose papers until he found the one he wanted. He lay it before Remy and smiled. "Your cousin came to see me before Gonzáles. I drafted his will. I'm certain that he left everything to you and Beatriz."

Remy felt his eyes widen as he examined the document. Remy watched him run his finger across the words to confirm it. "Yes," he finally announced. "It's just here."

Remy drew a deep breath of relief. Elijah had lost his life, but in doing so, he'd saved Remy's. It was that one buoyant plank adrift in the ocean after a great wreck. All Remy had to do was reach out and grasp it. His eyes raced to the bottom of it where they found Elijah's scratchy signature. It was there. "Eight thousand acres ought to make a good start," he said.

Austin reached for the document. "I seem to recollect a different figure," he said, and he poured over the legal description. "Yes, here it is. More than forty thousand, it seems."

"What!" Remy was in shock. "How'd that ignorant bastard get title to forty thousand acres?"

Austin looked at him as if he were disappointed in his reaction. "He wasn't so ignorant after all," he said. "Johnson was a shrewd businessman as well as a fine farmer. He paid off his note with Spanish gold. Where he got it, I've no idea."

"I've got a notion," Remy said wryly.

"When that was done, he bought adjacent tracts with cash. All recorded with good title. His herd grew with his farm. He traded horses and cattle in Louisiana for cash. He smuggled tobacco and whiskey, too, or so I was told. It wasn't any of my business. He lived up to his part of the bargain. I lived up to mine."

Remy slid the paper back around and read it again. Now

he knew where the money had gone. The corners of his mouth cracked in a wide grin. "And you'll record this all legal-like?"

"Yes," Austin clipped. "Yours and all the others. There's much to do, as I said."

"Then I'll be goin'."

"So soon. You look tired. Stay and rest. We'll talk a while of the old days."

"Are you kiddin'?" He rose from the table, shook Austin's cold hand, and started for the door. "I got me a place, Austin. I'm gonna go work it."

Chapter Thirty

He slept little on the trail back to the Menchacas', but at least he slept. He saw himself riding out of the ashes for the open country of the West. He would probably never own anything like Rancho de la Cruz, but then again, he'd never needed that much land anyway. Forty thousand acres was more than plenty. His luck had not failed him, and neither, he would always remember, had Elijah.

When he reached the ranch, he went first to see Beatriz and Elena Marie. He'd spent his days under the stars planning again. He would take Picosa and the others to Elijah's grant. His mind was putting the pieces together to see how they would fit. Beatriz would not look well, he knew that, but the news would lift her. They had a future together after all.

His mind had turned often to Kills White Bear and Maguara. He knew the Comanche would not trade the boy away. He sought an answer for Carlito's return, but his mind did not provide one. Still, he would try. That was the one end that remained loose. All the others, for better or worse, were either tied or torn off.

Beatriz's cousins were cold to him when he arrived. He did not know why. Surely, they did not blame him for what had happened. Anastasia Menchaca, the wife of Don Felix, accompanied him in silence as he made his way to Beatriz's room.

"Is something wrong, Doña Rosa?" he finally asked her.

"Wrong?" she seethed. "Yes, I would say something is wrong. Your wife comes to us half-dead, but this does not stop a man like you from seeking pleasure from her. She's been sick to her stomach for two weeks. You should be ashamed of yourself, you foolish man! As if she doesn't have enough to worry about. You could've killed her!"

"I got no idea what you mean."

"No?" She opened the door and allowed it to swing open. The curses she had for him dissipated into smiles for his wife. Beatriz lay on the bed with Elena Marie. Her color had returned, but she still looked sickly. Her eyes brightened at the sight of him. In his hand, he held a letter from Austin confirming the transfer of Elijah's land. She would be thrilled at the news, he knew, but when the door shut behind him he had another question.

"What's that woman fussin' about, Beatriz?"

She looked at him sadly. "I'm pregnant," she said, and then she turned away.

BOOK FIVE

—◆—

The Feud

1837

Chapter One

Remy gently laid the clay pot of ashes into the dark earth. He'd sent two vaqueros to Goliad to collect them. Who or what they were he had no idea, but he wanted to bring Elijah home and this was the closest he could come. The Mexicans had burned the bodies as they had at the Alamo.

A carved oak plank marked the name, birth date, and the day his cousin had died. In the corner they'd erected an altercito to honor the lives of Don Carlos Amarante de la Cruz and his wife. They lay together in the family plot in Béxar. Remy knew that place was full.

Remy shoveled the last of the dark and stony soil around the pot with a homemade spade, patting it carefully into a swollen mound. When he finished, he turned to Quelepe.

"I miss him," Remy said. Quelepe nodded in silence. "I never thought that stubborn son of a bitch could really die. It ain't the same aroun' here without his whinin'."

"He loved you," Quelepe told him. "He spoke of you often."

"Cussed me, more'n likely."

"Sometimes, yes," Quelepe admitted, "but always with the deepest affection."

Remy attempted to picture what that would sound like. He couldn't do it. But Elijah, as he well knew, had a special knack for insults, and no one practiced it more. He took what comfort he could from Quelepe's memories.

Remy knew he owed much of the success of that year to that curious, fossilized old man, who now counted seventy-one years in Texas. Despite his age he'd kept Elijah's ranch together. The cattle ranged on green pastures, and the fields, prepared by slaves, were ready for spring. Elijah had told Quelepe that if he did not return, he should expect his cousin to come and together they could decide what should be done. Remy arrived in a whirlwind, the same old look of hunger in his eyes, and Quelepe claimed that he could not have been happier.

All of what Remy saw encouraged him just as Austin had said it would. In land there was always hope.

Diego Picosa, now healed, came with his kin, along with seven other campesino families, at Remy's request. Quelepe said that Elijah had once owned thirteen slaves, most of which he'd kept hidden from Remy for obvious reasons. Seven had gone south at the Mexicans' invitation of freedom, but six had stayed on with Quelepe. Beatriz insisted that Remy free them all, but they chose to remain just the same and work for the same wage as Remy's vaqueros. Remy understood the basis for their decision. Like him, they had nowhere else to go. And like him, the land was all they knew.

For Remy that first spring was the hardest. The dog-trot cabin of which he and Elijah had once been so proud would not do. Beatriz never once complained, but Remy felt the need to duplicate as closely as possible what they had lost the year before. He would have resurrected Rancho de la Cruz, which he learned had been split and sold twice, if he could.

One of the vaqueros was a skilled mason. The rest, Remy included, could learn. They built a house of limestone and oak on the bluff above the old cabin, and then a wall around it that encompassed a well, grain stores and corn cribs, a barn for the horses, and rows of smaller wood houses for the help. He knew the Comanche still raided that area relentlessly. He also valued the lives of his family and those of his workers. He wanted them all safe behind that wall.

Construction halted to plant corn and cotton, and to work the spring calves. During those first months, Remy paced the floors of his Elijah-less cabin. Quelepe always shadowed him with cups of strange teas and elixirs to quiet his anxious mind. None of them worked. When Quelepe wasn't around he drank whiskey to numb the pain.

While Remy's homestead took shape, the Republic around it began to form as well. Houston had swept the election as he predicted he would, but as a consolation he had named Austin as his secretary of state. Austin accepted and set to work as always, but by December of 1836 he had passed on. The entire Republic, Houston included, grieved at the loss of this great and quiet man. But Remy believed he grieved more deeply than any other. He'd lost his friend and mentor, the link between past and present, in a year when he'd lost just about everything else. That first spring was new, but lonely. Cold rain fell on the cold earth.

When the Texas army continued to trouble him, Remy heard that Houston did as General Washington had done in similar circumstances. He could not pay them off—there was no money. So he simply furloughed all but six hundred indefinitely. If the rest were needed, the government would call. In the meantime, they were free to return home with empty pockets.

Remy watched events as closely as he could. Recognition by the United States, much less annexation, continued to elude the Texians. The institution of slavery, Remy knew, was the greatest impediment, not only to the Americans, but to the British as well, who were also worried about jeopardizing their significant investment in troubled Mexico. Jackson, despite his hidden agenda, remained aloof out of political necessity, and so Sam Houston scrambled to build an independent nation with the tools at hand. There weren't many.

But the Republic staggered on just as Austin had predicted it would. The government issued its first currency, the "star buck," and though it initially stumbled, it held its value well enough. Near the ruins of Harrisburg, a new capital city rose. To the chagrin of many it was called Houston, flying the flag of the lone five-point star, as did the seats of the Republic's twenty-three counties. The Texas navy (four small vessels and a few privateers) prowled the gulf, and young, unpaid Rangers fought on the frontier for their own homes and families. The Mexicans continued to threaten but did not invade.

The President plodded precariously through the muddy

streets of his booming capital among loud invitations to duel and whispered threats of assassination. It seemed to Remy that when Houston vanquished one enemy at San Jacinto, he made dozens of others at the same time. Some were jealous of his fame, some could never trust him, others just hated him outright. Houston ignored them all and plowed on. At nighttime, according to many accounts, he drank.

Remy met with problems of his own. Though things had miraculously calmed, Remy was never free of the burden of that disastrous, stormy year. He and Beatriz had suffered so completely that he knew their lives would never be the same. Their wounds had left deep and obvious scars. It used to be that he could take one look at her and know what she was thinking. They had once been that close. Now there were darker regions harbored in places he could never reach. Her eyes hid them from him. They could share the same room and the same bed, but not the same soul anymore. Much to his agony, she had drifted from him.

He'd loved her as much as he ever had, and he felt certain that she tried with all her heart to return it, but he knew that grief and pain had taken their toll. Elijah, Don Carlos, and their two sons were gone, and with them had gone Remy and Beatriz's youth and the simple joy of being alive. They no longer played together. She refused their long, morning rides; they never sat by the fire in the evenings and just talked. She offered excuses and kept to herself. Wherever Beatriz went (and she hardly went anywhere) Elena Marie went with her. She would not let the child from her sight. And Remy found himself the odd man out, more and more isolated with his loss.

He spent his days with his vaqueros and the endless nights with Quelepe and some strange, bitter tonic in his hand, pacing the warped floors. The old man's stories no longer enchanted him. There were other, more practical things on his mind now.

He hoped that in time, Beatriz would reach out to him as she once had, air her pain, share her misery, and know that she wasn't alone, because Remy hurt so terribly, too. Despite his best efforts, the loss consumed him. And he believed it hadn't stopped there. In his heart, he sensed it had consumed his marriage as well. What was once so good between them was gone, and even Beatriz must've known. Remy knew neither one had the strength to speak the words.

And if Beatriz's retreat alone wasn't enough to plague that first year of recovery, Remy had to watch her stomach swell. She quietly took care of herself as she had with all of her children. To him, this seemed strange. Remy didn't really know how she should act with this baby, but to treat it like one of the others didn't seem right to him. She never spoke of how she'd become pregnant, and Remy could not bring himself to ask. But it was on his mind always, and she must've known.

Remy thought Beatriz might act as if her pregnancy was somehow normal, but he never could. Every time he thought of it, it was as if a small and healing wound was ripped open. The child she carried belonged to the murderers of his children. He could think of it in no other terms.

Once the grave was covered, Remy leaned on his shovel to reflect on his work. "While we're at it," he said, "you ought to tell me where you wanna be buried."

"So soon?" Quelepe asked. "What's the hurry? I've got years to go yet."

"You never know," Remy said. "Your old head looks like it's done wore out three bodies already. You best think about what you want done." He cast his eye to the silent, stone house. "I'd pick a spot for me and Beatriz if she'd ever talk to me again."

Quelepe rarely commented on his marriage, and he failed to do so now. He just raked the ground with his toe and finally said, "There's no need for you to pick a place, Remy."

"How's that?"

He said it again. "There's no need."

"What the hell's that mean?"

"You won't die in Tejas, my friend."

This struck Remy as particularly strange, even for Quelepe. The old mestizo was a "seer" and still made predictions. Remy was damned if every now and then the old buzzard wasn't right. Just the same, Remy couldn't see himself going anywhere. His plan was simple. He intended to sink his roots in that rocky soil and hold tight. Somewhere on that ranch they'd lay him down. He was sure of that. He didn't want to know how or why Quelepe could say such a thing. His only instinct was to deny it. "I'll prove you wrong, old man."

Quelepe looked at him with those dark eyes. "I hope you do," he said. "I just see what I see. There's trouble ahead."

Remy poked the snout of the shovel into the ground. "It don't take a soothsayer to know that," he said bitterly. "Either come up with some goddamn details, or keep your fool notions to yourself. I don't need no more worries."

Quelepe, obviously regretting what he'd said, left Remy to himself.

Remy sat beside the empty grave until the sun set. Tomorrow, by God, he'd set his own marker beside Elijah's, Quelepe be damned. But now it was time to go inside and eat another quiet meal with his wife and child. Soon the baby would be born. He had yet to decide what to do about it.

Chapter Two

Kills White Bear was content with the season. The raiding was going very well. The line of whites was neither moving west nor even staying put. They were retreating eastward from whence they came. The lands of the Cherokee, Caddo, Delaware and Shawnee were at risk now, and that suited him and the rest of the People. These Indians were not welcome on the southern plains. Their enemies, the Lipan Apache and the Tonkawa, were but a fragment of what they had been and therefore no longer threatening. These tribes had embraced the whites, even ridden with them against the Nemenuh, and in doing so had wrought their own destruction. Kills White Bear knew the diseases of the whites took whatever warriors the Nemenuh could not reach with their arrows.

The People were never stronger, nor more confident. They had risen from the plague. The Méxicano soldiers were gone. Austin was dead, as was his treaty with Maguara. The Tejanos, as they now referred to white Texians, feared the Nemenuh as they feared no other and rightly so. Kills White Bear raided their ranches relentlessly, stealing their big American horses which all Nemenuh prized, took what women and children they wanted for captives and killed the rest—man, woman and child. It was warfare as Kills White Bear understood it and as it had been since the dawn of their kind. The Nemenuh were the People, all other races were something else—something lesser—and deserved whatever fate the Great Spirit willed. The white bear's warning left no room in his heart for pity.

Kills White Bear watched as the Penateka ripped and shredded the frontier with Méxicano knives, Nemenuh arrows and American rifles, and left it behind them in flames. It was the only warning, he knew, the Tejanos understood.

Yet, despite the bloodshed and unmitigated violence the Nemenuh unleashed, all information available to Kills White Bear told him that the whites were still coming in greater numbers than ever before. They balked at the Colorado before the Nemenuh threat, but they were still coming. And he knew there could be but one response.

Kills White Bear lay resting when the little Méxicano found him. He saw that the boy's nose and mouth were bloodied. As soon as the lodge flap closed behind him, the boy collapsed into tears. It pleased Kills White Bear that this boy had come to him with his troubles. He pulled him to his shoulder, and gently stroked his dark hair.

"Why the tears, Little Eagle?" He had named him this because of his sharp, black eyes and his tenacious spirit. If Kills White Bear's hope had a name it was Little Eagle.

"I was playing kick-the-ball with the other boys," the boy whimpered. "When I won, they beat me."

Kills White Bear understood. Nemenuh boys were hard on captives, and they were particularly vicious when it came

to the one he had adopted. Jealousy, he thought. They'd
come close to drowning him down by the river, they burned
him with coals to awaken him, he had to fight for his food.
They were testing his courage, but the little Méxicano had
persevered. He was as tough as any of the other captives,
and more so than most. In better than one year's time, he
had learned their language and their ways, and now proved
that he could master both. The other boys of Maguara's
camp couldn't bear it.

Kills White Bear wiped the blood from his face and
stroked his cheek. When the boy responded by putting his
bruised arms around his waist, Kills White Bear's heart
melted.

"Rest with me," he said. "In a little while Kills White
Bear will go out with you and watch you beat them again.
Then we'll work a little with your bow. You're still a bit
wild, I think."

The boy sniffled. "Can I borrow a horse?" he asked.

Kills White Bear stepped out of the lodge pointing to his
herd of several hundred. "Which do you choose?"

It seemed Little Eagle already knew. "The chestnut sorrel," he said without further contemplation or delay.

Kills White Bear was pleased. The horse was one of his
favorites, a good choice. "It's yours today and forever," he
said. "And five more besides."

He saw that Little Eagle was ecstatic. "Will you make
me a saddle?" he asked.

"No," he said, and the boy seemed confused. "But I'll
teach you to make one." The smile returned.

"And then we can ride?"

"All day and all night if you like."

They went out to gather the materials they needed.
Other people might have thought Kills White Bear was
foolish to give the captive boy horses. Most of them that
had been there for that short a time ran as soon as they
could. But Kills White Bear knew that Little Eagle wasn't
going anywhere. He'd come a long way in just four seasons.
His conversion was surprisingly complete. He never spoke
of his Méxicano family any more. He never used his Spanish tongue. Kills White Bear was certain that this boy was
content to live with the Nemenuh.

In that child's young body he had a son again, and he treated him accordingly. Life seemed full. Those boys were right to be jealous. Little Eagle would grow to be a great warrior. They could do what they liked to thwart him, it would have no effect but make him stronger. Some day Kills White Bear knew that they would follow the Little Eagle as their fathers followed him.

Chapter Three

B eatriz's screams tormented him. He'd gone out on the pastures with his horse in search of peace, but the wind in the valley funneled her cries to his aching ears. Why something as natural as birth was so excruciatingly painful was a mystery to him. But in this particular case, he thought he understood. This child, he thought, was anything but natural.

He wanted to be with her as he had with his younger two, but he couldn't do it. Quelepe was there, and Picosa's wife and two other campesinas. They could deliver the bastard child. Remy walked alone out on the summer grass, a jar of bust-head whiskey in his hand. He waited, it seemed, for hours. He never once heard her call his name.

When the sky turned violet in the east he heard the baby cry for the first time. He sat, cross-legged, facing the river which he could not see. But he heard the water run, and the warm breeze rustle the leaves of the cottonwoods and pecans. His horse nudged him several times until at last he reluctantly rose.

"All right, goddamnit," he complained, "I'm goin'."

He rode to the porch of the stone house and waited there. He heard the sound of hurried steps and a woman humming. Picosa's wife came out for fresh water.

"It's a boy, Don Remy!" she said smiling and re-entered. Remy remained mounted, waiting. At last, Quelepe stepped out with the child, wrapped in soft cloth, in his arms.

"Is she all right?" Remy asked him.

"Yes. The child was breech. It was a difficult birth. But your wife is fine. She's resting."

Remy dismounted and stepped on the porch. Quelepe offered him the baby, but he walked past into the door and through the house until he came to his wife's bedroom. The women were still wiping the blood from her thighs. Crumpled and bloody sheets, stained with summer sweat, were balled up on the floor. Beatriz looked emaciated and pale. They daubed her forehead with cloths dripping with cool well water. Remy sat beside his wife on the bed and put his hand to her brow. She felt cold and it frightened him.

"You sure she's all right?" he asked them quietly.

They nodded. "She'll be fine," one said.

With the worry gone, his former mood returned. "Has she seen the child?" he asked stiffly. The women looked blankly at each other before one answered.

"No."

"Good," he said, and even he realized the tenderness was gone from his voice. He walked back out to Quelepe, who held the child up for him to see in the morning light. Its eyes were coal black, set deeply in thin slits across a wide head. It looked oriental as far as he could tell, except for its dark curly hair and dark skin. If it had Beatriz's features, he couldn't see them. Remy knew without looking that it had none of his.

The infant reached for his finger, but Remy pulled it away. The whiskey burned in his empty and knotted gut. The rest of him felt cold. He'd been up all that night, and had slept little for the last ten. He stared at the baby. It was innocent, he knew, but that changed nothing. Beatriz hadn't seen the child. She wouldn't know. It would soon be over and he told himself he could live with what he was about to do.

He snatched the baby from Quelepe's arms, stripping the blankets from its pink body. He gripped it by the ankles with one hand and flipped it and the child howled. Without a word, he walked toward the river, the baby screaming with every step. Without a word, Quelepe followed. Remy heard the old man's steps crush the dry summer grass behind him.

There was no hesitation when Remy reached the river's edge. In one motion he arched his arm forward and released the child. It flopped into the water like a flat rock, the river's current quickly concealing its point of entry as if it felt the shame that Remy did not. The screaming stopped. The Comanche had taken his sons, Remy had taken theirs. What else could he do?

Remy stood there watching the river run as Quelepe shot past him and leaped into the dark, shallow water. He frantically searched the bottom with both arms until his face told Remy that he felt the child. He seized it, and brought it from the muck into the air. He took the shirt from his back, and wrapped it carefully around the child, clutching it to his chest, soothing it as best he could. Remy listened to it cough at first, then he saw the water spray from its screaming mouth. Quelepe looked up at him as he stood defiantly on the bank. Right was right. Quelepe did not understand. He hadn't seen what Remy had.

"What kind of man would do something like this to a baby?" Quelepe demanded. His expression was one of horror and rage, yet Remy remained unfazed.

"It ain't hers," he said, "and it ain't mine. I don't want it, Quelepe. You let it go. We'll tell her it was still-born."

Quelepe remained in the river holding the infant. He shook his head. "No," he spat. "I won't do it."

In an instant, Remy jumped furiously into the river as Quelepe moved away toward the opposite bank. Remy lost his footing on a submerged log and fell. He shot up from the murky depths yelling, water spraying from his mouth. "Look at it, Quelepe! Take a good look! It's a goddamn Comanche! They raped her!"

Quelepe shook his head. "She was not raped, Remy! Only one warrior loved her. The man who saved her life."

"That ain't true!"

"It *is* true. She told me. She would've told you if she thought you'd understand."

This he did not want to hear. "Are you sayin' she loved that man?!"

"No," Quelepe replied, slowly shaking his head. "I'm sayin' she wanted to live. She chose to sleep with one man while other captives were raped by dozens. He protected her, and this," he said, turning the baby to face him, "was the price. Beatriz did what she had to do. Don't curse her for it, Don Remy! Enough damage has been done."

"I won't have that bastard in my house, Quelepe!"

"And why not? What has he done to you?" Quelepe pleaded with him now. "Don't you see? This child is what I am, Remy. I have the blood of *los indios* in my veins. Am I not a man? Am I not good enough to live with you?"

"It ain't the same, Quelepe!"

"It is the same. It's the *very* same. It's not what he is; it's what he can be." He paused a moment and then repeated, "He is like me."

"An' he won't have it any easier. Not in Texas. People'll take one look at that boy and *know* he's Comanche. They'll dog 'im to the end of his days. He's got no place in this world."

"He does if you give him one. This is Beatriz's child. Regardless of what happened, it came from her. What's hers is yours. She'll love it as she's loved the others, and you must find a way to love it also."

Remy shook his head. "Give me one good reason why!"

"Because she'll never have another one," he said.

Remy was stunned, but only briefly. If he was furious before, he was now in a rage. He let it take him. "Is that one of your bullshit predictions?" he bellowed so angrily that saliva dripped from the corners of his mouth. " 'Cause if it is, I'll drown your ass with his."

"No," Quelepe answered defiantly. "Her womb was destroyed with this child's birth." He held the baby up to Remy. "If you want a son to replace those lost, this is your one and only chance. I suggest you seize it. I know Beatriz will."

Remy's anger was gone. His head fell into his hands and he said nothing. He felt his tears drip between his fingers. There would be no more young of his blood. He heard Quelepe wade out of the river, pass him and start back to the house. He felt now that he should explain himself.

"You don't know what it's like to lose a child, Quelepe. You don't know how bad it hurts."

Quelepe turned back. "No?" he answered, the child cradled to his chest. "I lost all of my children to cholera. I lost Elijah to the war. And now, Don Remy," he added, and Remy clearly marked his sadness, "I think maybe I've lost you as well."

Remy turned his back to face the river.

"Think about what I said when you're sober," Quelepe told him. "The man who did this evil thing was not you. I'll say nothing to Beatriz and you'll have another chance." He caught his breath. "But know this, Don Remy. Old Quelepe values life more than anything in this sad world. I'll protect this child's with my own. You may never love it, but you'll never harm it. Not as long as these lungs draw air. This I swear on your cousin's ashes."

How long Remy stayed out there he didn't know, but he was certain the river was rising and the current grew more swift.

Then he understood what Kills White Bear had meant. He was the one who had raped Beatriz, and that was why Remy had what Kills White Bear wanted. They'd traded sons, now half-brothers. It was the devil's joke. The tears stopped. He should've been thinking about Beatriz's health, or how to incorporate the child he could not destroy into their broken lives. He should've felt ashamed for what he'd tried to do. That, he knew, was what should've been on his anguished mind.

But what he thought of was revenge. Kills White Bear had cursed him, and Remy wouldn't rest until the favor was returned. Jack Hays commanded the Ranger station in San Antonio, and Hays had often asked him to ride against the Comanche. They had forgiven him for the mistake in the Concho Valley. In fact, they respected him for going after his family where no white man had gone before and lived to tell the sordid tale. Hays had told him that he could use a man like Fuqua. He was unlucky, Hays had said, but he was also gallant. Remy'd said that he had his hands full at the time, but now he would go with Hays at the very next opportunity, and then again and again until he killed Kills White Bear.

He might get Carlito back, and he might not. He would try. But he could stay out there on that river until he sprouted cypress roots and duck's feathers, and he could never love that bastard child. Never.

1840

Spring

Chapter Four

Kills White Bear knew the Rangers were coming and so picked his ground carefully. He had come to revenge a punishing raid by this same company only days before. Thirty Penateka had died and the demoralized survivors had come to him. Their cause became his. It was deep winter, and the Penateka were camped in their southernmost range. The wind was cold and the grass was dead, but Kills White Bear danced with his warriors while he waited for the full moon.

They'd raided four ranches west of the old town the Méxicanos called San Antonio, which Kills White Bear knew would bring the Rangers. He rode to the Nueces Canyon and waited for them there. The Rangers rode in small companies usually of less than twenty men. He would meet them on the plains with a hundred buffalo-robed warriors and destroy them all.

Exactly one year before, an army of white Tejanos, led by the Nemenuh's blood enemy Chief Castro and his Lipans, had ventured into the San Sabá valley and struck against a Penateka camp. Shocked that the Rangers were now attacking them in their own country in the dead of winter, Kills White Bear had rallied his warriors, stampeded their horses, and forced them to retreat. These Rangers had failed to run off the Nemenuh horse herds as they attacked and had not attempted to kill women or children.

When he realized the camp was not at risk, Kills White Bear was free to assault them on ground of his choosing.

It was a mistake they would soon regret, but if they learned something from it, Kills White Bear did as well. Only four years had passed since the Tejanos defeated the Méxicano Father, and despite relentless raiding by the Nemenuh, the sanctuary of the Comanchería was no longer safe. To decimate this particularly savage company of Rangers on the Nueces would make it so again, and he made absolutely certain that all of his band understood the importance of this battle's success. They were fighting, he told them, for their homes and their land.

When the scouts brought the news to his ears that the Rangers were in sight, Kills White Bear sent a party of ten to meet them. They were to fire on the Rangers and then retreat to this place where ninety more waited. The Rangers would surely follow. Once caught in the jaws of ambush, their destruction would be swift and complete. He promised his people victory and watched as the designated warriors rode east.

He soon heard the sound of the guns in the distance. Experience told him that it was Nemenuh rifles being fired. The whites withheld their own. This worried him, but soon enough he saw his warriors returning. Behind them rode the Rangers.

Kills White Bear formed his men in the half-moon formation of his father's father. When they had them on open ground they would dash out, surround them, draw their fire, and then cut them down as they reloaded. It was a strategy that had worked since the time of the Spanish. The Ranger captains were brave, he knew, but also very young and foolish. They did not seem to understand how easily they could die. Today, on this cold, gray and windy day, he was certain they soon would.

When the time was right, Kills White Bear signaled his warriors, who swept down like a north wind, clinging to the sides of steaming horses, on the startled Tejano Rangers. Very quickly they encircled them where they had no cover as he had planned. Kills White Bear was surprised to see that the whites did not panic. They simply dismounted and lay prone on the ground to fire their rifles. Time had taught Kills White Bear to respect their marksmanship, but his swarming warriors provided no target.

Well out of range, he carefully watched the plume of smoke pour from the Tejano barrels one by one, and quickly evaporate into the wind. He recognized the war chief Jack Hays and then was startled when he saw one more face that he knew. Fuqua had ignored his warning. It was just as well. When they had all shot and were frantically reloading, Kills White Bear signaled his men to dash for the heart of their ground. It would not take long.

Kills White Bear had expected them to close tight, maybe kill their horses for cover on that barren plain, and stand off his warriors as best they could. Instead, they instantly remounted, leaving their rifles where they lay, and rode directly toward his swarming warriors with pistols in their hands. Each Ranger singled out one warrior, overtook him with his big American horse, and shot him dead.

Kills White Bear watched in horror as a dozen warriors fell. The rest, confused, scattered. Enraged, he rode among his men to rally them. This was the last of the whites' resistance, he told them. They had to turn and take them now. He wheeled his own mount to lead them, but when he did he saw that the Rangers had not stopped to reload. They were still coming straight for them. Many times Kills White Bear had wondered if the whites were crazy. Now they confirmed it. He still had better than eighty warriors mounted, armed and angry. He regrouped and steadied them, and then hurled them again at their enemies.

Then it happened. The Rangers again picked individual targets and shot them point blank from the saddle before they could nock an arrow. Then they cocked the hammer on the pistol and did it again. And then once more. Kills White Bear was stunned, but he saw that the nerve of the others was broken.

For the first time in forty winters he saw fear on the faces of his people. War cries succumbed to howls of panic as they turned and fled. For the first time not one mounted warrior attempted to rescue the bodies of the dead and dying. It was the worst act of cowardice Kills White Bear had ever seen. He was confused and disgusted, but that was not the end of it. He also felt something that he'd never felt before. He was also afraid. To be defeated when one had the numerical advantage was the worst kind of bad medicine. Yet he knew he did not fear the white man. He feared the magic that gave them guns that fired once for each finger. The spirits had abandoned him on this most important day, and that unnerved him as no other thing could. No portent had warned him that something had changed. His religion had allowed him to bait his own trap. He'd led his men to be slaughtered and he knew then that the contest was no longer even and no longer natural. For the first time in his life he saw the enormity of the white threat.

There was nothing to do but run. Those magic guns would kill him as easily as they killed all the others. He turned west for the Devil's River and raced for his life.

He traveled for hours before he'd traveled enough. The dust in his mouth had a bitter taste. He stopped only when darkness fell.

Chapter Five

Kills White Bear was among the many mourners when Maguara found him. The despair of the People was great and complete. The dark shadow of death had fallen upon many of the Penateka's finest. As he cried with them, the wives of the dead warriors cut off their hair, ripped their best clothing, and slashed their skin and breasts with knives. They killed the horses of the dead warriors as their tears fell in pools of blood. The death shrill of the women filled his ears as they piled the weapons of the dead warriors in the center of the camp and burned them all. It was the worst disaster to strike his people since the great fever had come. He chanted with them, for as far as he was concerned what had happened to their husbands, brothers and sons was all his fault. For Kills White Bear the disgrace was complete. He was beside himself with grief and doubt.

Maguara led him to the council fire where the elders waited. He asked what had happened, and Kills White Bear, unable to hold back his tears of sorrow, told them all everything. In the end, he said, there was no real explanation for what had gone wrong. The Rangers had fallen within his grasp and they'd fought their way out with guns that shot forever. It was the unnatural work of demons. When the spirits turn against you, he said, all is lost. He no longer knew what to do, but he could no longer lead warriors in battle. He'd lost as many as he'd taken from Fuqua. He was shamed and he knew it.

Kills White Bear expected the council to panic, instruct the medicine men to seek out a solution, to fast until a vision provided an answer. But there was none of this. Maguara and the others listened calmly to what he said, and then Maguara spoke for all of them.

"This has happened before, Kills White Bear," the old man began. "Once our enemies had guns and the People had none. In those dark days our losses were heavy and our misery was great. At that time our grandfathers feared as Kills White Bear does now. They thought that demons had allied with our enemies. But we soon got guns and learned to use them. The problem now is the same as it was then. The whites have something that we don't have. But it has nothing to do with magic, and Kills White Bear is not to blame. It's but a thing, made by a white man's hand. And what the Nemenuh need, they'll soon have. What we need is time."

Maguara's confidence slowly restored his own. The Spirit Talker's words soothed him. While he listened the elders discussed the problem at length. It was soon decided that the entire tribe would migrate north, well out of range of the Tejanos. The People knew the plains like no other and the plains would still hide them. At the same time a delegation would ride to San Antonio and see the Tejano Father.

Their relentless raiding, they knew, had not been without effect. Over the last four winters they'd taken well over two hundred white captives and killed many times that number. They still had something the Tejanos desperately wanted and they decided that they would trade it for peace. At the same time, others would go in search of the guns that shot forever. A long-term truce would be preferable, but if the People could not come to terms with the whites, the talks would still buy them the time they needed, and they would be ready when the wars resumed.

As Kills White Bear listened to the elders make their

plans, his sense of despair began to lift. His faith in his people was restored. The elders did not fear the news, they simply responded to it. Their thread was not snapped, it was only twisted in a new and different knot. This would soon be undone. The question that remained for him was what he should do to help. He asked, and he waited.

Maguara brought the pipe to his face and bathed in its smoke. Then he handed it to Kills White Bear and told him to inhale deeply and the answer would come.

"The loss of so many saddens me," he began slowly. "But the look in Kills White Bear's eyes saddens me even more. I've known his heart since it beat in the chest of a quiet boy. I always knew it was the heart of a warrior, and a warrior he'll remain."

"He'll fight," Kills White Bear vowed, "but he'll not lead. Not anymore."

"Then you might as well not eat," Maguara said, "or breathe the air. Where Kills White Bear goes others will always follow. It's his destiny, and destiny cannot be changed. He thinks he's ruined the nation? What he's done is saved it. The lesson was expensive but invaluable. The Rangers are coming to this camp next, and then to the camps of the Nokonis, the Yamparika, the Quahadi, and the rest until no Nemenuh rides the plains. That is what the whites wish. Now that we know, we can save our women and children where otherwise the Rangers would've killed them in their sleeping robes. When we talk to the Tejano Father he'll pull them back and we will be saved. Kills White Bear must think of what happened in these terms."

Kills White Bear's throat tightened when he heard such words. "Kills White Bear is honored to know these things. Yet Maguara's wisdom does not still the cries of dying warriors in Kills White Bear's ears. He sees their blood on the prairie grass. These brave men, whom he's known since they left their mothers' womb and opened their bright eyes to our world, followed Kills White Bear and died. Out of fear for his own life, he left them behind to their fate. Surely their bodies lay bleeding on the earth, and their prayers went unheard. He knows the Rangers cut the hair from their heads and so they can never enter the Happy

Place. Without proper burial, their spirits wander lost on the plains forever. For the first time, Kills White Bear showed his back to the enemy. In the shadow of such shame, he cannot stand. He's lost faith in his *puha*. His disgrace is complete. He is broken." When he'd finished he hung his head.

The elders began rumbling when they heard this. Maguara listened carefully as the others spoke. Together they decided which course he must take and the Spirit Talker explained it in detail to him.

"Kills White Bear must renew himself in the moons to come. He'll neither take a part in the peace talks, nor will he search for the guns. He should go and see the medicine man Black Dog, and together they'll go in search of a new vision and a new way. The women will build him a sweat lodge alone out in the canyons. He'll fast and purify himself. His spirit guide will come and console him as we've tried to do. The White Bear will soon heal and his *puha* will return just as surely as warm blood still flows in his veins. The People will call his name when the time comes and he'll be the first flash of lightning the whites see from the storm that gathers on the plains. His voice will be our thunder. Old Maguara will live to hear Kills White Bear roar again."

The Spirit Talker's hand fell on his shoulder. "Rest, brother. You are loved here."

Chapter Six

Beatriz was in the courtyard playing with the children when Remy stepped out on the porch. He was dressed for another campaign, in a mix of vaquero and leatherstocking clothing and gear. But now there was one distinct difference. Over the last two years Samuel Colt had manufactured a thousand Holster Model Patterson .36 caliber five-shot revolving pistols. Remy and the other Rangers had ordered them as soon as they heard a repeating pistol was available. Soon the guns were known as the "Texas" Patterson, Colt's tribute to his first and best customers. Remy

had bought two of them, and they rode on opposite hips
in holsters Quelepe had fashioned from the finest tanned
leather.

Beatriz glanced at him, knowing by his appearance that
he was about to leave again. The smile she had for the
children vanished for him.

"Again, Remy?" she asked in disgust. It didn't matter to
him. Of all the times he'd gone with the Rangers, this one
was the most important.

"I'll see ya'll soon," he said, and he mounted his waiting
horse. Picosa, who would accompany him, was already waiting. Beatriz stood with her arms crossed, distant, but she
allowed Elena Marie to run to him. She climbed up the
stirrup and he pulled her up the rest of the way. "Daddy
loves you, sweetheart. You be a good girl and mind your
Mama."

"I will, Daddy," she said, those sharp, white, little teeth
chopping the words. He hugged her tightly and set her back
on the ground. "Bring me somethin' from San Antonio."

"You bet."

Then he saw that Beatriz nudged the toddler forward.
"Say goodbye to your Pa, Joaquin." The boy waddled
toward him with his little brown arms raised over his head.
Remy jerked the reins of his horse and rode out. Without
looking at his wife, he knew she was livid.

"I won't be here when you return, Remy!" she called
to him. He stopped his horse immediately and turned to
face her.

"And where would you go?" he asked.

"I have relatives in California." He was frequently reminded of that.

"And how would you get there?"

"Any goddamn way I can, gringo!"

Whenever she was angry with him he was a gringo, and
he was a gringo just about every day. "The Mexicans won't
let you cross through their country. The Comanche won't
let you cross theirs. I'd think about that if'n I were you."

"I've thought about nothing else," she said, and it stung
him. He looked angrily at the boy. It was the easiest and
surest way to retaliate.

"Of course there's certain benefits to bein' a captive of

the Comanche, ain't there, Beatriz?" To have just up and slapped her would've been more merciful.

"Get out!" she screamed. "Just get out!"

He pointed a lone finger at his wife. "I'll be back with Carlito. You git yourself ready to see our son. You an' I are gonna make a home for him again—a happy home, goddamn ya. You set your mind to that, woman." And then he spurred the horse and rode on.

Picosa rode beside him rolling two cigarillos. He stuck one in his mouth and handed the other to Remy. He lit his with the flintlock powder flash of his pistol, puffed it until it glowed, and then gave it to Remy to light his.

"Why will you not accept the child, Don Remy, and end this misery?" he asked in Spanish. "He's a fine boy."

"Oh I accept him, Diego. I accept him for what he is."

"That's a start, I guess," Picosa said.

"And it's also the finish. I'll have my own boy back soon. Beatriz'll come aroun' after that."

"Yes, she will," Picosa said, "with an axe in her hand, I think."

Remy snorted as if amused, but there was nothing funny about the deterioration of his marriage. The bastard child was an impassé between them. She treated him like a monster because he could not love the thing that had destroyed them. She lived in the casa mayor. Remy, by his choice, slept outside of the wall in the cabin he and Elijah had built all those years ago. Quelepe stayed with Beatriz and the children. He hoped the return of his oldest son would change all that. There was a chance they would pull together to reorient Carlito. When he came back and she'd cooled off, he would try once again to make things right.

Carlito, now ten years old, had been with the Comanche for four years. Remy was coming to terms with the loss when a strange thing happened. Three Comanche chiefs had ridden to see Colonel Henry Karnes at San Antonio asking for peace. Houston would've been thrilled, but Houston was no longer President of the Republic. By law he could not succeed himself. Mirabeau Buonaparte Lamar, the "hero" of San Jacinto and fervent anti-Houstonian, had swept the election. He ran on a policy of education, western expansion, and, most importantly, advocacy of a war of extermination against immigrant and native tribes alike. The Cherokee and other eastern nations had already been forced out of East Texas. It was a bloody business in which many innocent Indians died. Most of the Caddo were also gone, and white farmers planted Indian fields before the ashes of their wigwams had grown cold. What was left of the Lipan Apaches and Tonkawa—and there weren't many—rode with the Rangers against the last threat on the western frontier. The Comanche alone remained to challenge the Republic of Texas.

The raiding had begun as a trickle in 1835. Most, but not all, of the Comanche had honored Austin's treaty prior to that. It seemed to him that the American breed of horses and the ransom paid for captives was too much temptation for Comanche braves. Over the last five years the raids had grown in frequency and violence until unmitigated war raged along the Colorado.

Ranger companies, Remy's included, were in the field almost all of the time. Far too often they'd come too late to do much else but dig graves for mangled settlers in their burnt fields. Each time it happened, Remy despised the Comanche a little bit more.

The Colt revolver changed all that. The Rangers took the war to the Comanche now, and this more than anything, he believed, was the reason the Indians had asked for peace.

Remy was not alone in his hatred of that vermin race. He knew that one would be hard pressed to find anyone in Texas who remained sympathetic to the Comanche. A good place to look, however, would be Sam Houston. But Houston and his policy of "peace through commerce" with hostile tribes was shoved out of the way, and Lamar hated the Comanche as much as any one of his electorate.

Lamar was nevertheless happy to sit down and discuss the Comanche grievances with them if that was what they wanted to do. Word had it that the government would offer peace on four fundamental conditions. The Comanche would recognize Texas sovereignty (as if that meant a damn thing to them), stay clear of the white settlements, and allow whites to appropriate land east of the buffalo range, which would provide the appearance of the requested line. Remy knew, as he believed everyone did, that this was not realistic and would soon lead to war. Settlers would inch closer to the amorphous boundary until they crossed it, and it would all begin again. It was a fool's bargain.

But to him the last condition was the most important. For the talks to begin, it was agreed that the Comanche would return all of the captives they had taken in the last five years. This was the great surprise.

Remy hated the Comanche with an unholy intensity, but he'd sit down and embrace the devil himself if it meant he could see Carlito again. Little Remy was dead and buried. But Carlito was a loose end. Not a day passed when he didn't think of him, and not a day passed when he didn't feel the pain. He'd fought with Henry Karnes in the war, and his comrade knew he had an interest in these proceedings, and so, as a favor, Colonel Karnes invited Remy to attend with the hopes of collecting his son.

Never before had so many Comanche agreed to sit down as a people and discuss terms for the end of hostilities. Everyone, it seemed, was tired of the relentless and constantly escalating violence. The Texians still remained in a formal state of war with Mexico. They welcomed the opportunity to deflect Comanche depredations south of the Río Grande. It bothered no one that Texian security would come at the expense of the Mexicans, who continually threatened. Only the Comanche were hated more. The government would strongly encourage the Comanche to continue raiding the Mexicans as they always had.

President Mirabeau Lamar could not meet with the Comanche himself, so he sent the acting Secretary of War and three companies of regular troops. It occurred to Remy even before he hitched his horse to the rail that this was no diplomatic mission. It had the rigid face of a military campaign. He queried a couple of officers he knew as they approached the stone building Don Carlos called the Casas Reales. Formerly the residence of the Spanish Governor of

Tejas, it had once served as a prison for Philip Nolan's doomed expedition forty years before, among other infamous uses. The Anglos of Béxar, he knew, called it "the Council House."

He didn't rest easy knowing the fate of his son was in those smooth and formal hands. Maguara, he knew, would not like it either. He went immediately to air his concerns to the three Texas colonels, whom he found seated together in the Council House, waiting. The Comanche had indicated that they'd arrive anytime in a ten-day period. There was the look of impatience on all three of the officers' faces. He didn't know any of them, but they'd heard of him. Less than a minute passed before Remy decided he didn't like them. They were strict and formal, Southerners all.

Remy quickly dispensed with formalities. He heard the sound of his spurs as they chinked on the packed earthen floor.

"Now what's the deal here, boys? I got a lot at stake and I don't see nuthin' but trouble."

Colonel Fisher spoke first. "How do you mean, Captain Fuqua?"

"There's soldiers everywhere for one thing. The chiefs agreed to a peace and they'll honor it. They'll see these troops and get the general idea that maybe you won't. That gets us off to a bad start. Then them officers out there tell me there'll be no exchange of gifts for the Comanche chiefs, and no ransom paid for captives. You can't do business with them like that."

The three officers looked at each other but said nothing until Fisher said, "We have our orders, Captain."

"I don't see how them orders allow for Comanche custom. Those are chiefs comin' here. Ya'll gotta treat 'em with respect. Certain things must be done. They'll bring gifts and they'll expect them in return. The captives they treat as spoils of war. They'll trade 'em, but they won't give 'em away. We've whipped 'em once, gentlemen. But they ain't beaten, not by a long shot. You can't treat 'em like they are."

"We shall respect our orders." Fisher held up a paper to Fuqua and followed along the words with one, bony finger.

"Gifts are to be dispensed with. No ransom will be paid. If the captives are not freely offered, we are to take the chiefs hostage until such time as they are." Then he looked back at Remy. "There'll be no compromise with the savages, Captain."

He spit, and then let them have it. "I bet you wouldn't say that if'n it were your boy they had."

"We sympathize with your position, it's just that . . ."

"I don't want your goddamn sympathy!" Remy snapped. "I want my son! You hold a gun to them chiefs' heads and they'll kill 'im, sure as hell! You gave your word, Colonel," he said, squinting his eyes. "You best keep it."

He could tell nothing that he said had any impact on these men. Three army heads were never as good as one in Remy's experience, and he figured these boys in particular didn't know shit about the frontier. There was an uneasy silence in which their expressions revealed to Remy how much they appreciated either a militiaman's disapproval or his threat—neither of which they gave a damn about, and then Fisher quickly changed the subject.

"Do you know the Penateka chief, *Mook-war-ruh*?"

"Maguara. Yeah, I know him."

"We understand he's to be their spokesman."

Remy rolled his eyes. They really didn't understand at all. The Comanche didn't have one voice. They had a thousand. "He can speak only for his band, and that's if they agree with what he says. You people have no idea how the Comanche operate. If you want a treaty, you've got to bring the whole damn Penateka tribe in to hear what you've got to say, and the Quahadi, the Nokonis, the Yamparika, the Kotsoteka, the Tenawa and the Tanima, too. Maguara's delegation is only the first step. You bait in one bird today and maybe the whole flock'll come in tomorrow. You give Maguara somethin', and he'll give you somethin', and then you'll go from there. I kin assure you that's what he's got in mind."

As he watched, the three colonels consulted with each other in hushed whispers. When they'd finished, Fisher turned again to him. "While things may not proceed as you'd like, we do have our orders, Captain. The army doesn't operate like the militia."

Remy scratched his groin. "Well, now, that I already knew."

"Yes, well, just the same, we were wondering if you'd stay on and help convey our demands to Mook-war-ruh. He'll need to understand that he's not dealing with the Spanish or the Méxicanos anymore. He's dealing with the Republic of Texas, and the Republic means business with the Comanche."

"I'm not sure you need me to convey that to Maguara," Remy said. "He'll know right off. But I'll damn sure stay. And I hope you boys'll be stayin' too. You're 'bout to poke your finger in the hornet's nest, and we're all gonna get stung." He pointed a lone finger out the door. "What's left of my family's out there, and the families of hundreds of other men." He spit on the floor. "We ain't seen much of the army out here these past four years of war."

Fisher stopped him there. "We thought we'd have the approval of frontiersmen to deal firmly with the savages. We don't see many as sympathetic as you."

Remy leaned on their rickety table. "I personally don't give a damn about the Comanche. Once they give me my boy, I'll help you hang every goddamn one of 'em. But you harm one of the remaining hairs on that old man's bald head under a flag of truce, and you'll destroy any chance of peace with the Comanche from here out. A hundred war parties'll ride under the next full moon. The frontier's gonna burn, gentlemen, and it'd be nice to know if the people that started the fire'll be aroun' to help us put it out."

"We understand your concerns, Captain Fuqua," Fisher said, "and we appreciate your assessment of the matter at hand. There'll be no bloodshed. The government simply intends to take a firm stance with the savages. We're dealing from a position of strength. The Comanche came to us. All will go well, I assure you. Your boy'll be returned."

"In ragged pieces most likely," Remy said, and then he turned to leave. "I'll be aroun', boys. You send for me when the time comes." He spit on the floor one last time and walked out. They didn't like him, he knew, and he didn't give a damn.

Chapter Seven

Remy was picking at his breakfast of *carne guisada* on the morning of March 19, when Picosa's elbow nudged his ribs. *"Mira,"* he said, and Remy looked. He saw two Comanche scouts ride proudly into town. He watched them speak with the soldiers and then ride back out. Remy crossed the street still chewing his tortilla to learn what was happening.

"What's the word, boys?" he asked, wiping his mouth with his sleeve.

"They're comin', Captain. Within the hour."

In half that time, the procession streamed into Béxar, with Maguara at its head. Remy counted sixty-five Comanche in all, dressed in their finest, which indicated to him how sacred they regarded the talks with the Texians. The fact that they brought their wives and children with them conveyed their trust. Remy already knew they were wrong on both counts.

Noticeably absent at first glance were the promised captives. The government had asked for the return of all two hundred whites. The Comanche brought only two, an Anglo woman and a young Mexican boy. Like most all older white captives, the female had been ravaged. That was plain enough to Remy. Her exposed skin was bruised, burned, scarring or scabbed. Her nose, burnt down to the bone, gave her an appearance that Remy could only describe as macabre. As shocking as she looked to the others watching, it was what Remy had expected. He knew there was no mercy for adult captives in plains warfare. Better to die, Maguara had once told him, than fall into the hands of your enemies.

The soldiers and citizens of Béxar who gathered to greet her gasped at first glance. Remy observed that they were both shocked and outraged by this young woman who attempted to hide her face from her own people without success. The more they crowded her, the greater her obvious despair.

Suddenly it occurred to Remy how fortunate Beatriz had been as a captive. She bore scars, yes; but at least she had not been disfigured. Though he thought he understood the Comanche mind better than most, their criteria for who would be spared and who would be defiled, who would live and who would die, remained an absolute mystery. While he sympathized with this woman and the others still held, he was thankful that his wife had been spared such cruelty. As much as it pained him to admit it, he knew Beatriz had benefited from Kills White Bear's touch.

Colonel Fisher and the others pulled the woman aside to speak with her first. She told them the scars they saw were but the surface of her misery. She'd been sexually humiliated by dozens. The women had beaten and tortured her. For entertainment, they held torches to her face to make her scream.

Colonel Fisher struggled to control his anger as the girl burst into tears. "Take me away from here," she shouted. "I want to be hidden from these prying eyes!"

She said she had looked at her reflection in a Comanche stream. She knew how she looked. That was still better, she said, than how she felt. There was no way back from this. She said she wished they'd killed her.

"And where are the others, Miss?" Fisher asked. Remy noted his tenderness. He'd not expected it.

"I know of fifteen more in the camp where I came from," she said sobbing, "but I saw others in other camps. I can't say how many. I understand Comanche now. They don't know that I do. They want to see what they can get for me. If it's enough, they'll bring in the rest one at a time."

"We'll see about that," Fisher seethed, and Remy saw him cut his eyes to the waiting Comanche. Already, he thought, the outcome looked grim.

The woman pleaded with him once more to take her away. Fisher sent her with some of the local ladies to bathe and dress her and treat her seeping wounds, and then marched off to deal with the Indians. Remy reached out and grabbed his arm.

"Easy now, Colonel," he cautioned. "You've seen for yourself what they've done to her. There's others out there facin' the same thing. Let's think about them."

Fisher paused, thinking a moment with his eyes closed. He was obviously aggravated. Remy saw that they all were. Then Colonel Fisher put his palm out between himself and Remy, as if he felt Remy was interfering. "Let's just see what they've got to say."

"There ya go," Remy agreed smoothly. Maybe Fisher still saw the bigger game. "Nice and slow's the way." As precariously as things had begun, Remy sensed that they now might go better. The soldiers, if nothing else, could appreciate the captives' predicament. He hoped it would temper their immediate relations with Maguara and the other chiefs.

Remy greeted the aging Spirit Talker, who stood calmly with the others. If the old chief had noted the venomous reaction of the whites at first sight of the ravaged girl, he made no sign. He sat proudly on his saddle, the breeze tossing the eagle feather stitched in what was left of his hair, waiting. Maguara nodded to Remy, but the old man refused to speak.

The tension of that first meeting was broken by a young boy's skill with a toy bow. By now people where throwing up coins for him to shoot out of the sky. It was as if the circus had come to town.

While much commotion was made over the girl, next to nothing was done about the Méxicano boy who had been brought in with her. Remy walked straight to him, and pulled him from the saddle.

"¿Estás bien, hijo?" he asked him. The boy, the light absent from his eyes, nodded slowly. "¿Donde vives?" Remy asked, and the child said the name of a village that Remy did not recognize. He waved Picosa over and flipped him a coin when he was near. "See to him, please, Diego. Clean 'im up and get a doctor to look at 'im. Then see if you can work somethin' out to get 'im home." When Remy looked up again, Colonel Fisher was emphatically waving him forward and Remy went.

The Comanche delegation was ushered into the Council House. Offered chairs, they chose to squat on the earth floor opposite the men they recognized as the Tejano war leaders. Their weapons rested in their laps. Maguara stared at Remy but still refused speech. Remy said in Spanish that they must all ask the spirits to guide this meeting, but Maguara answered only in the Comanche tongue. Remy then understood. Though Remy was not a soldier, he was still an enemy in Maguara's eyes, and the Spirit Talker would not acknowledge him. There was nothing more Remy could do but listen, and hope.

Since Maguara would not speak in Spanish, an interpreter, a former captive of the Comanche, was brought in. At the same time, Remy saw one of the other colonels whisper into the ear of one of his subordinates, who quickly left the room. Remy heard the shuffle of hurried feet and the chink of weapons being rustled outside.

Colonel Fisher should've begun as Remy had, with some sort of eloquence that alluded to this great occasion. This, he knew, is what the Comanche expected. Instead, Fisher immediately demanded to know why the other captives had not been brought in as agreed.

If Maguara perceived Fisher's hostile tone, he did not show it. He calmly responded that he had brought in the only one he had. Remy cringed. Maguara, who marked it well, then said that there were certainly more captives, but many of them remained in Comanche camps which operated beyond his control.

Remy understood that Maguara was explaining band structure, as he'd tried to do. "We talked about that, Colonel," he interjected. "Today's just a start." The interpreter did not translate what Remy said. Maguara took it from there.

"The Tejano chief is wrong to worry," he explained through the interpreter. "The other captives can be had soon enough. We have agreed to provide them and we will. But they are ours, as the horses are ours, and we will not give them away any more than we would give you our horses so that we would not make war. We will accept sugar, coffee, flour, blankets, ammunition, powder, and vermilion for the return of your people. And there is one thing more: we want the guns that shoot for each finger."

He delayed here to study Remy. Then he went on. "When Maguara's old eyes see these things in his warriors' hands, the captives will be brought to Béxar in the first moon that follows. Maguara gives his word."

Remy recognized the look of supreme confidence on the chief's face. He'd prepared Fisher and the others for what the Comanche would request. What he needed was a moment to discuss a counter offer with the colonels. The guns they could never give them, of course, but what was wrong with the other things? If the government wouldn't provide them, Remy and the citizens of San Antonio could scratch something together. They could ransom some of the captives, if not all. Before he could suggest alternatives, Maguara said one thing more.

"How do you like that answer?" It had the distinct ring of arrogance. Maguara did not understand the white mind, even when he was looking at angry white faces.

Fisher erupted. "I do *not* like your answer!" Maguara recoiled from the harshness of the delivery. "I told you not to come here again without your prisoners. You've come against my orders. Your women and children may depart in peace, and your braves may go and tell your people to send them in. When those prisoners are returned, your chiefs here may likewise go free. Until then we'll hold you as hostages!"

Maguara appeared muddled by this abrupt tone, but things must've become clear when soldiers rushed in and lined the walls of the Council House. When the interpreter failed to convey this last directive, Fisher ordered him to do so at once. He staunchly refused, the color draining from his face. It seemed to Remy that only he and this other man in the middle knew what would happen if the Comanche understood the terms.

Remy, unnerved, stepped between the officers and the bewildered Comanche chiefs. "Don't do this!" he begged. "You see how captives are treated on the plains. That's how it is, and you can't change it. These men'll die before they let it happen to them. Colonel, I beg you. Don't let him translate that statement, and send them troops back out."

By now the chiefs were rumbling. They looked at each other, eyes flashing, and then to the soldiers. Maguara called out to Fuqua. "What's wrong?" he asked him in Spanish. He had no idea what was happening. It was as

Remy had said. They never expected violence of any kind to occur under a truce. To them, it was unthinkable.

"Stay calm!" Remy ordered him in Spanish. "Do nothing and you're safe."

Then Fisher attempted to move Remy out of the way. When he would not go, Fisher ordered two sentries to restrain him. Remy felt hands grip him at his biceps, and then abruptly snatch him backwards until he met the stone wall. Maguara's eyes followed him, his head cocked. Fisher turned then to the interpreter.

"You tell that woman-killin', child-rapin' son of a bitch exactly what I told you to tell 'im and you do it now!" Still the man remained silent. "*Do it*!"

Remy watched in horror as the interpreter quickly blurted the words to the stunned Comanche and then dashed out the door. Instantly the thirteen Penateka chiefs howled their cries of war, gripped their weapons with desperate but steady hands, and leaped at their would-be captors. Remy shouted, "No!"

The peace talks erupted into a free for all—red men against white. The first to die was the sentinel who barred the door. Then Remy heard someone shout for the soldiers to open fire. The little house boomed in a thunder of yellow and white lightning flashes. Balls ricocheted under the instant shroud of hot, white smoke, and bloody knife blades clinked against limestone, ripped against leather or tore at the flesh of screaming men. Remy yanked free and dove for Maguara to hold him until it was over, but the old chief shoved him aside and stabbed another Ranger captain before he was shot down. He fell dead, wild-eyed, face to face with the scrambling Remy.

"Oh, no," Remy moaned. "Oh, no." But this was just the beginning.

Another Ranger was wounded in the leg by a stray bullet, but snatched a rifle from one of the chiefs, put the barrel against his head and yanked the trigger. Before that man fell with most of his brains exposed at the center of gushing blood, the Ranger clubbed another with the stock.

Everywhere around Remy soldiers and warriors fell dead, dying or wounded. The constant percussion rocked the floor under him. He could no longer see from the veil of smoke, and yet the blind fire continued and particles of red powder cinders stung his face and arms.

Then the door burst open, and the surviving chiefs leaped through it, screaming to the others outside. Remy crawled out after them. By now, he'd drawn his own pistol to defend himself.

When the Comanche women and children heard the screams of their husbands and fathers, they grabbed their own weapons and turned on the people they had previously amused. People appeared shocked to see them fight every bit as viciously as their warriors. The boy who had shot coins out of the air now turned his toy bow and sunk an arrow into the chest of a circuit judge. The judge fell stone dead.

The soldiers shot the savages down, all of them, in the streets, but in the process, they shot innocent bystanders scrambling for safety. The soldiers were equally as dangerous as the Comanche then. Remy saw people of all races fall. Comanche children were blown nearly in half, lying in the street in grotesque and bloody configurations as their wounded mothers crawled toward them crying in the blood and dust until they were shot down unmercifully. The screams and gunfire rang in Remy's aching, muffled ears.

Picosa had run to the sound of the guns and there found Remy. Together they ran down unarmed Comanche women and children and hustled them into the safety of a vacant store. "Lay still," Remy told them in Spanish, "and you won't be harmed." Soldiers came to guard them, and Remy and Picosa ran on to save others. Not once did Remy fire his gun.

It was over when there were no more Comanche to kill. Thirty-three chiefs, warriors, their women and children lay dead. Thirty-two women and children, many of whom were wounded, were led away to jail. Seven white men were laid out stiff in the streets, and ten more were seriously wounded. The army could not have made a bigger mess of things.

Colonel Fisher darted about the smoking, bloody streets, like a chicken when it sees the hawk's shadow, giving orders, sending men out to scout the plains, calling for San Antonio's only surgeon, and restoring order as best he could after he'd decisively destroyed it.

Remy singled him out in the confusion. He used Don Carlos's method to display his disgust. "Happy now, Colonel?"

Despite the appearance of control, Remy saw that the officer was shaken. "I had no idea they would react that way. No idea whatsoever."

"Yeah, you did, you dumb son of a bitch," Remy sneered. "I told ya so myself." Remy whistled for his horse and the animal came running, the reins dragging the ground between its hooves. Remy looked again at Colonel Fisher and said, "Your education just cost me my boy. I won't forget it. Someday, when you ain't wearin' that uniform, me and you's gonna settle up."

"Don't give up hope, Captain," he said. "We now have captives to trade for the others."

Remy glared at him. "And who're you gonna talk to about tradin' 'em, Fisher? What Comanche would ever sit down again with you? You got no idea what you've done. Your men shoot pretty good with women and children. We'll see how they do on the frontier against the warriors that're comin' to avenge these people you slaughtered here today." With that said and festering, Remy turned away and mounted.

"Where you goin', Fuqua?"

"Home, Colonel," Remy answered, surprised that he had to ask. "As fast as this horse can carry me, I'm goin' home. I only hope I can beat the Comanche there." He pointed his finger. "Me an' you'll visit again," he said.

Chapter Eight

They split at the river. Picosa flew north to round up the vaqueros on the distant pastures; Remy arrived at the main house in his own flurry. He ordered everyone to stop what they were doing and hear what he had to say. Little flecks of tobacco flew out his mouth as he spat his orders. He assigned every person a task and then said, "Do it now."

One look at his face and Beatriz understood. She helped Remy secure the casa mayor as she'd done since she was a child. She organized everything, much better than he ever could. She thought to bring the chickens in for eggs and the cows for milk. She ordered racks of peppered beef and cured turkeys from the smokehouse. The *campesinos* and blacks huddled within the walls, and the great doors and windows were shut and bolted. At night, the lamps were to be turned out. Armed vaqueros would slowly walk the lonely walls in shifts.

In the buzz of frantic preparations, Beatriz's path crossed Remy's. There, in front of them all, he grabbed her and caressed her rib to rib. He felt her heart pound against his in the way it hadn't done since her captivity.

"Listen, woman," he told her, his eyes locked on hers. "I love you, ya hear? I don't care about the past, I don't know about the future. But, I love you. Wherever you go on this earth, I'll follow. *¿Sabes?*"

She searched his eyes, wanting to believe him, he knew. "And Joaquin?" she asked crisply. He was more than ready to capitulate.

"We ain't gonna see Carlito again," he said. "I got no hope for it after what's happened. Joaquin's our only son; our only hope for a son. I kin see that now. I'm sorry that I couldn't before. I'll raise him as my own." She hesitated. "I swear it," Remy said.

Beatriz slapped her arms around him and hugged him tighter than she had moments before. He could feel her chest heave against his as she sobbed, the release of four years of pain. "I love you, husband," she cried.

"I'm sorry," Remy muttered, his mouth pressed against her hair. "I didn't know how to act. I was heartbroke."

"Chist," she whispered as she drew back and put her finger to his lips. "I forgive you. I knew someday you would open your eyes."

Remy picked her up in his arms and kicked open the parlor door. It had been as easy as that. What a fool he'd been! How many years had he wasted? He turned back to his astonished workers. "We're safe for the moment," he said, not really certain that they were. "Ya'll keep on doin' what you're doin'. When Picosa comes in, see that he posts a watch. Doña Beatriz and me's busy with preparations of our own."

Before he could turn away, Quelepe stepped forward with that ridiculous grin. "What?" Remy barked, his right eye twitching in irritation.

"Never give up hope of Carlito, Don Remy. I saw you two together in a dream."

Quelepe's timing was typical. Why this now, he thought? "Hush up, ya old fool! I don't want to hear that kind of half-cocked shit no more. You go round up them goats, maybe butt heads with the billie, and then see to it that them horses have plenty of hay." The old man looked a little sheepish, and even Beatriz did not come to his aid. "Go on! Git! The Comanche are comin'!"

Then he felt the palms of Beatriz's hands caress his scraggly cheeks. She pulled herself to him and kissed him, and he could barely hold back the tears of joy. As sure as he knew he'd lost his oldest boy forever, he knew he had a wife again and life would stumble on.

He yelled to no one in particular. "Watch them babies for a while, somebody," and then he kicked the door closed and carried his giggling wife upstairs.

Chapter Nine

Kills White Bear thought he heard the sound of wailing on the wind. He emerged naked from the sweat lodge, having been there for a week. The dream had finally come only the night before. All that day he'd done nothing but consider its significance. Now something had happened, and he mounted his horse which was staked nearby and swept the bare hills to Maguara's camp.

As he came closer he was certain some disaster had struck. He sprinted on the horse now and rushed in. Maguara's wife was in the center of camp surrounded by dozens of mourning women.

"What's happened?" he asked, and she told him. Thirteen chiefs were murdered, and twenty more besides. The rest were taken hostage and would be killed after twelve days from where the sun stood if the white captives were not returned.

The camp erupted into howls of despair. The mourning rites began immediately. Bodies were maimed, the sacred locks of hair cut from their trembling heads. Horses belonging to the dead chiefs were killed, and would be killed for the next two days until thousands lay dead on the plains for the buzzards.

There was nothing Kills White Bear could do for the helpless captives. The Nemenuh turned on them in a rage and killed them all with slow fires and dull knives. Only their screams could be heard above the constant shrill and wailing of the grief-stricken tribe.

"Who will lead us?" he heard people shout all around him. As Kills White Bear moved among his stricken people to comfort them, all eyes turned to him. In the face of disaster, he realized that Wolf Eyes' prediction had come true.

With the death of Maguara and the others, Kills White Bear quietly ascended as Principal Chief. With the next breath he took, his power returned. His people were waiting. He would demand blood for blood.

Kills White Bear dreamed of a concerted action and knew such a campaign must be meticulously considered and planned. He understood his people's thirst for revenge. But Maguara had taught him caution. He advocated initial restraint while the medicine men sought omens and portents to guide them.

He realized soon enough that he could not control the young warriors. Leaving the rites of mourning to the women, many rode immediately to San Antonio to accost the soldiers, but they soon returned saying the army would not oblige until the unilateral twelve-day truce had run out. Why they would honor one and not the other was a mystery to Kills White Bear, but it kept his headless warriors from destroying themselves. When the soldiers would not fight them, they turned to raiding the frontier for the remainder of the spring.

Against so many small, mobile and utterly motivated war parties, the Rangers were useless. It was hit and run, in the old way. Following the Tejanos' example, the People took no captives. Kills White Bear saw blood on the rising full moon.

One by one, the parties returned to Kills White Bear's camp with horses, mules, guns, ammunition, blankets, flour, sugar, coffee, and fresh, bloody scalps. Their rage had been vented to some degree, he thought, but was far from spent. Young, hot-headed warriors took their dead elders' place in council. Kills White Bear recognized that the leadership of the Wasps now had a rash and wild face. They insisted on knowing what Kills White Bear planned for the Penateka's revenge, and he relied on eloquent oratory to calm them. "We must be patient," he told them, "and we must go north."

The council erupted in dissent and rebuttal. The young warriors lashed out at him, calling him a coward. It was a stinging insult and one that had no place in the council where cool heads had always prevailed in any crisis, but Kills White Bear overlooked it, as he'd seen wise Maguara do.

He had other, more distant designs. As Principal Chief, he explained, he had the power to strike the camp and would now exercise it. They would follow the buffalo north to the high plains all the way to the Arkansas, and heal. Those who disagreed could do as they wished, but the bulk of the tribe, he promised, would follow him. If the young men wanted to war with the Tejanos, they would have to do so alone.

He told his warriors he wanted their revenge to have real impact. He said that small war parties were no longer the way against the horde of intruders. In the north country he would find another one.

"Come with me now," he urged them. "Before the fall rains come, we'll return to this country and wage war like the Tejanos have never seen. There'll be no whites alive to weep at their destruction. Their country will again be ours. But there is much for us to do. Our wounds still bleed."

Their doubtful expressions told him he'd not yet won them. But he could neither share his spirit vision with them, nor could he reveal his recent dream; to do so would nullify the power of both, and they were desperately needed.

In the sweat lodge he had a vision of dead Tejanos lying about a burning town. The air there was humid, and gulls drifted over the carnage for scraps of food. He saw waves wash ashore leaving bodies behind as they retreated again to the sea. It would soon come to pass, and he knew it just as surely as he knew hot blood still flowed in his powerful veins. It gave him a confidence wise men could sense in his oath of revenge. At dawn, they would strike camp and leave that place of sadness and anger. "You'll have your blood," he promised those angry faces, "when the time's right."

Chapter Ten

J ack Hays pushed the band of his hat high above his brow. Gritty salt lined his forehead. His face and neck were sunburned deep red. His eyes constantly searched the hills that lay west.

"Hell, Fuqua," Hays said. "The Comanche just ain't out here no more."

"No, Jack," he answered, spitting. "They ain't."

"Well, if nuthin' else them Wasps is chiefless after that Council House deal. By all accounts them was young warriors that raided, and maybe they're raided out. I reckon maybe the rest lost their nerve and skedaddled for the Rockies."

Remy took a big swig on his canteen, wiped his parched lips with his sleeve, and then shook his head. "They ain't chiefless, Jack," he said flatly.

"Who's left?"

"Buffalo Hump and Piava, for two. Kills White Bear, the one you call Black Heart, will most likely take Maguara's place."

"Who's that?"

"The son of a bitch we chased out of the Nueces Canyon," he said, and then added, his voice low and rough, "the man that raped my wife and killed my boys."

Remy felt Hays study him for a moment before he responded. "Oh, yeah." There was a passion in the way he said it. "I remember that lucky bastard. We liked to powder-burn him. Don't git your knickers in a twist, Captain Fuqua. Black Heart'll git what's comin' to 'im. I'll run into that son of a bitch some day and when I do, I'll bring you his head. That's a goddamn promise."

"Don't you touch it, Jack," Remy said. "When you find him, the first thing you do is send for me. Ya hear? He's mine."

"I hear," Hays said. "Don't look like it'll be this year though."

Their shadows fell long across the dried grass. The sun had already set. Everything was golden. In the distance, Remy heard the coyotes howl. Mourning doves flew from the river to the roost to wait for the new dawn. A nighthawk floated over the dark line of live oaks, and a whitetail buck silently emerged, ears out wide, from the black brush. The deer turned back as two does stepped out behind him. The cicadas engaged as if they were cued. What was missing, Remy knew, was the Comanche.

"I wouldn't be too sure, Captain," he said. "I'd keep your scouts out on the San Sabá for the balance of the summer if'n I was you. When you don't see the bastards is when it's time to look. It ain't over yet. They'll be back with the buffalo."

"I think they're broke, Fuqua. Me an' you shot 'em up good last winter. The Council House Fight took what the Colts didn't. They've sufficiently avenged themselves in my view. They might not want no more of us."

"I hope you're right, Jack," Remy told him. "But I don't think so. They're up in the north makin' medicine. When they find it, they'll be back and there'll be hell to pay." Then he called to his men. "Let's go home, boys. There ain't nuthin' for us to do out here."

1840

Summer

Chapter Eleven

The summer grass was green, the hunting good, and the weather cooler, dry and breezy on the high plains. When they weren't hunting buffalo, the People rested in the heat of the long days. At night, they danced for hours until their legs failed them, and then they sat together—warriors, women and children—to rest, by large fires roaring beneath the sparkle of uncountable stars. They comforted one another with traditional songs, moving oratory, oaths, and blessings. Each day they moved a little further from the pain of Maguara's massacre. Under the free air of the night sky, the tribe grew stronger. They were healing.

Kills White Bear did not lead the Wasps alone. Another war leader from another band of Penateka emerged to fill the void with him. He was called *Pohchanah-kwoheep*, Buffalo Hump. They discussed their mutual problems at length, and Kills White Bear was encouraged to learn that his brother saw things as he did. Together they planned a war of retribution to the escalating rhythm of the tribal drums.

At Kills White Bear's request, Black Dog and the other shamans had gone into the mountains to seek visions. Initial communication reported that all signs were good, and the confidence of the tribe climbed with its spirit.

Kills White Bear waited for the waxing moon, the time when the coyotes were the most active and successful hunters. Maguara had taught him that it likewise marked the period of optimum compromise and cooperation between human beings. The waxing moon united a man's will and spirit. Kills White Bear would soon call on them both.

He sent runners to the other bands to tell them that the Penateka were in need. Since the time of his grandfather interaction with the bands had been infrequent at best. Fuqua had been unlucky indeed. Kills White Bear understood that his time among the Nokonis had not been wasted. He saw things as few did, he understood the ways of others. He knew that all the bands had become self-sufficient, self-sustaining, intermarried and distinct cells that no longer needed each other to thrive since they had acquired the horse and followed the perpetual buffalo. But Kills White Bear also understood that what made the People strong also made them weak. They were too independent for their own good. Their enemies the whites, on the other hand, it seemed, moved as one.

Among the bands, their culture, customs, and rites all varied to some degree. But their history, language, and blood were still the same. Kills White Bear envisioned a Nemenuh confederacy of some thirty thousand strong to ride south and turn back the evil tide. To accomplish this, he had to convince the separate tribes that the People— all the People—were threatened. He knew it would not be easy.

The Quahadis, the Antelopes, refused to come as he'd anticipated. They were loners, far removed from the Wasps' troubles. His cousins, the Nokonis, the Wanderers, spent that summer living up to their name. They were so scattered that an appeal to them was useless. Other bands were either far to the north hunting buffalo, or in the deep south raiding the Méxicanos—both well beyond the range of his runners.

But the Kotsoteka and the Yamparika were camped at the headwaters of the Arkansas near the trading fort of the American William Bent. Kills White Bear learned that these Nemenuh had graciously received his runners and returned word that their cousin would be honored to come among them and speak his mind.

Then the Méxicano agents appeared on the plains. They came to Buffalo Hump and Kills White Bear expressing great sorrow for the loss of the chiefs and respected them with gifts which Kills White Bear distributed among his people. Though he considered them enemies, the Méxicanos told him that the Tejanos had also drawn their blood, and their quest for revenge equaled that of their Comanche brothers. The Méxicanos proposed that, together with the Nemenuh, they could still drive Tejano devils from the land. When this was done, the Méxicanos would draw the line solidly at the Colorado, and the buffalo range would forever belong uncontested to the Nemenuh as long as the wind blew and rivers ran.

Such an alliance appealed to both young civil chiefs. Kills White Bear turned to the Méxicanos and asked them specifically what they had in mind.

They said they had spies throughout Tejas, and that the army, militia and the Rangers were everywhere looking for the Comanche. The absence of the raiders and the heat of the summer sun would soon drive them away. When the spies confirmed that all was again quiet, the Comanche should come due south to the coastal town of Linnville, where the Tejanos stored many valuable goods that might interest them. They would be met there by a force of Méxicano soldiers, who would come by water, and from there they would turn east together and sweep the Tejanos across the Sabine as the Méxicano Father had intended to do the year before. The Comanche could take whatever bounty they wanted. They could kill as many Tejanos as required to avenge the massacre at the Council House. Before the first cool breath of winter, no Tejano would walk the Méxicano earth.

Kills White Bear thought first of his dream. In it he'd seen this place called Linnville that the Méxicanos described. It was not on the coast, it was on Lavaca Bay in the land of the Karankawa, but he trusted the power of his vision and knew the Nemenuh could make it come true. Buffalo Hump enthusiastically conveyed a similar opinion, and Kills White Bear assured the Méxicanos that they could depend upon the Nemenuh to do their part.

He lit the stone pipe and then passed it to them. "Send word to Kills White Bear's ears when all is ready," he said. "And the Nemenuh will come."

Chapter Twelve

Buffalo Hump stayed with the tribe to continue the celebration of renewal. Kills White Bear, in the company of his young adopted son alone, rode north to see his cousins.

They honored his arrival with a feast and dancing. When that was finished, the councils of two bands gathered to listen to what he had to say. Kills White Bear waited for the commotion to settle, and then he addressed a hundred chiefs, elders, shamans and war leaders. He felt the spirit of Maguara fill him as he stepped into the circle to speak.

"Kills White Bear's heart is glad," he began, his great voice booming in the still, dry air, "to see the Kotsoteka and the Yamparikas together in peace in the valley of the Arkansas. These ears have already heard of the Great Peace between our beloved cousins and their enemies, the Cheyenne and Arapaho. Kills White Bear sees thousands of war ponies grazing on green grass, the women's bellies full of fresh meat, and laughing children running naked through the camp playing children's games. The buffalo are more than the stars of the sky, and the deer are not afraid. These things comfort Kills White Bear because he has not seen them in his own country for the last four winters.

"Tears flow like a river from the women of the Wasps. Our hearts are black from the burning of our lodges. Our children do not play games. Where we once heard laughter, we hear only the screams of the dying and the thunder of white men's guns. There is no peace in the south.

"The Wasps sat down with the Tejanos as you did with the Cheyenne and Arapaho. To trust them was a grave mistake. Our chiefs were murdered under the white flag. Their women and children died with them in the streets of Béxar, where no grass grows.

"This summer the Wasps have shared your land with you, our beloved cousins. The Penateka are grateful that your hearts are open to us and you know that in your country there is enough for all. That is the ancient and true way. But if the Kotsoteka or the Yamparika came to our

country, we could not return the favor. The Tejanos take
our land from us, and the Tejanos do not share.

"We Penateka were once the largest and strongest of the
bands. We were the body, and you the arms. In the past,
when the Kotsoteka and the Yamparika had trouble with
their enemies, they came to the Penateka for help. Kills
White Bear sees that we are now the weakest, and we must
come to you.

"Soon the Wasps will return to our land and make war
on our enemies. The rivers will run with Tejano blood until
the Wasps have their revenge and our land is again safe
for our children. We invite you, our cousins, to ride alongside us and help us claim what is ours, for the prizes of
war will be great and your young men can win honor."

Kills White Bear paused, expecting to hear war whoops.
There was only silence. Then, one of the Yamparika chiefs
rose to speak.

"The Yamparika sympathize with our cousins," he
began. "They have talked of this matter since we first heard
Spirit Talker and the other chiefs were slain. We have also
spoken with Bent, the American. It was he who arranged
the Great Peace with our enemies, and now we sleep at
night. Bent tells the Yamparika that it would not be wise
to wage war against the Tejanos. He asks us, why should
the Yamparika smoke out the bees if one can't taste the
honey?"

Kills White Bear answered. "The Yamparika do taste the
honey. They raid the Tejanos as they please, and the Penateka, in turn, take the blame. Soldiers ride into our country
and punish the Penateka for Yamparika raids. The Wasps
ask the Yamparika to ride with us and ensure there is
honey for all."

The old chief shook his head. "Bent is the friend of the
Yamparika. His words are wise, and he tells us to turn our
heads away."

Kills White Bear responded. "And who is Bent but another white man? Like you, the Wasps once saw the Tejanos as one tribe, and the Americans as another. And yet,
we know the Tejanos were born of American fathers. They
call themselves two names to confuse us, but they share
one blood."

Kills White Bear turned away from one chief to address them all. "My cousins, ask yourselves where are the Cherokee? The Delaware? The Kickapoo? And the Shawnee?" His voice grew quiet. "Kills White Bear knows. The Americans drove them from their homes for their sons the Tejanos to kill. These tribes ran like rabbits into land the American Father does not want. Now the whites turn their eyes to the hunting grounds of the Wasps, and Kills White Bear is not surprised to hear that Bent tells their cousins to turn their heads away. Is this man your friend? Is this man wise? No. He wags the black tongue of the Tejanos behind a liar's smile. He feeds you with one hand, while he hides a bloody knife in the other. He says, leave the Wasps to their fate, when he knows the same waits for you."

Here he paused, moving from face to blank face. They were moved. "Hear me, my cousins!" he thundered. "The Wasps do not come crying to ask that you fight for them. They are warning you that the time has come to fight for yourselves. Hurry to their side before it's too late." He threw his head back to the stars. "The night is falling on the Nemenuh."

This time a heavy-set, stern-faced Kotsoteka chief rose. "And where are your chiefs?"

"They are murdered," he sneered.

"And yet the Wasps ask the Kotsoteka to follow when they can't be led."

"Kills White Bear leads the Wasps, as does his brother Buffalo Hump; we are both proven in war. Kills White Bear was chosen by Maguara's own hand to lead in his place. He was called to the council at sixteen winters when the voice of the white bear took his. He's led his warriors many times against the Lipans, Tonkawa, Méxicanos, and Tejanos. He is Black Heart," he said, pounding his chest once with his fist, "the warrior with a price on his head because the Méxicanos fear him. His name is known in camps he's never seen. Before he came to this one your own people called him *Par-riah-boh*, the Principal Chief of the Penateka. He will lead, and he will conquer."

"Kills White Bear's memory is short," the Kotsoteka answered. "Mine is longer. At the beginning of this year,

word came to these ears that Kills White Bear led a party
of eighty warriors against fourteen Tejano rangers. Half of
your number died. The rest fled, and Kills White Bear left
his dead and wounded behind. Is this the leadership the
Kotsoteka can expect?"

The challenge shook Kills White Bear. His gut twisted
in knots. His first instinct was to lash out and humble the
portly Kotsoteka, but he had a greater purpose and had to
shove his pride aside. "What you say is true," he answered,
his voice quiet, yet steady. "Kills White Bear lost those
warriors and Kills White Bear alone accepts the blame. Yet
he gained an understanding that the Kotsoteka and the
Yamparika do not have. War is changing in the south. Kills
White Bear discussed it with Maguara and Bloody Knife
long before they were murdered. Their wisdom lives on in
Kills White Bear's head alone. The Tejanos are devils, and
raiding is no longer the sport it once was. But Kills White
Bear knows what to do. Your warriors have a choice. They
can learn from Kills White Bear and live, or they can learn
from the Tejanos and die."

The Kotsoteka chief pressed him. "And Kills White
Bear, who showed his back in battle, would teach Kotsoteka warriors?"

Impatience got the best of him. This time he answered
in anger. "Kills White Bear is the only one who can teach
them." Then, in response to this insult, he angrily ripped
his hunting shirt from his body and tossed it to the flames.
He raised his arms above his head and faced the gathered
bands. The flames illuminated the vicious scars on his chest,
back and arms. "Kills White Bear asks if this is the chest
of a coward?"

The faces in the crowd froze, astonished at the violence
carved on his war-chewed flesh. The old men stared va-
cantly, while the young men gasped in awe. Some looked
coldly at their elders as they began to chant their respect.
"Warrior! . . . Warrior! . . ." Even they knew that such a
body could never boast, and never lie.

When the chanting subsided, Kills White Bear continued
with new vigor and new pride. "This body," he began,
"speaks for itself. Kills White Bear turned his back only

once, and that was to come and warn you, his cousins. He lived so that you may also live."

And then the Yamparika chief stood once again. "You've come here, where there are no Tejanos. Why not stay here? There's room for us all. We have peace on the high plains. The Yamparika will not go looking for war for war's sake. To do so is madness. Kills White Bear's youth betrays him. The Yamparika will raid the Méxicanos as we always have, and leave the Tejanos alone, as Bent advises. This is what the Penateka should do. Stay with us, Kills White Bear, and grow old."

Kills White Bear brought his fingers to his temples and rubbed them. He threw his head back, and sighed. Then he looked again at the gathered warriors and threw his arms out to them. "And if Bent came to you and said, 'Yamparika, stay here in peace and be quiet, I only want to take the air,' could you live? To surrender our land to the Tejanos would be the same, for without it, the Penateka would die of shame. The snows of winter need not fall on Kills White Bear's head for his eyes to open. The years no longer offer him wisdom; they promise him the death of the nation that he loves more dearly than his own life." He steadied himself, eyes scanning the enthralled crowd.

"Kills White Bear showed his back one time," he said, "but he'll never show it again! He knows there is no peace with the Tejanos, and Bent thinks only of them. First they take Wasp land, then they take yours! For the gray hairs to do nothing but cling to lies is true madness!"

Now he heard the warriors rumble. He was winning them. One last warning, he thought, and they were won. "War waits for the Wasps in the south. Kills White Bear tells you that there is no other way. When the Tejanos are gone, the Kotsoteka and the Yamparika can come into our land and share it with us again as they've always done. The Wasps will welcome you as brothers."

He paused here and then shifted his tone. "But if the Penateka fall, the other bands fall with them. If our thread unravels, your backs are also bare. Watch carefully what becomes of us, my cousins. If we can't take your warriors, let us take your prayers. The Penateka will go and fight for the People to the death! Kills White Bear swears it!" He looked intently along the circle of watching eyes. "And if we die, you die!"

He watched as the two chiefs of both bands looked at one another. The Yamparika spoke for them both.

"We've heard Kills White Bear's words," he said, "and our hearts go out to him. We will talk it over and see if our minds follow. What he asks is no easy thing. We ask for time."

"That we do not have," Kills White Bear said. "Already we've waited too long. Maguara once thought as you do and you see how his patience was rewarded." He waited. Nothing. No one else spoke. "The time, my cousins," he whispered, "is now."

He stepped out of the circle. He reached for Little Eagle, and the boy took his hand. Together they walked to their horses, mounted and rode quietly out of the camp.

Before they had traveled far, Kills White Bear heard the sound of galloping hooves on the plains behind them. He turned and waited as Yamparika, Kotsoteka, and even some Kiowa warriors overtook them. There must have been a hundred or more. Their faces were young and eager.

"Our chiefs are old and fat," one Kotsoteka said. "They have many horses and many wives and have lost the taste for war. Not so for us. We heard Kills White Bear and understand his troubles. His enemies are ours. We'll follow him south to defeat the Tejanos. We ask for nothing but the chance for honor."

"And you'll have it," Kills White Bear promised, "and much more besides."

Chapter Thirteen

Kills White Bear assumed responsibility for the campaign's logistics. The tactics were left to Buffalo Hump. By late July, their force was gathered, provisioned and blessed by the shamans. By Kills White Bear's estimate, they had over four hundred warriors, far less than what he wanted, but adequate just the same.

Kills White Bear envisioned an extended campaign, as

he knew the Wasps of his grandfather's time had once had in the wars with the Spanish. The women and the children would follow their husbands and sons into war. These, he knew, would not only feed and shelter his warriors, but could also be depended upon to fight with them should the need arise.

Kills White Bear warned his young men of the pistols that shot forever. When they saw them, they should withdraw *en masse* to cover and fend off the short-ranged pistols with concentrated rifle fire. The Nemenuh had not been able to find pistols of their own, so Kills White Bear advised his men that the only way they could be had was to pry them from the cold fingers of dead Tejanos. This, he explained, was priority.

When all was done, Kills White Bear struck his camp and rode alongside Buffalo Hump at the head of one thousand.

Once they left the relative safety of the central hills, Buffalo Hump chose to travel only at night. Kills White Bear knew surprise was everything, and his people intended to strike deep into south central Texas. They spent their days hunkered in great thickets of oak, cedar, and pecan trees. They rode with the rising moon until the break of dawn.

By the August moon, they skirted south of San Antonio. Full of soldiers and bad medicine to boot, they were glad to leave it behind. From there, they turned east, toward the town called Gonzáles, which Buffalo Hump widely circled. Then they paralleled the Guadalupe River, slipping like snakes through the dry coastal prairie grass on the way south.

Kills White Bear was ecstatic. Never before had so many penetrated so deeply. Rear guard riders brought him the news. Not one Tejano had seen the signs on the sun-baked earth. They could strike without warning, and soon they would.

Chapter Fourteen

Remy could not sleep in the summer heat. He slipped from Beatriz's side and walked barefoot out to the well. The cool water soothed his sweating brow as he looked up to let the droplets roll past. The skies overhead were dark and clear. He marked the position of the stars and judged that the sun would rise in three hours. In four, it would already be hot. By mid-afternoon, the very air would hum and even the oak trees would appear to waver. No wild animal moved in the daytime heat. Even the birds refused to sing. The grass beneath the oaks and weeping pecans was pressed flat by cattle frantic for shade. Only the buzzards rode the thermals, circling the bellowing cattle as if they were certain the calves could never last another day. The Colorado no longer flowed. Pools of stagnant, cloudy water, thick like jelly with algae, bordered by sand and sun-bleached gravel, remained for the stock to drink. The weeds along the bank, their leaves curling, bowed before the fury of the August sun. Ticks, red-bugs, horses, and dragonflies still prowled the burnt grass. The rest of the insect tribes had surrendered a month before. It was the slow time, with short, exhausting work days and long siestas in any shady spot that promised the first breath of breeze. The land not only refused to support life, it threatened it.

Even the Comanche, Remy knew, would never travel this time of year. But Ranger companies still sporadically scouted Hayden Edwards' plateau for signs of them anyway. All summer long, there were none. Remy and his volunteers had quit the field in late May to see about his family and ranch, but he knew young Jack Hays and Ben McCulloch never had. These men kept watch over the scorched frontier.

The rooster crowed. Remy sat on the porch smoking a cigarillo and watched the sky break blood red in the east. The sun came up almost white. It would be hotter today than the day before. Only a storm in the gulf could save them now, and he hoped the clouds were gathering out there somewhere under a south wind. He longed to smell the sweetness of rain in the air. By mid-September, he thought, the rain would come and with it, the Comanche.

Remy heard a rider in the distance. He saw the puff of dust before he saw the man and horse. He recognized him as Josiah Sledd, one of McCulloch's men. Sledd bolted from the lathered and blowing stallion.

"Mornin'," he said, and walked straight to the well. He drew the bucket to his face and drank deeply while the horse moved to the trough. Remy sat in his underwear, legs crossed, the cigarillo dangling from his chapped lips. Sledd yanked the pail from his face and spit on the dusty ground.

"We got trouble, Captain Fuqua," he said, wiping his mouth with his sleeve.

"What sort?"

"Comanche. McCulloch cut their trail just west of Plum Crick. They're headed south."

This got his attention. "South? Why in hell would a raidin' party head south? McCulloch's read it wrong. I'll ride out directly and have a look-see for myself."

"It ain't no raidin' party, Captain" he said.

"What else could it be, Sledd?" Remy asked, resting his elbows on his knees. "McCulloch probably cut a cattle trail. Rancher moving his stock south to water and river grass, more'n likely. Ain't a drop or a green blade up on the plateau. Hunters always see what they're huntin'."

Sledd shook his head. "Cattle don't leave a hundred cook fires in an oak grove. They don't leave raw bones sittin' next to 'em neither. The grass is mashed flat a hunerd yards wide. It ain't cattle, and it ain't just a war party. The whole goddamned tribe's on the move."

Remy was not convinced. "If that were true, they'd have hit any number of farms and ranches along the Guadalupe. Ain't nary a one been touched. Not that I've heard of."

"McCulloch ain't really had the occasion to visit with 'em about their plans. He says to gather your company and join him on the road to Victoria. They're headed that way."

None of this was good news, not in the height of summer. "All right," Remy said. "But this better be what he says it is."

"It's worse," and he threw the bucket back for another deep gulp. "I'd be obliged for the loan of a fresh horse."

"Take one," Remy said.

Sledd moved for his. "Not that one," Remy told him.

Chapter Fifteen

At first, the Tejanos must've thought they were Lipan coming to trade. Kills White Bear could not understand this mistake. Only the People wore bonnets of buffalo hide and horn on the war path. Their faces were painted red and black. Their intent should've been obvious, but the Tejanos had let them come too close. When they saw it was the Nemenuh, it was too late.

Buffalo Hump ordered his horde to surround Victoria, while individual raiding parties assaulted it. They cut down Tejanos in the fields and in the streets before their fire was returned. Béxar had taught them the cost of fighting the whites like this, and they soon withdrew south of the town with their bounty, which included several hundred horses and mules.

At dawn, Buffalo Hump turned back and attacked the city again. They'd lost warriors, and Victoria had not yet sufficiently paid. More of the Tejanos died, and this time the warriors set fire to the big, wooden lodges. Buffalo Hump would have stayed there another day to see the town reduced to ashes, but Kills White Bear reminded him that this was not their destination. They had a grander scheme than this.

"The victory," he reminded his colleague, "lies on the coast. Kills White Bear has seen it. We leave this village bleeding, my brother. When the Méxicanos come, it will die."

Chapter Sixteen

Remy pushed his men well after midnight until they cut the headwaters of Arenosa Creek. There he pitched his cold camp. His men gnawed jerked venison and hard corn bread and sucked their gourds dry, taking turns to watch over hobbled horses.

Before dawn they were up and mounted without a word, following the Comanche. An hour after daylight, the line of trampled grass and brush fanned out into a stretch a half-mile wide. Remy knew that from this point forward the slaughter had begun.

He spaced his men accordingly, warning each to keep his eye peeled. The Indians were traveling with women and children, some on foot. He'd seen their tracks. Soon they'd overtake them.

They came across pools of dark, cracked blood and fresh graves dug nearby. Remy's pace instinctively quickened. Soon he saw the forms of men in the distance. Rangers, he thought. Captain Zumwalt's Lavaca-based men were digging a shallow grave when he reached them. He saw the victim, a man he did not recognize, a deep gaping powder-burned wound in his chest. The soles of his feet had been sliced away, and were deeply imbedded with grit and chaff. They'd made the poor bastard walk until he apparently could walk no further. Then they shot him dead, scalped him and rolled on.

Remy's immediately thought of the destruction of his men, particularly the Tonkawa, on the Concho four years before. Such creative torture, he thought, resembled the touch of the war chief Kills White Bear, and the opportunity to catch him bloody-handed on the coastal plains energized him. He would advance faster now.

"Who's ahead?" he queried Zumwalt.

"McCulloch and Tumlinson. Between us we've got a hunerd and twenty-five men on the trail. More comin' every hour. McCulloch sent word east and west."

"Tumlinson?" Remy said. "Why didn't he stay in Victoria? This trail leads right to it."

"Because they've already been there," Zumwalt said. "Tumlinson slipped out at night for help."

"We best get along, don't ya reckon?"

"We're a-comin' as fast as them Mexican ponies'll carry us. We only stop to bury somebody, and we stop most every hour."

Remy turned to his men, most of which he saw were staring at the dead man. "Let's git!" he said, and they rode on.

Chapter Seventeen

Kills White Bear saw the town in the distance. His warriors had sacked and burned every ranch and farmhouse between Victoria and where they now stood. They killed those they did not take captive. They stole the horses and speared the cattle for sport.

The captured horses now numbered well over two thousand by his estimate. They trailed behind to a point that he could no longer see. It was all going very well, and he and Buffalo Hump now smelled the salt air in the wind. Kills White Bear closed his eyes, matching his vision with what he'd just seen. The two were the same. This town, he knew, they would burn to the ground, and he assured the worried Buffalo Hump that they had nothing to fear.

"And what did you see after that?" Buffalo Hump asked him.

The question was a good one. "Nothing," he answered, and instantly it troubled him. But there was something else. "Do you see the Méxicanos?" he asked and Buffalo Hump scanned the horizon, answering that they were not yet in sight. As far as he could tell, the Tejanos were going about their strange daily business as Tejanos usually did. There was no sign whatsoever that the Méxicanos were a threat to them. The village would be easy to take.

"It's no matter, brother," Buffalo Hump told him. "They're

not needed for what we must do. Let's make a vision come true. The Méxicanos will come."

Kills White Bear watched as Buffalo Hump again arranged his warriors in the shape of the half moon. When they were ready, they raced for the town and engulfed it. Five men, three white and two black, died in their barren fields. They took a couple of women, one in a strange, impregnable vest of bone around her waist, and strapped them unceremoniously to the backs of sweating mules. The rest of the whites rushed to the water, taking to their strange, fat canoes, and paddled out of range of the Nemenuh rifles. When all were driven out, Kills White Bear and his warriors searched the town.

The Méxicanos had not lied about what waited for them in this place. The stores were fat with goods. Foodstuffs, pots, pans, ammunition, guns, even a repeating pistol or two, were found and quickly loaded by Nemenuh women, who were expert packers. They found strange clothes, bolts of colored cloth, which they tied to the tails of their horses, and fine blankets in the stores. Warriors wearing hats that rose the length of a man's knee above their heads lanced cattle with glee. The women walked about with a device that opened widely, shading them from the sun. They spent the balance of the day toying with gadgets, packing what they wanted and destroying the rest. He watched some of the young men catch baby alligators to bring back as proof that they had warred all the way to the coast.

Amidst the joy and laughter of riches beyond his people's imagination, Kills White Bear fumed. There were no Méxicanos, and he knew the Nemenuh could not wait. The warriors were blind in their celebrations. There had never been a raid as successful as this one, but without the Méxicanos it remained little more than just that. Kills White Bear had hoped for a war of extermination that he knew then would not come. This was the reason his vision had ended here at the coast. He took nothing from this place, and when the sun hung in the west, he ordered his warriors to burn it and went looking for Buffalo Hump. He found him equally distraught.

"They lied to us, Brother," Buffalo Hump lamented. "We're deep in the enemy's country, and the Méxicanos will not come."

This treachery posed a number of serious problems. "The only thing to do," Kills White Bear said, "is to abandon the goods and the horses, split into two dozen parties, and follow the sun west to the Nueces canyon. From there, we can move north where few of the Tejanos will follow. The young men should stay behind and detain the soldiers, while the rest disappear in the thickets."

Buffalo Hump pointed to their people, busy loading a hundred slow-footed mules in the golden glow of the fires. Women argued over pots and pans while the warriors ran wild. "I promised them bounty, Kills White Bear."

"Not this much!" he argued. "We could never move fast enough with all this."

"I didn't know this would be here, and I didn't know the Méxicanos would lie. But I won't deny the People the spoils of war. They lost their husbands, friends and fathers. They've suffered the heat. The Tejanos owe them what they've taken. Buffalo Hump could never ask them to leave it behind."

"Then you've doomed them," Kills White Bear answered angrily. "The scouts say the soldiers are closing."

"I've thought of this," Buffalo Hump said. "We should not scatter and flee west. We should turn back as one against the Tejanos and put our feet back on the same trail that led us here. We'll not rest until we reach the hill country. We're rich with fresh horses, guns, and ammunition. We'll travel as the buffalo do, and any that oppose us will meet the horns of the gathered bulls. The Tejanos could not keep us out, and, the Great Spirit willing, they won't keep us in."

Kills White Bear felt Buffalo Hump's hand fall on his shoulder and gently squeeze it. "Follow me, brother, and live."

Kills White Bear put his disappointment aside and gathered his people. He realized he'd been a fool to trust the Méxicanos. Had his warriors concentrated on the northern settlements, such a force would've wiped them from the skirt of the Earth Mother. Now the Wasps were running for their lives. The greatest war party in the history of the Nemenuh was wasted. If they survived, he swore he'd skewer the Méxicanos' snake tongues with a dull stick in their own rocky earth.

Chapter Eighteen

The initial skirmish did not last long. One of McCulloch's men died when his party stumbled into a flanking wave of Comanche horsemen. Remy realized these warriors protected the main column, which was now mysteriously returning north *en masse* by the same route by which they had come. His men and horses were exhausted after days of hard riding in the wake of the Indians. Now they'd turned and ridden right past them. Had the main body swung on his and McCulloch's men, they could have easily crushed them. When they did not, Remy realized that they'd lost their taste for war. The Council House Fight, he thought, had finally been avenged. They were running now.

Loaded with stolen horses and supplies from two towns and a dozen ranches which they did not seem inclined to abandon, they would make slow progress. By the time he conferred with McCulloch, he'd made up his mind what he would do.

"Beats all I ever saw, Fuqua," McCulloch told him. "We can't stop 'em."

Remy thought differently. "We kin cut 'em off."

"They won't stay together, Captain."

"Yeah, they will. If'n they were going to split off, they'd have done it by now."

Remy could see McCulloch was considering what he'd told him. "Hell, with fresh horses, we could dig in somewheres north of 'em."

"Damn right, Ben," Remy nodded, "and recruit three times our number on the way. We'll lay up somewheres and whip 'em good."

"Where?" McCulloch wondered, and Remy's mind instantly retraced the Comanche route. In the beginning they'd crossed what the settlers called the Big Prairie, a

grassy flat lined with heavily wooded tributaries of the San
Marcos River. Perfect for an ambush. He turned to McCul-
loch at the very moment McCulloch's jaw started to move.
They said the words together.

"Plum Creek."

Chapter Nineteen

The mules refused their burdens in the heat. Frustrated
warriors shot them where they stood. Kills White Bear
looked back at the littered trail of broken chests, rolls of
calico cloth and colored ribbons that flitted in the breeze.

In the distance, he could see the Rangers. Shots rang out
continuously, and his harried column could not rest unless
they turned back to kill the Tejanos who chased them. At
first it was only a few weary Rangers, and Kills White Bear
urged Buffalo Hump to swing back and destroy them and
thus buy them some time. But their warriors were committed to their prizes, only abandoning them when the mules
took their last step. Now soldiers followed as well.

It was no use to consider alternatives. Kills White Bear
knew there was wisdom in Buffalo Hump's decision, and
he would not defy it. His brother knew the strengths of his
people, and he also knew their weaknesses. He intended to
keep his word. Buffalo Hump had said the Tejanos would
not attack them if they stayed together, and so far, he'd
been right. They were not threatened by the few that followed. Their rifle fire meant nothing to Kills White Bear.
His vision had told him clearly. Kills White Bear would not
die in battle.

He smiled when the rear scouts advised both him and
Buffalo Hump that the soldiers were riding their horses to
death. A day more in the summer sun, he thought, and all
the Tejanos would be on foot. The Nemenuh, who understood the needs of horses if not mules, could travel easily
for two more nights without stopping. On the third, they
would rest in their own country.

Chapter Twenty

Remy reached Plum Creek on August 11. He and McCulloch were met by Jack Hays, Matthew Caldwell, Big Foot Wallace, the Hardeman brothers, Kit Ackland, and Jesse Burnham, all men who had come to manhood fighting the Comanche. Each had brought more with them that shared the same grim history. Remy counted ninety-three faces, including his own.

Out there somewhere was Edward Burleson and eighty-seven Bastrop volunteers. With him, they were told, were Chief Placido and his Tonkawa. Placido had but fourteen warriors under his command, but the scouts said that they had run thirty miles on foot at the opportunity to draw the blood of their enemies. The image of those sweating, panting warriors told Remy how deeply they hated the Comanche. Only he hated them more.

The regular army was represented by two men: Major General Felix Huston and his aide. As far as Remy was concerned, this was plenty.

Remy and McCulloch recounted the atrocities to date: the burning of towns and ranches; the toll of their slain neighbors; the mutilated women and lanced babies. The light in these men's eyes dimmed. They'd all lost kin and friends to the savages. When the Comanche came, they vowed to destroy them once and for all.

Remy wasn't thinking in such collective terms. Soon, he thought, he'd stand over Kills White Bear's body, and the cloud that had shadowed him for four years would be burned away in the smoke and dust under the relentless August sun.

General Huston attempted to discuss tactics. Remy and the dozen other Ranger captains simply refused. The Comanche would come, and they'd kill them. Contingencies? No need. This was the battle for which they had waited years. The Comanche would seldom stand against an army. Raiding was their choice, and Remy knew it was a wise one. When they came, you counted your losses and buried the dead and waited helplessly for the next time. He knew that though all of those men had felt the sting of the Wasps, many had never seen a Comanche face. Soon they'd see over a thousand. He recognized the coming battle as a singular opportunity.

There would be no warning, no offer to parlay, no attempt to trade for captives. Remy understood implicitly that they had not gathered to punish the Comanche, they'd come to exterminate them. It would be blood for blood where a little river crossed a big plain that could no longer be shared. Tomorrow, Remy said grimly, one race would rule Texas.

For Remy's part, there was but one caveat. His son, now ten years old, might be among the Comanche. They could kill whomever they wanted, he said, but he'd be obliged if they'd keep an eye out for Carlito. Those present understood, and Remy knew the word would be spread: Fire on red skin, but look for white.

At daylight Remy heard the scouts return. The Comanche were coming. Matt "Old Paint" Caldwell, a man of many years and about three skin tones, emerged as the Texian's leader. In less than twenty minutes, Remy and the other men with horses were mounted. He checked his revolver for dry powder. In August, it always was. He handed his extra revolver to Picosa, who thanked him silently with a nod.

"Cuidado, viejo," he told him. "When this is over, I wanna see a smile on that ugly face."

"Until that time, gringo," Picosa answered, checking the cylinders of the Colt, "your only view, as always, will be of my backside. I avenge my patrón, Don Carlos, this day. And no man can keep me from it."

"Just don't be a fool, goddammit, Diego. Ya got a family at home."

"Oh, it's Diego when I'm your warrior. But Picosa the cabron when I'm in your pastures."

"It's Picosa the cabron pretty much every day, I reckon." He reflected a moment and then thought what the hell. I'll say it. "Look, I never had much of a Pa. I was fond of Don Carlos and miss 'im a little each day, but he aggravated me more than anything else. I don't believe I ever measured up as far as he was concerned. You probably don't look back on things like I do, but I've always looked up to you. What I know about ranchin', I learned from you. There ain't a man in this world I respect more. Your hair's gray and greasy, but I'd like to see you keep it just the same. You be careful out there, old man."

"I'll see you in your grave, Don Remy."

"Uh, you ain't bin talkin' to that weasel Quelepe, have ya?"

"Picosa never listens to fools, except maybe one. And though that white man may be loco, Picosa trusts him with his life. For a vaquero, there's no greater measure."

It was an honor such as he'd never had. He'd waited years to hear it. He thought it would never come, not from that salty, savvy mayordomo. Remy reached for him. "Give me your hand, Diego." He did, and they clasped each other firmly. "*Cuidado, viejo.* We're gonna build us a hell of a ranch over Kills White Bear's grave when this is over."

"To the old days and that aggravating Don Carlos, Don Remy," Picosa said, lighting a last cigarillo. *"Buena suerte."* And then it was time to go.

They gathered in silence as the dust cloud rose toward them in the south. Caldwell stepped forward.

"Boys," he said, "there's eight hunerd to a thousand Injuns yonder way. They have our women and children prisoner. They burnt the coast to ashes. They've already kilt several good men. They have repulsed the Rangers below. We are but ninty-three strong, and I believe we can whip hell out of 'em.'' He paused, and his eyes scanned them all. "Boys, shall we fight?"

They all answered in one sustained cheer.

"Now, I say we give command of this outfit to General Huston. He's the highest rankin' feller aroun', and the onliest one that's got a purdy uniform. We kin all see 'em better when the dust gits up.'' Remy laughed. "Boys, gratify me by votin' aye.''

"Aye!" Remy called as the others did, too. Huston assumed command and quietly ordered ninety men to press forward against what looked like the entire Comanche nation. Before long, riders overtook them. Remy heard them say that Colonel Burleson and his men were closing on the scene. Huston wisely waited.

Through the limbs and choked brush, Remy saw them. They wore their finest, the ribbons of Linnville fluttering from their horses' tails. Soon enough, they'd hang by them.

The light of day brought new worries. Kills White Bear saw that the procession was spread too thinly. Too many warriors were occupied in driving the stubborn mules and weary pack horses. The rest were busy helping their women and children or watching captives. The rear guard was still harried, and there were not enough scouts riding ahead or on the eastern flank, the most likely source of a strike.

But the spirit of his people was high. At dawn, the men began singing while others swooned to their songs. The white man's mules were a curse, but the warriors were far from weary. All medicine was good. Buffalo Hump had chosen wisely, considering that he would not leave the white man's things behind.

The land ahead unfolded in his mind. There was but one more large open prairie to cross in the Tejanos' country. Once past it, they would follow the river until they came to the hills that fed it. There they would be safe. The soldiers who followed would no longer be a threat because the heat of the day would soon finish them. If not, before the sun set, he himself would turn with a handful and cut them down while they cried for water.

There was no time for celebration when Burleson's men arrived. Huston ordered the running Tonkawa warriors to tie white rags around their arms to distinguish them from the Comanche. Then he arranged two hundred men in a hollow, open-ended square formation. Burleson on the right, Caldwell, Remy's command among them, on the left. The Bastrop men formed in the rear behind Huston's aide. When all was ready, Huston waved them forward, and Remy and Picosa silently picked their way through timbered creek bottoms and heavy brush for the open ground beyond. In the direction where the dust rose, he heard the rumble of twelve thousand hooves.

There was something else, and Remy cocked his ear to listen. He thought he heard singing.

Kills White Bear heard the beating breasts of the mourning doves as they darted overhead for the west. It was already too hot for so many birds to be moving to water or feed. These, he knew, had been flushed from the oaks where they had roosted for the day. He turned his head eastward, in the direction from which they'd come, and he saw the heads of men and horses drifting quietly through the tall, burnt grass of the flat. These, he knew, were not their pursuers. His voice boomed across the open expanse.

"*¡Los Tejanos!* One last gift for my warriors!" Before the words had left his mouth, the bravest of the young men wheeled their mounts to charge. Kills White Bear held them. "Remember first the women and children, and also

the guns that shoot forever. Take cover together in the
oaks, my brothers, between our enemies and our families.
If the Tejanos come, they'll fall."

This time they listened, but the Tejanos did not advance.
Instead, they halted a little out of rifle range and dismounted in the old way. This confused him.

When Remy heard the order, he was livid. "What's this,
Huston?!" he bellowed, waving his pistol in the air. The
general knew nothing of Ranger tactics and even less about
the Comanche's. "Let's run 'em down!"

There was no reaction and the column stood still, waiting. Remy could see the Comanche caballada moving
northwest, the women and warriors scrambling behind it.
Though he could not see them, he knew the hills were not
far away. A line of rifles had formed to shield the escape
and buy the tribe the time they desperately needed. The
Rangers would never catch so many on open ground again,
and Remy knew it.

"Goddamn," Remy spat to Picosa. "This battle's gone to
hell in a hand basket ever since the army got here."

The stalemate was more than the Kiowa and young Nemenuh could bear. They hopped on their horses and dashed
for the Tejanos, quickly encircling them. Kills White Bear
could hear the taunts of his warriors as they fired on the
whites.

He knew the victories of the recent past blinded even
the men he held in the oak thicket. He recognized the
impulse to join the men on horse.

"Do you want to kill," he asked them, "or be killed? If

it's victory you want, wait with Kills White Bear. If you want to die young, ride with fools. The choice is yours."

He watched briefly as his warriors retied the reins to their ankles and clutched their rifles in their hands. If the whites charged together, he was certain they could hold them in the open ground and cut them to pieces. There would be nowhere for them to run.

There was a Kiowa warrior wearing a breastplate no Tejano bullet could penetrate. His medicine was strong, and all the Nemenuh knew it. Kills White Bear watched as he pulled out of the whirling circle, and charged the Tejano line. They fired on him, and Kills White Bear could hear the thud of the balls as they found their mark. Yet the Kiowa turned, his horse prancing, and faced the warriors in the oaks.

"Do you see, my brothers? They cannot kill me! And they can't kill you! There's nothing to fear!"

Remy studied the craziest warrior out of so many strangely dressed ones as he charged them three separate times. Then he turned to Picosa. "Get yourself a rest, *cabrón*. That armor flies up when he stops to turn. When you see that son of a bitch yank them reins, you fire for his ribs."

Remy watched as Picosa lay prone on the ground and engaged his set trigger. Sure enough, the Indian returned, this time coming closer before he stopped to shout. Just as his mouth started to move, Remy heard Picosa's hammer fall.

It stunned Kill White Bear to see the Kiowa's body knocked clear of the horse and crumple to the warm earth. This was the worst kind of bad medicine, the sort he'd seen in the Nueces Canyon earlier in the year. But it would not shake him as it had then. His heart ached that such a fine man was wasted, yet he knew his strategy remained sound.

As his eyes moved up and down the line, he could sense that his warriors no longer shared his confidence. "The Kiowa did not listen," he told them. "Now you must. He made a mistake, and we can't afford another. Hold this line until Buffalo Hump has taken your wives to safety. The Kiowa's death means nothing. When Kills White Bear falls, it'll be time to run."

One warrior spoke. "I, Red Hawk, knew that Kiowa. He was my friend. I must claim his body."

"No," Kills White Bear responded. "Not now."

"It must be now," he answered, and he mounted and dashed out for it. Kills White Bear saw the Tejanos cut him down. Then another tried, and another, until half a dozen went at once and managed to collect the bodies of the slain.

His warriors inspected the dead Kiowa's shield. There were several dents but no hole. The Tejano bullet had passed through it but left no sign. It was evil. The howls went up as the warriors' resolve crumbled and Kills White Bear knew he was powerless to soothe their raging fears. Before he could say anything else, some were already mounted.

"If we run," he warned them, "they'll kill us."

One of them jerked the reins of his horse and turned it northwest. "They'll kill us either way, Kills White Bear. Two days before these ears heard you yourself say that we should scatter. Now is the time. Save yourself for another day if you can."

Chapter Twenty-One

R emy heard the Comanche's wail and instantly knew, as all the Rangers did, that they'd just lost their nerve. The captains hastily conferred with Huston in that animated fashion Remy'd seen in the past, and then Huston gave the order to charge. By the time the word reached his ears, Remy had his men mounted and dashing for the oaks.

Out of the corner of his eyes, he saw that the rest had quickly followed.

The initial charge was not without cost. Remy lost three men to rifle fire, but the rest charged on into the thicket. The few Indians that defended the line were broken immediately. The ones that were not shot were run down by excited and foaming horses. Remy noticed where their frantic hooves had torn their flesh.

Once past the front line, he saw where Caldwell and Burleson had turned their commands toward the main column of fleeing Indians. Remy reloaded his pistol and led his men there. Behind them, they left only the dead.

He saw that Caldwell had reached the main body and dispersed it. The Comanche now raced for the thickets of the river bottom, quickly bogging down in the spongy earth. Remy formed a phalanx of rifle fire and shot the savages down as they frantically kicked their stalled horses. The quick ran across the massed backs of mules and horses and disappeared into the brush where other Texian guns waited. Through the dust, the confusion and the screams of men and horses, Remy's mind remained clear. His soul was as worn and hard as the calluses on his hands. The warm blood that dripped from his face was not his. The smoke in the air smelled of rout. He knew the Penateka were broken.

The battle was over, but the killing went on. Soon enough, they saw the fate of the captives. They'd been arrowed, lanced, and shot down as the Rangers broke through the rear guard. Victory complete, Remy thought that the violence should have ebbed. But when the Texians caught first sight of dead, mutilated women, it actually escalated. Remy knew the Comanche would have hell to pay. The debacle of the Council House Fight had taught the rangers that there was no way to handle adult Comanche prisoners, and so it was the unspoken understanding that they'd take none.

The surviving warriors fled along the river for the hills and the Rangers followed. Remy had emptied the cylinders of his Colt four times in the pursuit. At the fifth, he stopped with Picosa to load and allow the horses to blow as his men rushed past. Nobody needed any orders anymore.

"Any sign of Carlito?" he asked. In his excitement, his fingers fumbled with the revolver. He was out of breath. Picosa shook his head. "How many did you kill?"

"I saw six fall," he answered, rolling a cigarillo, "not counting the first."

"I shot nine," Remy said, "but not the one I wanted. I know that bastard's here somewheres."

"Enough, Don Remy." Picosa was breathless. "The horses are winded. Many Comanche are dead. The rest are running for their lives. Let fresh men hunt them now. Our part's done."

Remy shook his head. It wasn't over, not by a long shot. "You go on back and rest if'n you like, old man. You done enough. My part ain't done till Kills White Bear's dead. I know I saw him there at the first. He's slipped by somehow. He won't be so lucky here directly, I'll grant ya that."

Diego shifted his saddle back squarely on his horse's back. "Where you go, Don Remy, Picosa goes also. You can't be trusted to go out by yourself."

Remy listened to his horse's labored breathing. He felt its lathered coat. It was cool enough. "Let's go if'n we're goin'. That pistol loaded?"

"No, it's too hot to even touch it. A minute more."

"There's no time, Diego. You go on back to camp. I'll catch up with the others."

Picosa shook his head and pulled his powder horn, shot pouch and new fangled percussion caps. They were a pain to manage on horseback, but Remy waited impatiently. "Let's ride, cabrón," Picosa said, and there was nothing to do but follow him.

They'd sprinted maybe two miles when Picosa jerked back his reins. Remy saw his squinting dark eyes cut to the west.

"There, Don Remy," he called, pointing the pistol barrel. "There's the man who killed Don Carlos."

Remy's eyes burned from the sweat and the dust and the mean glare of the sun, but he discerned the figure of Kills White Bear in the dusty distance well enough. He was alone, watching from the peak of a rounded knoll. Naked to the waist, Remy clearly saw the white claw marks on that red skin. The bear's cape was lashed to the savage's saddle.

Without a word, Remy sank his spurs in the stallion's ribs.

Chapter Twenty-Two

When his line had broken, Kills White Bear gathered whom he could after the Tejanos passed over, and began harassing them from the rear. Most of his warriors had fallen anyway. When the main body of his procession had been disbursed, there was no longer anything to guard. He could not stem his despair, and he lost the will to run. He waited on the high knoll for a Tejano ball, but it had not come.

He knew the cost of this failure. He knew he'd lived to see the sun set on the Penateka. It was, he thought, the blackest fate. For him, life was over even if his broken heart still beat. He knew that the hills of the San Sabá, the country of his birth, were lost.

Then he saw two riders racing on his position. One was an older Méxicano man whom he thought he recognized but could not place. Of the other, he was more certain. It was Fuqua.

All thoughts of death vanished at the sight of one last challenge. He quickly assessed his position and decided how it would be done. Today his old enemy would die, or he would.

When they were close enough, Kills White Bear wheeled and ran his horse downhill to the nearest thicket. It was but an island of brush. As soon as he entered it, he stopped, dismounted and turned back to watch.

Sure enough, the two men separated to opposite sides of

the thicket. When the Tejanos saw that he had not emerged from the other side, they would return. The Méxicano could track him. He was pretty sure that Fuqua could not. He tethered the horse, slung his rifle strap over his shoulder, and carried his bow through the dense cover, skirting the edge of the thicket where the Méxicano had gone. Soon enough, he heard the sound of slow moving hooves of a single rider. He nocked an arrow and waited.

The Méxicano had a pistol. Soon, he thought, it would be his.

Chapter Twenty-Three

Kills White Bear saw him clearly. The Méxicano had stopped, studied his moccasin tracks on the ground and then cocked the hammer on his pistol. It was too late for precautions, he thought. Kills White Bear silently pulled back the bowstring, anchored his fingernail to the crack between his teeth, and waited for the Méxicano to lean into the clear lane where he knew his arrow could fly cleanly to its mark.

The Méxicano sat motionless on the back of his horse for what seemed an eternity. Kills White Bear whistled. Then the animal startled and stepped once, and the Méxicano's frame filled the opening. Kills White Bear let the string slip from his fingers and he saw the fletching disappear into the man's chest. He heard the shaft clatter on the ground well behind him, and he knew then his arrow had passed through the man's lungs and body. He would not live long.

When Kills White Bear stepped out of the thicket, he saw the Méxicano had lost his pistol in the fall. He was sitting up, coughing, his eyes moving from his wound to Kills White Bear, whose steps crushed the brittle summer grass beneath his feet. There was a knife in the Méxicano's bloody fingers and a snarl on his bloody lips. Kills White Bear stepped before him to watch him die.

"Ven, bastardo," the Méxicano growled thickly. His voice was weak and his lungs rattled as he struggled for breath. His mouth was choked with both mucous and blood. *"Tengo algo para tí."*

"And I have a gift for you as well," Kills White Bear said, and he kicked the Méxicano square in the mouth, rocking him backwards against the ground. Despite his pain, the man lashed at his ankles in wide, sloppy swaths until Kills White Bear stepped on his wrist. Then he knelt beside him and pressed his knife blade against his throat. "You'll follow Kills White Bear's tracks no more," he promised, and in one motion he split his thick, dark and whiskered skin from ear to ear. The blood gushed beneath the Méxicano's open and wild eyes. His mouth moved, but there was no sound, save the gurgling of blood in his throat.

Then Kills White Bear snatched him by the hair and scalped him. When the flesh was free, he rose and held it in front of the dying light of the Méxicano's dark eyes.

He took the pistol first. He checked the condition of the Méxicano's horse. One glance told him that his was still better. He checked briefly to see if Fuqua was yet upon him, and then if the Méxicano's pistol was loaded. The gun felt warm and heavy in his hand. He cocked the hammer and worked the cylinder to familiarize himself with its unusual operation. Soon enough he understood it. He realized that the little brass caps must somehow take the place of the flint spark, and he fumbled through the dead Méxicano's pouch to find where he kept the extras.

When he had them, he had everything. He'd waited months to get his hands on a gun like this. It was power. It was life. And he would soon use it to kill Fuqua and then many others after him. He yelled loudly to celebrate this little victory knowing his enemy would soon follow.

Chapter Twenty-Four

Remy's panic turned to fear when he heard Kills White Bear shout. No shots had been fired. There was nothing to do but ride to the sound of that fading voice.

Kills White Bear had been in that thicket they'd passed earlier. Remy thought it foolish to separate from Picosa. But they'd done it without thinking, and when they realized that the Indian had held, they did it again. Picosa must've looped back to try and flush him out. Remy knew he should post himself at the other end and wait, but he couldn't do it. He trusted Diego's instincts, but he trusted his own more. He circled back, moving far too quickly with such dangerous quarry, to locate Picosa. When he found him, they'd both withdraw after they set the brush on fire up-wind. That was the only safe way. Then he'd heard the war whoop.

When he cleared the point and could not see Picosa, he shuddered in alarm. Not two minutes passed before he came upon Picosa's grazing horse. He leaped from his stallion and rushed through the weeds until he found Picosa's body.

"Diego?" he cried, kneeling. "Diego?" He was gone. "Goddammit!!!"

He saw the tracks, remounted and followed them briskly. He wasn't worried about ambush. He did not call out for others to come with him. What he feared most was bringing Picosa's body home to his wife and children. First he'd avenge him. That was the easiest thing. Then he'd find the courage to face Picosa's family.

Kills White Bear sat atop the high ground and faced east, waiting for Fuqua. When he heard hooves approaching from the opposite direction, he was startled. Fuqua, he knew, was not that quick and not that clever. This was a Nemenuh. He cocked the Méxicano's pistol just in case he was wrong.

A voice called to him. He heard it clearly. "I am here, Wolf Eyes," he answered. The lone rider approached in silence. Kills White Bear had never seen him in the daylight before. He looked ghastly.

"Where are your people?" Wolf Eyes asked him.

"Dead or soon to be," he said.

"Who will lead them?"

"They won't be led," Kills White snapped bitterly. "All

of this could've been avoided had they listened. They clung to their spoils more dearly than they did their own lives. When it came time to fight the Tejanos, they ran from them instead like rabbits. They were cut down in the confusion like we do the buffalo. There was nothing I could do."

"And now?"

"I wait for my enemy," he said, cutting his eyes to watch.

"That is not wise. Gather your people in the hills, Kills White Bear. Prepare them for another day."

Kills White Bear glared at the spirit. "You have advice for me now, Wolf Eyes! Where were you before this disaster when I was praying for wisdom? Hundreds of my warriors lie dead. What is there for Kills White Bear to do but die fighting? I want the man that comes more than any."

"You're not a child, Kills White Bear," Wolf Eyes scoffed. "You're the Principal Chief. Your people are lost and crying for you. Put your personal feuds aside and go tend to them. There'll be another day, I swear it."

Kills White Bear cringed in disgust. His disappointment soured his every thought. "Tell me about another day, Wolf Eyes. Let these tired ears hear. Can we save our land? Can we live as we have?" The spirit had no answer. "I no longer think so," Kills White Bear said. "I need to be warned, not consoled."

"Very well," Wolf Eyes answered. His voice was low. "I have but one warning for you today, Kills White Bear. If that man comes, he'll kill you. His is the blood feud, fire for fire. If you truly want to die, wait in this place for that man. He'll take the hair from your head, and the limbs from your body. You'll never enter the Happy Place. Lead your people, Chief, or die in shame. The choice is yours. Decide quickly. He comes."

Kills White Bear didn't fear Fuqua, but his spirit guide swayed him from the narrow-mindedness of revenge. He thought again of the women and the children scrambling into the hills. The Tejanos could never kill them all. He was the one remaining *Par-riah-boh* of the Penateka. If his people ever needed him, they needed him now. "Where should we go?" he asked.

"Wherever you can."

Chapter Twenty-Five

Kills White Bear circled his rearing horse, whooped loudly, then dashed for the cover of the cedar breaks. Remy leaned low against the stallion's neck and followed. "I'm comin', Kills White Bear!" he hollered in Spanish. "You hear me? I'm comin'!"

The cedar boughs stung his face, but it was nothing to him. When Remy cleared the break, he saw that the Comanche had crossed a little flat and was headed for the river. Remy swung hard to the east to cut him off.

When Remy's horse plunged in the river, Kills White Bear turned and whipped his own mount forward in a splash of white water and foam. Remy's horse moaned, attempting to drink between loud blowing, but Remy whipped it hard against its neck. "If you've ever loved me, you gotta run!"

The stallion stumbled on the clay bank that rose from the river and went down hard. Remy held fast to its back. "Git up, now! Yah!" The animal staggered to its slipping feet, shook the clay from its coat and stumbled over the driftwood and vines that choked its path.

Once out of the bottom, there was nothing but open prairie for better than two miles, Remy guessed. Here he would catch him. He raked the ribs of the stallion so sharply with his spurs that he knew he'd torn its hide. He would make it up, he thought. After he caught that Indian, the horse could rest for a month. Quelepe would mix up some salve. The best of Remy's grain stores would be his.

Remy and the stallion shot across the open flat. The animal seemed to understand and responded. Together they closed on Kills White Bear. When Remy could see the drops of sweat slipping down the bones of Kills White Bear's back, he raised the Colt straight-armed and fired. Nothing. The second shot only clicked and he cursed it. He thought he saw a tuft of horse hair blow free from the hip on the third, but the Indian pony ran on. The fourth shot was rushed and therefore wasted. For the fifth, he would wait until he was close enough to powder burn the bastard's skin.

He heard a rattle in his horse's chest, but Remy was too near to quit. He lashed the horse once more with his free hand. The horse screamed but ran on.

Kills White Bear reached the end of the flat and shot uphill for a stand of live oaks. The shift in elevation broke his momentum; Remy practically stuck the barrel of the pistol in the Indian's back. He cocked the hammer one last time and screamed at the man he would kill. Before he could pull the trigger, the stallion fell.

Remy flew over its neck, and smashed hard on the earth. He jumped up and aimed the pistol again, but it was too late. Kills White Bear had passed into the safety of the trees.

Remy ran to his horse. "Git up, now, dammit! A little more and we got 'im! Don't fail me!" Remy jerked the reins but the horse refused to rise. It continued to lie on its side, pawing at him with his front leg as if to apologize for its weakness. When Remy saw how badly it was hurt, he forgot all about the Comanche chief and knelt beside it. He saw bloody foam bubble from its nostrils and mouth. Its eyes were bloodshot and glassy. It breathed deeply, broken. Remy knew the vessels in its lungs had burst from the heat and the pressure. It would soon drown in its own blood.

Remy stroked its head until the animal grew still. He said the same thing over and over. "I'm sorry. It's my fault."

The last shot in the revolver entered the horse's brain and it died instantly. It was the second friend he'd lost in the course of an hour. Not once had those sad eyes blamed him.

Chapter Twenty-Six

Remy limped into camp and let the saddle slip from his aching shoulder. The others sat around the fire, telling stories of what they'd done that day. He learned that although there were many Rangers wounded, there were but two killed. One white man and Fuqua's "Meskin." Remy saw that Picosa's body had been wrapped in calico cloth, soaked through with blood from his head and chest. The sight of it chilled him.

The soldiers told him that they had counted close to ninety Comanche bodies. There were more out there some-wheres, they told him, but they saw no point in looking. The dead were left where they fell.

"If'n you need another horse, Captain," one of the younger men said, "there's plenty to be had. Mules, too. The folks the Injuns stole 'em from don't need 'em any-more."

"I'll ride Picosa's," Remy said quietly, reaching for the coffee pot.

"He was one pretty fair Meskin, I'd say, Captain Fuqua."

Remy cut his eyes at the youth. "He was a man, son. And don't let me hear nobody say no diff'rent."

In the silence that followed, Remy heard the clink of a whiskey bottle tipped against his tin coffee cup. He nodded in thanks. Cold cornbread soon followed and he nibbled it slowly. He heard commotion in the thicket behind him.

"What's all that racket?" he asked no one.

"Oh, them Tonks is all fired up to beat hell," a Bastrop man answered. "I've been over there twice to shut 'em up, but they won't hear of it."

"Let 'em be," Remy said. "It's their right. They fought like hell. They ain't got much to celebrate anymore."

Remy asked for one more sip of whiskey, and the man offered him the jug. "For Diego," he said, and Remy thanked him again.

"For Diego," Remy repeated, and he drifted off alone in the direction of the Tonkawa.

It was a sight that surprised him when he thought nothing else could. Designs smeared in blood covered sweating, tat-tooed bodies as they danced around a roaring fire. Remy stood and watched, listening to crack of the fire. Placido, chief of the Tonkawa, saw him and motioned for him to sit near. Remy did so, as he had once with Maguara in what he knew now were simpler times. He took his place as Placido studied him in silence.

"Why the sadness in your eyes, Fuqua?" he finally asked him in Spanish. "Our enemy was defeated today. None of my warriors fell. Many Comanche scalps hang from our lances. The Tonkawa came on foot, but tomorrow they'll leave on fine Comanche horses."

Remy thought about how to respond. With the Indians he could speak openly and there would be no shame. It was the feature he admired most about them. They were whole men, who expressed their joys and their sorrows before each other. Tears flowed when they should, and Remy felt his own coming.

He spoke in Spanish. "Fuqua was born angry into a cold world. Winter by winter it grew worse. Now that he's a man, it is a rage. His gray hair comes and all he thinks of is revenge. It's a disease that dooms him and all of those near."

Placido nodded slowly, his eyes glistening against the roar of the flames and said, "Tell me more, great warrior."

Remy took a hard slug of the whiskey and went on. "Once Fuqua was the friend of the Comanche. He lived in his place, the Comanche in theirs. There was peace between us. Then the Comanche came to Fuqua's camp and killed his children and stole his wife. When he won her again, she was with Kills White Bear's child. Since that time, Fuqua's hated this man like no other and he swore to kill him at all costs. This was what Fuqua was thinking of when the war cry went up this day. In his anger, he looked only for his enemy and not for his friends. When he looked back, Fuqua lost a man he held dear to his heart, and then his favorite horse through his own foolishness, and Kills White Bear still lives. There can be no victory, Placido, in such loss."

Placido puffed the pipe and handed it to him. "In my time," the old chief said, "there would have been two hundred warriors around the fire to celebrate the scalp dance. Now there are but fourteen. Placido is pleased to offer these young warriors victory, but his heart, like Fuqua's, is also black. Placido knows the white men killed his people. Our children die young coughing from strange diseases that choke out their breath. Our land is gone. Placido knows there's no future for the Tonkawa. What we were, we will never be. In his heart, he hates the whites." He paused to consider what he'd said. "Is this wrong, Fuqua?" Placido asked.

"No," Remy answered. "Fuqua has the blood of two worlds, and lived happiest in yet a third. He feared the

whites, and ran from them. But they soon caught up with
him and destroyed his world, and forced him to live again
in theirs. His eyes have seen the evil of the whites. Placido
is not wrong to hate them. In his heart, Fuqua hates
them, too."

"And yet," Placido continued, "when the whites came to
Placido's camp and said, 'Come with us to make war on
the Comanche,' he was glad to do it. As much as he hated
the whites, he hated the Comanche more. His warriors
came running and killed many. Old Placido took two scalps
of his own."

"It was the same for Fuqua," Remy said. "He smelled
the blood and was drawn to it."

Remy could see the old chief understood. But Placido
told him that even in victory he had not forgotten the pain
of loss. It followed him like a shadow as he stepped across
the graves of his own young sons. Once, he said, the Tonkawa planted crops under the sun and spent their days
playing with children. The Tonkawa had enemies, yes, but
they had many friends and relatives. Their thread was
strong and tight. Life was rich and unspooked game was
everywhere. None of this was so anymore.

With the Spanish, Placido said, came continual war. It
was unholy, unnatural, unceasing. When the Spanish left,
the Méxicanos came. And in their wake the whites, and
they were the worst. Tonkawa fields were left untended
and their children screamed for food. Always, he said, the
Tonkawa were busy on the warpath. Everywhere they went,
they found rifles raised against them. Blood flowed in each
of the four seasons. There was no cycle anymore, only del-
uge and death. It became, he said sadly, the way of the
world.

Remy drew hard on the jug and passed it to Placido,
who was grateful. "Fuqua is tired, Placido," Remy said.
"Where can his body find peace?"

Placido said that when he was Fuqua's age, he searched
high and low for such a quiet place. While looking, he
found only war. Many Tonkawa fell. Those who rode the
warpath with Placido rode no more. He had but two hand-
fuls of warriors around his fire, and to these he clung with

all the power that remained in his failing arms. It would not be long, he knew, before these too would slip away.

In this country of war, he said, hatred sustained them as corn and melons once did. Placido could see that it had sustained Fuqua as well. What choice do they have in this place where their long thread unravels and the earth stands still in darkness? To survive is victory now, and the great warrior Fuqua had won another day. The cost meant nothing because all men must die. The spirits of his dead brothers do not complain. It would be an honor to die with Fuqua and all living men knew it. Those who have fallen knew it, too. Fuqua, he said, was right to live as he had.

Remy thought a moment before answering. "Fuqua hears Placido's words. They comfort him. But the night is long and lonely. Where six men once stood, now Fuqua stands alone. Those that died in the struggle were his brothers. They followed Fuqua and they are no more. The fire of his anger has consumed him until only ashes remain. His heart is black with grief."

Placido told him that his suffering is what made Remy what he was. Pain was everything in a man, and Placido and Fuqua were great men. The blade of the knife must be burned before it will hold its edge. But this, he said, should be done one time only and then the knife should be sheathed. If left in the fire, even the finest steel would be ruined. The time had come, he said, for Fuqua to step away from the flames and live. War was a young man's game, and Fuqua was no longer a young man.

Placido said he knew the sun was setting on the Tonkawa. They would soon go to their fate from which they could never turn back, each with a rifle in one hand, and a tomahawk in the other. It would be war to the very end, and rightly so. He had no regrets, and he was not afraid. Their way of life was worth dying for. Placido and his warriors, he said, would soon die screaming.

Placido said that he believed Remy traveled the same narrowing path, but for different and strange reasons. The Tonkawa were battling outside demons while Fuqua fought with those within. Fuqua said he hated white men, and in saying so he hated what he was. If this were true, peace could come for every warrior, but it would never come for

Fuqua. His enemies, the Comanche, would soon die as the Tonkawa were dying. It was but a matter of time. Who, Placido asked, would Fuqua fight then?

Fuqua, Placido said, was a white man in a white world. He clasped his hands together and said that the two should naturally mesh as his fingers did. Peace would come for Fuqua, but would Fuqua embrace it? This was the choice he must make. If he continued to live like the Tonkawa, he would die like the Tonkawa. The time had come to set his anger aside and leave Kills White Bear to his own fate. There was, he said, no other way. Fuqua's wife and remaining children were waiting for him. He must turn away from the fire and go.

Remy sat before Placido, pondering what he said. The wind blew cool after the evening rain, and Remy breathed the clean air deeply. "Fuqua knows a wise man when he hears one," Remy said. "He's not heard many. He'll do what Placido suggests."

"Good," Placido said. "This pleases me." Then he nodded toward his whirling warriors. "Tonight Placido does not celebrate the death of the Comanche as much as he honors the dead among his own nation. Dance with us, Fuqua, in honor of those lost to you. Those were good days you shared together. Thank the Great Spirit for the opportunity to gain honor and still walk the Earth Mother with your pride and a beating heart. There are few that have seen what you've seen and still live. You are a man. And you have the strength to walk away from war. The years bring wisdom. Let this be your guide now."

Placido handed Remy the jug, and he tipped it back. "Dance with us, and remember what we were when the earth was young. Restore your spirit for the struggles to come. Take heart, Fuqua, for the night is coming. And in darkness, there is the peace you seek. Placido wishes you good years between now and then. They are there for you if you want them. For you, there is the promise of joy. Dance with the Tonkawa tonight, Fuqua, and then tomorrow leave the Tonkawa behind. You'll not hear us weep."

Placido signaled a warrior, who soon came to him with a piece of steaming meat. "Eat, Fuqua," he said. "It'll give you strength and courage."

The old chief watched as he bit it. Pork, he thought. They'd butchered a hog. It had the flavor of oak and the aroma restored his hunger. He quickly ate it, and washed the meat down with the whiskey.

Then he took off his shirt and boots and joined the dancers as Placido had urged. They marked him with ashes and blood from an urn as he twirled among them. Soon he no longer cared if any of the other Texians observed him. He was hypnotized by the swaying flames, the warmth of the whiskey, the beat of the drums, the chanting of warriors and his own movement. He danced faster and faster until sweat covered his body. He glanced at Placido, and the old chief was watching him, a big smile on his face. Remy's grief was gone, and he sensed that possibly his rage was gone with it.

When day broke, they were still dancing and Remy was free.

1846

Chapter Twenty-Seven

When Kills White Bear received word of the council, he knew he must go. The *Tahbay-bohs*, the Americanos, had adopted the Tejanos as the Méxicanos once had, and now they wanted to speak with all of their red children about the new law. They had come, Kills White Bear was told, to find peace. He already knew it would be impossible to find.

The Caddo, Wichita, Kichais, Tonkawa and other remnant tribes accepted the new terms without complaint or reservation. What else could they do? They'd bent their knees long ago to the Tejanos. But despite the wars and sickness that had claimed so many of Kills White Bear's generation, the Nemenuh, twenty thousand strong by his estimate, still held most of the southern plains.

But the Penateka had lost their hills. Rangers had pursued them relentlessly after the disaster at Plum Creek, and hundreds more of all ages and sexes died running with wounds in their backs. There was little for Kills White Bear to do but abandon the land of his birth and take his people far to the north, above the Red River, where the other bands were still strong and the Tejanos would not follow.

The *Tahbay-bohs*, through their agent, Neighbors, a man most of the northern Nemenuh trusted, promised hope. He had brought the two commissioners before them, and Kills White Bear, though remaining cautious, was anxious to hear their words in the place the Tejanos called Comanche Peak.

Kills White Bear accepted his gifts graciously, as he saw the other chiefs do, and sat quietly. Then the white men told him what he wanted to hear. The American Father wished them to have their home on the plains as long as the rivers ran and the wind blew. This they could do on certain conditions. They must accept the word of the American Father and submit to his will. Fugitives on the run from the American Father in their country must be turned over to him at his request. White captives must be returned, as well as any horses stolen from the Tejanos. They must trade only with men who held the American Father's papers and no other. And there was one more: they must stay west of Tejano settlements and leave them in peace.

Kills White Bear stood and introduced himself, making it clear that despite his rank he spoke for one man only. He said that they wanted their land above all other things, but the conditions of the American Father would be hard for the civil chiefs to enforce. The young men craved prestige, and the terms for which the American Father asked denied them access to it. Still, he said, these terms could be agreed to if the American Father gave them what the Tejanos never would. There was an end, he explained just as Maguara had once done to him, in moving away from an advancing frontier. The west did not go on forever, as white men seemed to believe. Already the People encroached on each other's hunting grounds. If the American Father truly desired peace, he must draw the line.

The other Nemenuh cheered. But the commissioners hemmed and hawed after Kills White Bear's words were translated. He'd seen that same reaction before whenever any Nemenuh spoke of the line, and he fully expected to see it again when he came to this place. The benefit was that the other chiefs had seen it, too.

He spoke in his own tongue to the other Penateka present. "Do you see, my brothers? It's like Kills White Bear told you. The Americans and the Tejanos are one and the same." And then to Neighbors in Spanish, "Tell them to come again when they have something to offer. Kills White Bear's ears are always open."

He left the trinkets where they lay on the ground and mounted. Without a word, Little Eagle and the other Wasp warriors followed.

Chapter Twenty-Eight

Kills White Bear led his people in search of the buffalo. The Wasps found them west of the Canadian River, in the high plains well above the Llano Estacado, and there the Wasps stayed. Kills White Bear's vision never once urged him to return to the San Sabá Hills where he knew the Rangers waited with fingers on the guns that shot forever. He hated the Tejanos as every Penateka did, but now he feared and respected them as the buffalo did a pack of wolves.

He thought the American commissioners wanted to draw the line. He could see it in their eyes. Something he did not understand must have prevented them from doing so. He assumed that they, too, feared the wrath of the Tejanos. It was, most likely, as it had been in the time of the Méxicanos. The devil Tejanos were beyond anyone's control. In the absence of signs and oracles, Kills White Bear would leave them in peace as a wise man does the hornets' nest.

Kills White Bear sheltered his people in the summer warmth of the high plains' grassy bosom. The waters of the

Canadian were still sweet and cool. Despite their losses and their grief, they still lived as they always had. He'd heard that the other chiefs present at the American Father's talks had touched the pen to paper. Though he refused, it was just as well that the others had. There was peace on the plains.

The war parties of other bands rested with them that summer. When Kills White Bear learned that they intended to raid the Tejanos, he shamed them in another direction. It was too late, he told them, for that. The American Father would not like it, and the Penateka would certainly pay for any blood the young warriors drew. The Tejanos had learned to hunt down and kill the Nemenuh, but they still could not distinguish one band from the other. Neighbors had asked that they give peace a chance and let tempers cool. If war came again, it would certainly be the other bands' responsibility. The Wasps were spent. In the meantime, the young warriors could raid the Méxicanos, as even Neighbors himself had suggested, and they would have their blood and honor. The wounded Penateka could live in peace, grow strong again on the fresh liver, marrow and tongue of the buffalo, and wait for another day. The wisdom of this even the rash, young men understood.

That summer made sixteen for Little Eagle. He came to Kills White Bear and asked his permission to go south with the raiding party.

"And who would lead?" Kills White Bear asked.

"Round Mountain," Little Eagle said.

"I'd follow an armadillo before I'd follow him," Kills White Bear told him, looking down his nose. "Make no mistake, my son. The man's a fool."

The boy frowned and kicked at the ground with his bare foot. "I no longer wish to stand in my father's shadow," Little Eagle said. Then he turned to Kills White Bear and stared. "I seek honor of my own."

"And what's your animal spirit, young warrior?" Kills White Bear asked. Little Eagle's frown turned to shame.

"I have none," his son admitted.

Kills White Bear thought back to the time of his own quest. There were no longer elder shamans among his band. The old mystics were gone. Younger men had taken their places as Kills White Bear encouraged them to do, but they were not proficiently skilled in the old ways to earn Kills White Bear's trust. He knew a young warrior's quest could not happen as it'd happened for him. He'd often pondered what he should do when Little Eagle's turn came. Now that it had, he decided the only thing to do was share his own medicine with this boy he loved so dearly. If successful, it would be his greatest gift.

He put his hand on Little Eagle's shoulder and squeezed gently. "I know a place in the old country," he told him. "Get your things and we'll go there together."

"It's too dangerous," Little Eagle protested. "You're the *Par-riah-boh*. The People need you."

"The Tejanos will never touch me," he said. "It was promised to me when I was your age. And if you come, they'll never touch you. Come with me to our home."

Kills White Bear was glad to see that familiar valley, even though the sun had scorched the hills brown. He rode first to a bluff, where they could see that the country never ended beneath that cobalt blue sky. He made an offering of smoked meat and water, and then knelt to pray. When he finished, he opened his eyes to see that Little Eagle was watching him.

"What're you doing?" the boy asked.

"This place has special meaning to me," Kills White Bear explained. "My wife and child are buried here. They died when I was young and happiest. I prayed to their spirits to look after you, my adopted son, because you walk beside me in my own child's place. I love you as I loved him."

Instinctively, Little Eagle reached for him and they embraced. Kills White Bear felt the stout shoulders of his son.
They were now taller than his own, and felt more solid.
This young Méxicano had mastered boys' games, the hunt,
and the horse. He rode for hours in the heat as the Nemenuh warriors do, without complaint. It had been years since
the boy spoke of his former life. Nemenuh memories had
crowded out the white. Little Eagle had grown true. This
boy he'd raised was now a man, with a man's agenda. There
were so many other things for Kills White Bear to worry
about these days. But the boy had no grandfather to teach
him as Cold Knife had taught him. He regretted how he'd
neglected Little Eagle. The wars had been the cause. He
would attempt to make up for it now that there was peace.

He pulled away gently. "Are you ready?" Kills White
Bear asked him.

"Yes."

"It'll not be easy."

"Nothing of any value ever is," Little Eagle answered,
and it pleased him. This boy was wise beyond his years.
They shared no blood, it was true, but they were one in
the same. He realized he'd been wrong to curse his fate
when it had blessed him with this boy's love. Nothing
meant more.

He pulled his medicine bag from under his breechcloth
and emptied its contents on the ground. He went through
each one and explained their significance, carefully replacing them all. Little Eagle took them for his own.

Then Kills White Bear drew a map in the dust. On it,
he marked the location of Wolf Eyes' grave. He explained
the procedure as the shaman Three Bears had once explained it to him. Little Eagle must bathe in the river to
cleanse himself and then go to the little bluff, stopping four
times only to smoke. He would stay four days in that place
without food or water. He should rise each morning and
sit facing the sun. He was to face west and watch it set.
Sleep if he could.

"What am I waiting for?" he asked impatiently.

Kills White Bear smiled at his anxious son. "For whatever comes," he said. "I'll be here, praying for you. Go
and do as I've told you, and believe."

For five days Kills White Bear waited. At first, he thought
mostly of his wife and the early days when he was happy.
That quickly turned to his troubles with the Tejanos. He
knew he'd inherited Maguara's world, with Maguara's
problems, and despite his prayers for a solution and the
hours he spent chanting with the comforting breeze of the
San Sabá valley blowing through his braids, no answer
came.

When he wasn't thinking of his people, he thought of his
son. He knew better than anyone how dangerous a vision
quest could be. His heart could not afford to lose another
as dear to him as Little Eagle.

When five days turned to six, Kills White Bear could
stand it no longer. He mounted his horse, crossed the river
and rode west. Rising again on the high ground, he
searched the horizon. His heart leaped when he saw the
lone form of his son threading his way through the cedar
brakes and tall grass, and he dashed toward him with the
treated stomach of a buffalo sloshing full of water in his
hand.

The boy was crying. He handed him the water and told
the boy to dry his tears. Despite his obvious thirst, he did
not drink. Kills White Bear knew without asking that it
obviously had not gone well. He was now worried that his
son's blood would not allow him the last and greatest step
toward Nemenuh manhood.

"Don't concern yourself, Little Eagle," he consoled him.
"Sometimes it takes more than one attempt for the vision
to come. We'll come again under the next moon."

"It came," he answered curtly. "You named me well. I
am White Eagle, with white feathers covering a Nemenuh
soul." He turned to Kills White Bear and showed him the
claw marks across his heart. "It was the eagle's gift," he
explained. "In exchange, I offered my life to the People.
I'll fight the Tejanos for the land with my last breath. We'll

either win the struggle or die. The eagle does not know the outcome."

Kills White Bear was thrilled at the news. Few were offered the eagle's spirit. He saw hope in his son's vision but was confused by the boy's tears.

"Why then do you weep, White Eagle?" he asked him tenderly. "We all must die. If you fall in battle against the Tejanos there is no reason to shed tears. It brings honor to your spirit. Our ancestors will welcome you to the Happy Place."

The boy wiped his tears from his face, and in doing so, Kills White Bear sensed his resolve return. "White Eagle will fight the Tejanos at his father's side for many winters to come. Many will fall to his knife. I'll die a war leader of the People. It is promised."

Kills White Bear was relieved to hear these words, but they failed to explain the boy's darkness. "Can you tell me what troubles you, then?" he asked.

"No," White Eagle said. "But I can say this. It won't be a white bullet that finds me."

Chapter Twenty-Nine

For ten years Sam Houston had courted the Americans. Twice in official capacity as the President of the Republic, and then God knows how many ways in shadier deals out of the public eye. It was in here, Remy knew, that Houston operated best.

In his first term, a desperate Houston had begged for admission into the American Union, only to be coldly rebuffed by the prevailing northern abolitionists. Lamar's administration turned away and looked west, dreaming of a Texian empire. But Houston's vision had never faded. In his second term, he'd treated the Americans like a jilted lover. It was their turn for desperation.

Remy understood that slavery was a weak argument against the American annexation of Texas. The truth was that the plantations were fated to remain east of the Colorado River. The hill country and the plains were too arid for cotton. Where slaves already worked, he knew, was where they'd stay.

But if the Americans wanted to expand from sea to sea, which was the talk Remy heard, they would have to incorporate Texas. If they did not, Texas would soon rival them for control of the Northern Hemisphere. War between the two, it was believed, was inevitable. Better to accept Texas as she was, warts and all, than to fight her later when she'd become as powerful as she promised. This, Remy believed, was at the core of the renewed and feverish negotiations.

Houston played both ends against the middle, of which Remy knew he was master. He sat with the Mexicans in one room, and with the Americans in another. Meanwhile, the British and the French waited in the wings. Americans were simultaneously arguing with the British over the Oregon territory. They could not bear European influence of any kind rooting just across the Sabine. The British, of course, were the worst. When the Americans caught wind that the British were stalling their negotiations, they, sabers rattling, again hinted of war with Texas.

In the end, Houston struck a favorable deal that had no equal in the American Union. No other state had entered as an independent Republic. No other territory had entered with half of its domain unsettled, and hostile tribes still sovereign on land claimed by the state. And no other state had presented itself with two disputed borders. In annexing Texas, Remy knew, the Americans had certainly annexed war.

Remy valued the advent of stable currency, good roads and reliable mail service. Some of the public debt was paid in the bargain, and Texas still controlled its most precious enticement, its exhaustive public land. But what Remy valued most in voting for annexation was that the federal government was now responsible for the defense of Texas. For him, that was the most attractive feature.

War with Mexico was inevitable. The Río Grande had always been disputed as the international boundary. Already in that year, American troops gathered below the Nueces to provoke hostilities and settle the question once and for all. In this, owing in part to Placido's advice some years before, Remy knew he would take no part. What interested him more, however, was that now the Comanche were Uncle Sam's problem.

American Indian policy was clear enough to him. Andrew Jackson had banished the eastern remnants to the wilds of the west, a region labeled on their maps as the "Great American Desert." It was thought that there was room for all out there where no white men lived, and there always would be. The great plains east of the Rockies would belong to the savages forever, and who would care?

Without having to ask, Remy knew that the Americans expected the Texas state government to cede the western buffalo range to the Comanche. This policy was formed without a working knowledge of the Texian mind. Eastern editorials tended to view the horse Indians as noble savages. Texians, who had fought them for decades, maintained no such illusions. Remy knew better than most that they had lost two hundred lives a year to the Comanche since the Indian wars had begun in 1836.

Through ranching, they could settle territory the Americans assumed to be uninhabitable, and moreover, they already were. Texas retained sovereignty over all of their public land, and they simply refused to designate one acre of it to the hated Comanche. Instead, the state government opened it to settlement, and the stout-hearted responded. There would be no reserve for the Comanche to use as a sanctuary for their bloody raids. Easterners did not understand how much blood had been spilled or how deeply the hatred ran as a direct consequence.

As far as any Texian was concerned, the Comanche could leave or they could die. The hill country and the plains beyond would yield to the bull and the plow soon enough. Remy knew this would lead again to war, and with annexation the Americans were obliged to respond. If they did not, Remy knew the Texians would. On the frontier it was just that simple, just that vicious, and just that cold.

But first there were the Mexicans.

Remy had traveled to Houston to file papers on new land, see his attorney and attend to some business with the brokerage house. There were no banks in Texas. The papers said there were now about two hundred thousand residents of the new state, and more were coming every day. It was, as far as Remy was concerned, the biggest mess he'd ever seen.

To him, cities were always miserable, and Houston was a miserable city. The people there were loafing, money-grabbing, murdering swindlers. None of them could've lasted a week on the frontier and obviously never intended to try. Gangs of whiskey-drinking, tobacco-chewing, apparently motherless boys ran through the muddy streets taunting passersby. Next to homes, churches, law offices, general stores, surveyors, wheelwrights, tanners, saddlers, and cotton brokerages stood innumerable saloons, grog shops, whore houses, and shanties where unshaven, wretchedly clothed and stinking drunks slept it off. There was no end to the gamblers—"knights of the green cloth" as Remy called them—or the charlatans, the fleecers, counterfeiters, thieves, and the pistol-toting, hotheaded, frontier scum that always followed the farmers after the land was conquered. For them, violence was not so much a necessity as it was a sport. Remy noticed a tote board to wager on the number of murders to occur in a week, and he had his confirmation. This, to him, was what cities meant. It reminded him of what New Orleans had been like when he was a boy, only he was certain it was far worse here.

For a rancher, however, prosperity meant money. The price of beef was high and rising. Immigrants bought his stock, and with annexation, new markets opened in the east. For the most part he bartered, as everyone did, but he used every scarce dollar he got his hands on to buy more land just to make sure he never became neighbors with the shiftless strangers that surrounded him.

Beatriz still talked of California, where she believed life remained as it once was before they'd lost Rancho de la Cruz. She'd accompanied him to Houston, riding near for comfort as they passed by the riff-raff of a hungry city. He knew without asking that she shared his view of its wickedness. A new breed had come to Texas. Austin would've been appalled at the sight of the unregulated, thoughtless, dingy sprawl. Texas would never be the same.

They rode to the *El Conquistador,* the finest hotel of which Remy knew, and stabled the horses. He went ahead and found his wife a cool glass of water. He sat her on the sofa while he made final arrangements with the clerk. Remy paid cash and was sliding the bills across the counter when he caught the man's eyes roaming his wife.

"What's the problem, feller?" Remy asked.

"The woman with you's a Meskin, sir?"

He turned briefly to look at Beatriz, and then back at the man. "You're far too astute to be a clerk, sir. What's that got to do with any goddamn thing?"

"We don't allow Meskins here, sir," he said formally, his eyes fixed on his counter.

Remy signed the register and spun it around for the clerk to see. He saw the man's pupils dart along the words he'd angrily scribbled. "Captain Remy Fuqua, Ranger Company, Bastrop County." When he was certain the clerk had finished, he slid his coat back over the horns of his Colts, replaced his wallet, and said, "I believe you'll consider an exception this time, won't ya, son?" His eyes bored through the clerk's.

He hesitated, and then managed a nervous smile. "I don't see why not, Captain."

"It's good that we agree," Remy said coldly. "Fetch my wife's things up to our room."

"I'll call for the boy."

Remy never moved back from the counter. "No boy. You."

"It's not my job, sir."

"It is now. Git your chincy ass a-shakin' up them stairs 'fore I stick a boot up it."

The astonished clerk did so without further delay, and Remy followed with Beatriz. The man placed their things, poured clean water into the bowl, and set out fresh towels. Remy asked him to wait just a moment as he reached into his pockets. "I got a tip for ya," he said. When he pulled out his hand, it was empty. "There's plenty of Mexicans in Texas. They was here 'fore you, and what's more, they're a whole lot better. You point that long, bony nose down at my wife again, I'll snap it clean off." Remy snatched open the door. "Now git, hoopsack! And stay scarce!"

The clerk shot out the door just ahead of Remy's foot. Remy wasn't as quick as he once was. He turned to Beatriz, who was washing her face and hands in the basin, and grinned. She came to Remy and hugged him.

"I'm sorry about that, *querida,*" he told her in Spanish.

"Oh, I don't care," she sighed. "Let's just do what we've got to do and leave this place. I hate it here."

He understood. Then she asked him, "I thought you said you'd be avoiding trouble from now on."

He smiled once more. "That," he said, "was no trouble."

He suggested that she rest and then prepare for dinner.

"Where could we go?" she asked him morosely.

"Anywhere we want," he answered, but she said it wasn't worth the aggravation. Bring something back, she told him, they'd eat it here where they wouldn't be bothered.

He went out and tended to his business, his wife's lament etched into his mind. When he returned he was fumbling with half a dozen thick, bulky books.

"What's this, Remy?" she asked him.

He laid them out one by one. "*Chitty on Pleading*, Martin's *Law of Nations,* Coke's *Institutes,* Brown's *Civil Laws* . . . an' this last little jewel here is Remy's new novel. I'll have to send the wagon back for the Texas Statutes. The bastards've already filled eight volumes."

"Law books!" Beatriz said, astonished.

"I'm gotta sit for the bar, honey," he explained. "I figure it's the only way."

"Only way for what?"

"You can't just hang these sons of bitches no more, Beatriz. First you got to try 'em, then you hang 'em. I'm gonna learn how." He threw back the drapes to reveal the clutter and clamor of the streets. "We can't leave Texas, Beatriz. It's our home. The thing to do is watch after it." He thumped one of the books. "Who knows? Might even run for office."

"*¡Dios mío!*" she exclaimed, exasperated. "A lawyer in the family! The shame, Remy! I'm glad Don Carlos didn't live to see this happen. It'd certainly have killed him."

"Maybe," Remy admitted, and again he looked out the window. "But that down there is part of what did." He sat down on the sofa and opened the first book. "Let's see. Page one. My goodness, this is small print. I should've known."

1849

Chapter Thirty

One March morning, Remy saddled one of his horses—it no longer mattered much which one—and rode over the ranch. Remy was now forty-three, and he was reminded of the cost of every difficult year by the throbbing joints of his stiff bones. He could no longer stomach the fire of a stallion. He rode geldings now. Cristóbal Picosa, Diego's oldest son, was at his side. Joaquin, whom Remy called "Jack," made three.

Remy dismounted and knelt to the ground to feel of the grass. "About another week or so, Cristóbal, and we can move 'em. If'n we get more rain, we'll need to drive the herd out to the thickets. When the heat plays out the high range, they can fall back to the river and summer on the lower pastures. That'll get us by till fall, and we'll go from there." He turned and faced the young vaquero. "That the way you see it?"

"Sí, Don Remy," Cristóbal answered. *"Está bien."*

" 'Fore ya'll drive 'em up there, course you'll need to cut out the yearlins' and brand the ones that ain't marked yet. Next month, after they get a chance to fatten up on the spring grass, we'll drive 'em north to Missouri. By the way, how's your English?"

"So-so," Cristóbal admitted, tilting his flat palm.

"You need to work on it, son. There's a good reason for it."

"And what would that be, Don Remy?"

" 'Cause you're the new mayordomo, that's why. Senator Houston got me appointed judge. I'm a goddamn politician now, may God help me. I got no time to look after things here like I should. You're takin' your daddy's place." Remy enjoyed Cristóbal's surprise.

"I didn't expect this, Don Remy," the boy said.

"You're twenty-five or so now, ain't ya? I was eighteen when me and my cousin started workin' this place, and neither one of us knew the first thing about it. We made out all right, and you'll do a hell of a lot better. You know the land and the cattle. There's no better vaquero in the county, and no man rides like you." Remy grasped the young man's hand. "Your Pa'd be proud of you, Cristóbal. He was my teacher, and now I'm yours. I'm happy to do right by you. You earned it. When we get back, you move your family into my old cabin. It's still the best one on the place for my money."

"Thank you, Don Remy," Cristóbal said. "I'll do my best."

"I know you will." Cristóbal's face looked pale. "What troubles you?" Remy asked him.

"Will the cattle buyers not take advantage of me, Don Remy?"

"Well, sure they will. They'll skin ya good first time or two just like they skinned me and everybody else in creation. They can't help it no more than a snake's got to slither. You'll learn better soon enough." The confidence Remy showed in Cristóbal did not comfort him.

"I mean, will they do business with a Mexican?" he asked.

"They will if they want my cattle," Remy quipped, "which they do. That's one of the reasons why I took the bench, son. I'm gonna make a place for Mexicans in Texas. It won't be easy, but it's the right thing to do. You belong here."

Then he turned to someone who maybe did not. He noticed that Jack wasn't paying the least bit of attention to what was going on. It was time to get his interest.

It had been years since he was openly cold to Joaquin. Remy was ashamed of his behavior in those days. He chalked it up to harder times and tried his best to make amends. He'd given Joaquin his name and introduced him in town and everywhere else as his son when he knew well enough that even the thickest brute knew better.

Remy believed that he'd spent enough time with Joaquin for a natural bond to develop. Remy saw no reason to fault himself when it didn't. Remy nurtured him as best he could, but though he called him his son he couldn't love him as one. He just couldn't. When his mouth said "son," his mind flashed the image of Carlito. Nothing Remy could do would change it.

Beatriz showered the boy with affection, as did Quelepe. This, Remy figured, was compensation for the cooler quality of his share. Remy had promised years ago to care for Joaquin as his own, and even Beatriz understood that he'd kept his word the best that he could, all things considered. She'd come to accept Remy's remote relationship with his adopted son. She, above all others, understood how much effort it took for Remy even to be civil when Joaquin, like any child, was mischievous, openly misbehaved or otherwise disappointed his father. Remy never raised his hand against the boy even though there were plenty of times when he thought he should. As the years passed, it was enough for Beatriz that there was peace between them.

As he grew older, Joaquin took on more of Beatriz's outward physical features. He'd grown tall, strong and handsome, with glistening black eyes and shiny dark hair.

He had good Hispanic color and grace. Remy sensed a hint
of Don Carlos when the sun caught him right. This was
providence, Remy thought, because although Mexicans
were not readily accepted in many corners of white Texian
society, the Comanche was an eternal outcast.

But the boy's soul, Remy believed, was Comanche. This,
more than anything, made him think that expecting the
child to adapt completely to their life was hopeless. Remy
saw a wildness in him that his mother's blood had not diluted. He did like to read, but there all socialization ended.
Joaquin thought more of hunting deer than ranching cattle.
He learned to ride like a vaquero, and that was the extent
of his interest in their world. He spoke English and Spanish
perfectly, but almost never used either. Instead, he practiced yelping like a turkey hen and bleating like a fawn,
among other sounds. All were reproduced with amazing
accuracy.

As soon as he learned to shoot, Joaquin was out after
game. He needed none of Remy's instruction, he just
seemed to know how. He rose hours before dawn and rode
alone, barefoot and shirtless, through the open country and
in the cedar brakes of distant hills. The boy feared nothing
in the wild. He would go all day without eating, preferring
to bathe in the river rather than use one of the family tubs.
He took a natural dislike to the odor of soap. Beatriz tamed
him as one tamed a raccoon—with regular nibbles of good
food in the palm of an open hand until a pattern was established. Joaquin would eat, kiss his mother sweetly on the
cheek, tell Quelepe of a large buck he'd seen and then go
again and hunt until he'd killed it. Racks of Joaquin's ant-
lers covered the barn. He came indoors only to sleep, and
only then in the winter. Many nights he sat by a fire with
his nose in a book out on the range beyond the sound of
his mother's anxious voice. Remy had to send the vaqueros
out to fetch him. He was never easy to find.

Beatriz must've sensed his wildness as well, and asked
sweetly for Remy to spend more time with the boy if he
possibly could. He was young, she said, and could be
molded. Of course, Remy acquiesced. This morning's ride
was part of that. He would do anything for her, and he

554   *David Marion Wilkinson*

certainly did not dislike the boy. For Beatriz's sake, Remy would try and bring him around.

Remy only knew one way to approach the problem. He would rely on the same methods by which he was raised. Though harsh, he judged them effective. If nothing else, the Scotch-Irish knew how to make a man out of a boy. If was for his own good if Joaquin were to survive in a changing world.

Remy reached over, grabbed Jack by the ear and spun him around. "Look here, boy. You watch this man and learn. *¿Comprendes?* Life ain't all huntin' and horse ridin' out in the hills like it's been up to now. You're gonna learn about them cattle and the farm. And you'll learn how to work, too. I grant ya that."

"Will I be your foreman someday, Captain?" the boy asked.

"You'll be what you'll be," Remy answered. "And I don't know what that is just yet. You've been behind your mama's skirt long enough. You should've been out on the range earnin' your keep long before now. But you're mine now and playtime's over. You're gonna work with the vaqueros, sleep with the vaqueros, and eat with the vaqueros till some of it rubs off. Book learnin' comes at night on your own time. You'll spend Sundays with your Ma and Quelepe. The rest of the time you keep your ass up, your head down, and your hands on leather, iron, or hide. Cristóbal, here's your jefe, and don't let me hear you ain't pullin' your end. *¿Me entiendes?*"

"*Sí, Captain,*" he said, rubbing his reddened lobe.

"All right then. Let's mount up and go home, boys. Breakfast is waitin'." Then he turned to Joaquin. "And you better eat good, young'n."

Before he spurred his horse, he caught the flash of Cristóbal's necklace. He reached over and grabbed it by its worn leather strand. It was a silver dollar.

"Where'd you get this, Cristóbal?"

"From the devil," he said.

Remy remembered, smiling as he let it go. He'd won the stallion only the week before he'd tossed the boy the coin, but he never knew he'd won Cristóbal at the same time. The world had come full circle, and it warmed him. How

Diego Picosa's life had blessed his. The old mayordomo, Remy thought, lived on in the new. "Might be a few more where that one came from," Remy said. "You wait and see."

Remy thought of the old days on the long ride home.

Chapter Thirty-One

Kills White Bear rode to the edge of the bluff above the Canadian River and looked down. Such a procession he'd not seen before, as White Eagle had warned when he led him there. Kills White Bear looked carefully before he said the word. "Americans," he pronounced, and the others agreed.

It was understood that the American Father had raised his long knife against the Méxicanos and defeated them in their own camp. Neighbors had explained that in the peace that followed, the lands to the west, from the Sabine to the Rockies and the great water beyond, now belonged to the Americans.

This, to Kills White Bear, was nonsense. The land the Americans said they owned was held by the Ute and the Apache, among many others. Though these nations were blood enemies of the Nemenuh and would always be, Kills White Bear admired and respected them. They would not yield their land any more easily than the Nemenuh had—not to the Americans and especially not to the Tejanos, and he knew it was curiously claimed by them both, though one was said to belong to the other. It was the same sort of madness about which the Spanish used to speak and then the Méxicanos that followed them. It meant nothing to him.

Hundreds passed below him. He viewed it as strange and wrong. The treaty provided for no line across which the whites should not step, but the Americans had told them that where no white men lived, no whites should go. These that crossed Nemenuh land did so without permission, in defiance of the agreement. The Americans had said nothing.

Though it appeared that they were only passing through to the west, Kills White Bear was still alarmed and angered.

Who these men were he could not say. They were not soldiers and they were not traders. They had no machines with them for making scars in the earth, they built no silly square lodges. But where grass once grew for the buffalo to graze, the earth lay bare and brown for others to easily follow. Penateka scouts reported that thousands had already passed that spring, and he counted three or four hundred more this day. How many would come tomorrow? How long before some of them decided to stay and the shady line again shifted west and the Nemenuh were no longer welcome?

The warm rays of the sun bathed his cheek as he wondered what should be done. The strangers were wise. They traveled together, tightly bound, all bearing arms. To rush them, he knew, meant disaster, and he could neither afford the loss of his young warriors nor more damage to the already wounded psyches of their wives and children. The People were precious. Forty-eight winters had brought wisdom to Kills White Bear. He understood his greater responsibility all too well.

He decided he would soon go to Neighbors and protest. He would send word to the American Father that his children were not obeying. For three years they'd had peace on the plains. If the American Father could not control the whites, the fourth would see the return of war. The Wasps, he knew, were ready again.

Of this plan, he expected little. The Americans would answer with lies, of course, but it might buy a little time and allow him to understand more about what was happening. He felt certain he could piece something together from the clamor of wagging white tongues.

They would also backtrack the travelers. There might be stragglers which could be overcome easily, or if nothing else, they usually left things behind that told part of their strange story. Any information was welcome, and Kills White Bear was desperate to know all.

He turned his mount east and followed the Canadian. The answer was out there somewhere, and he resolved to find it.

Soon enough they found stragglers. But there was no need to kill them. They were dead and buried in shallow, spiritless graves. He ordered his warriors to unearth them in order to learn the cause of death. Had they killed each other, or had an arrow from one of the other bands pierced these black hearts?

While the young men dug, Kills White Bear rummaged through the discarded wagon. There were pots and pans that he'd not seen before, probably used for cooking. He also found their strange implements, shovels, pickaxes and contraptions that made no sense, and also casks of liquid silver. Then it struck him. He'd seen things like this among the Méxicano camps they'd raided in mountains of Zacatecas. These were the tools of strange men. Such people craved gold and silver like other men breathed air. Somewhere west of the Comanchería they must have found it. It was, he knew, the worst kind of curse. It made fools out of devils, and he understood then that many, many more would be coming before the snow fell that year.

His warriors called his name, and he went to them. The body was laid out and stripped bare. Its hair was brown and the teeth looked strong, but the skin was inconsistently aged and wrinkled. There was no wound on the front side, and when Kills White Bear kicked it over, he saw no wound in back. Disease.

He moved upwind out of caution. Experience taught him to fear, but when he saw no pock marks, the only sign of the white pestilence that he recognized, he was comforted to some degree. Just the same, he would take no chances.

He saw that some of the young men were trying on the man's boots and clothes.

"Leave them," he ordered. "Evil spirits are near. Burn everything and we'll go. Kills White Bear has what he came for."

His party was still some time from camp when the sun fell. Kills White Bear had spent the balance of that afternoon rehearsing what he would say to Neighbors. He should meet with other young civil chiefs of the Wasps, advise them of what he'd seen, and perhaps they'd go together as a show of force.

He pulled out of the line and stopped to look back. The

color of the land at sunset was at its richest, and even in his troubles he had not forgotten. He saw then that one of the young warriors had not obeyed him. He was wearing the shirt of the dead man.

Chapter Thirty-Two

Women brought fresh grilled buffalo meat to his lodge that evening. It was his favorite, and he had felt the pangs of hunger earlier on, but now he turned his head away.

"Does this not please you?" White Eagle asked.

"I don't feel well," he answered. "I'll eat when I rise."

"In that decision father, you're alone," White Eagle said, tearing the first bite with his teeth.

Kills White Bear watched as his son ate ravenously. He heard the smack of White Eagle's lips as he slipped beneath his buffalo robes. The sound of it, along with the acrid aroma of the smoked meat, nauseated him.

"Why do you linger?" he asked his son, irritated. "Do you not have a wife?"

"I do," he answered, his mouth full. "But, I'll stay with you as long as you feel poorly."

"I'm blessed," Kills White Bear said, and he lay down on his robes.

He awoke some time later. His bowels sounded like a gathering storm and there was the immediate urge to discharge them. Before he reached a suitable place, he vomited clear fluid simultaneously with a fierce emission from his bowels. There was nothing strange in what he'd eaten over the past few days, and what he'd just eliminated did not feel or smell right. The odor was ghastly. He went to the fire pit and took a burning ember of oak in order to examine his stools. He found pools of cloudy fluid with strange white particles, like maggots, mixed in. It was odd. He tossed the wood back into the fire on his way to his lodge. He noticed his hands were trembling. The short excursion had exhausted him.

He lay down but could not sleep. His bowels still cramped, but now the rest of his body joined them. A fever fell upon his brow, and his skin felt cold and clammy as sweat beaded from every pore. He put his hand to his heart. It beat rapidly, as if he were running, but also very faint. He felt drained, and when the urge to vomit and defecate came again, as it did so often, he had to crawl out of his lodge. When he felt weakest, he called out to his sleeping son.

White Eagle sprang to his side, and in the darkness he saw him wipe the sleep from his eyes. "What's wrong?"

"I'm sick. Go and find She Denies It and ask her to bring her medicine bag."

When he returned, White Eagle stoked the fire so that they could have light. She Denies It arrived and examined him.

"Your skin is blue, like three others who rode with you. You've eaten something that disagrees."

"I've eaten nothing," he told her, and she held her hand to feel of his breath.

"Strange. You have a fever, but your breath is cold." Then she pressed her palm to his chest. "I feel no beat," she said, "and your skin is freezing." She reached for his robes to cover him but he kicked them off.

"I'm burning up," he complained.

"That's not possible. Rest quietly. I'll see what I can do."

What medicines she gave him he could not keep down. Others sent for her throughout the night, and she went back and forth relentlessly. Kills White Bear sensed her stress. When day broke, his discharges were dark green and he could no longer stand.

She Denies It tried to pour water down his throat, but he did not want it.

"How goes the camp?" he asked, and he heard his own voice tremble like an old man's.

"Many are sick. Some are already dead. The others are leaving."

The news frightened him. "They must not go. The evil

rides on the wind. If they leave, it'll ride with them. They'll take it to the other camps."

"I can't stop them," she said.

"I can," he insisted. "Help me up." Then he turned to his son. "Gather them for me, White Eagle. I must make them understand."

Some came, but they kept their distance. He told them what he'd told She Denies It, and she confirmed to them that the first to fall had ridden with Kills White Bear. Two had not made the night.

One woman stepped forward to speak for the rest. "You're unlucky, Kills White Bear. I'm sure it'll pass soon enough, but I'll not risk your fate. I'm going to my cousin's camp until all is well here. If you live, I'll follow you again."

"Don't go," he urged her, but he fell to his knees and vomited the green mucous to the sound of the crowd's gasps and the women's shrilling. There was no stopping them after they'd seen that. His band scattered to the four winds, and the evil, he feared, traveled with them.

ħ

For seven days and nights, Kills White Bear lay in his lodge while the fever raged. The skin around his bones withered before his eyes, and his ears were full of women's wailing. If he pressed his fingers against his flesh, it remained indented.

White Eagle did not spend one day in sickness. He tended first to his father night and day, and then, at White Bear's request, to the others who had fallen. Soon his own wife, Kicking Bird, succumbed and that was the last Kills White Bear saw of him.

The dead, Kills White Bear was told, were dragged downwind of the camp. Already the stench was overwhelming. There were not enough of the healthy remaining to bury them, and so they lay stacked together in lifeless rows like wood.

In the end, it was worse for his camp than smallpox had ever been. When he was strong enough to walk about his camp, the misery overwhelmed him. A quick count confirmed the worst of his fears. Half of his people lay dead.

And if that was not bad enough, runners from the other bands brought the news to his pounding skull. The evil had hunted them down, too, and killed them as they lay in their lodges.

"How many?" Kills White Bear cried.

"At least half," the runner answered, "including all civil chiefs that I know. The People's grief is great. Come and comfort us when you can. We all look to you."

Kills White Bear felt his body tremble with rage. More than three years of peace had been wasted. Entire families had been wiped out by the whites' silent killer. Three generations died in the course of days and not one shot was fired. This, he knew, was the end, but he could never speak of it.

The runner waited for his reply.

"I'll see to my own dead first, my friend. Then I'll come to you and yours. Tell the People that Kills White Bear lives. The claws of the evil clung to his back, but he was strong enough to cast it off. His body is weak from the struggle, but his spirit remains unbroken. When the dead are buried, he'll move to some clean place and start anew. All are welcome at Kills White Bear's camp. He will feed them and clothe them, and wipe the tears from their eyes. His prayers go out to all."

Before they parted, Kills White Bear caught a glimpse of his son. In his arms, he carried the lifeless body of his young wife.

He sent White Eagle, who needed a purpose to assuage his grief, with a small party to hunt buffalo while he himself went on to see Neighbors. It was then that he learned the name of the evil. Cholera, the whites called it. The Nemenuh knew it as death.

He soon learned that it had not only taken half of the Peneteka. The rest of the bands, save the Quahadi, who hunted far to the north when the sickness came, lost half of their number as well. When he knew and understood, the impact of it rocked his wasted, hollow frame. Ten thousand Nemenuh were no more.

Chapter Thirty-Three

When the fall rains came, what was left of the Penateka gathered under Kills White Bear's strengthening arms. He was the last *Par-riah-boh* of the Wasp band to walk the weeping face of Mother Earth. They'd all come to him as he'd asked, and though he comforted them as best he could, he had no answers for them. Waves of miners kept rolling through their country, and no Nemenuh had to be warned to stay clear. He watched them pass by the thousands, untouched, while the chants and orations of young, inexperienced shamans prayed for signs until they fell, exhausted. Nothing came, and Kills White Bear knew he was alone to face whatever presented itself in the wake of such a disaster.

When he returned to his camp from the sweat lodge, he saw their horses waiting. Warriors milled about the council fire while their chiefs waited patiently inside for the last Chief of the Penateka. Kills White Bear entered his lodge, shoulders back and head erect, all eyes upon him as he took his place.

"It makes my heart sing to see you well, my brothers," he said. "Welcome. Peace to you all."

The Chief of the Yamparika answered.

"We came not to speak of peace, Kills White Bear. Ten winters ago, Kills White Bear came before us to ask for our help. The Yamparika did not see what he saw. They did not listen and turned away. Now we see the warning of Kills White Bear come to pass. White men travel our country as if they own it. Behind them they leave evil that kills in the night and leaves no tracks for our warriors to follow."

Kills White Bear nodded. "It comes as no comfort to

him that his words proved true. He does not gloat in his wisdom. He only weeps for the dead."

The spokesman continued. "What else can the Yamparika do, but also weep? But there remains the question of the People's response. And if our grief is great, our rage is greater. Our young men are hungry for revenge."

"Then let them eat," Kills White Bear said.

"If Kills White Bear will ride again against the Tejanos, who we know brought this evil to us, the Yamparika will follow. And the Kotsoteka, the Quahadi, the Nokoni, the Tenewa, and the Tanima will also follow. Our allies the Kiowa will come as well. All will follow and make war on the Tejanos until they are driven from the plains. The honor to lead belongs to the man with the stout heart of the white bear."

Kills White Bear stood and closed his eyes. It was the moment he had waited for since the time of his vision. At last, the People were united against their common foe. They finally understood. Yet he knew that for the Penateka, it'd come too late.

"Kills White Bear knows," he began, "that the time for war has come. It pleases him to see his cousins string their bows and sharpen their knives. He knows it's not too late for the People."

He threw his head back to the heavens. "But when he came to you with tears in his eyes, half of his people already lay dead. Half again died this past summer." He turned to face his guests. "For fifteen winters, we've known nothing but war. The Penateka fought alone. Those days have passed, and Kills White Bear is glad to see it. But while it strengthens his spirit to know that the Nation is still strong, he knows the Wasps are weak. Kills White Bear can't abandon them for the warpath and fight the Tejanos with their cries of hunger in his ears."

"What should be done?" the Yamparika asked. "The whites killed us with fever just as certainly as they put a knife to our throats. Such treachery should not go unpunished."

"Kills White Bear agrees," he said. "Yet the years of war have taught him things that others do not know. If the People ride together on the warpath, the Tejanos will crush us. They are too many, and we are too few. Why spend ourselves in one campaign? It's but a repeat of Buffalo Hump's mistake in the great coastal raid." He paused to breathe, his voice louder when he spoke.

"Kills White Bear's scouts tell him that the American soldiers are building forts as the Spanish once did. If so, they are easily avoided. The Tejanos expose their open chests to us, awaiting our arrows. Split one force into a hundred. Big, American horses are waiting. Scalps are waiting. Captives are waiting, and the Tejanos value nothing more. If the Rangers come, avoid them at all costs. But we should burn land that surrounds the Colorado until even the Tejanos don't want it. When the grass again grows green, the Nemenuh will walk it alone."

The warriors whooped, and it cheered him. He reached for White Eagle, who was sitting near. "I offer you my son, White Eagle, as our war chief. His medicine is great, greater than my own. What Penateka are able will ride with him to follow you."

He raised his hands, the wind of the prairies in his hair.

"There can be no peace with the Tejanos, brothers. The American Father turns his head away from our sorrow. When he turns it back, his Tejano children will lie dead at his feet, bleeding. It is my vision, and it is my prayer. Go and make war on the Tejanos with my son. The Great Spirit gave us this land, and no man can take it from us. Kill them as they've killed us. Offer them blood for blood. Kills White Bear's heart goes with you when his body can't. His love bathes you like a warm breeze."

Kills White Bear spent that evening alone with the chiefs making medicine while the warriors of all bands danced to the beat of the drums and the chanting of brave women. The moon was three quarters and waxing, the time when all power grows. A lone wolf howled in the hills. The signs were good again.

At dawn they feasted together and sang arm in arm. Kills White Bear saw to it that old bonds were renewed and new ones formed. At his request, feuds were forgiven and debts released. Enemies embraced each other like brothers.

By mid-morning, the war parties quickly scattered south across the plains. Some to the Brazos, some to the Colorado and the Trinity, others still to the ranch country above the Río Grande. Kills White Bear mounted his finest horse and escorted them from his camp. He returned alone, thinking that it would happen just as he always knew it could. The cholera had pulled them together and nothing could pull them apart. Maguara would've been pleased.

Chapter Thirty-Four

Remy listened with his ear resting on his hand for what seemed like a day. This attorney had obviously been told beforehand that Remy was a frontiersman and new to the bar, what one might call a cornstalk lawyer. Far from humbled by his rough edge, Remy was actually proud of it. He'd read all those tedious books carefully, absorbing them all, and greater men than he had come by the legal profession in the very same roundabout way.

This popdick for the plaintiff took Remy's brief education to task. He wore Remy out with flowery language, out-of-state citations, frequent references to the Magna Carta on up, finally winding down, or so Remy hoped, with an *ad hominem* attack against the adversary's client. Remy was certain that the defendant, a hapless homesteader, was wholly ignorant of the fact that he was being insulted. There was just too much chaff flying around to see the grain. What this "wind-seller" wanted, Remy knew, was the defendant's land.

Remy'd already whittled a piece of white pine first into a saddle and then a spur. Shavings littered the floor. One or two little flakes hung in his beard. For the sake of courtly appearance, he shaved every third day whether he needed it or not. This was day three. His spittoon was full to the brim and he chewed on. The lawyer never drew a goddamn breath.

Defense counsel should've objected long ago, but since the defendant had probably paid his attorney's fee in hogs and spotty, thin-shelled chicken eggs, he hadn't retained the best. If this stick-in-the-mud wouldn't object to such a line, by God, Remy decided he would.

He rapped his gavel on the oak plank three times. "Enough of that, now, counselor. The court is surprised that the Old Testament has not been cited seein' how every other goddamn thing in creation has."

The attorney, clearly irritated, answered stiffly. "I was gettin' to that, your honor, when the court decided to try the defendant's counsel's case for him."

"Well, *somebody's* got to," Remy said, staring at the groggy-eyed lawyer for the homesteader. Remy was certain that he'd hit the jug a time or two over the noon hour. He turned back to the plaintiff lawyer. "Get to the point, man," Remy asserted. "Five minutes more of wind and this little cracker-box courthouse'll blow over."

He started right back where he left off. Remy reached for a new piece of wood. This time, he thought, he'd whittle a horse.

Before the first shavings hit the floor, Remy regretted his decision to sit on the bench for a number of reasons. He'd come to hang murderers, horse thieves, and bandits. He rarely saw them. By far, the majority of disputes he adjudicated involved tedious questions of land titles, just like the one he was presiding over now. Slick, southern-bred lawyers sniffed out the cracks in Spanish and Mexican land grants scribbled on crumbling paper, and the titles issued during the Republic's reign were equally faulted and obscure. Many tracts were never actually surveyed. Some of the frontiersmen in Remy's area, though they'd lived on their land for years, had never bothered to file. Land was cheap, but improved land was especially attractive, and the speculators wanted whatever they could take to sell again to lazy newcomers. It was at the root of all the cacophony that surrounded him daily.

Remy's sympathy lay with his neighbors, farmers and ranchers just like him. In Remy's mind, the ambiguous Texas Constitution had attempted to protect the small freeholder and debtor, and he ruled accordingly. Legalities aside, and he frequently shoved them that way, what mattered most to him was the intent of each disputing party. Did they want to work the land, or flip it? Both meant profit in Texas, but only one was truly right. And if the farmer's claim wasn't right, he could at least compromise in Remy's court, keep some of his land, work hard to buy more and know better next time. The land syndicates of Houston and Galveston, oftentimes fronts for eastern companies funded by Yankee money, were frequently disappointed when Remy's gavel fell.

But it wasn't the caseload in his court that troubled him most. It was the renewed violence on the frontier that made him feel he was wasting his time and talents. All his efforts were for naught if the homesteaders were being murdered. The federal government, apparently appalled by the Rangers' vicious participation in the Mexican War, had cut all funding to the fabled companies. It seemed that some of the Rangers had remembered the Alamo and Goliad once more as they fell upon the hapless Mexicans. Without federal money, the bankrupt state had little choice but to disband them. For three years, it had made little difference. Now at the close of the fourth, the Comanche had returned to the settlements, and the frontier burned as it never had before.

Remy monitored the newspaper accounts closely. Over two hundred had died or been taken captive in that one year alone, and the army set in forts, wringing its hands. Their dismay over the horrendous and bloody violence that erupted everywhere made them appear timid or afraid. Remy knew this was not the case. They simply had no idea how to respond to the swift and rushing red tide. This was their weakness, and Remy knew no one sensed it more acutely than the Comanche. And no one knew how to use it better.

Remy planned to use whatever influence he had with the state government to recall the Ranger companies at all costs. Jack Hays had been lured off in search of California gold, but dozens more rough and ready young frontiersmen lurched forward, eager to take his place. They knew exactly what to do. The army could either learn from them, or stay out of their way.

Remy carefully etched the horse's mane before he blew it clean and sat it proudly on the bench. The jury foreman, who Remy knew happened to be the first cousin of the defendant, and owed him money to boot, nodded his head in admiration of Remy's craftsmanship. For a slick, big-city lawyer, plaintiff's counsel had not conducted an extensive *voir dire*. Next to his cousin, Remy was certain, sat his wife's brother-in-law. Oh, well, he thought. Justice is blind. Remy nodded back, and rapped the gavel a second time. Cut off in mid-speech, the plaintiff's lawyer's cheeks puffed blood red.

"We ain't gettin' nowhere fast, counsel," Remy declared, slicking back his hair. Beatriz had bought him some rectified bear oil—all the rage—to hold it in place, which it did with dignity. But Remy was damned, however, if it didn't get a little musky after the second day. "The court's gonna save us all a little time," he said, wiping his hand on the bench. "Where is the law—the Texas statutes, mind you— to support your contention? That's the only thing I've heard lackin' these last two days. An' by God, I do mean the *only* thing."

The attorney stood angrily and flung open his dark coat. Remy saw that a dagger was sheathed over his breast. "Here is the Texas law, your Honor!"

"I understand you now, sir," Remy said calmly as he reached under his robe, borrowed from a Methodist minister (not much work for them around there) until he fondled the familiar bone grip of his Colt.

Remy slammed the pistol loudly on the bench to the snickers of his jury. The barrel faced out. "And here's the Constitution! Case dismissed! You best scat for Houston City and like it!"

Then he turned to the defendant. "Plant your corn and cotton in the spring, Johnson. But spend your winter mindin' your affairs. Might be wise to visit the land office with a fresh survey in hand." Then he addressed the rest. "The Comanche are loose in the country. See to your loved ones and draw in the latch strings at night. The Governor'll call up the Rangers directly, I'm certain. Until then, mind you and yours. This court's adjourned. The bench's only regret is that I didn't do it yesterday before this hair oil turned on me." He slammed the gavel down one last time, and then tossed it behind him.

The clerk scribbled as quickly as he could. Remy leaned over and spoke to him. "Clear my docket, George. I'm goin' home."

"Yes, sir, Judge."

Remy's mind then turned to the record. It had a peculiar way of haunting him. "You didn't write down that last little bit, did you?"

"Every word, your honor."

"Not about the pistol, though?" he asked, eyebrows raised.

"Oh, yes, sir. Proudly."

Remy clucked his tongue against the roof of his mouth. "You're a little too damn efficient for my liking, George," he told him. "Oh, well, the hell with it. That weasel can appeal the decision if he likes. He'll have to pick a better jury than this to win that case. It looked like the defendant's family reunion." Remy gathered his things and prepared to leave. His clerk came to him again.

"Some of the court would like to bow our heads before we part, Judge. We're prayin' for rain to bust the drought."

Remy never stopped what he was doing. "As long as the wind blows out of the west in Texas, George, it won't do any good to pray. Try again in September when God's got a better chance. Put out the lamps on your way home."

Chapter Thirty-Five

Cristóbal and his vaqueros were working the yearlings in the big corral when Remy arrived. He was worn thin, and hungry. He briefly checked to see that everything was in order. It looked as if Cristóbal had done a fine job. The only thing missing, at first glance, was Joaquin.

"Where's Jack?" Remy asked, still mounted. Cristóbal kicked at the ground with the toe of his boot before he answered.

"He's not here," he finally said.

"Now that I can see," Remy said, rubbing his eyes. "Where the hell is he? Out in woods somewheres under a cedar?"

"Resting. In the barn."

"Restin', hell. You gettin' any work out of 'im, Chris?"

"Oh, yes, Don Remy," Cristóbal said, never looking at him. "The boy works hard."

Remy closed his eyes, sighed, and slowly shook his head. "Your Pa told me a lot of things I didn't like, but he never lied to me." He opened his eyes. "If you want his job you won't either. Now I'm askin' again, and I expect a straight answer. Is Jack pullin' his weight on the ranch?"

"No."

"That's what I figured." He dismounted and handed his reins to a young vaquero. "You say he's in the barn?"

Cristóbal said nothing, but nodded his head.

"All right," Remy snapped. "I'll take care of it. Ya'll done a good job roundin' up them cattle. See that they get plenty hay after ya'll are through. Bring in the rest of the men off the range and make sure everybody stays behind the fence from now till the new moon. Post two men in shifts all night, and keep your powder dry. I'll be back directly."

Remy was tired and irritable. He knew that now was not the best time to handle Joaquin, but he hadn't chosen it. He'd made it quite clear what was expected of his son. Joaquin had defied him, and Remy resolved to make him think twice before he did it again.

He marched to the west side of the barn and threw open the doors. Sunlight fell on the haystack that cradled Joaquin, a book between his knees, a half-eaten apple in his mouth. The boy snapped up, but it was too late. Remy barred any hope of escape.

"There you are, you half-breed son of a bitch!" he sneered between his clenched teeth. "Nobody under my roof is idle, you hear me! I'm gonna teach you somethin' even you kin understand!"

He snatched a set of reins from the wall, and gripped the bit in his hand. Then he wrapped the leather around it until only about three feet hung loose. When he turned back his own shadow loomed large and black against the knotty pine planks. Its image did not distract him for long. He saw that while the boy cowered before him, he did not try to run. He rolled to his side instead and braced himself, his knees drawn to his chest. The book fell to the ground face down and the apple rolled off into the dust.

Remy raised his arm above his head, the muscles in his head tight, jaw locked, and crashed it down. Stiff, cracked leather snapped against bare skin and the boy shrieked in pain.

Remy had already drawn his arm back to strike again when he suddenly lost all momentum. Joaquin's scream struck him cold. The sound of it echoed in his scrambled mind until it mixed with another voice. In that short pause he recognized it. It was the forgotten cry of his youth. He froze as it reverberated louder and louder until only his boy's voice remained. He shook his head, but he still heard it clearly, pleading for the help that never came. He closed his eyes, saw his uncle standing over him, an angry man over a frightened boy, a skinny lash clenched in his callused hand. He again felt its sting and then the tingling warmth of his swollen, raw flesh as the next blow fell. He could feel the warm blood running down his back. How he'd hated his uncle. He still bore the scars. He remembered now.

The reins slipped from Remy's hand. He shuddered, breathed deeply. He thought of his agony, the bitterness, the humiliation and the misery, and where all these had driven him. There was no excuse—not then, and certainly not now. He could not do to this boy what'd been done to him. It was, he realized, the final step in Placido's dance.

"Git up, Jack," he said quietly. "It's over."

The boy uncoiled and turned to him, his dark eyes blazing. There was not the first trace of a tear; this boy was a fighter. It was then that Remy finally saw himself in Joaquin. He hoped he'd never see it again.

He extended his hand. "Take it, Jack," he murmured. "I'm so, so, so very sorry. I'll never beat you again. I swear."

Joaquin seemed confused by this about-face. Remy stood still, waiting patiently for the boy to come to him. The anger in Joaquin eyes slowly gave way to a deep longing. When Joaquin's hand finally reached for his, Remy grasped it and drew the boy's body to his. He reached around Joaquin's back and squeezed. The fresh scent of youth, like spring rain, filled his head.

When he felt Joaquin's arms clutch him tightly, he knew it was not too late. Remy would waste no more time fending off this boy's affection, he would nourish it. His tears welled up until he felt the first of them roll down his cheeks. He could not stop them and he did not try.

"Never again," he promised him. "It'll be diff'rent from now on."

"I know what you want," Joaquin told him, "and I'll do it."

"It don't matter, Jack," Remy said, smudging the tears from the boy's cheek with the heel of his hand. "Do what you can. We'll get by."

He heard footsteps behind him, and he turned together with the boy. It was Beatriz. Never had he seen her so angry, and never had it vanished as quickly. She seemed awed by what she saw.

"It's all right, Beatriz," Remy told her quietly. "We're all right."

She tossed the stick of oak—no doubt meant for him—against the wall of the barn and joined them. "Good, Remy," she whispered, as sweet and true as the first time he'd heard her call his name. "You've made me very happy." It was a voice from his past that he welcomed. The rest, he hoped, were gone.

When they turned to leave, Remy saw Quelepe. The old Méxicano had stood in the sunlight watching it all.

"I bet you didn't see this comin', did ya, ya old goat?"

Quelepe looked at him and smiled. "Who could?"

1855

Chapter Thirty-Six

Remy sat rocking next to Beatriz that sunny, Sunday afternoon. He'd come in early and bathed to spend some time with her as had become his habit. Of course, she'd been to mass with the children that day. She'd napped when they got home and looked fresh to him. The old oak glider squeaked as they shifted back and forth. They just sat and talked, enjoying the shade and whatever breeze came their way.

A lone rider appeared on a fine dapple-gray. As he grew closer, Remy recognized him. It was Jasper Starkes' middle boy, Anson.

"Afternoon, Judge Fuqua," Starkes greeted him after he'd tethered his horse and slipped through the gate. He took off his hat and bowed slightly and awkwardly to Beatriz. "Ma'am?"

"Howdy," Remy said. "What brings you out here?"

"I come t'visit," Anson stated in a thick drawl.

"Have ya now?" Remy asked. He looked at his wife, whose dark eyes studied the man before they turned to him, silently asking the question. "Well, get out of the sun, young Starkes," Remy said. "Sit up here with us and visit away. I'll draw a little cool water from the well."

"Much obliged, Judge," the man answered, and he sat quietly. "Hot today, ain't it?" he said to Beatriz.

"Very hot," Beatriz agreed flatly.

"We could use a little rain, couldn't we?"

"Rain is good," she said.

When Remy returned with the ladle, the mystery was over. Elena Marie stepped out in a starched white dress. Remy had to squint his eyes just to look at her. One of her mother's flowers rested above the ear in her chestnut hair. She was a little taller than her mother, perhaps a little thinner, and there was no mistaking those dark, brooding de la Cruz eyes. But the olive tone of her skin was close to Remy's. And her hair reminded him of his mother. She glowed golden in the afternoon sun, its rays outlined the sun-bleached blonde streaks of her dark, honey-colored curls. She was, Remy thought, quite striking.

Remy looked at his wife. "Why do I get the notion that this ain't no surprise visit?" Elena Marie smiled bashfully and took her place at her mother's feet. Beatriz watched her intently, her expression blank. She said nothing.

"You ain't told 'em?" Anson asked Elena, a little disappointed when Remy saw his daughter shake her head no. "Well, I reckon it's up to me, then," Anson began. He turned to Beatriz first. "Mrs. Fuqua, your daughter's quite dear to me. In fact, I love her. I believe she cares for me, too. I've come to ask ya'll both for her hand."

Remy considered a response carefully. This was his only daughter, and his only blood child. Starkes was a good boy, came from a good, honest family. A little dense maybe, maybe a little crude, a number of rough edges certainly, but a decent enough fellow just the same. Of course, he thought his daughter could do much better, but if this is what she wanted it was fine with him.

Before he could say anything, Beatriz excused herself and entered the house ahead of a slamming door. When she came back, she had a full glass of whiskey in one hand, and a hand-rolled cigarillo in the other. It was scandalous behavior, shocking daughter and suitor alike, but Remy knew Beatriz was greatly disappointed. She sat there puffing away in jerky movements. Elena Marie would not look at her. Good choice, Remy thought.

Remy thought it might smooth things over a little if Beatriz heard from her daughter.

"Is this what you want, Elena?"

"Yes, Papa," she bubbled. "Very much."

He turned to the boy. "How'll you keep her, Starkes?"

"Your daughter kin pretty much keep herself, Judge," Starkes replied. "But, I saved up for a quarter league of land not far from my Daddy's. I own a few head of cattle, and soon I'll own some more. I'm a good farmer, too, at least when the rain cooperates a little better. I know what work's all about. Always have. I cain't do for her like she's used to, God knows, but I kin love an' honor her and give her a good home."

A good enough answer for Remy. "Now you heard this man, Elena. It won't be easy."

"I don't care, Papa," she said, her face bright with the passion of youth. Remy had seen the very same expression when he'd come to Beatriz's tent all those years ago and swept his future wife away from her father. "I'll work hard and do my share. I always have. I won't be far from you and Mama."

"Anywhere but here's too far for your Mother, honey. But we both knew this day was comin' sometime." This was for Beatriz's benefit and he turned to her. "We just didn't think it'd be today." Then he made the biggest mistake a lawyer could make. He asked her a question when he didn't know what her answer would be. As soon as he'd said the words, he regretted it. "What do you say, Mother?"

Beatriz exhaled a plume of smoke and then slurped a little more whiskey. She shuddered as she swallowed. She never looked at Starkes. *"¿Habla español, joven?"* she finally asked.

"No, Ma'am," he said, looking a little puzzled. "I don't talk no Meskin." Beatriz cringed. "Elena here kin teach me directly."

"My daughter is a . . . 'Meskin,' señor!" She said it like he did, her lips curled for emphasis as she bobbled her head in parody. That whiskey must've gone straight to her head.

"She ain't all Meskin," Starkes allowed, "and even if'n she were, it don't bother me none. Love is blind, Ma'am."

Maybe, Remy thought, but his wife damn sure wasn't. Starkes spoke of Elena Marie's race as if it were a birthmark or blemish to be overlooked. Beatriz had heard him well enough. Outwardly cold, she was quietly smoldering within. She held her nose, drained the last of her liquor and fought to swallow it. She wanted to gag, Remy knew, but her pride wouldn't let her.

"You're Catholic?" she asked when she could speak again, her eyes slightly askew.

"No, Ma'am," Starkes drawled. "I reckon I'm a Baptist, or some such, it's hard to say."

Beatriz dashed out her cigarillo in the now empty glass of whiskey. *"¡Sangre de Cristo! ¡Un gringo Bautista!"* And this was only the beginning. She stood, mumbling in Spanish to herself, and paced back and forth. Sometimes she didn't look too steady. Finally, she disappeared into the house, babbling everywhere she went. Remy thought none of it was fit to translate for the confused Starkes. The deeper she went, the louder she spoke. Remy had no choice but to take it from there.

"Well, looks like we'll need a little more time to kick it aroun' yet, Anson," Remy said casually, like they were speaking again of the weather. "You go on home. I'll send word to ya when we know somethin'."

Starkes stood still, he jaw set, facial muscles quivering. The poor boy wasn't angry, he was in pain. "I love her, Judge," he said with conviction.

"I know, son," he told him. "I know." Remy rose. "Close the gate on your way out."

Elena Marie, furious with her mother's rudeness, stormed off to her room. But Remy knew damn well his daughter was not surprised. Why else would she not have warned her? He told Elena through the locked door to calm herself and be patient. They'd figure something out directly.

Beatriz was still cursing the world when he found her. Tobacco smoke engulfed the room. She gripped an uncorked bottle of whiskey by the neck like a dead chicken, its contents sloshing all over her favorite carpets. She'd have shot him if he'd spilled the first drop. She kicked her finest, hand-carved furniture out of her path. A small table, imported from Laredo, soared through a stained glass window. Through war, revolution, Indian raid, illness, drought, the first gray hair she'd found on her head, he'd never seen her in such a state.

"Now, Beatriz," he began tenderly, his open palms before her as a sign of peace.

"*¡Me lleva la chingada!*" she cackled, like a drunken vaquero on payday. Remy recoiled in shock. It would've been far less riskier for him, he thought, to talk to a tornado. For some reason his mind recalled what he always believed was her finest attribute among so many. Beatriz was a damn good shot.

"We gotta talk, honey."

"What's there to talk about?" she snapped in Spanish, swaggering. "The gringo wants a *Meskin* girl! Why should he not have ours?"

"Beatriz," Remy begged. "Please."

"I spent years attending to that foolish girl," she snarled

between clenched teeth, eyes darting. "I nurtured her the way my mother nurtured me. I taught her all the songs of my youth. I sent her to school with her relatives. We made all the festivals in Béxar and Laredo. It was always dangerous and hard, but I wanted her to know her people. She was acquainted with all the young men of the finest ranchero families in south Tejas. When they came to court her properly, she was cold to them and turned them all away. A new invitation arrived only yesterday. It was not even opened. She could've had anyone she wanted, and she picks this dirty, white farm-boy. A Baptist of all things!" She wrung her hands. "I've failed my father and my blood!"

"Don Carlos prob'ly said the same damn thing about me."

"You know damn well he did. But he was wrong, and I'm right. Things are different now. You'd know that if you weren't a fool."

Remy tried to reason with her. "You can't make her love someone else, Beatriz. It's as simple as that. She's twenty-two years old. You were sixteen when we married."

"And I had a head on my shoulders," she said tersely, her face flush and stiff. "Elena Marie obviously does not. She's blind to the way the world's changed. Things are not the same for her as they were for me. I couldn't make her see it!"

Remy couldn't follow. "See *what*?"

The bottle went up, gurgled, and then went down. The overflow spotted the rug. Cigarillo ashes followed. "What she is! Where she belongs! What's at stake! She's thrown it all away."

"No, she hasn't," he insisted, however delicately. "She loves that boy, white or not, and you've got to let her go."

Her eyes now trained on his, flashing. "That's easy for a white man to say, Remy. It's not your culture that crumbles."

"Whites don't have much in the way of culture, Beatriz. There ain't no time for it. We just work, and do."

"And that, you *cabrón*," she snapped, "is supposed to comfort me?" That was the nicest thing she said to him for the balance of that day and the one that followed. From then on he did not argue with her. Her understood her bitterness, and simply let it run its natural course.

On the third day she came to him. Her anger was gone, and so, thank God, was the whiskey. "All right," she said. "All right."

Remy, Cristóbal, Joaquin, and three others drove the stock, both horses and cattle, to Starkes' place. Jack rode ahead, and had Anson open his corral. They separated the animals as the dust flew in the air. When the gate closed on them, Anson Starkes came to Remy.

"What's this, Judge?"

"That's your answer, son. Comanche style. Send your Mama 'round to the ranch. She an' Beatriz can work out the details. We're thinkin' maybe next spring."

Starkes hollered and threw his hat in the air. "I wuz worried sick, Judge. Things didn't look too good."

Remy thought they looked like what they were. "Beatriz'll come aroun' in time, providin' of course she sees you do right by my daughter. An' I best not hear no diff'rent. Don't you raise your hand to her, you hear! You do, an' it'll be my turn for a surprise visit."

"That's not my way, Judge," Starkes said, and Remy liked the way he delivered it. "I'll treat her like a queen."

"And I wanna have babies bouncin' on my knee by this comin' Christmas. I want that clearly understood."

"I'm ready to commence with that as soon as it's good and right." There was a light in his eyes and a grin on his lips. Remy didn't care for either.

"I wouldn't appear too anxious just yet, Starkes," Remy warned mordantly. "An' you best not jump the goddamn gun! She's my only daughter. I don't want no details, I just want results." Remy shook his finger at him. "Christmas, and not a day before."

"I understand," the boy said, ashamed of his eagerness.

Remy slipped his hand under his vest and produced a thick envelope. "Here's the rest of the dowry."

He watched as Anson thumbed through the crisp Yankee bills. "There must be a thousand dollars here!"

"Ever seen money like that before, son?" Remy asked him.

"No, sir."

"And ya never will again, either. Not from me. Buy yourselves some land up river near my spread. It'll work out in the end."

Starkes shook his head, shoved the money back into the envelope and handed it to Remy. "I can't take it, Judge. I want your daughter, not your money."

This Remy liked. The boy had spirit. Remy nudged it back with the toe of his boot. "You git both in the bargain." He leaned forward in his saddle until his shadow fell across Anson's face. "The best of marriages ain't easy, Starkes. I'll give ya'll every advantage that was given to me. I owe my daughter that. You make her a nice home, Starkes. And then you work hard, through the good and the bad, to keep it happy. I promise you that you'll see plenty of both. That's all I kin tell ya."

"Much obliged, Judge," he said as he shoved the envelope into his pocket. He seemed ashamed to accept it, and Remy took this as a good sign. "You kin rely on me."

"Believe me, I am." He turned to his vaqueros. "Let's go, boys. Our work's done."

Before he wheeled, Starkes caught his horse by the bit.

"I hear you're runnin' for the legislature next election."

"You heard right."

"I'll vote for ya."

"Oh, you'll do more than that," Remy said, and rode out.

Chapter Thirty-Seven

The white agent, Neighbors, had asked Kills White Bear to count his people. Runners went from lodge to lodge, each carving their figures into one bleached, bison scapula bone. When the last runner returned, Kills White Bear tallied the marks. Less than one thousand Penateka still clung to the Earth Mother.

For the first time since the great coastal raid, Kills White Bear saw hope for his people. The American Father again promised peace on the plains. At long last he would draw the line—Maguara's undying dream of salvation—separating his red children from his white, and then raise his long knife to keep each in his own country. Kills White Bear could not believe it when Neighbors sent word that the American Father finally had heard the Wasps' cries. His vision of blood had served its purpose. The exhausted Penateka had won a place. Neighbors said the American Father had pressured the Tejanos to provide reservation land. At night, he heard the old women chant his name around dying fires.

Neighbors promised them the region that surrounded the Clear Fork of the Brazos, a land of green prairies and rolling hills, thick woods and sweet water. It was the winter home of the buffalo, and the deer were thick. It would serve them well.

Of course, Kills White Bear had many questions. Neighbors talked in terms Kills White Bear did not understand. The agent explained to him that their reservation home would be five leagues, or twenty thousand acres. This meant nothing to him, but he promised Neighbors he would bring his people to see it with their own eyes.

Now that they'd drawn the line, Kills White Bear became leery of it. But Neighbors cautioned him that it had been won by the American Father at great cost. He loved his red children and would embrace all who put their rifles away and settled within its boundaries. The rest, Neighbors told him, would be hunted down as they'd never been hunted before. New soldiers were coming. One way or another, the agent warned, there would be peace.

Kills White Bear knew that Neighbors spoke the truth, but his own experience had taught him that the American Father held the paper in one hand and the knife in the other. This time the only difference was that they offered him what he'd always said the Penateka must have. He put his misgivings aside, gathered his people, and rode with new hope to the Clear Fork to see the home he'd won.

Neighbors was waiting for him when he arrived. Kills White Bear greeted him and they sat together on a blanket. Neighbors proudly unrolled the map. Kills White Bear studied it a moment, following the rivers with his finger to find the place where his feet now stood. It became clear enough to him that the Waco, Tawakoni, Wichita, Caddo, and Tonkawa were now located just one day's ride from where he sat. This troubled him. Not only were their enemies close by, it also appeared that they'd not been given much land. But he knew that these tribes together did not equal the number of Penateka present. These skulking, farming Indians had not won their land as the Penateka had.

Kills White Bear moved his eyes along the line that marked the reservation. It was small, of course, but large enough to accommodate a shifting camp. Now he questioned the specifics.

"And this," he asked, "will be our home forever in Texas?" Neighbors indicated that it was. "And between what rivers marks our country east and west?" There was no reason to inquire as to the northern boundary. It was known that the Red River marked the end of the Tejanos' country. His cousins among the four other bands, still numerous and strong, held it firmly. Kills White Bear's people were still welcome among them.

Neighbors' expression puzzled him. "What you see marked is the boundary, Kills White Bear," the agent explained. His voice sounded quietly apologetic.

"For a camp it's adequate," Kills White Bear said. "But our hunting ground must also be marked. I see nothing here. We need but little." He scratched his own line between the Brazos and the Colorado, a generous concession, he thought, but a fraction of their traditional range. Many would be unhappy with such a line, but he understood bet-

ter than most that the Wasps were also but a fraction of
what they once had been. To live they needed peace.

He laid the quill down on the blanket and slid the map
to where Neighbors could see and understand that the Penateka were not greedy. "This is all we ask," he said. "In
the spring and summer, we'll be far to the north. Tell the
American Father the Penateka are sworn to peace. Kills
White Bear's people will stay on our side of the line. He
swears it."

Neighbors did not even glance at the map. Kills White
Bear watched as he rubbed his face with his hands. He
looked tired, and spoke again only after exhaling loudly.

"You don't understand, Kills White Bear," he said, and
he indicated the original mark on the Clear Fork, "This is
to be your home summer and winter, forever. It's all you
need, and all they'll give you."

Kills White Bear was stunned. He waved his hand toward
the waiting Wasps. "Do you not see, Neighbors, how many
people I've brought you? This country is good, there's
much game, but a month of hunting by so many, and the
game will be gone. The buffalo come and go, and we must
follow them."

"No," Neighbors said. "When the buffalo enter your
land, you may hunt them. But when they leave, you can't
follow. The American Father'll give you cattle to eat, and
corn and other grains. In the spring, I'll teach you to grow
your own."

Kills White Bear felt a lump in his throat. He rose from
the map, allowing the wind to crumple it. "The American
Father wishes for us to live in one place, and make scars
in the earth like our enemies the Tonkawa? Is this what
these ears hear?"

"I know it'll be hard at first, Kills White Bear. I'll help
you all I can. If you want to live, you must change to the
new way."

"It seems to me, Neighbors," Kills White Bear said, "that
the American Father does not know our heart and our
ways." He shoved the map to him with his toe. "Show him
the line I've drawn, and explain the depths of our sacrifice
for peace. His line will never do. We must talk again and
soon."

Neighbors stared at him solemnly. "The talking is over, Kills White Bear," he said. "Soldiers are coming. To live in peace, the Penateka must stay within these lines. You have no choice."

Kills White Bear shook his head. "That's not living, Neighbors, and that's no choice. All the American Father asks of the Nemenuh is that we cease being Nemenuh. I know every river and every wood from the Arkansas to the Río Grande. I was born on horseback, and went in all directions from which the four winds blow. I'll give up all of that for the plains between the Brazos and the Colorado. I bent my knee to speak with you, but it's quickly straightened should the warpath call. We were never vanquished and won't be treated like we were." He breathed, and stiffened. "The American Father threatens me with blood. I was born in blood. I'm not afraid to die in it. He asks for peace." He shot out his finger toward the map. "I've shown you the price. The trade I offer is more than fair. Tell him this for Kills White Bear."

He turned to the others crouched near, hope on their faces, and spoke to them in their own tongue. "The chiefs of my youth would never have led me to this place, and I can't lead you. They offer us land that we can ride in half a day's time in which to live, hunt, and die. They take away the buffalo and give us the cow. They take away the flowers, wild roots, and berries of the plains and give us a plow. If we don't touch the pen to their paper, they'll come and hunt us again until they kill us all. Your choice is simple. You can die here strapped to the ass of an ox, or die on the plains hunting buffalo. I'm the last chief of my tribe, but my tribe is gone. Kills White Bear has made his decision. You must make yours."

"What will Kills White Bear do?" one asked.

"He'll kill white men until they kill him and he wins the right to leave this awful world with honor. When I sit beside my ancestors in the Happy Place, I can look them in the eye and say Kills White Bear did not lead his people to this sad country to eat from the white man's hand. He died like a man in the old way, with the warm sun on his shoulders, the wind in his hair, and a bloody knife in his hand."

And then he told Neighbors that there could be no peace with such treachery. He told him that he knew Neighbors was not to blame. It was the greedy Tejanos who were behind it and many of them would soon pay.

Unless the White Father agreed to his terms, it was the last time, he told the agent, that he'd sit with the white men and speak of peace. This was his third, last, and most bitter disappointment. The line that he'd prayed for came too little, too late.

Chapter Thirty-Eight

That winter was harsh, and many fell ill with cough and fever, and many more died of starvation. Kills White Bear no longer had the strength or the means to provide for them all. The weak, the sick, the very old, the very young and the disgruntled conspired against him. There was food and a warm fire, they argued, waiting for them at Neighbors' camp on the Clear Fork. They said Kills White Bear would lead them to a miserable death, and he did not deny it. Nor did he attempt to sway them as they organized to leave his camp. He divided the best of his horses and what little meat he had among them. He sent White Eagle and several other warriors to ride with them to see that they arrived safely. There were no longer any shamans to bless their journey, but Kills White Bear said that they left with his prayers. The white man's road would be hard, he warned them. But his heart wished them well.

The day after the dissenters left, Kills White Bear circulated among his warriors to count them a second time for a different purpose. For him, it was a grim task. Families were split in two. Wives and children left husbands and fathers. One Penateka hand did not trust the other. The thread was ripped apart and fragments scattered. The circle was broken forever.

The toll gave him nothing but the number of bodies available for a war that he knew would never end. Life as he knew it was over. His vision was a curse. Half of the Penateka had turned away from the prairie to camp beside Neighbors. It broke his heart.

The rest would sit with him quietly and watch the snow fall. They no longer made medicine, they did not seek signs. Kills White Bear was now convinced that the Great Spirit no longer looked down on them. Why else had their world turned so cold? The north wind cut through the limbs of bare, shaking trees, howling at him on sleepless nights. He called to Wolf Eyes to bring him wisdom. He never came. It was then that Kills White Bear understood the finality of his situation. The magic of his life was gone.

If the grass grew again in the spring—and he was not sure that it would—he would lead his warriors south to make war. He was no longer fighting to make a home for his people. He had none.

If the spring came, he would put down his responsibilities as chief and pick up his guns and pistols. There was nothing to win and nothing to lose, and he resolved to fight accordingly. He would pass from this life as violently as he'd entered it, and in the process, take as many of his demons with him as he possibly could. In a world without choices, it was his only path, and he embraced it in bitter silence.

That long winter no fire could warm him. If his prayers were answered and the spring did come, it would be his last. Once, when the wind grew still in the dead of a cold, starlit night, he thought he heard the spirit of the white bear laughing.

1856

Chapter Thirty-Nine

The Delaware had led them to the Comanchería. They'd come just as Neighbors promised they would. Word had it that the bluecoats had split forces after they crossed the Red River and began their descent, like locusts, southwest. Some occupied the old presidio near the Llano River that the Americanos called Fort Mason. Others went to the Clear Fork of the Brazos and built anew. Though they constructed these forts, they did not stay in them. Kills White Bear stalked them as the fox does a jackrabbit. The difference was that he did not possess the strength to pounce.

These soldiers were like no other Kills White Bear had seen. Regardless of the weather or the days they spent on the trail, their uniforms were clean and polished, and they wore strange feathers in their hats. They had the hated pistols, but they also carried short-barreled rifles that loaded quickly from the breech. They rode fine, tall, muscular American horses, and sometimes even brought the thunder guns with them onto the plains. They scoured the land like demons; the Delaware interpreted the signs. Whenever they came across unshod pony tracks, they turned and followed them to their source and laid waste to any Indians they found.

They fell first on the Lipan Apache, and then the Waco and Kickapoo. Most of the survivors of these nations already lived on Neighbors' reservation. Those who did not, whether they raided or not, were hunted down and killed. The fate of these warriors meant nothing to the Nemenuh. But Kills White Bear could see that the Penateka were next.

The raiding had gone remarkably well the year past. Though Kills White Bear knew the whites were still coming, they dared not drive one wooden stake in the plains that lay west of the Colorado. The warriors of all bands raided relentlessly, but his feet never left the warpath.

In keeping with his advice, the raiders hit and ran, always avoiding mass companies of either Rangers or soldiers. The bulk of the other free bands resided deep in the north, out of harm's way.

Very quickly, Kills White Bear realized that the bluecoats would not cross the Red River. This was all he needed to know.

In the fall of that year, the bluecoats attacked them at dawn in their camp on the Concho. Kills White Bear saw his warriors fall to the smoke of their carbines and the flash of their sabers. He scattered the survivors to the brush, and he himself was running when he saw White Eagle collapse

from his saddle. Blood marked a wound in his back. Kills
White Bear screamed in horror as he unloaded one cylinder
of his eight gauge double barrel—the weapon he now favored—into each of the two soldiers closest to White Eagle's body, and they both fell dead in the dust. A ring of
warriors formed behind him, and in their covering fire, he
went to collect the body of his son. He was still breathing
as they disappeared together and raced north for the Red
River.

For seven days, Kills White Bear cared for his son with
medicine and prayers. On the eighth, when he saw that
White Eagle would live, he organized another party of survivors in the thinning ranks of his warriors. At dawn, he
circulated among the camp to organize them. When he
came back with his weapons, ready to ride, he saw that
White Eagle, a trickle of blood seeping from his healing
wound, was mounted with the other warriors. His courage
was a testament to the others. Together, hand in hand, they
rode off.

It went on like this throughout that year and into the
next. Always the sound of guns echoed in Kills White
Bear's ears. The Nemenuh and the Tejanos tore at each
other, with the soldiers always on their burning trail. One
by one, he buried his warriors wondering when the day
would come when they'd bury him.

Then, as quickly as they had come, the bluecoats left.
Scouts went out and returned. The forts, they confirmed,
were abandoned. They'd gone northwest, they learned, to
the Utah country.

Kills White Bear laughed maniacally when he heard the
news. When they had the Wasps hanging only by the width
of a bloody blade, they let them go. They'd hounded them
to the edge of the abyss, but did not have it in them to
push them over. White people were so strange, and so foolish. What made them strong also made them weak. And it
would be the Tejanos who'd pay for their crimes. Kills
White Bear swore it to the few he had left.

1860

Chapter Forty

When the bluecoats left, the Rangers came again. They rode confidently, provisioned for an extended campaign. The fighting that followed was as fierce and bloody as any Kills White Bear had ever seen. Exhausted, he took his band of warriors north of the Red River to collect themselves in sanctuary. But this time, the Rangers forded the river without a pause and ran them down. The plains were swept by fire, blood, and hatred more intense than the August sun. Death was everywhere.

Kills White Bear watched as the Rangers fell on camp after camp of the other, more remote bands. As he expected, they now killed men, women, and children. His cousins were shocked, demoralized, and outraged, but he, above all other warriors, understood. It was a humiliation the Penateka had known for years, and it lay at the core of his undying hatred. His warning had come true, and the war chiefs of the other bands came to him for advice. His response was always the same. The weak and the weary could go to the Indian agents, but the brave hearts must stay on the warpath and exact blood for blood. For two winters, it was this way. The People were wasted, and wave after wave of Tejano Rangers came.

Warriors died by the hundreds in those mean seasons and left no sons behind to take their place. Very quickly, Kills White Bear saw the northern bands depleted as his own had been. But the raids, fueled by the Nenemuh code of revenge, continued.

In the fall of that bloody year, the plains grew quiet. The Rangers had suddenly withdrawn. No one understood or trusted it. Inexperienced shamans sought signs, and the warriors danced.

Even Kills White Bear had to admit that things were strange. There'd been a drought that summer past; the locusts had descended in black clouds. The deer were dying, their stiff tongues dyed black. The moon had blocked the rays of the sun and for a time, day became night. Everything his people saw boded ill, and they trembled before him.

Kills White Bear spent his nights alone riding the rolling hills, wondering why no Tejano bullet had found him. He'd given it every chance, and he was old and tired. His hair was now white, and his body scarred and cold. Why, he despaired, was he still here? Had he not done all that was expected of him? What evil surprise waited for him next? He rolled his head back on his shoulders to watch the night sky and then he saw it: the burning star and its trail of fire behind it.

Maguara's comet had come again like an old friend, and Kills White Bear understood the silence then. He knew then why the Rangers had gone so mysteriously. He sent word to all the remaining war chiefs that he had a message for them, and two days later they met under that same sky.

"Rest, honored cousins," he told them, "and take heart. This is no supernatural evil that befalls us. Feed your stomachs, mourn your dead, and sharpen your weapons. Our homes are calling to us to return and claim them. The whites have fallen one against the other, and that is the only reason the Rangers have pulled their blades from our throats. The hands that killed our people will now kill their own. The fire that consumed our nation will now consume theirs. Rest and make ready. Kills White Bear, last Chief of the Wasps, hears the undefended southern plains beckon. He will answer and fight on. Those who have courage, follow him."

1861

Late Winter/Spring

Chapter Forty-One

Against the advice of his wife, Remy rode alone to Austin that cold day late in January. Beatriz feared for his life, and rightly so. He had been threatened many times over the past year. He came, he told himself, out of his sworn duty to his electorate. Beatriz told him this was absurd since none of them were talking to him anyway. His legislative term would expire in the fall, and his party made it quite clear that he would not be returning to the Capitol. Nevertheless, he decided to speak his mind on this one last occasion, regardless of the consequences, and retire to his ranch with the satisfaction that he had done what he thought was right. He already knew what would happen. The convention was but a formality.

The streets of Austin were choked with people on the day the assembly was to convene. Stump speakers harangued on every corner. Bonfires raged, their flames engulfing books by despised northern authors and perishable goods manufactured by tainted northern hands. The air was crisp and very still. Pungent smoke hung close to the winter ground like a shroud. Remy waded through it to the Capitol.

Violence had erupted all around him in the year past, not only along the disputed borders of Texas, but also in its heart. Northern-born teachers were hounded from Texas schools. Yankee seamen were mobbed at coastal ports. A minister from Kentucky, who had already made it clear that he believed in the Bible's endorsement of slavery, cautioned his congregation against the flogging of blacks. His flock answered with seventy lashes to his back, nearly killing him. In Dallas, three black men were lynched without a trial and without cause. In Fort Worth, three whites were hanged about that same time, solely on the suspicion that they'd tampered with slaves. Rumors of slave uprisings, abolitionist raids, well poisonings, and political assassination fanned the flames of a frantic people that Remy had seen smoldering for years. Kindling was abundant in that year of drought; the election of Abraham Lincoln provided the torch.

For one to hint of his neighbor's ties, either real or imagined, to the north, or to speak one word of reason in the Yankees' favor was enough to encourage the most dangerous and hostile suspicions. Frequently it went much further than threats. Farms and homes were burned and honest people were waylaid and murdered. Many so marked for violence sold out for whatever they could get and scrambled for distant California in the hope that the madness of Texas would not follow.

Whenever Beatriz suggested that they leave, too, Remy angrily reaffirmed his vow to stay in Texas forever. This country, he reminded her, was the land of her birth, and her father's and his father's before him. It was their home and would always be. Against great odds and adversity, they'd managed to sink their roots deeply in that bloody clay soil. It was unthinkable to him to let it all go now and run. Though his position was conservative and controversial, he was convinced, he told her, that his history had earned his family a safe place. They would cling to their land and let the storm blow over, as Don Carlos had always preached, politics be damned. As bad as things looked, he told her, they'd both seen much worse.

The political unrest in Austin, capital of Texas since 1850, was greater than in any other town along the western frontier. Remy wrapped the collar of his duster closely around his neck, clenched his teeth to brace himself and rode into town against the icy winds.

He paused before a crowd gathered to hear a local Baptist minister. The man, portly, waistcoat two sizes too small, was fiery and spoke well, mesmerizing the people assembled. For a time, he held Remy, too.

"Don't take my word for it, folks," he told them. "Hear the word of God. I quote from the Book of Daniel, of the prophesy foretold, Chapter Eleven, verses six through nine. Bear with me, folks. I know it ain't the Sabbath. In the interest of brevity, I paraphrase:

"And the Kingdom of the South shall be strong, and one of their princes will have dominion, and his dominion shall be a great dominion. And in the end of years, the Kingdom of the South shall join themselves together, and they shall come to the King of the North to make an agreement; but the words shall not retain the power of the arm, neither shall the agreement stand. But out of the branch of the Southern Kingdom's roots shall one stand up in his estate, which shall come an army, and shall enter into the fortress of the King of the North, and shall deal against him, and shall prevail."

The minister lifted his eyes from the Good Book. "Hear the word of God, my brothers, and do not be afraid."

Remy watched as the man's gaze fell on him. "I see Judge Fuqua there! We've caught the ear of a dissenter. Welcome, law-giver. What say ye to the prophesy of Daniel?"

Remy spat, and steadied himself in the saddle. "I say read 'em the rest, Reverend."

"How's that?"

"The rest of the chapter, Brother. Read 'em the rest." When the minister hesitated, Remy walked his horse through the center of the crowd, and it parted before him. When he reached the minister he snatched the open Bible from his hand.

A man named Baldwin had published a book called *The Armageddon,* in which the author maintained that the Bible foretold of the South's coming success. The book enjoyed great currency in Texas, at least among the religiously inclined. Remy took it upon himself to consult his own King James and consequently formed a different opinion.

"Let's just read it like it is," he told them. "Judge for yourselves." He held the book up for them all to see, and then drew it back to his chest. "The Book of Daniel, Chapter eleven, verse thirteen: For the King of the North shall return, and shall set forth a multitude greater than the South's, and shall certainly come after certain years with a great army and many riches.

"Verse fifteen: So the King of the North shall come, and

cast up a mount, and take the most fenced cities, and the arms of the South shall not withstand, neither his chosen people, neither shall there be any strength to withstand.

"Verse twenty-five: And the King of the North shall stir up his power and his courage against the King of the South with a great army; and the King of the South shall be stirred up to battle with a very great and mighty army; but he shall not stand, for the Kingdom of the North shall forecast devices against him.

"Verse twenty-seven: And both these Kings shall be to do mischief against the other, and they shall speak lies at one table; but neither shall prosper: for the end will come at the time appointed."

Remy closed the book, handed it back to the blustering Baptist and swung around to face the sullen crowd. *"But neither shall prosper,"* he repeated. "What's there to fear in that, ya dumb sons of bitches?" he asked them dryly and then quietly rode on.

Late in December, 1860, South Carolina had voted to secede. She was either joined immediately by her Southern sisters or soon would be. Remy had no doubt of that. Now, due to the frenzied efforts of merchants, lawyers, and young politicians—barking war dogs all—it was Texas' turn to decide.

Remy sat quietly as the phrasing of the Secession Ordinance took shape. He realized there was little use in debating its provisions. Remy agreed with practically every one. It was the supposed solution that he opposed.

The Convention decided upon six reasons for secession:

The general government of the United States had administered the western territories in such a way as to exclude the influence of the South. This was true; slavery was outlawed in the west.

The disloyalty of the people of the North and the imbecility of their leadership had created incendiarism and out-

lawry in Kansas. This Remy considered partially true.
Abolitionists had preached violence, and John Brown,
among others, had listened. But Remy knew that the zeal-
ots did not speak for the entire North, they simply shouted
louder just like they did in Texas.

The Union had failed to defend Texas against both Mexican bandits and Indians. This was certainly true, but the
army had never faced the viciousness of either element before. Warfare on the frontier, be it against horse Indians
or fierce Mexicans, was something new, just as it'd been
for the Ranger companies when they were first formed. The
Yankees were learning their hard lessons.

The ordinance further stated that the Northern people
had become inimical to the South and to their beneficent
and patriarchal system of African slavery, preaching the
debasing doctrine of the equality of all men, irrespective of
race or color. Now here, Remy thought, was the true curse
of slavery. There were now one hundred eighty-two thousand slaves in Texas alone—almost half the Anglo number.
While ninety percent of the population owned no slaves,
no one wanted to live next to them as equals. The South,
Remy knew, saw no place in their society for the people
they had uprooted. They preferred slavery to any alternative and now would have to fight for it.

The slave-holding states had become a minority, unable
to defend themselves against Northern opposition. This was
true, but also just. Other nations had phased out slavery in
peace, and Remy believed the same could occur in the
South. He lived well without slaves, and others could make
the same adjustment. It was a matter of time and patience,
and it seemed to him that both had run out in Texas.

The extremists of the North had elected as president and
vice president two men whose chief claims to such high
positions were the approval of all the above wrongs. These
men were pledged to the final ruin of the slave-holding
states. Remy had a problem with this. It was unfortunate,
of course, that Lincoln had been elected. The North had
put forth a "Black Republican" to answer sectionalism with
sectionalism. A strong nationalist candidate, a master of
compromise and diplomacy, a healer—an Andrew Jackson
perhaps—would have been preferred. No such man had

emerged. But Lincoln was sworn to uphold the Constitution and was therefore bound by it. He could irritate and obstruct the South if that were truly his wish, but he could not attack and destroy it. Remy knew the South was safer in the Union than outside of it. But the ordinance adopted did not speak of that. Houston, on the other hand, often did, but he was drowned out as a traitor to his own people. Remy stood with his old commander, and the same label applied.

Remy sat in his chair as the final provisions were read before a packed House and gallery. Each of the delegates, representing their neighbors from the Red River to the Río Grande, was then called by name to vote. He heard two dozen "ayes" before he heard his name. "Fuqua."

He rose before the House to deliver the answer he'd practiced a hundred times before now. The gallery was hushed. He was the first to speak before he voted. They waited to hear what he would say.

"Mr. Speaker," he began, "I offer this house the wisdom of two men who marked the passage of my long years. Their words have guided my path to this day, and I won't turn away from them now. Stephen Austin, the true founder of this state, rose from his deathbed to warn me that it is far easier to destroy a nation than to build one. His words haunt me as I watch the storm gather here. Secondly, I remember the words of my father-in-law, Don Carlos Amarante de la Cruz. When I, a white man, entered a Mexican's house, our cultures clashed as violently as our troubled nation's do now. We soon came to blows, but before blood was drawn and our family ruined, this noble man said that, while it was right to argue, we must never fight. We made that house our home, and I've never forgotten those words of peace and compromise. This house would do well to consider them now."

The House erupted in hisses and taunts. The speaker pounded his gavel to restore order. When all was quiet, the chief delegate turned again to him. "The time for speeches has passed," he snapped. "Aye or nay, Fuqua. Let's get on with it, man."

Remy raised his voice in response. "It doesn't surprise me that this House can't interpret wisdom when it's offered. I've

given you my answer! I still hear the echo of Mexican cannon
fire from the fields of San Jacinto ringing in my ears. Twenty-
five years have passed, but I'm still not deaf to reason. I know
what war looks like! Soon you'll all have your own view. I
warn you in advance that you'll find it ugly."

The gallery shouted him down. "The North won't fight!"
"Peaceable secession!" He heard one voice clearly.
"Hang 'im!"

Remy turned to the gallery. "What're you people afraid
of? The voice of one man? You'll soon hear the screams
of thousands! Your hisses'll not drown out the thunder of
the Northern guns! Your jeers rock this house today, but
the Yankees'll tear it down around you tomorrow. The
blood of our sons will flow like a river. Right or wrong, the
Union is our only shelter."

He looked at the angry faces perched in the balcony.
"You say, hang me? What's there to fear from me? I'll not
raise my hand today against this state for which I proudly
fought, and I won't raise it tomorrow against my own kind
when this house leads Texas to war and ruin. Not now!
Not ever!"

"Aye or Nay!" the Speaker insisted, "or you'll be passed
over!" He pounded the gavel until its handle snapped.

Remy thundered his reply. "Do you need to hear the
words! Who would listen? In the name of God and Texas
I vote No! No! And Hell No!"

Remy sank to his seat against the deafening roar of protest and the flash of burning eyes. The crowd grew quiet
again only when the next name was finally called. He was
out of breath, his heart was nearly beating out of his chest.
He was drowned out and defeated, but he'd said what he'd
come to say. Out of the corner of his eye, he saw Sam
Houston watching him.

Houston, the old Jacksonian, a believer in the mystique
and destiny of the Great Experiment, had argued with his
last breath for Unionism in the Senate debates in Washington. Appalled by what they considered his traitorous efforts, the state political machine had yanked him home
from the Capitol. Undaunted, Houston ran for governor
that hot summer, frequently peeling his shirt from his
sweating back, on a populist, party-less platform in 1857.

He lost. He ran again in '59 and won, and sat before this Assembly as its reluctant, powerless governor. Unionism, Remy knew, had finally ruined the old warrior. Fate and the fervor of the times had shoved him aside.

Houston had sat calmly whittling when Remy's turn had come to vote. Now that he was seated again, Remy's gaze fixed on his, and Houston nodded in approval. That was the last he'd ever get that day. But it was also the proudest of his life.

"Aye!" was the next answer, the next and the next, and so on amidst the few "No's" until the name of James Throckmorton was called. Remy could see that this man would speak also.

"Mr. President, Judge Fuqua spoke well enough for me. In view of the responsibility, in the presence of God and my country, unawed by the wild spirit of revolution around me, I vote no!"

The gallery drowned him out in derision. Remy watched him spring to his feet again. "Mr. President, when the rabble hiss, well may patriots tremble!" and he sat down. Remy wished that he'd said that. Abuse came in waves from the gallery until even the delegates themselves shouted them back down, and the black toll went on. In the end, only six others had voted with Remy.

As news of the tally spread, the gallery shouted in victory. The delegates stood and embraced each other while they turned their backs to him. Pistols were fired in the house, he heard rifle shots in the streets. Everywhere people were celebrating. Before the Speaker had touched his pen to the document, a procession of women carried a magnificently hand-stitched Lone Star flag to take the place of the Stars and Stripes. The referendum would be offered to the people now, and Remy, like everyone else present, knew how they would vote.

Remy filed through the exuberant crowd, those closest to him turning cold and hostile until he'd passed. Everywhere, dark eyes followed him. At last he ran into a group that did not disperse. "Excuse me, fellers," Remy said.

"There ain't no excuse for a traitor like you," said the ugliest one. Remy recognized him after a moment's recollection. This was a land man who had brought a claim before Remy's court. He'd found against him and was proud of it. He realized then that this particular confrontation wasn't about politics, it was revenge.

Remy's stomach knotted as he struggled to control his anger. This man wasn't worth it and Remy made sure he knew. "I know you, boy," Remy said. "I know your kind. Scum like you don't bother me no more. You ain't worth the lickin' you deserve for insultin' me. You're here today and gone tomorrow. Your kind don't leave no tracks."

The man ejected a syrupy stream of tobacco juice on the floor. Remy saw that it splattered on the cuffs of his pants. "Might've left one," he said through those dirty teeth, his gray eyes fixed on Remy's. "Your case has been attended to, Fuqua. Mark it. It's true."

"What's that supposed to mean, you slacker?"

"You'll soon see, Fuqua. There ain't no place in Texas for you no more."

Remy snatched the man by the collar and shoved him against the wall. "I won't hear talk like that! I believe in the law, and I don't think it'd be wise to shake my faith today. You or anyone of your grog shop associates set one foot on my land and I'll hack it off! I swear it."

He studied the man's dull eyes. They told him nothing except that there was no fear. "I'll be waitin' for you!" This Remy delivered as an oath.

"Relax, Judge," the man said with a strange assurance. "I know your place very well. You'd be pleased to recollect that I once had a claim thereabouts. But yew won't see me aroun' there no more. And remember that I was with yew here today. Might be important 'fore long."

"Don't you threaten me, boy! I'll make quick work of you!"

"It's no threat," he snapped. "It's a fact. You'll get what's comin' to ya if you ain't already, but I don't have to do nuthin'. Ya done it to yourself. I just made sure the right folks knew about it, and that'll be the end of yew, sure as hell."

"We'll see about that, Mister," Remy seethed, and he released him.

"Yes, we will, Judge," he sneered maliciously. "We damn sure will."

Chapter Forty-Two

Remy stood with Sam Houston and five others before the blank eye of the camera. The flash briefly blinded him. When he opened his eyes again, the breeze had blown the white, bitter smoke over them all, where it lingered. Houston fanned it from his face, and then stepped away. He turned to Remy and said, "There now! Solid evidence contrary to the popular opinion. I was still alive on this day." He coughed dryly. "Join me for refreshment, won't you, Judge?"

They walked side by side down Congress Avenue, Houston lumbering with a pronounced, unsteady limp, his face grimacing from the pain of the ankle shattered twenty-five years before, until they reached a watering hole not unknown to Remy. Houston's cough persisted. His chest rattled and wheezed as he exhaled. He looked drawn, pale, and old. He paused at the door, and it was then that Remy noticed the dark stains on the thigh of the general's trousers. When he removed his coat, Remy saw another on his shoulder. The old wounds, he knew, were weeping again.

"Now it's well known, Fuqua," Houston announced, "that I quit barrooms in 1845, and that I only patronized them in a small way before that." Remy laughed. "Nevertheless," he continued, "this joint comes highly recommended by drunkards whose opinion I still value." He paused. "Politicians every one, I assure you," he added.

"Suits me," Remy said.

Not a head turned as they made their way to the bar. Remy watched as the governor ordered an anemic ginger water and a shot glass of good Kentucky bourbon whiskey. Remy bought the rest of the bottle and they turned together from the bar.

"Best to sit in the light," Houston said, "don't you think?" Remy figured Houston's life had been threatened, too. His suggestion was probably wise, and Remy followed him.

They sat together in the corner, their backs to the wall.

Houston propped his ankle in the seat of an empty chair and rested his cane against his leg. The table was sufficiently illuminated by a nearby window. Remy filled his glass and sipped it.

"Tough in there today, was it not?" Houston said.

"It was what I expected, General."

"Nevertheless, I'm proud of you," Houston told him. "It takes a big man to stand up to a mob like that. In some ways, you remind me of me." He brought the glass of ginger to his lips and paused. "And that's not good."

Remy grinned. "I would've thought there'd been more than seven to vote against secession. The goddamn war dogs stacked the House. Where were the planters from the Brazos? They don't want this."

"No," Houston agreed, "but they're afraid to do what you just did. They think they can stay home and count their money and all of this'll go away. Those men have every quality of a dog, save fidelity. Of course, I thought we'd do better just the same. I can't express my disappointment. The war dogs have no idea what they've done."

Remy watched as Houston studied the glass of whiskey before him. He reached for it, and Remy reached for his hand.

"I thought you swore that off when you were baptized," he said.

"It's true. I took the covenant in the river on a cold, November day. All my sins were washed away, or so the good reverend told me. My first thought was of those poor fish." He slipped his hand from under Remy's. "Don't fret yourself, Fuqua. Houston's bowed but not broken. I haven't sipped a drop since '51." He brought the glass to his nose and breathed deeply. "But I still savor the aroma so. There's nothing like the smell of good whiskey."

Satisfied that he'd not be a part of any moral backsliding, Remy returned to the business at hand. "What will you do now, Sam?"

"I'll fight the referendum tooth and nail," the old man vowed with those steely blue eyes. "It must get by the people first, and my name still means something to them."

"And if it passes?"

"Then I'll obstruct the secessionists every way I can and

buy time. I'm the elected governor of this state. There's the matter of legality for the convention to jump first. They won't push me aside as easily as they think."

Remy maintained no illusions of such futility. "You can't stop 'em. If secession passes, they'll join the Confederacy and they'll come to you to take the oath."

"I'll never do it, Fuqua," Houston answered crisply. "I took another oath, and I'll stand by it to the very end."

"You'll have to. We all will."

"I won't," he said, and he was adamant.

"What, then?"

"I'll reform the Republic, the Southern Confederacy be damned. We voted today to leave the Union and nothing more. We stood outside the United States before, and we can do it again. I've spent a considerable amount of time in the east. I know the Northern people. There'll be no 'peaceable secession.' They'll crush the South before they ever let her go. Texas must stand apart, and leave the secessionists to their fate. All I need is a little time while I formulate a diversion to draw the Texians away from civil war."

Remy leaned forward in his chair. "What sort of diversion?" he asked him.

"Why, the invasion of Mexico, of course." He'd said it as casually as if he were announcing that he planned to cross the street.

Remy was dumbfounded. "What?!"

Houston stared at him blankly. "Don't look so shocked, Captain. It's the most obvious course."

"That's treason," he said curtly.

"Yes, it was. Yesterday. But tomorrow, after secession, we'll call it a matter of national interest. No Texian'll blink twice. Already the cream of the Ranger companies gather. I've asked the Secretary of War to provide me with modern arms in the name of national defense. The Yankees may buy that. When we have the guns, we'll ride against northern Mexico in the name of bringing order, and at the same time, provoke hostilities."

Remy shook his head in disappointment. "That's dead wrong, General."

"Wrong?" Houston asked him. "What is *wrong*? I only

see hard choices. I tell you that war is inevitable, Fuqua. The question is do we want it here or in Mexico?"

"Think of those people, for God's sake! They've suffered enough."

"I have," Houston said. "The Mexicans've had fifty governments in forty years. The masses'll not notice if a white face shows itself in the Halls of Montezuma. Only a few must die. In the end, Mexico will be saved from herself. Their suffering can only end under our flag. History will never fault me, and there's more to gain than territory."

"Like what?"

"The Union, man!" He spoke it like a creed. "Expansionism is not dead. Already there are designs on Cuba and Central America. But Mexico's the real prize. The United States may pull herself together to face a common foe. The war at home is avoided, a rival falls, and Democracy marches on to conquer new land. America controls the continent more completely than even Jackson ever dreamed. And the Mexican people will embrace us as their savior."

Remy polished off the last of his glass and corked the bottle. "Where you're goin'," he said calmly, "I can't go. I've done what I can for the Union. I don't believe you start one war to stop another, General, and I want no part of your damn schemes."

"Not schemes, Fuqua," he countered. "They're only dreams."

"Call it what you will, Houston. It's still ugly." He glared at the governor. "I'm a simple man. I don't see what you see, and I'm damn proud of it. My hands, Sam, are bloody enough." He pushed his chair back and rose. "My constituents, God love 'em, tell me that my seat's suddenly vacant. Word is they're fittin' me for a hemp necktie. If they ask, Governor, tell 'em they can find me at home playin' with my grandbabies."

Houston sat rigid, expressionless, and pale as Remy stood. His eyes were vacant. Then he grabbed his arm. The first thing Remy noticed was an obvious shift in his voice. "Sit, Remy," he pleaded. "For God's sake, please sit. You're so goddamned hot-headed that I'm surprised you didn't vote with those other idiots."

Remy looked at the arm that held him. "It's time for me to go, General."

"There's no reason to go," he protested, gripping him tighter. "I'm old, and I'm tired and my country's gone to hell. After all we've been through together, can you not bear a little ranting? I can't invade Mexico, and I can't afford to lose another friend. Sit with me a while longer, Remy," he said. "I beg you."

With some reluctance, Remy sat back down. Houston released him. "You had me goin' there, General," he said as he pulled the cork from his bottle. "You've always been full of surprises, but this was your best."

Houston managed a smile and sipped his ginger. "That was no surprise, Captain. It was policy until one minute ago."

"I know for a fact that I didn't change your mind."

"No, of course not," Houston said, waving his hand. "I've been yelled at all my life for my convictions. I'm used to it." His tone shifted. "But when you rose to leave I felt the lights dim a little. My heart skipped a beat, and for a moment I did not have the strength to grip this glass." His gaze turned to the distance. "I'm old, Remy. I know I'm dying."

"Don't talk like that, General."

"It's true, I feel it. My world's crumbling, and I'm too weak to stop it. I'll die in exile, a broken man. I can see that now. There'll be no invasion of Mexico, and Texas'll join the Confederacy before the end of the month. Civil war follows as sure as night follows day. I know I won't live to see the end of it."

Remy sat there, watching him sadly. His cheeks sunk against his bones as he spoke. He looked almost frail. The man seemed to age before his eyes. The glow was gone.

"You and I've seen war, Fuqua," Houston told him. "But we've not seen a war like this one. 'Peaceable secession,' my arse! Texas'll drown in her own blood. Hundreds of thousands of my people will die."

He asked if Remy truly judged it immoral to invade Mexico. For his part, he said, he didn't think twice about it. Where his nation was threatened, he didn't allow morality to get in his way. He saw, he said, only what Jackson had taught him to see.

His hand steadied. "In my day, by God, the nation came first! I could've easily won Mexico. It's still clear in my mind, and only I could have done it. If I were ten years younger, I'd have provoked a war a month ago and the western world would change! I see it vividly in the dimming light. I'm the last of my kind, Fuqua. I make nations!" Then his voice grew quiet. "But just now, as you started to leave me, I realized I'd waited too long. The moment came, I sensed it, but like a fool I let it pass me by. It's my last and most deeply regretted mistake. This body no longer responds to this great will. The error has cost me Texas."

Remy really didn't know what to say. He pitied this old, wounded, arthritic man. Houston must've seen it in Remy's eyes. His own flashed angrily. His response was immediate, and Remy shuddered at the return of that booming voice.

"Don't look at me like that, man! You shame me! I won't have it! Don't take this image of me away—that of my darkest day—when you leave this room. I'm sick, and poor and I'll soon be powerless. History'll sweep me aside with a footnote. My enemies'll see to that. But this is not the picture I want you to hold when you leave this old man whose sand has run out. What you see here is not Sam Houston!"

Remy wanted to soothe him. "You'll be remembered, General. Always."

The general snapped back. "But not like this, in defeat! I have another image in mind!" He closed his eyes for a moment. When they opened again, a smile had come. "You were with me, Fuqua, on that day back in April in '36. We were beaten, and on the run. Do you remember?"

"I do, General," Remy said quietly, almost a whisper. "Very well."

"And then Santa Anna made one mistake. I could smell it, and only I understood how to squeeze out every advantage. In the afternoon I rallied men who had threatened to hang me that same morning. They tell me that I'm no Andrew Jackson. Jackson be damned! Even his will was no match for Texians. Merciful God, what a race!"

"You're preachin' to the choir, General," Remy said. "I was there."

"Then you saw me mount that white charger, pull my sword from its sheath, and lead those men to victory! 'Hold your fire, men,' I told them. 'Hold your fire.' I still hear it so very well. Twice my horse was shot out from under me, my boot was full of my own blood, but I rode on at the front of my line. Before the smoke cleared, I knew I'd changed history. In twenty minutes, I made a nation! Do you remember, Fuqua?"

"Sure I do," Remy said, nodding with pride.

Houston's gaze gripped him now. Those gray eyes glistened. "Nothing," he cried, "no enemy, no illness, no misfortune, can ever take that moment away from me! When you think of Sam Houston, Captain Fuqua, I want you to think of him on that day. It was my finest."

He reached for Remy's hand and grasped it. The general's fingers felt cold and callused. Remy could feel them tremble. "Will you do me this one last favor, my old friend? It would mean so very much to me."

"Of course I will, General. I've never forgotten, and I never will. I was proud to serve under you then, and now."

Houston closed his eyes and bowed his head. A smile came to his lips. "Thank you," he muttered. "Thank you."

Chapter Forty-Three

As he rode on, Remy wondered if he should try to ride out the war as Don Carlos had advised him to do years ago. He knew his heart couldn't be in this one. But straddling the fence hadn't done Don Carlos any good, and from talking with General Houston, he realized that he wouldn't profit by it either. If he wanted his land, he would have to fight for it. Nothing had changed. If Placido still lived, Remy thought, even he would not fault him. He hadn't gone looking for war, war had come looking for him.

Joaquin would enlist, he felt certain of that. He and Beatriz had sent the boy to the military academy in Bastrop. Houston's boy was there now. Since graduation, young Jack had taken an interest in the land, it was true. But when war broke out, the ranch wouldn't hold him any better than Remy's uncle's farm had once held him. The trick, Remy thought, would be to detain him there a while as things took shape.

Remy thought he might go to Houston's old ally, Ashbel Smith, and agree to form his own company with the understanding that they'd be stationed on the frontier and fight at home, as Houston had suggested. The Northerners may threaten, but the Comanche were already astir. Even the government, whatever government, might understand that. He'd keep one eye on Texas, the other on Jack.

He thought of how the ranch should be managed in his inevitable absence, what precautions to take, where to put their money so it'd be safe—those sorts of things. But in the end all of these considerations gave way to the pending confrontation between him and Beatriz. There was no way he could tell her and avoid blood. She never did understand why he'd become a lawyer and then a judge. She hadn't spoken to him for a month when he entered politics. She was almost indifferent to the secessionist furor. His stand for Unionism was lost on her, and he understood why. Her people were still not included. But she understood the violence and threats he received from his own people well enough. She'd heard them ever since white people settled in Texas. She'd seen them turn on Don Carlos, who was innocent. He knew the fact that they'd turned on him was no surprise to her. That he was willing to fight for them would be the shocker.

Remy thought he'd try to put it to her this way. He was still fighting for their land and still fighting for her place in it. If the South won, he would be a part of it. He and Beatriz's fortunes would rise with the Confederacy. If the North won, God only knows what would happen, but he'd have the respect of his own people because he'd done what a man in his position was expected to do. Sooner or later, he and Beatriz could go on as they had or maybe better.

On the other hand, if he did nothing they'd be cast out as Don Carlos was, and everything they'd worked for would be lost. Already it was happening to others, and he couldn't bear to see it happen to him. He loved his land and his life, and he thought that, at fifty-five years of age, he was too old to start over. The fire, the hunger, was gone and even she could see it. His only choice was to cling to what they had, a lariat in one hand, a rifle in the other. The way it'd always been.

When Texas joined the Confederacy, he would publicly announce that he'd taken the unavoidable oath. That would stop the threats and his family would be safe. Then he'd raise his command and patrol the frontier and be thanked for it. He would go to war only when war came to Texas. For him, it would first and last be a defensive campaign. Anyway, that is what he'd tell her, and when he did, he'd make sure old Quelepe was near so that he could patch his wounds. With just a little luck and a little time, he knew he could ride it all out. He had always been so damn lucky.

Gray settled into black when night fell; the wind grew still. The winter cold bit his fingers as they gripped the cracked leather of the reins. Everything was quiet save the squeak of his tack when he heard the snap of branches under careful hooves and the rustling of dry, brittle brush. Out of habit he drew the Gump from its scabbard, cocked it, and lay it gently across his lap. From then on, he watched everything and listened closely. What he heard was most likely a browsing deer, he thought.

He soon crested a long rise, saw immediately the orange glow pulsating beneath the metallic blanket of impervious clouds. He paused for just an instant to study it. Fire. On the river. Near his place. And he was at least ten miles away. He lashed the horse with the reins and galloped for his home. As he grew closer, he was certain he heard shouting.

He abandoned the trail to travel as the crow flies, driving the groaning horse through thickets of live oak, dogwood, greenbriar, cypress and cedar that shrouded the river bot-

tom. Thorned vines raked across Remy's cheek, but he
rode on. He let the gelding, darting and wheeling, pick its
own way through the blank. Remy leaned low against its
lathered neck and held tight. When it came to the bluff
over the little creek, it leaped across in one long bound,
stumbling briefly on the loose gravel on the opposite bank.
Remy hung close, and whipped it again until it found its
feet. The chill no longer bit him. All Remy felt from then
on was the beating of his frantic heart. He knew then he'd
made his choices too late. It had happened again.

Remy crashed out of the brush above the river onto the
open pasture nearest his home. When he saw it plainly, all
momentum ceased. He stopped there and stared. For the
third time in his life he returned to face utter destruction.
There should've been cattle all around him. There were
none. The barns, the sheds, the outbuildings, the homes of
the vaqueros and Elijah's cabin were all engulfed in flames.
They could not burn the wall, or the big house, but they'd
obviously tried. Smoke billowed from glass-less windows,
the limestone above them was stained black with cinders.

It was a sight he should've anticipated. He'd heard the
threats, he knew what was happening to other people, and
he always knew it might happen to him. When he saw the
glow he'd tried to prepare himself. He knew they'd gotten
him, and they'd gotten him good.

Every instinct told him to go on. Put out the fires, attend
to the wounded, bury the dead, swear revenge blood for
blood. Fight! That was what his heart demanded. But his
mind knew better. The image before him simply overwhelmed any impulse, and despair extinguished his smoldering rage. All he could do was stand there, keep his
distance and hang his head. They'd whipped him.

Most of all, he did not want to ride in there and find the
body of his wife. If she was in there, he resolved to bury
her. Then he pictured himself sitting next to that fresh

grave with the Colt to his head, his finger on the trigger; he could hear his brain beg him to pull it just a little this one last time. His mother had done it, the precedent was set, and Remy knew he could do it, too. This time there was no way out, and no place to go.

And then he heard a man's voice. It screamed in Spanish for the vaqueros to man the well and form a line to the house. It snapped Remy from his hopelessness and he whipped the horse one last time to coax it through the burning gate. He saw that his skin flashed red from the fire. The people were alive and they were fighting it—black, white and Méxicano together—and Remy resolved to fight it, too.

The first man he came to was Starkes, black with smudge, the whites of his eyes glistening against the flames.

"Where's my wife?" Remy shouted.

Starkes did not look at him. "You shoulda kept your mouth shut, Judge! You brung this on yourself. My place's next."

"I asked you a question, goddamn ya! Where's Beatriz!"

"Aroun' the back, savin' what she can. She's all right, Judge. She was with me and my wife when they came." When his bucket was filled, he ran off to the house. He paused briefly at the porch and turned again to Remy and stared at him. He threw the water without looking. Remy left them all and ran to find Beatriz.

When he saw her, when he confirmed that she was alive, when he heard her ordering the others to save what they could, he found the first measure of calm in that chaos. All was not lost as long as that woman lived.

She looked at him and rattled in Spanish. "Remy! Quickly! The furniture!" And he followed her skirt, part of which he saw was burned away, and entered the inferno with her. From now on until she drew her last breath, Remy would be by her side. The whole world could burn, he thought, and the flames would never touch them. Not while they were together.

By daybreak it was over. What could be saved lay in a blackened pile. The rest, all of it, had burned. Everything save the stone was reduced to smoldering ashes.

When they'd done all they could do, Beatriz looked to the wounded. She laid them away from the house in the sun, fed and watered them, spread a little butter on their burns. There was not enough to go around. Remy saw to the dead. Some of the men were already rebuilding a shed to house them from the winter wind. They were coping.

Joaquin had slipped away at dawn with Picosa and two other grim young vaqueros. Remy knew without asking that they followed the tracks of the murderers. He said nothing and let them go. It was what he would do if he were their age and had their spirit. His rage had passed on to them. True justice in Texas had always relied on the gun. Remy's relied on Joaquin's.

Ten white raiders had hanged nine of Remy's own, six Mexicans and three blacks. Remy and one of his vaqueros cut them down one by one and buried them. They dug nine fresh graves in the rocky, black earth. Most of the vaqueros had been out on the ranch that day. They'd seen the flames and rode in. Always armed, they'd managed to ball off the murderers. As soon as that was done, they'd cut Quelepe free. He still kicked. After that, they attended to the fire.

Remy sent most of the vaqueros and blacks and their families to Starkes' place. They were to go and protect it and themselves; one man was to return with a wagon. All of Remy's had been burned. A few others volunteered to stay behind with Beatriz and Elena Marie to do what must be done.

Beatriz sat tirelessly with Quelepe's head in her lap, stroking his hair. Remy sat by her side to give her a fair chance to tell him what a fool he'd been.

"I'm sorry," he told her. "I never thought it'd come to this. I thought I could reason with 'em. I'd forgotten how mean they were. It's my fault." But she said nothing. Instead, she spread her free arm around his shoulders and pressed him against her.

"I'm proud of you, husband," she gently said in Spanish, "but it's time to go." Just like that. There was no anger, no blame, no resentment. She just said what he knew was right. There was no other moment that he could remember when he loved her more. It was just time to go.

He lifted his head from her shoulder and nodded. "I know," was all he said.

When Quelepe heard Remy speak these last words his eyes opened and searched for him. "Don Remy?" His voice was dry and raspy. "Is that you?"

Remy put his hand to Quelepe's ancient, scraggly cheek. "I'm here, old man."

Quelepe grabbed his hand, his fingers felt cold. "I fought for our land, Don Remy. At first, I welcomed them as I would any stranger, but then I saw the evil in their eyes and I knew why they'd come. I fought them, Don Remy, with the last of my strength, but there were too many. I want you to know that I did not give in."

"Rest quiet, Quelepe," Remy said, pulling his hand away to press it against Quelepe's rising chest. "I know you did what you could."

Quelepe rubbed his rope-burned throat. "They beat me with a rifle butt and knocked me senseless. I watched them hang the others and then they came for me. I did not cry out."

"Well, you cheated 'em, Quelepe," Remy said. "You're too damn skinny to hang. All gristle. If it'd been me, I'd have tied a rock to your ass."

Beatriz's wary expression told him, no more jokes. Quelepe closed his eyes again. "Don't be afraid, Don Remy. Against the flames of the great house, I saw you and Beatriz old and happy in some other place. Your people'll have turned against you as people do, but God will not forsake you. It'll be as I've told you. You won't die in Tejas. You still have your courage and you still have your luck. In the west, that's all you need."

Remy looked over the ruin of his ranch. "Well, we're just gonna go see. I grant ya that."

Quelepe reached for his hand. *"Adiós, mi hijo,"* he whispered.

Remy gripped it. "You ain't goin' nowhere but California, you old fool."

Quelepe shook his head. "Shut up, Don Remy, and listen for once. Only you would argue with the dying. Lay me to

rest in your place, next to Elijah, and go with open arms
in peace. What belongs to me now belongs to Joaquin. Tell
him I love him."

"He knows, Quelepe."

"You tell him!" the old man commanded, his eyes glistening. "It's all right to say the words, Don Remy. I can
say them. I love you, and I love Beatriz. I'll miss you both
dearly. You'll rise from this, I promise you."

"We love you," Beatriz told him.

"There's one thing more," he muttered, his glance lost
to the distance. "Out there on the plains somewhere is
Carlito, young and strong as you, Don Remy, once were. I
see him clearly." He chest rattled, he struggled for breath.
"He no longer knows who he is. He runs wild with the
Comanche. I don't know what'll happen, but I know this.
If you can tame him again, like you did the great stallion,
he is yours forever." He gasped. "Joaquin will know his
brother, and you'll have another son. It'll not be easy, but
nothing ever is. *Cuidado,* my friends. Go with God."

Then his eyes waxed over and he slipped away. Remy
let go of the hand when it no longer gripped his. Remy
dug his ninth and final grave while Beatriz prepared Quelepe's body. The last of the old ones was gone.

As

It was nearly midnight when Joaquin returned. Remy
watched him as he sat by the coals, a poncho around his
shoulders, his rifle in his lap. Without a word Joaquin unsaddled his horse and drew a little water from the well.

"Hot coffee by the fire," Remy offered.

Joaquin spit out the water and reached for a cup. Remy
filled it for him, and Jack squatted by the fire to drink it.
When he offered nothing, Remy asked.

" 'Ya'll find 'em?"

Joaquin sipped his coffee and then stared at him. "We
found 'em," he said. "Camped down by the river south of
Austin. Blind drunk."

"Anybody see ya?"

"No one that lived."

"Ya'll shot ten men?"

"Naw, we shot four. The rest we hung," he said, and he took another sip of his coffee. "An' they're still hangin'."

"Ya'll leave any sign?"

"Nary a one. Took care of it myself."

Remy studied him a moment. Joaquin appeared steady, a little too steady maybe. Those dark eyes mirrored the low flame of the coals. Remy saw pain. "You all right?" he asked him.

"Yeah, I'm all right," Joaquin said. "They got what was due, I reckon."

Remy nodded once. "Sounds like they did," he said.

Jack turned from the fire and stared at Remy. "I didn't care for it much, Pa. At least, not like I thought I would when we rode out of here all in a huff."

Remy refilled his own cup. "Good."

Chapter Forty-Four

Thirty-five years of accumulated wealth fit into two borrowed wagons, the gaps between each squeaky oak plank sealed with straw and pitch for the river crossings as Diego Picosa had done. There was nothing anyone could do about the goddamn dust.

As Remy and his family prepared to leave Texas in March, 1861, Texas delegates voted one hundred and nine to two to join the Confederacy. All state officials were ordered to take the oath of allegiance. Remy heard that Sam Houston had sat in the Capitol's basement and whittled while they called his name three separate times. True to form, he refused to speak the words. He was removed from office.

Beatriz set about her tasks with the vigor of a woman half her age. Texas was no longer a home to her. She preferred starting over with nothing in California to living with money and property here. Her enthusiasm inspired his, and he saw to his own affairs.

He couldn't find a buyer for his land. Refugees never

could. But his money was there in the brokerage houses of Houston at his disposal, and his cattle, what was left of them, still chewed their cud on the winter grass. Before the raid he'd had thousands. Sensing weakness exactly where it was, thieving cowboys stole what the raiders hadn't scattered. Remy took fifty of the best that remained; the rest roamed wild as they always had.

He offered his men allotments of his land. They each refused. The vaqueros chose to stay with him. Some of the blacks sought their freedom in Mexico with Remy's blessing. The rest packed up for the journey west. He deeded the entire ranch to his daughter, who vowed to stay, and Remy sadly wished her well. It nearly killed Beatriz to leave Elena Marie behind, but she accepted it as she had all other disappointments. Their daughter had her own life now, and two daughters of her own to raise. These were the hardest to leave behind.

Remy ran an ad in the Austin paper to buy him the time they needed. It said briefly that he could no longer stand against the rising crimson tide. He'd fallen for a principle as Houston had, and he was proud of his company. It should please his enemies to know that they'd run him out. He thanked his neighbors and constituents for years of friendship, trust and good will. It remarked that they were all fine people, easier led than goats, and accomplished arsonists as long as the grass was dry. They need not come again, it said, the Fuquas were truly going. The secessionists could go to hell and wait for Jeff Davis to meet them there. They would get, it said, what was coming to them. Unfortunately, the rest of the country would get it with them. It was no misfortune to him that he'd not be there to see it happen. They'd see their homes smoking soon enough. The best and the bravest were either dead or gone, and now the Fuquas were going, too. It ended with "God Bless Texas and God Damn You."

While Remy and Beatriz made their preparations, they met others on the run. Some had been burned out, the rest just figured they soon would be. Remy welcomed them all. On the barren plains there was strength only in numbers.

They left mid-April, just before the May rains and just after Beauregard's Confederate battery fired on Fort Sum-

ter, and rode northwest into the hills. They forded the Pedernales, the Llano, and the San Sabá until they reached the
Colorado at its most westward turn. That led them to the
mouth of the Concho, and they paralleled it in the ruts of
the U.S. overland mail route. At the fork, they joined with
another party, refugees from Dallas.

With Cristóbal and Joaquin as outriders, Remy led
them west.

1861

The Last Summer

Chapter Forty-Five

Kills White Bear heard his stomach grumble as he watched
them below. There were far too many, he knew, for the
sort of gnashing, tearing confrontation he would've so enjoyed. Less than twenty warriors followed him this day. Fe-
vers, plague, bluecoats and then the relentless Rangers had
all seen to that. Kills White Bear was connected to his country
by the sheerest thread. Yet, he knew that the spirit of the
Nemenuh was most defiant at its now exposed core.

In many ways it was easier now. The soldiers had gone,
and all but a few Rangers remained on the plains, and these
stayed behind the walls of forts. His Wasps picked their prey
as the hawk picks his hare, falling on them just as quickly,
with talons just as sharp, and then vanished, untouched.

Their many recent victories had encouraged his warriors.
Morale soared as the fortunes of war shifted. For the first
time in four winters of battle and death he heard his warriors talk of their future as if they actually had one. Kills
White Bear kept his own cynical counsel. But he could not
deny that the plains had opened to them just as Maguara's
comet had promised.

The question for him now was, what would they do with them? They were so few, so hungry, so weak. Where, he wondered, would the Great Spirit lead them now?

In his heart, he knew the answer. Even if he never saw another white man in his country, he knew the Penateka had slipped past the point of return. The Wasps, he knew, were a withering arm of a dying body.

But he did see white men rolling across the prairie toward the setting sun, a dozen different parties in one moon's time. Their river flowed east and west, without end. For Kills White Bear it was a grim reminder of the whites' greatest power—the power of numbers. He knew this alone was what had defeated him.

The soldiers were gone today, yes. But they'd return tomorrow. And when they did, they'd see what he saw. The Penateka's river had run dry. That previous spring—the spring that had promised a Great White War, brother against brother—the Wasps were but a trickle. It would take but one more hot and bloody summer under the gun and even that pitiful stream would sink into the dust and never return.

The Great Spirit had chosen this hard path for him, and he knew he could not turn away from it even in the summer of his sixtieth year. He was an old man now, and should've been doing what an old man does. But there was no place for him to sit and reminisce over the stories of his youth, and no one to hear them. He lived on the back of his war pony.

The albino bear had marked his chest in blood for a dark purpose. His fate was cruel, but he accepted it without complaint. It would be left to the other bands to regenerate the Nemenuh nation. For his cousins he still had hope, for his brothers he had none.

Twenty-five winters of war had broken his heart but not his spirit. Rage still smoldered in an empty chest. He still had strength in those cracked, spotted hands. He knew the sclera of his eyes were red and clouded, but they could still follow his enemy's trail. His nose still sniffed out weakness, and he smelled it now as the white wagons rumbled awkwardly below.

Each day he rose without song or prayer and painted his body for war—his pock-scarred face red and his broken heart black. For him the end would come only when the accursed Tejanos put a bullet through him. Any that rode with him could expect the same. What he wanted most, and he made this clear, was to die and end the misery of a life that had lost every purpose but one.

When he saw that another wagon train had come, he recognized only another chance to finish this cruel contest with honor. For three days he and his warriors had followed them. He held the young men, now rootless and wandering, from their rashness while he studied the whites patiently with his genius for war. Where he saw white, he also saw red.

He summoned White Eagle and the others to sit before him as he drew the plan of attack. He detailed every position, considered every contingency, explained when to press them and when to back off. They would pick at the stragglers first to frighten the rest. They would taunt the main body at night so they could not sleep. They would threaten them between water holes to delay and demoralize them. When the water ran out, they would slice them into quarters and cut them down in the heat of the summer sun one man at a time. They would strike like lightning and kill who they could. They should let the horses take the whites' bullets because they could easily be replaced. It was the Wasp warriors who were precious in these last campaigns.

He was proud of their courage, he told them. Not many warriors would take on such a risk. But if it could be done, Kills White Bear affirmed that he could do it. Kills White Bear was on the hunt again, and he saw that his warriors were honored to follow him to the end of the bitter trail.

Chapter Forty-Six

Nights were spent in a tight circle, the tongue of one wagon chained to the next, four men on guard on two-hour shifts. Remy swore to whip any son of a bitch he found asleep, and they seemed to understand that he meant it. There was nothing he could do about the two herders he'd lost. The Indians had hit them that quickly. But the other two he lost were goddamned fools, secessionists who were "better voters than fighters," as the saying went. They'd run from the war they'd wanted, but they'd run the wrong way. Remy buried them where he found them, marking their shallow, dusty graves with a single stone.

Remy didn't know these bastards who had decided to harass them. There weren't supposed to be any Comanche this far south this time of year. But the ones who were out there were damned determined. He saw that right away. Remy's people did not have far to go before they were in New Mexico and Apache country, and Remy knew the Comanche would not dare follow. New Mexico was still garrisoned with United States troops, and the powerful Apache were blood enemies of the Comanche.

But Remy knew that relief was closer than the Río Grande. Fort Stockton was nearby with good water and state troops. It also linked the stage line between San Antonio and El Paso, and would be more heavily traveled than the overland mail route. A little further and the Comanche threat was behind him for good. Remy chose that over going back for water and giving ground he'd already won. The stifling heat and his slow, defensive progress soon made him regret it.

They were moving too slowly over gravelly roads, and he heard the soured water sloshing in the near-empty barrels. The horses and cattle could get a little moisture off the morning dew on the grass, and he knew the Longhorns could go days without water. But where could the sunken-eyed children get a drink? This was on his mind always.

They were four days from water in one direction, and five days in the other, at least according to the map provided with the Texas Almanac. Remy paced the perimeter until midnight and was up again at four. They ate what they had, and at first light the men unchained the wagons as their wives watched over them with determined faces and cocked rifles. These were good people, he thought. Tough. Gritty. They'd make it.

An hour after daylight, the oxen teams were hitched and the wagons rolled on west. Remy sent the best of the single men along with Cristóbal, Jack and his vaqueros to ride ahead and ferret out any ambush. Not an hour passed when he didn't hear gunfire. If it wasn't ahead of him, it was on the flanks. The Comanche, as always, avoided a pitched battle. It was hit and run, a war of attrition and of the greater will. He had to draw the train tightly together and wait for the outriders to respond. Their horses couldn't bear the strain, and after a while neither could he.

It went on like this for three long days. The day before, a day in which they'd not traveled more than five miles, the water had run out. At night he heard the babies crying. Beatriz left his side to do what she could do. The first of the horses died and the screams of thirsty children drowned out the yipping coyotes. There was not a hint of rain in the night sky, and not one blink of lantern light in the black void that lay west between them and Fort Stockton.

He knew he should've waited at the water hole and held off the Comanche until his boots wore out.

Kills White Bear heard the cry of babes on the night wind, yet they did not trouble him. He'd heard the cries of hundreds in his own camps, and the Tejanos had silenced them quickly enough. The thirst of these would soon be quenched in that same cool manner.

White Eagle and four others would detain the scouts. Kills White Bear and his men would wait to hear the shots, and then rush the train. They would not find white men in their sights just yet. They would aim for the oxen now and the wagon wheels would sink into the dust. Their father the sun would do the rest. There were no Rangers to help these people now. Two days more and it'd be done.

Chapter Forty-Seven

The Comanche had baited the outriders too far from the main body. Remy cursed Joaquin, who damn sure should've known better. But they were hot and tired and crazy with thirst. If nothing else, even Remy knew how easy it was to make a mistake.

It was, he knew, what the Comanche had planned. He

stopped the train right there among howls of protest and
told them they best draw up tight and wait.

They didn't have to wait long. Twenty or so warriors hit
the flanks in a blur and not one provided a clear target.
They shot from under the necks of their ponies. Remy
heard the thud of the bullets as they plowed into the meat,
muscle, and bone of groaning oxen. They fell, knees first,
to the dust. Red blood bubbled from dry, powder-white
noses. In twenty minutes, half the teams lay still in the dust.

With the oxen gone, Remy altered his strategy. They had
to split up. He asked for ten volunteers to ride for Fort
Stockton. Picosa was first to raise his hand and Joaquin
second, but Remy shook his head. He needed them there.
Six of his vaqueros and four of the others said they'd go,
and they switched their saddles to fresh horses, Remy's
included. He gave them Mexican silver to pay any price.
Two days there and one day back. They needed an escort
and oxen. "Send the water ahead," he told them. "We'll
hold the Comanche off well enough."

At dawn Remy rose to the sound of approaching hooves.
He hadn't slept an hour. He adjusted his eyes to the dis-
tance. A single Indian rode at the head of a party of ten.
They came within three hundred yards and stopped dead.
Distinctly he saw ten bodies drop from ten horses and then
the Comanche just stood there waiting.

Remy's eye was drawn to the white cape that rode on
the saddle behind the leader. He should've known.

He went first to Joaquin. "You stay with your mother,
you hear? You don't leave her side."

Joaquin nodded. "Where're you goin'?" he asked.

"I gotta talk to somebody," Remy said.

Beatriz heard him well enough and didn't like it. "Before
you talk to anybody, Remy, you talk to me."

He wouldn't tell her that Kills White Bear had come for
them. "Now don't you fret, woman," he said with a feeble

grin. "I'm gonna buy us some time, maybe cut a deal. You tell the others to gear up to travel light. At sundown, we'll make for the fort together. It's what I should've done two days ago. We'll come back for the wagons."

He pulled one of his Colts from his holster, spun it around and handed the bone grip to her. "You keep this close, now, Beatriz." Then he turned to Joaquin. "If somethin' happens—and I don't think it will—you know what to do, don't you?" This had nothing to do with replacing his leadership. What he meant was that under no circumstances should Joaquin allow his mother to be taken alive.

His son's eyes studied his. Remy knew he understood him very well. "Yeah," Joaquin finally said, "I know. What're ya gonna say to 'im, Captain?"

"Somethin' he likes, I hope. Ya'll stay calm. I might know that son of a bitch out there."

As he watched, Beatriz slid his Pa's Christian Gump rifle from that old crusty scabbard.

"Is it Kills White Bear?" she asked him.

"Naw, honey," he lied, and he hoped it was convincing. "He's too old for the warpath. This is probably just some young hothead feelin' his oats."

"Don't be afraid, Remy," she said as she re-primed the pan and snapped the battery back down tightly. "I'll watch over you."

"What's there to be afraid of?" he asked her. "They remember me. It's just a little misunderstanding between old friends."

Kills White Bear shielded his eyes to discern the wavering object that approached. Soon enough he made out the form of a lone Tejano rider. He rejoiced when he saw that it was Fuqua. Now he understood how they'd done so well under his constant pressure. He thanked the Great Spirit for allowing his greatest enemy to fall within his slipping grasp. It was his last and greatest gift.

But then something else struck him, an unexpected complication. He would have no part in turning a son against his father. It was the worst kind of bad medicine, and Kills White Bear knew better than any what sort of damage such an omen could do. He turned to White Eagle, who stood ready, watching all.

"Circle the train and watch the rear," he ordered. "This man may sacrifice himself so that others might live."

He could see that his son was confused. "Where could they go?"

Kills White Bear attempted to mask anxiety with irritation. "Nowhere if you're watching. Now go."

White Eagle argued with him as he knew he would. "We've beaten him. I deserve to hear him plead."

"You'll hear nothing but the sound of my quirt against your back if you don't do as you're told. Battle's not the time to argue. Ride on, warrior."

When White Eagle hesitated, Kills White Bear raised his hand. In front of the other warriors it was an insult, he knew, but one that could be repaired. In anger, his son jerked the reins of his pony and did as he was commanded.

With that done, Kills White Bear could savor the moment for which he'd waited a lifetime. Already he could smell the blood.

Chapter Forty-Eight

Remy holstered his remaining pistol and ran his horse nose to nose with Kills White Bear's, and only then did he jerk back the reins. The two stallions butted one against the other until Remy's horse reared. He let it kick the Comanche's mount until Kills White Bear was forced to pull the smaller mustang back. As always the argument was territorial, but the confrontations were man against man. One's spirit was the first weapon drawn. Remy needed Kills White Bear to understand that he was not afraid.

Remy stared in silence for some time, and then turned his gaze to the scalped bodies of the men he'd sent out the night before. They lay naked and bloody. Their hearts had been ripped out of their chests. The sight of it sickened him—he'd practically raised some of those boys—but he didn't show the first trace of emotion. Slowly he swung his head back to face his enemy's mocking stare.

"¿Qué quieres, Mata Oso Blanco?" he demanded. It was a low, gravelly growl.

Kills White Bear answered harshly in a voice Remy hadn't heard in over twenty years. It instantly struck some distant chord, like the crack of a whip. "What I want, you can't give me," he said, his words dripping with spite. "But you can pay for my remorse."

Remy spat tobacco juice at the hooves of the Comanche's horse, and then shook his head. "You need to pay me what you owe."

The muscles in Kills White Bear's clenched jaw quivered as he heard Remy's words. He lunged forward in his saddle. "You were paid, Fuqua."

"I was paid half by Kills White Bear, the black liar!" Remy spat leering. "You cheated me! Maguara said one thing and Kills White Bear did another. Now I claim the rest of our bargain, an' an old lie becomes the truth."

Kills White Bear leaned back, absorbing Remy's insults, his face like stone. Remy went on. "The price for your redemption is my life, and that of the people who depend upon it. Let us pass in peace, Kills White Bear. We're leavin' your country. You gain nuthin' from our deaths."

The Comanche's response was immediate. "That's true enough, Fuqua. I gain nothing. But I profit a little from your loss. The Earth Mother does not weep for me, and she'll not weep for you. I owe you nothing but pain, and that debt only I'm willing to repay." He delivered his answer, firm and final, and then added, "I hate you, Fuqua, and everything your black hand touches."

Those words washed over Remy in the hot breeze. He had his answer. This man—the murderer of his children, the defiler of his wife, the man who'd taken Don Carlos from him, and then returned for old Picosa, the man he'd chased on the day he'd ridden the great stallion to death—said that he hated him. Remy was proud of it! One way or another the deaths of thousands were on this man's hands. For three decades, Kills White Bear alone had hemmed in an entire nation at the Colorado with terror, fire, and blood. Farms, ranches, villages, and even towns, the result of years of sweat and toil, lay in silent ashes. The destruction of Linnville was so complete that it was never rebuilt.

And Remy, when he was just a boy, had saved his miserable life and thereby damned his own. Now, at the end of his days in Texas, with fourteen more dead and the rest dying, he'd asked one last time for peace. Kills White Bear denied him, and again pledged hatred as if it were something new and wondrous. So be it, Remy decided. So be it.

He felt the old rage begin to swell. The only question that remained was what was the best way to use it. His fingers trembled, the hair bristled on the back of his neck. He knew he could not dance with Placido on that day. He unleashed his own hatred, certain that with one more black memory he could surpass that of his glaring enemy. But what the years had taken in strength they had repaid with wisdom. The lives of others depended upon what he was about to do. He deliberated for a moment more in the sun and then made his choice.

"I welcome your hatred, old fool! It's like the rain on dry grass. My life for yours."

Kills White Bear said nothing until Remy saw the malignant smile grow on his lips. "Get down and die, Fuqua," he said grimly.

"The bargain first," Remy demanded. "Let these other innocent people pass. Our quarrel is not theirs. They're leaving your country and they won't return."

Remy saw that this caught Kills White Bear's interest. "Where do they go?" he asked.

"West. Beyond the mountains to the great water. They run from war."

"Is that where one goes?" Kills White Bear smirked. "I wished that I'd known it. I'd have led my people there long ago."

"Wherever you lead your people, Kills White Bear, war'll follow as sure as the coyote follows the blood trail of a wounded bull." Remy wiped his mouth with his wrist. "And Fuqua's glad of it. It's what you deserve. I see no place for you here. I've not forgotten that you're the murderer of children."

Remy could see this last piqued the Comanche. "I killed according to the law of the feud, Fuqua," Kills White Bear said proudly, his head back. "The sun, the moon, and the mountains bear witness. They understand the ancient code. Blood cried for blood. These eyes have seen a nation die. My own children perished in my arms, screaming to the last, and I swore then to avenge them. It was my right, and my honor! I killed your son, your father, your friends, your people—every one I could—and was glad to do it. My only regret is that I didn't kill you when I had the chance. If I had, those people," he said as he pointed to the distant wagons, "would've already been dead."

It was Remy's turn again and he leaped at the opportunity. "I'll give you another chance, you son of a bitch! I'm here; and I'm waitin'! It's the same as it's always been. If you want my ground, you take it!" He leveled his glance. "But first the bargain, Kills White Bear. Let your warriors hear the words. Soon they won't hear any more from you."

Kills White Bear, lips pursed, shook his head. "No bargain, Fuqua. You've nothing to trade. First you die, then they die."

Remy understood him well enough. It was time for the dig, the medicine breaker. He knew exactly what it must be. "But if you finish with me, I got one more surprise for you, coward." He turned and pointed in the distance to Joaquin, who stood mounted. "Your own blood vows to draw yours. Your son is mine. If I don't kill you, he will. And then where'll your spirit go?"

Kills White Bear did not flinch. "Ah! There's yet another twist to this story, devil! Someone who once belonged to you now belongs to me. One word from my lips and he'll take your life in the blink of an eye!"

This was a bluff and Remy knew it. He saw no white man riding with Kills White Bear. The Rangers had reliable reports that the Comanche had murdered all white captives after the Council House Massacre twenty-one years ago. Quelepe was mistaken. Remy knew Carlito was long dead.

That conviction returned his mind to the business at hand. Another dig or two to shame him in front of his warriors, and it would be time.

"What's the word," he grimaced, "and I'll speak it! I've

never been afraid of you! You ran from me once and before it's over you'll wish you'd run again. I challenge you, coward! Don't you hear? Fuqua sees the eyes of the doe deer in your head. I smell your fear. I offer you my life for my people's. Take it if you can." He slipped his knife from its sheath, its reflection fell across Kills White Bear's scowling face. "Draw your blade, old man, and watch your blood run! You'll die today!"

"So be it!" Kills White Bear yelled, and he leaped from his horse a little before Remy jumped from his. Kills White Bear turned to his warriors. "Stand back, and let what will happen happen. When I kill him, you can have your blood."

All Remy wanted was to kill this man. He lunged at him twice, and the Comanche dodged him. Then Kills White Bear came for him.

They gripped hand to hand in a sweaty embrace. Remy could smell the bear grease of his braids, the sweetness of his oiled skin and the stench of his hot breath. He yanked his arm free and pounded him twice in the head with his fist. Kills White Bear staggered back, shaken, but did not fall. Remy pounced again and the Comanche kneed him solidly in the ribs.

Breathless, Remy backed off to gather himself but Kills White Bear was on him again. What strength this old warrior possessed! Remy couldn't restrain his arm, and he felt the sharp burn as the savage's blade sliced his abdomen. He screamed in pain so loudly that his enemy must've thought it was over. When he stepped back, Remy slugged him as hard as he could. Kills White Bear crumpled before him, dazed.

Remy, his shirt cut open and his waist drenched in blood, swung the blade of his knife back against his forearm and moved in for a lethal sweep. One quick motion across the throat was all he needed, and the opportunity was there. He moved to seize it, his stare cold.

But then he heard the sound of galloping hooves approaching. He pivoted toward Kills White Bear, and even the old warrior held up his hand to stop this rider. This was not in the bargain, he seemed to say. But it was too late. Remy felt the thud of blunt iron against his temple.

There was the bitter taste of metal in his mouth, and despite all effort to the contrary, he sank to his knees, and wavered. In his confusion, he thought he heard the faint sound of another distant horse on the run.

His image cleared of the man before him. He wore only a breechcloth, his sweating chest rose and fell in the afternoon sun. He turned against Remy, the tomahawk raised in a muscled, sweating, glistening arm. He uttered something in a language that Remy could not understand. But the voice Remy heard was his. And the eyes, those blazing eyes, belonged to Beatriz. The man who was about to kill him was Carlito.

Remy rubbed his bleeding head, struggling for speech in the confusion. He saw that Kills White Bear had risen and attempted to stop Carlito. Even his enemy did not want this. Carlito shrugged away, arguing with him, and then he came again toward Remy. He felt the sting as the warrior snatched a handful of his hair. Remy could not raise his hand against him. His throat lay open to this final thrust. It was then that Remy leaned back against the tightness of his son's grip and stared into those dark, sparkling eyes.

"Carlito?" he gasped desperately, but not out of fear. His son cocked his head like a dog that hears a strange noise. "Don't you know me, son?" Remy said in Spanish. "I'm your Pa."

Remy knew it was his only chance, his last chance, to connect with him. There, under the sun, with his throat bare and open to steel, he thought maybe the tie between them was too strong for the years apart to sever. That boy, he knew, had once loved him so dearly.

Remy used Carlito's hesitation to try and strengthen it a little more. "I'm your Pa, Carlito," Remy said again, this time as gently as he could and the words would still ring true.

Carlito's muscled arm fell, and he looked to Kills White Bear for confirmation. It was the first time that Remy had ever seen the old Comanche truly shaken. Remy marked the horror in Kills White Bear's eyes. He begged Carlito in the Comanche tongue as Remy heard the thunder of hooves shake the ground around him. Remy knew Kills White Bear had admitted the truth, and his warriors howled when they heard the startling news of abomination, that fate had pitted son against father. Everything stopped dead but the wind and the heavy, hollow beat of frenzied hooves.

Remy looked at his son, shocked that Quelepe's last and strangest prediction had come true. Carlito was alive. He held out his hand and it looked as if his son would take it. "Come to me, Carlito," Remy beseeched him. "It's all right."

Then Remy saw Joaquin's body fly through the air and collide violently with Carlito's. They both fell hard to the earth, separated, and then popped up to face each other. Carlito's prior confusion vanished with this newest challenge. He whooped loudly to confirm his malicious intent. Joaquin did not falter. When Carlito stepped once toward him, Joaquin stepped twice. One step further by each and they locked.

The other warriors drifted back in horror as brother fell against brother. Even they seemed to understand the tragedy. Equally proportioned and evenly matched, it was the most violent and vicious struggle Remy had ever seen.

He heard Kills White Bear yell to stop it, and Remy yelled, too. Their pleas only escalated the *melee*. They gnashed, gnawed and slashed at each other like lions, until their blood sprinkled Remy's face. All he could think to do was scream.

What he thought first was thunder was actually the agonized voice of a frantic Kills White Bear. Remy knew they were both the losers in this last contest. Thirty years of war had boiled down to its rawest essence, and now brother fought brother for the plains that belonged to neither tribe. Remy gave way to the most intense, indefensible fear. His whole body trembled in terror as it had the night he watched his parents die. He knew his future was about to be wasted.

"Stop 'em, Kills White Bear!" Remy yelled, but he saw that the Comanche knew of no way to intervene. He could only watch, as Remy did, as their sons tore each other apart. The other warriors would not touch them as if they were warded off by some taboo. Even Remy didn't know which one to grab. They were committed absolutely to each other's destruction.

Then there was that terrible sound. Remy had heard it a hundred times in the wars. It was the dull thud of steel ripping deeply into flesh and then bone. Joaquin shrieked loudly and sank to his knees with a deep groan. Carlito's knife was imbedded to the handle in his chest. Carlito twisted it once more and only then let it go.

Joaquin fell backwards to the earth, stunned. His frightened eyes fixed first on Remy, the pain contorting his face, his hand tugging at the knife which he could not free. Then he said, "I'm sorry, Pa." His lips formed the words without the faintest sound. "I'm sorry." Then his dark eyes lost their focus and their lids closed.

Everything grew still. Remy heard nothing but the sound of Joaquin struggling for breath. He scrambled on his knees to Jack's side and gathered his head in his lap, the bone-handled knife rose and fell with his bloody chest. "It's all right, Jack," Remy whispered. "Your Pa's here."

He turned from Joaquin to look at Carlito. He stood raised, bloody, defiant, his sweating chest heaving with pride, ready to strike again. Kills White Bear called to him and Carlito looked away. Remy caught a glimpse of the despair in Kills White Bear's eyes. Then he saw Kills White Bear drop his weapons from his hands. "Enough," the old Comanche muttered in Spanish.

The word was hollow and hopeless, too little too late. The old Comanche knelt beside Joaquin and put his hand against his cheek. "Enough."

Remy nodded, and tossed his own weapon away. A dead calm fell over the plains. Remy pressed his hand against Joaquin's wound to stop the gushing blood.

An instant later, he heard the sharp clap of lead against flesh. Carlito shuddered violently above him. The ball ripped through his chest, a ribbon of blood two feet in length traced its path as it exited Carlito's back. It sprayed from his chest and rained on Remy. Remy then heard the roar of the rifle as it echoed across the barren hills.

Carlito staggered back, attempting to steady himself, but Remy knew there was no use. He said something in Comanche to Kills White Bear. It went unanswered. Carlito's dark eyes rolled back in his head, and he was dead before he hit the ground. Red blood poured from the ugly hole in his heart.

Remy snatched his head to the east. In the distance, he could see Beatriz lying prone, the barrel of his Gump rifle resting solidly on a fallen yoke, the taper of her skirt flapping gently in the breeze, as she rammed the rod into the bore to reload it.

The brief silence that followed was shattered by Kills White Bear's thunderous wail. Remy watched as the Indian left one son to collapse by another. His tears fell whole to the ground, encapsulated by dust. He threw sand in his braids before he sliced them off and pitched them away. Then he raked the blade of the knife across his scarred chest and smeared his blood with Carlito's.

Remy was sick with grief but could not cry. He loved Carlito, he knew, but he could never match Kills White Bear's awful display. The Comanche withered before him. His warriors scattered to give him room. They did not attempt to speak amidst such howling.

Joaquin's groan snatched him from that state of shock. This one lived, and Remy would do all he could to save him. He gathered his son in his arms and scrambled the three hundred yards to take him to his mother.

Beatriz, Remy knew, understood what loss was all about. But she fought this one with every ounce of courage and calm. There was a doctor among them, and she called his name. He came and examined the boy, who now lay in her lap.

"I believe he's lucky, Mrs. Fuqua," the doctor said. "It ain't in the heart. I'll pull it out. If the artery ain't cut, and we kin stop the bleedin', your son might live."

"Do it now, doctor," she said without hesitation. "I'll hold him." Then she told the boy in Spanish how much she loved him. He lay still in her lap, too weak to wince as the knife was extracted. The doctor poured whiskey on his flesh, burning him, and Remy watched as Beatriz pressed the flat of her palm to the wound. Blood oozed between her fingers.

She looked up at Remy. "I can stop it, husband. He'll live. Do what you've got to do so we can make Fort Stockton."

Remy didn't know where Beatriz found her faith. He didn't think there was a chance Joaquin could live. He rose nonetheless to do what his wife had asked. That's all he thought of now. One of the men grabbed his arm as Remy passed by. "What now, Captain?"

"I don't know," he said, and walked back out on the plains where more misery waited. One son dying and one son dead.

Then he turned and looked at the people that watched him. He knew the fight was over. The Comanche would leave this evil place and never return. He would soon do the same. "Hitch up what teams we got left, goddamn ya," he barked. "An' unload them wagons. We leave within the hour."

Chapter Forty-Nine

As Remy re-crossed his steps, he thought he should go ahead and kill that bastard anyway. The bitter, tragic end of this thirty-five-year nightmare was Kills White Bear's fault. Remy's misery made it hard for him to think of anything but revenge. It was the one response, Remy knew, that he and Kills White Bear both understood. The Comanche would expect Remy's bullet in his brain. He pulled the Colt from his holster and cocked it. None of the other warriors made the first move to stop him. Even they knew, Remy thought, that this was what Kills White Bear wanted.

But when Remy reached him, when he saw Kills White Bear rocking with the body of his son in his lap, when he heard the sad rhythm of that lonely song, he knew he could do no such thing. He uncocked the pistol and put it away. He stopped when his shadow fell across them both.

"Kills White Bear," he called quietly. The Comanche never moved, never looked. "My people can't stay out here in the sun no more. But I'd like to help ya bury my boy. Maybe say a few words."

Now the Comanche turned to look at him. Already the fire of those eyes had burned out. "Say what you will,

Fuqua, and then go. But I won't bury this young warrior like a white man. He belongs in another place."

Remy looked at the hairless, bullet-scarred body of his son. He saw the eagle's feather woven into his single braid. The dark locks, matted with blood, glistened with bear grease. Remy saw then that it was true that this body belonged in another place. That fact alone added insult to injury. "I oughta kill ya for what ya done."

"You already have," he said, and he turned away. Then he yelled to his warriors, and instantly they rushed off. Remy feared for what might happen next. Perhaps he'd misread the Comanche. He'd done it before.

But when they returned, they carried full buffalo stomachs of sloshing water, one held between two riders. They laid them at Remy's feet and then rode away to keep their distance. Remy waved for Cristóbal and two others to come and collect them. When the water was loaded and gone, he thanked the Indian for this one act of mercy.

"There's a water hole," Kills White Bear told him, "deep, clear and cool, to the north. I don't know why you passed it."

" 'Cause I didn't know it was there."

"What does a white man know about the plains?" Kills White Bear muttered. "You can reach it before the sun sets. My warriors'll show you where it can be found."

Remy thought about it and decided otherwise. "We're goin' the other way."

The Comanche shook his head as if disgusted by Remy's decision. "You won't make the other way," he said. "Kills White Bear has seen to that. Take the water as my gift of life, save your wounded son, and then leave me, Fuqua. You're safe now to go where you will. It's nothing to me anymore."

Remy marked the position of the sun and knew he had to go. He removed the crucifix Beatriz had hung on his neck before they were married and placed it carefully around his son's. Kills White Bear shifted a little to give him the room. Remy rose to stand over Carlito's body a little longer.

"I can thank you for the water," he said, "but I can't thank you for this. I'll never get over what you took from me. Our paths may cross again, and when they do I'll settle with you."

Kills White Bear did not seem bothered by his threat. He didn't even acknowledge it. "Ah, Fuqua," he said so quietly, Remy strained to understand, "my path grows short. What can you do to me that's not already been done? As a boy I had a vision. It spoke to me just as clearly as you do now. It told me war was coming, but it never told me what the cost would be. Here, in my arms, lies the most painful reminder."

He closed Carlito's ghastly eyes. "I know this man I hold belongs to you. The world, and everything in it, now belongs to you. But why do you blame me for clinging to mine? I fought for my home."

"And I fought for mine."

"And yet the joke," Kills White Bear said sadly, his glassy eyes focused on nothing, "is that neither of us can keep it. We tore each other apart to make the way for others whose names we'll never know. Now you go your way, and I go mine; each has scarred the other, and for what?"

He stroked Carlito's cheek. "I know your heart, Fuqua. I know this man I took was your son. But he was also mine. I raised him. I fed him. I taught him. I loved him. I watched him grow into a leader of men. He was everything to me, and I could not have been prouder of what he became. I kept him from harm, but I couldn't keep him from his fate. And I won't keep you from yours. Shed no tears for this one, Fuqua. He lived the best of lives. I swear it."

Kills White Bear paused a moment, and swallowed hard. "It was your woman, his mother, who killed him, no?"

Now Remy's tears came. "I don't wanna talk about it no more, Kills White Bear. It won't do no good."

"There is no good, Fuqua. Not for the Nemenuh. And this dead warrior carried a Nemenuh's heart."

Remy did not turn away.

"Go, Fuqua." It wasn't as much an order as it was a plea. "I'll see our son's body is prepared, with honor, in our way. Let there be peace between us here at the very last. A warrior's life is measured by the power of his enemies. There were none greater than you. I honor your courage. But our struggle ended when this boy drew his last breath. Take my blood child and go. If he lives, the heart of Kills White Bear beats on in a New World that he leaves cursing."

He lay Carlito to the ground and straightened him. He wiped the blood from his body, and crossed his arms at his chest. "Our paths will never cross again," he said.

As Remy watched, Kills White Bear wrapped their son in his white cape and carefully laced it with leather. He loaded the body on the back of a painted mustang and mounted his own horse.

Remy needed to know one more thing. "What'd he say to you there at the last?" he asked him.

"He said it was exactly as his vision had warned him. He knew what would happen, yet he came to defend me. Such was his heart." Kills White Bear threw back his head, the tears streaming down his cheeks.

Kills White Bear gathered the reins of his horse and mounted it. He left his weapons where they lay. He turned and looked at Remy once more. "There was a time," he said, "when I could've beaten you. All of you. My vision told me what to do so clearly." The breeze swept his long, gray hair across his face. "No one listened," he said. "Now, no one can."

These were the last words he spoke. It was fitting that they were defiant. Remy watched him put his heels to the horse, its rear hoof stepping on the stock of his rifle and snapping it in two, and disappear into the brush. Not once did he look back.

Chapter Fifty

There was no need for Kills White Bear to speak of his decision to his warriors. They already knew. It took him three days to reach the hills that overlooked the San Sabá. He never ate. He never slept. He stopped only to graze the horses. It was these times that he sat singing the song his grandfather had taught him when he was just a boy:

Oh, Sun, you live forever

But the Nemenuh must die—
Oh, Earth, you live forever
But the Nemenuh must die—
There was not a day in sixty winters, he thought, when he hadn't heard it sung.

He removed the stubborn rocks from the grave. There was nothing but a few fragments of dried bone and withered hide until he lowered White Eagle's body to take its final place beside Morning Song and Red Sun. Then he replaced the stones and sat above the grave to wait for the setting sun.

Day became night and then night day. The hours meant nothing. When he finally heard the sound of footsteps, he was too weak to stand. He waited until the man came to him.

"Good day to you, Penateka Chief," Wolf Eyes greeted him.

"Is it still the day, Wolf Eyes? I can't tell anymore."

"It is the day, my friend," he said. "The sun is setting." He sat beside him. "I've come to discuss your future."

Kills White Bear scoffed at this. "What future?"

"The one you've earned. I'm proud of you. You fought well."

"Well, Wolf Eyes?" he asked, his eyes closing. "In my time we lost everything. I was beaten."

"We lost everything, it's true. But you, Kills White Bear, were never beaten."

Kills White Bear looked at him. Wolf Eyes' hand reached for his and he grasped it and held it tightly. "Walk with me a little way," the spirit said.

"I can't walk," Kills White Bear told him.

"You can this last little bit. There's strength in those limbs yet. Lean on me. I've come to help."

They walked north, uphill it seemed to him, toward the creeping darkness. After they'd traveled a little ways, Kills White Bear saw the brilliant light of a great council fire. "What nation is this?" he asked.

"Yours," Wolf Eyes told him. "The fire burns for you."

Now he felt uncertain, a little afraid. Wolf Eyes sensed his hesitation, and begged him to move on. As they came closer, the fire's heat broke the chill of the night air. He felt stronger from it and took his arm from around Wolf Eyes' shoulder to walk alone. He sensed Wolf Eyes drift from him, and he passed on, drawn to the warmth. He had the sense that he belonged here.

Forms solidified at the edge of darkness. Rows of unrecognized warriors lined both sides of that green and grassy path. As he passed them by, they called his name, while those behind him cheered it. He heard the voices of people he could not see swell in the darkness, gathering until it was a roar. His strength returned. He walked faster now, almost a trot. At the last, he was running.

When he reached the fire, he recognized the faces gathered around it. His mother and father were there, his sisters, his cousins, his friends and comrades, Maguara and the other great chiefs of his youth. They all welcomed him, but Cold Knife, his beloved mentor, spoke the words of greeting. How he'd missed them all. He remembered now as he stood next to the glow.

He looked at his body in the fire's light. His skin was again firm and deep bronze, his chest again chiseled and solid. The hair that fell across his shoulders was deep, full, and shining black. All his scars were gone save the one the bear had marked on his chest when he was just a boy. He made fists with his hands, and watched the muscles in his arms respond as they had when he was in his prime. The spirits had returned his youth.

Four people stood between Kills White Bear and the fire with their backs to him. Three turned together and reached for him. It was Morning Song, their son, and daughter, all as beautiful as the day before smallpox came and took them away. He clutched each so tightly that he felt the beating of their hearts.

There was but one remaining, and Kills White Bear was curious to see who it was. He reached to turn him, but this last one swung to him first and hugged him more tightly than the others before. Kills White Bear felt the arms of White Eagle caress him. The last to welcome him was the dearest. Now, the tears of joy came. They were all together again.

His adopted son broke away to point to the plains below unfolding in the golden light of a breaking dawn. The grass was vibrant green as far as his sharp eyes could see. The buffalo milled quietly like the shadow beneath a great cloud. Horses grazed by the thousands in the hills above them. It was a world that he thought he'd never see again. "It's all yours," White Eagle told him, "forever."

Their earthly thread was broken, but the Great Spirit had not forgotten his promise to the Nemenuh. There was a time, now forgotten, when Kills White Bear had doubted. There was no denying it now. Kills White Bear had lost one world but gained another. The reward was worth the years of pain, struggle and unending war. There was meaning to his way of life after all. He'd fought for it to the very end and the swelling voice of eight hundred generations cheered him in gratitude. He'd won a place and nothing else mattered.

In the distance, above the roar of multitudes, he heard the distinct growl of the great albino bear. One spirit honored another.

Chapter Fifty-One

Remy and his party left Fort Stockton well provisioned. They traded for fresh oxen and horses and hired a smith to repair the wagons. Things went better after the new start.

They slipped through the Wild Rose Pass for Fort Davis. From there they traveled to El Muerto Springs and then on to Van Horn's well. In the middle of August they came to the Río Grande at Fort Quitman and traveled it north to Fort Filmore. There they forded the river, and on that September day, Remy left Texas behind forever.

The crossing never struck him like he thought it would. Long ago he'd learned the value of land. His aunt had once told him that land was everything, and he'd lived, fought, and killed by that hard law. So many others had died. His own price could not have been higher. He'd buried three generations in that dark, brooding soil and then left it all for a place he'd never seen and where he was certain he would not be able to name the trees. But none of that

mattered anymore as they rose from out of the river bottom
for the high country that lay west.

At fifty-five years of age he still saw a future ahead of
him. In new country, he'd find new hope.

Beatriz was with him, Joaquin was healing, Remy's own
cuts had already scabbed over and itched like he had fleas.
He still had a little money in his pocket and he still heard
the Longhorns bellow when an impatient vaquero's whip
fell across their backs. He'd lived in three nations and he
was young enough, he hoped, to live yet in a fourth, if
California went her own way. Flags had never mattered
much to him.

But now he saw land as a commodity, like money and
tools and even horses, a means to an unconscious end. He
realized it was the dream that had sustained him, and he
would carry it easily from Texas to California. The challenge would be there, the risk, the promise of years of toil,
but it was the dream that would make the coming struggle
all worth while.

As long as Beatriz was there to share it, it didn't matter
where they went. The life they'd known in Texas they'd
know again somewhere else. The harsh years had taught
him how precious it was, and how fragile. He'd soon learn
the names of strange trees. Now, with the Río Grande behind him, he slept at night.

In the morning, before his breakfast, he'd dance just a
little by himself to remind himself of the pain Placido had
urged him to leave behind all those years ago. Now even
Remy was glad his enemies had burned him out. They'd
freed him of the terrible burden of blood and soil. He was
no longer rooted to his own destruction. He could breathe
again, hold his wife near, and hope. No law this time, no
politics. He'd work the land and not be too damn attached
to it. That had always been his mistake. He knew better
now.

One morning he tied his horse to the rear of the wagon
and took his place beside his wife. They didn't need him
to lead anymore. Beatriz held the reins and Remy rode.
The road was not so bumpy once they left Texas.

Often he'd reached in to test Joaquin's brow for fever.

It was gone. Then he turned to watch the country unfold before him. He held Beatriz's free hand in his.

"We did it," she told him. Her face was beaming, full of the old color, vigor, and determination.

"Well, we're damn sure doin' it, anyway."

"I feel good, Remy," she said. "Very good."

"So do I, sweetheart. So do I." It'd been years since he'd said this, and many more yet when he'd truly felt it. He saw her eyes search his barren neck.

"Where's your crucifix, Remy?" she asked him.

He had his answer ready. "Ah, Beatriz, I must've lost it in that scuffle. I'm sorry. I know it meant the world to you."

"I don't care," she said. "I'll get you another. You need all the help you can get." She smiled at him as she did the day she'd won him. She looked so much younger to him in the western sun. Their ranch took shape in his mind from the corner of that warm, loving smile. All he had to do was build around it, get a good hat for the California sun, come inside when the California rain fell, and watch the slow years pass, but not too closely. Life was the miracle he'd mistaken for land, and he would cherish it from now on.

And he would never tell her who she'd killed that day on the plains of west Texas. He loved her too much to cause her any more pain. That grief he'd bear alone for the rest of his days. She would never know.

Author's Afterword

Anyone who wonders about the impact of European diseases on Native American cultures should consider the following:

The Aboriginal Population of Central Mexico:

YEAR	EST. POPULATION
1518	25,200,000
1519	Cortes Conquers Mexico
1532	16,800,000
1548	6,300,000
1568	2,650,000
1585	1,900,000
1595	1,375,000
1605	1,075,000

Sherburne F. Cook and Woodrow Borah. *Essays in Population History*

"For among the tribes which have not employed vaccination smallpox is as destructive today as it was in Europe before the time of Jenner; at that time 50,000 persons are said to have died of this disease in England alone. In 1837 smallpox attacked the Mandan Indians (relatives of the Dakota [Souix] inhabiting the Missouri River Valley); within a year only twenty-seven individuals remained out of the population of 150,000."

Henry M. Lyman, M.D., et al. *The New American Family Physician*, 1899.

Texas' betrayal broke Sam Houston's heart. When the Civil War began in earnest, Houston nevertheless formally declared not for the Confederacy, but for his beloved Texas and the South. Houston's eldest boy, Sam, Jr., was seriously wounded at the Battle of Shiloh and listed as killed in action. A Union medical officer found the boy's body and Bible, each shot completely through, and took both to a Union chaplain, who happened to be one of the signers against the Kansas-Nebraska Bill and, as such, a staunch admirer of Sam Houston. He read Margaret Lea Houston's inscription to her son and promptly assumed personal charge of the boy's recovery. When he was well enough to travel, Sam Houston, Jr., was returned to his family.

Sometime in 1862, Sam Houston's buggy was stopped by a Confederate provost marshal, and its occupants ordered to produce their passports. Houston replied, "San Jacinto is my pass through Texas," and he rode on.

Popular support swelled for Houston as the war took its toll on Texas just as he had predicted. He was urged to run again for governor in the 1863 election, yet it appears that he had lost interest. His physical condition was likewise no longer up to the challenge. He had lost weight since the beginning of his exile, and had developed a persistent cough. He succumbed to pneumonia in July of 1863, the same month of Lee's debacle at Gettysburg, the turning point of the war Sam Houston had tried so desperately to avoid.

After the war for Texas independence, Juan Nepomucena Seguín, the Tejano veteran of several major campaigns, restored order to his home community of San Antonio de Béxar. One of his first acts was to bury the ashes of the destroyed Alamo garrison with honor.

Seguín left the military to enter politics and was elected to the Texas Senate in 1838. He worked tirelessly for positive relations between Tejano and Anglo Texians. Always daring, he often rode with the famed Texas Ranger Jack Hays on expeditions against the Comanche.

When he understood that there could never be peace with Mexico, and that both predominant Mexican political factions—the Centralistas and the Federalistas—intended to reconquer Texas, he warned officials of the Republic accordingly. Convinced that an invasion was inevitable, Seguín, then mayor of San Antonio de Béxar, ordered the evacuation of the city. When the Mexican army did arrive,

one of its commanders publicly announced that Seguín was
a Mexican supporter. He never overcame the resulting
stigma, and in 1842, he felt compelled to emigrate back
to Mexico.

Given the choice by Santa Anna of either serving in the
Mexican army or going to prison, Seguín reluctantly rode
with General Woll against his old Texas comrades. He was
universally denounced throughout the Republic as a traitor
to his nation.

After the Mexican War of 1848, Seguín asked for and
received permission to return home to Texas. The valiant,
much-maligned Tejano hero died in Nuevo Laredo in 1890.
The city of Seguín, Texas, was named in his honor. It
thrives to this day.

Forever allied to the Texians, the Tonkawa Chief Placido
rode with them in several campaigns against their mutual
foe, the Comanche. Despite his proven loyalty, he was nevertheless banished with his entire Tonkawa nation to the
Indian Territory in 1859. His refusal to aid Union sympathizers during the Civil War eventually cost him his life.
He fell to his old Comanche enemies in a battle at the Fort
Sill Reservation.

His charges harassed and murdered on their Clear Fork
Reservation by white settlers, Robert Neighbors under-
stood that pacified tribes could never live in peace in Texas.
He urged the Bureau of Indian Affairs to move all reserva-
tion nations, including the Comanche, to the Indian Terri-
tory. In September, 1859, after being forced by Texas
Rangers to leave their livestock behind, they crossed the
Red River to the Cache Creek Agency into what is now
Oklahoma.

Neighbors returned to Texas and was immediately shot
dead in the back.

The last free Comanche, a Quahadi band led by the half-
breed Quanah Parker, surrendered to reservation life on
June 24, 1875. Thus ended the longest, bloodiest and most
vicious struggle between a Native American nation and the
pioneer descendants of European immigrants. The Coman-

che wars, lasting over fifty years, shaped three generations of Texans.

No Amerindian nation native to Texas was ever granted a reservation within the present day boundaries of the state.

According to T.R. Fehrenbach's *Comanches: The Destruction of a People*, a survey at Cache Creek in 1910 counted only 1,171 Nemenuh, of all bands, in residence. An anthropologist estimated in 1931 that only ten percent of the Nemenuh at Cache Creek were of pure blood.

—David Marion Wilkinson
Austin, Texas
December, 1993–August, 1996

Acknowledgments

I would like to thank Professor Neil Foley, Department of History, University of Texas at Austin, for sharing his "Texas Until 1845" (History 320L) course with me. His lecture series provided a sturdy framework as I began to research the period, and some of the selections cited in the Preface to this novel were gratefully borrowed from his required readings.

Additional research suggestions were graciously offered by Dr. Arnoldo De Leon, Professor of History, Angelo State University; Dr. Donald E. Chipman, University of North Texas; Dr. Frank de la Teja, Southwest Texas State University; Dr. David J. Weber of Southern Methodist University; Dr. Daniel J. Gelo of the University of Texas at San Antonio; and Dr. Andrew A. Tijerina and Dr. Joe S. Graham, both of Texas A & M—Kingsville. I had candid and fruitful telephone conversations with Dr. Weber, Dr. Graham, Dr. Tijerina, and especially Dr. de la Teja in my search to understand Tejano culture and ranching operations in Mexican Texas. I came to these acknowledged scholars and experts as an unpublished, unproven novelist and yet none of these men ever once treated me as such. They were all very generous with their time and expertise, and I remain grateful. Also, I owe an acknowledgment to Mr. Norm Flayderman, the world's foremost authority on historic arms. I wrote him for help, and he answered straight away.

Special thanks to Mr. T.R. Fehrenbach. I relied heavily on the research and opinions expressed in his works, *Lone Star* and *Comanches: The Destruction of a People*, both of which have no equal as far as I am aware. Mr. Fehrenbach also took the time to respond twice to written questions. Always supportive and kind, I'm honored to express my sincerest thanks for his assistance and interest.

I am pleased to acknowledge my debt to the following sources: Donald E. Chipman's *Spanish Texas: 1519–1821*, an excellent one-volume study of a truly remarkable period, and one from which I was pleased to quote in the preface of this novel; Arnoldo De Leon's *The Tejano Community, 1836–1900* (Dr. De Leon is a recognized pioneer in the study of his rich culture. Don Carlos Amarante de la Cruz, the mayordomo, Diego Picosa, and the mystic mestizo, Quelepe Ortiz, share Dr. De Leon's knowledge with the readers of *Not Between Brothers*); Joe S. Graham's *El Rancho in South Texas*; Sandra L. Myer's *The Ranch in Spanish Texas: 1691–1800*; Jovita Gonzalez's unpublished Master's thesis, *Social Life in Cameron, Starr and Zapata Counties* (1930).

Roberto M. Villarreal's unpublished Master's thesis, *The Mexican American Vaqueros of the Kenedy Ranch: a Social History* (1972) and Jack Jackson's *Los Mestenos* brought El Rincon's Rancho de la Cruz to life. Don Worcester's *The Texas Longhorns* convinced me that the Texas breed probably had some degree of English blood, and I yield to same. Jo Ella Powell Exley's (Editor) *Texas Tears and Texas Sunshine* brought a uniquely feminine perspective to the pioneer experience. I thought her choices of accounts of frontier life were excellent, and I wove them in wherever I could. Stephen L. Hardin's *Texian Iliad* laid the foundation of the war, and the author was kind enough to share a quotation with me. Remy's participation at Gonzales, Concepción, the siege of Béxar and finally San Jacinto were drawn from Mr. Hardin's account. *Texian Iliad* is the best, most recent and most complete work on the Texas Revolt. To be sure I had it right, I also consulted Jeff Long's *Duel of Eagles* and James W. Pohl's *The Battle of San Jacinto* among others; Richard R. Stenberg's "The Texas Schemes of Jackson and Houston, 1829–1836" (*The Southwestern Social Science Quarterly*, Dec. 1934) convinced me that the Texas Revolt was more sticky than Sam Houston ever publicly admitted. I also acknowledge Donaly E. Brice's *The Great Comanche Raid*. Kills White Bear and Remy Fuqua follow in Mr. Brice's tracks, and he knew the country well. Ernest Wallace and E. Adamson Hoebel's *The Comanches: Lords of the South Plains* is the richest account I could find of Kills White Bear's culture and heritage; W.W. Newcomb, Jr.'s classic *The Indians of Texas* fleshed out the doomed Karankawa and Coahuiltecan nations, as well as the Tonkawa, who survived; and there is no better book on the Texas Republic than William Ransom Hogan's work of the same name. Remy borrowed his eye for detail. What is good about *Not Between Brothers*, the sometimes stormy marriage of fact and fiction, was built on the foundation laid by the above-mentioned writers, historians and sociologists. What is faulted is my responsibility alone.

I am especially grateful for the following primary sources: Nelson Lee's "Three Years Among the Comanches" (*Captured by the Indians*; Frederick Drimmer, Editor) (He saw what Remy did.); *The Adventures of a Frontier Naturalist: The Life and Times of Dr. Gideon Lincecum* (I was amazed at the vigor, intelligence, humor and courage of this remarkable man.); John Holland Jenkins' *Recollections of Early Texas* (Mr. Jenkins was a neighbor of the fictional Remy Fuqua and Elijah Johnson. He also fought at Plum Creek, and, like Remy, lived beyond it with wisdom.): Jos Enrique De La Peña's *With Santa Anna In Texas*, which provides the Mexican perspective on the Texas campaign. I found my title in the editor's (Carmen Perry) footnotes, as excerpted, I believe, from a speech by Santa Anna to his reluctant troops. Lastly, I am indebted to Noah Smithwick's *The Evolution of a State*. It is a wonderful book by a wonderful man. Remy Fuqua's fictional journey often parallels Mr. Smithwick's very real one. I reviewed many first-person accounts, of both men and women pioneers, but these were the most complete and delightful of which I am aware. I admire all of these people. Their kind is gone forever.

I am also indebted to the late J. Frank Dobie, who saw a cultural niche and filled it amply with color, interest, intelligence, humor and love. I read *Coronado's Children*, *The Mustangs*, *The Longhorns*, *Jim Bowie: Big Dealer,* and *A Vaquero of the Brush Country*. Hopefully, you'll sense the touch of these works throughout mine. He taught me about the instincts of wild horses and cattle, but more about the spirit and grit of the people who tamed them. Dr. Dobie was without peer, and is sorely missed in Texas. I wish we could have had a drink together in his back yard. It would've been late before he got shed of me.

I'm grateful to Peter Cowley, M.D., and Kirby Stewart,

M.D., for explaining, in laymen's terms, thank God, the ravages of smallpox and cholera as these sections were drafted. Thanks to J. Mack Barham, M.D., for reviewing them for accuracy once they were complete. I felt it was important for the reader to understand the holocaust of European diseases on indigenous people, and these three able physicians helped me do it.

I am fortunate that R.C., Mildred and Bobby Zesch have shared their land and life with me for these past six years. Sections of this book were written in the little cabin that faces south toward Calf Creek to catch the summer breeze, not too far from where Bowie and his brother held off a party of enraged Lipan, Caddo and their allies. I had pack-rats only for reviewers in those days. Three years ago, I'd started *Brothers* without a true beginning. I sat over a campfire speaking with R.C. Zesch about many things until we came to his own history, at which time he first told me the tragic story of his rancher parents. It struck me, as I hope it will strike you, and so Remy's violent story begins exactly where Mr. Zesch's did that warm, summer night. R.C. overcame it, as Remy does, to walk proudly on his portion of the earth, and rightly so. He earned it. Thank you, Zesches, for everything.

I feel fortunate to have assembled such a fine group of readers. They are: G. Mike Pugh, Amarillo, Texas; Lisa Minton (what an editor), Sally Sanchez, Mike Peebles, Barbara Minton, Chandler Ford, Donna Lee, Katherine McCulley and R. Louis Bratton, all of Austin; Kay Wilkinson and Jim Bradley of Dallas, Texas; John Holmgreen of San Antonio; fraternity brothers T. Rex King and Ashley Walker of Mt. Pleasant, Texas; J. Mack Barham, M.D., Monroe, Louisiana; "Deputy" Bob Campbell, Bozeman, Montana; E. Barham Bratton of Wimberley, Texas; Mary and Johnnie Wilkinson of Houston; Bobby and Sherri Zesch of San Angelo, Texas; and most of all, fifth-generation Texan Aline Jordan, who slugged it out with me draft by wretched draft. She threatened to string me up if I didn't get it "right," and I never once doubted her. Thanks, Aline, for the terror.

It was to my good fortune that the manuscript found its way to Robert H. Thonhoff, historian, award-winning writer and current president of the Texas State Historical Association. He reviewed the manuscript, called me with good news, and then later sent twenty-three legal pages worth of corrections. I was honored by his gracious participation in the project. Nothing meant more to me than for a man like Mr. Thonhoff, a curator, defender and lover of the Texan heritage, to give this book a nod of approval.

I'm dearly grateful to my in-laws, the Brattons, who gave me the first "respectable" job I've ever had, and then allowed me to slip out of the office (without pay, of course) to attend Dr. Foley's class on Tuesday and Thursday afternoons. Thank you all for your kindness, generosity, support and encouragement. A paycheck twice a month was also nice.

I'd be remiss if I neglected to mention my high school English teachers Margaret Stork and Freda Katz. Together, they've inspired countless young lives. They certainly inspired mine, and I've never forgotten. I'd also like to thank Robert F. "Bobby" Frese, Jr., former senior editor at Doubleday and Taylor, now I think the owner of a retail outlet in Birmingham, Alabama. He read my first two novels years ago and rejected them both. But he took the time to tell my why, which is the same thing as telling me how. He likewise encouraged me, by letter and by phone, at a time when I needed it most, and I'm pleased to mention his kindness and friendship here, at my very first opportunity.

Thanks to Barbara and Roy Minton, Emily Minton Carsey and all the Minton clan for twenty years of friendship and encouragement.

Special thanks to Elizabeth C. Lyon, M.A., of Eugene, Oregon. She never listened to my whimpering ego as she rubbed my nose in the basics of novel construction. She began as my teacher, and quickly became my friend. I could never please her, but I began to wonder who could. For the struggling writer, however, I'm certain that there is no better place to turn. She is the one true lighthouse beacon along that stormy, rocky, wreck-strewn coast. Thank you, Elizabeth.

For better than a decade now I've been fortunate enough to work under the editorial direction of Dr. William J. Scheick, Professor of English at the University of Texas at

Austin. He saw something in me that I never saw in myself, and then nurtured it with patience, understanding and care. He has been my teacher, mentor, critic, confidant, defender, advocate and friend. For ten years he said the same thing: "Fewer words, David. For God's sake, fewer words." Thanks, Bill, for everything. You don't know how much it meant to me to have someone like you in my corner. At long last, the debt is paid.

Thanks to my mother, Johnnie Wilkinson. What I know about courage and character, I learned from her example.

I'm pleased to acknowledge the outstanding contribution of Robert Rorke, my BOAZ editor. A lifetime resident of Brooklyn, New York, and a fine writer in his own right, he quickly established himself as the enemy of my longtime allies: verbosity, lethargic prose and melodrama. Accordingly, I hated Robert from the very start. In the end, however, this acerbic, over-educated Yankee taught me a great deal about this tedious craft. *Not Between Brothers* is largely what it is because of Robert's firm, caring, red ink-stained hand.

I can't say enough about Tom Southern and Elizabeth Vahlsing, the twin visionaries of BOAZ. Their integrity, wisdom and grace elevated *Not Between Brothers* beyond where I could ever have taken it. In a world where the publishing industry is increasingly dependent upon harsh market laws and the blockbuster mentality, the future of the art form belongs to the stubbornly intrepid. In a word, that is the independent heart of BOAZ, and may God and good fortune favor those with the courage to dream and dare. I feel extremely fortunate that we found each other. They plucked this toad from the murky pond of obscurity and treated him like a prince. Thank you both.

Thanks to the ubiquitous Bob Riley, our mutual friend, for bringing us together.

And lastly, a word of gratitude, love and devotion to my wife, Bonnie Dale Bratton, to whom this novel is dedicated. Her faith never wavered even when my own did. I defined my image in those dark, brooding, mysterious eyes. She is everything to me, as Beatriz was to Remy. With English, German and Cherokee blood, her roots have thrived in

Texas for five generations where they hold tightly to this day. Our two sons proudly make six. Spur up, boys. The future's your wilderness. Don't be afraid.

—D. Marion Wilkinson
Austin, Texas
August, 1996

TO GUARD WHAT HE HAS GAINED . . .

Remy Fuqua came to Texas with little more than the clothes on his back. Only his force of will enabled him to marry into the powerful Mexican family of Don Carlos de la Cruz. In a few years, he'd gone from poor orphan to wealthy rancher. Now a husband and father, Remy would kill to protect all that he has gained.

TO AVENGE WHAT HE HAS LOST . . .

The Penateka warrior Kills White Bear had witnessed the near destruction of his people. Smallpox, ravaged hunting grounds, and the encroaching settlers have decimated his tribe's way of life. For Kills White Bear, there can be no peace with the Anglos, or the Mexicanos.

MAN WAGES WAR

Now, the destinies of these two extraordinary men will cross—as the United States, Mexico, and the Plains Indians wage war over the Texas landscape. . . .

"The best-researched fiction readers are likely to find . . . a rattling good story about well-drawn characters living in perilous times."
—*The Amarillo News-Globe*

"This historically rich yet imaginative tale of Texas from the 1820s to the 1860s starts off strong and gets stronger." —*The San Antonio Express-News*

"An epic, sprawling page turner that's as big as the Lone Star State . . . wonderfully written . . . a great read . . . a great book." —*Studio Tulsa KWGS*